WARLORD OF MARS™

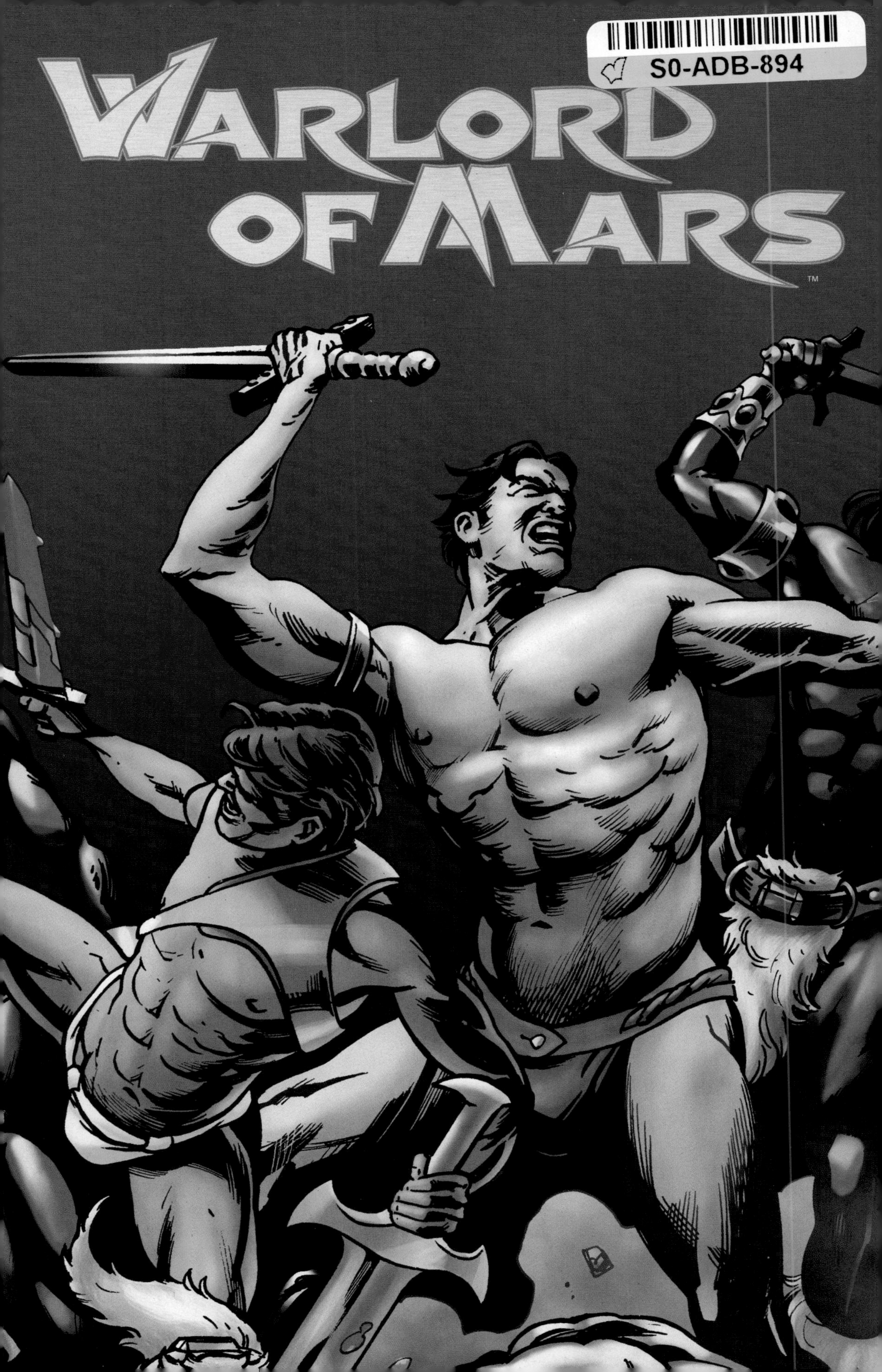

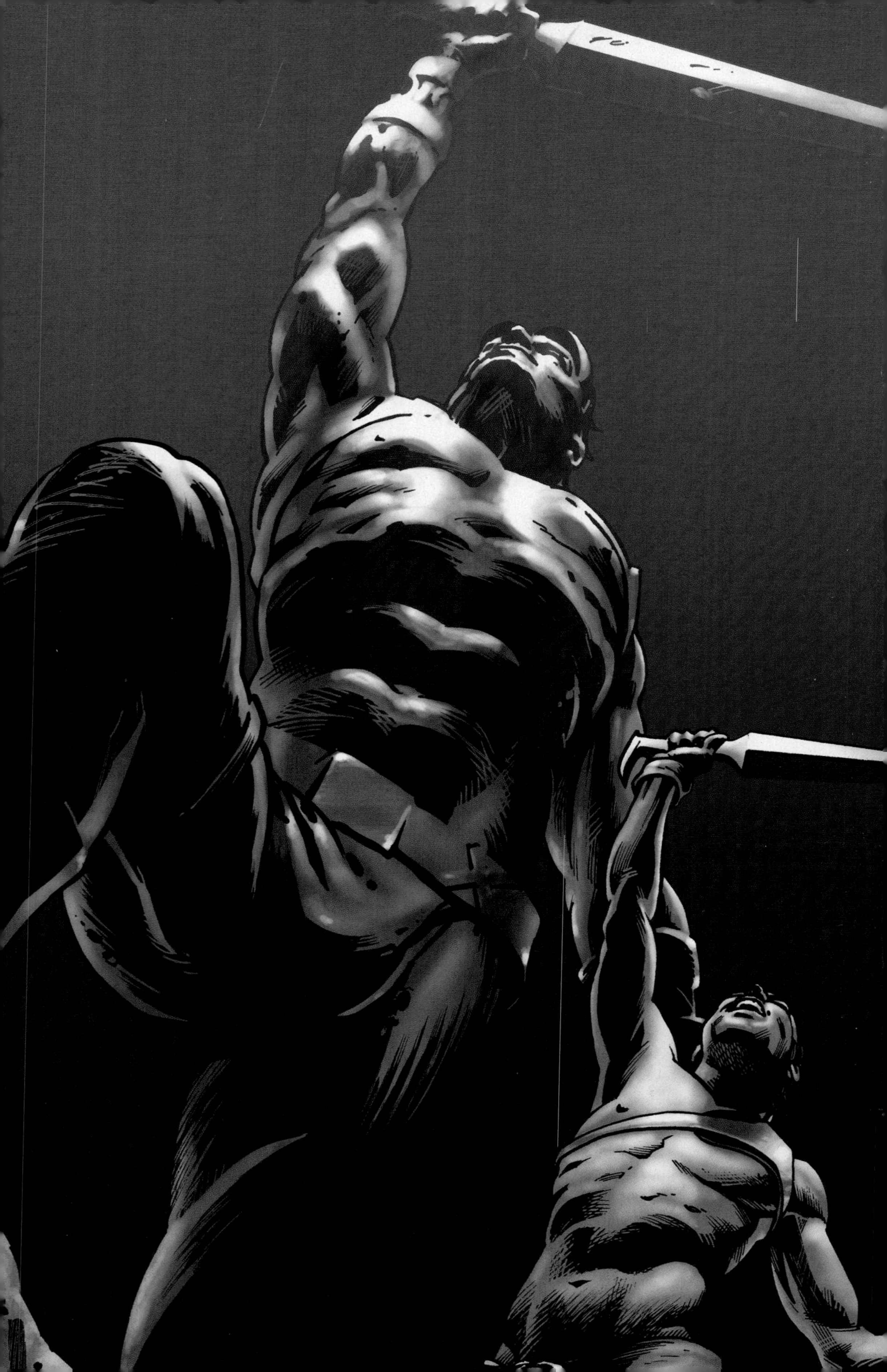

WARLORD OF MARS™

based on the stories of

EDGAR RICE BURROUGHS

written by

ARVID NELSON

illustrated by

STEPHEN SADOWSKI (#10-12)
EDGAR SALAZAR (#13-18)

colored by

SHANE ROOKS (#10-12)
MAXFLAN ARAUJO (#13)
MARCELO PINTO (#14-18)

lettered by

MARSHALL DILLON

collection cover by

JOE JUSKO

collection design by **JASON ULLMEYER**

This volume collects issues 10-18 of Warlord of Mars by Dynamite Entertainment

DYNAMITE®
Visit us online at **www.DYNAMITE.net**
Follow us on Twitter **@dynamitecomics**
Like us on Facebook **/Dynamitecomics**

Nick Barrucci, President
Juan Collado, Chief Operating Officer
Joe Rybandt, Editor
Josh Johnson, Creative Director
Rich Young, Director Business Development
Jason Ullmeyer, Senior Designer
Josh Green, Traffic Coordinator
Chris Caniano, Production Assistant

First Printing
ISBN-10: 1-60690-336-5
ISBN-13: 978-1-60690-336-0
10 9 8 7 6 5 4 3 2 1

WARLORD OF MARS™, VOLUME TWO. First printing. Contains materials originally published in Warlord of Mars #10-18. Published by Dynamite Entertainment. 113 Gaither Dr., STE 205, Mt. Laurel, NJ 08054.

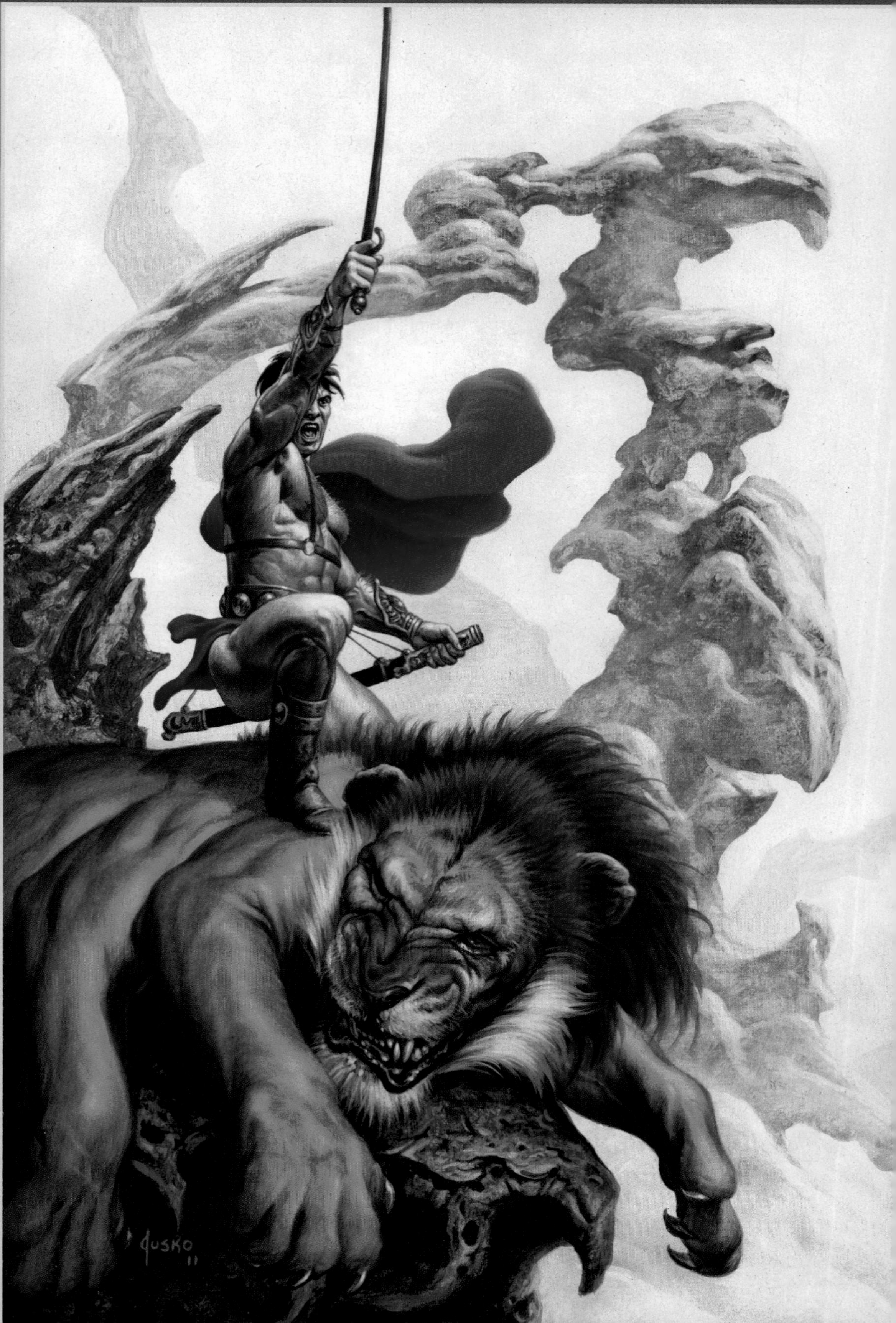

John Carter departed Mars as mysteriously and suddenly as he arrived. He would not know the joy of witnessing his son, Carthoris, bursting the shell mere days after his father's disappearance.

Aside from incubating in eggs, Red Martians are like Earthlings in every anatomical detail. They emerge from their shells able to walk, with their psychic abilities fully developed. It is not uncommon for a Barsoomian child to be capable of speech a mere fortnight after the hatching.

Carthoris developed at rapid pace, even by Martian standards, a fact attributed to his Earthly heritage.

Dejah Thoris and her young prodigy were faced with a gruesome mystery: the Caretaker of the great Atmosphere Factory that sustains all life on Barsoom was horribly slain just before Carter disappeared.

The Caretaker possessed a magnificent amulet set with a unique, multi-hued gem. This priceless insignia of his office was not found with his corpse. But the artifact's whereabouts would not remain a mystery for long...

E.R.B.

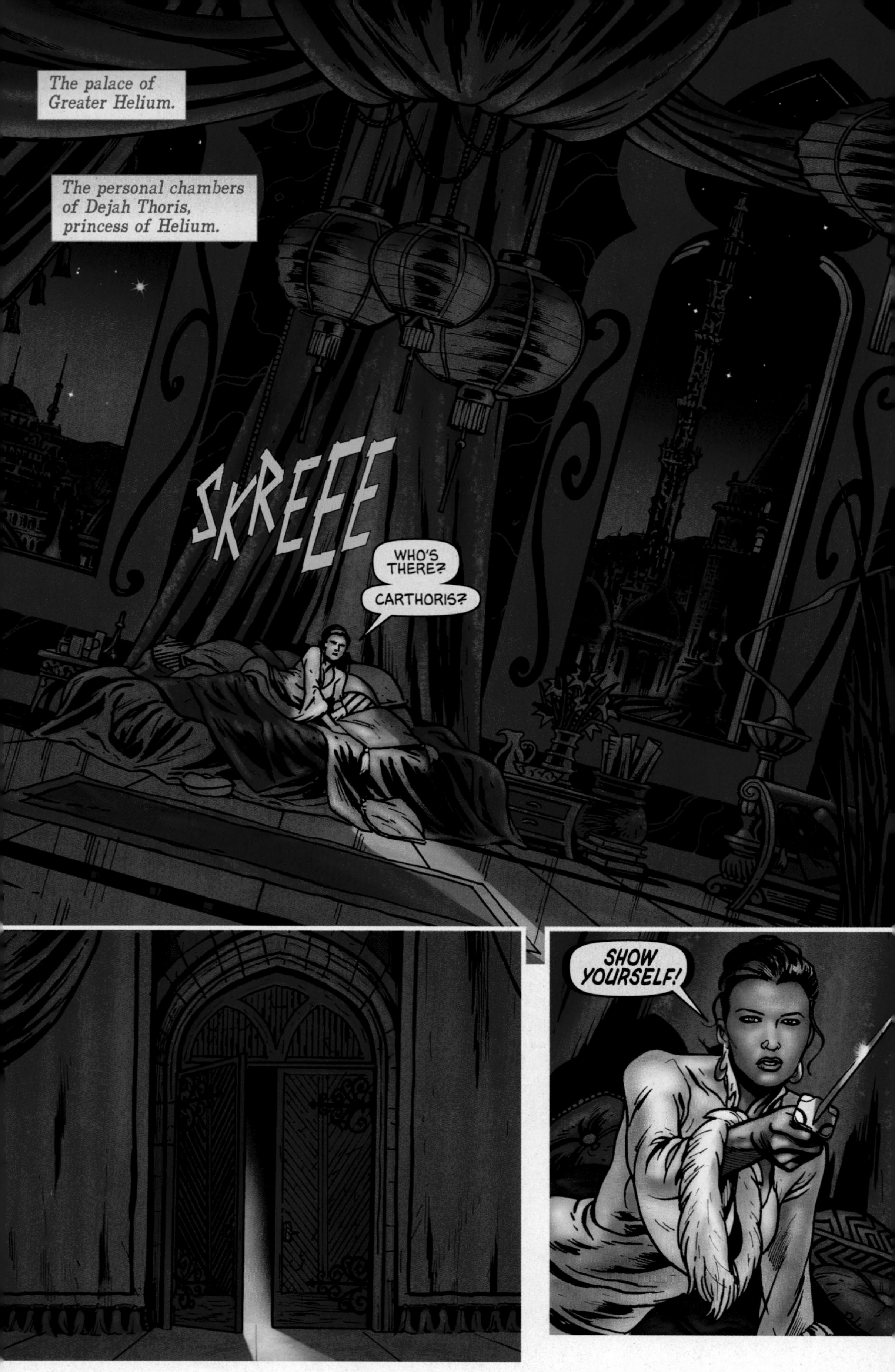
The palace of Greater Helium.
The personal chambers of Dejah Thoris, princess of Helium.
SKREEE
WHO'S THERE?
CARTHORIS?
SHOW YOURSELF!

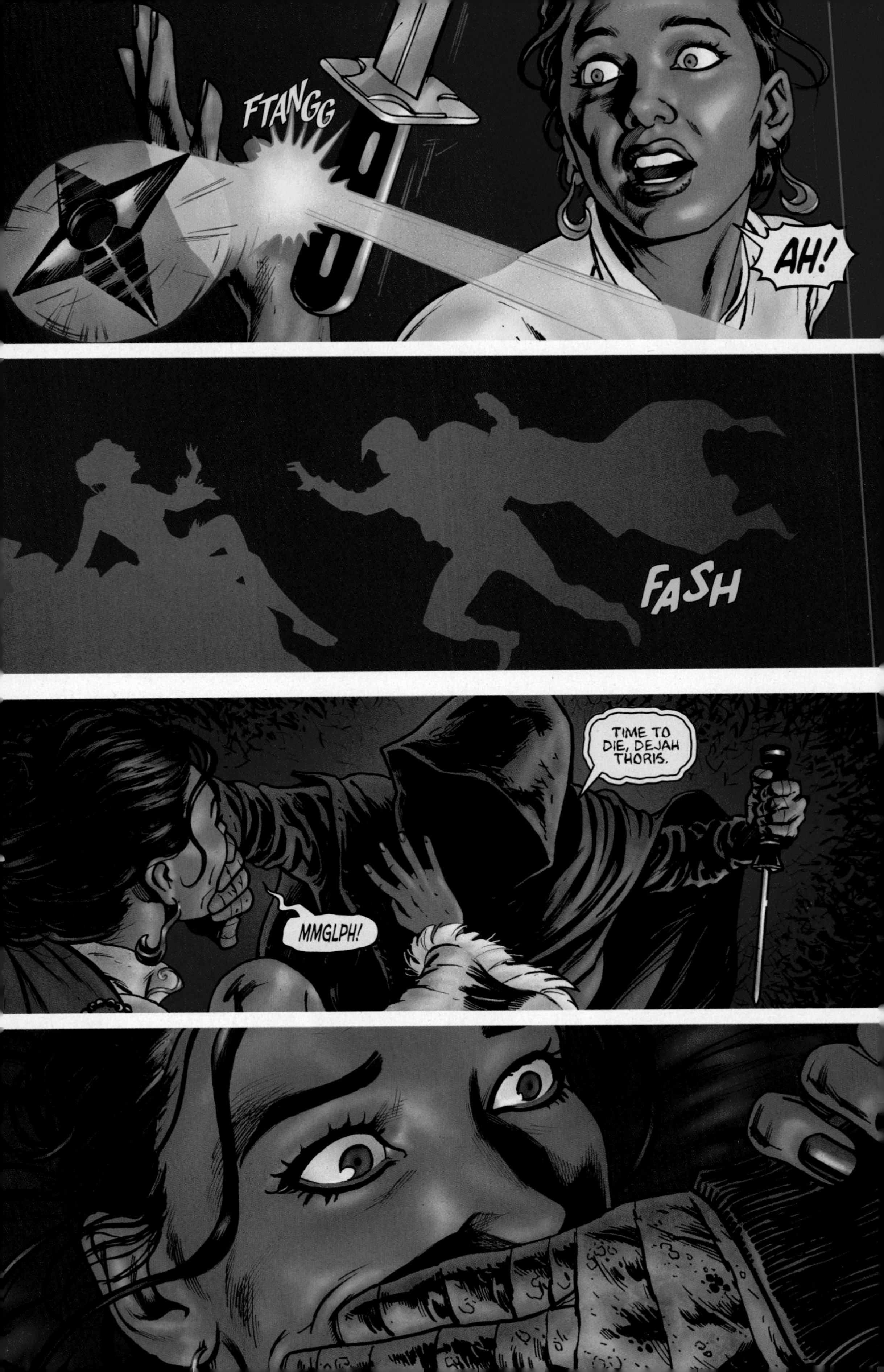
FTANGG
AH!
FASH
TIME TO DIE, DEJAH THORIS.
MMGLPH!

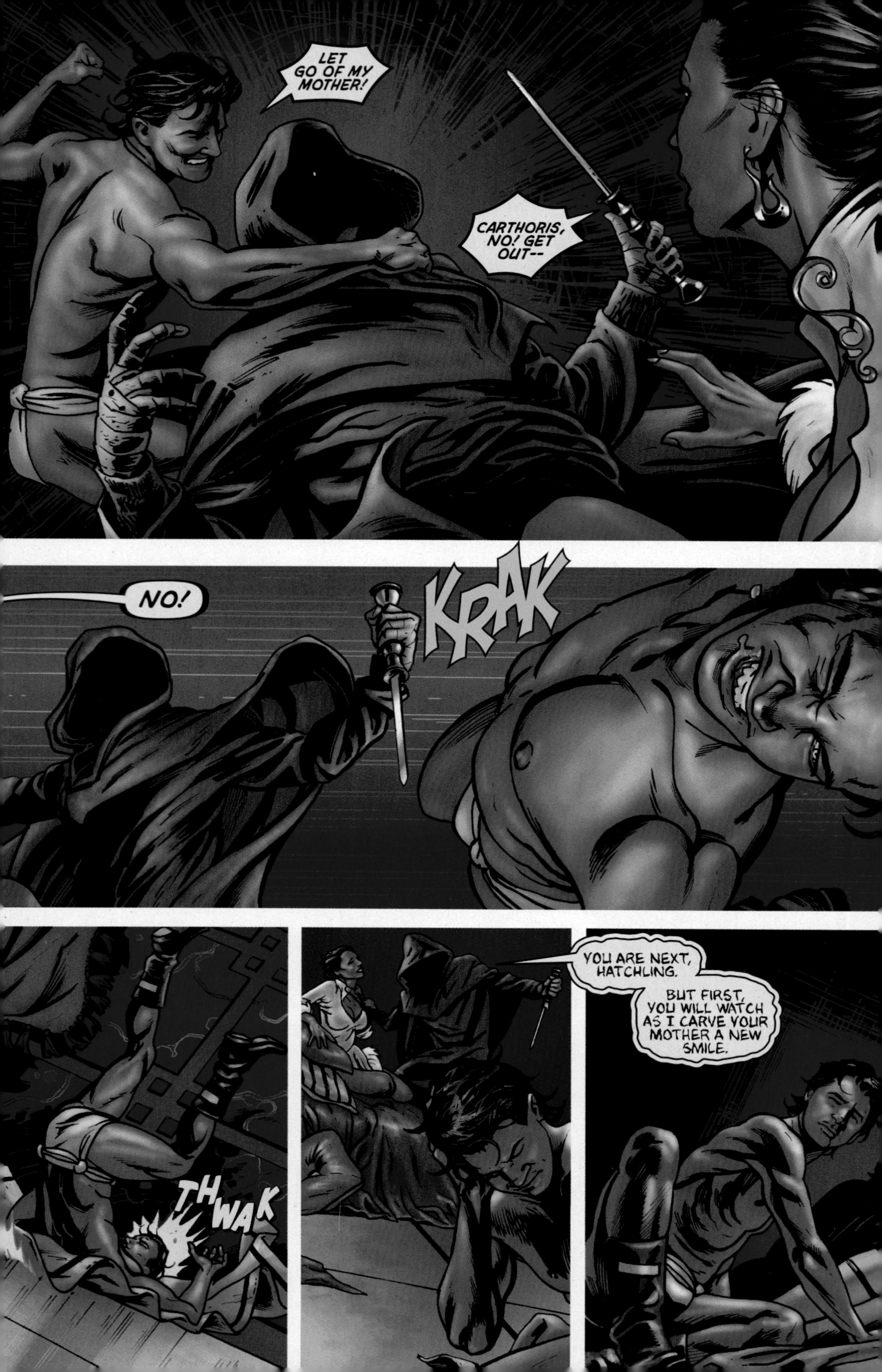
LET GO OF MY MOTHER!
CARTHORIS, NO! GET OUT--
NO!
KRAK
THWAK
YOU ARE NEXT, HATCHLING.
BUT FIRST, YOU WILL WATCH AS I CARVE YOUR MOTHER A NEW SMILE.

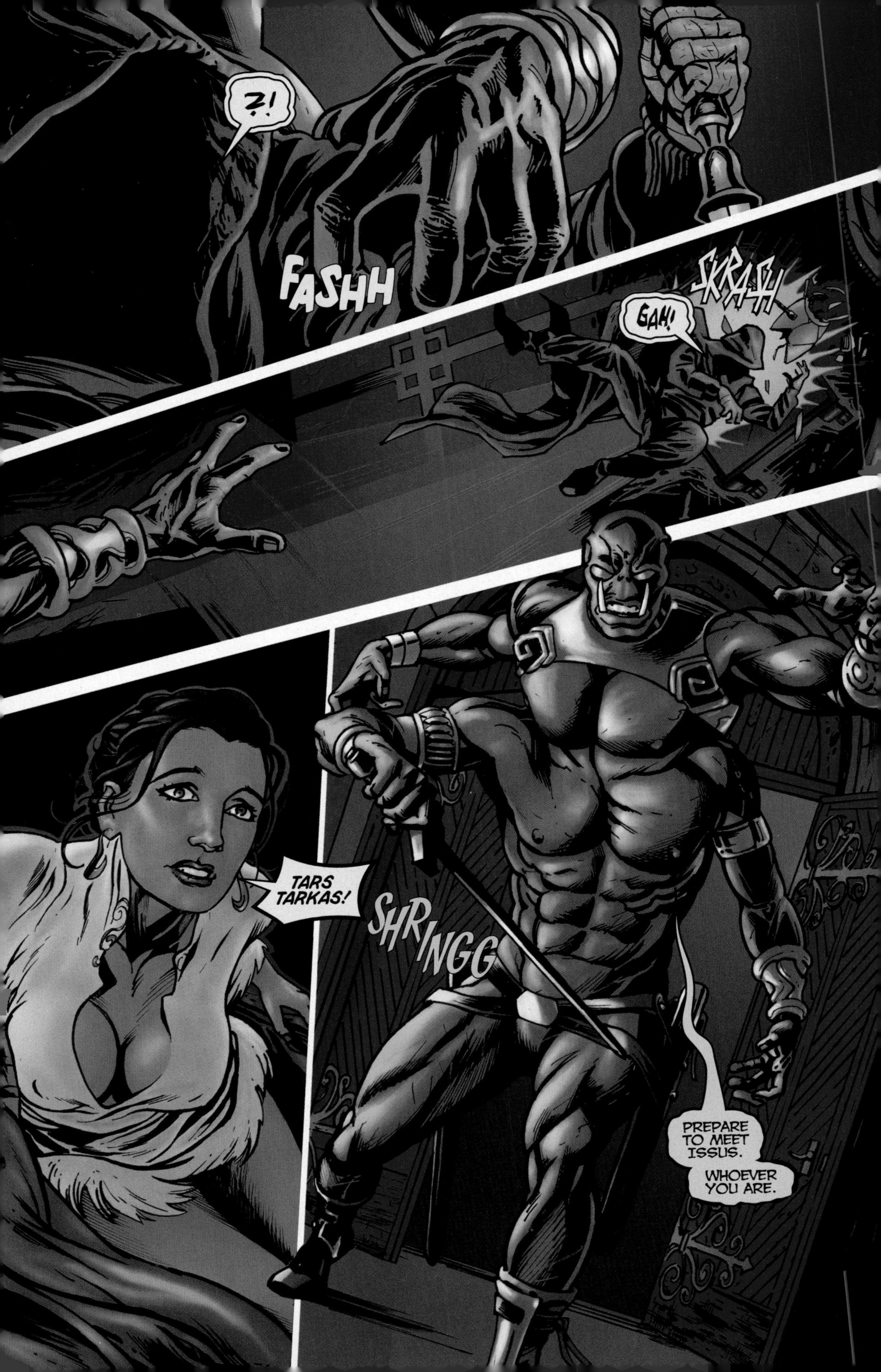
?!
FASHH
SKRASH
GAH!
TARS TARKAS!
SHRINGG
PREPARE TO MEET ISSUS.
WHOEVER YOU ARE.

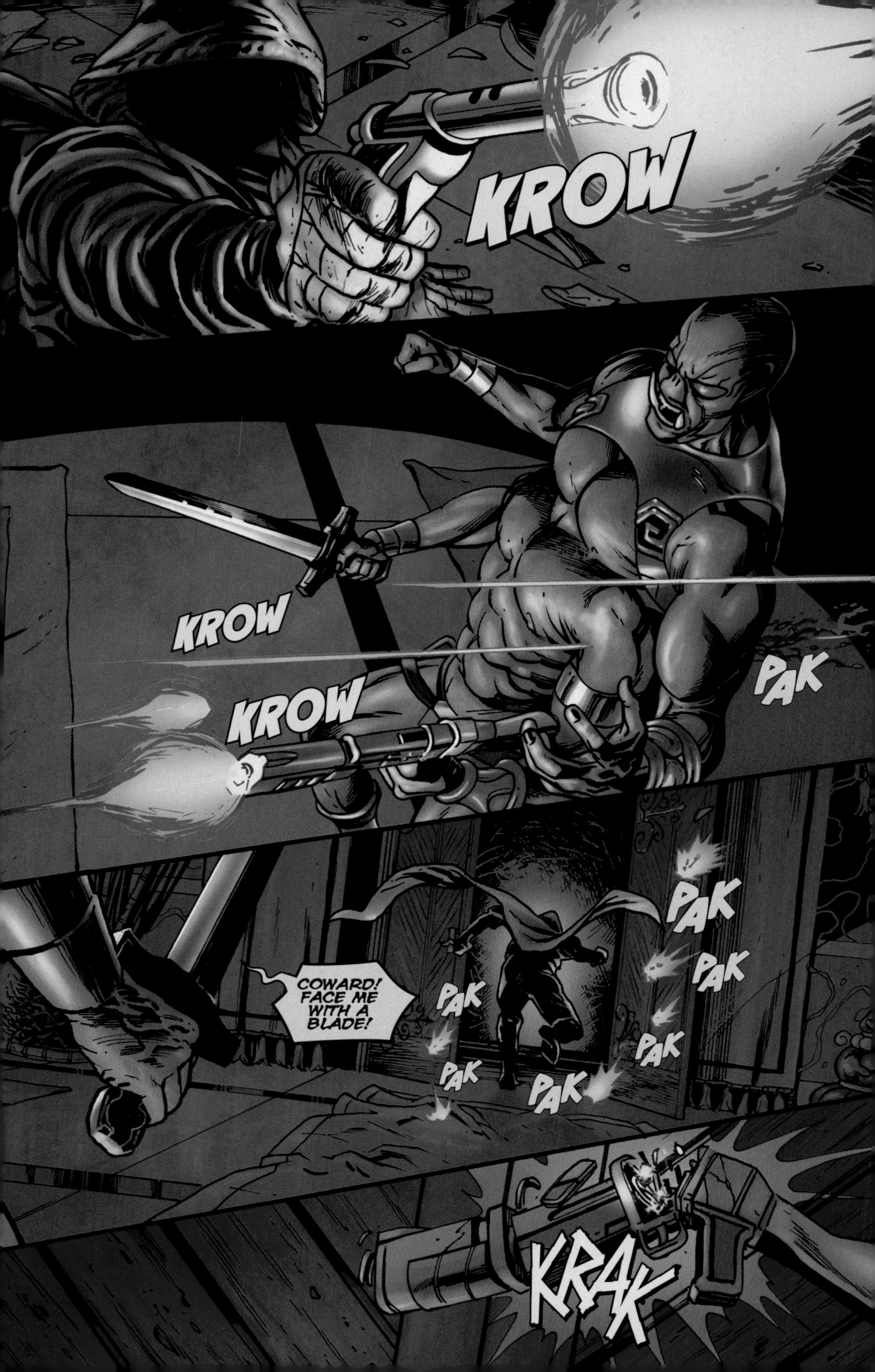
KROW
KROW
KROW
PAK
COWARD! FACE ME WITH A BLADE!
PAK
PAK
PAK
PAK
PAK
PAK
KRAK

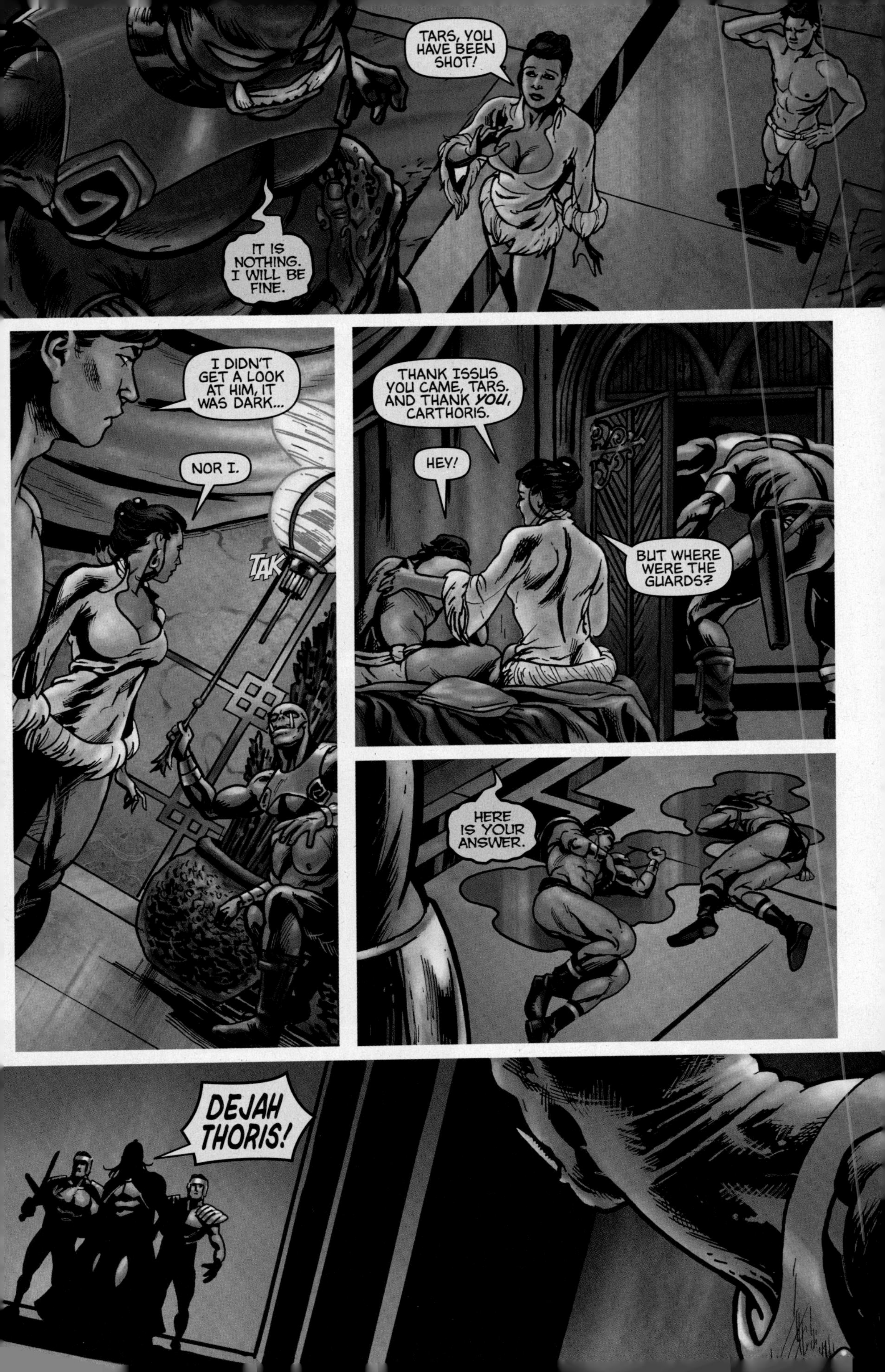
TARS, YOU HAVE BEEN SHOT!
IT IS NOTHING. I WILL BE FINE.
I DIDN'T GET A LOOK AT HIM, IT WAS DARK...
NOR I.
TAK
THANK ISSUS YOU CAME, TARS. AND THANK YOU, CARTHORIS.
HEY!
BUT WHERE WERE THE GUARDS?
HERE IS YOUR ANSWER.
DEJAH THORIS!

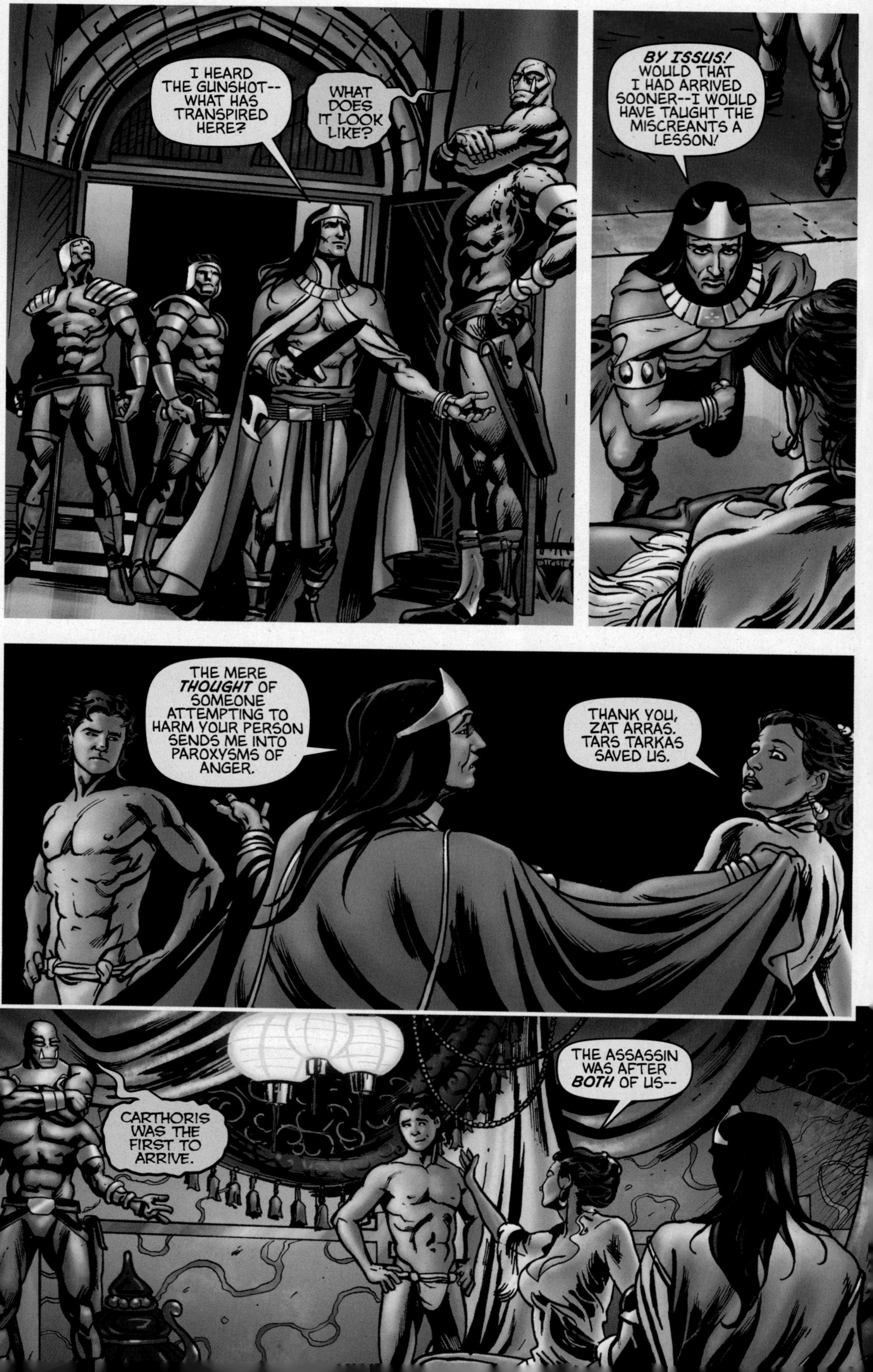

I HEARD THE GUNSHOT-- WHAT HAS TRANSPIRED HERE?
WHAT DOES IT LOOK LIKE?
BY ISSUS! WOULD THAT I HAD ARRIVED SOONER--I WOULD HAVE TAUGHT THE MISCREANTS A LESSON!
THE MERE *THOUGHT* OF SOMEONE ATTEMPTING TO HARM YOUR PERSON SENDS ME INTO PAROXYSMS OF ANGER.
THANK YOU, ZAT ARRAS. TARS TARKAS SAVED US.
CARTHORIS WAS THE FIRST TO ARRIVE.
THE ASSASSIN WAS AFTER *BOTH* OF US--

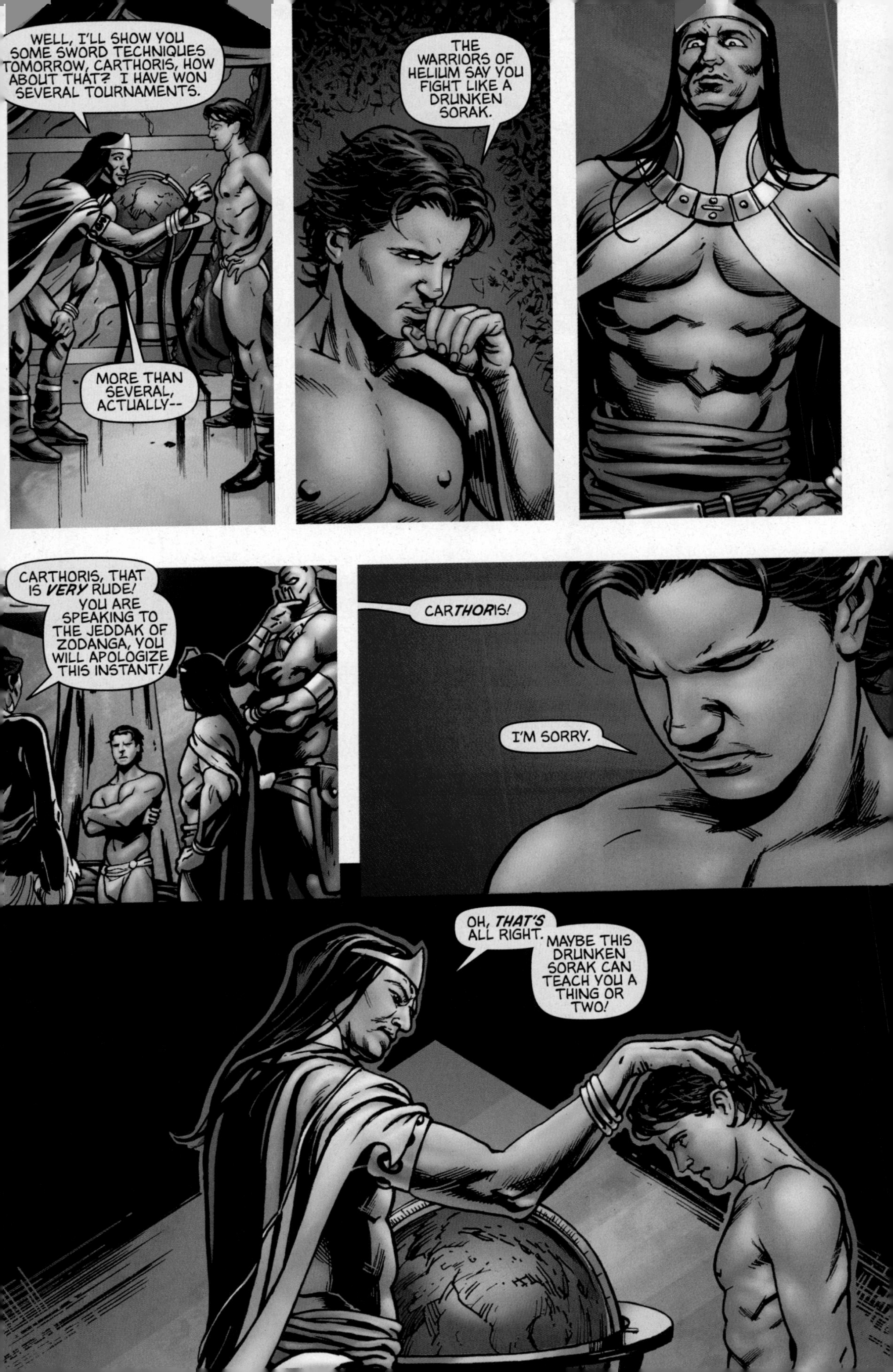
WELL, I'LL SHOW YOU SOME SWORD TECHNIQUES TOMORROW, CARTHORIS, HOW ABOUT THAT? I HAVE WON SEVERAL TOURNAMENTS.
MORE THAN SEVERAL, ACTUALLY--
THE WARRIORS OF HELIUM SAY YOU FIGHT LIKE A DRUNKEN SORAK.
CARTHORIS, THAT IS ***VERY*** RUDE! YOU ARE SPEAKING TO THE JEDDAK OF ZODANGA, YOU WILL APOLOGIZE THIS INSTANT!
CAR***THOR***IS!
I'M SORRY.
OH, ***THAT'S*** ALL RIGHT.
MAYBE THIS DRUNKEN SORAK CAN TEACH YOU A THING OR TWO!

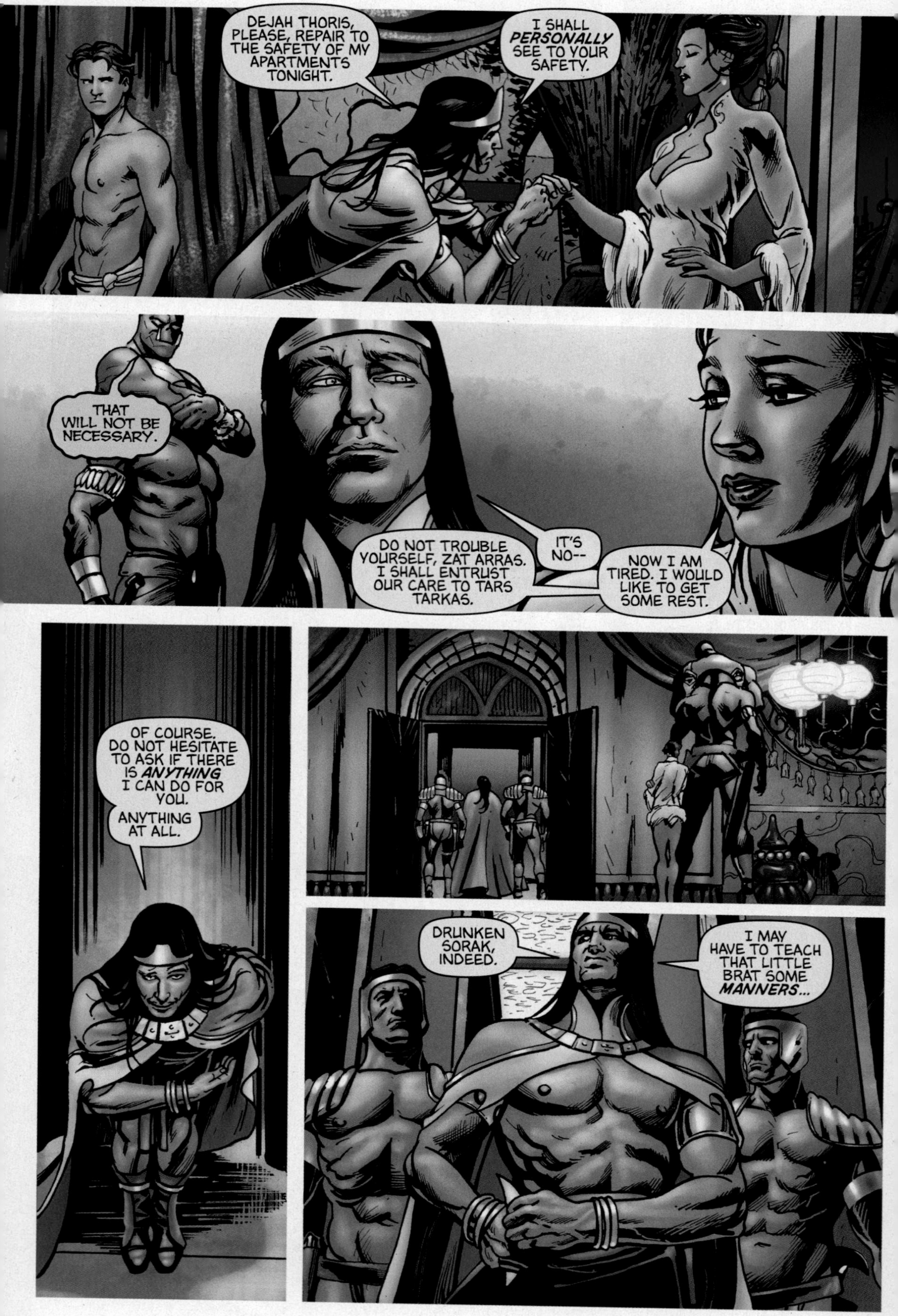
DEJAH THORIS, PLEASE, REPAIR TO THE SAFETY OF MY APARTMENTS TONIGHT.
I SHALL PERSONALLY SEE TO YOUR SAFETY.
THAT WILL NOT BE NECESSARY.
IT'S NO--
DO NOT TROUBLE YOURSELF, ZAT ARRAS. I SHALL ENTRUST OUR CARE TO TARS TARKAS.
NOW I AM TIRED. I WOULD LIKE TO GET SOME REST.
OF COURSE. DO NOT HESITATE TO ASK IF THERE IS ANYTHING I CAN DO FOR YOU.
ANYTHING AT ALL.
DRUNKEN SORAK, INDEED.
I MAY HAVE TO TEACH THAT LITTLE BRAT SOME MANNERS...

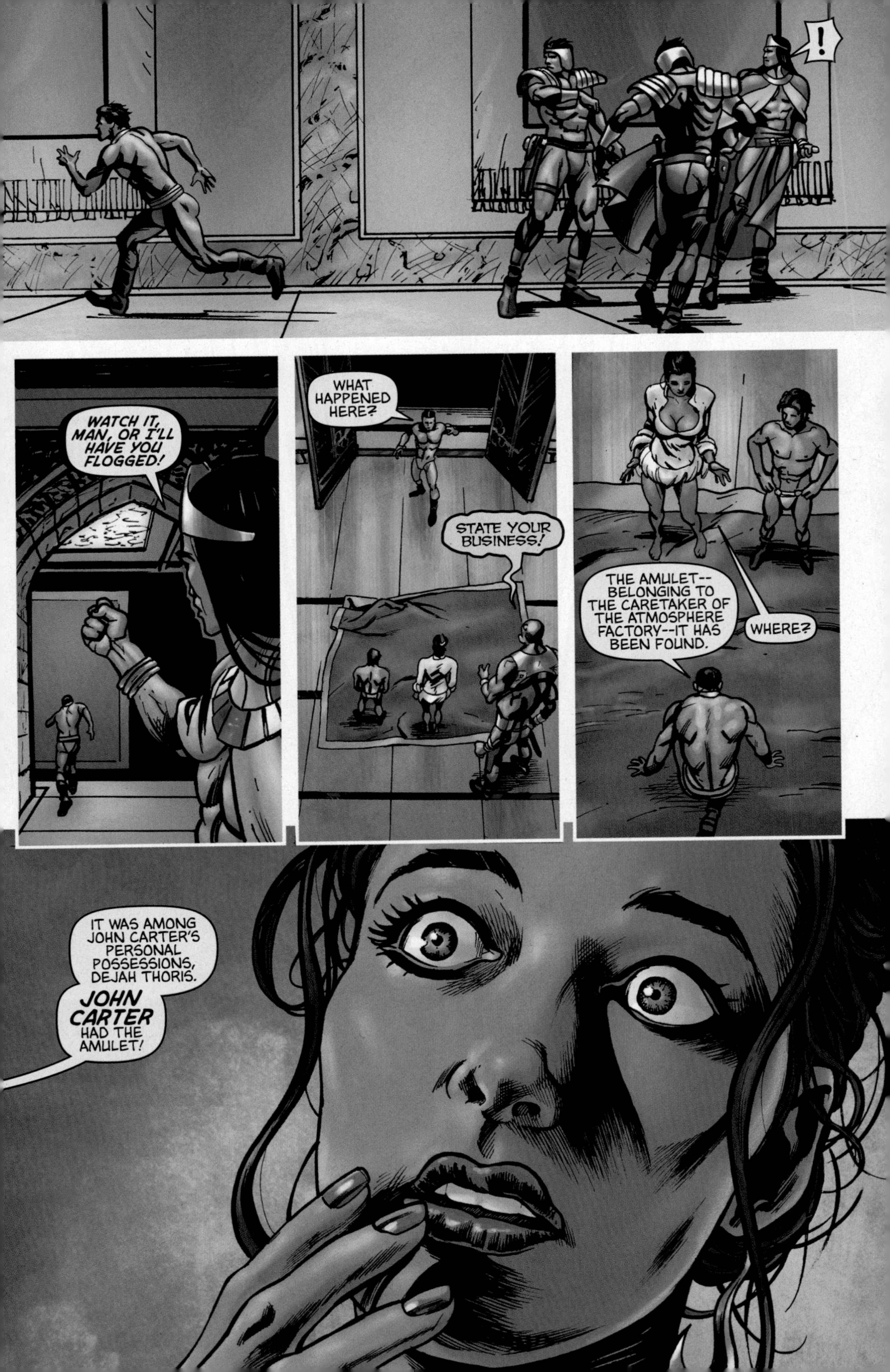
!
WATCH IT, MAN, OR I'LL HAVE YOU FLOGGED!
WHAT HAPPENED HERE?
STATE YOUR BUSINESS!
THE AMULET-- BELONGING TO THE CARETAKER OF THE ATMOSPHERE FACTORY--IT HAS BEEN FOUND.
WHERE?
IT WAS AMONG JOHN CARTER'S PERSONAL POSSESSIONS, DEJAH THORIS.
JOHN CARTER HAD THE AMULET!

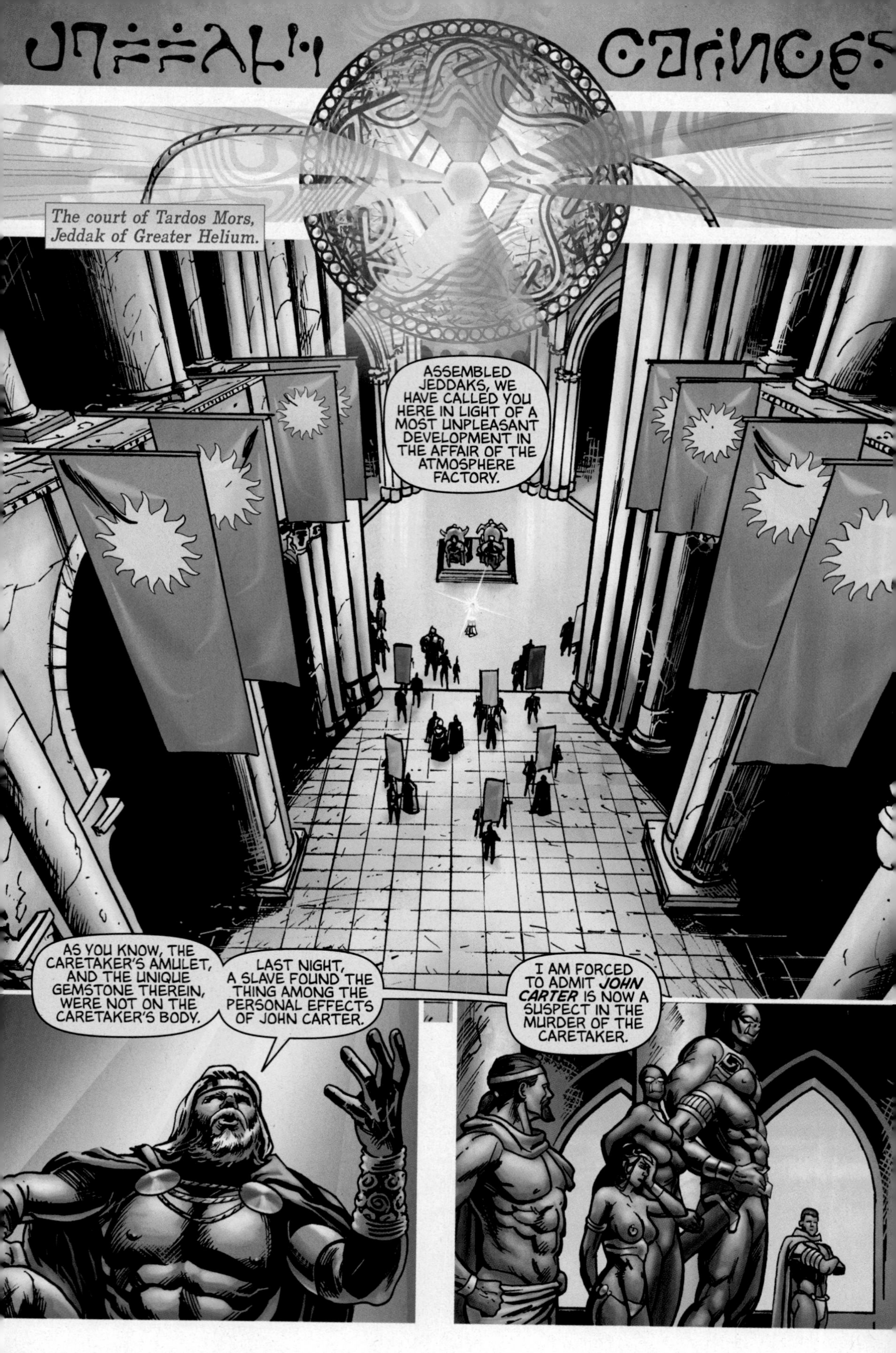
The court of Tardos Mors, Jeddak of Greater Helium.
ASSEMBLED JEDDAKS, WE HAVE CALLED YOU HERE IN LIGHT OF A MOST UNPLEASANT DEVELOPMENT IN THE AFFAIR OF THE ATMOSPHERE FACTORY.
AS YOU KNOW, THE CARETAKER'S AMULET, AND THE UNIQUE GEMSTONE THEREIN, WERE NOT ON THE CARETAKER'S BODY.
LAST NIGHT, A SLAVE FOUND THE THING AMONG THE PERSONAL EFFECTS OF JOHN CARTER.
I AM FORCED TO ADMIT *JOHN CARTER* IS NOW A SUSPECT IN THE MURDER OF THE CARETAKER.

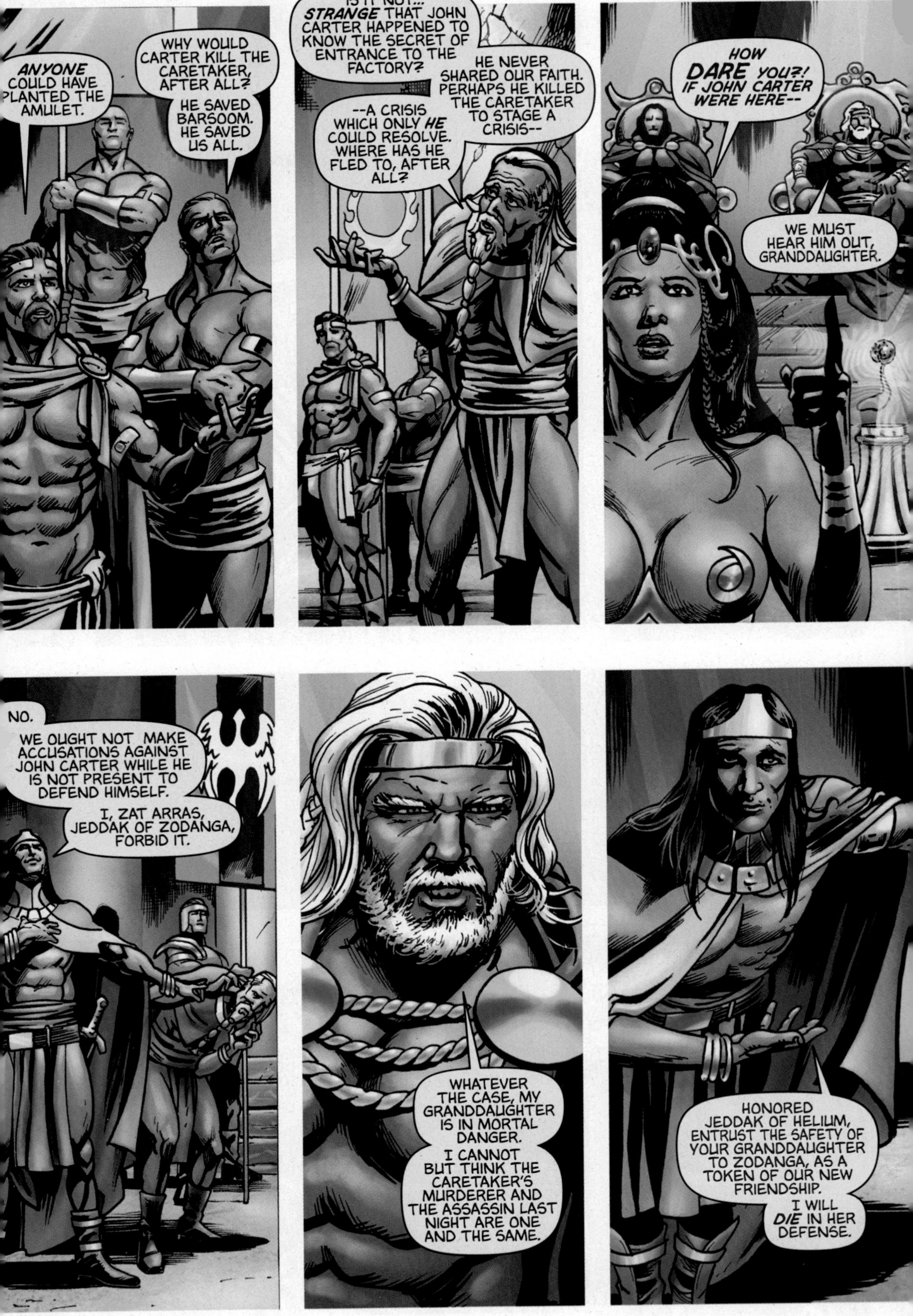
ANYONE COULD HAVE PLANTED THE AMULET.
WHY WOULD CARTER KILL THE CARETAKER, AFTER ALL?
HE SAVED BARSOOM. HE SAVED US ALL.
IS IT NOT... STRANGE THAT JOHN CARTER HAPPENED TO KNOW THE SECRET OF ENTRANCE TO THE FACTORY?
HE NEVER SHARED OUR FAITH. PERHAPS HE KILLED THE CARETAKER TO STAGE A CRISIS--
--A CRISIS WHICH ONLY HE COULD RESOLVE. WHERE HAS HE FLED TO, AFTER ALL?
HOW DARE YOU?! IF JOHN CARTER WERE HERE--
WE MUST HEAR HIM OUT, GRANDDAUGHTER.
NO.
WE OUGHT NOT MAKE ACCUSATIONS AGAINST JOHN CARTER WHILE HE IS NOT PRESENT TO DEFEND HIMSELF.
I, ZAT ARRAS, JEDDAK OF ZODANGA, FORBID IT.
WHATEVER THE CASE, MY GRANDDAUGHTER IS IN MORTAL DANGER.
I CANNOT BUT THINK THE CARETAKER'S MURDERER AND THE ASSASSIN LAST NIGHT ARE ONE AND THE SAME.
HONORED JEDDAK OF HELIUM, ENTRUST THE SAFETY OF YOUR GRANDDAUGHTER TO ZODANGA, AS A TOKEN OF OUR NEW FRIENDSHIP.
I WILL DIE IN HER DEFENSE.

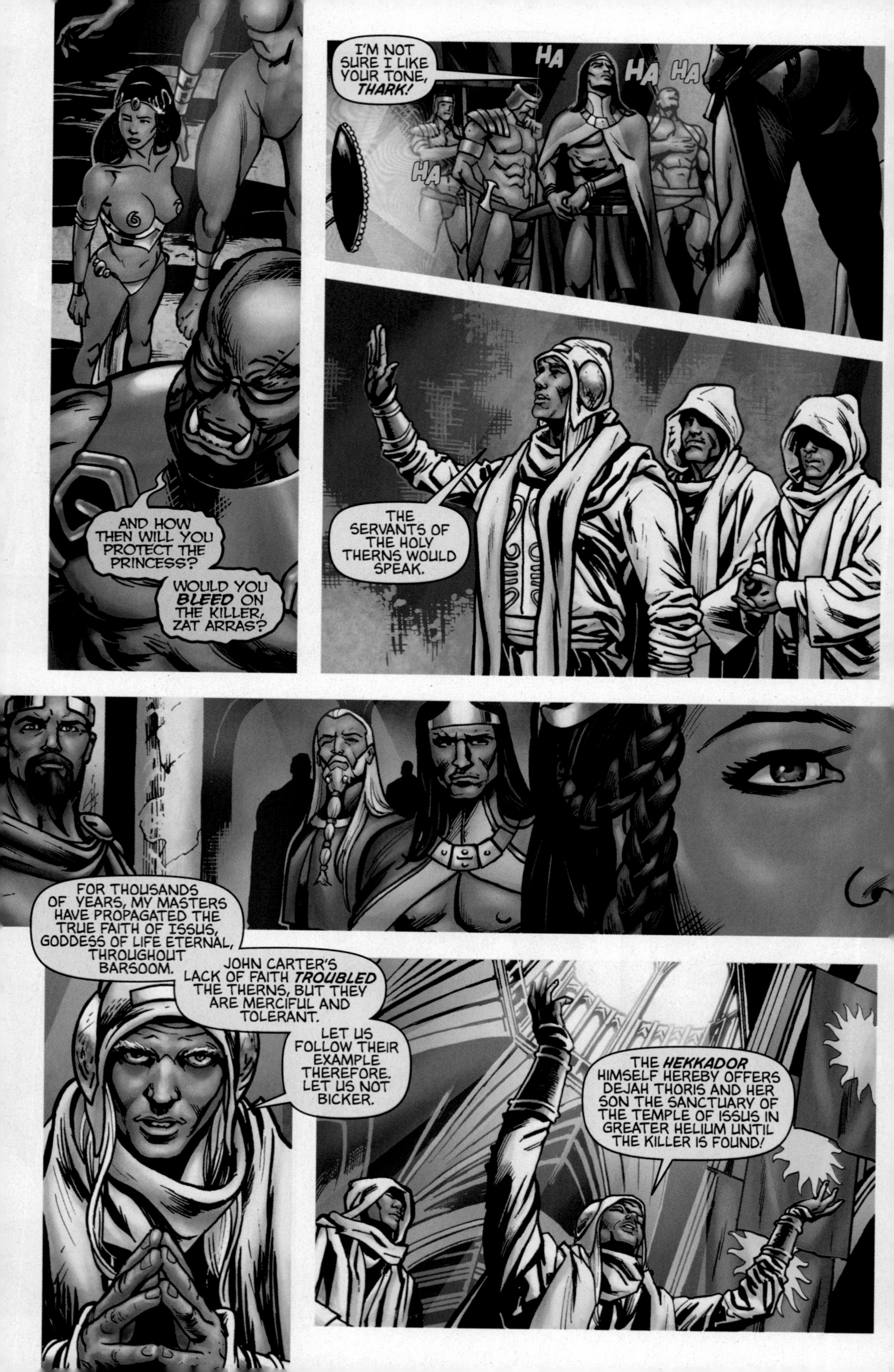

AND HOW THEN WILL YOU PROTECT THE PRINCESS?
WOULD YOU BLEED ON THE KILLER, ZAT ARRAS?
I'M NOT SURE I LIKE YOUR TONE, THARK!
HA
HA
HA
HA
THE SERVANTS OF THE HOLY THERNS WOULD SPEAK.
FOR THOUSANDS OF YEARS, MY MASTERS HAVE PROPAGATED THE TRUE FAITH OF ISSUS, GODDESS OF LIFE ETERNAL, THROUGHOUT BARSOOM.
JOHN CARTER'S LACK OF FAITH TROUBLED THE THERNS, BUT THEY ARE MERCIFUL AND TOLERANT.
LET US FOLLOW THEIR EXAMPLE THEREFORE. LET US NOT BICKER.
THE HEKKADOR HIMSELF HEREBY OFFERS DEJAH THORIS AND HER SON THE SANCTUARY OF THE TEMPLE OF ISSUS IN GREATER HELIUM UNTIL THE KILLER IS FOUND!

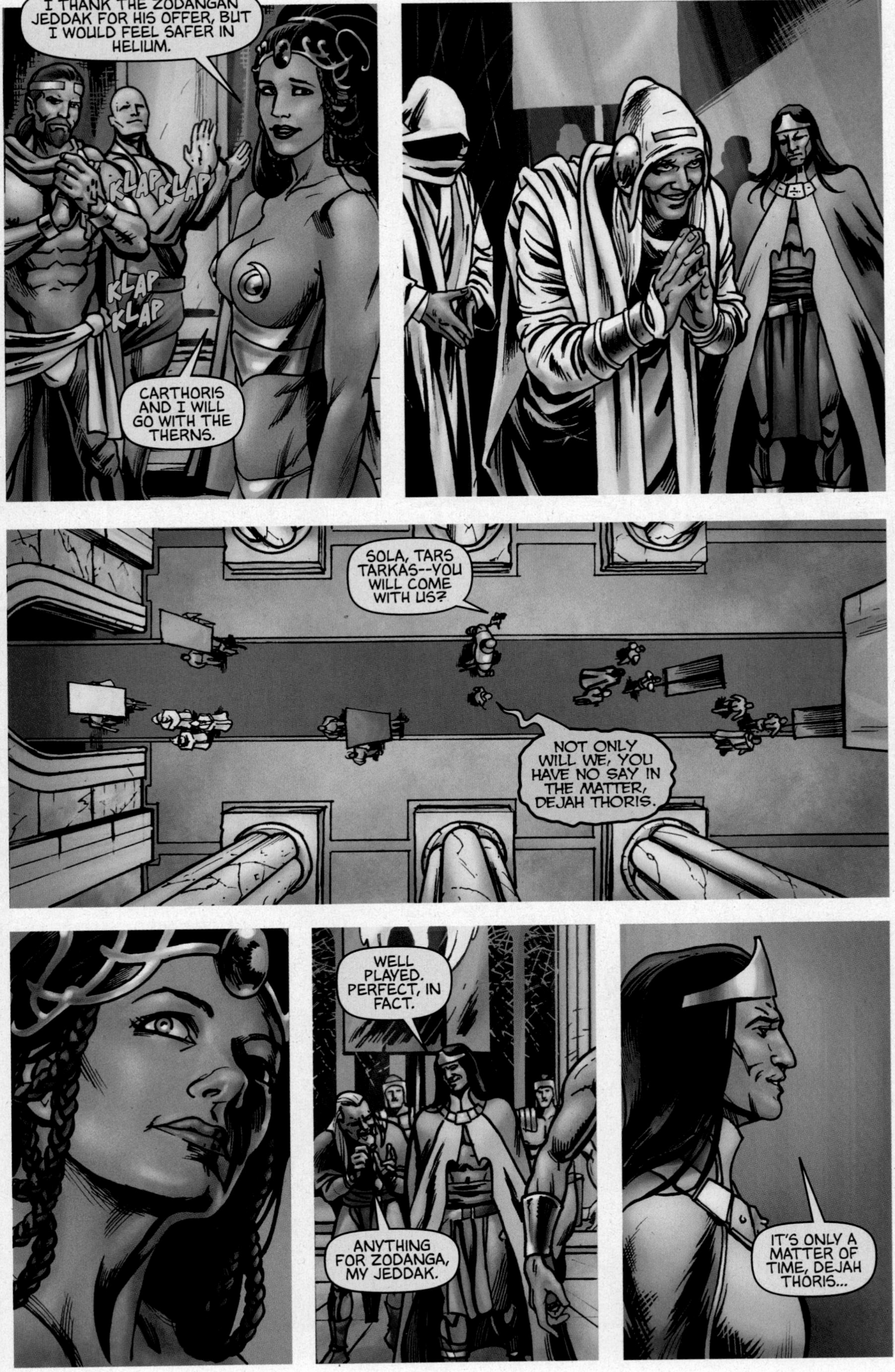
I THANK THE ZODANGAN JEDDAK FOR HIS OFFER, BUT I WOULD FEEL SAFER IN HELIUM.
KLAP KLAP
KLAP KLAP
CARTHORIS AND I WILL GO WITH THE THERNS.
SOLA, TARS TARKAS--YOU WILL COME WITH US?
NOT ONLY WILL WE, YOU HAVE NO SAY IN THE MATTER, DEJAH THORIS.
WELL PLAYED. PERFECT, IN FACT.
ANYTHING FOR ZODANGA, MY JEDDAK.
IT'S ONLY A MATTER OF TIME, DEJAH THORIS...

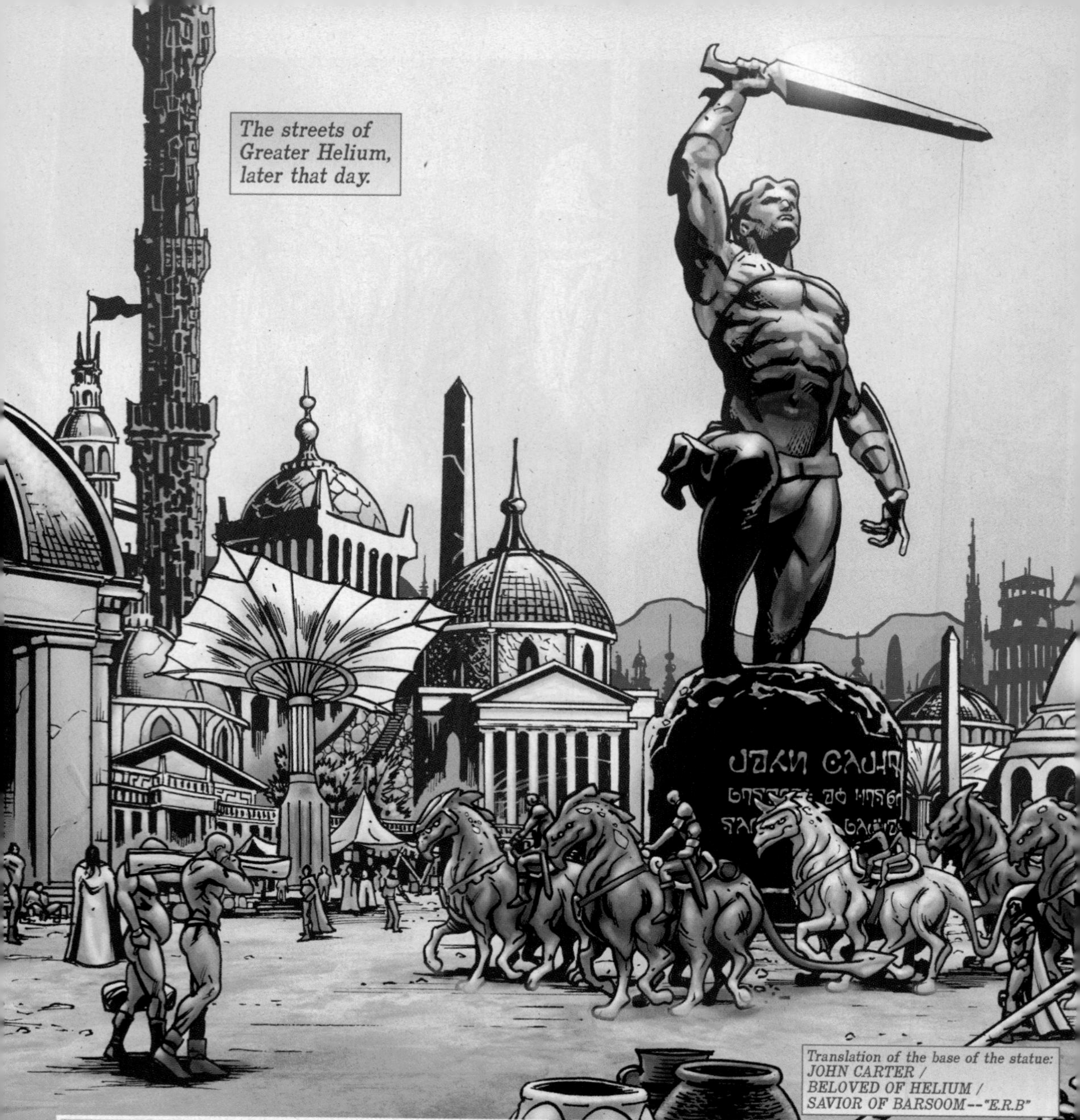
The streets of Greater Helium, later that day.
Translation of the base of the statue: JOHN CARTER / BELOVED OF HELIUM / SAVIOR OF BARSOOM--"E.R.B"

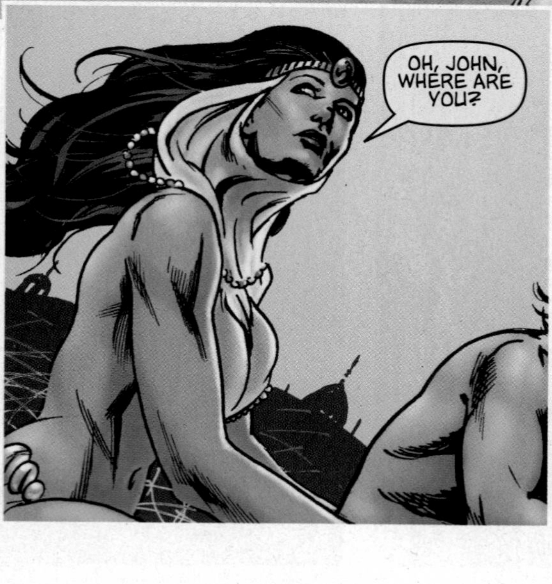
OH, JOHN, WHERE ARE YOU?

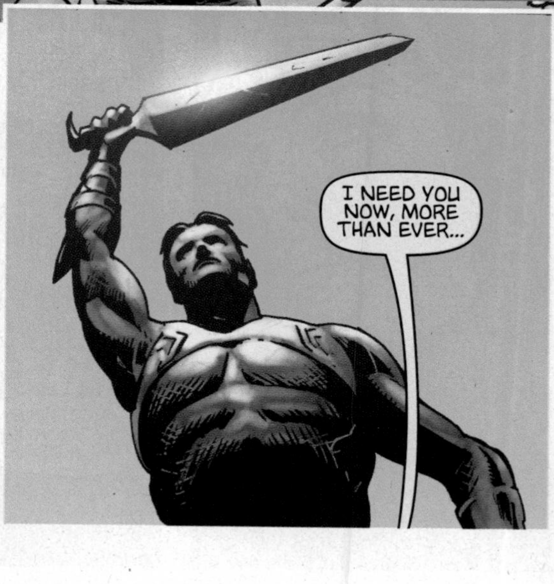
I NEED YOU NOW, MORE THAN EVER...

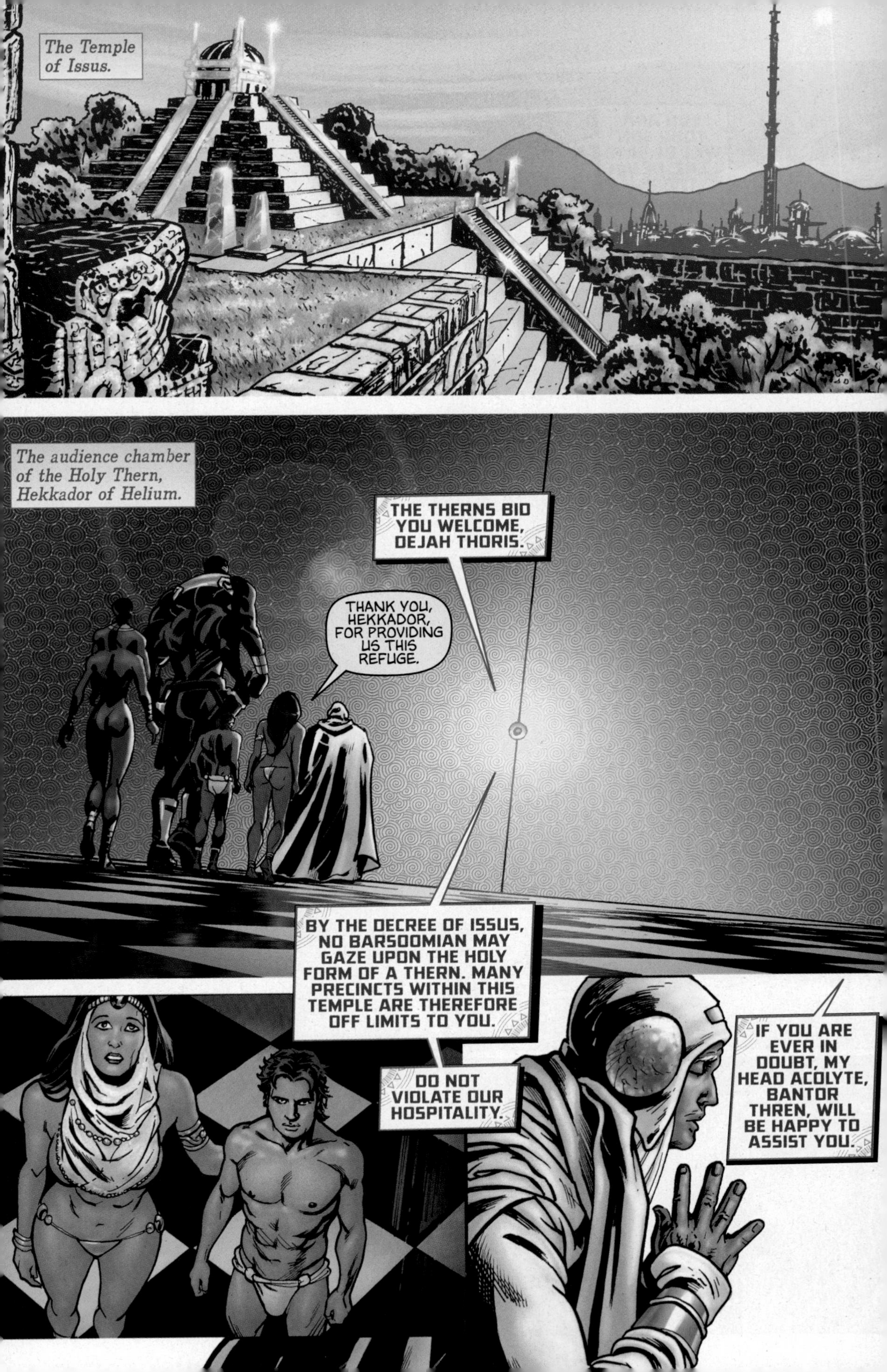
The Temple of Issus.
The audience chamber of the Holy Thern, Hekkador of Helium.
THE THERNS BID YOU WELCOME, DEJAH THORIS.
THANK YOU, HEKKADOR, FOR PROVIDING US THIS REFUGE.
BY THE DECREE OF ISSUS, NO BARSOOMIAN MAY GAZE UPON THE HOLY FORM OF A THERN. MANY PRECINCTS WITHIN THIS TEMPLE ARE THEREFORE OFF LIMITS TO YOU.
DO NOT VIOLATE OUR HOSPITALITY.
IF YOU ARE EVER IN DOUBT, MY HEAD ACOLYTE, BANTOR THREN, WILL BE HAPPY TO ASSIST YOU.

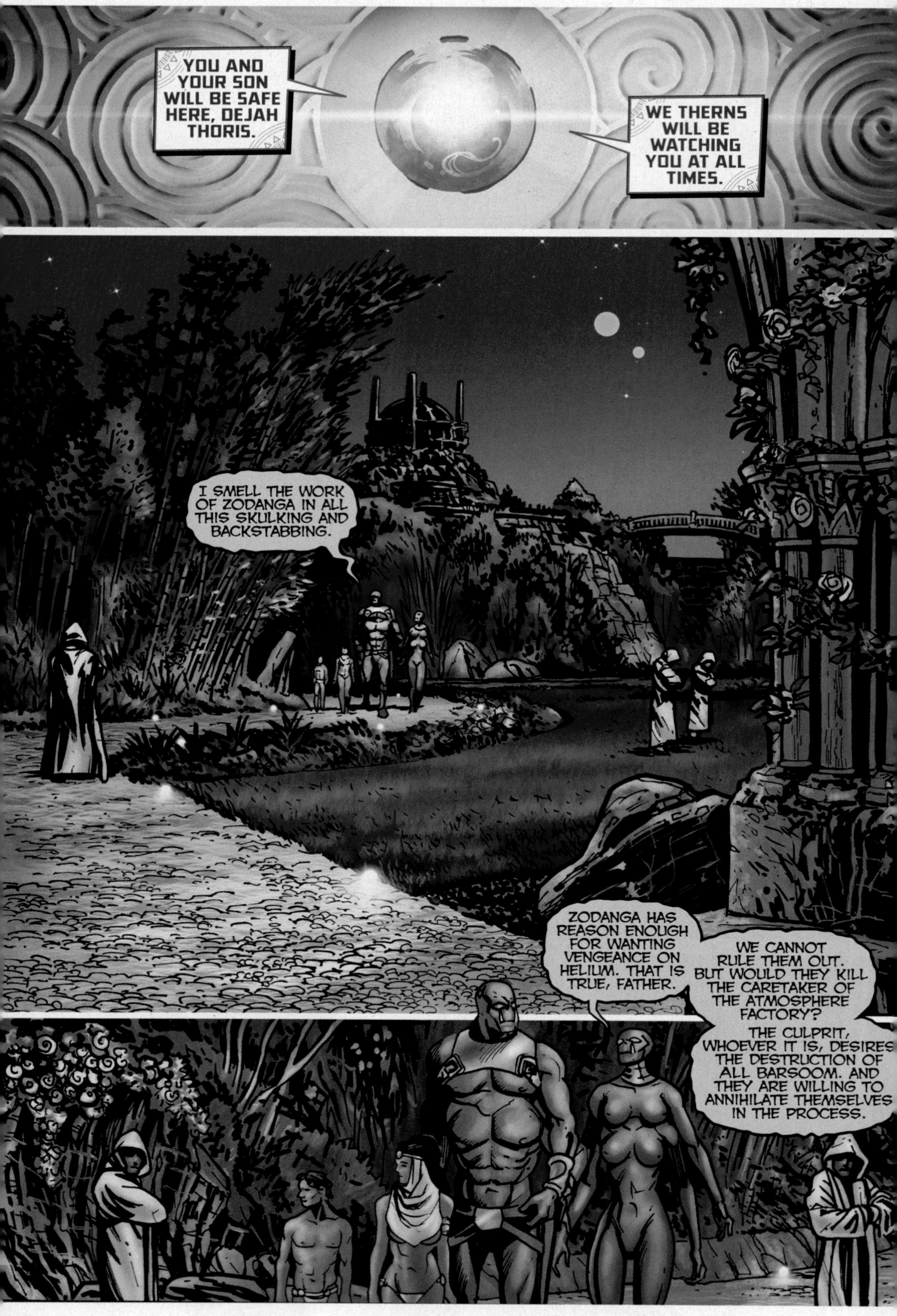
YOU AND YOUR SON WILL BE SAFE HERE, DEJAH THORIS.
WE THERNS WILL BE WATCHING YOU AT ALL TIMES.
I SMELL THE WORK OF ZODANGA IN ALL THIS SKULKING AND BACKSTABBING.
ZODANGA HAS REASON ENOUGH FOR WANTING VENGEANCE ON HELIUM. THAT IS TRUE, FATHER.
WE CANNOT RULE THEM OUT. BUT WOULD THEY KILL THE CARETAKER OF THE ATMOSPHERE FACTORY?
THE CULPRIT, WHOEVER IT IS, DESIRES THE DESTRUCTION OF ALL BARSOOM. AND THEY ARE WILLING TO ANNIHILATE THEMSELVES IN THE PROCESS.

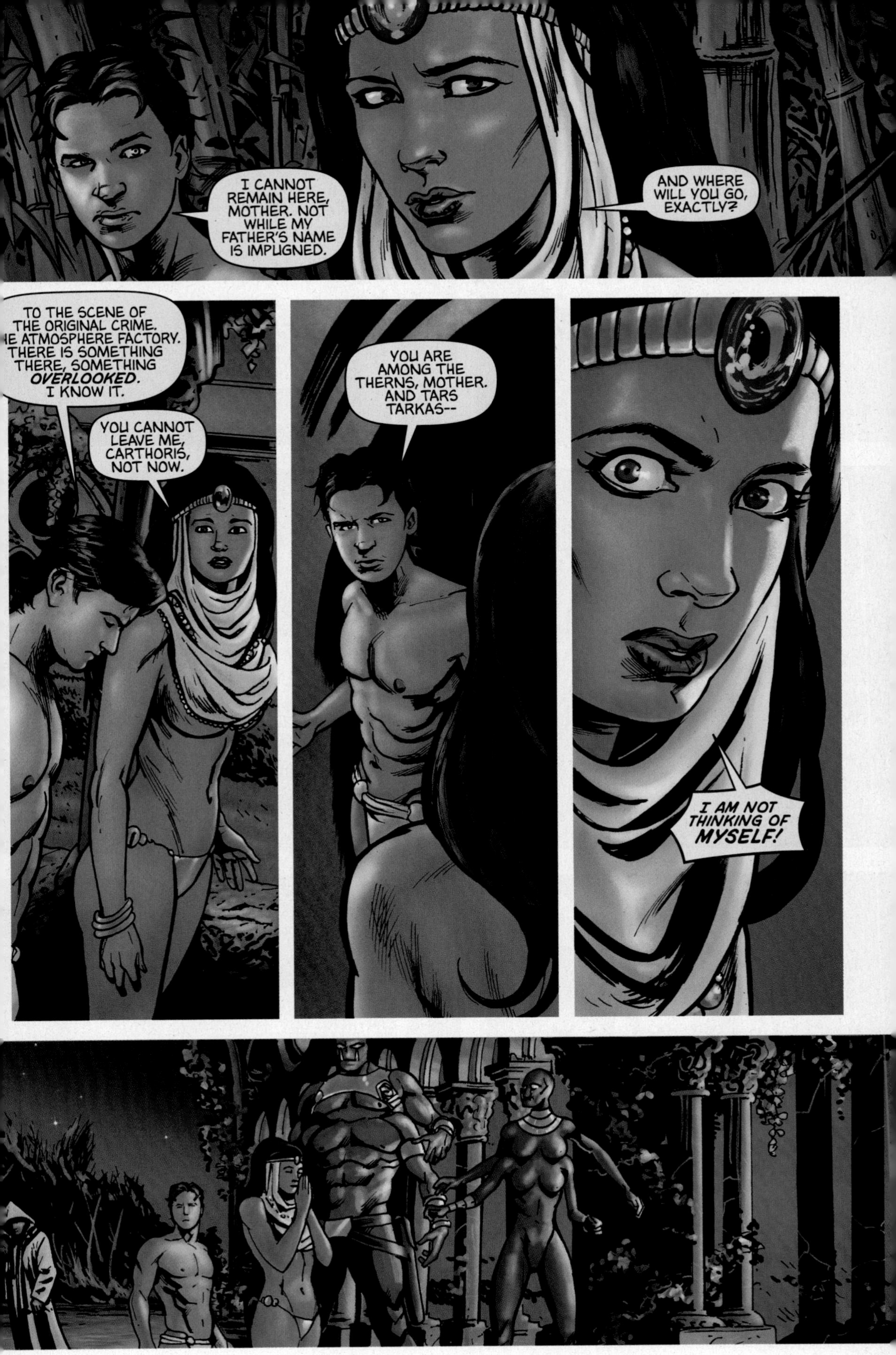
I CANNOT REMAIN HERE, MOTHER. NOT WHILE MY FATHER'S NAME IS IMPUGNED.
AND WHERE WILL YOU GO, EXACTLY?
TO THE SCENE OF THE ORIGINAL CRIME. HE ATMOSPHERE FACTORY. THERE IS SOMETHING THERE, SOMETHING OVERLOOKED. I KNOW IT.
YOU CANNOT LEAVE ME, CARTHORIS, NOT NOW.
YOU ARE AMONG THE THERNS, MOTHER. AND TARS TARKAS--
I AM NOT THINKING OF MYSELF!

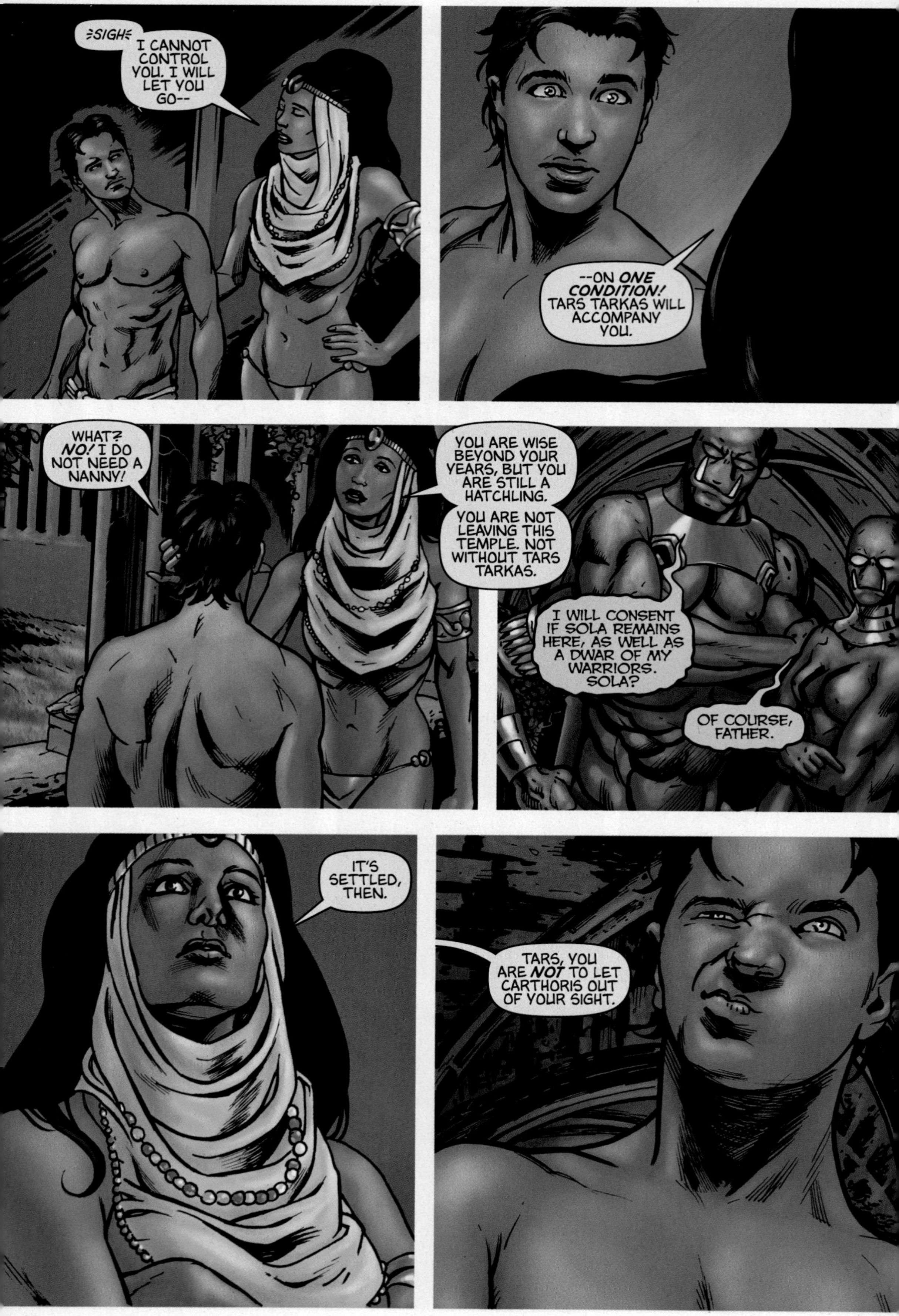

SIGH
I CANNOT CONTROL YOU. I WILL LET YOU GO--
--ON ONE CONDITION! TARS TARKAS WILL ACCOMPANY YOU.
WHAT? NO! I DO NOT NEED A NANNY!
YOU ARE WISE BEYOND YOUR YEARS, BUT YOU ARE STILL A HATCHLING.
YOU ARE NOT LEAVING THIS TEMPLE. NOT WITHOUT TARS TARKAS.
I WILL CONSENT IF SOLA REMAINS HERE, AS WELL AS A DWAR OF MY WARRIORS. SOLA?
OF COURSE, FATHER.
IT'S SETTLED, THEN.
TARS, YOU ARE NOT TO LET CARTHORIS OUT OF YOUR SIGHT.

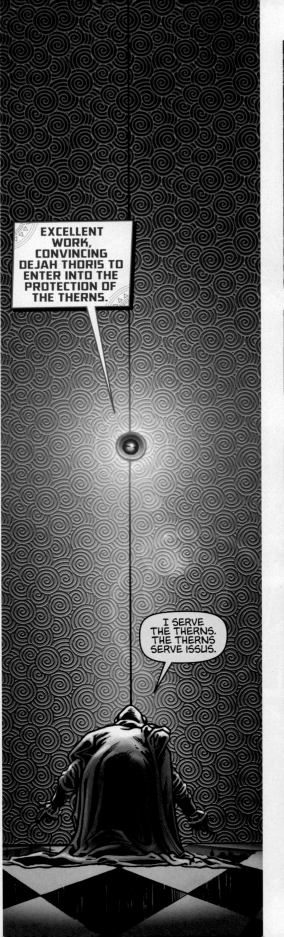

EXCELLENT WORK, CONVINCING DEJAH THORIS TO ENTER INTO THE PROTECTION OF THE THERNS.

I SERVE THE THERNS. THE THERNS SERVE ISSUS.

MATAI SHANG, THE FATHER OF THE THERNS, HAS TAKEN AN INTEREST IN THE HELIUM PRINCESS.

HE MAY ASK HER TO JOIN HIM IN THE PARADISE OF THE VALLEY DOR.

I WILL SELECT YOU TO DELIVER THE TIDINGS SHOULD THAT COME TO BE.

I AM UNWORTHY OF SUCH AN HONOR!

YOU HAVE SERVED ME WELL, BANTOR THREN. SOON, IT WILL BE YOUR TIME TO TRAVEL UPON THE ISS AND KNOW THE PARADISE OF DOR.

HOLY HEKKADOR, I HAVE NO GREATER DESIRE.

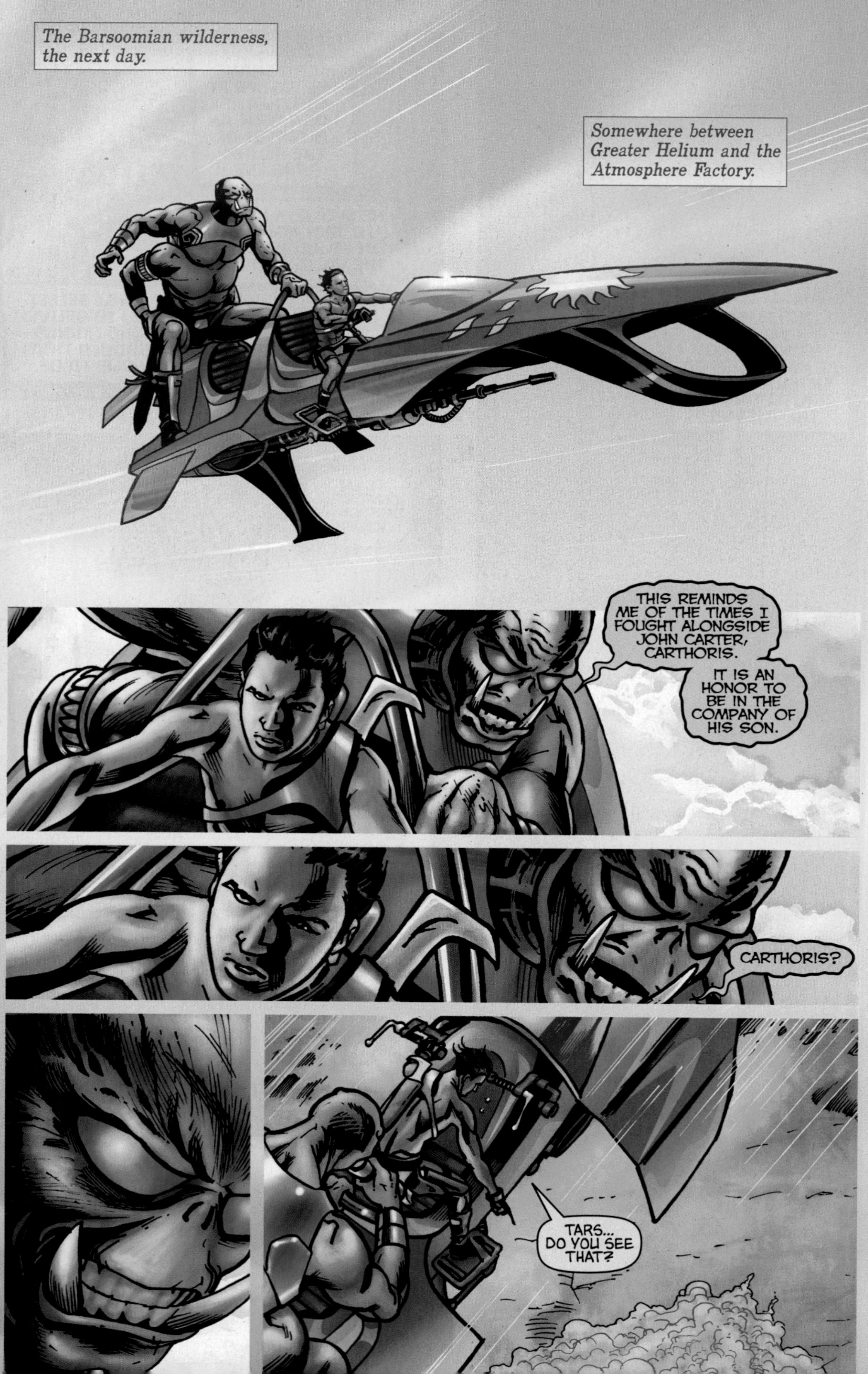
The Barsoomian wilderness, the next day.
Somewhere between Greater Helium and the Atmosphere Factory.
THIS REMINDS ME OF THE TIMES I FOUGHT ALONGSIDE JOHN CARTER, CARTHORIS.
IT IS AN HONOR TO BE IN THE COMPANY OF HIS SON.
CARTHORIS?
TARS... DO YOU SEE THAT?

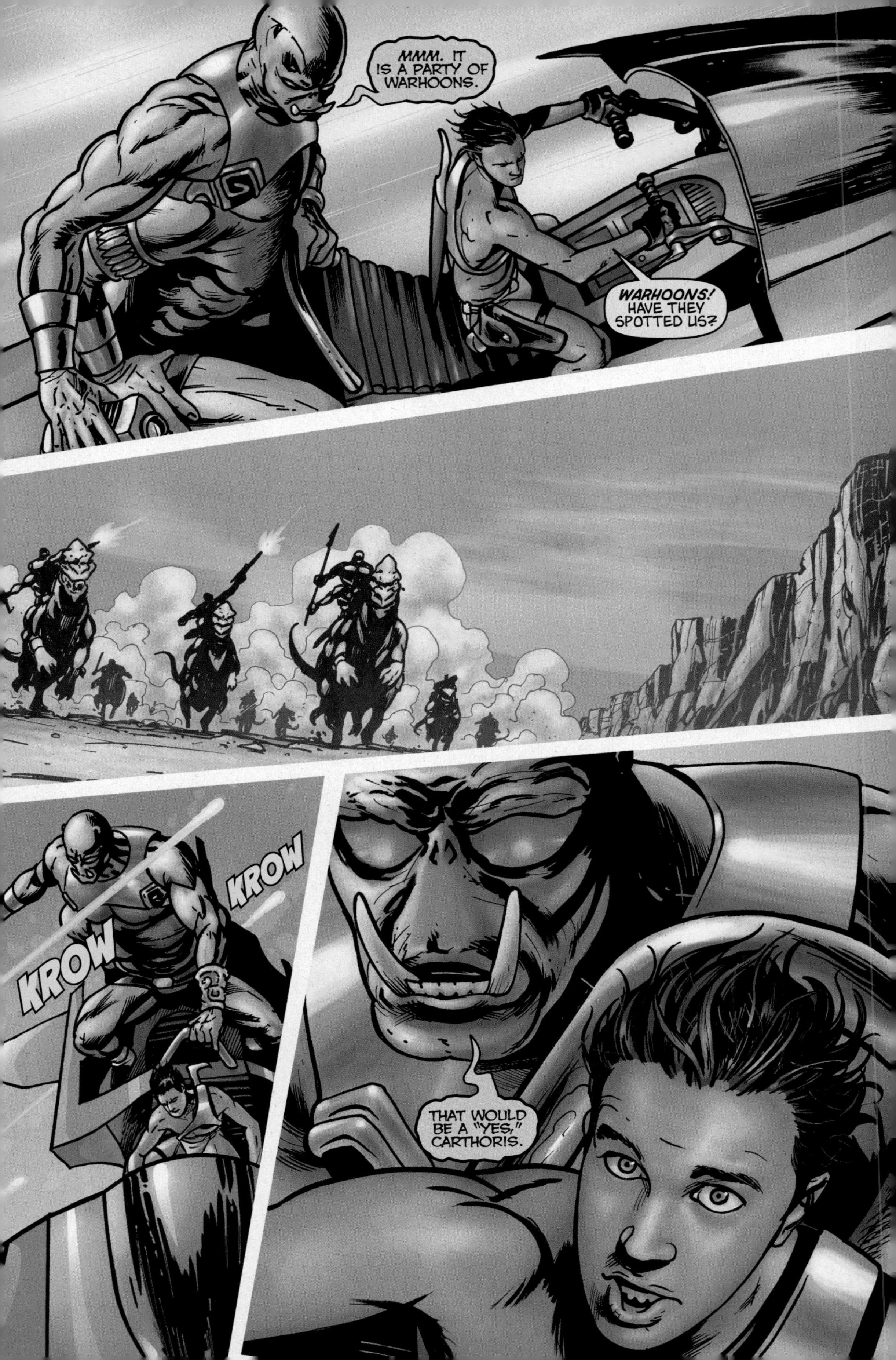
MMM. IT IS A PARTY OF WARHOONS.
WARHOONS! HAVE THEY SPOTTED US?
KROW
KROW
THAT WOULD BE A "YES," CARTHORIS.

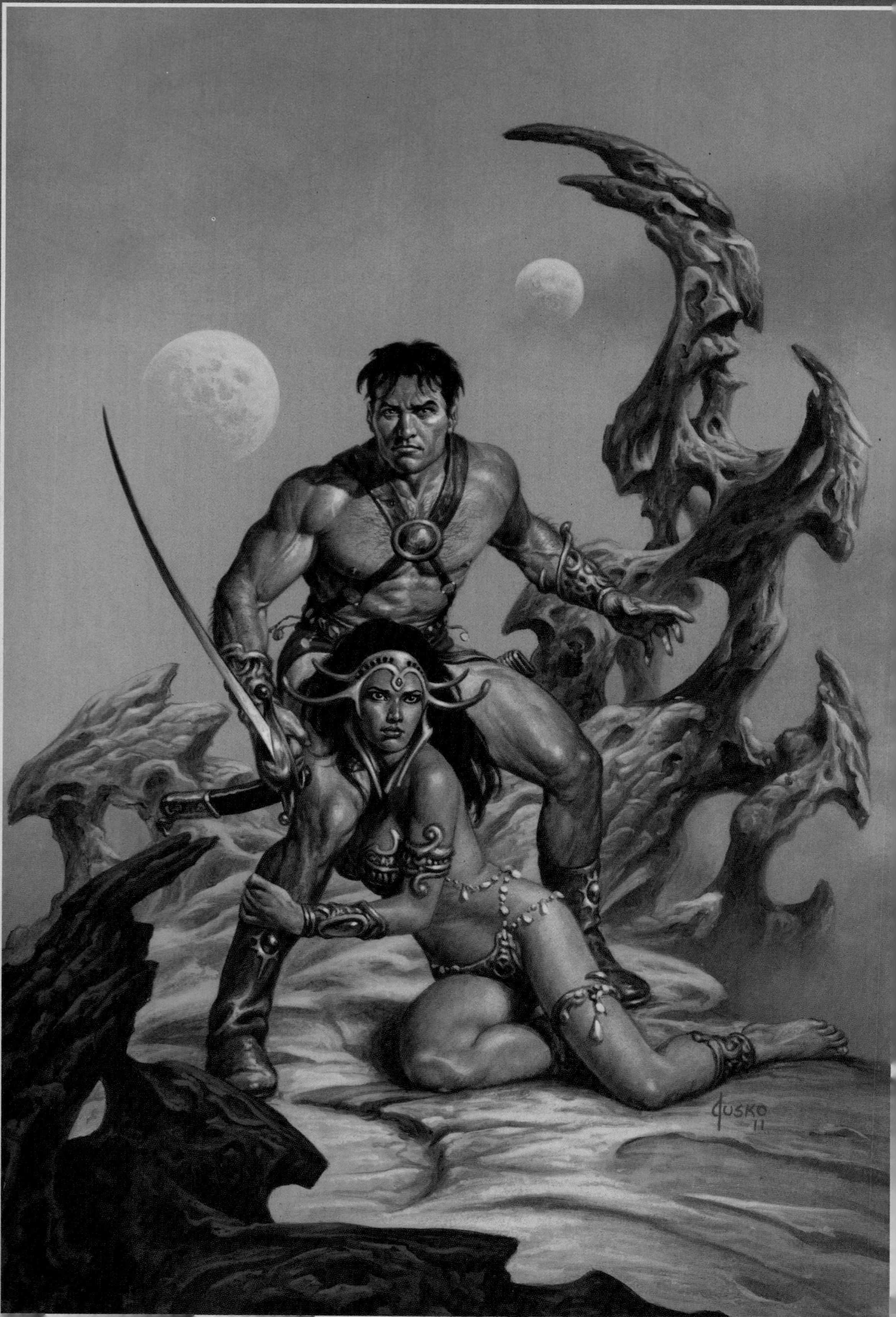
JUSKO

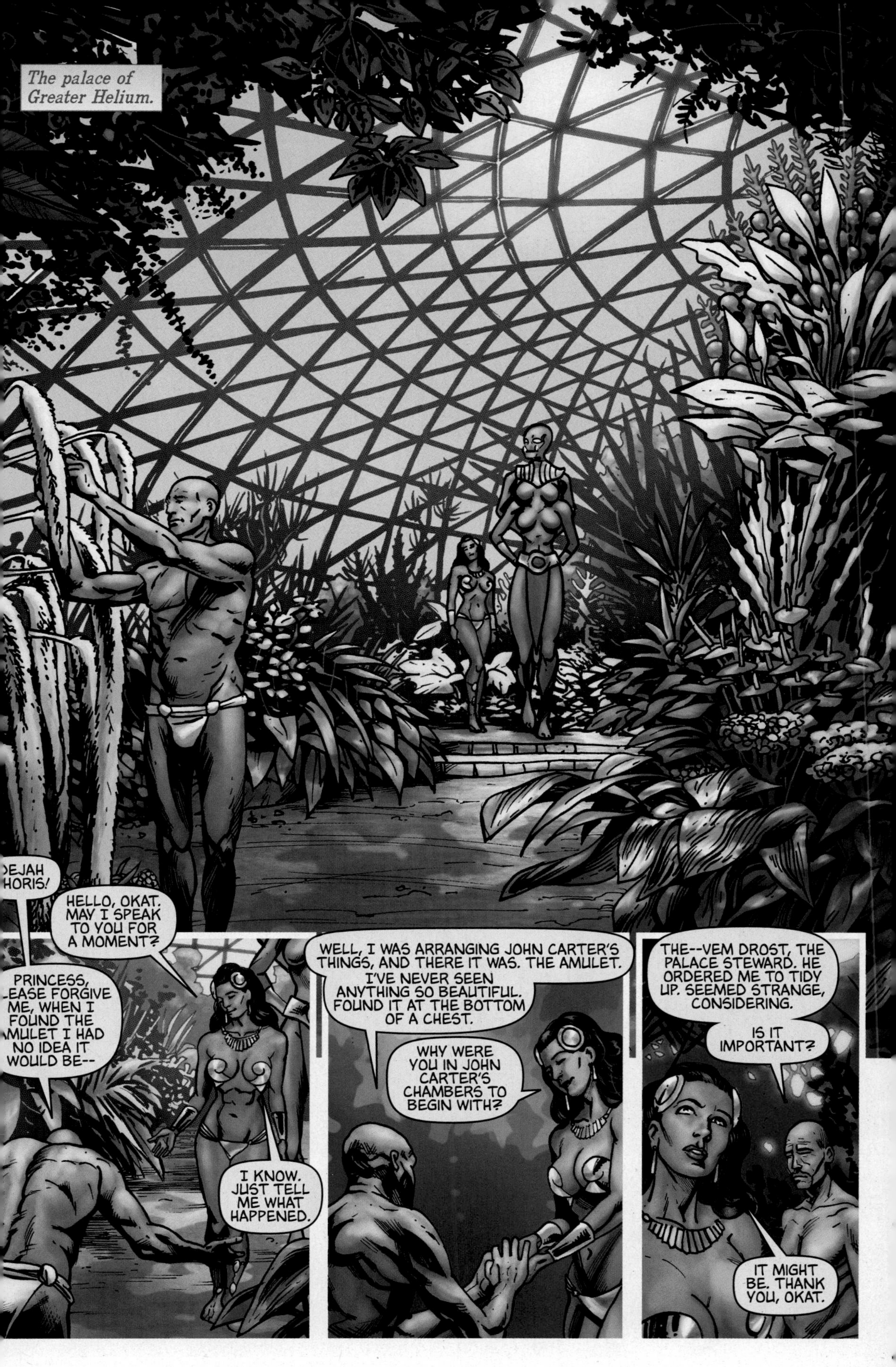
The palace of Greater Helium.
DEJAH THORIS!
HELLO, OKAT. MAY I SPEAK TO YOU FOR A MOMENT?
PRINCESS, PLEASE FORGIVE ME, WHEN I FOUND THE AMULET I HAD NO IDEA IT WOULD BE--
I KNOW. JUST TELL ME WHAT HAPPENED.
WELL, I WAS ARRANGING JOHN CARTER'S THINGS, AND THERE IT WAS. THE AMULET.
I'VE NEVER SEEN ANYTHING SO BEAUTIFUL. FOUND IT AT THE BOTTOM OF A CHEST.
WHY WERE YOU IN JOHN CARTER'S CHAMBERS TO BEGIN WITH?
THE--VEM DROST, THE PALACE STEWARD. HE ORDERED ME TO TIDY UP. SEEMED STRANGE, CONSIDERING.
IS IT IMPORTANT?
IT MIGHT BE. THANK YOU, OKAT.

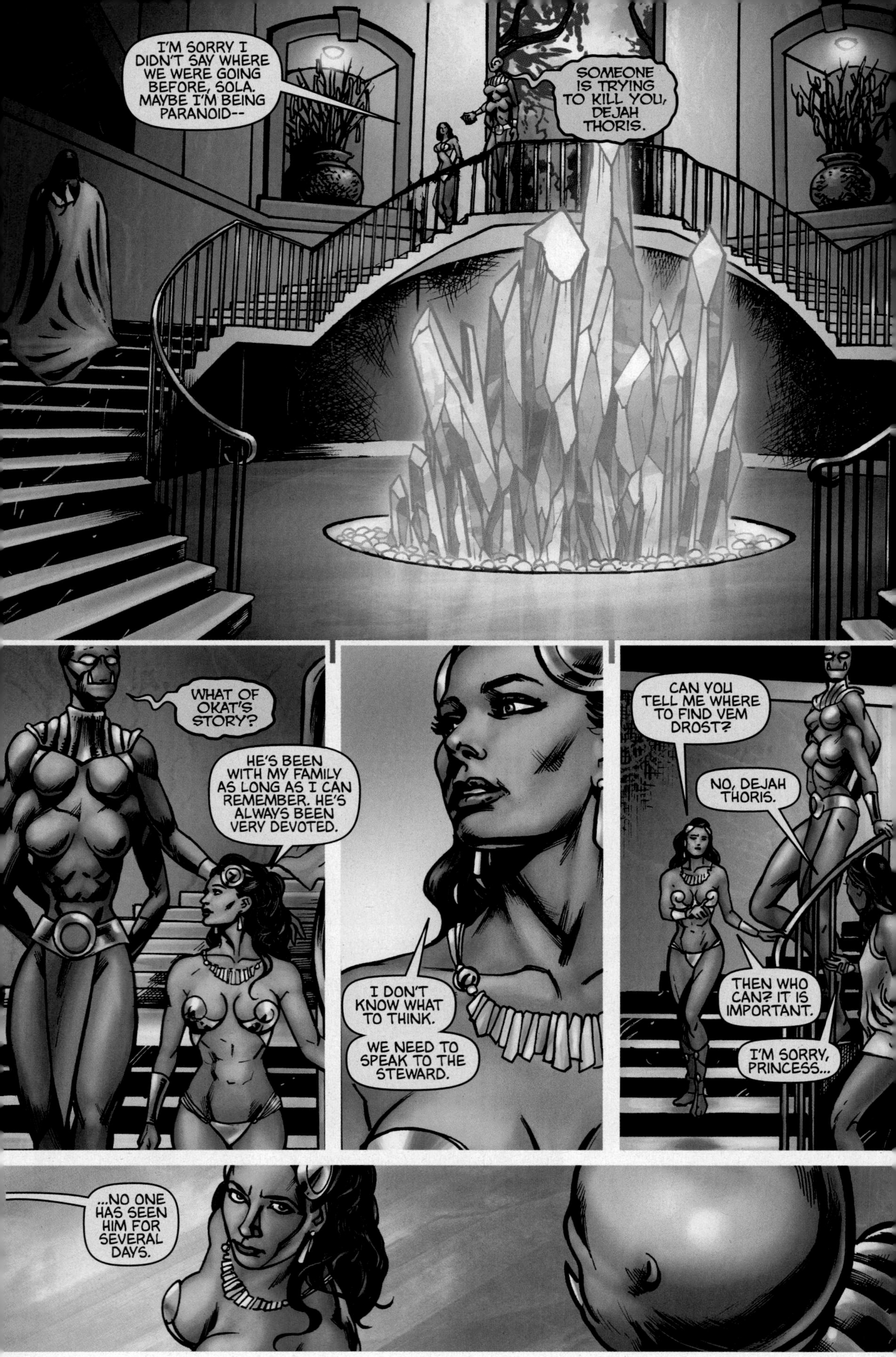
I'M SORRY I DIDN'T SAY WHERE WE WERE GOING BEFORE, SOLA. MAYBE I'M BEING PARANOID--
SOMEONE IS TRYING TO KILL YOU, DEJAH THORIS.
WHAT OF OKAT'S STORY?
HE'S BEEN WITH MY FAMILY AS LONG AS I CAN REMEMBER. HE'S ALWAYS BEEN VERY DEVOTED.
I DON'T KNOW WHAT TO THINK.
WE NEED TO SPEAK TO THE STEWARD.
CAN YOU TELL ME WHERE TO FIND VEM DROST?
NO, DEJAH THORIS.
THEN WHO CAN? IT IS IMPORTANT.
I'M SORRY, PRINCESS...
...NO ONE HAS SEEN HIM FOR SEVERAL DAYS.

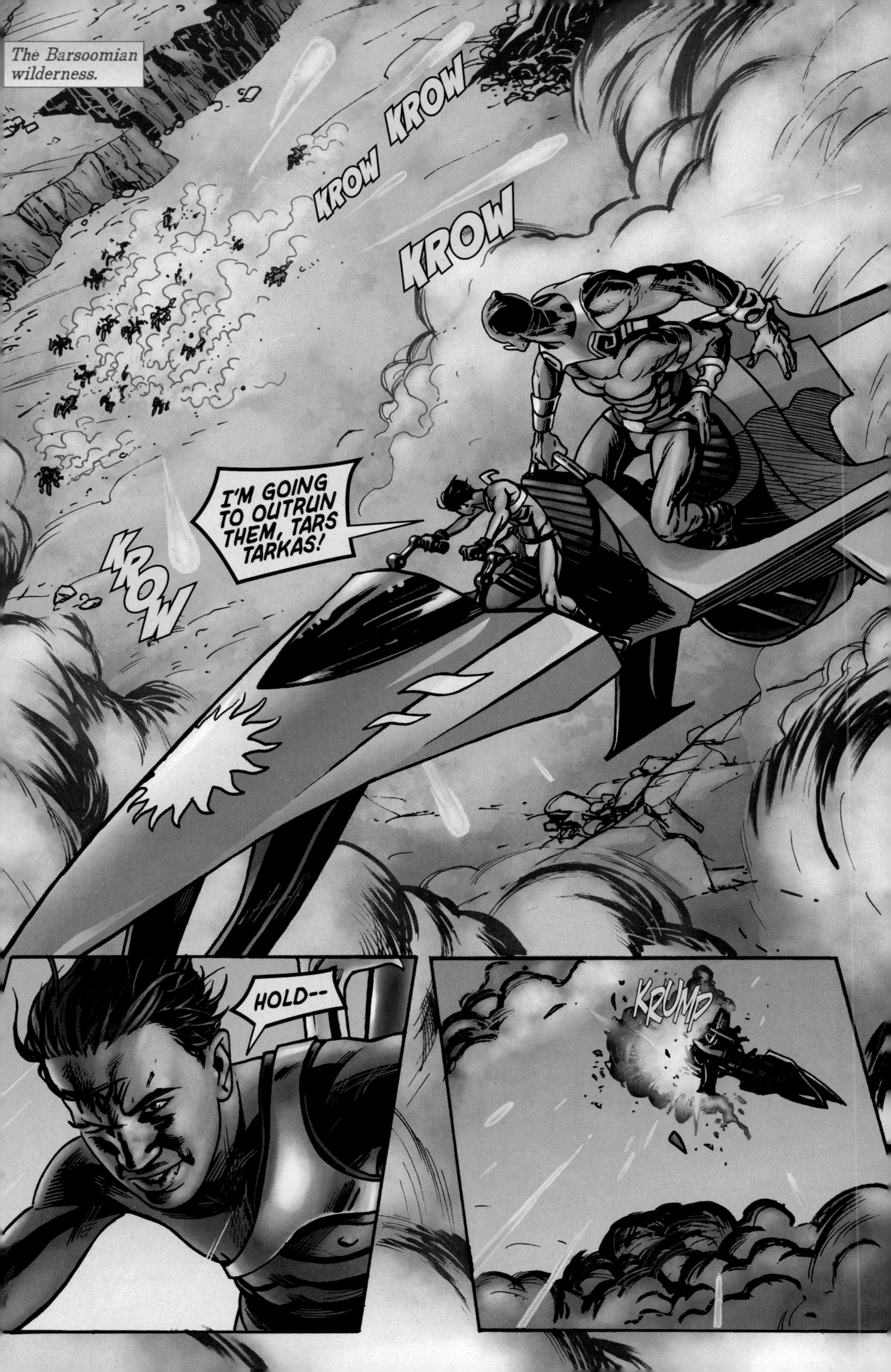
The Barsoomian wilderness.
KROW KROW
KROW
KROW
I'M GOING TO OUTRUN THEM, TARS TARKAS!
KROW
HOLD--
KRUMP

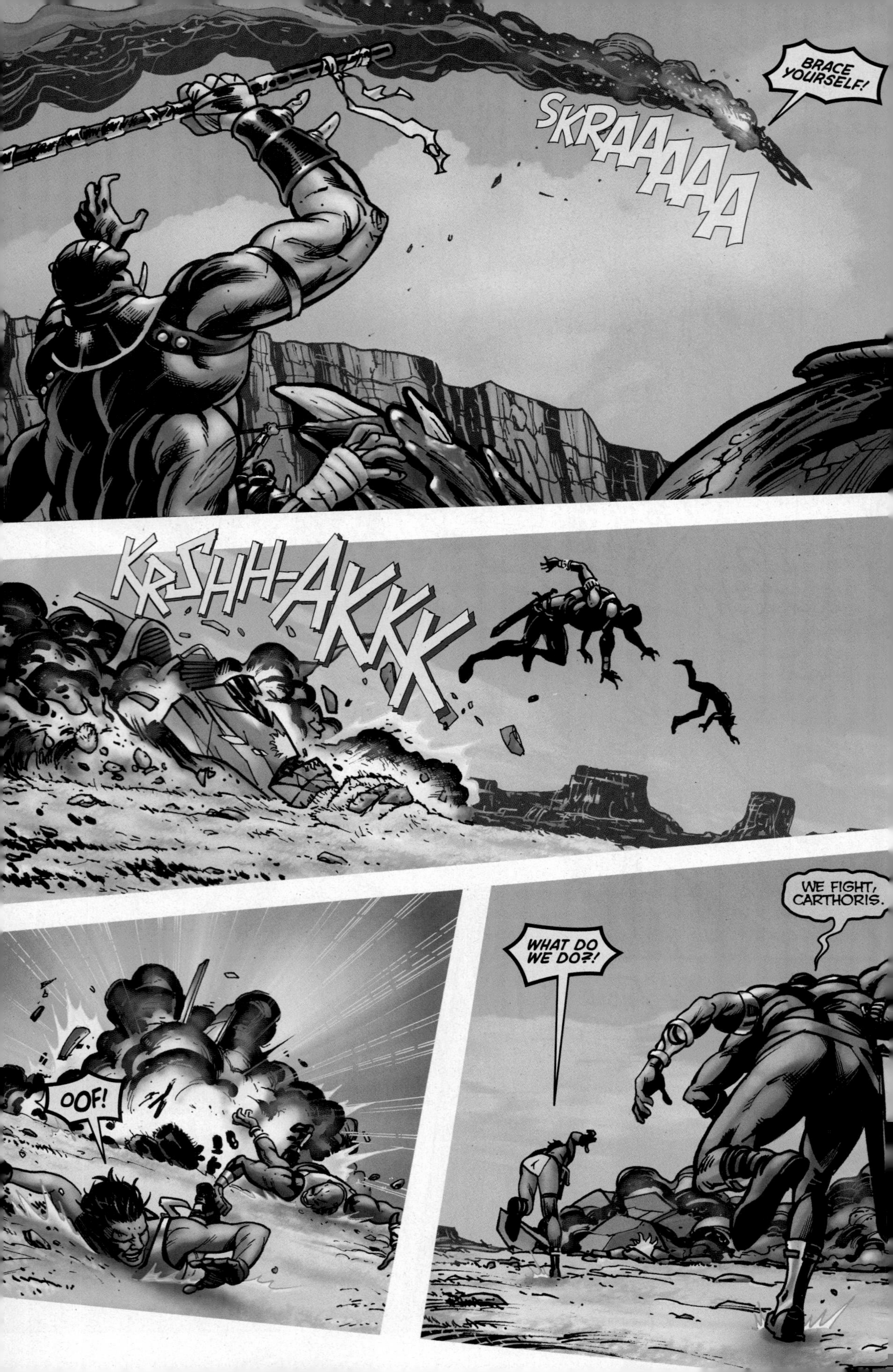
BRACE YOURSELF!
SKRAAAAAA
KRSHH-AKKK
OOF!
WE FIGHT, CARTHORIS.
WHAT DO WE DO?!

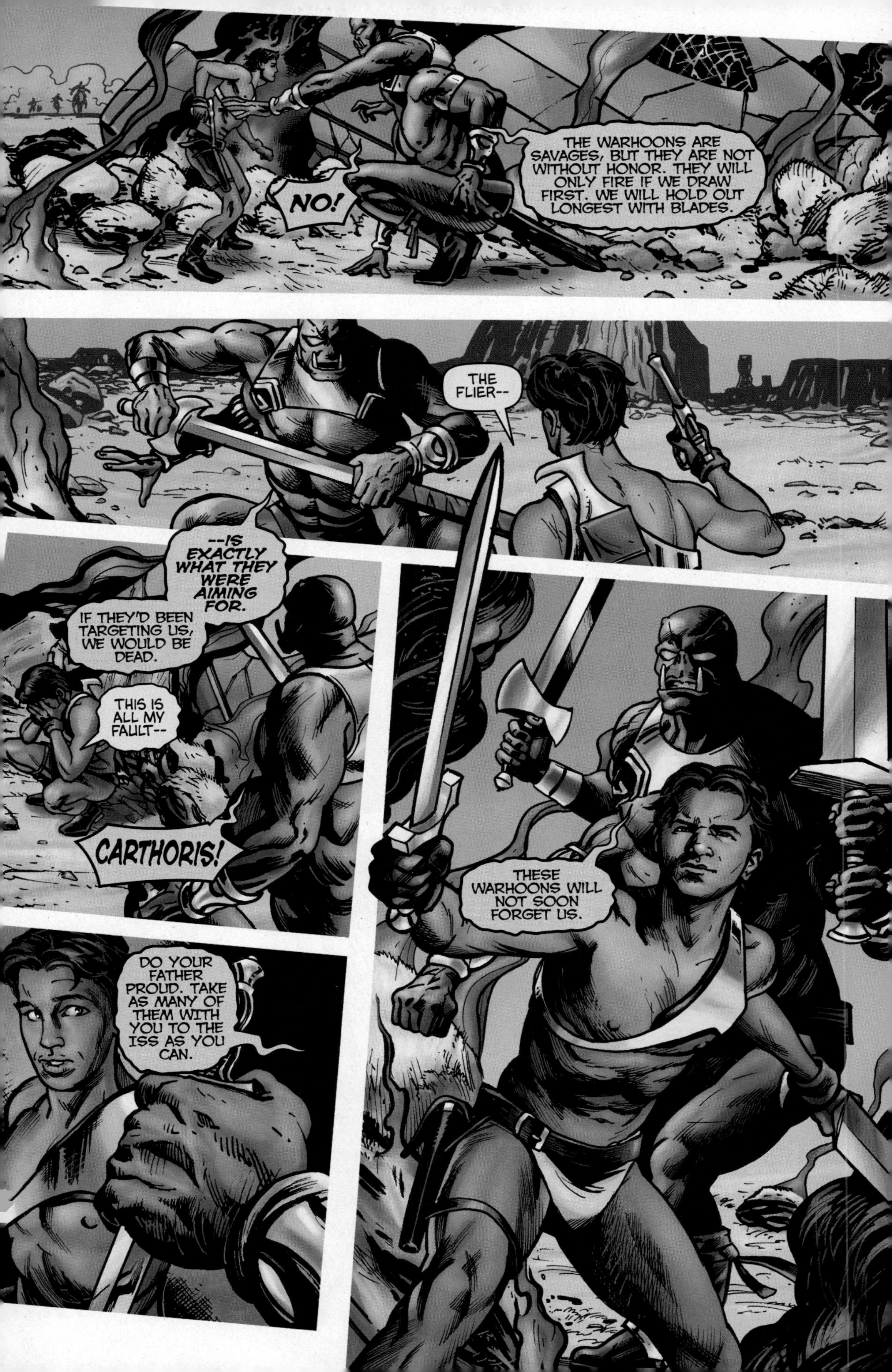
NO!
THE WARHOONS ARE SAVAGES, BUT THEY ARE NOT WITHOUT HONOR. THEY WILL ONLY FIRE IF WE DRAW FIRST. WE WILL HOLD OUT LONGEST WITH BLADES.
THE FLIER--
--IS EXACTLY WHAT THEY WERE AIMING FOR.
IF THEY'D BEEN TARGETING US, WE WOULD BE DEAD.
THIS IS ALL MY FAULT--
CARTHORIS!
DO YOUR FATHER PROUD. TAKE AS MANY OF THEM WITH YOU TO THE ISS AS YOU CAN.
THESE WARHOONS WILL NOT SOON FORGET US.

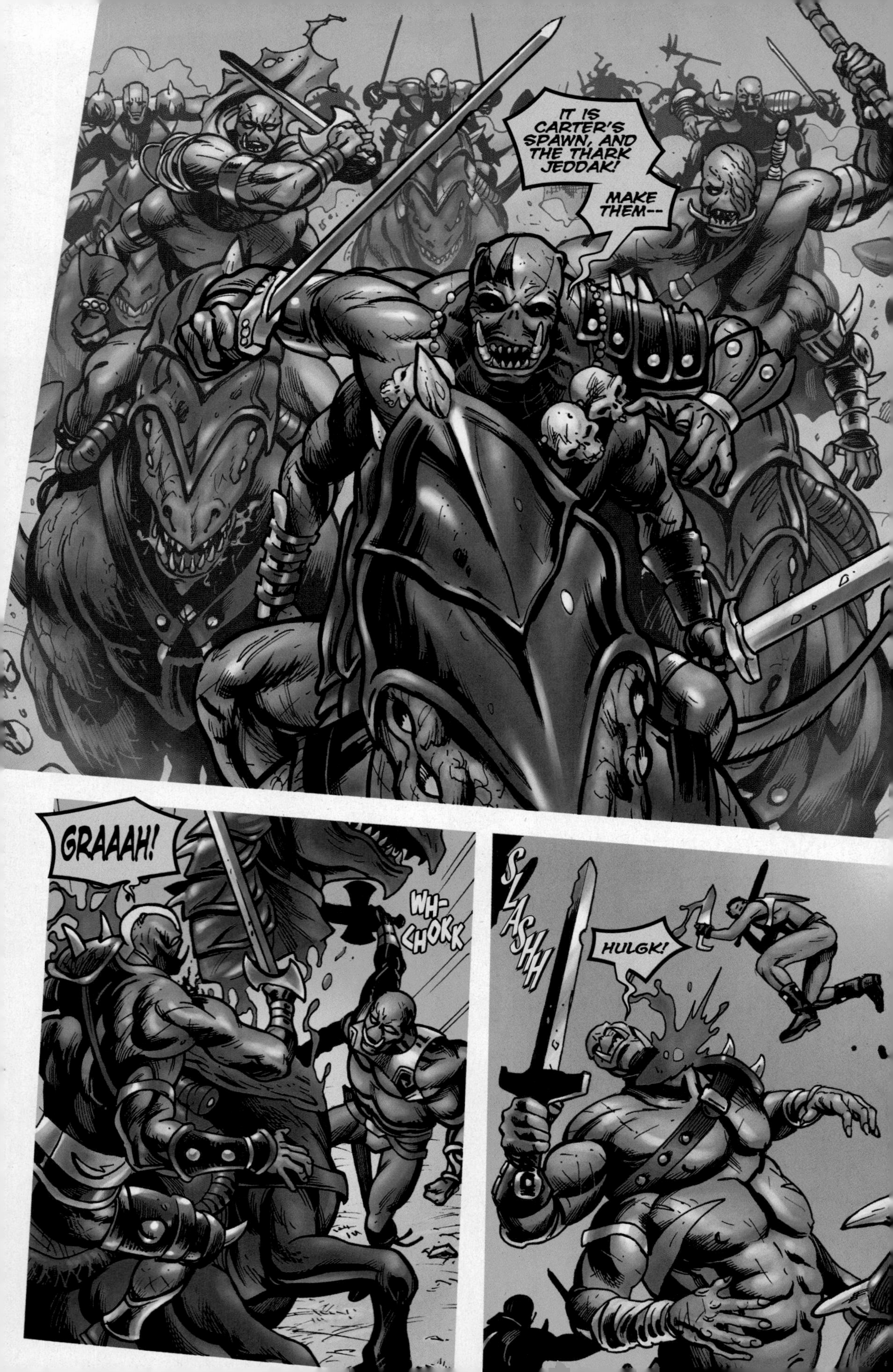
IT IS CARTER'S SPAWN, AND THE THARK JEDDAK!
MAKE THEM--
GRAAAH!
WH-CHOKK
SLASHH
HULGK!

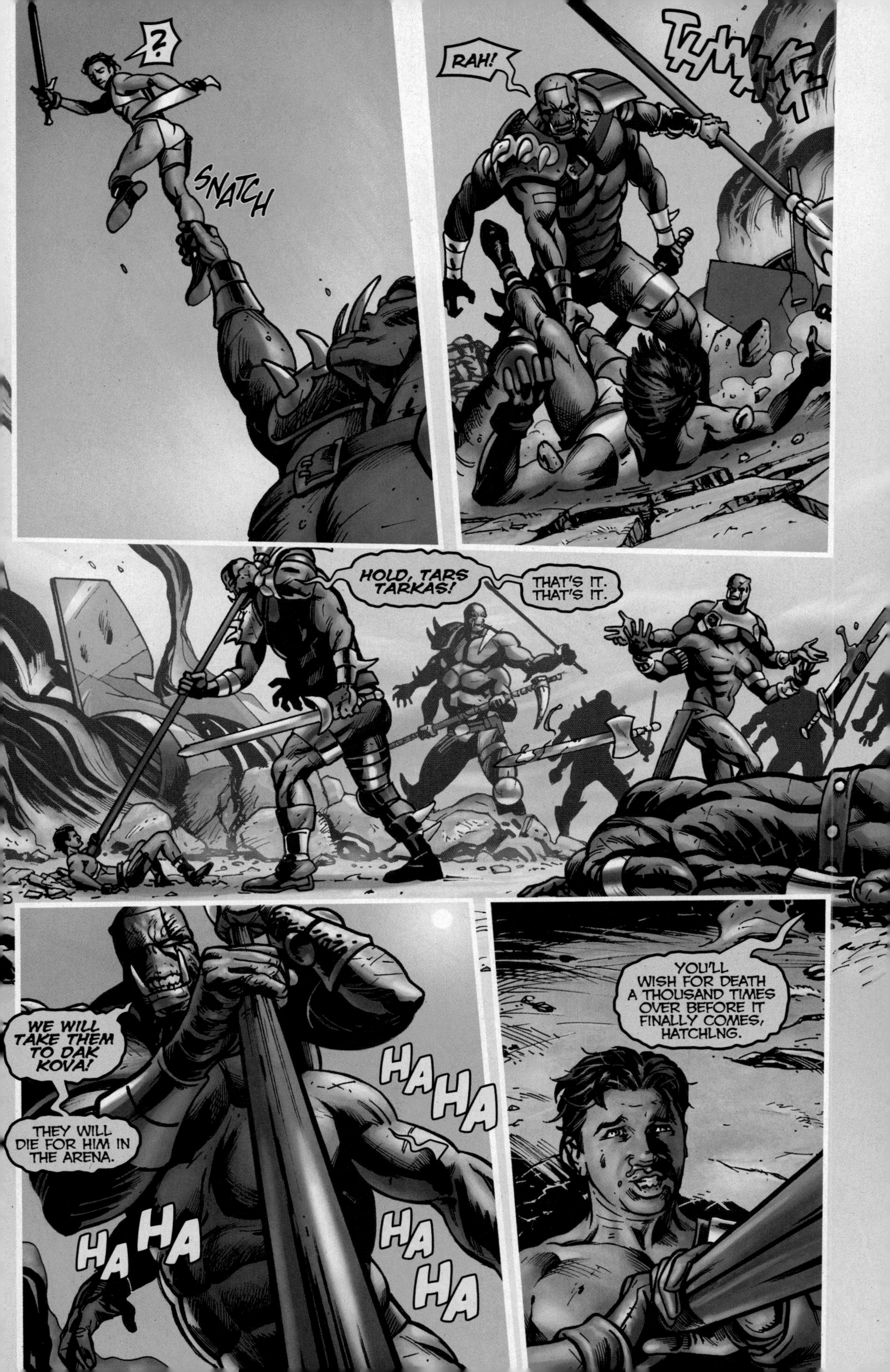
?
SNATCH
RAH!
THWAKK
HOLD, TARS TARKAS!
THAT'S IT. THAT'S IT.
WE WILL TAKE THEM TO DAK KOVA!
THEY WILL DIE FOR HIM IN THE ARENA.
HAHA
HAHA
HAHA
HAHA
YOU'LL WISH FOR DEATH A THOUSAND TIMES OVER BEFORE IT FINALLY COMES, HATCHLNG.

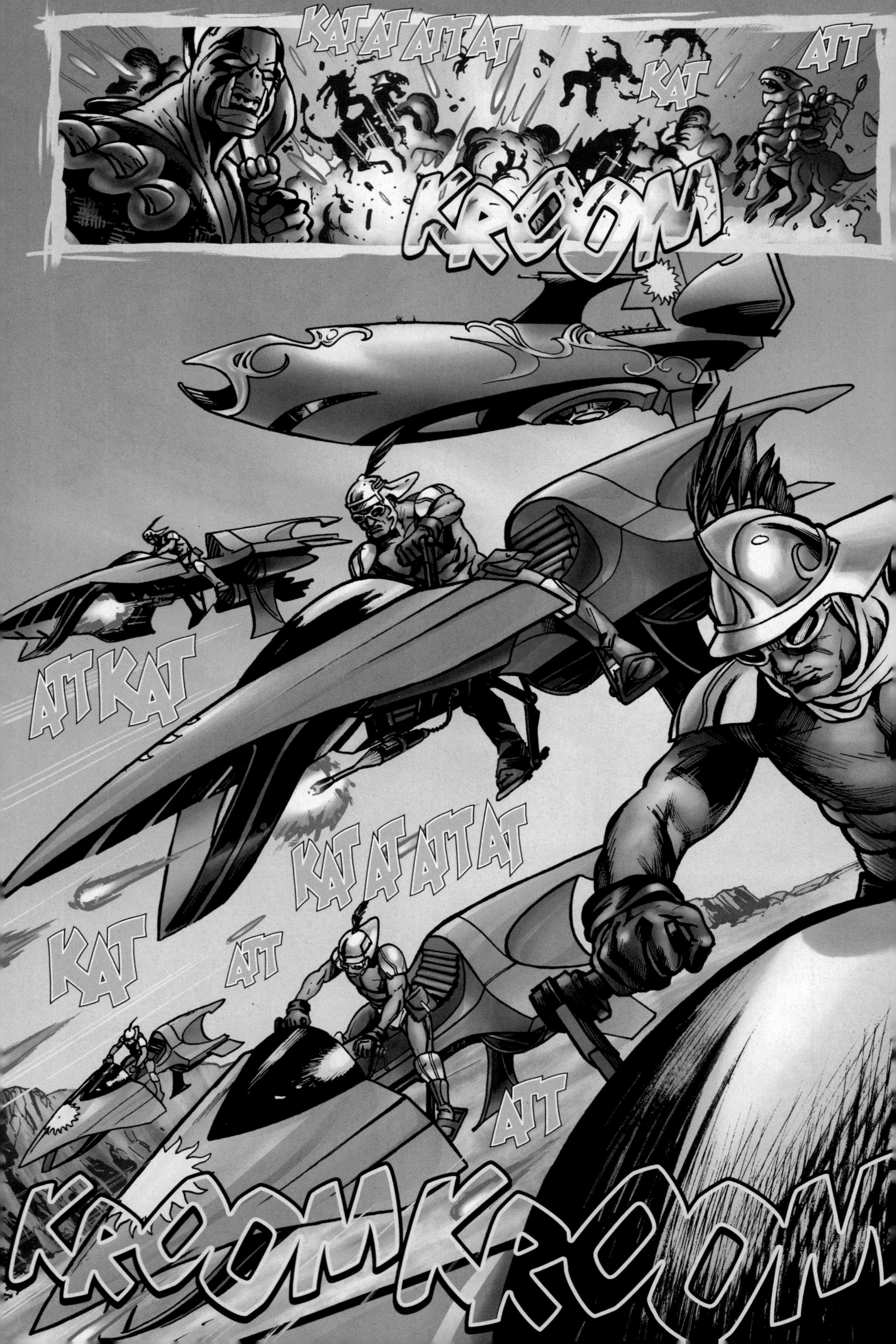
KAT AT ATT AT
KAT
ATT
KROOM
ATT KAT
KAT AT ATT AT
KAT
ATT
ATT
KROOM KROOM

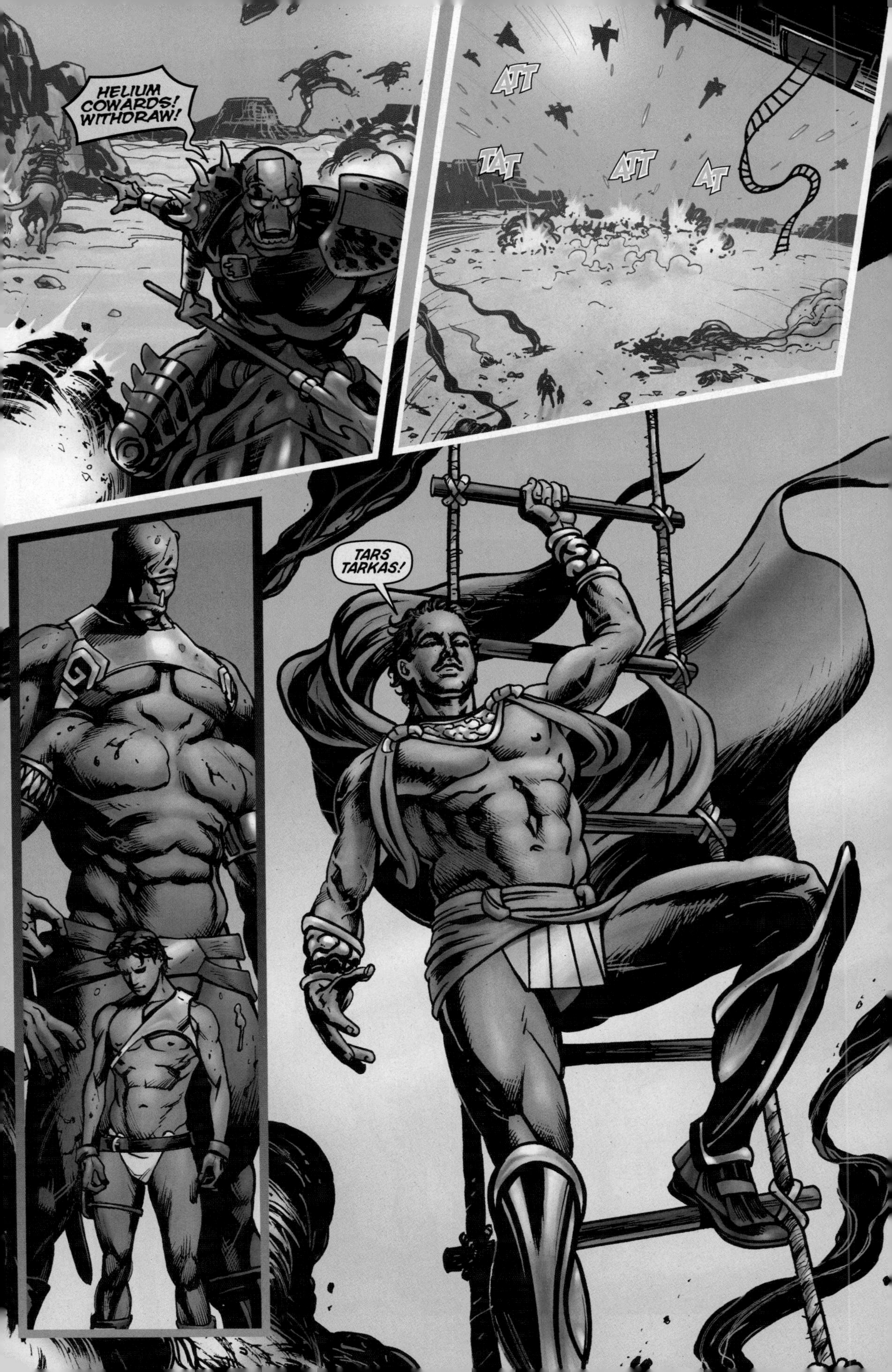
HELIUM COWARDS! WITHDRAW!
ATT
TAT
ATT
AT
TARS TARKAS!

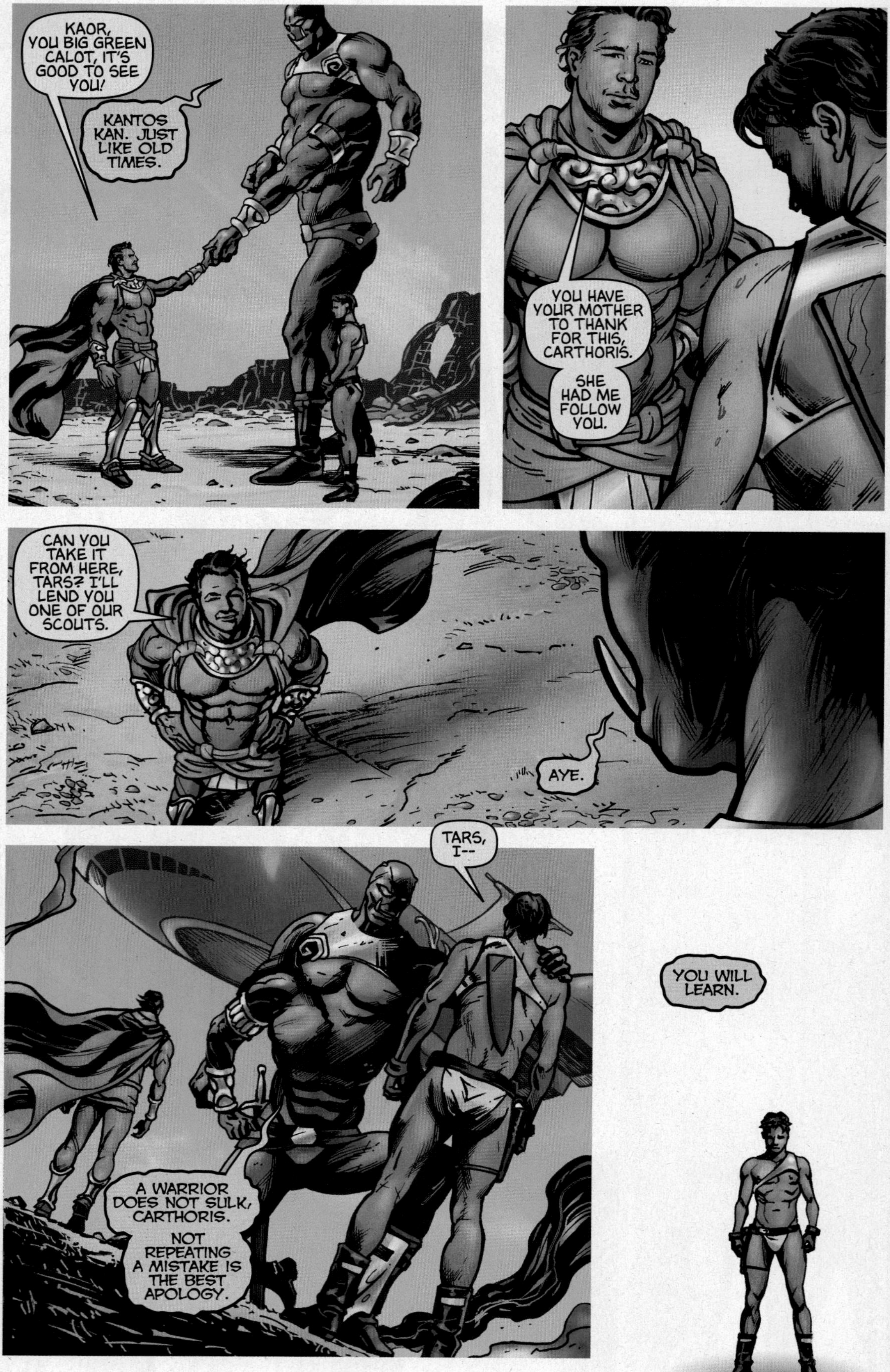
KAOR, YOU BIG GREEN CALOT, IT'S GOOD TO SEE YOU!
KANTOS KAN. JUST LIKE OLD TIMES.
YOU HAVE YOUR MOTHER TO THANK FOR THIS, CARTHORIS.
SHE HAD ME FOLLOW YOU.
CAN YOU TAKE IT FROM HERE, TARS? I'LL LEND YOU ONE OF OUR SCOUTS.
AYE.
TARS, I--
A WARRIOR DOES NOT SULK, CARTHORIS.
NOT REPEATING A MISTAKE IS THE BEST APOLOGY.
YOU WILL LEARN.

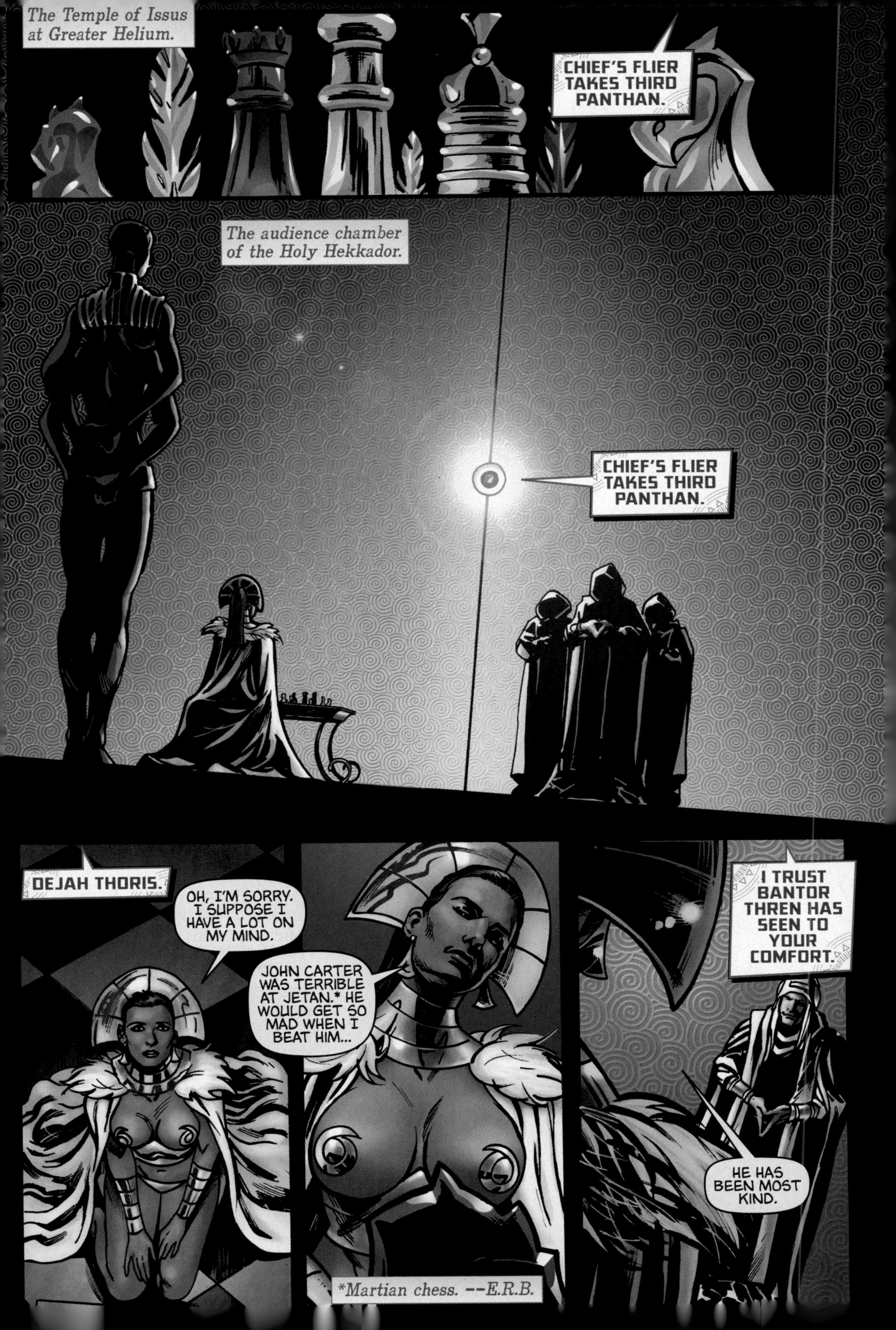

The Temple of Issus at Greater Helium.
CHIEF'S FLIER TAKES THIRD PANTHAN.
The audience chamber of the Holy Hekkador.
CHIEF'S FLIER TAKES THIRD PANTHAN.
DEJAH THORIS.
OH, I'M SORRY. I SUPPOSE I HAVE A LOT ON MY MIND.
JOHN CARTER WAS TERRIBLE AT JETAN.* HE WOULD GET SO MAD WHEN I BEAT HIM...
*Martian chess. --E.R.B.
I TRUST BANTOR THREN HAS SEEN TO YOUR COMFORT.
HE HAS BEEN MOST KIND.

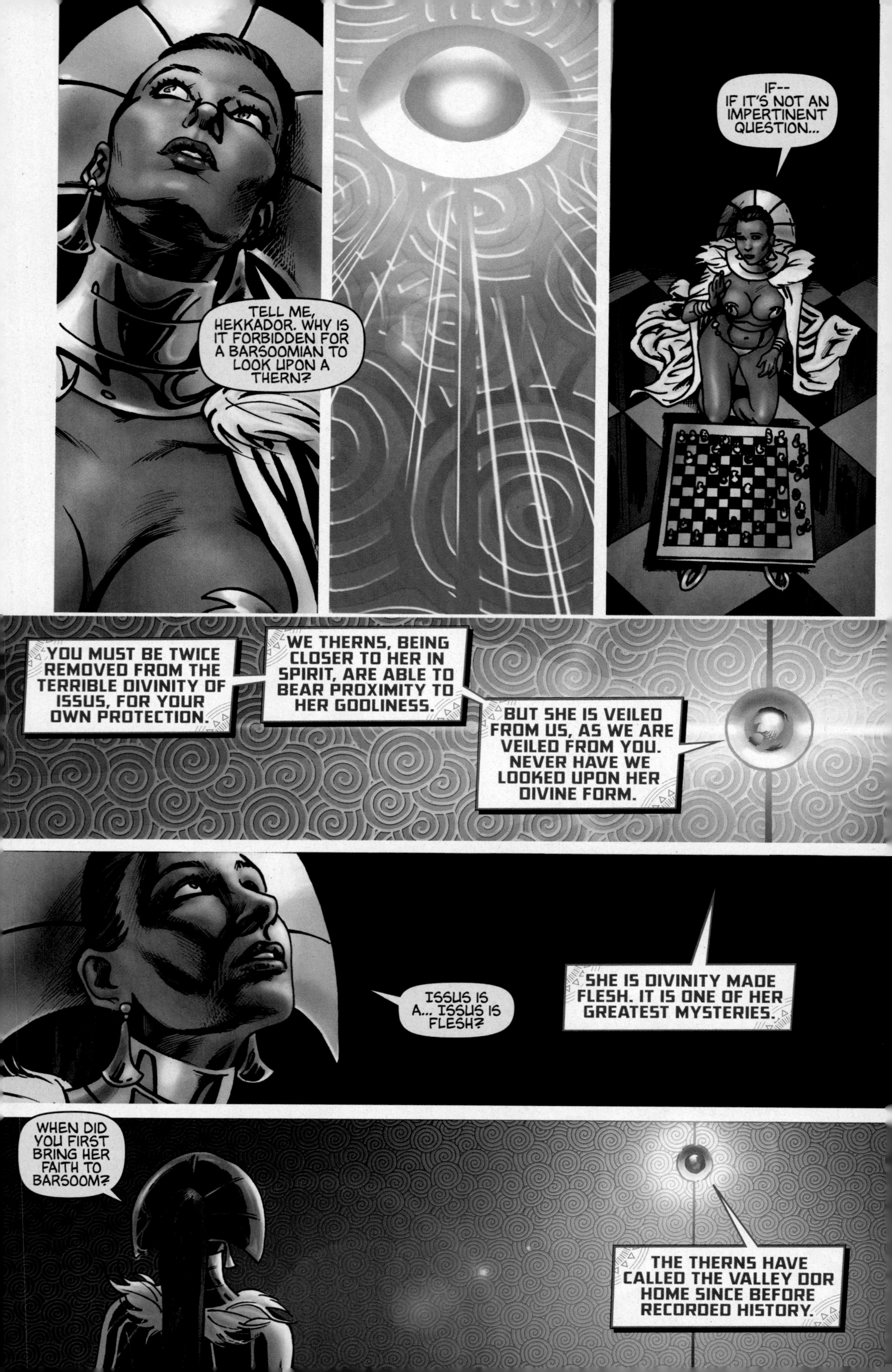
TELL ME, HEKKADOR. WHY IS IT FORBIDDEN FOR A BARSOOMIAN TO LOOK UPON A THERN?
IF-- IF IT'S NOT AN IMPERTINENT QUESTION...
YOU MUST BE TWICE REMOVED FROM THE TERRIBLE DIVINITY OF ISSUS, FOR YOUR OWN PROTECTION.
WE THERNS, BEING CLOSER TO HER IN SPIRIT, ARE ABLE TO BEAR PROXIMITY TO HER GODLINESS.
BUT SHE IS VEILED FROM US, AS WE ARE VEILED FROM YOU. NEVER HAVE WE LOOKED UPON HER DIVINE FORM.
ISSUS IS A... ISSUS IS FLESH?
SHE IS DIVINITY MADE FLESH. IT IS ONE OF HER GREATEST MYSTERIES.
WHEN DID YOU FIRST BRING HER FAITH TO BARSOOM?
THE THERNS HAVE CALLED THE VALLEY DOR HOME SINCE BEFORE RECORDED HISTORY.

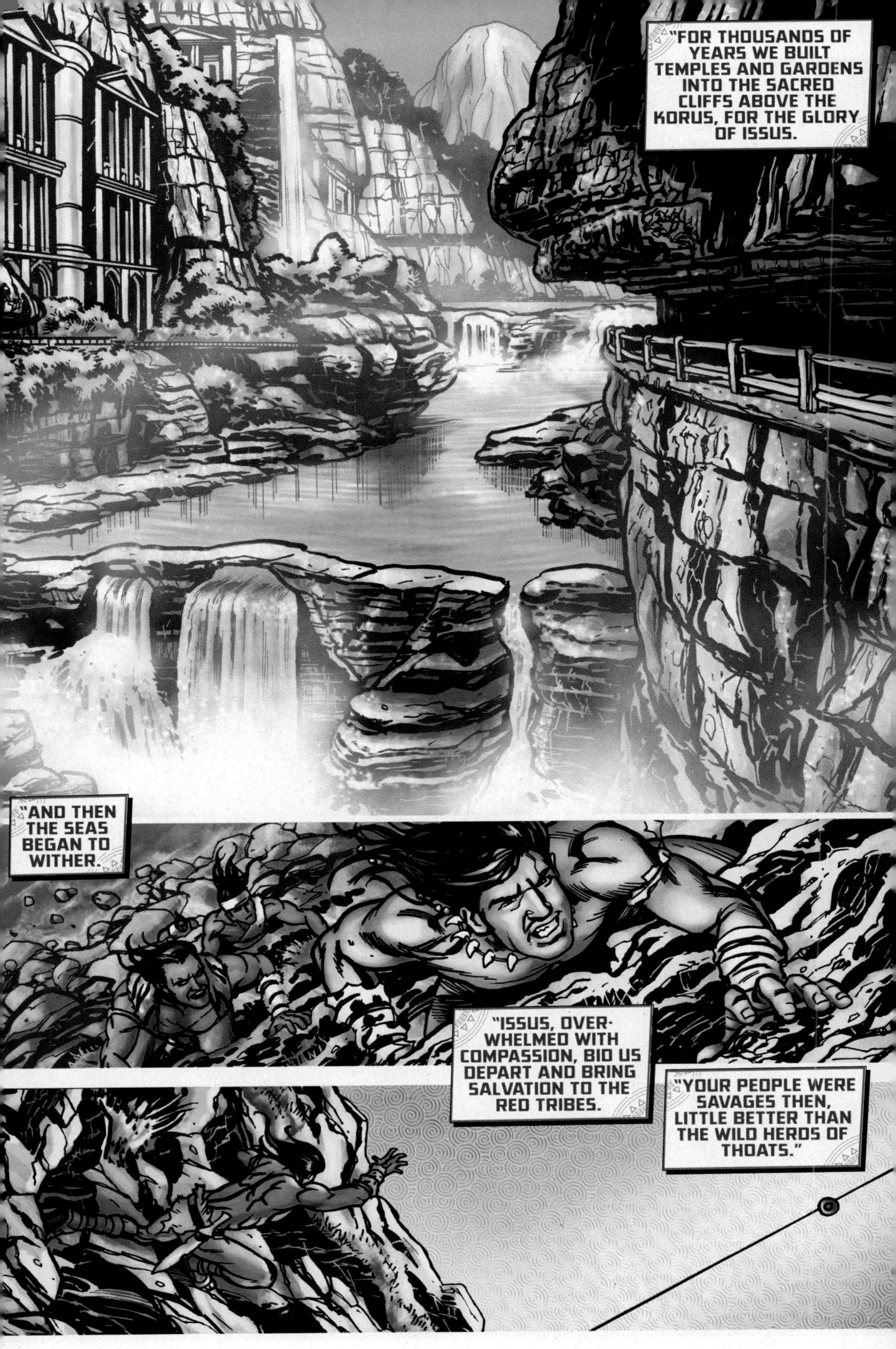
"FOR THOUSANDS OF YEARS WE BUILT TEMPLES AND GARDENS INTO THE SACRED CLIFFS ABOVE THE KORUS, FOR THE GLORY OF ISSUS.
"AND THEN THE SEAS BEGAN TO WITHER.
"ISSUS, OVER-WHELMED WITH COMPASSION, BID US DEPART AND BRING SALVATION TO THE RED TRIBES.
"YOUR PEOPLE WERE SAVAGES THEN, LITTLE BETTER THAN THE WILD HERDS OF THOATS."

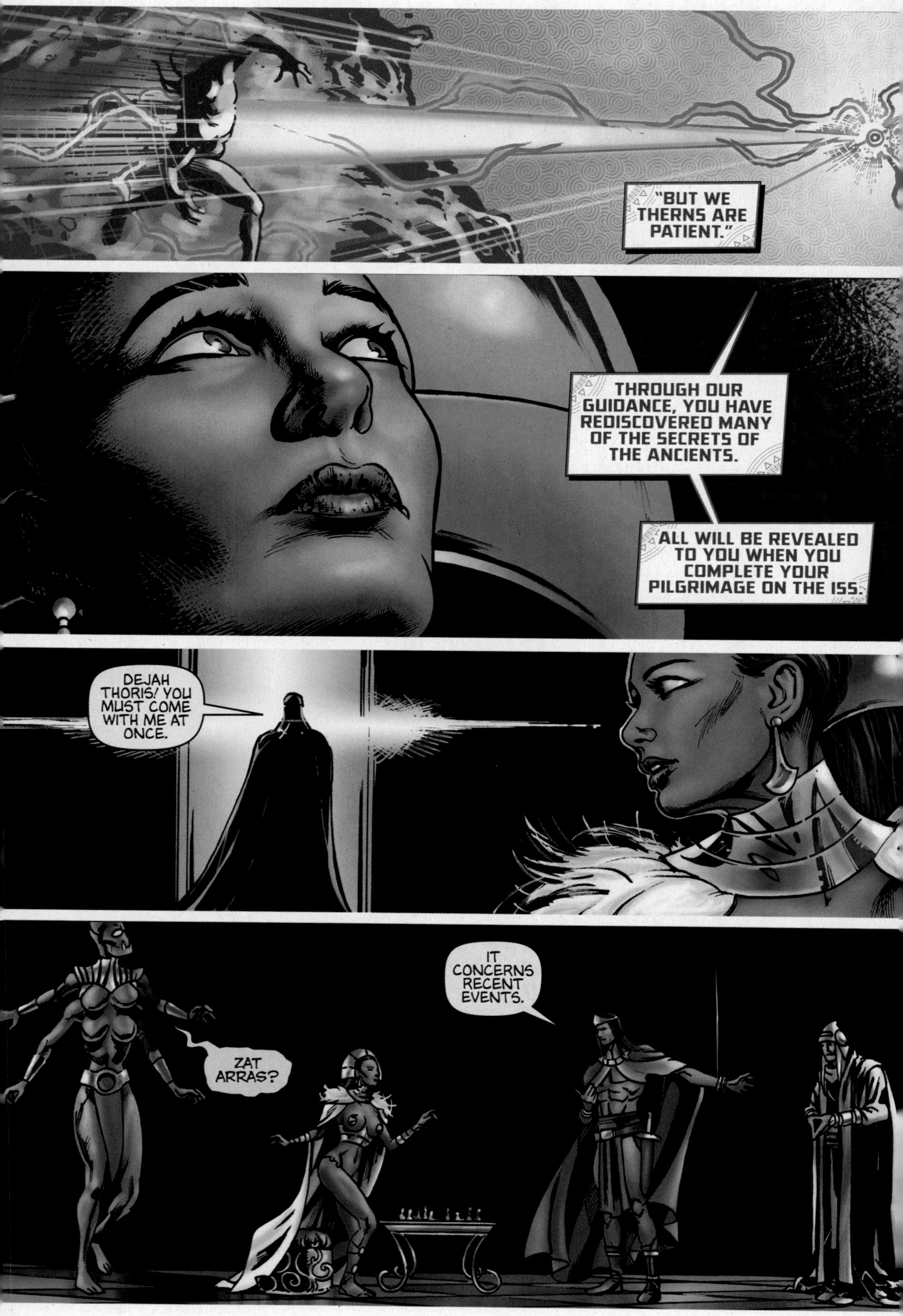
"BUT WE THERNS ARE PATIENT."
THROUGH OUR GUIDANCE, YOU HAVE REDISCOVERED MANY OF THE SECRETS OF THE ANCIENTS.
ALL WILL BE REVEALED TO YOU WHEN YOU COMPLETE YOUR PILGRIMAGE ON THE ISS.
DEJAH THORIS! YOU MUST COME WITH ME AT ONCE.
ZAT ARRAS?
IT CONCERNS RECENT EVENTS.

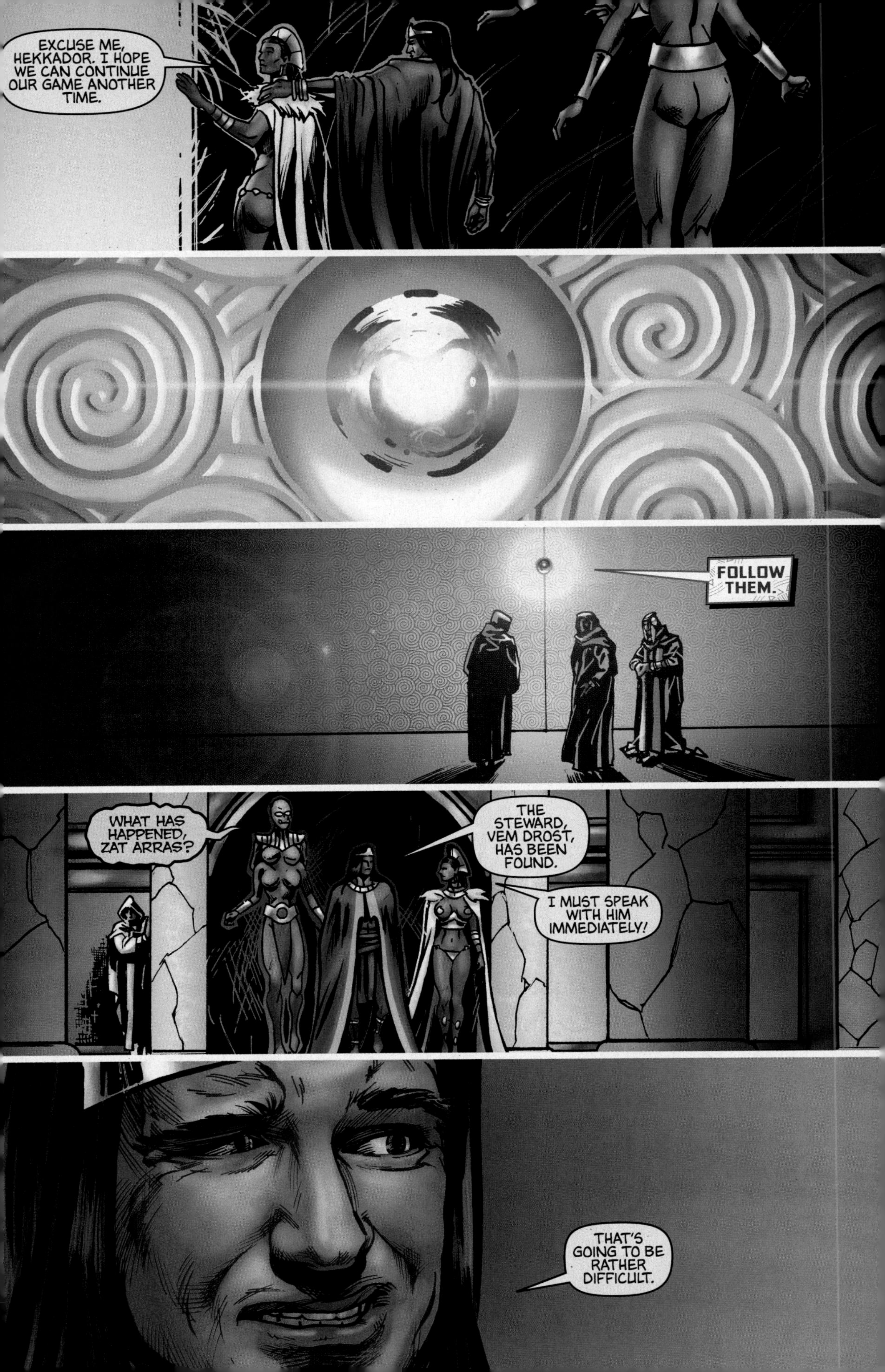
EXCUSE ME, HEKKADOR. I HOPE WE CAN CONTINUE OUR GAME ANOTHER TIME.
FOLLOW THEM.
WHAT HAS HAPPENED, ZAT ARRAS?
THE STEWARD, VEM DROST, HAS BEEN FOUND.
I MUST SPEAK WITH HIM IMMEDIATELY!
THAT'S GOING TO BE RATHER DIFFICULT.

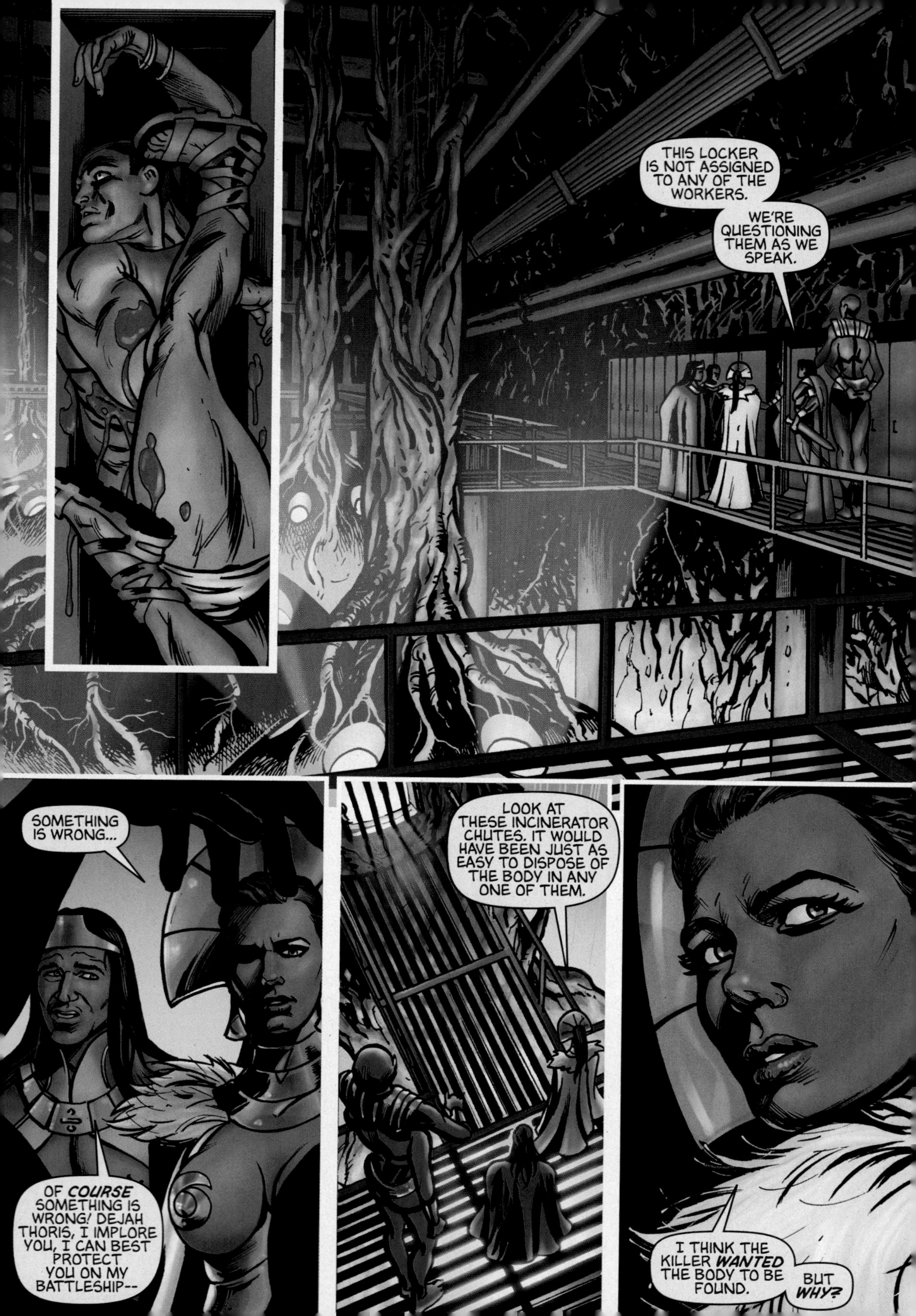
THIS LOCKER IS NOT ASSIGNED TO ANY OF THE WORKERS.
WE'RE QUESTIONING THEM AS WE SPEAK.
SOMETHING IS WRONG...
OF *COURSE* SOMETHING IS WRONG! DEJAH THORIS, I IMPLORE YOU, I CAN BEST PROTECT YOU ON MY BATTLESHIP--
LOOK AT THESE INCINERATOR CHUTES. IT WOULD HAVE BEEN JUST AS EASY TO DISPOSE OF THE BODY IN ANY ONE OF THEM.
I THINK THE KILLER *WANTED* THE BODY TO BE FOUND.
BUT *WHY?*

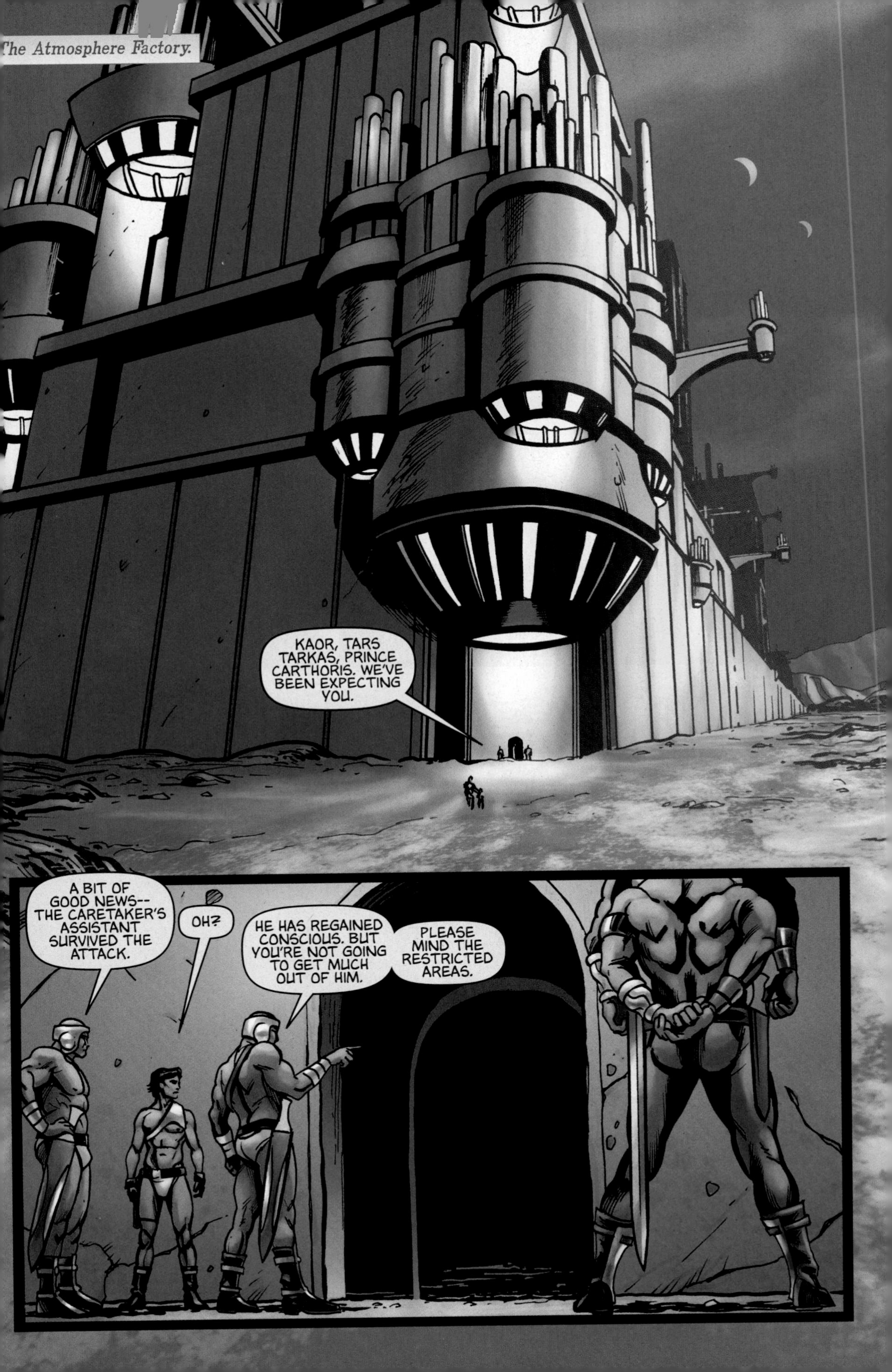
The Atmosphere Factory.
KAOR, TARS TARKAS, PRINCE CARTHORIS. WE'VE BEEN EXPECTING YOU.
A BIT OF GOOD NEWS-- THE CARETAKER'S ASSISTANT SURVIVED THE ATTACK.
OH?
HE HAS REGAINED CONSCIOUS. BUT YOU'RE NOT GOING TO GET MUCH OUT OF HIM.
PLEASE MIND THE RESTRICTED AREAS.

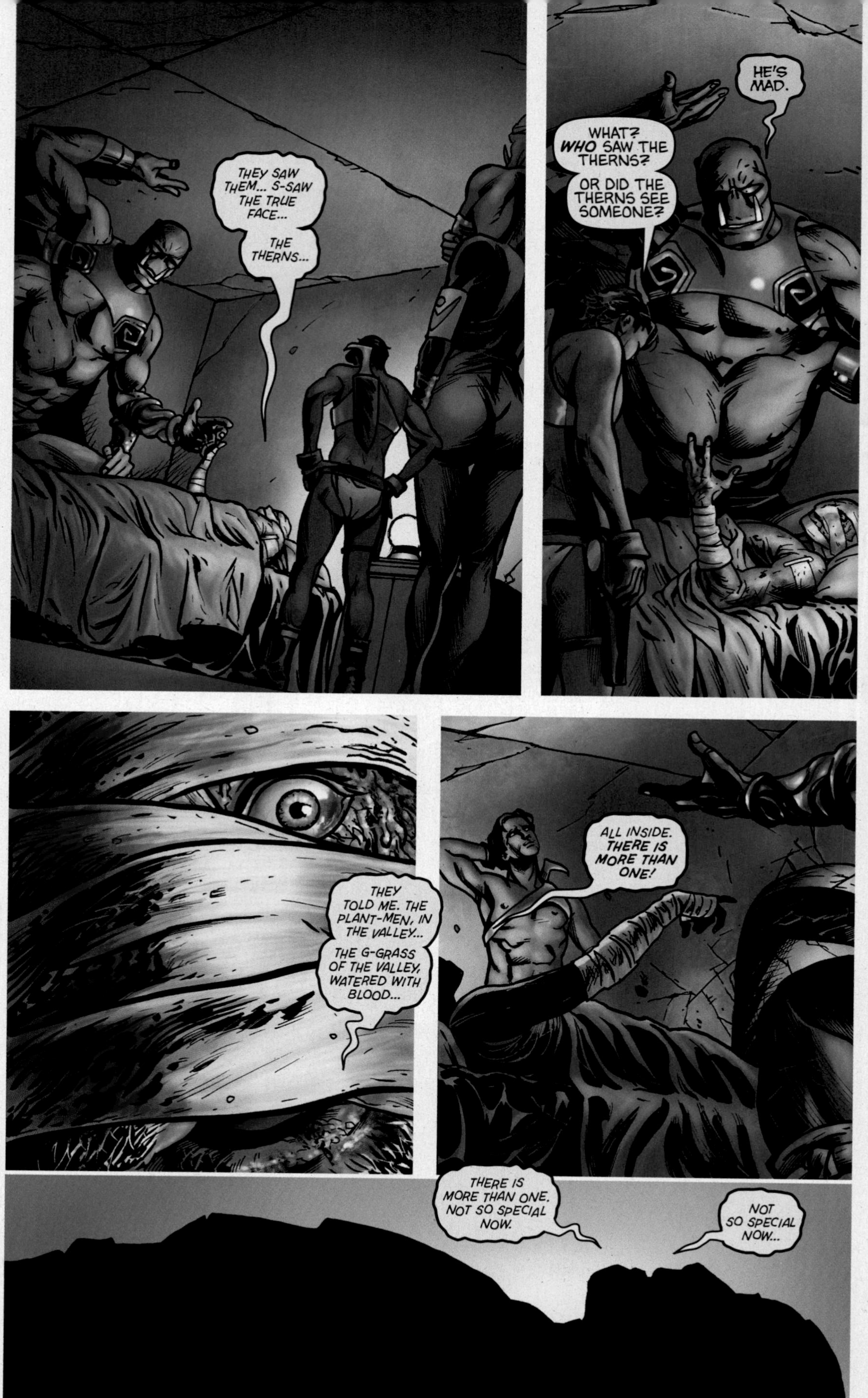
THEY SAW THEM... S-SAW THE TRUE FACE...
THE THERNS...
HE'S MAD.
WHAT? WHO SAW THE THERNS?
OR DID THE THERNS SEE SOMEONE?
THEY TOLD ME. THE PLANT-MEN, IN THE VALLEY...
THE G-GRASS OF THE VALLEY, WATERED WITH BLOOD...
ALL INSIDE. THERE IS MORE THAN ONE!
THERE IS MORE THAN ONE. NOT SO SPECIAL NOW.
NOT SO SPECIAL NOW...

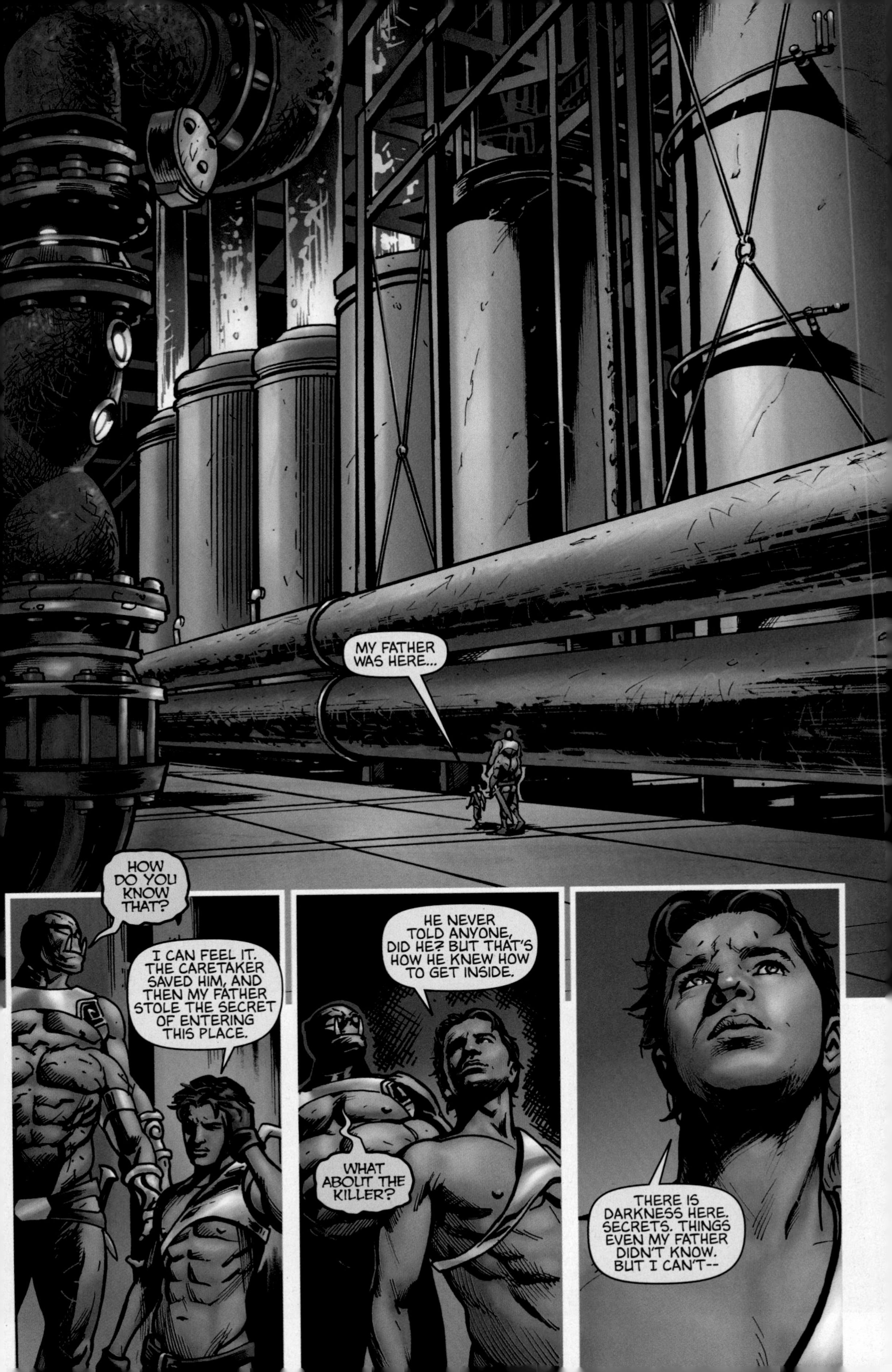
MY FATHER WAS HERE...
HOW DO YOU KNOW THAT?
I CAN FEEL IT. THE CARETAKER SAVED HIM, AND THEN MY FATHER STOLE THE SECRET OF ENTERING THIS PLACE.
HE NEVER TOLD ANYONE, DID HE? BUT THAT'S HOW HE KNEW HOW TO GET INSIDE.
WHAT ABOUT THE KILLER?
THERE IS DARKNESS HERE. SECRETS. THINGS EVEN MY FATHER DIDN'T KNOW. BUT I CAN'T--

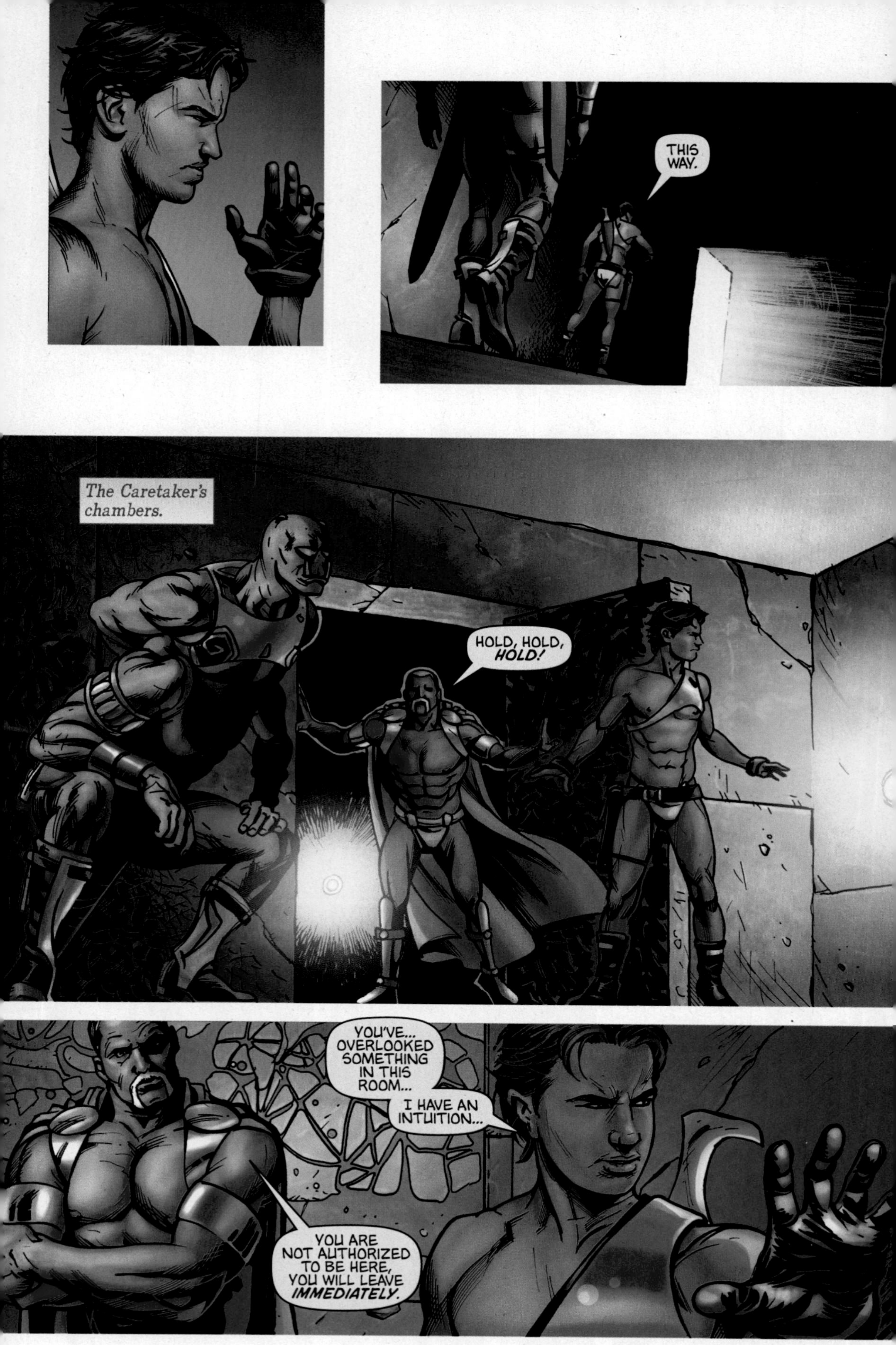
THIS WAY.
The Caretaker's chambers.
HOLD, HOLD, HOLD!
YOU'VE... OVERLOOKED SOMETHING IN THIS ROOM...
I HAVE AN INTUITION...
YOU ARE NOT AUTHORIZED TO BE HERE, YOU WILL LEAVE IMMEDIATELY.

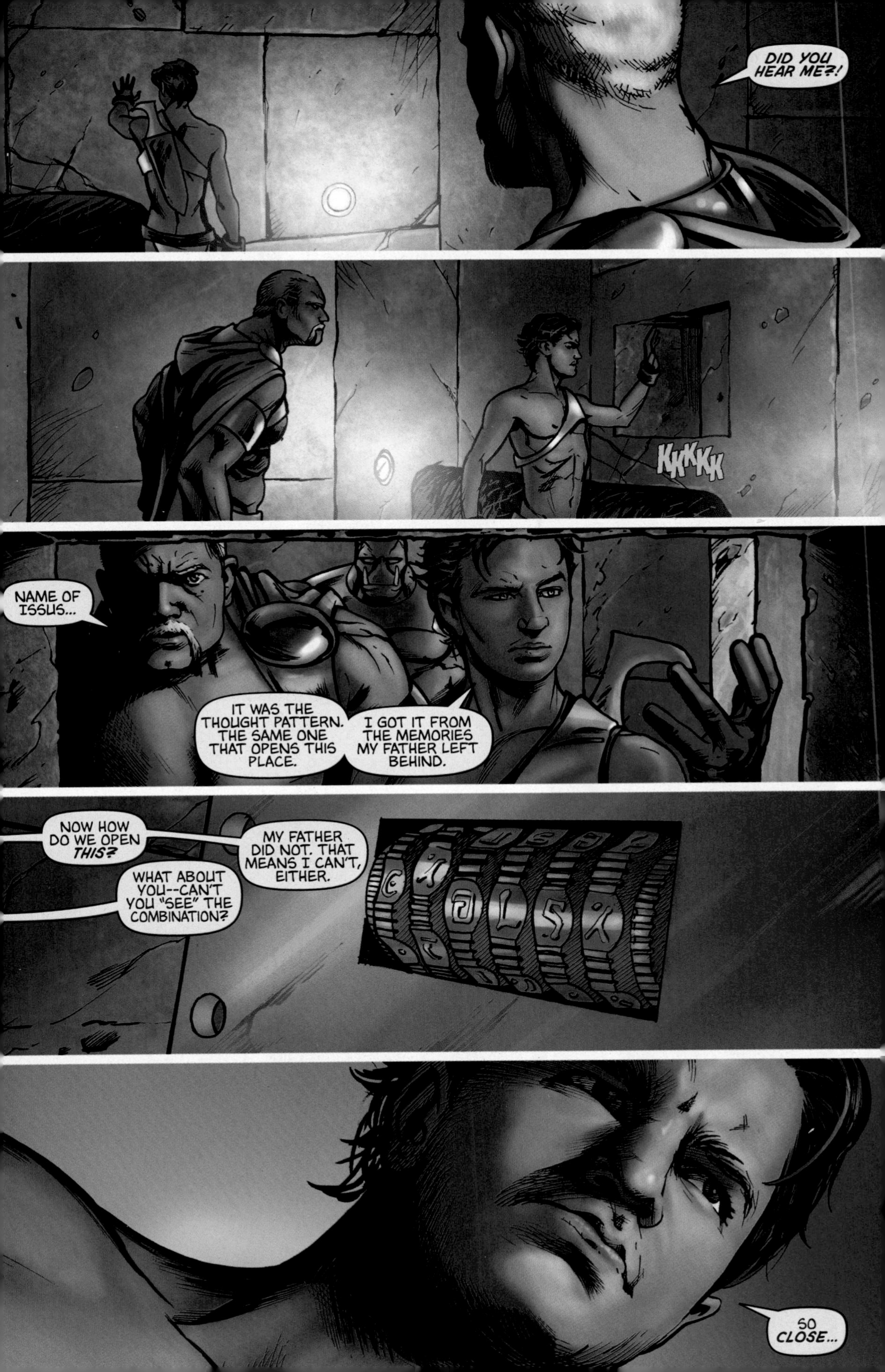
DID YOU HEAR ME?!
KKKKK
NAME OF ISSUS...
IT WAS THE THOUGHT PATTERN. THE SAME ONE THAT OPENS THIS PLACE.
I GOT IT FROM THE MEMORIES MY FATHER LEFT BEHIND.
NOW HOW DO WE OPEN *THIS?*
WHAT ABOUT YOU--CAN'T YOU "SEE" THE COMBINATION?
MY FATHER DID NOT. THAT MEANS I CAN'T, EITHER.
SO *CLOSE...*

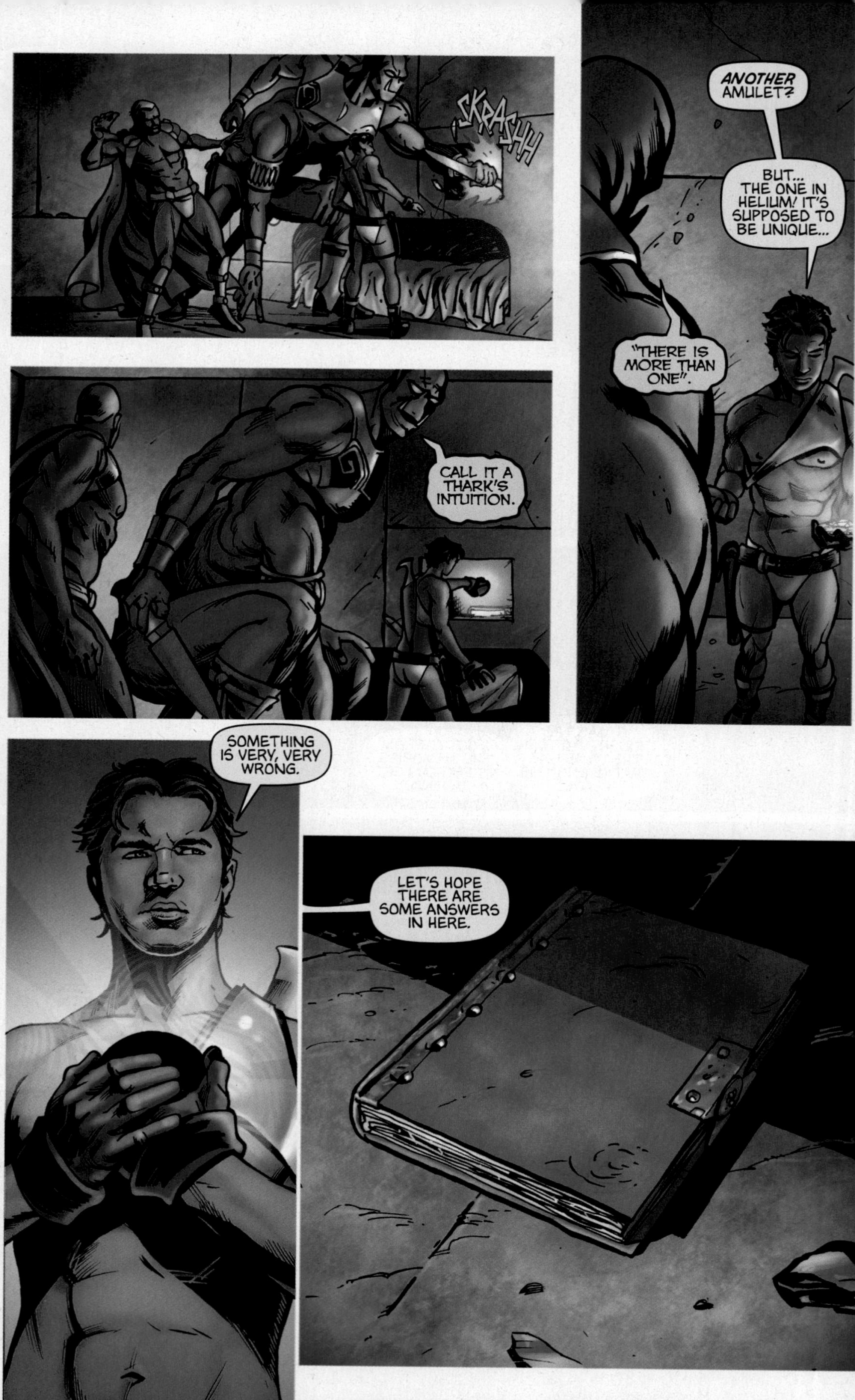
SKRASHH
CALL IT A THARK'S INTUITION.
ANOTHER AMULET?
BUT... THE ONE IN HELIUM! IT'S SUPPOSED TO BE UNIQUE...
"THERE IS MORE THAN ONE".
SOMETHING IS VERY, VERY WRONG.
LET'S HOPE THERE ARE SOME ANSWERS IN HERE.

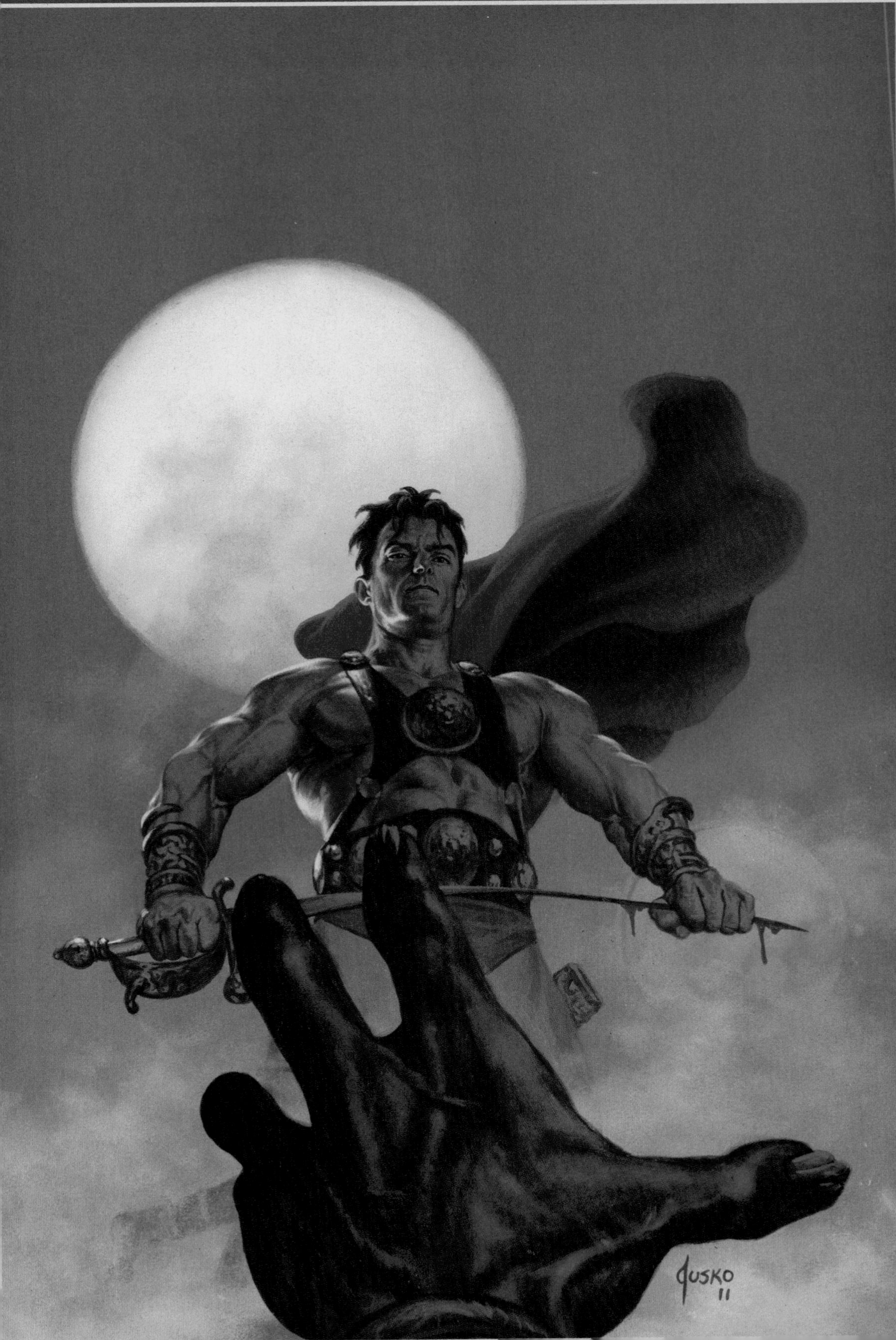
JUSKO
11

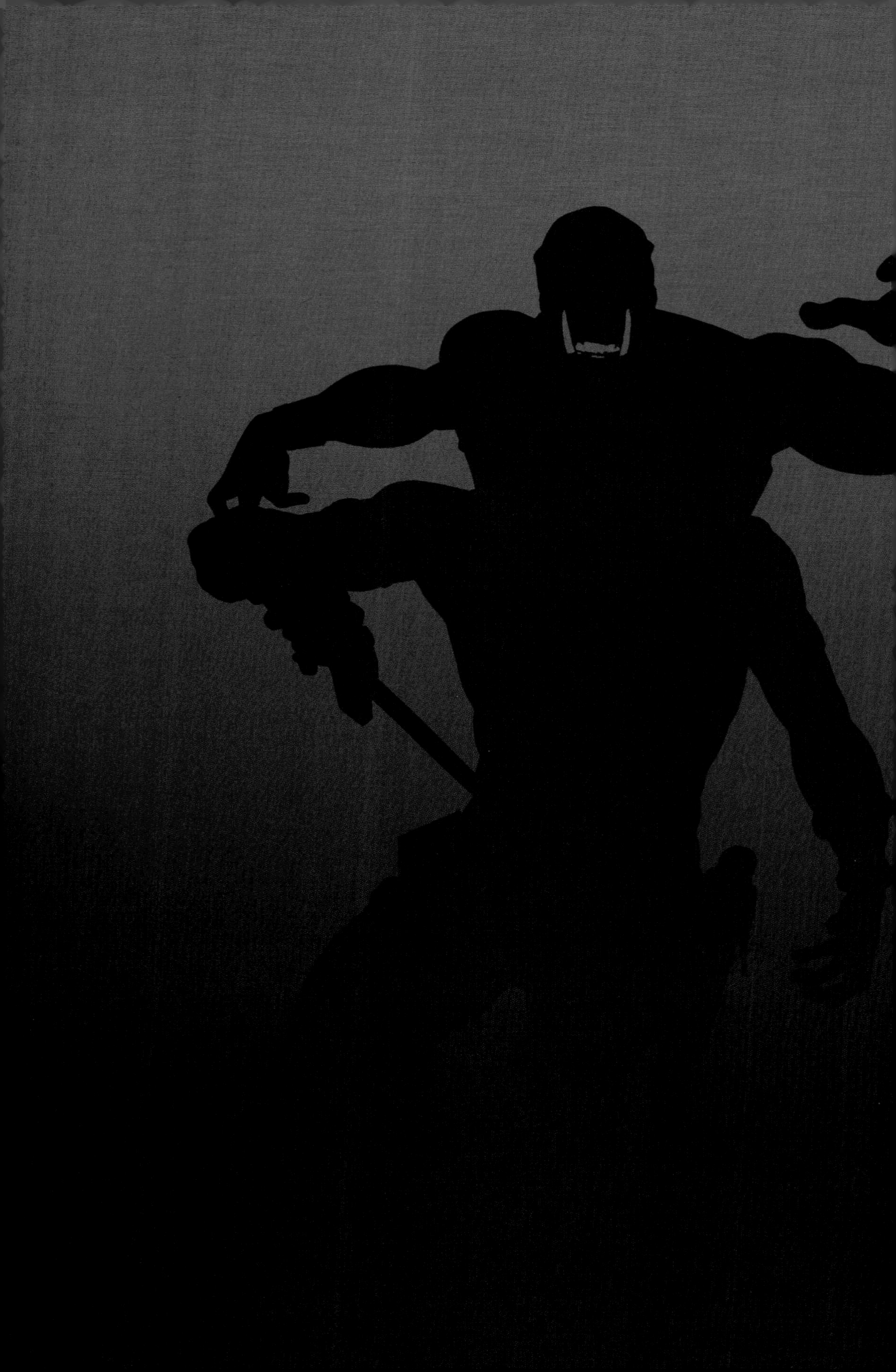

The palace of Greater Helium.

GOOD NIGHT, ZAT ARRAS. THANK YOU FOR NOTIFYING ME ABOUT VEM DROST.

DEJAH THORIS, THIS TIME I INSIST. YOU *WILL* ALLOW ME TO ESCORT YOU--

GOOD NIGHT.

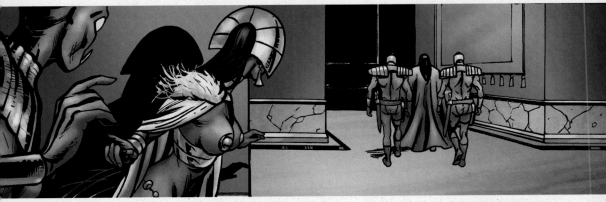

YOU REALLY ARE TIRED!

WE'RE NOT GOING TO SLEEP, SOLA.

WE'RE *NOT?*

I JUST HOPE IT'S NOT TOO LATE.

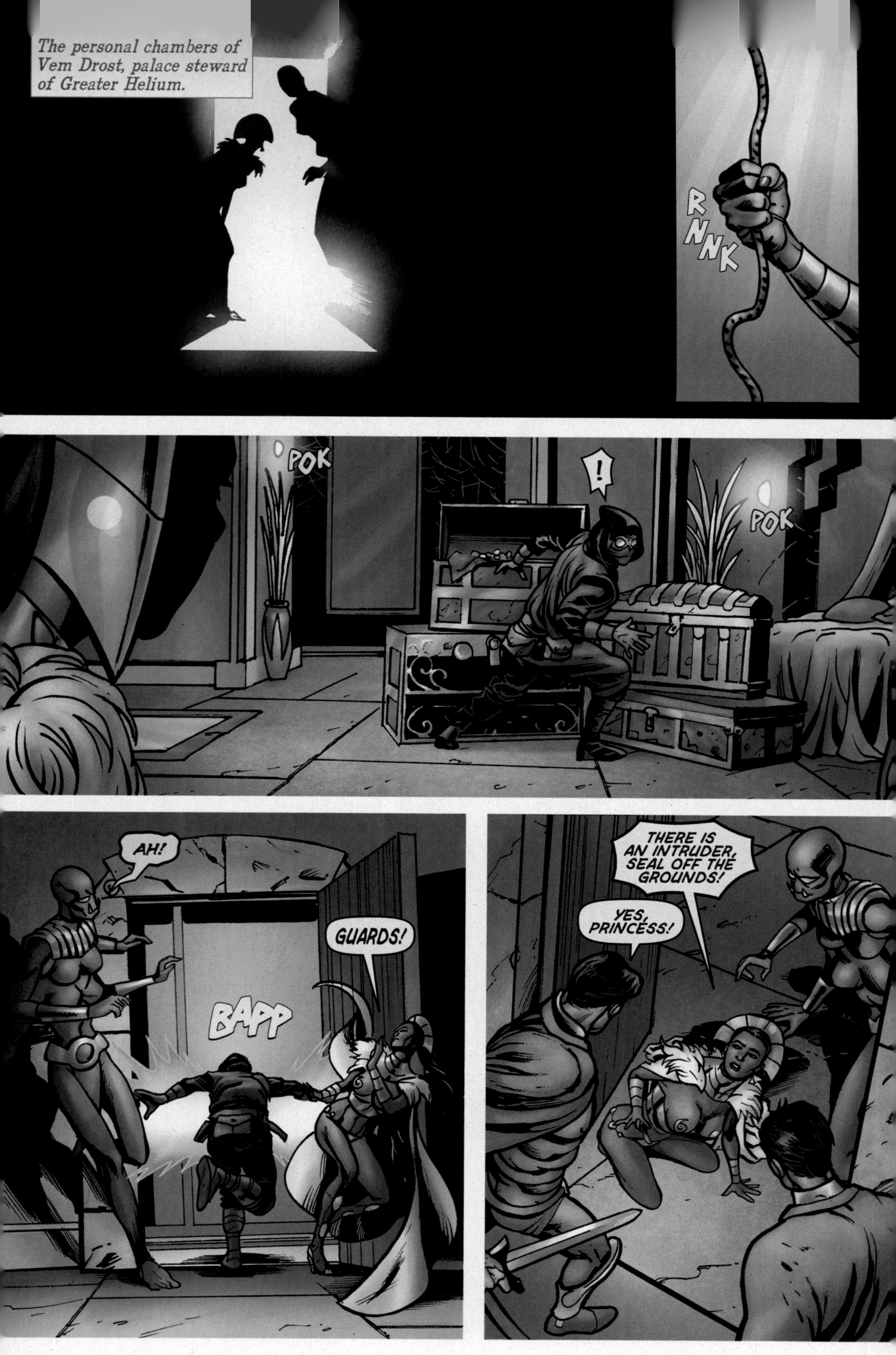
The personal chambers of Vem Drost, palace steward of Greater Helium.
RNNK
POK
!
POK
AH!
GUARDS!
BAPP
THERE IS AN INTRUDER, SEAL OFF THE GROUNDS!
YES, PRINCESS!

I DO NOT THINK THAT WAS THE ASSASSIN.

NOR I. AND WE MAY BE THANKFUL FOR IT, OR WE WOULD BE DEAD.

LOOKS LIKE VEM DROST WAS PLANNING A TRIP.

A LONG ONE AT THAT.

HERE'S SOMETHING!

WHATEVER'S INSIDE, IT'S HEAVY...

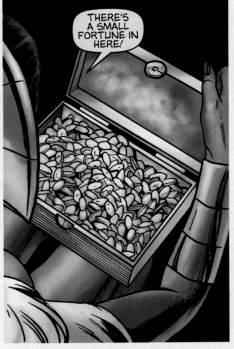

THERE'S A SMALL FORTUNE IN HERE!

THESE ARE ZODANGAN COINS...

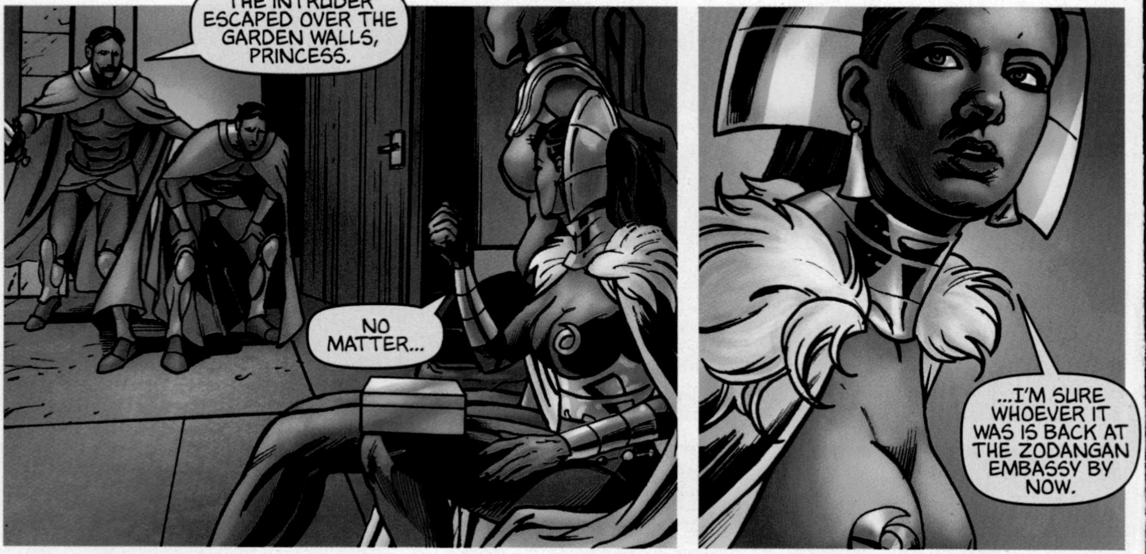
THE INTRUDER ESCAPED OVER THE GARDEN WALLS, PRINCESS.
NO MATTER...
...I'M SURE WHOEVER IT WAS IS BACK AT THE ZODANGAN EMBASSY BY NOW.

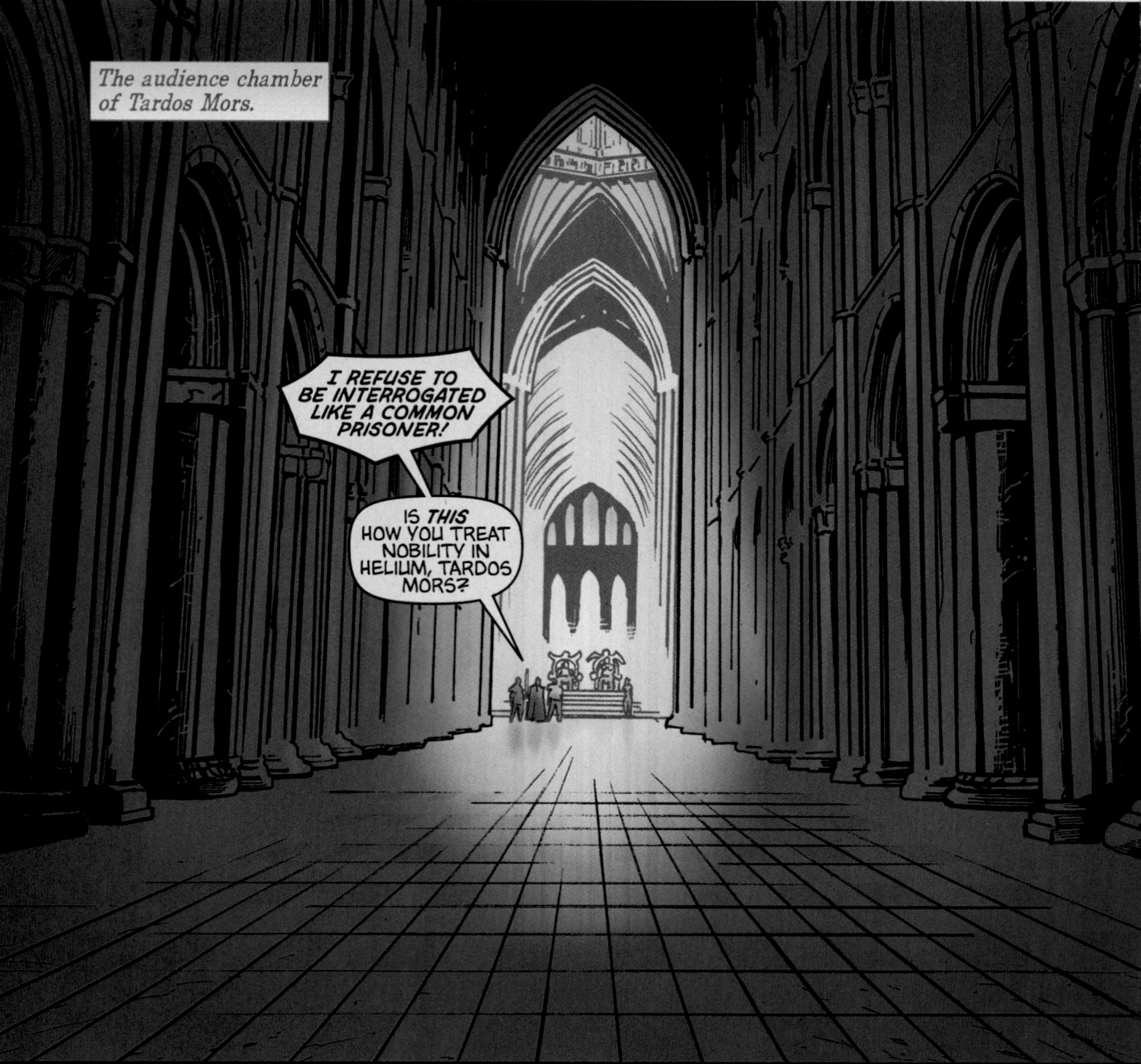
The audience chamber of Tardos Mors.
I REFUSE TO BE INTERROGATED LIKE A COMMON PRISONER!
IS THIS HOW YOU TREAT NOBILITY IN HELIUM, TARDOS MORS?

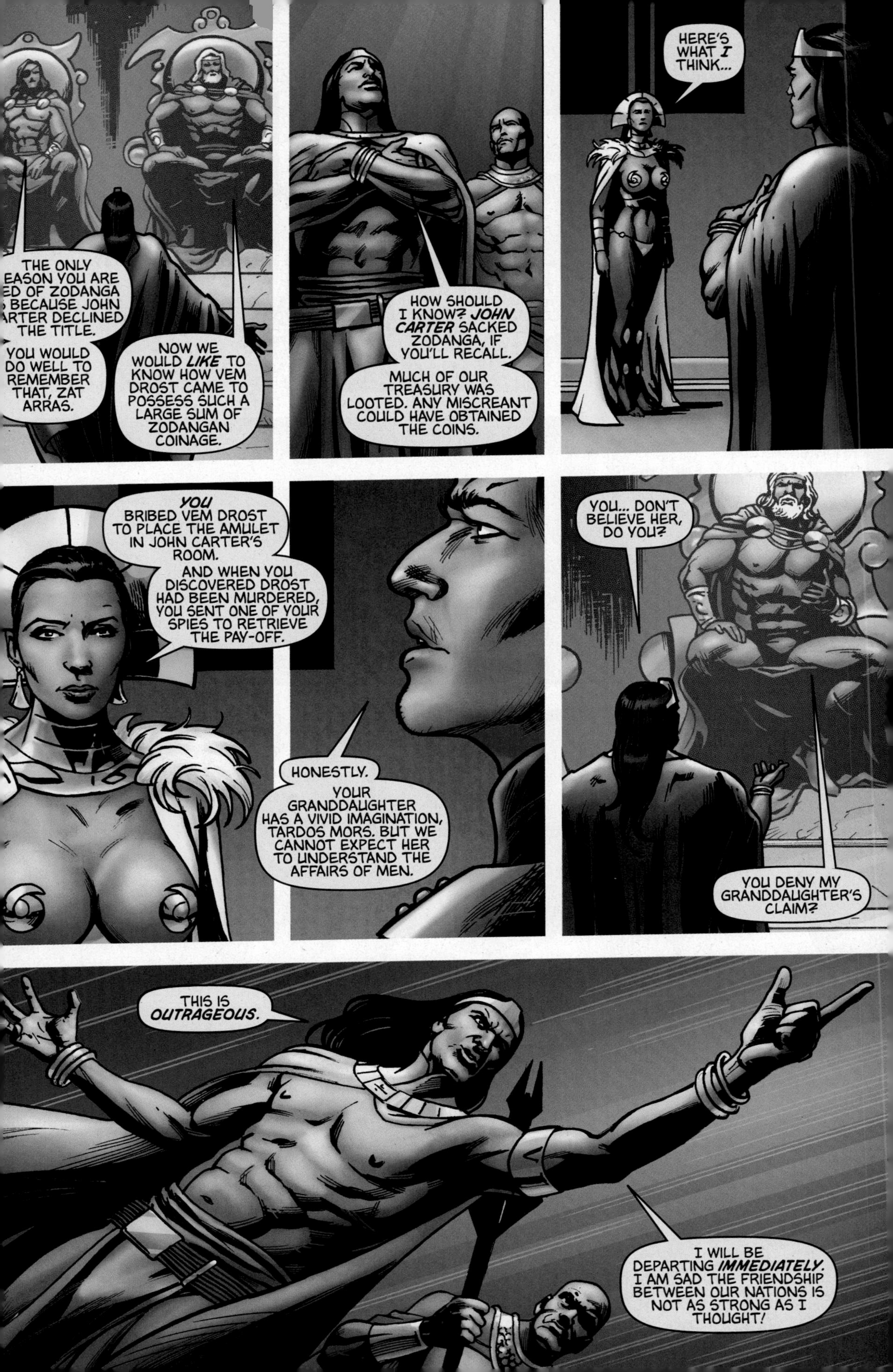

THE ONLY EASON YOU ARE ED OF ZODANGA BECAUSE JOHN ARTER DECLINED THE TITLE.
YOU WOULD DO WELL TO REMEMBER THAT, ZAT ARRAS.
NOW WE WOULD *LIKE* TO KNOW HOW VEM DROST CAME TO POSSESS SUCH A LARGE SUM OF ZODANGAN COINAGE.
HOW SHOULD I KNOW? *JOHN CARTER* SACKED ZODANGA, IF YOU'LL RECALL.
MUCH OF OUR TREASURY WAS LOOTED. ANY MISCREANT COULD HAVE OBTAINED THE COINS.
HERE'S WHAT *I* THINK...
YOU BRIBED VEM DROST TO PLACE THE AMULET IN JOHN CARTER'S ROOM.
AND WHEN YOU DISCOVERED DROST HAD BEEN MURDERED, YOU SENT ONE OF YOUR SPIES TO RETRIEVE THE PAY-OFF.
HONESTLY.
YOUR GRANDDAUGHTER HAS A VIVID IMAGINATION, TARDOS MORS. BUT WE CANNOT EXPECT HER TO UNDERSTAND THE AFFAIRS OF MEN.
YOU... DON'T BELIEVE HER, DO YOU?
YOU DENY MY GRANDDAUGHTER'S CLAIM?
THIS IS *OUTRAGEOUS*.
I WILL BE DEPARTING *IMMEDIATELY*. I AM SAD THE FRIENDSHIP BETWEEN OUR NATIONS IS NOT AS STRONG AS I THOUGHT!

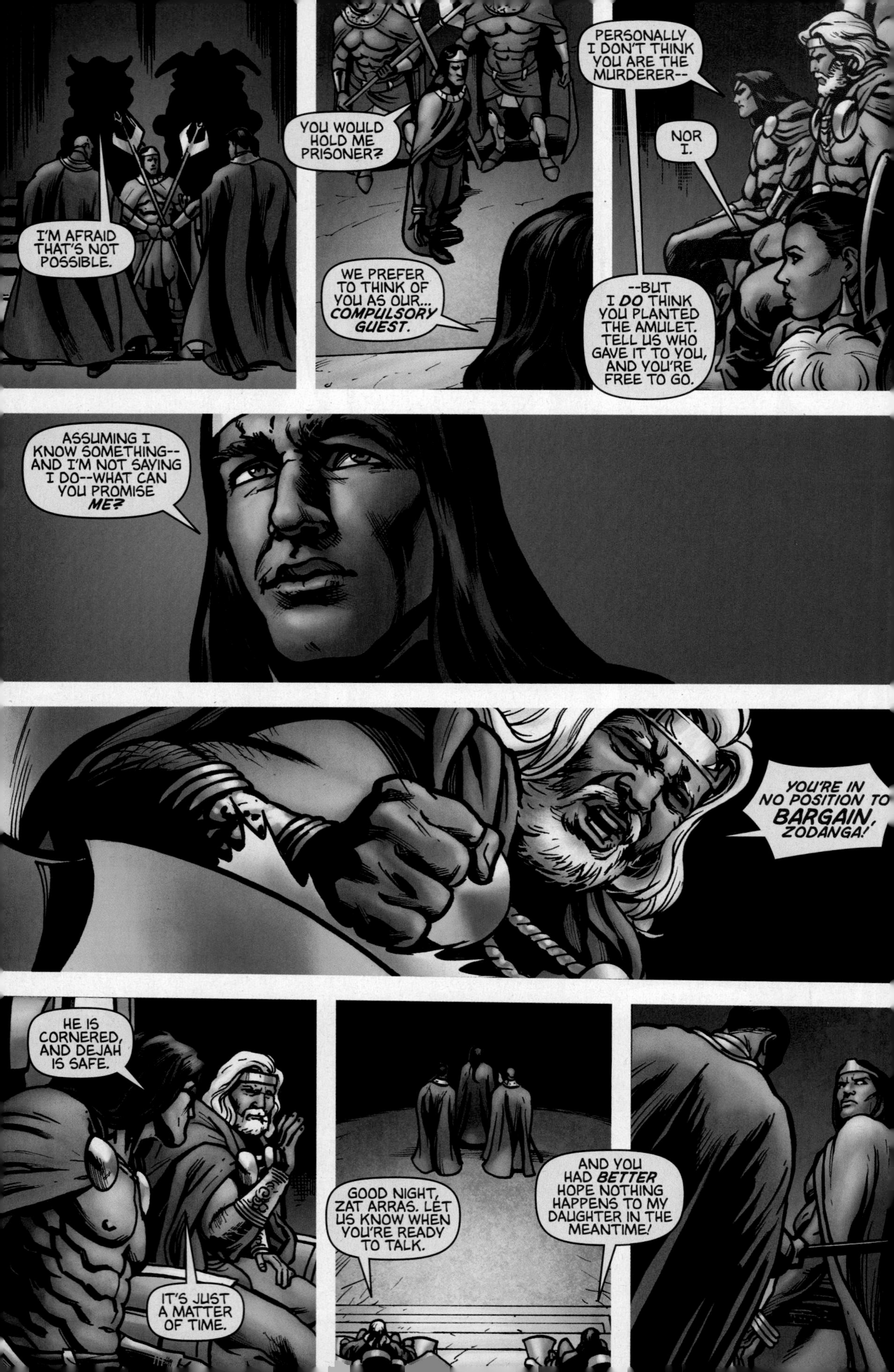
I'M AFRAID THAT'S NOT POSSIBLE.
YOU WOULD HOLD ME PRISONER?
WE PREFER TO THINK OF YOU AS OUR... COMPULSORY GUEST.
PERSONALLY I DON'T THINK YOU ARE THE MURDERER--
NOR I.
--BUT I DO THINK YOU PLANTED THE AMULET. TELL US WHO GAVE IT TO YOU, AND YOU'RE FREE TO GO.
ASSUMING I KNOW SOMETHING-- AND I'M NOT SAYING I DO--WHAT CAN YOU PROMISE ME?
YOU'RE IN NO POSITION TO BARGAIN, ZODANGA!
HE IS CORNERED, AND DEJAH IS SAFE.
IT'S JUST A MATTER OF TIME.
GOOD NIGHT, ZAT ARRAS. LET US KNOW WHEN YOU'RE READY TO TALK.
AND YOU HAD BETTER HOPE NOTHING HAPPENS TO MY DAUGHTER IN THE MEANTIME!

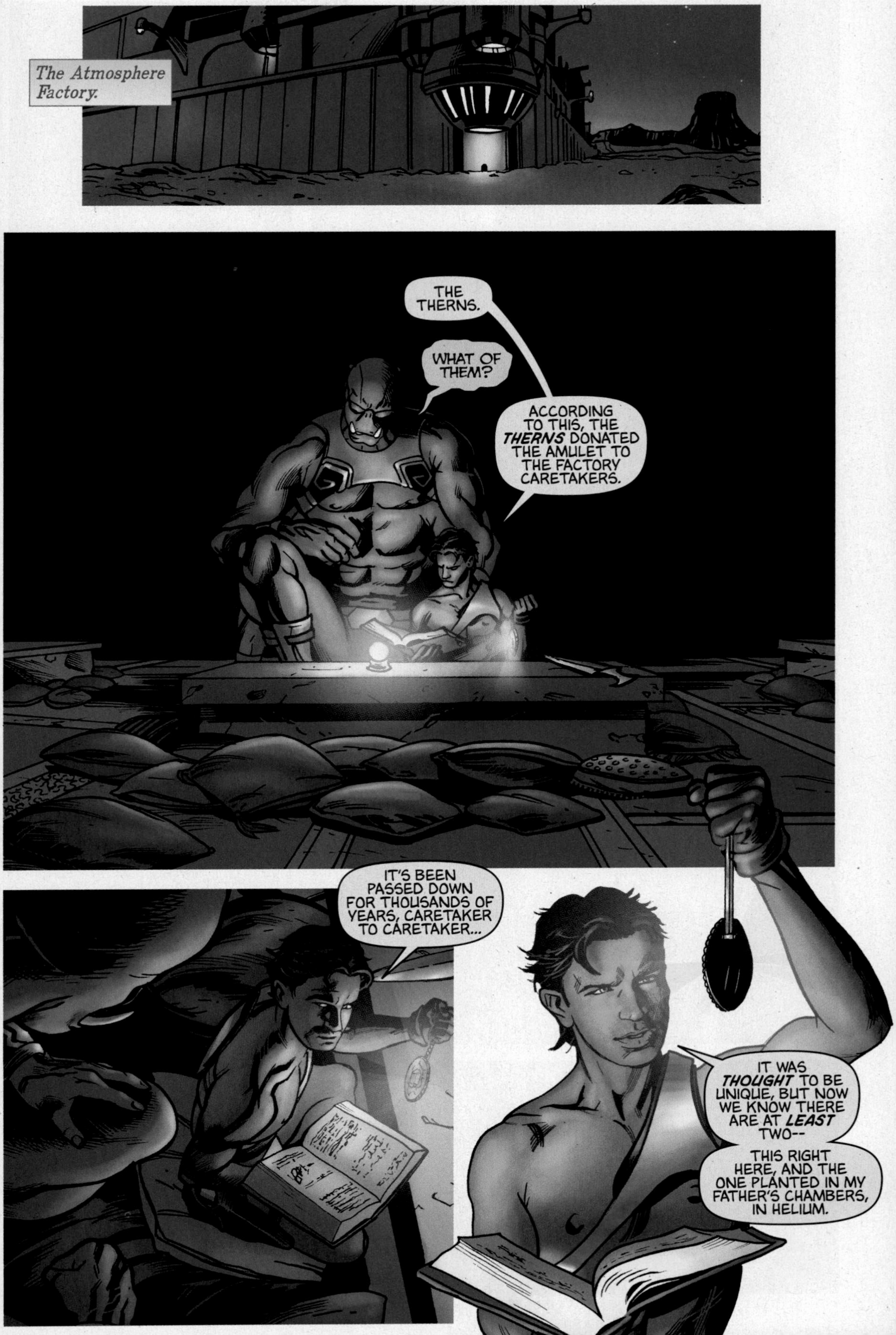
The Atmosphere Factory.
THE THERNS.
WHAT OF THEM?
ACCORDING TO THIS, THE *THERNS* DONATED THE AMULET TO THE FACTORY CARETAKERS.
IT'S BEEN PASSED DOWN FOR THOUSANDS OF YEARS, CARETAKER TO CARETAKER...
IT WAS *THOUGHT* TO BE UNIQUE, BUT NOW WE KNOW THERE ARE AT *LEAST* TWO--
THIS RIGHT HERE, AND THE ONE PLANTED IN MY FATHER'S CHAMBERS, IN HELIUM.

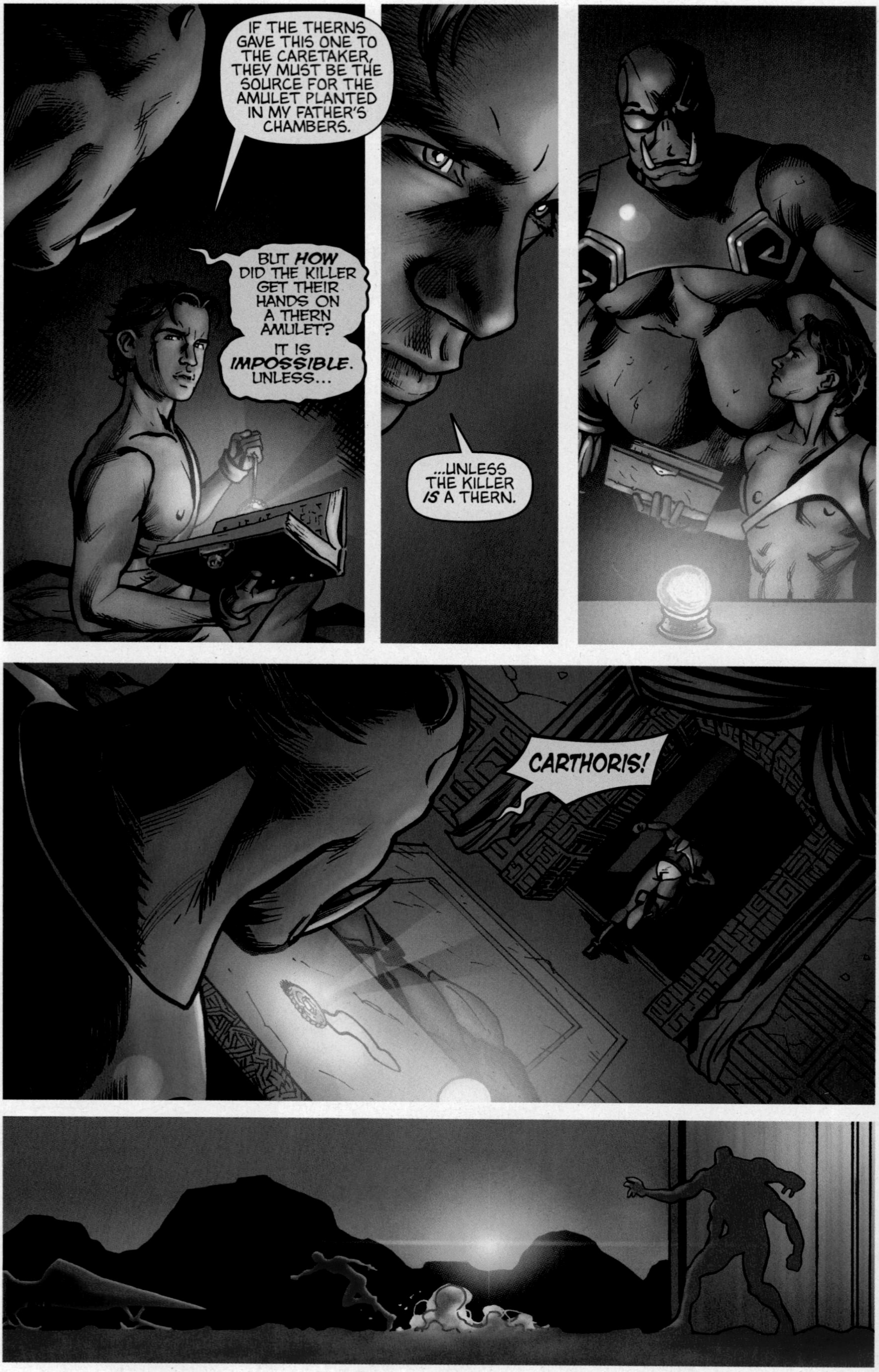
IF THE THERNS GAVE THIS ONE TO THE CARETAKER, THEY MUST BE THE SOURCE FOR THE AMULET PLANTED IN MY FATHER'S CHAMBERS.
BUT HOW DID THE KILLER GET THEIR HANDS ON A THERN AMULET?
IT IS IMPOSSIBLE. UNLESS...
...UNLESS THE KILLER IS A THERN.
CARTHORIS!

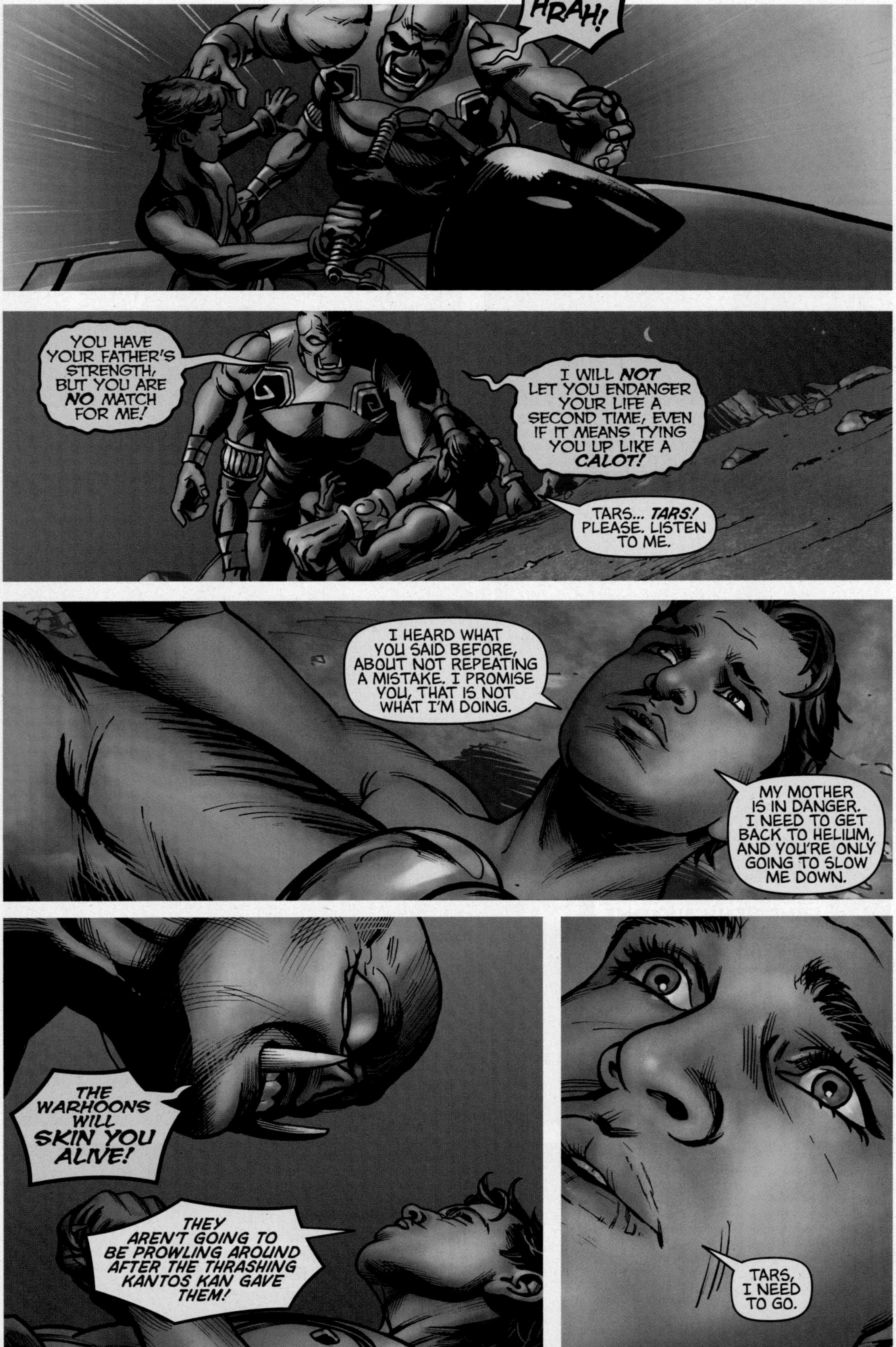
HRAH!
YOU HAVE YOUR FATHER'S STRENGTH, BUT YOU ARE NO MATCH FOR ME!
I WILL NOT LET YOU ENDANGER YOUR LIFE A SECOND TIME, EVEN IF IT MEANS TYING YOU UP LIKE A CALOT!
TARS... TARS! PLEASE. LISTEN TO ME.
I HEARD WHAT YOU SAID BEFORE, ABOUT NOT REPEATING A MISTAKE. I PROMISE YOU, THAT IS NOT WHAT I'M DOING.
MY MOTHER IS IN DANGER. I NEED TO GET BACK TO HELIUM, AND YOU'RE ONLY GOING TO SLOW ME DOWN.
THE WARHOONS WILL SKIN YOU ALIVE!
THEY AREN'T GOING TO BE PROWLING AROUND AFTER THE THRASHING KANTOS KAN GAVE THEM!
TARS, I NEED TO GO.

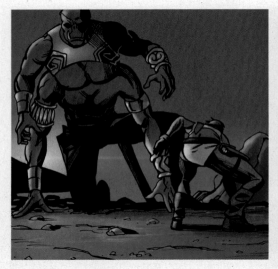

VRE EE

The Temple of Issus at Greater Helium.

DEJAH THORIS, PLEASE COME TO MY AUDIENCE CHAMBER. I MUST SPEAK WITH YOU.

CAN IT WAIT, HEKKADOR? I AM TIRED.

I AM AFRAID NOT, PRINCESS.

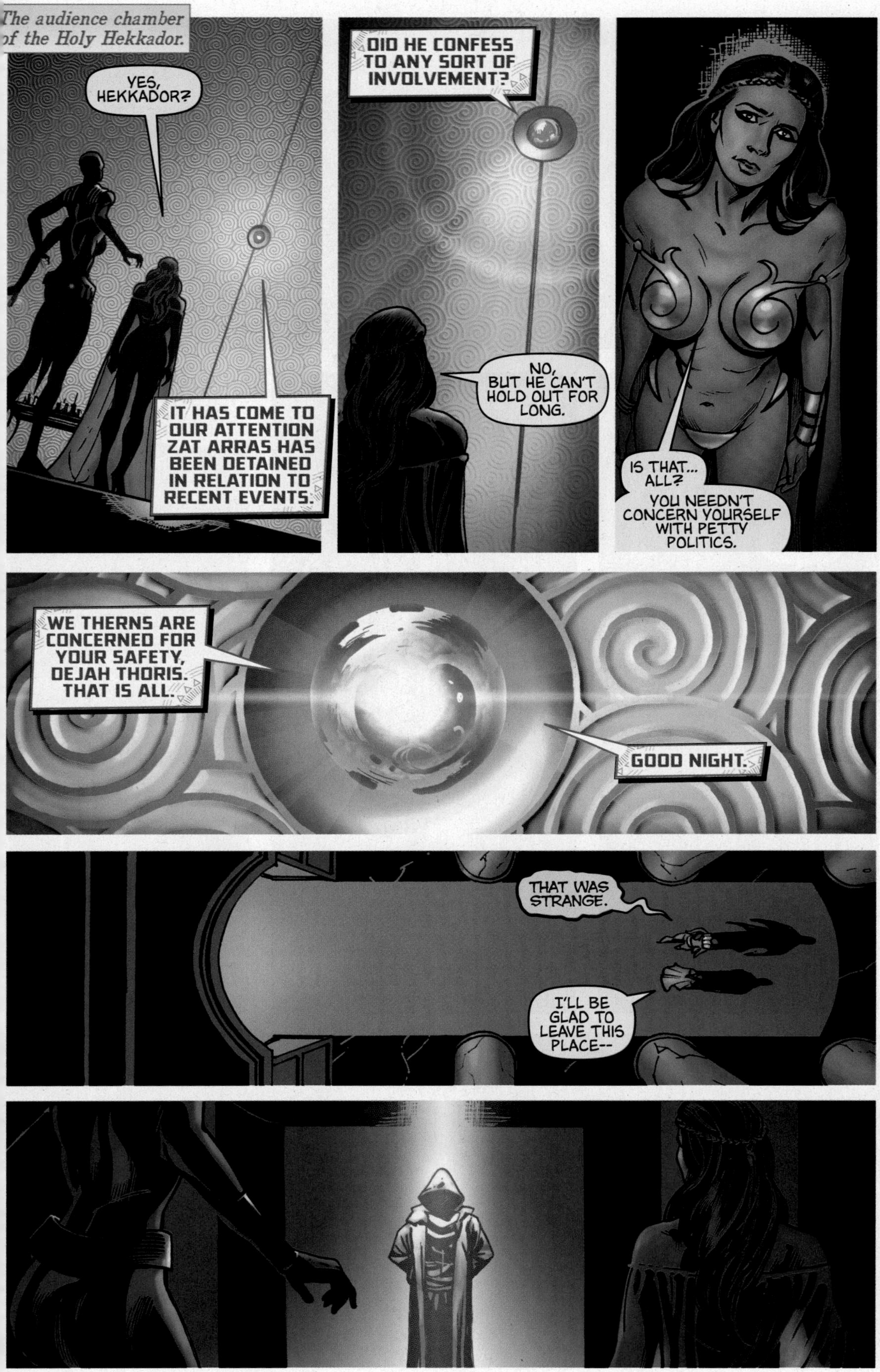
The audience chamber of the Holy Hekkador.
YES, HEKKADOR?
IT HAS COME TO OUR ATTENTION ZAT ARRAS HAS BEEN DETAINED IN RELATION TO RECENT EVENTS.
DID HE CONFESS TO ANY SORT OF INVOLVEMENT?
NO, BUT HE CAN'T HOLD OUT FOR LONG.
IS THAT... ALL?
YOU NEEDN'T CONCERN YOURSELF WITH PETTY POLITICS.
WE THERNS ARE CONCERNED FOR YOUR SAFETY, DEJAH THORIS. THAT IS ALL.
GOOD NIGHT.
THAT WAS STRANGE.
I'LL BE GLAD TO LEAVE THIS PLACE--

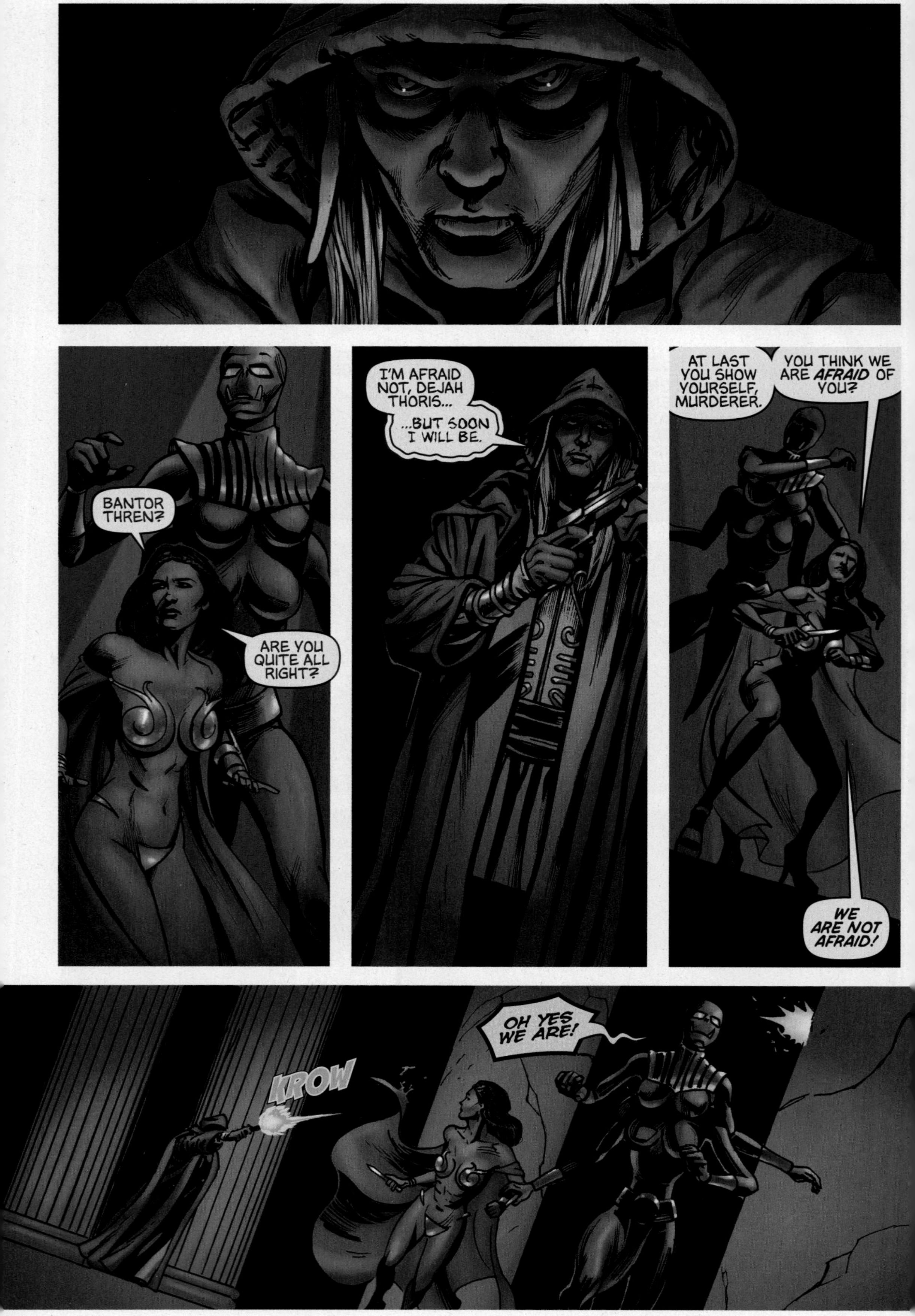
BANTOR THREN?
ARE YOU QUITE ALL RIGHT?
I'M AFRAID NOT, DEJAH THORIS...
...BUT SOON I WILL BE.
AT LAST YOU SHOW YOURSELF, MURDERER.
YOU THINK WE ARE *AFRAID* OF YOU?
WE ARE NOT AFRAID!
OH YES WE ARE!
KROW

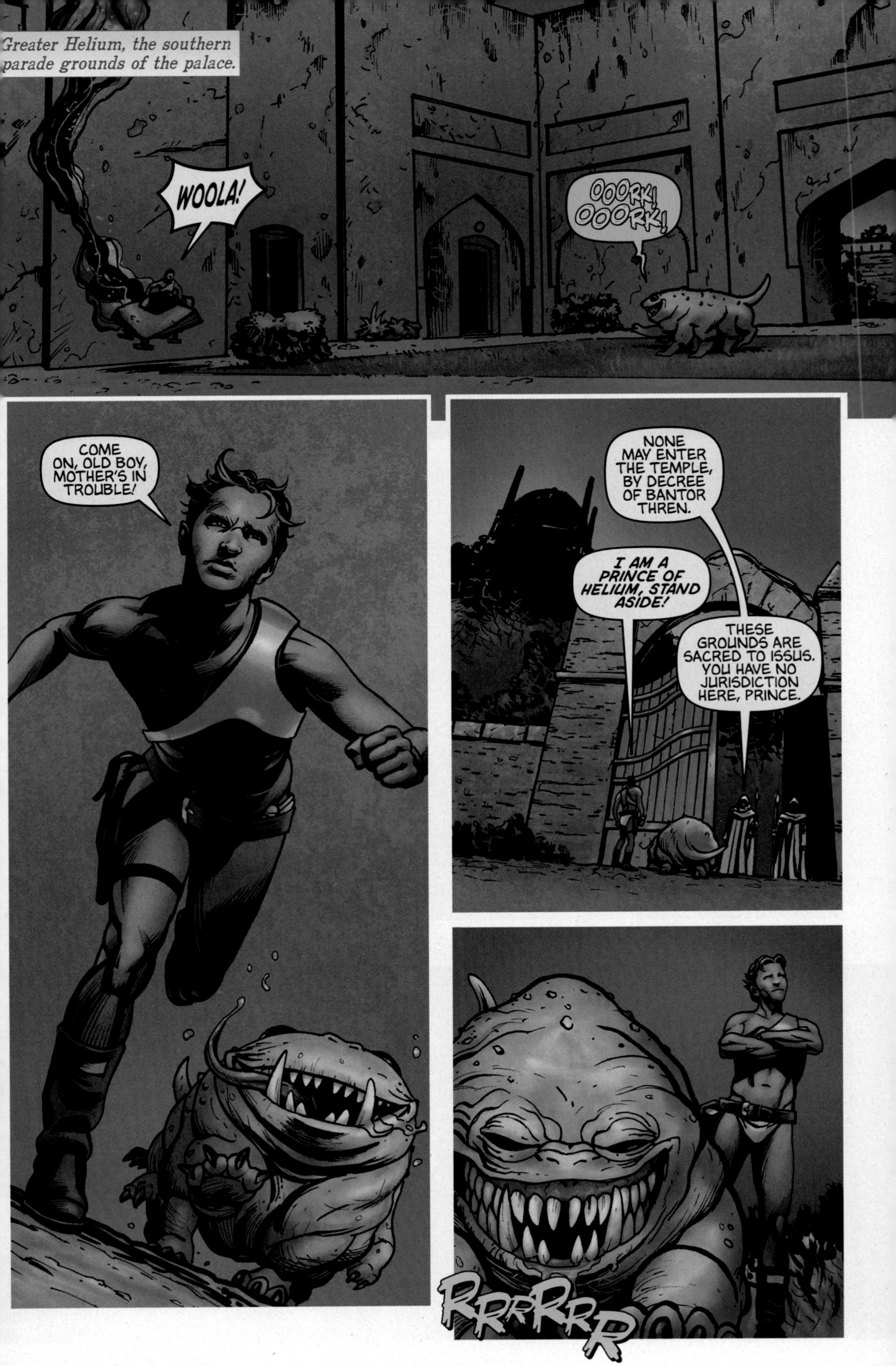
Greater Helium, the southern parade grounds of the palace.
WOOLA!
OOORK! OOORK!
COME ON, OLD BOY, MOTHER'S IN TROUBLE!
NONE MAY ENTER THE TEMPLE, BY DECREE OF BANTOR THREN.
I AM A PRINCE OF HELIUM, STAND ASIDE!
THESE GROUNDS ARE SACRED TO ISSUS. YOU HAVE NO JURISDICTION HERE, PRINCE.
RRRRRRR

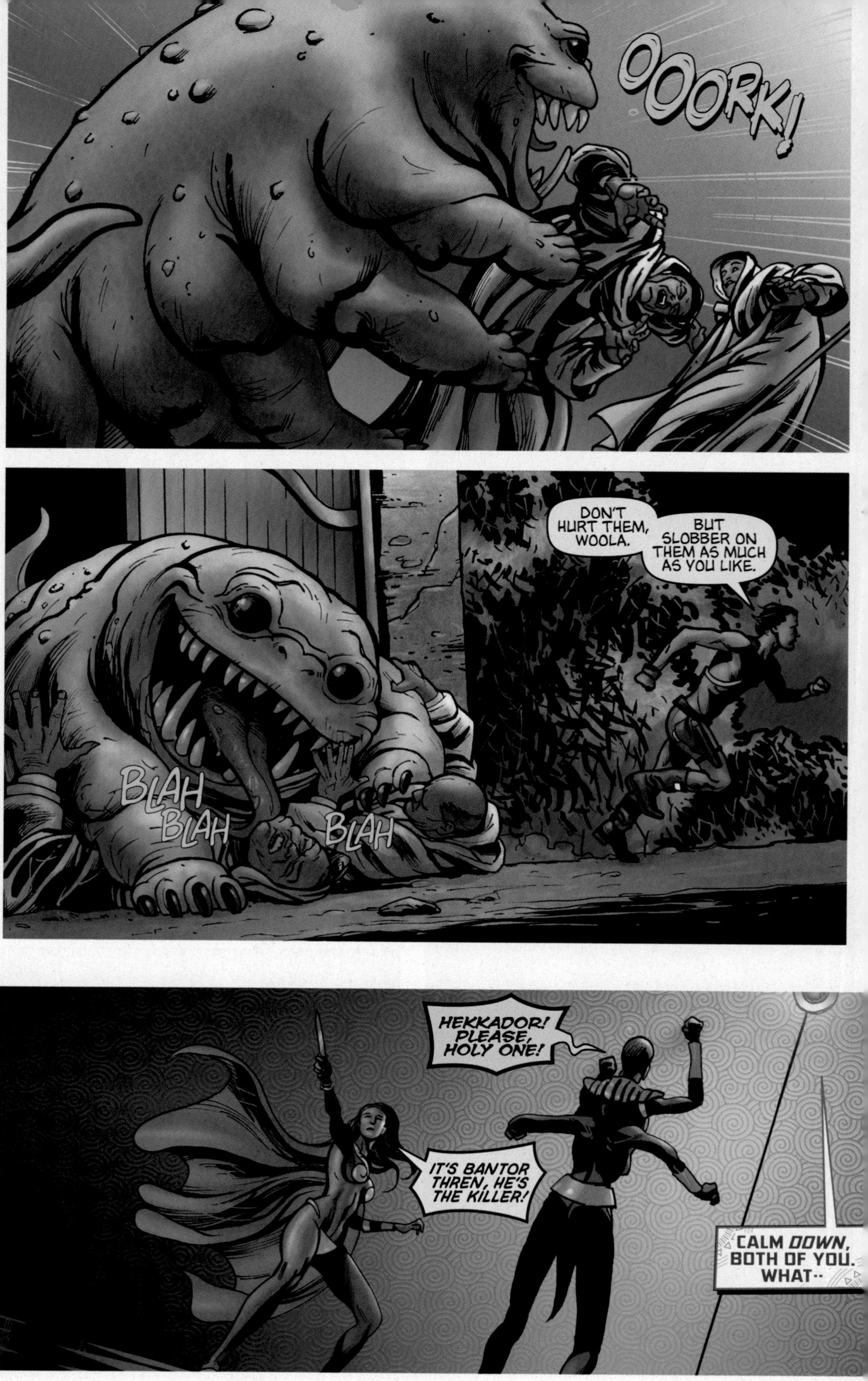
OOORK!
DON'T HURT THEM, WOOLA.
BUT SLOBBER ON THEM AS MUCH AS YOU LIKE.
BLAH BLAH
BLAH
HEKKADOR! PLEASE, HOLY ONE!
IT'S BANTOR THREN, HE'S THE KILLER!
CALM DOWN, BOTH OF YOU. WHAT--

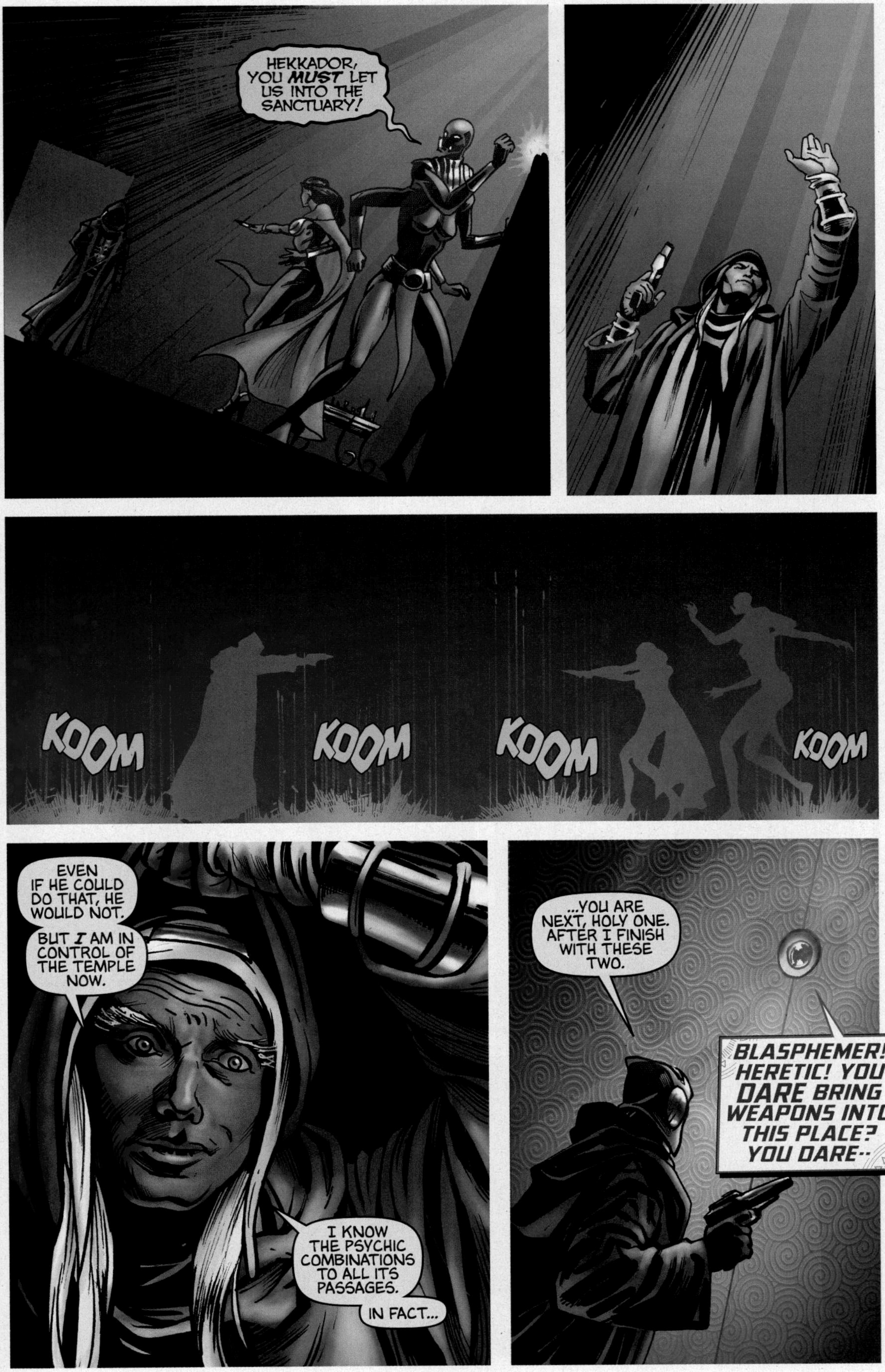
HEKKADOR, YOU MUST LET US INTO THE SANCTUARY!
KOOM
KOOM
KOOM
KOOM
EVEN IF HE COULD DO THAT, HE WOULD NOT.
BUT I AM IN CONTROL OF THE TEMPLE NOW.
I KNOW THE PSYCHIC COMBINATIONS TO ALL ITS PASSAGES.
IN FACT...
...YOU ARE NEXT, HOLY ONE. AFTER I FINISH WITH THESE TWO.
BLASPHEMER! HERETIC! YOU DARE BRING WEAPONS INTO THIS PLACE? YOU DARE--

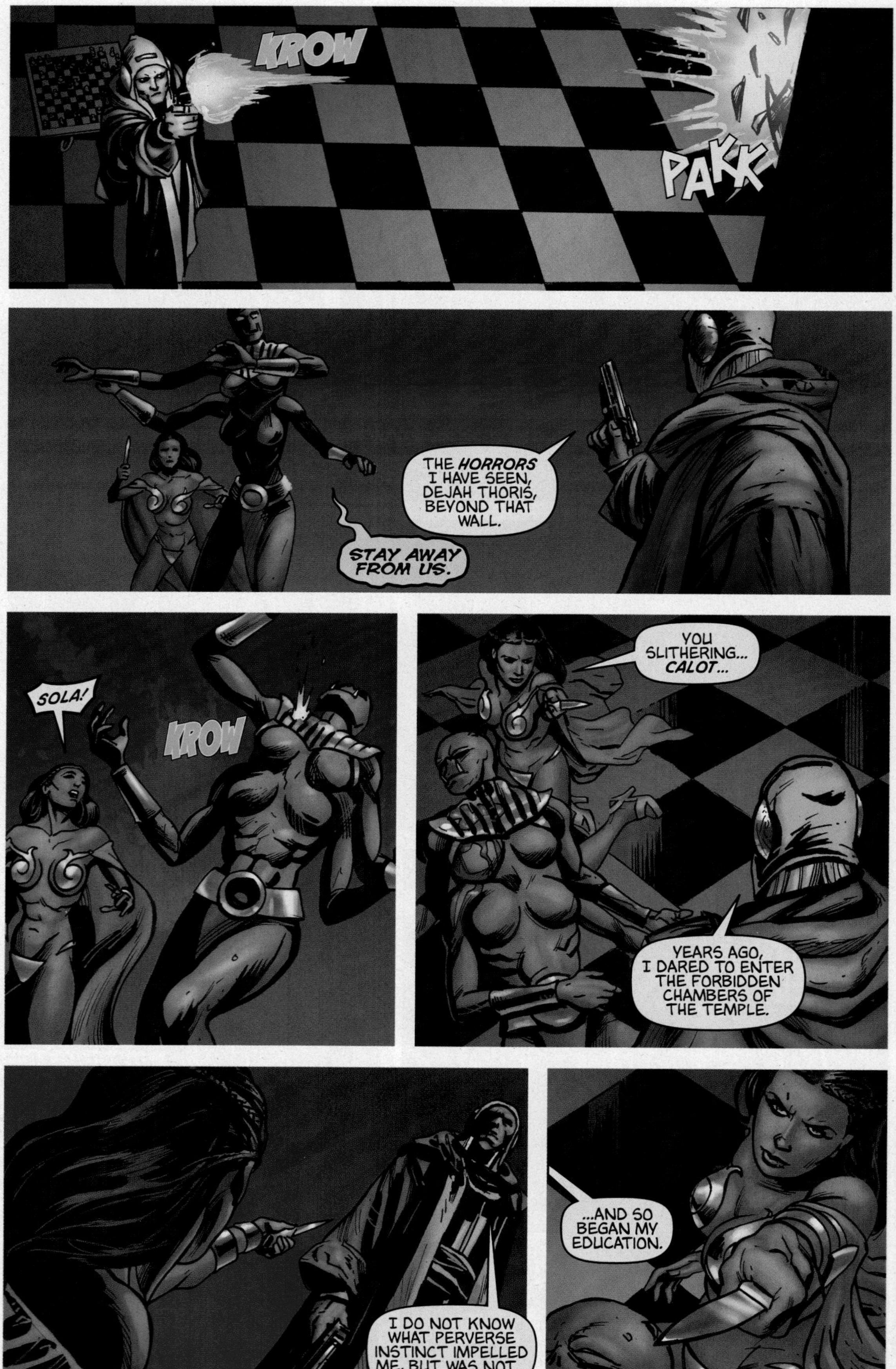
KROW
PAKK
THE HORRORS I HAVE SEEN, DEJAH THORIS, BEYOND THAT WALL.
STAY AWAY FROM US.
SOLA!
KROW
YOU SLITHERING... CALOT...
YEARS AGO, I DARED TO ENTER THE FORBIDDEN CHAMBERS OF THE TEMPLE.
I DO NOT KNOW WHAT PERVERSE INSTINCT IMPELLED ME, BUT WAS NOT... SO DIFFICULT...
...AND SO BEGAN MY EDUCATION.

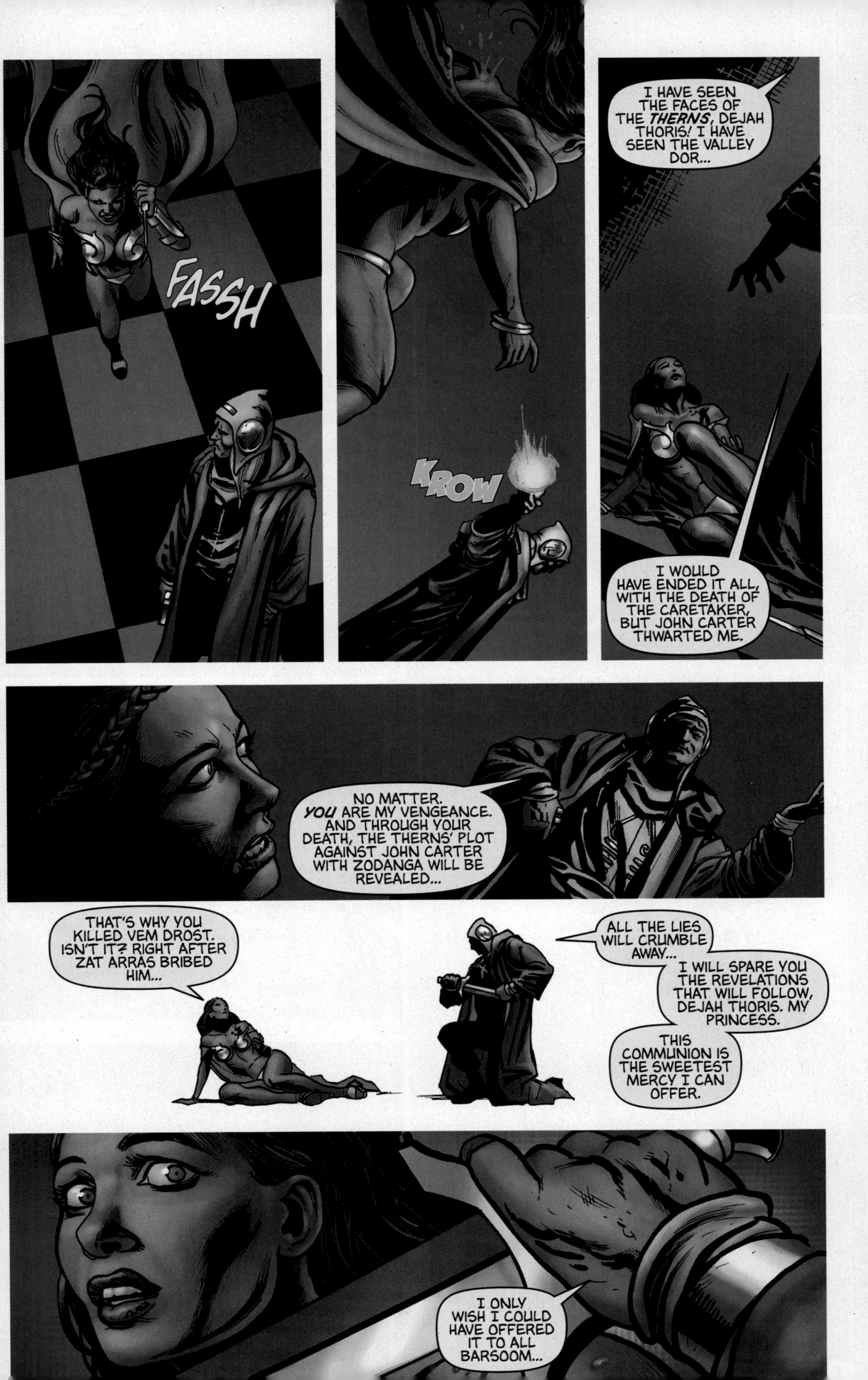
FASSH
KROW
I HAVE SEEN THE FACES OF THE *THERNS*, DEJAH THORIS! I HAVE SEEN THE VALLEY DOR...
I WOULD HAVE ENDED IT ALL, WITH THE DEATH OF THE CARETAKER, BUT JOHN CARTER THWARTED ME.
NO MATTER. *YOU* ARE MY VENGEANCE. AND THROUGH YOUR DEATH, THE THERNS' PLOT AGAINST JOHN CARTER WITH ZODANGA WILL BE REVEALED...
THAT'S WHY YOU KILLED VEM DROST. ISN'T IT? RIGHT AFTER ZAT ARRAS BRIBED HIM...
ALL THE LIES WILL CRUMBLE AWAY...
I WILL SPARE YOU THE REVELATIONS THAT WILL FOLLOW, DEJAH THORIS. MY PRINCESS.
THIS COMMUNION IS THE SWEETEST MERCY I CAN OFFER.
I ONLY WISH I COULD HAVE OFFERED IT TO ALL BARSOOM...

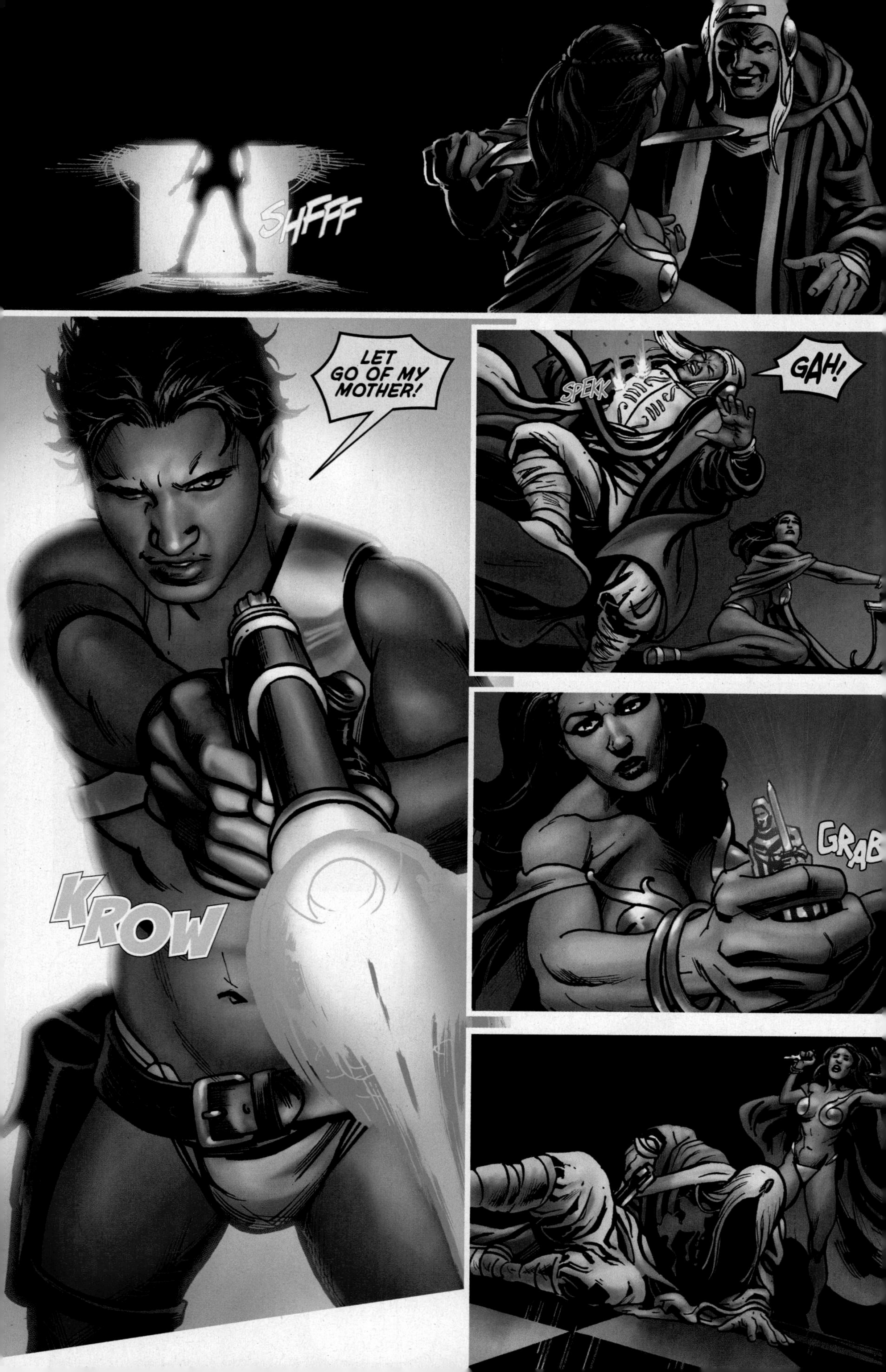
SHFFF
LET GO OF MY MOTHER!
KROW
SPEKK
GAH!
GRAB

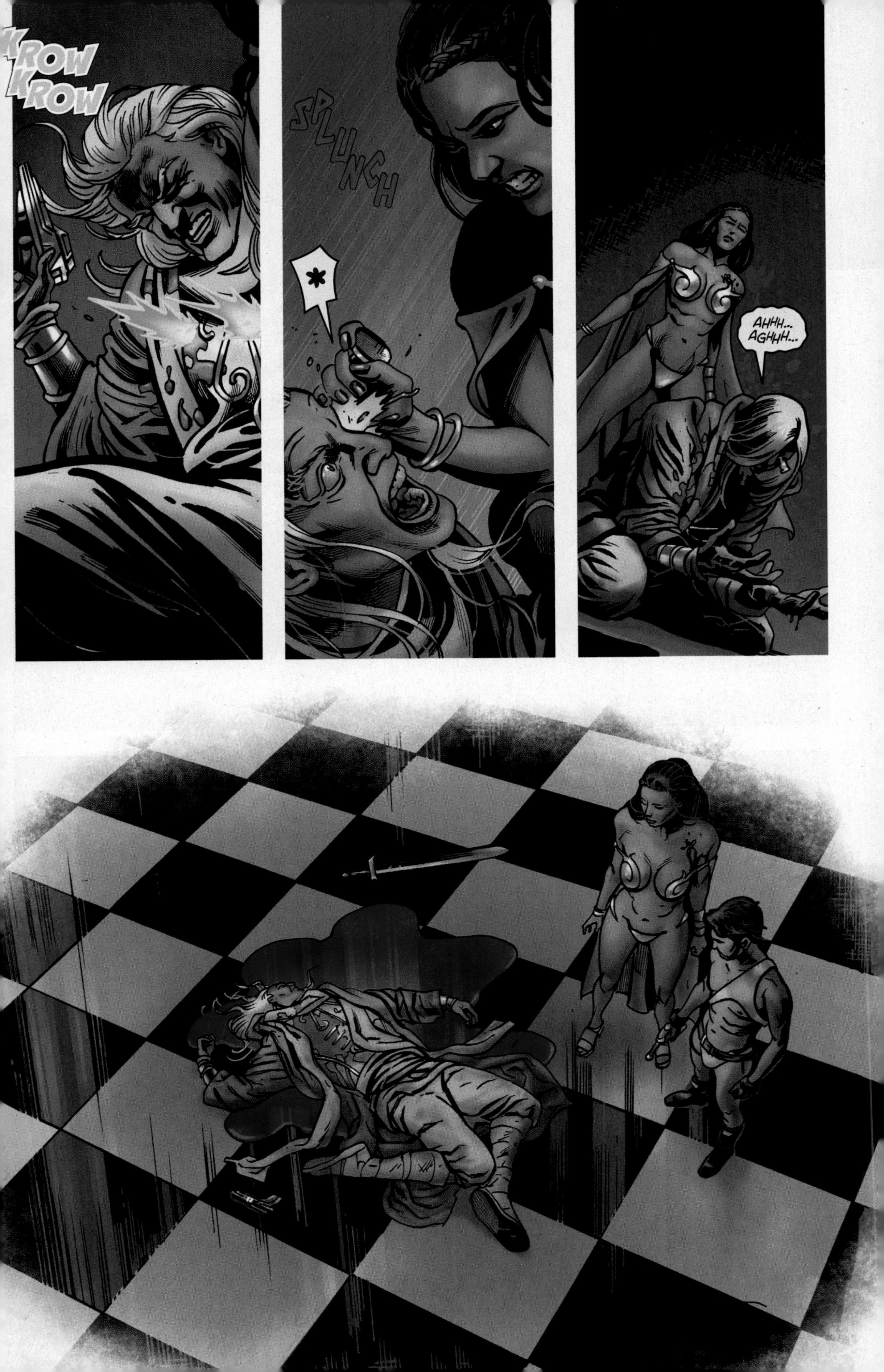
KROW
KROW
SPLUNCH
*
AHHH...
AGHHH...

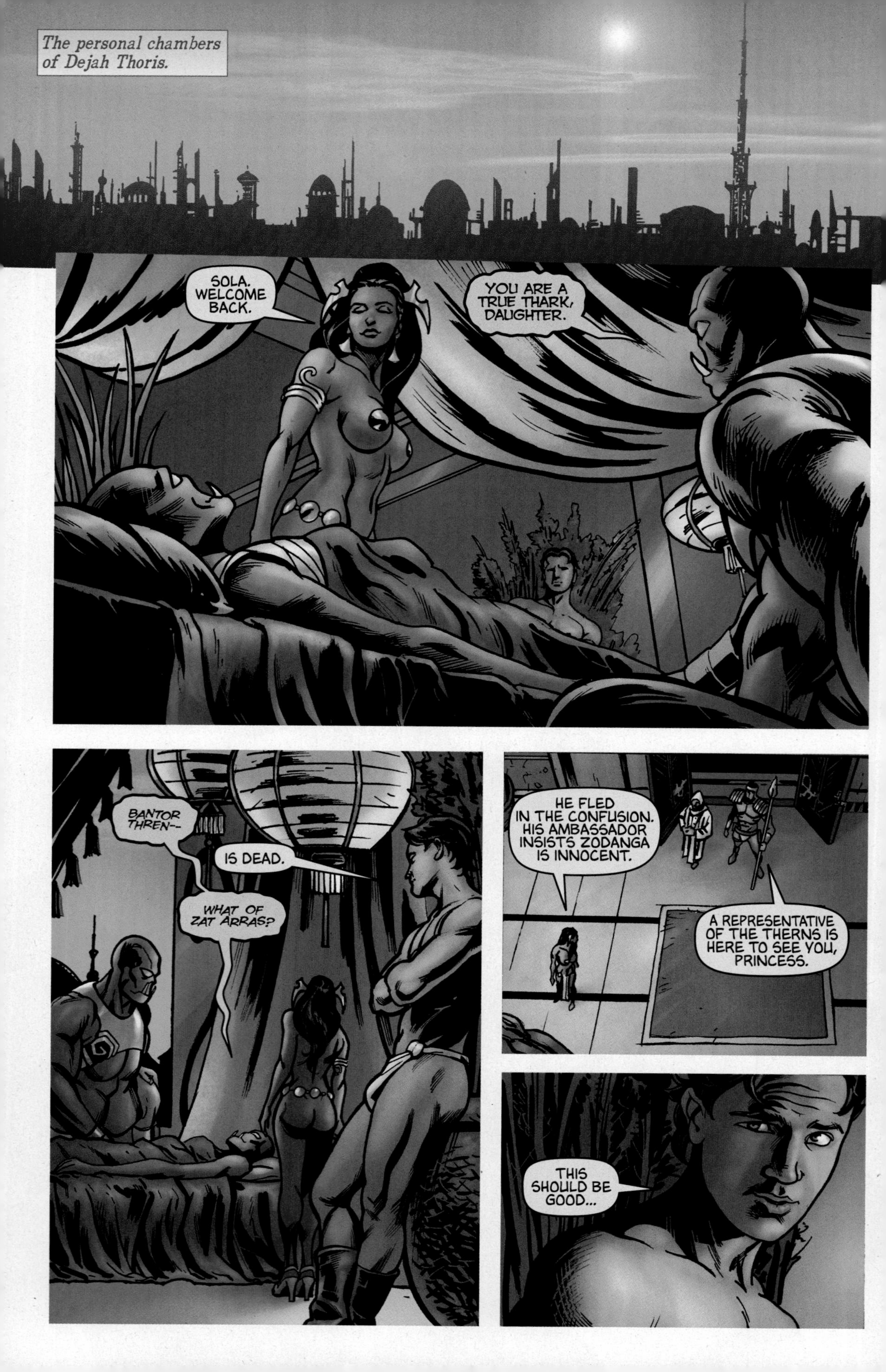
The personal chambers of Dejah Thoris.
SOLA. WELCOME BACK.
YOU ARE A TRUE THARK, DAUGHTER.
BANTOR THREN--
IS DEAD.
WHAT OF ZAT ARRAS?
HE FLED IN THE CONFUSION. HIS AMBASSADOR INSISTS ZODANGA IS INNOCENT.
A REPRESENTATIVE OF THE THERNS IS HERE TO SEE YOU, PRINCESS.
THIS SHOULD BE GOOD...

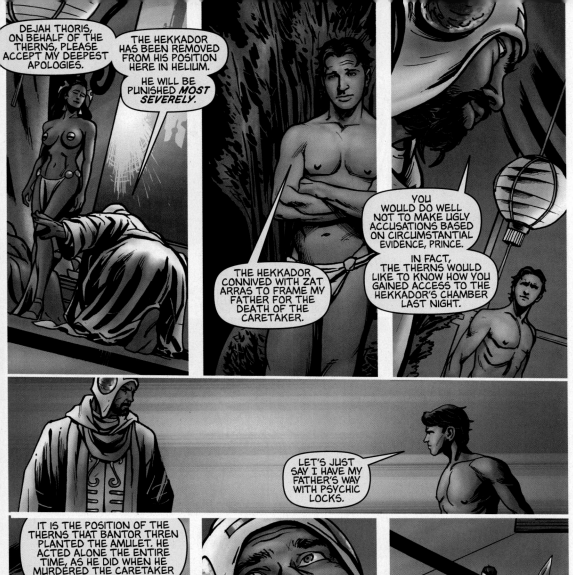

DEJAH THORIS, ON BEHALF OF THE THERNS, PLEASE ACCEPT MY DEEPEST APOLOGIES.

THE HEKKADOR HAS BEEN REMOVED FROM HIS POSITION HERE IN HELIUM.

HE WILL BE PUNISHED *MOST SEVERELY.*

THE HEKKADOR CONNIVED WITH ZAT ARRAS TO FRAME MY FATHER FOR THE DEATH OF THE CARETAKER.

YOU WOULD DO WELL NOT TO MAKE UGLY ACCUSATIONS BASED ON CIRCUMSTANTIAL EVIDENCE, PRINCE.

IN FACT, THE THERNS WOULD LIKE TO KNOW HOW YOU GAINED ACCESS TO THE HEKKADOR'S CHAMBER LAST NIGHT.

LET'S JUST SAY I HAVE MY FATHER'S WAY WITH PSYCHIC LOCKS.

IT IS THE POSITION OF THE THERNS THAT BANTOR THREN PLANTED THE AMULET. HE ACTED ALONE THE ENTIRE TIME, AS HE DID WHEN HE MURDERED THE CARETAKER OF THE ATMOSPHERE FACTORY.

HE SAID... HE SAW THE THERNS, THE VALLEY DOR...

THERE IS NO QUESTION THREN GAINED ACCESS TO THE FORBIDDEN PRECINCTS OF THE TEMPLE.

THAT IT DROVE HIM MAD SHOULD SURPRISE NO ONE.

SURELY NONE OF US BELIEVE THE RAVINGS OF A MAN WHO SOUGHT THE DESTRUCTION OF ALL LIFE ON BARSOOM?

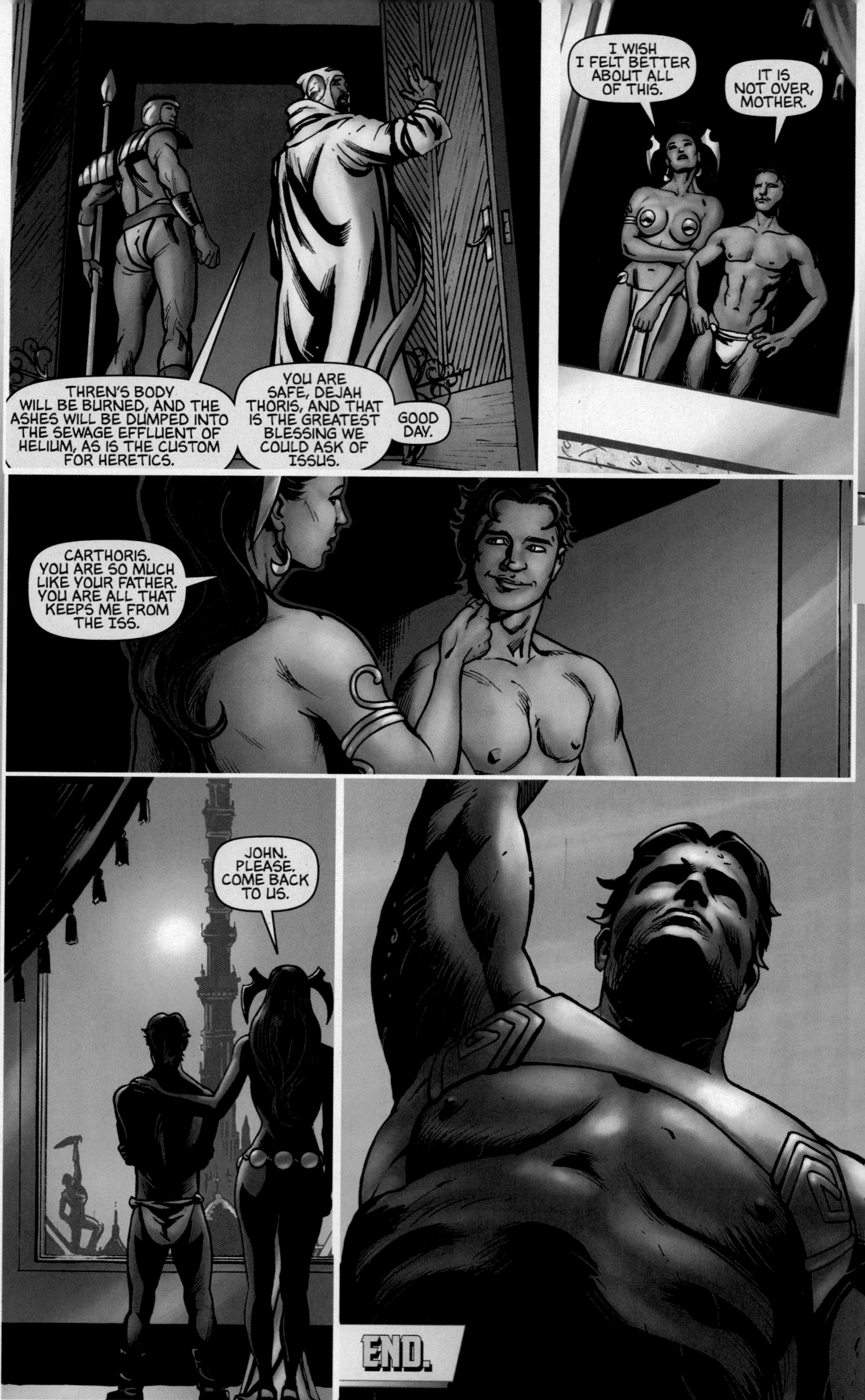
THREN'S BODY WILL BE BURNED, AND THE ASHES WILL BE DUMPED INTO THE SEWAGE EFFLUENT OF HELIUM, AS IS THE CUSTOM FOR HERETICS.
YOU ARE SAFE, DEJAH THORIS, AND THAT IS THE GREATEST BLESSING WE COULD ASK OF ISSUS.
GOOD DAY.
I WISH I FELT BETTER ABOUT ALL OF THIS.
IT IS NOT OVER, MOTHER.
CARTHORIS. YOU ARE SO MUCH LIKE YOUR FATHER. YOU ARE ALL THAT KEEPS ME FROM THE ISS.
JOHN. PLEASE. COME BACK TO US.
END.

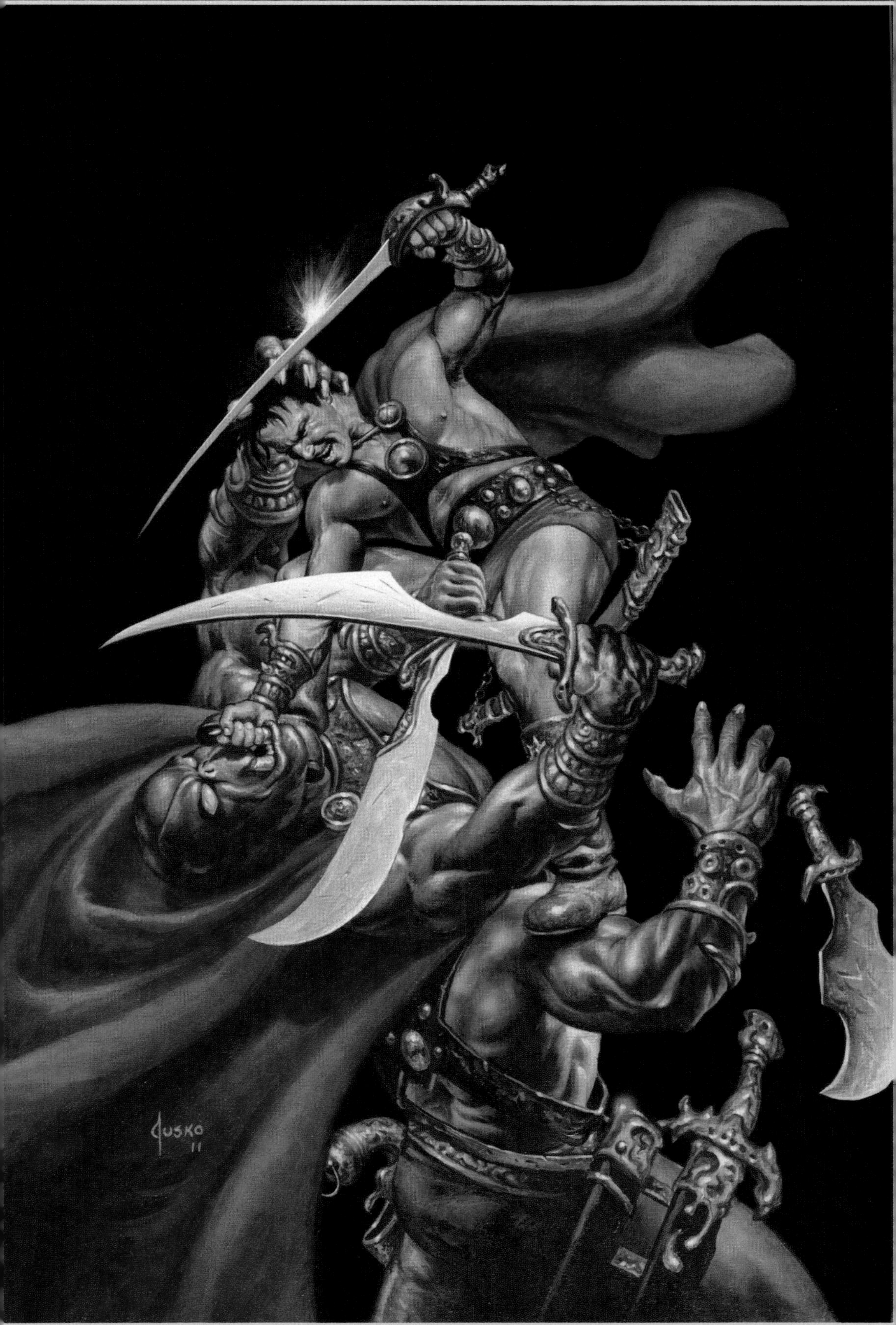
JUSKO
11

GODS OF MARS PART ONE:

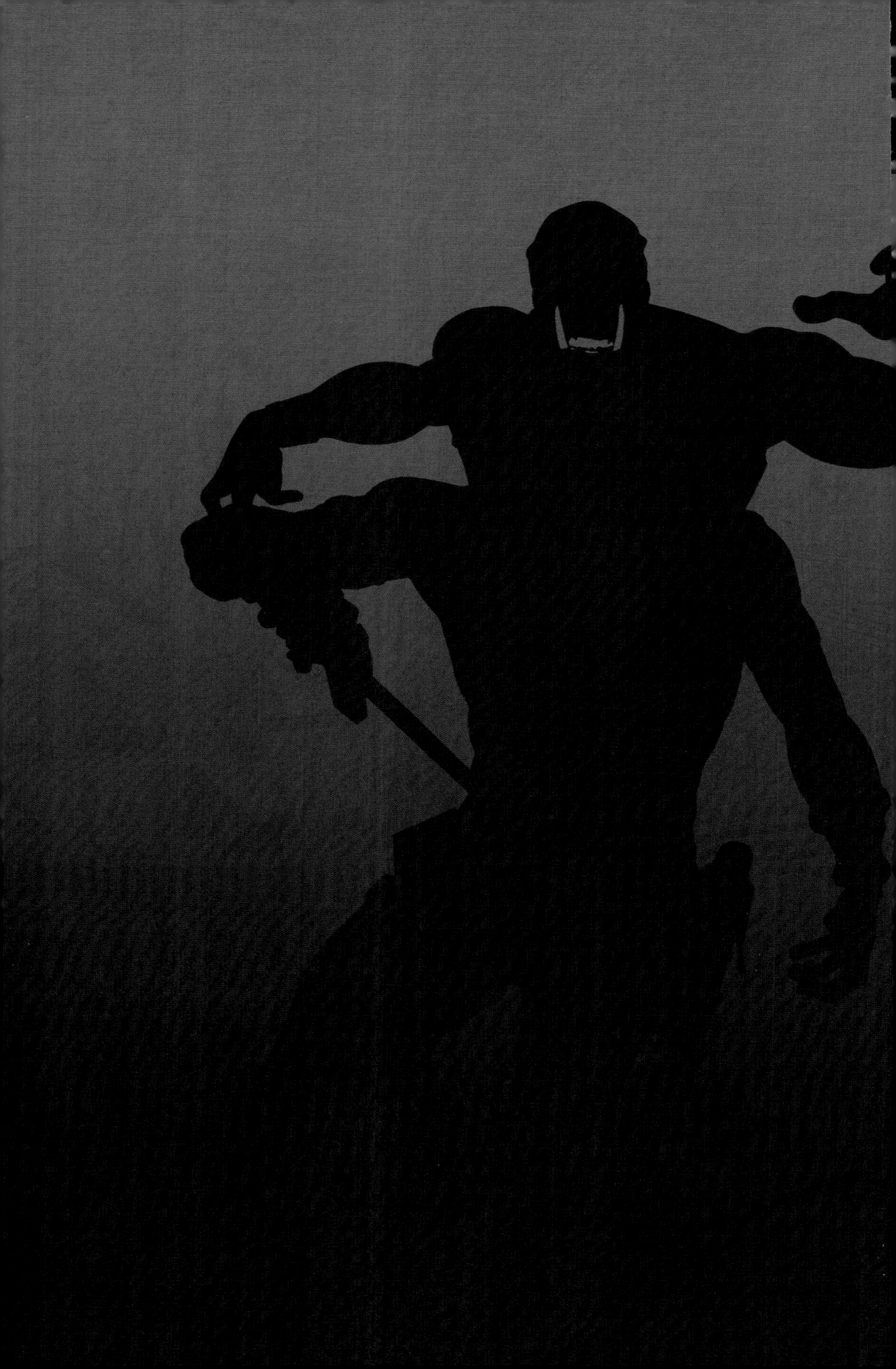

Twenty-one years had passed since I had laid the body of my great-uncle, Captain John Carter of Virginia, in that strange mausoleum in the old cemetery at Richmond.

Often had I pondered the odd instructions he had left me, especially his direction that he be laid in an open casket, and that the bolts of the vault's door be accessible only from the inside.

I had read the remarkable manuscript of this remarkable man, who remembered no childhood and could not even offer a vague guess as to his age; this man who had spent ten years upon Mars, fighting for and against the green and red men, and who had won the beautiful Dejah Thoris, Princess of Helium, for his wife.

Often I had wondered if John Carter were really dead, or if he had returned to Barsoom to find he had opened the atmosphere plant in time to save the dying planet on that far-gone day that had seen him hurtled ruthlessly back to Earth.

Had he found his black-haired Princess and the son he had never known? Or had he been too late, and gone back to a living death upon a dead world?

Thus was I lost in speculation until one sultry August evening when old Ben, my body servant, handed me a telegram. Tearing it open I read:

> 'Meet me to-morrow Hotel Raleigh Richmond.
> JOHN CARTER'

I took the first train for Richmond the next day and within two hours was being ushered into the room occupied by John Carter.

Apparently he had not aged a minute. His eyes were undimmed, and the only lines upon his face were the lines of iron determination that always had been there.

'Well, nephew,' he greeted me, 'do you feel as though you were seeing a ghost, or suffering from too many of old Ben's juleps?'

'Juleps, I reckon,' I replied. 'But maybe it's just the sight of you again that affects me. You have been back to Mars? And Dejah Thoris? You found her well and awaiting you?'

'I have been to Barsoom again, but it's a long story, and I must return. I have learned the secret, nephew. I may traverse the trackless void at will.

'I have come because my affection for you prompted me to see you once more before you pass forever into that other life I will never know, and, though I have died thrice and will die again to-night, I am as unable to fathom as you.

'Even the therns of Barsoom, that ancient cult which for countless ages has been credited with holding the secret of life and death, are as ignorant as we. I have proved it, though I near lost my life in doing so; but you will read it all in the notes I have been making during the three months I have been back on Earth.'

He patted a swelling portfolio that lay on the table.

'I know you believe, and I know the world, too, is interested, though they will not believe for many years; ages, even. Earth men have not yet progressed to where they can comprehend the things I have written.

'Give them what you wish of it, but do not feel aggrieved if they laugh at you.'

That night I walked down to the cemetery with him. At the door of his vault he turned and pressed my hand.

'Good-bye, nephew,' he said. 'I may never see you again, for I can never again bring myself to leave my wife and boy while they live, and the span of life upon Barsoom is more than a thousand years.'

He entered the vault. The great door swung slowly to. The ponderous bolts grated into place. The lock clicked. I have never seen Captain John Carter of Virginia since.

But here is the story of his return to Mars on that other occasion, as I have gleaned it from the notes which he left for me upon the table of his room in the hotel at Richmond.

—E.R.B.

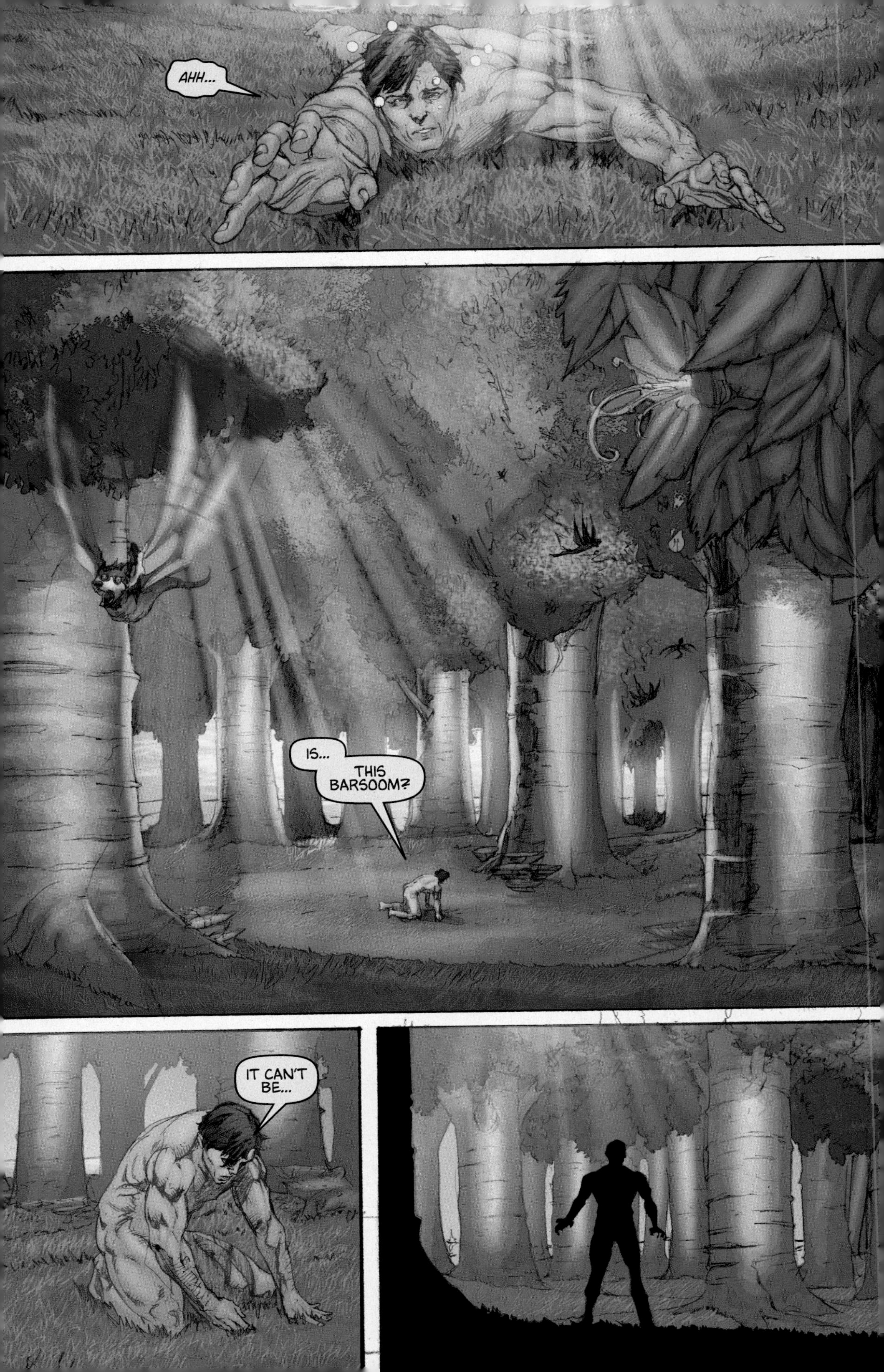
AHH...
IS...
THIS BARSOOM?
IT CAN'T BE...

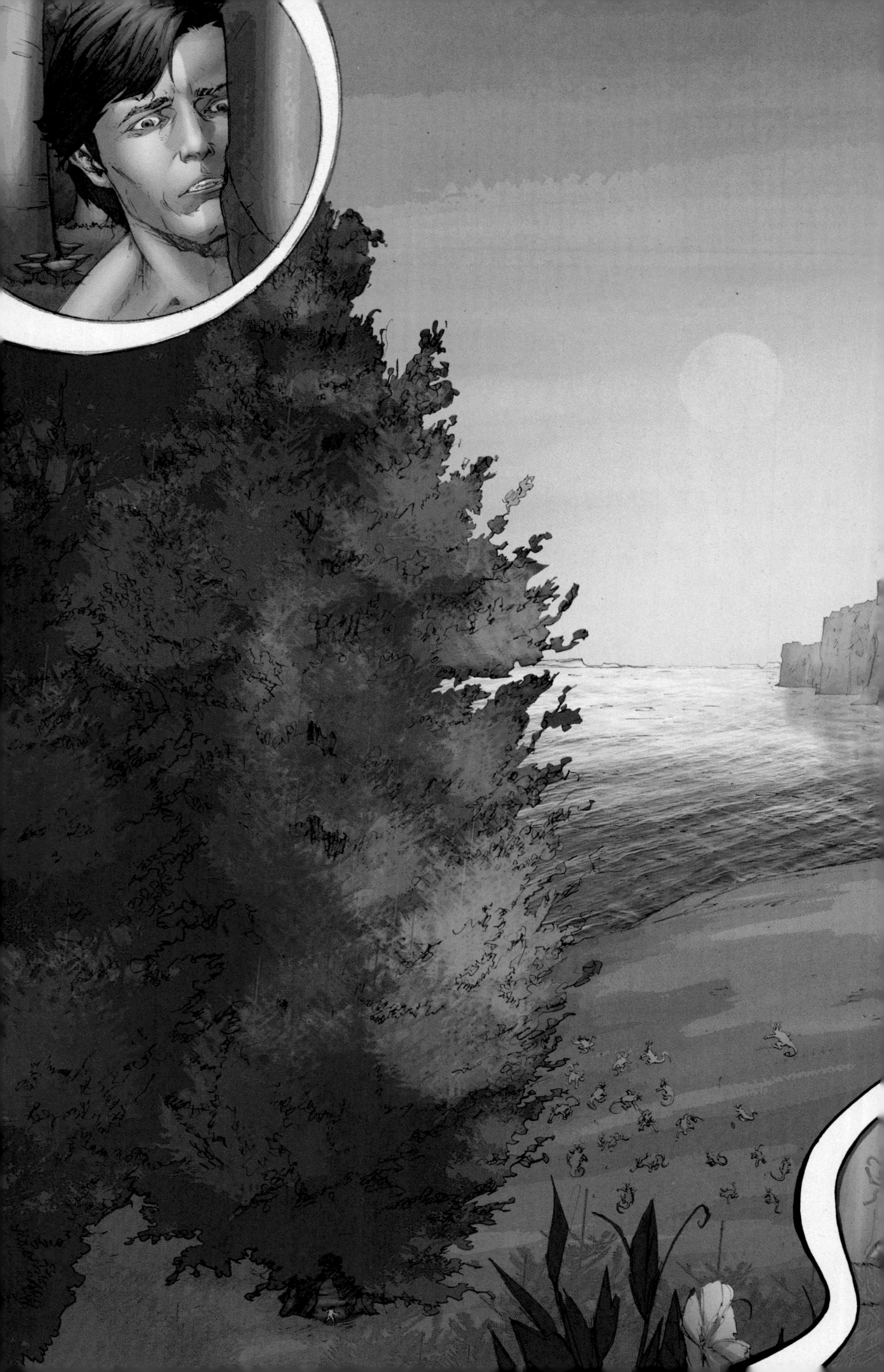

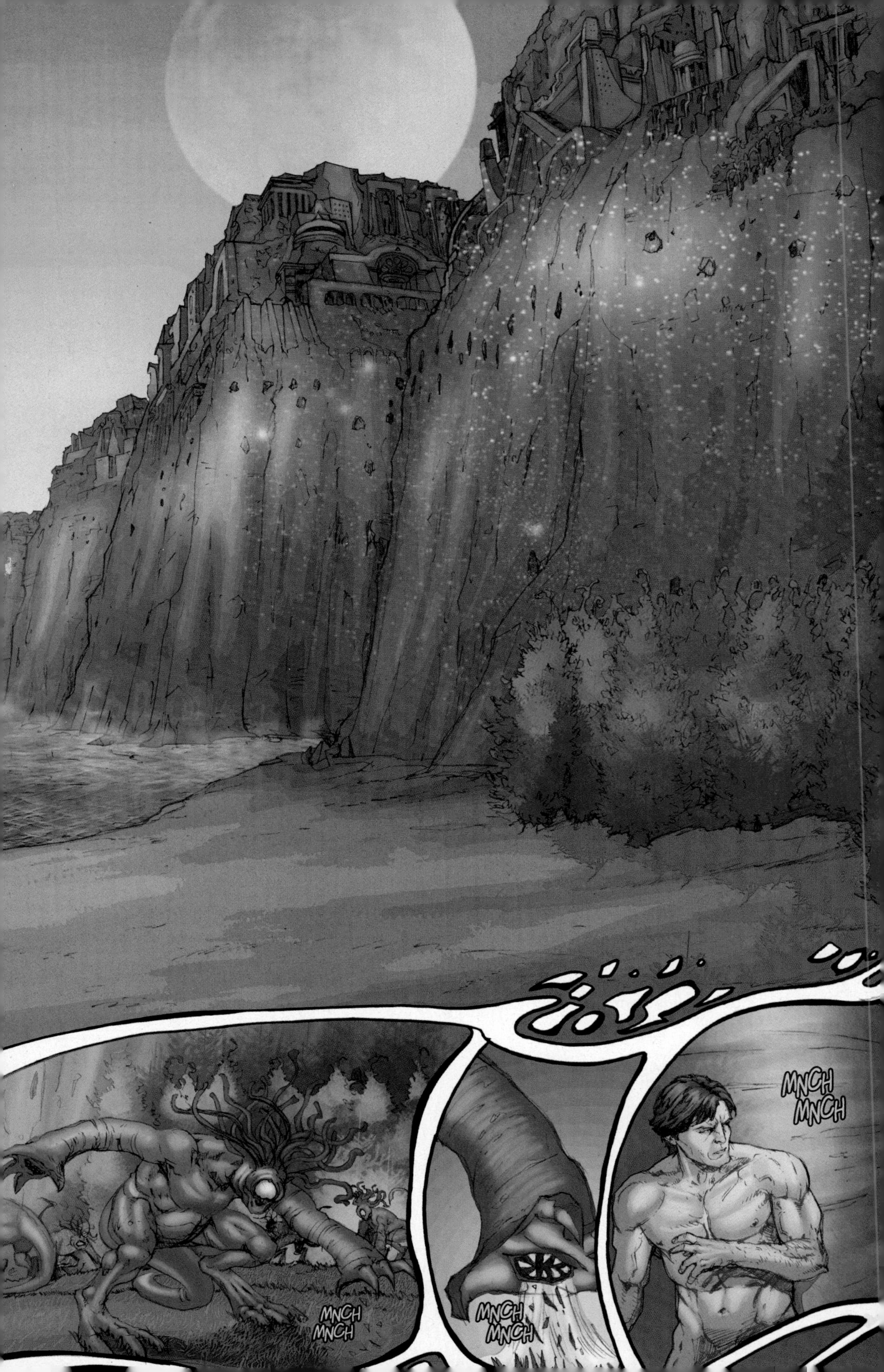
MNCH
MNCH
MNCH
MNCH
MNCH
MNCH

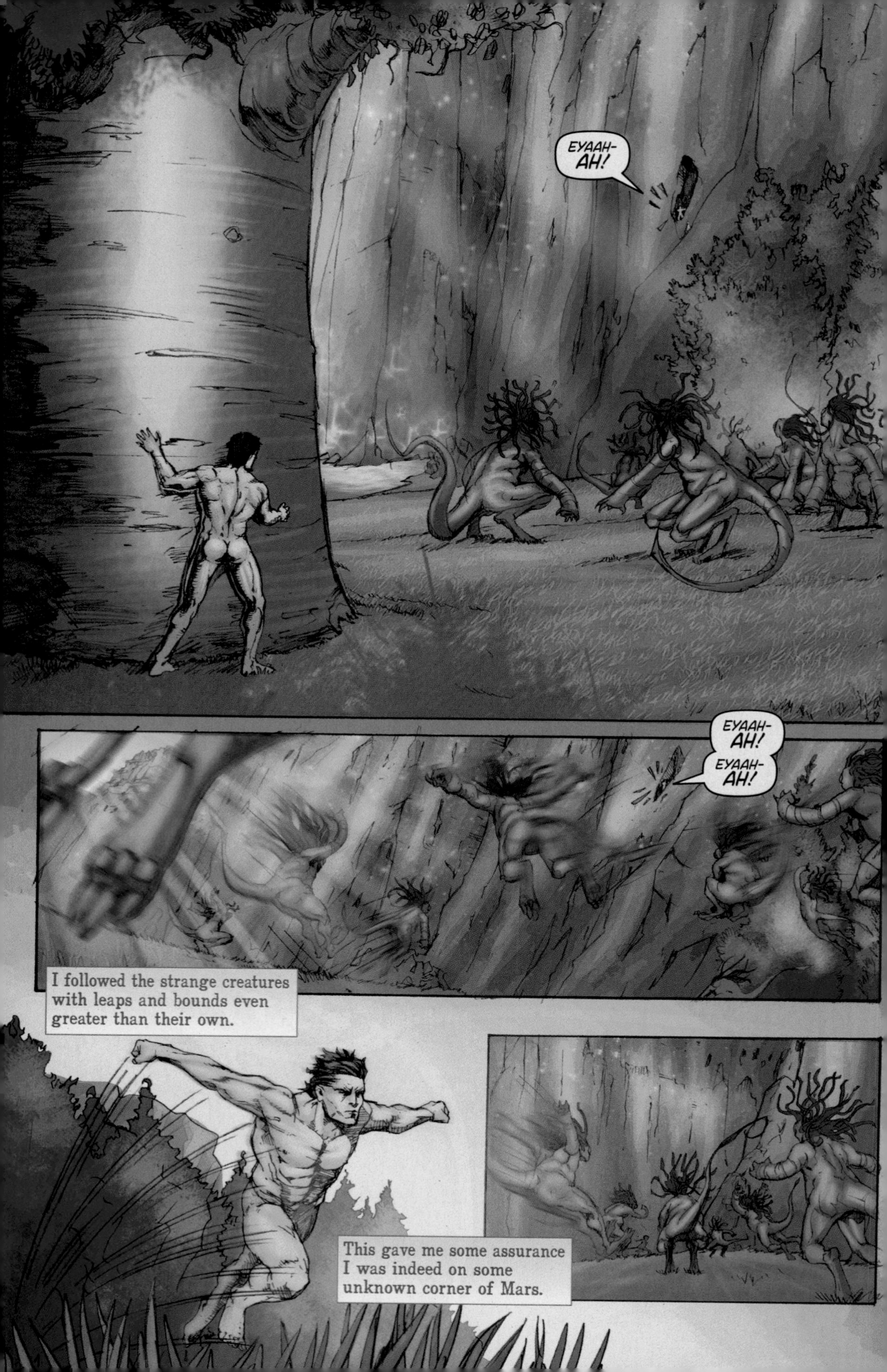
EYAAH-AH!
EYAAH-AH!
EYAAH-AH!
I followed the strange creatures with leaps and bounds even greater than their own.
This gave me some assurance I was indeed on some unknown corner of Mars.

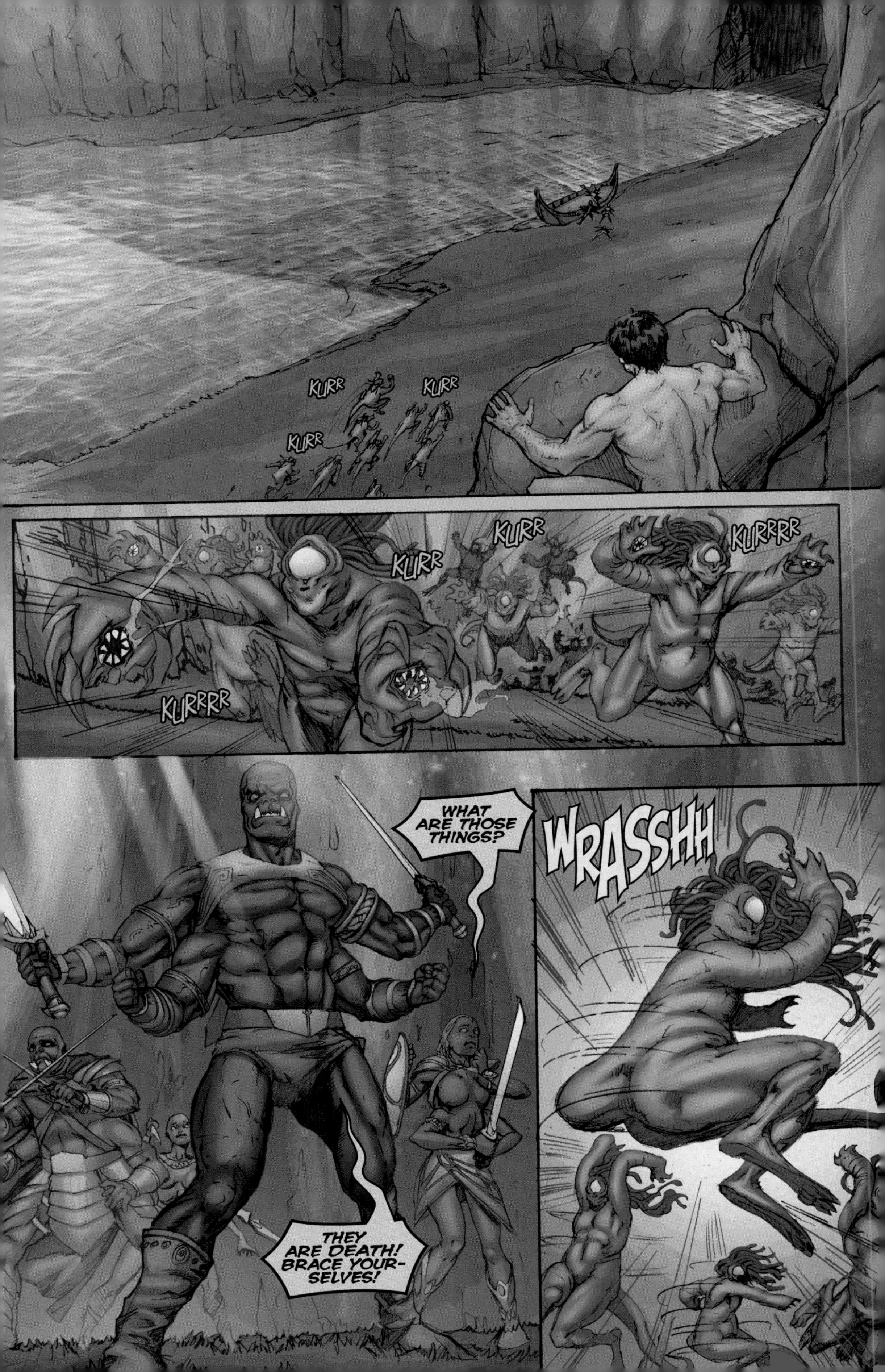
KURR
KURR
KURR
KURR
KURR
KURRRR
KURRRR
WHAT ARE THOSE THINGS?
THEY ARE DEATH! BRACE YOUR-SELVES!
WRASSHH

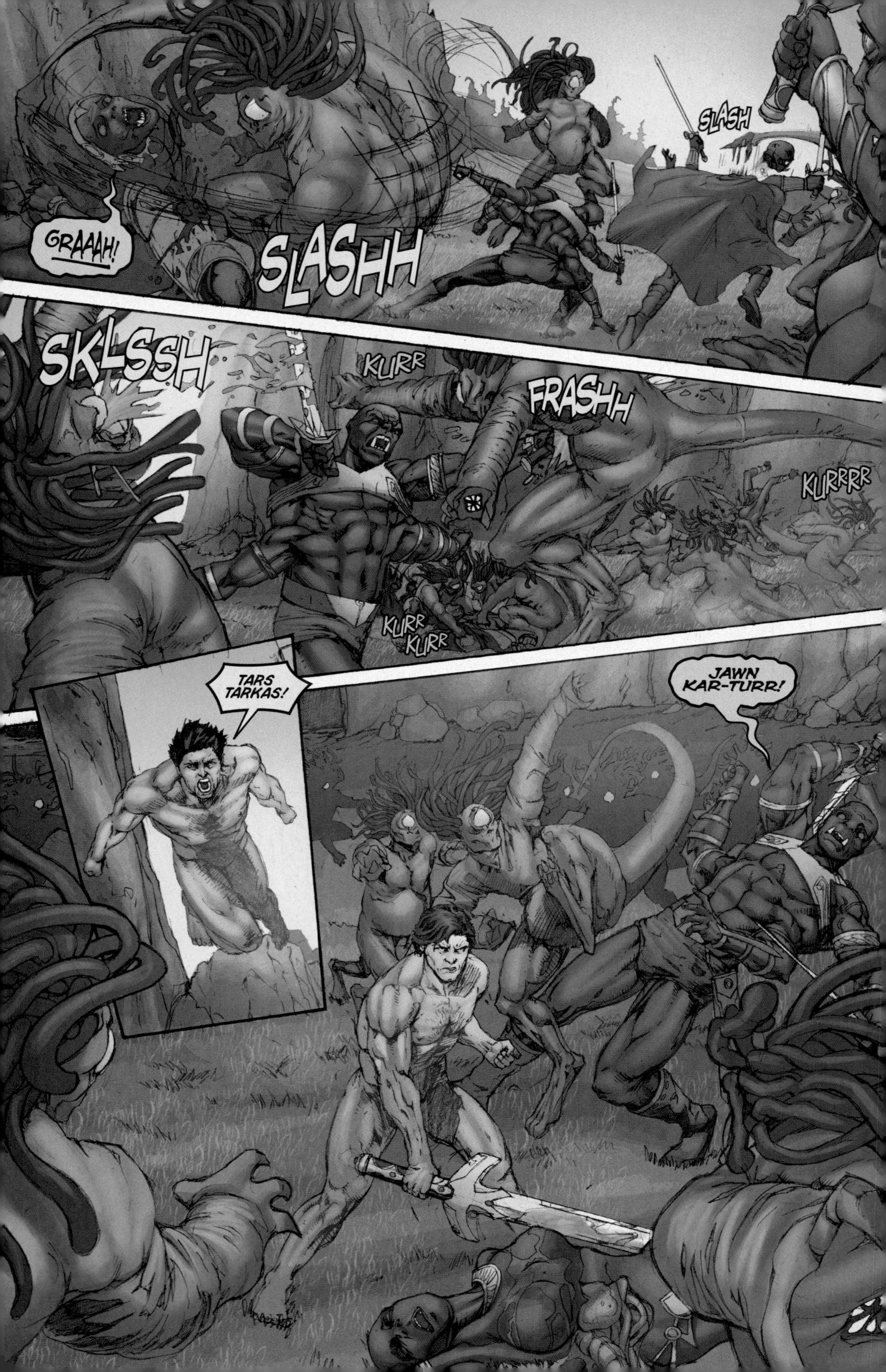
GRAAAH!
SLASHH
SLASH
SKLSSH
KURR
FRASHH
KURRRR
KURR
KURR
TARS TARKAS!
JAWN KAR-TURR!

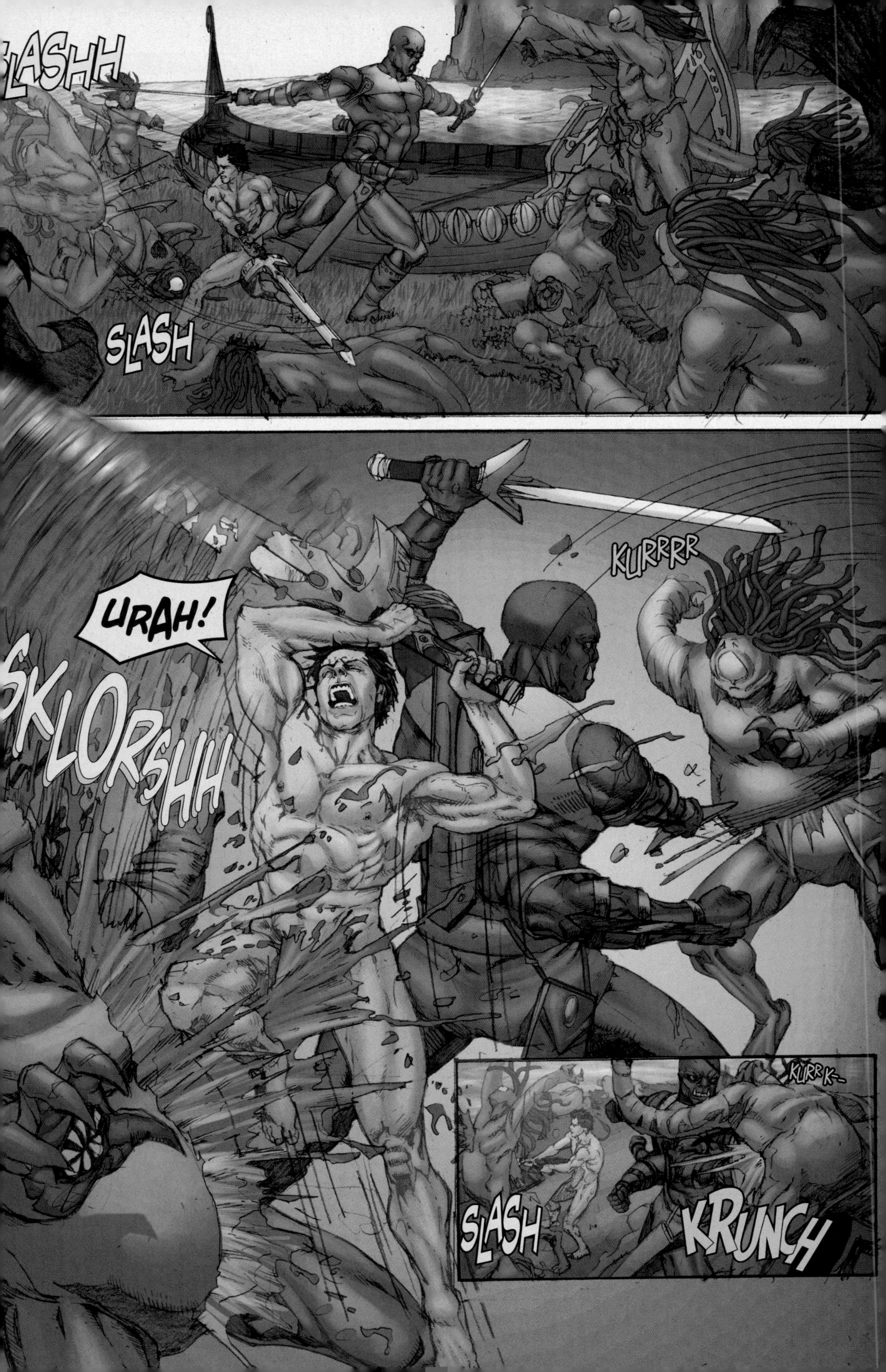
SLASHH
SLASH
URAH!
SKLORSHH
KURRRR
KURRK-
SLASH
KRUNCH

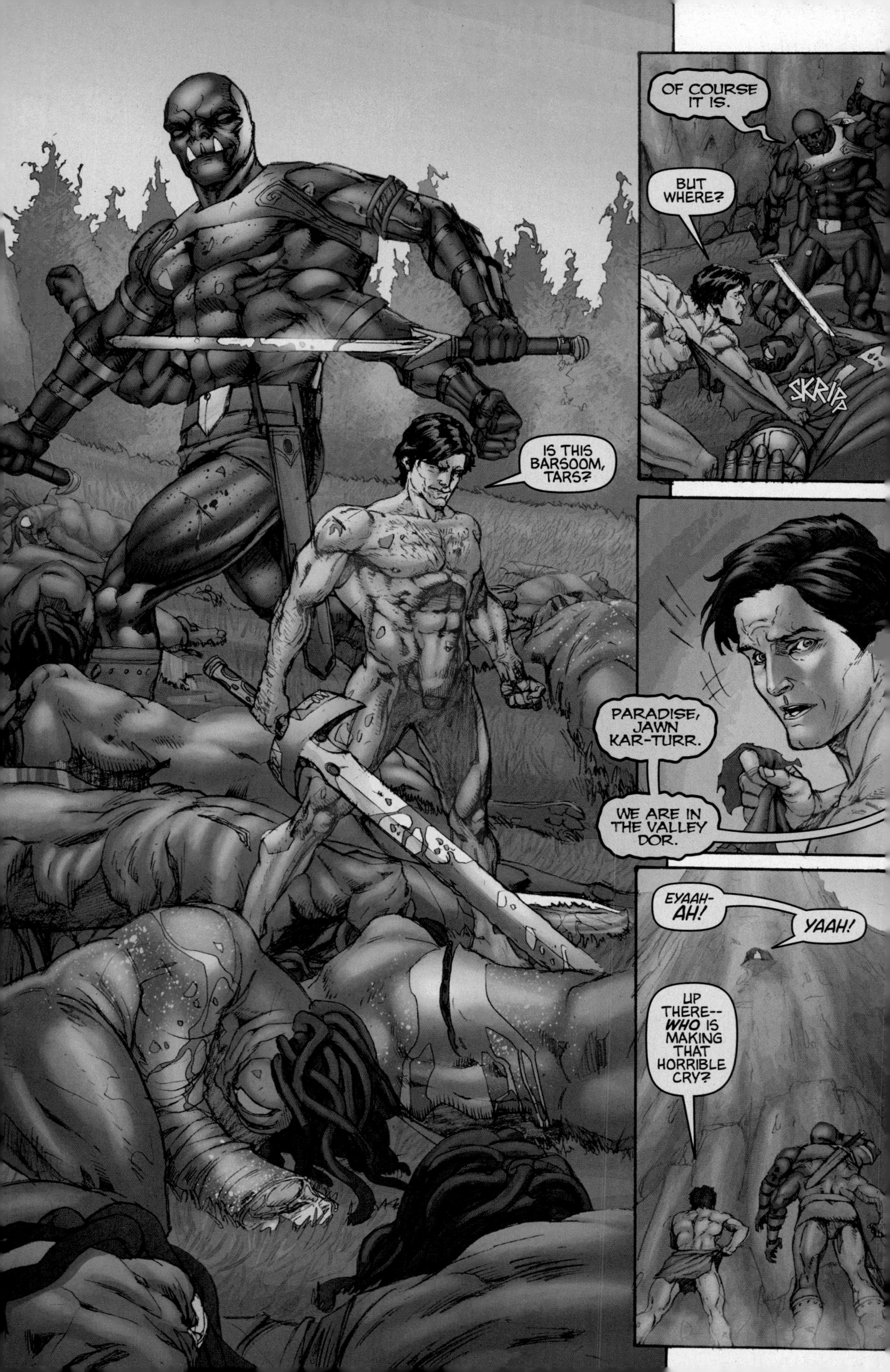
IS THIS BARSOOM, TARS?
OF COURSE IT IS.
BUT WHERE?
SKRIPP
PARADISE, JAWN KAR-TURR.
WE ARE IN THE VALLEY DOR.
EYAAH-AH!
YAAH!
UP THERE--WHO IS MAKING THAT HORRIBLE CRY?

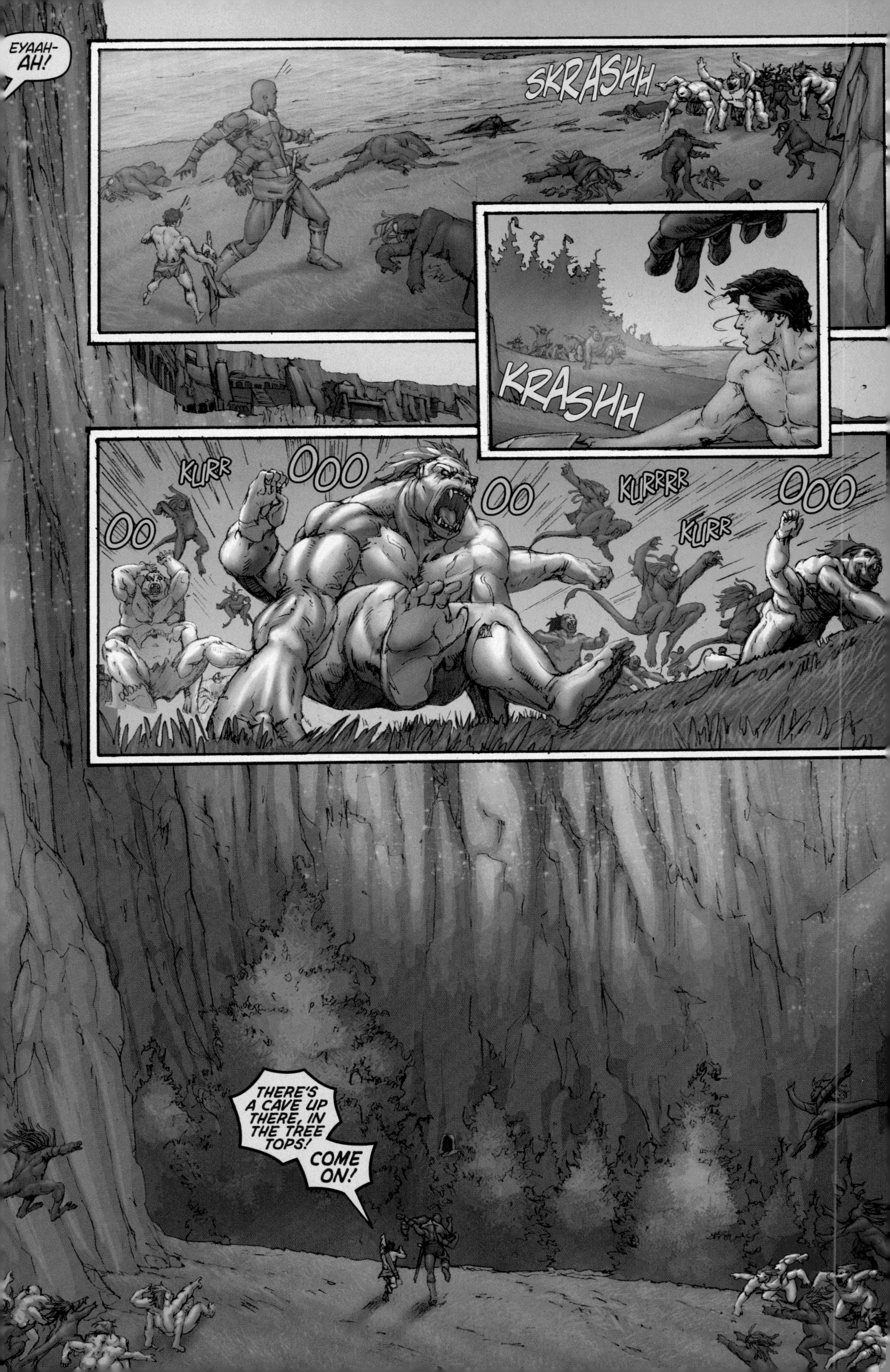
EYAAH-AH!
SKRASHH
KRASHH
OO
KURR
OOO
OO
KURRRR
KURR
OOO
THERE'S A CAVE UP THERE, IN THE TREE TOPS!
COME ON!

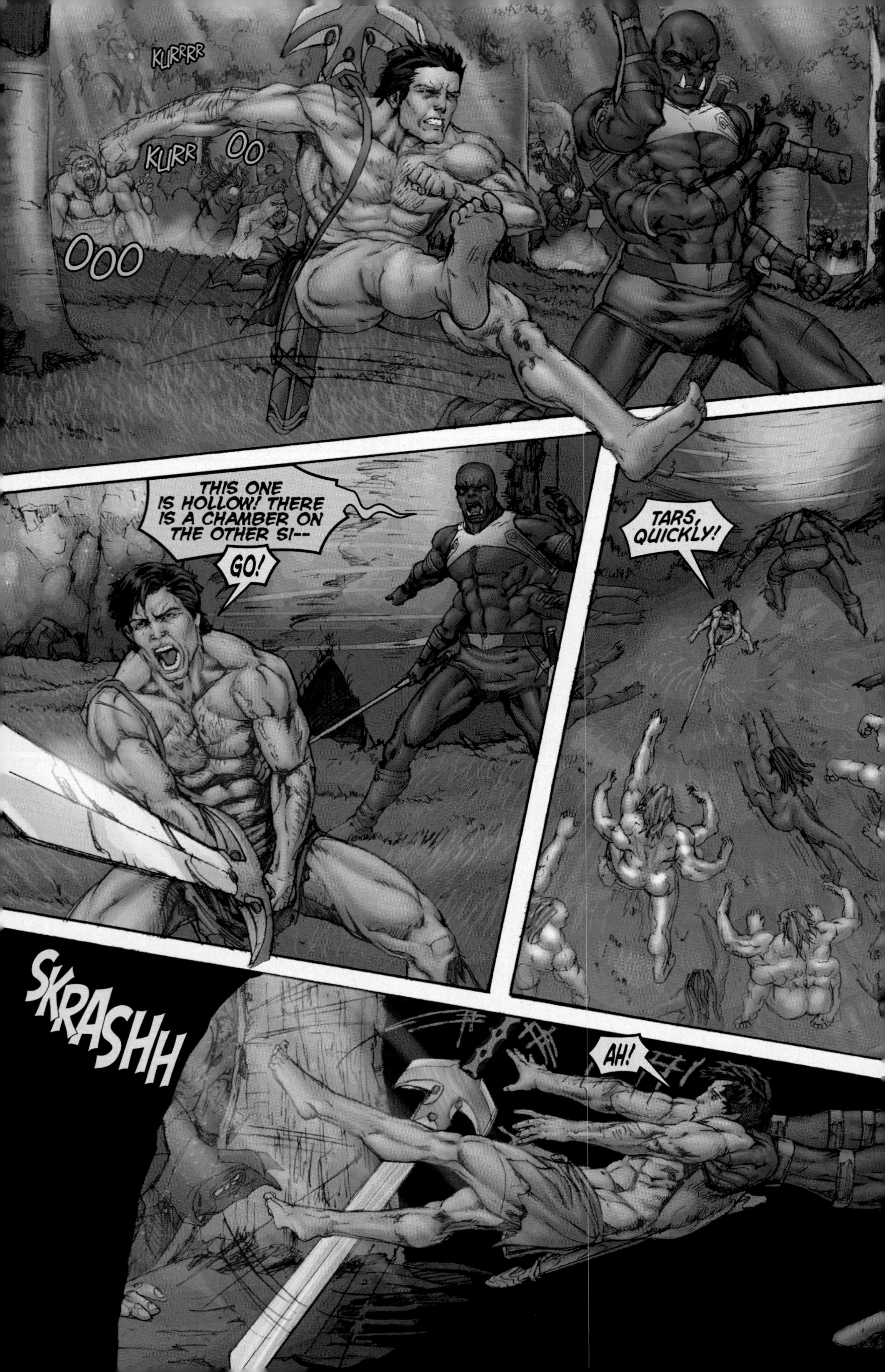
KURRRR
KURR
OO
OOO
THIS ONE IS HOLLOW! THERE IS A CHAMBER ON THE OTHER SI--
GO!
TARS, QUICKLY!
SKRASHH
AH!

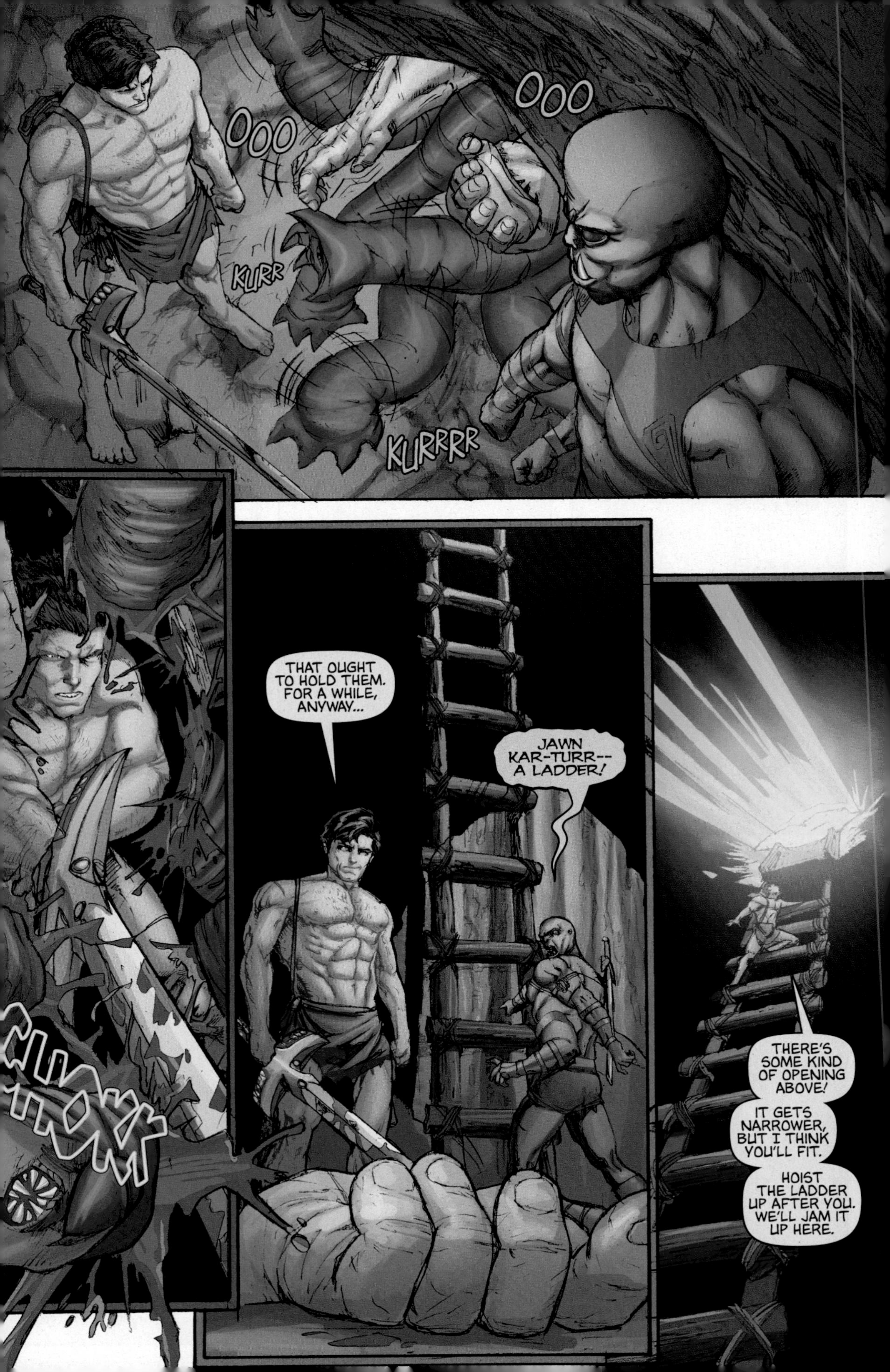
OOO
OOO
KURR
KURRRR
THAT OUGHT TO HOLD THEM. FOR A WHILE, ANYWAY...
JAWN KAR-TURR-- A LADDER!
THERE'S SOME KIND OF OPENING ABOVE!
IT GETS NARROWER, BUT I THINK YOU'LL FIT.
HOIST THE LADDER UP AFTER YOU. WE'LL JAM IT UP HERE.

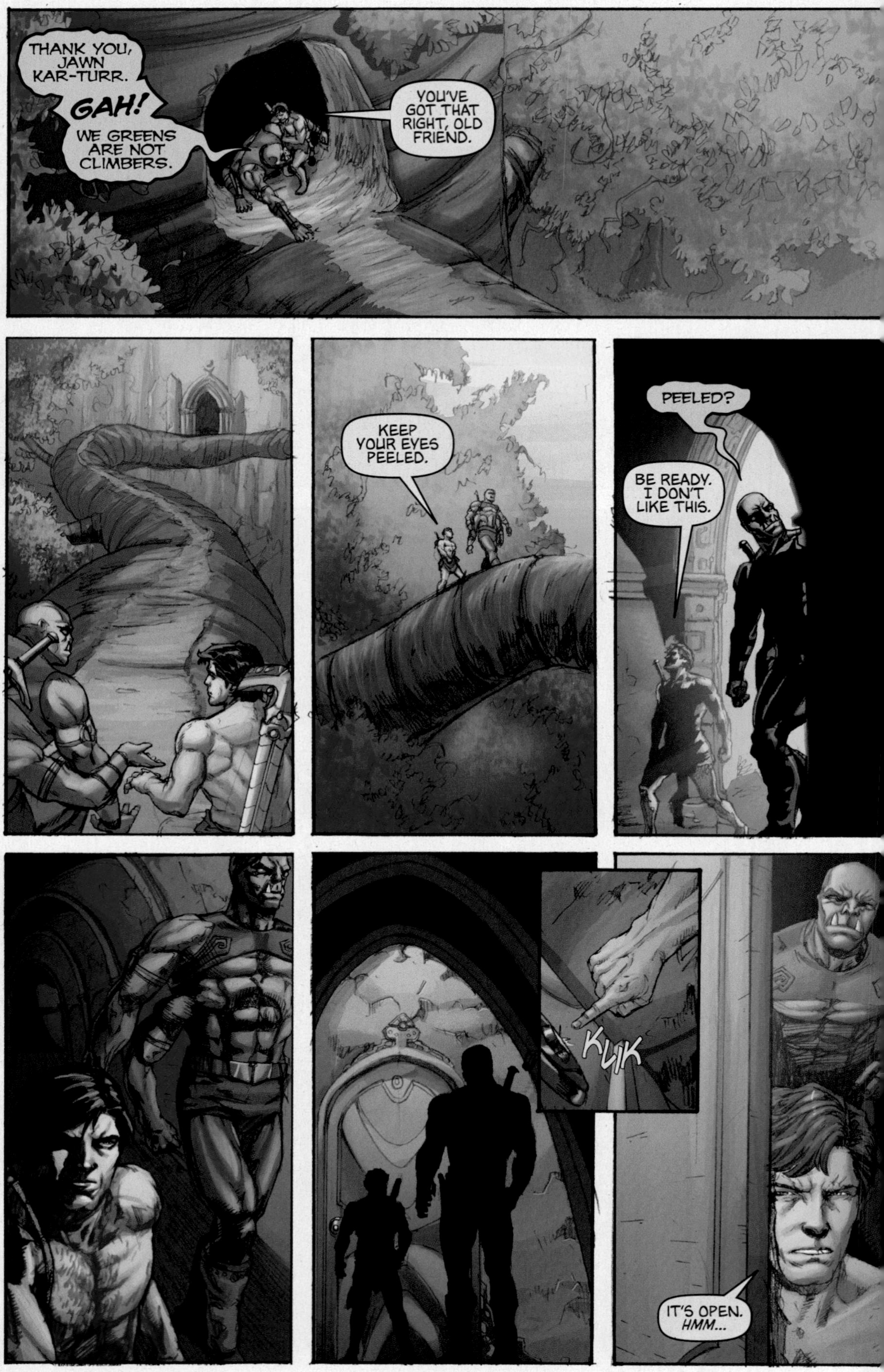
THANK YOU, JAWN KAR-TURR.
GAH!
WE GREENS ARE NOT CLIMBERS.
YOU'VE GOT THAT RIGHT, OLD FRIEND.
KEEP YOUR EYES PEELED.
PEELED?
BE READY. I DON'T LIKE THIS.
KLIK
IT'S OPEN. HMM...

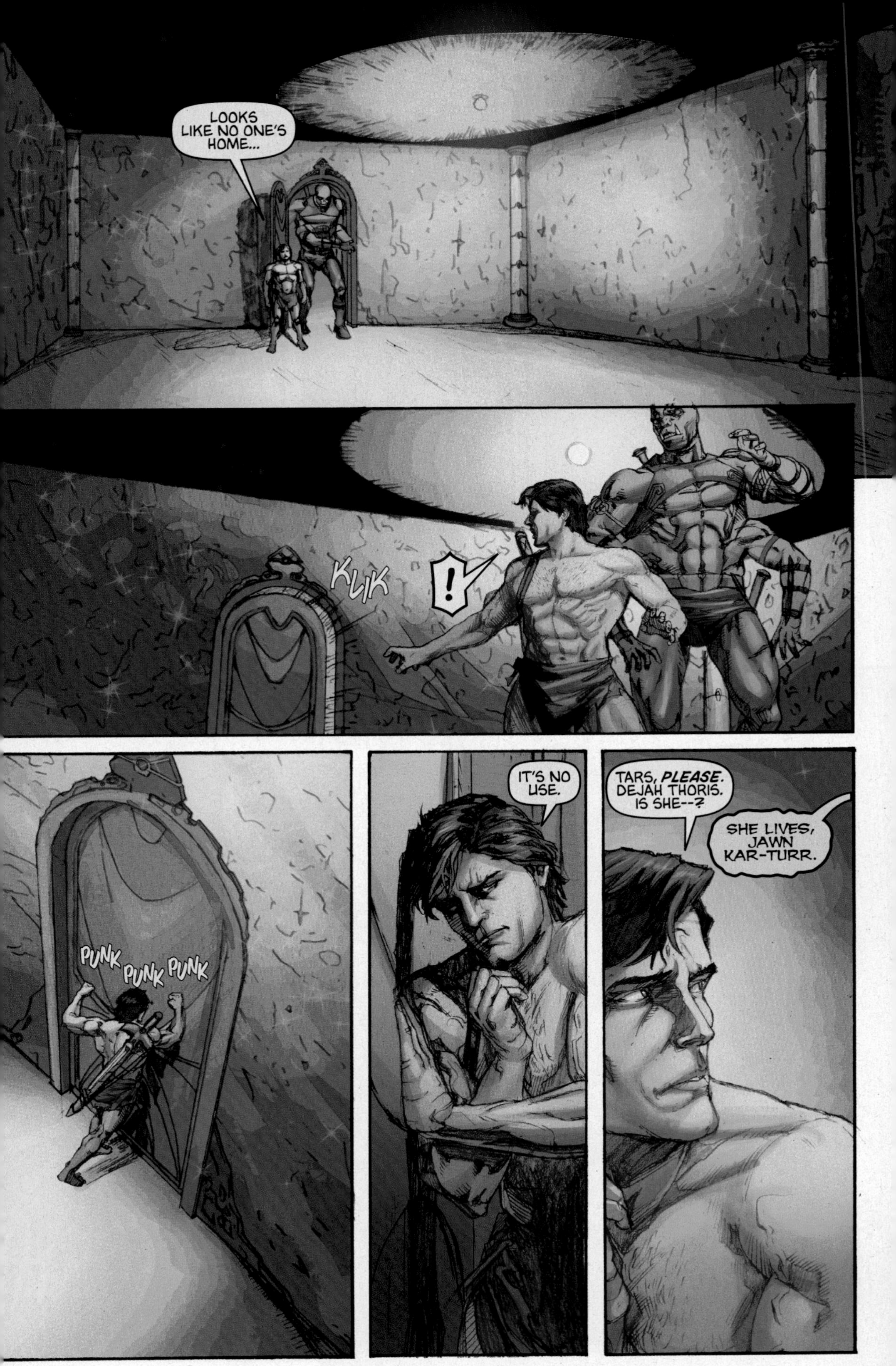
LOOKS LIKE NO ONE'S HOME...
KLIK
!
PUNK PUNK PUNK
IT'S NO USE.
TARS, *PLEASE*. DEJAH THORIS. IS SHE--?
SHE LIVES, JAWN KAR-TURR.

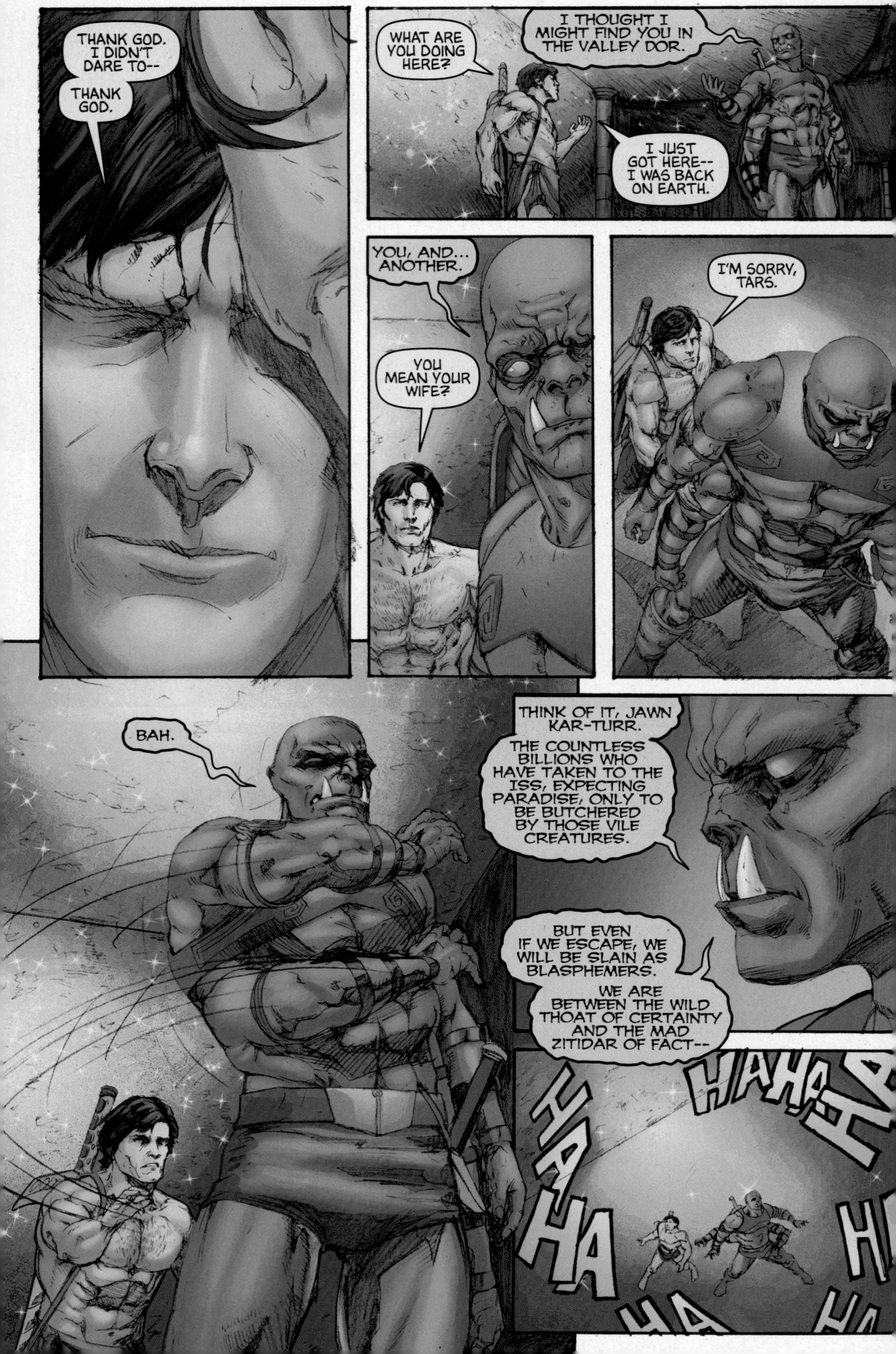
THANK GOD. I DIDN'T DARE TO--
THANK GOD.
WHAT ARE YOU DOING HERE?
I THOUGHT I MIGHT FIND YOU IN THE VALLEY DOR.
I JUST GOT HERE-- I WAS BACK ON EARTH.
YOU, AND... ANOTHER.
YOU MEAN YOUR WIFE?
I'M SORRY, TARS.
BAH.
THINK OF IT, JAWN KAR-TURR.
THE COUNTLESS BILLIONS WHO HAVE TAKEN TO THE ISS, EXPECTING PARADISE, ONLY TO BE BUTCHERED BY THOSE VILE CREATURES.
BUT EVEN IF WE ESCAPE, WE WILL BE SLAIN AS BLASPHEMERS.
WE ARE BETWEEN THE WILD THOAT OF CERTAINTY AND THE MAD ZITIDAR OF FACT--
HAHAHA
HAHA
HA

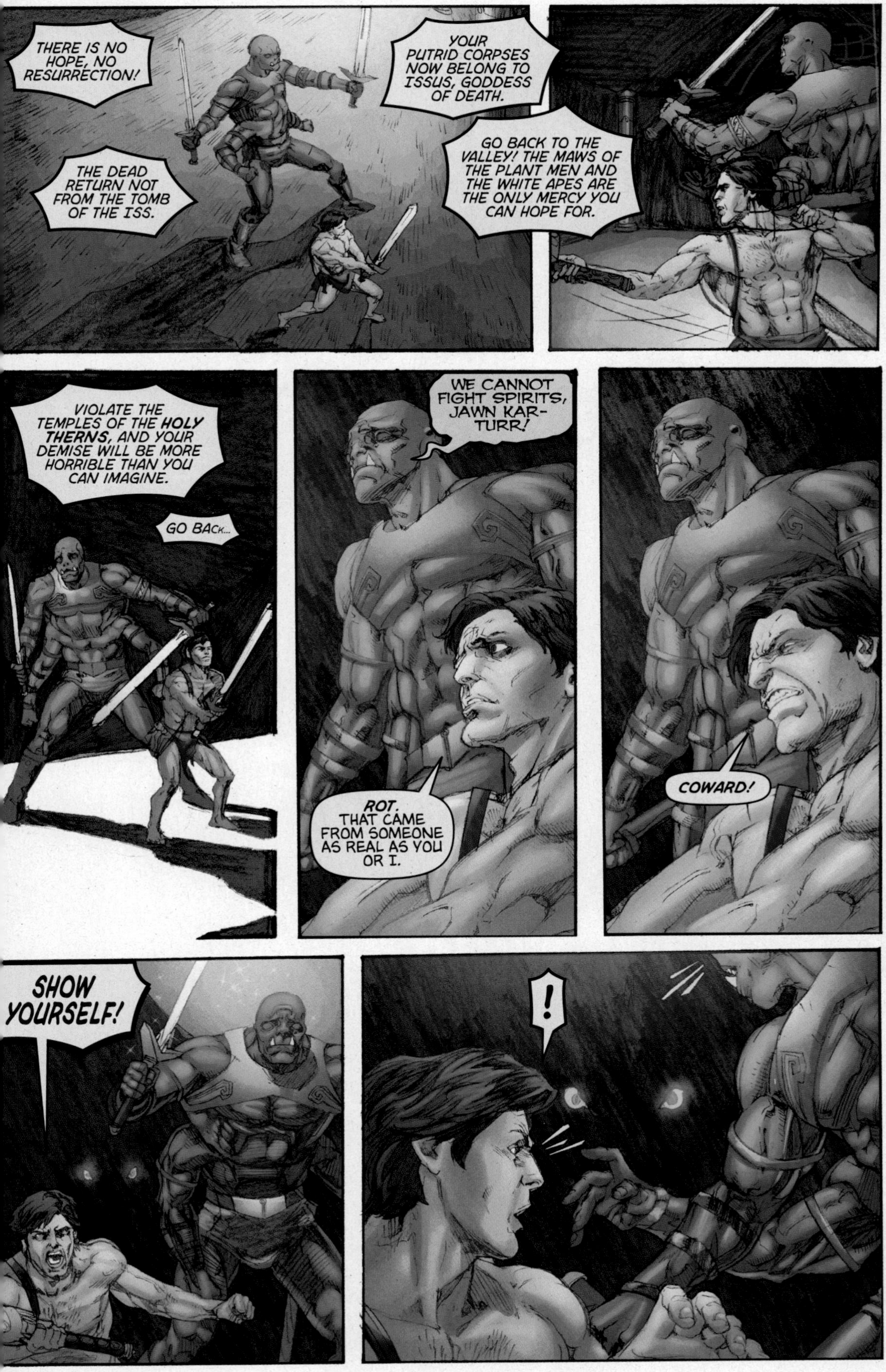
THERE IS NO HOPE, NO RESURRECTION!
THE DEAD RETURN NOT FROM THE TOMB OF THE ISS.
YOUR PUTRID CORPSES NOW BELONG TO ISSUS, GODDESS OF DEATH.
GO BACK TO THE VALLEY! THE MAWS OF THE PLANT MEN AND THE WHITE APES ARE THE ONLY MERCY YOU CAN HOPE FOR.
VIOLATE THE TEMPLES OF THE HOLY THERNS, AND YOUR DEMISE WILL BE MORE HORRIBLE THAN YOU CAN IMAGINE.
GO BACK...
WE CANNOT FIGHT SPIRITS, JAWN KAR-TURR!
ROT. THAT CAME FROM SOMEONE AS REAL AS YOU OR I.
COWARD!
SHOW YOURSELF!
!

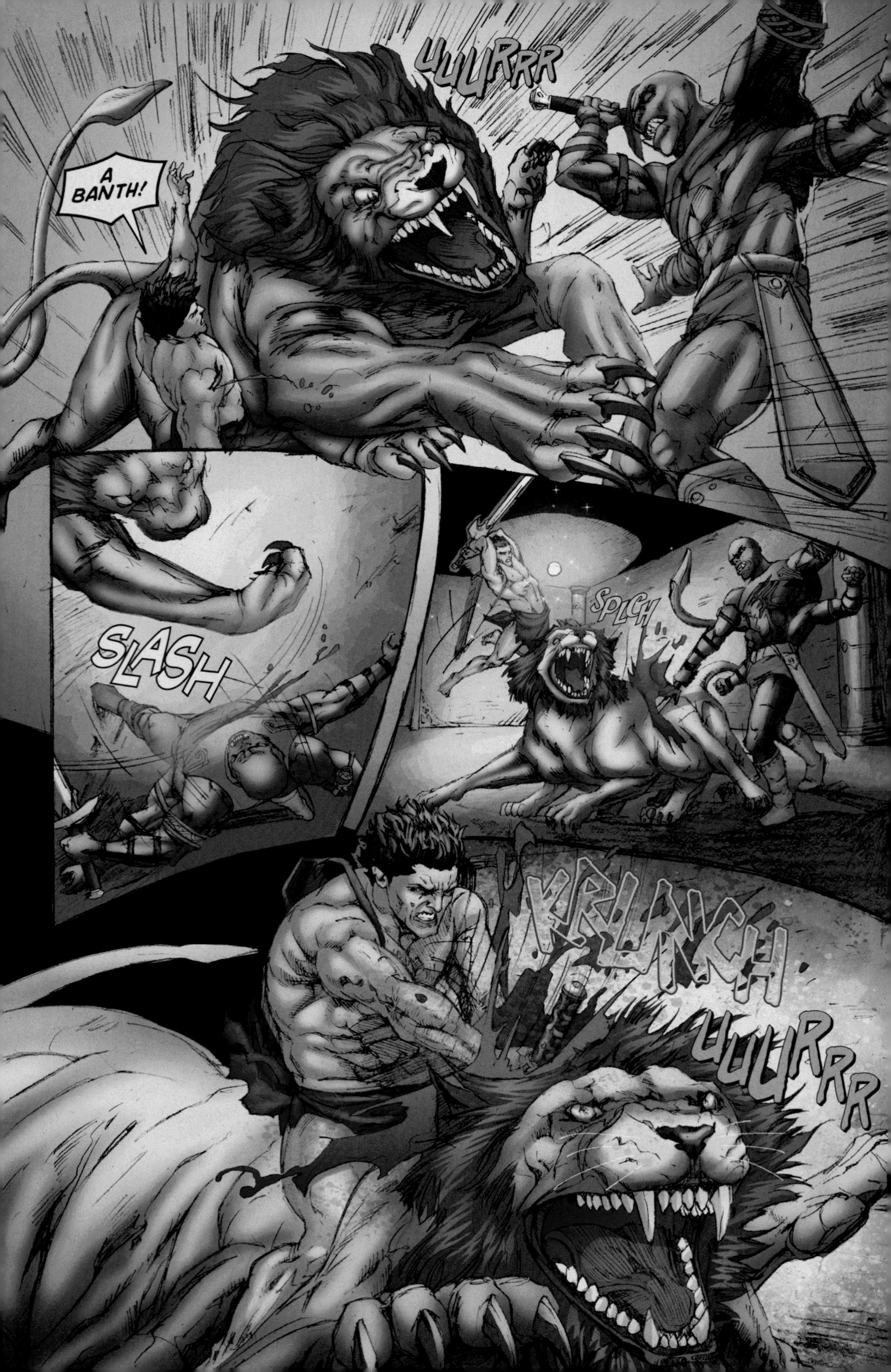

A BANTH!
UUURRR
SLASH
SPLCH
KRUNCH
UUURRR

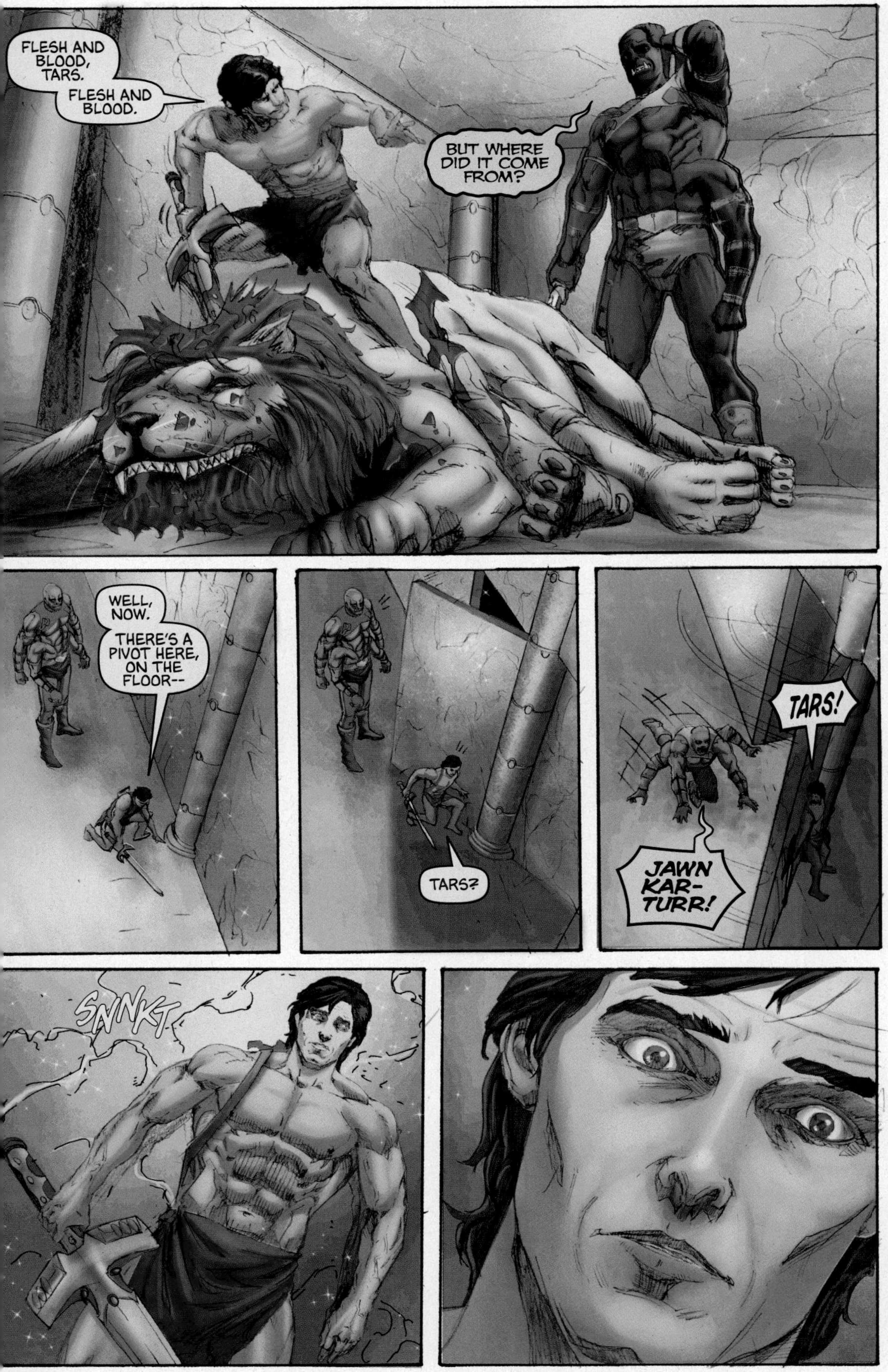
FLESH AND BLOOD, TARS.
FLESH AND BLOOD.
BUT WHERE DID IT COME FROM?
WELL, NOW.
THERE'S A PIVOT HERE, ON THE FLOOR--
TARS?
TARS!
JAWN KAR-TURR!
SNNKT

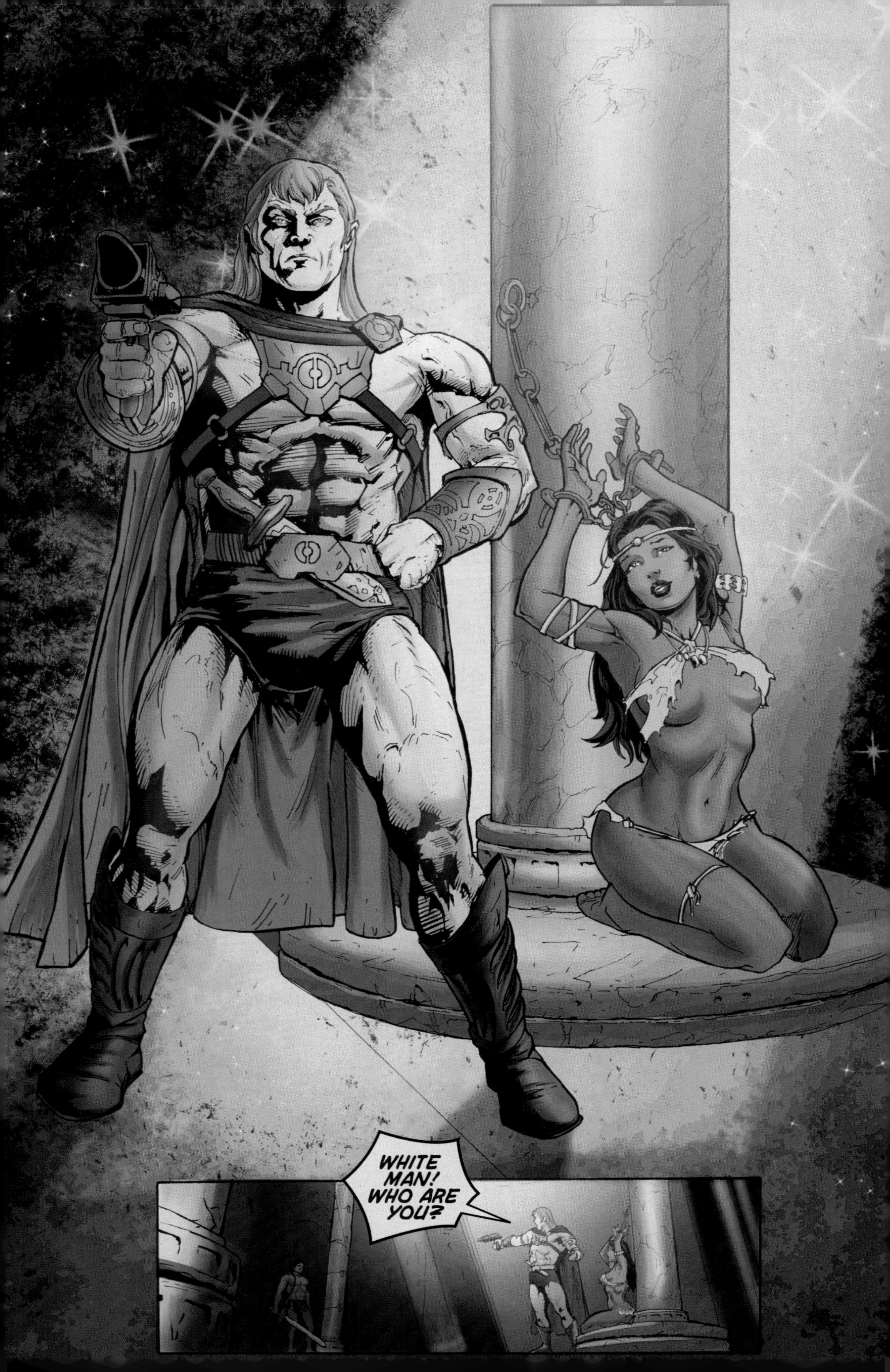
WHITE MAN! WHO ARE YOU?

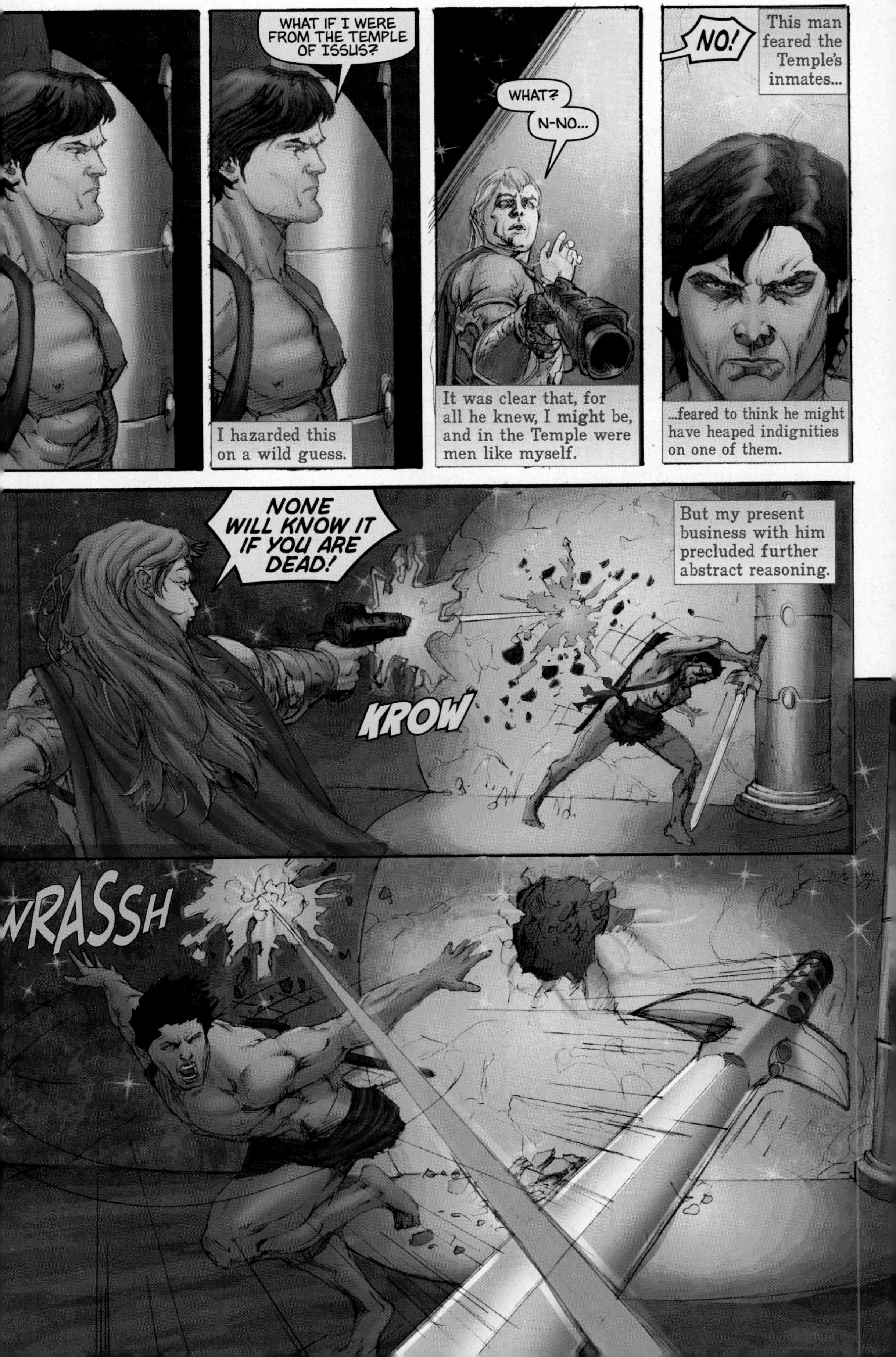
WHAT IF I WERE FROM THE TEMPLE OF ISSUS?
I hazarded this on a wild guess.
WHAT?
N-NO...
It was clear that, for all he knew, I **might** be, and in the Temple were men like myself.
NO!
This man feared the Temple's inmates...
...feared to think he might have heaped indignities on one of them.
NONE WILL KNOW IT IF YOU ARE DEAD!
But my present business with him precluded further abstract reasoning.
KROW
WRASSH

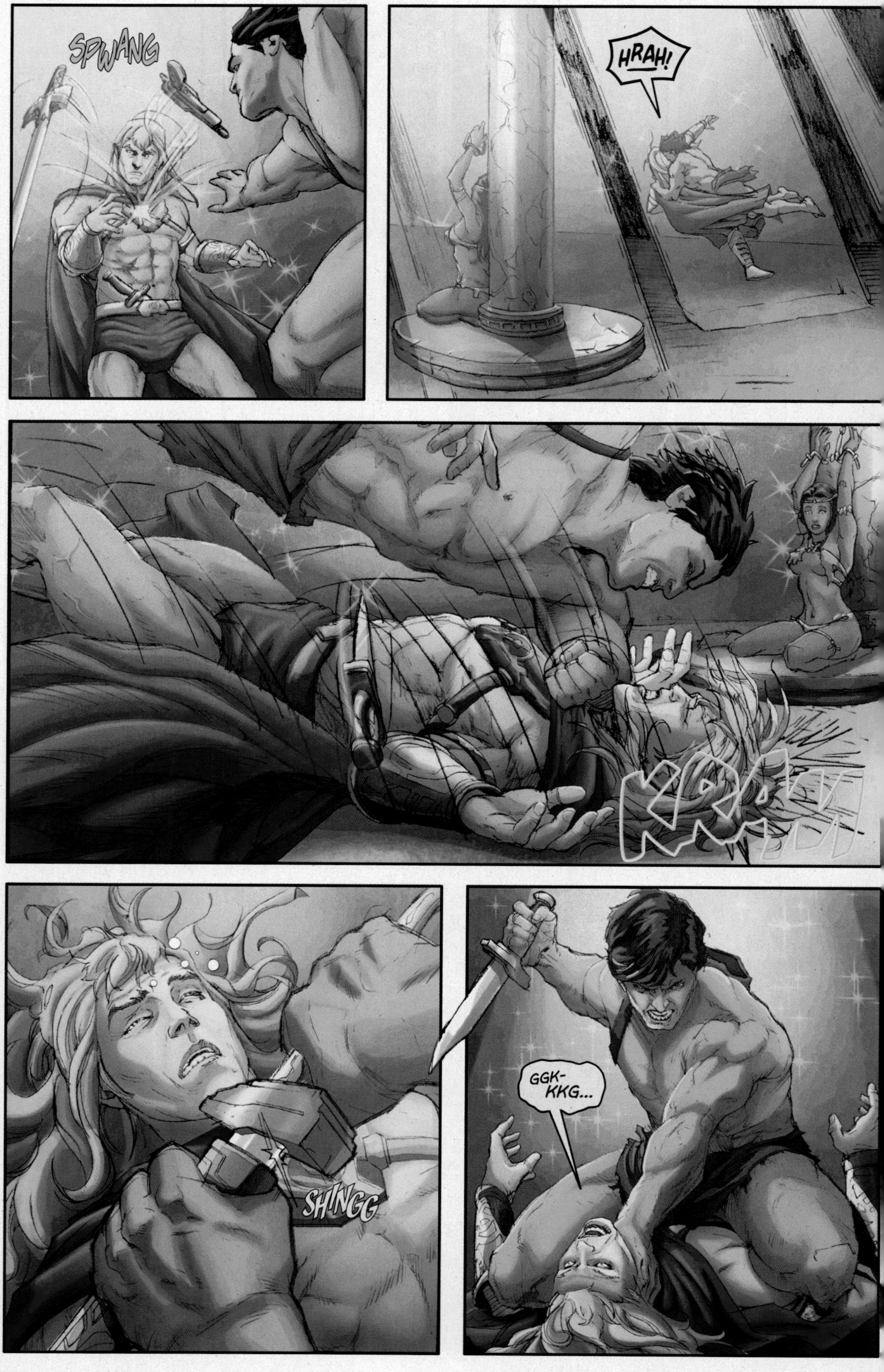
SPWANG
HRAH!
SHINGG
GGK-KKG...

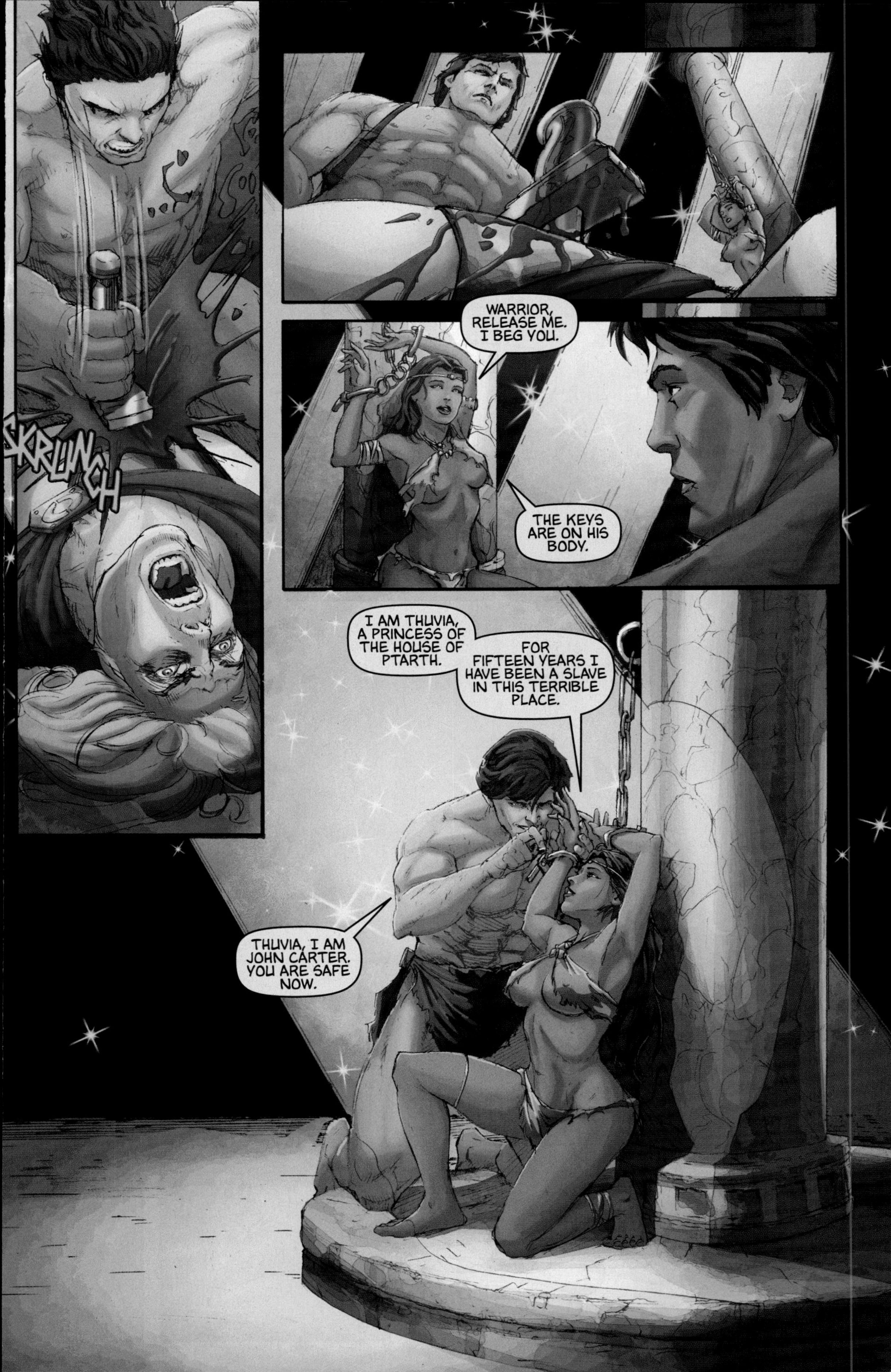
SKRUNCH
WARRIOR, RELEASE ME. I BEG YOU.
THE KEYS ARE ON HIS BODY.
I AM THUVIA, A PRINCESS OF THE HOUSE OF PTARTH.
FOR FIFTEEN YEARS I HAVE BEEN A SLAVE IN THIS TERRIBLE PLACE.
THUVIA, I AM JOHN CARTER. YOU ARE SAFE NOW.

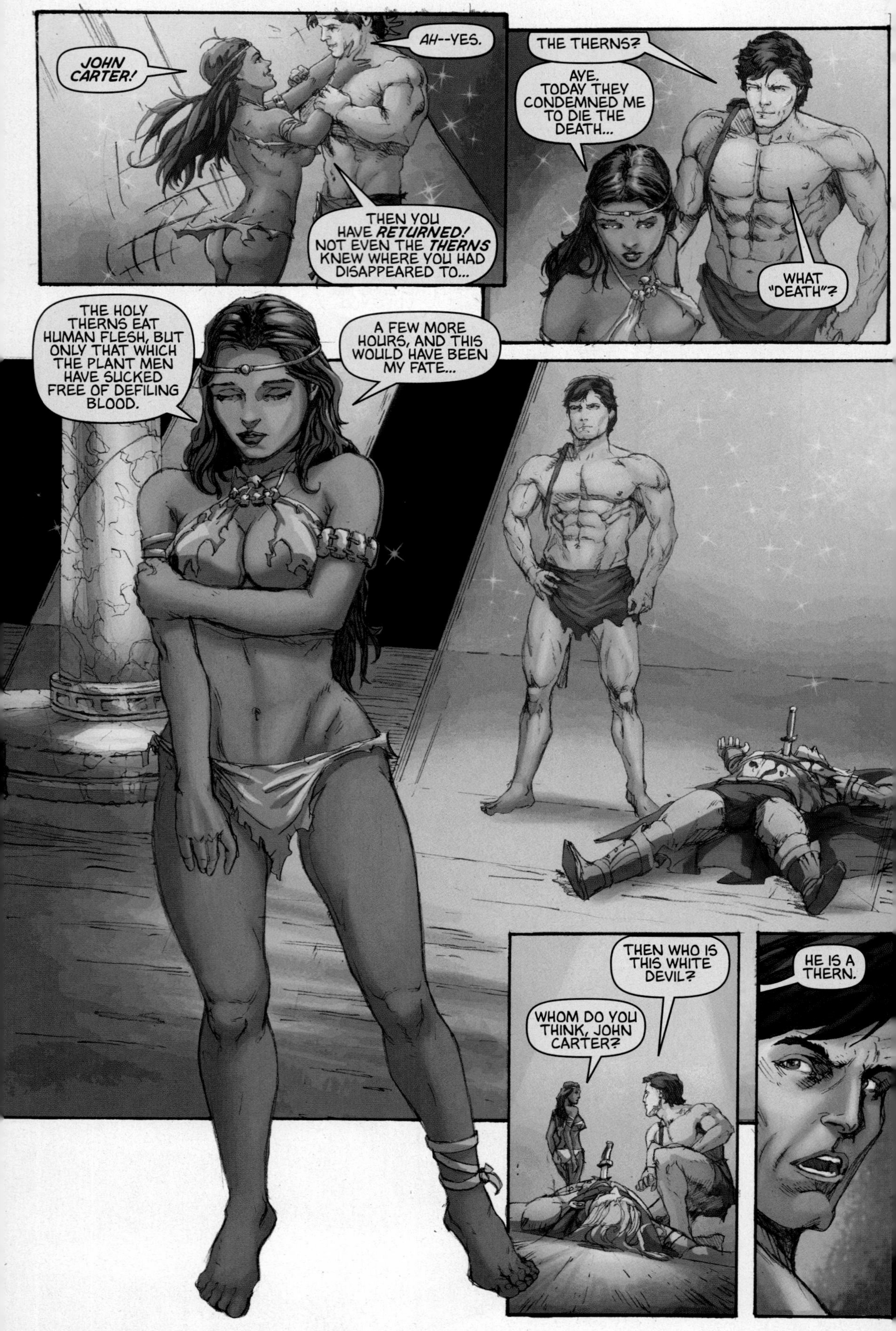
JOHN CARTER!
AH--YES.
THEN YOU HAVE RETURNED! NOT EVEN THE THERNS KNEW WHERE YOU HAD DISAPPEARED TO...
THE THERNS?
AYE. TODAY THEY CONDEMNED ME TO DIE THE DEATH...
WHAT "DEATH"?
THE HOLY THERNS EAT HUMAN FLESH, BUT ONLY THAT WHICH THE PLANT MEN HAVE SUCKED FREE OF DEFILING BLOOD.
A FEW MORE HOURS, AND THIS WOULD HAVE BEEN MY FATE...
THEN WHO IS THIS WHITE DEVIL?
WHOM DO YOU THINK, JOHN CARTER?
HE IS A THERN.

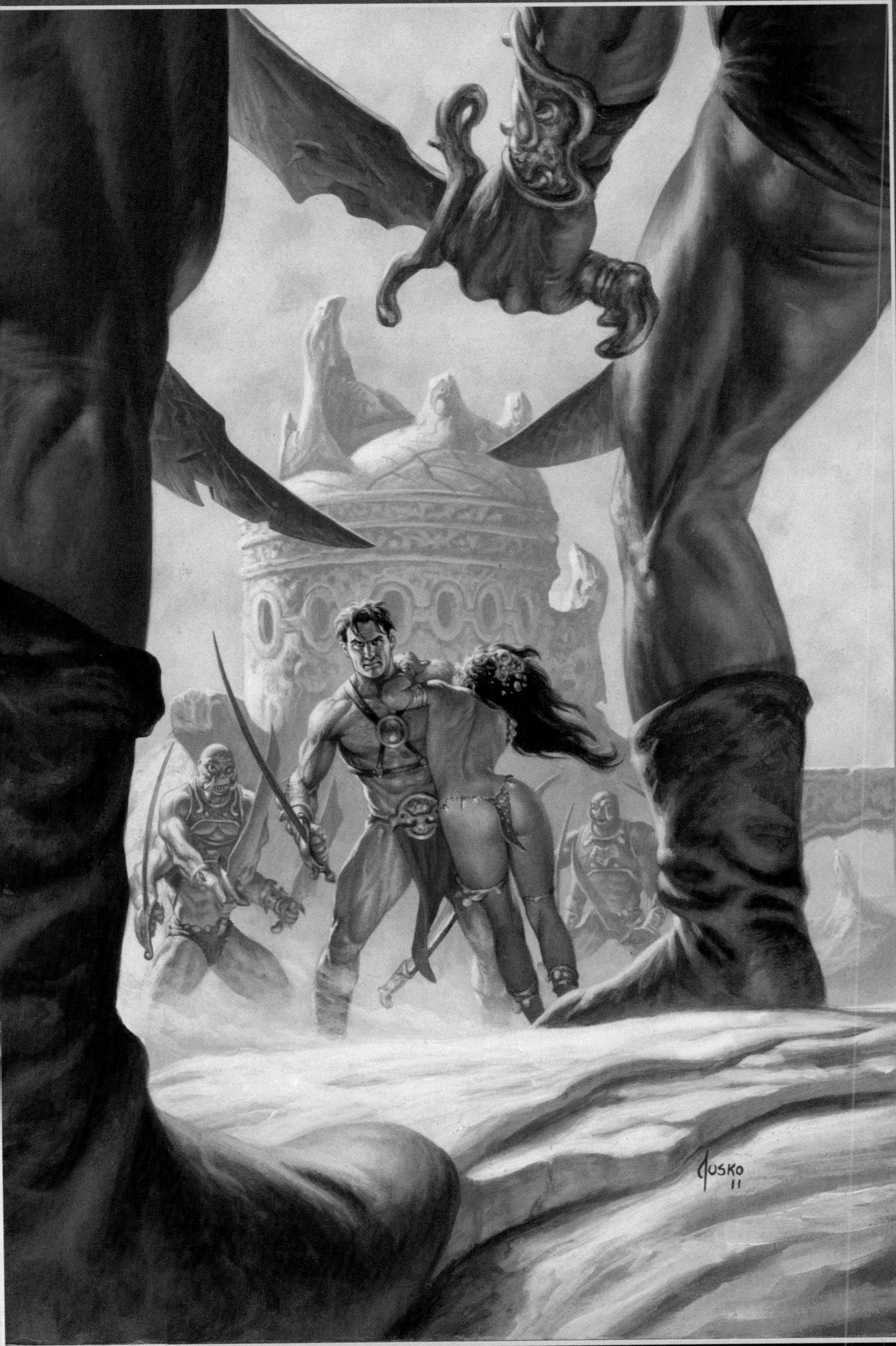
JUSKO
11

GODS OF MARS PART TWO:

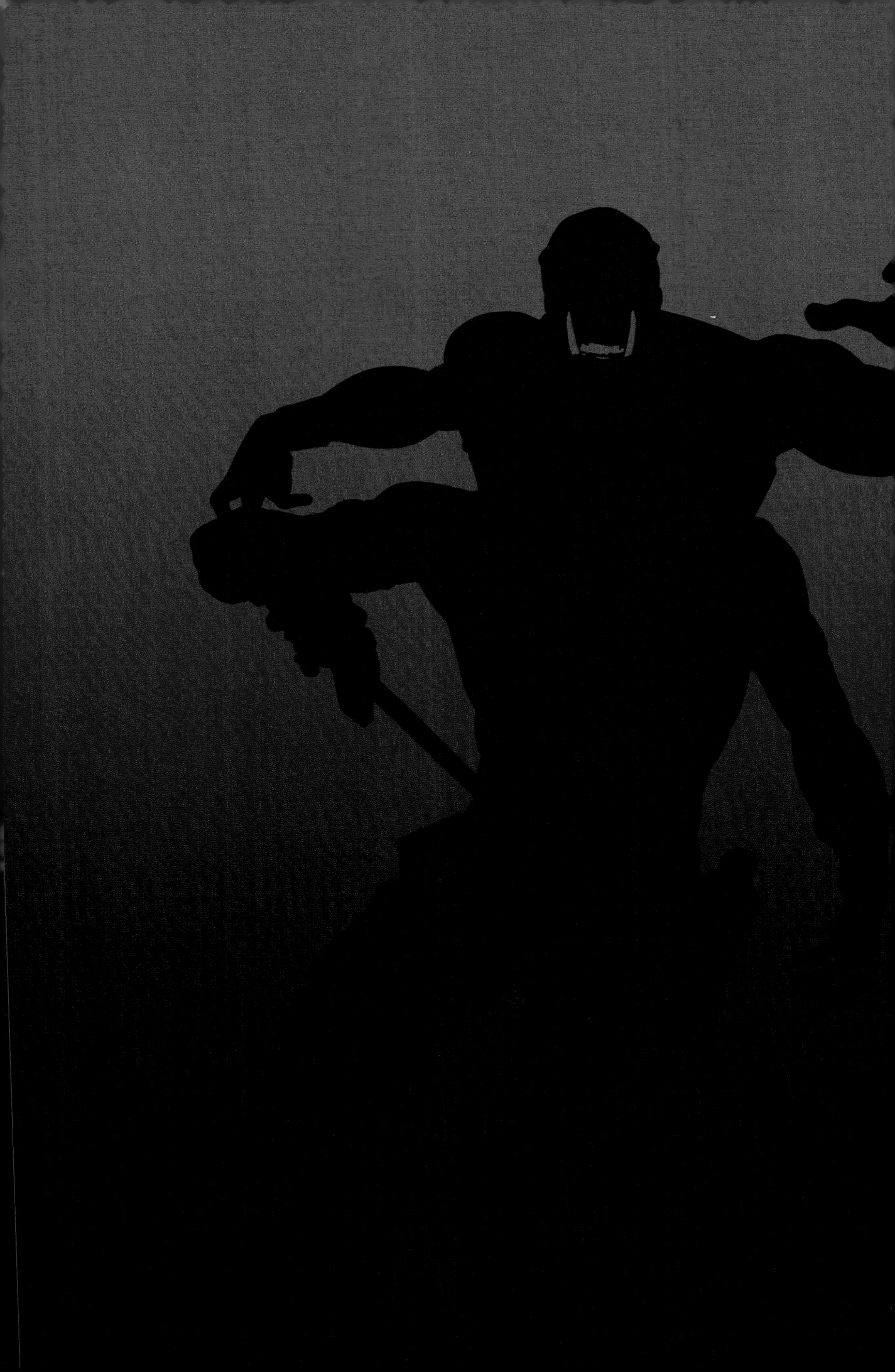

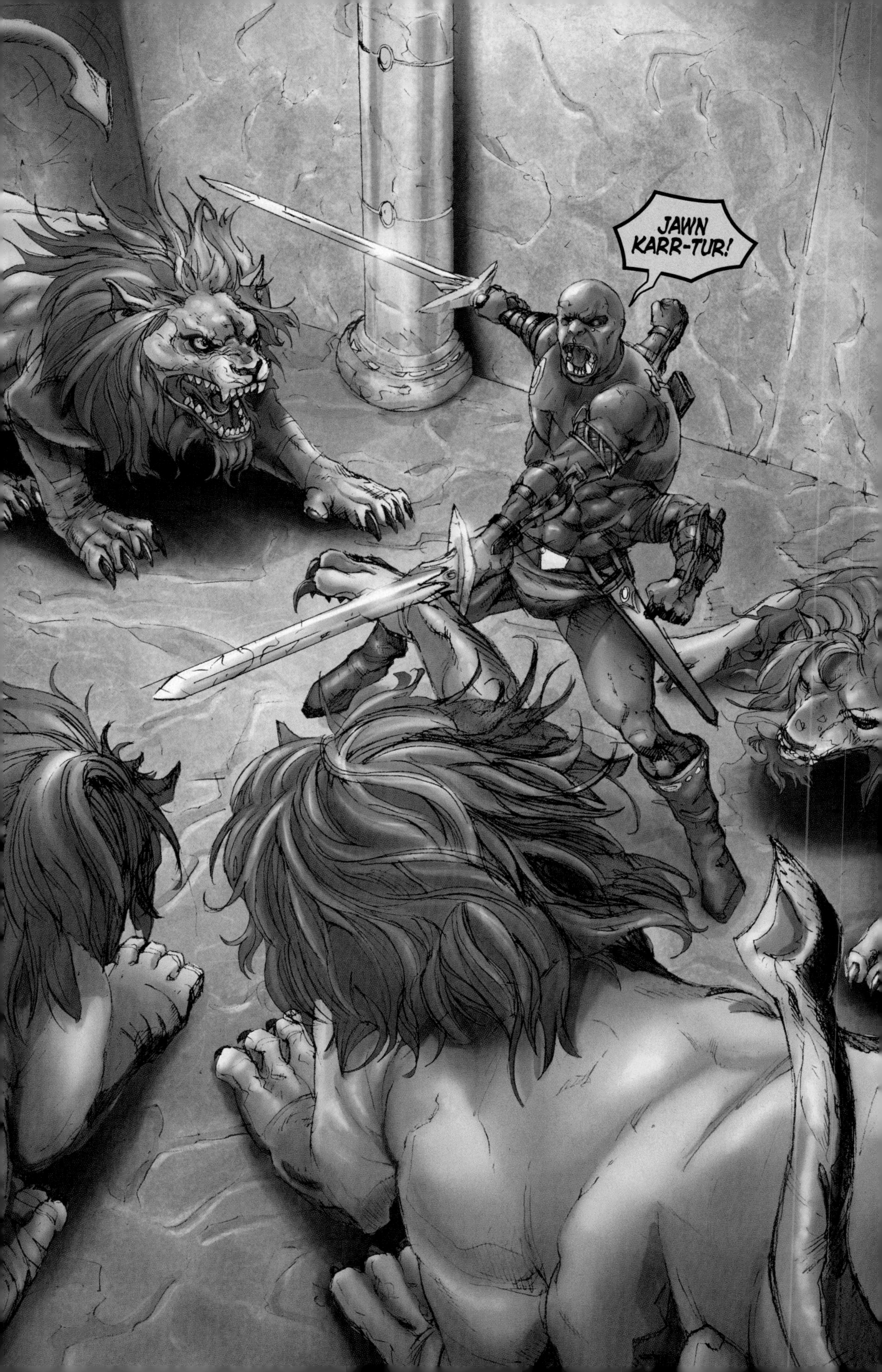
JAWN KARR-TUR!

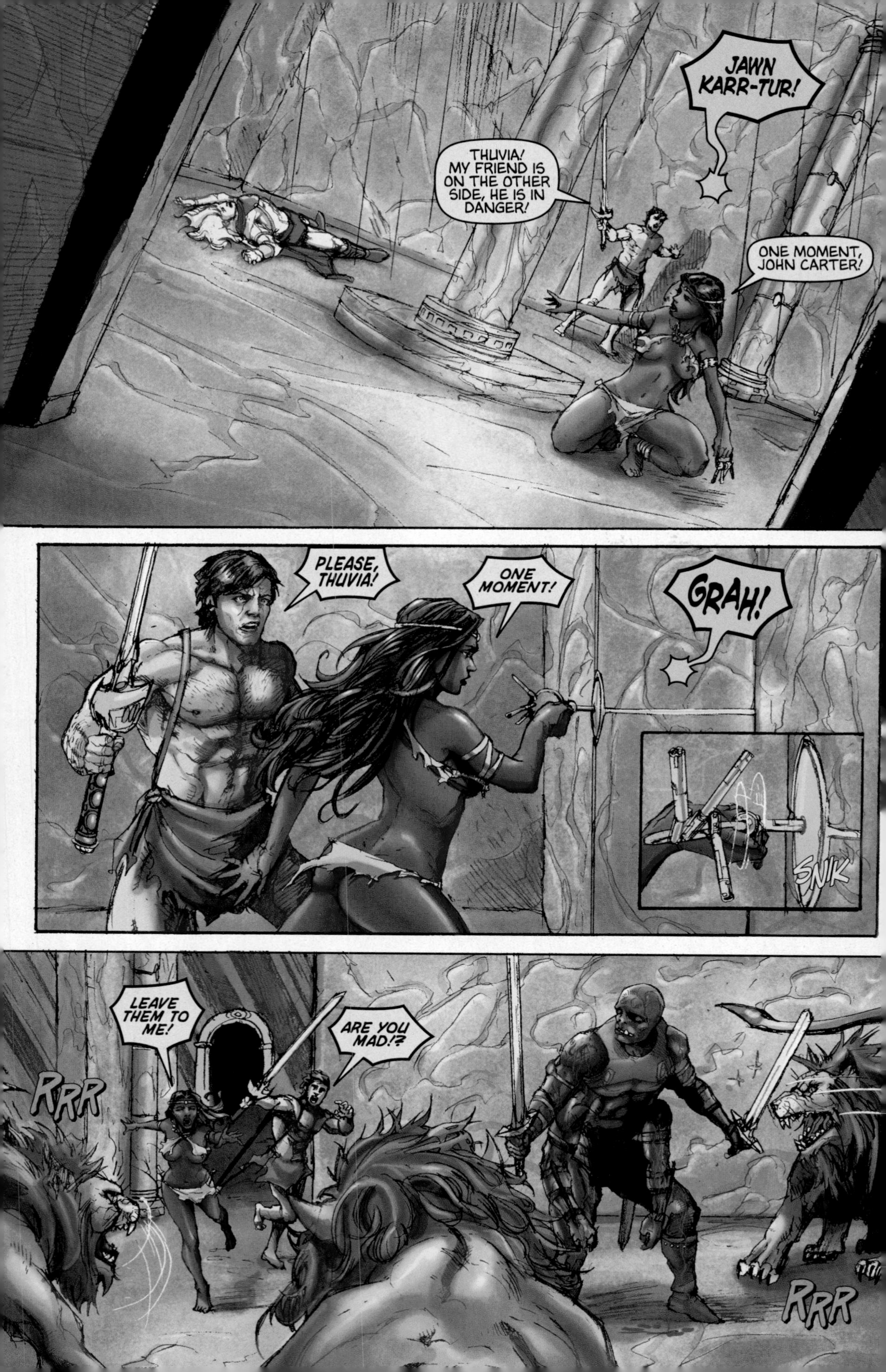
JAWN KARR-TUR!
THUVIA! MY FRIEND IS ON THE OTHER SIDE, HE IS IN DANGER!
ONE MOMENT, JOHN CARTER!
PLEASE, THUVIA!
ONE MOMENT!
GRAH!
SNIK
LEAVE THEM TO ME!
ARE YOU MAD!?
RRR
RRR

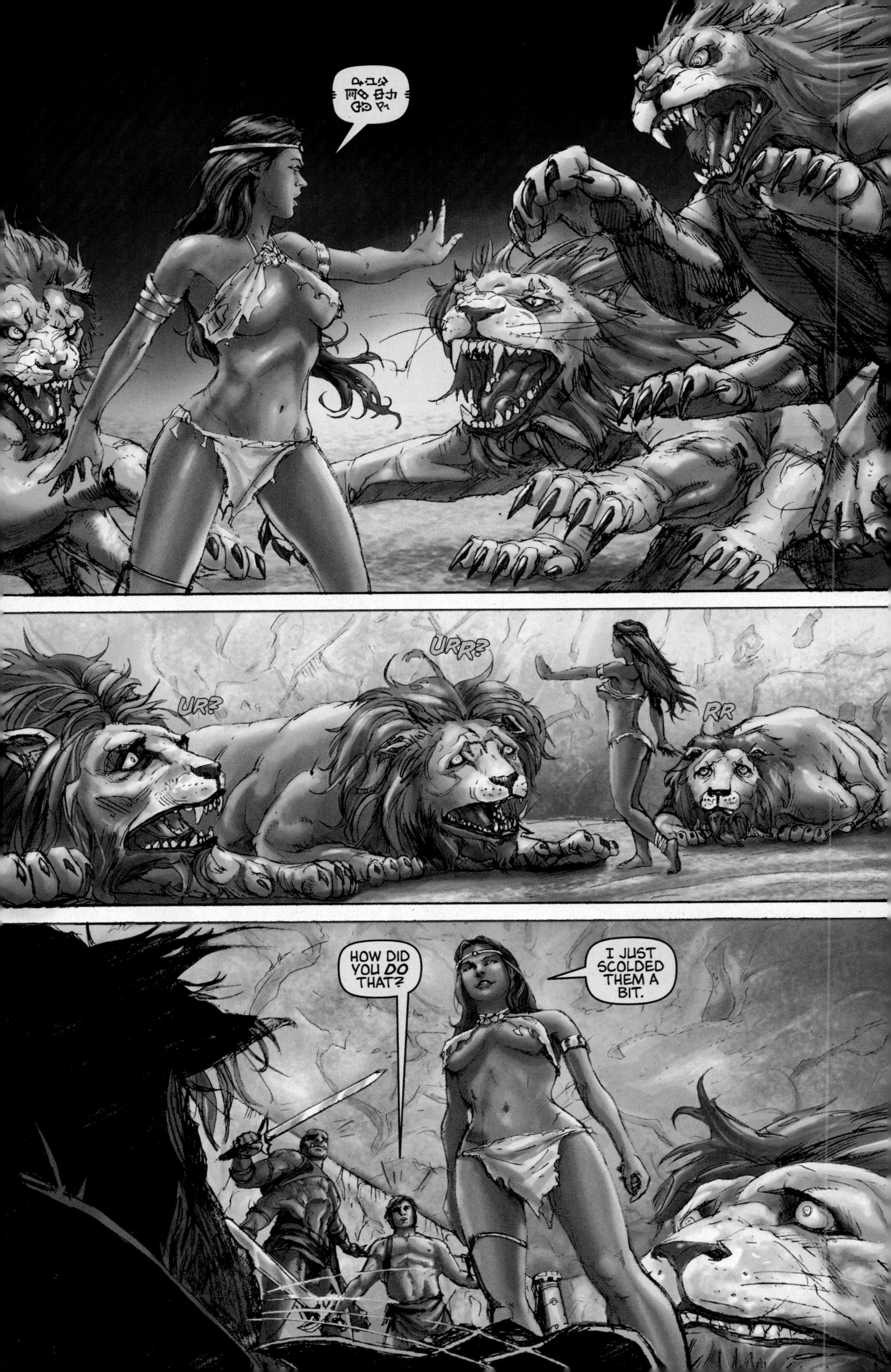
UR?
URR?
RR
HOW DID YOU DO THAT?
I JUST SCOLDED THEM A BIT.

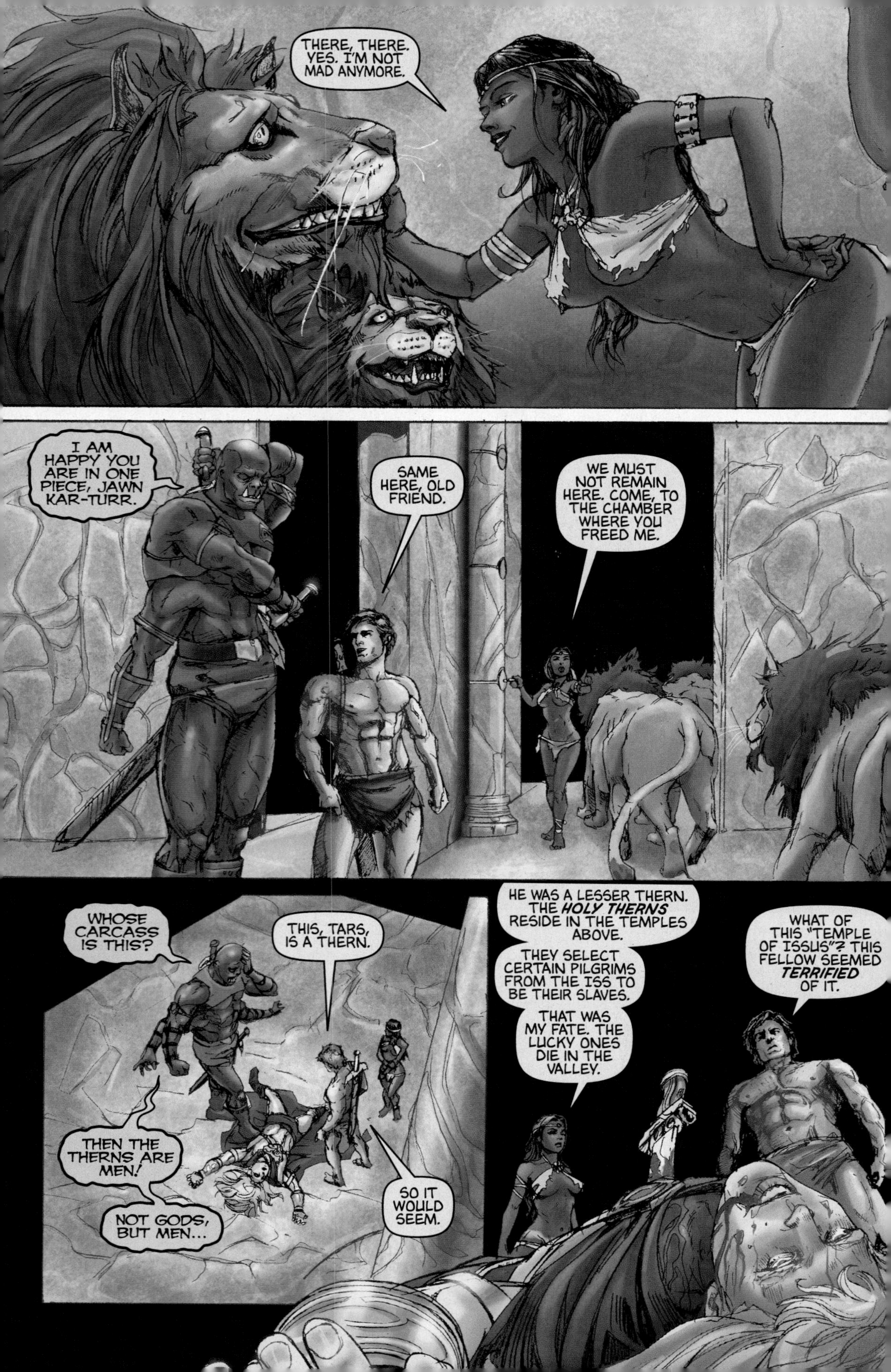
THERE, THERE. YES. I'M NOT MAD ANYMORE.
I AM HAPPY YOU ARE IN ONE PIECE, JAWN KAR-TURR.
SAME HERE, OLD FRIEND.
WE MUST NOT REMAIN HERE. COME, TO THE CHAMBER WHERE YOU FREED ME.
WHOSE CARCASS IS THIS?
THIS, TARS, IS A THERN.
THEN THE THERNS ARE MEN!
NOT GODS, BUT MEN...
SO IT WOULD SEEM.
HE WAS A LESSER THERN. THE *HOLY THERNS* RESIDE IN THE TEMPLES ABOVE.
THEY SELECT CERTAIN PILGRIMS FROM THE ISS TO BE THEIR SLAVES.
THAT WAS MY FATE. THE LUCKY ONES DIE IN THE VALLEY.
WHAT OF THIS "TEMPLE OF ISSUS"? THIS FELLOW SEEMED *TERRIFIED* OF IT.

THE TEMPLE IS TO THE THERNS WHAT THE VALLEY DOR IS TO THOSE OF OUTER BARSOOM--

--A PARADISE OF FLESHLY DELIGHTS. ALL THERNS TRAVEL THERE AT THE END OF THEIR LIVES.

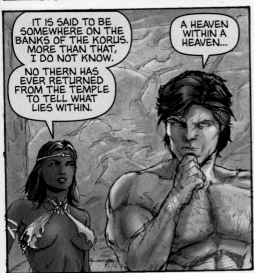

IT IS SAID TO BE SOMEWHERE ON THE BANKS OF THE KORUS. MORE THAN THAT, I DO NOT KNOW.

NO THERN HAS EVER RETURNED FROM THE TEMPLE TO TELL WHAT LIES WITHIN.

A HEAVEN WITHIN A HEAVEN...

I'VE HEARD OF A RED MAN ESCAPED FROM HERE, HUNDREDS OF YEARS AGO.

IF HE DID IT, SO CAN WE.

THAT IS ONLY A LEGEND, JOHN CARTER.

THESE CAVES ARE *CRAWLING* WITH THE LESSER THERNS AND THEIR SLAVES--

--BUT THE *REAL* STRUGGLE WOULD ONLY BEGIN ONCE WE REACHED THE CLIFF TOPS.

THE HOLY THERNS HAVE BEEN BUILDING THEIR STRONGHOLDS ALONG THE OTZ MOUNTAINS SINCE THE BEGINNING OF TIME.

AND A MILLION OF THEIR WARRIORS POPULATE THE TEMPLES WITHIN.

WE ARE DEAD.

FINE BY ME. BACK ON EARTH, I'VE DIED TWICE.

THUVIA, WE HAVE THE *RIGHT* TO ESCAPE FROM THIS VILE MOCKERY OF HEAVEN. WE HAVE TO *TRY.*

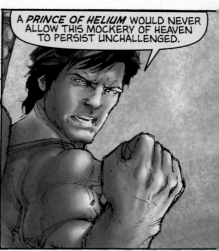

A *PRINCE OF HELIUM* WOULD NEVER ALLOW THIS MOCKERY OF HEAVEN TO PERSIST UNCHALLENGED.

AND WHAT IF WE *DO* ESCAPE? OUR OWN PEOPLE WOULD PUT US TO DEATH AS HERETICS AND BLASPHEMERS.

A PRINCE OF HELIUM SHOULD KNOW BETTER THAN TO MAKE SUCH A SUGGESTION.

I WAS WRONG, THUVIA-- ESCAPE IS NOT OUR *RIGHT*, IT IS OUR SOLEMN *DUTY.* WE *MUST* WARN ALL OF BARSOOM.

I... HAD NOT THOUGHT OF IT THAT WAY. I WOULD GIVE MY LIFE A *THOUSAND* TIMES IF I COULD SAVE A SINGLE SOUL FROM THIS PLACE...

THAT'S IT! AND PEOPLE MIGHT BE MORE INCLINED TO ACCEPT THE TRUTH IF IT CAME FROM *ALL* OF US.

THIS IS TARS TARKAS, JEDDAK OF THARK.

WHAT SAY YOU, TARS?

TO THE GATES OF THE TEMPLE OF ISSUS, TO THE BOTTOM OF THE KORUS--I GO WHERE JAWN KAR-TURR LEADS. I HAVE SPOKEN.

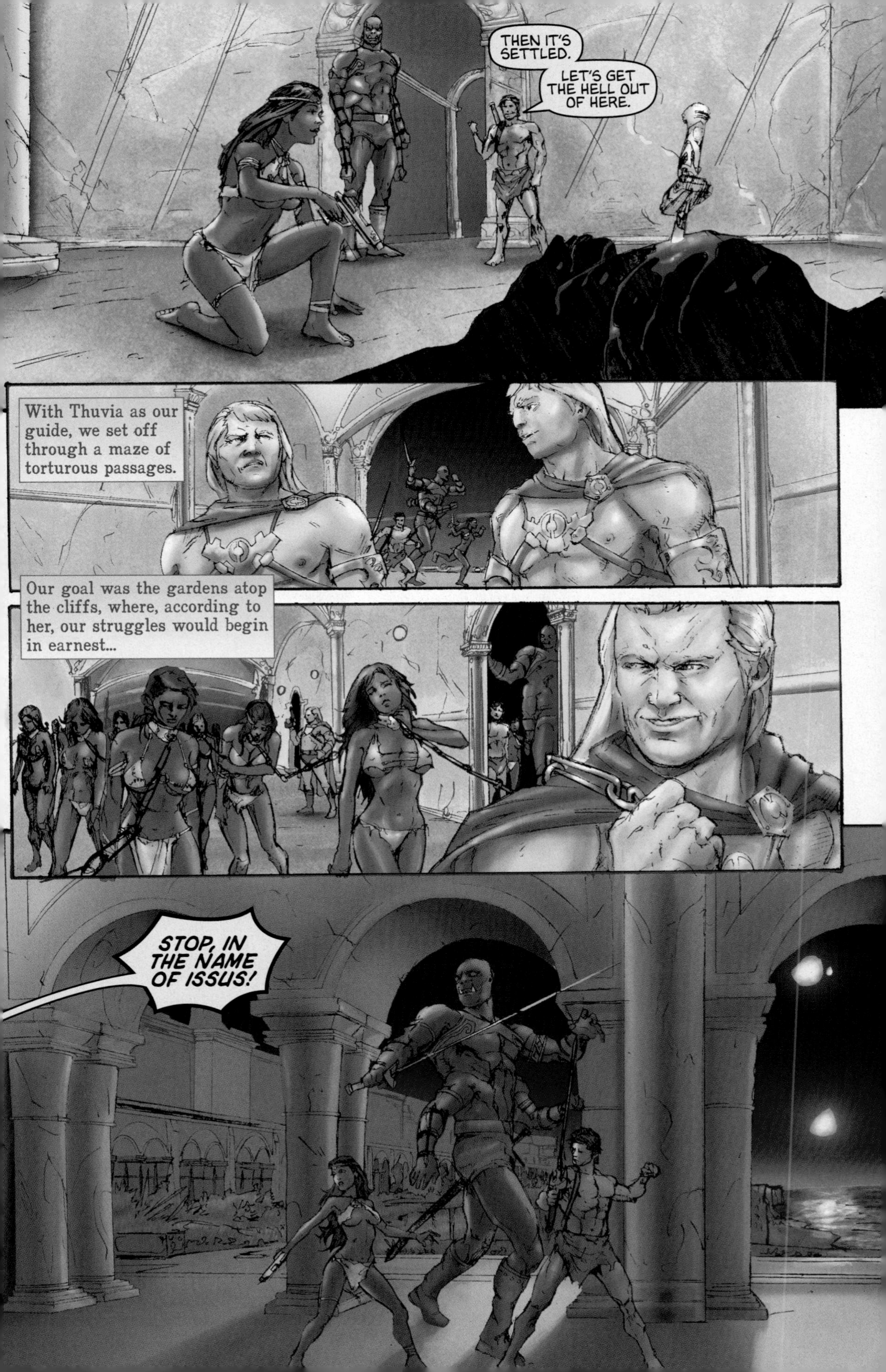
THEN IT'S SETTLED.
LET'S GET THE HELL OUT OF HERE.
With Thuvia as our guide, we set off through a maze of torturous passages.
Our goal was the gardens atop the cliffs, where, according to her, our struggles would begin in earnest...
STOP, IN THE NAME OF ISSUS!

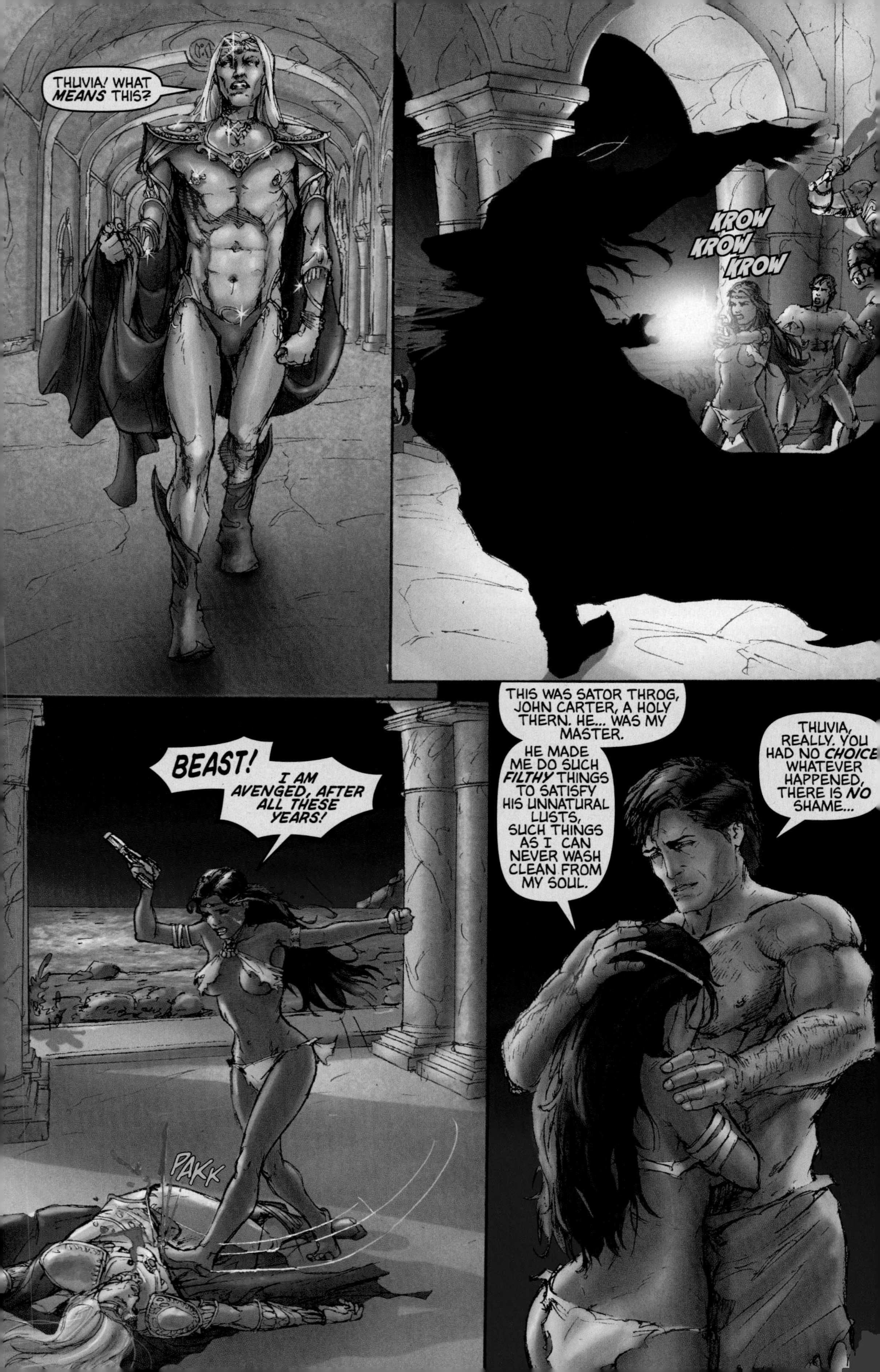

THUVIA! WHAT *MEANS* THIS?
KROW KROW KROW
BEAST!
I AM AVENGED, AFTER ALL THESE YEARS!
PAKK
THIS WAS SATOR THROG, JOHN CARTER, A HOLY THERN. HE... WAS MY MASTER.
HE MADE ME DO SUCH *FILTHY* THINGS TO SATISFY HIS UNNATURAL LUSTS, SUCH THINGS AS I CAN NEVER WASH CLEAN FROM MY SOUL.
THUVIA, REALLY. YOU HAD NO *CHOICE*. WHATEVER HAPPENED, THERE IS *NO* SHAME...

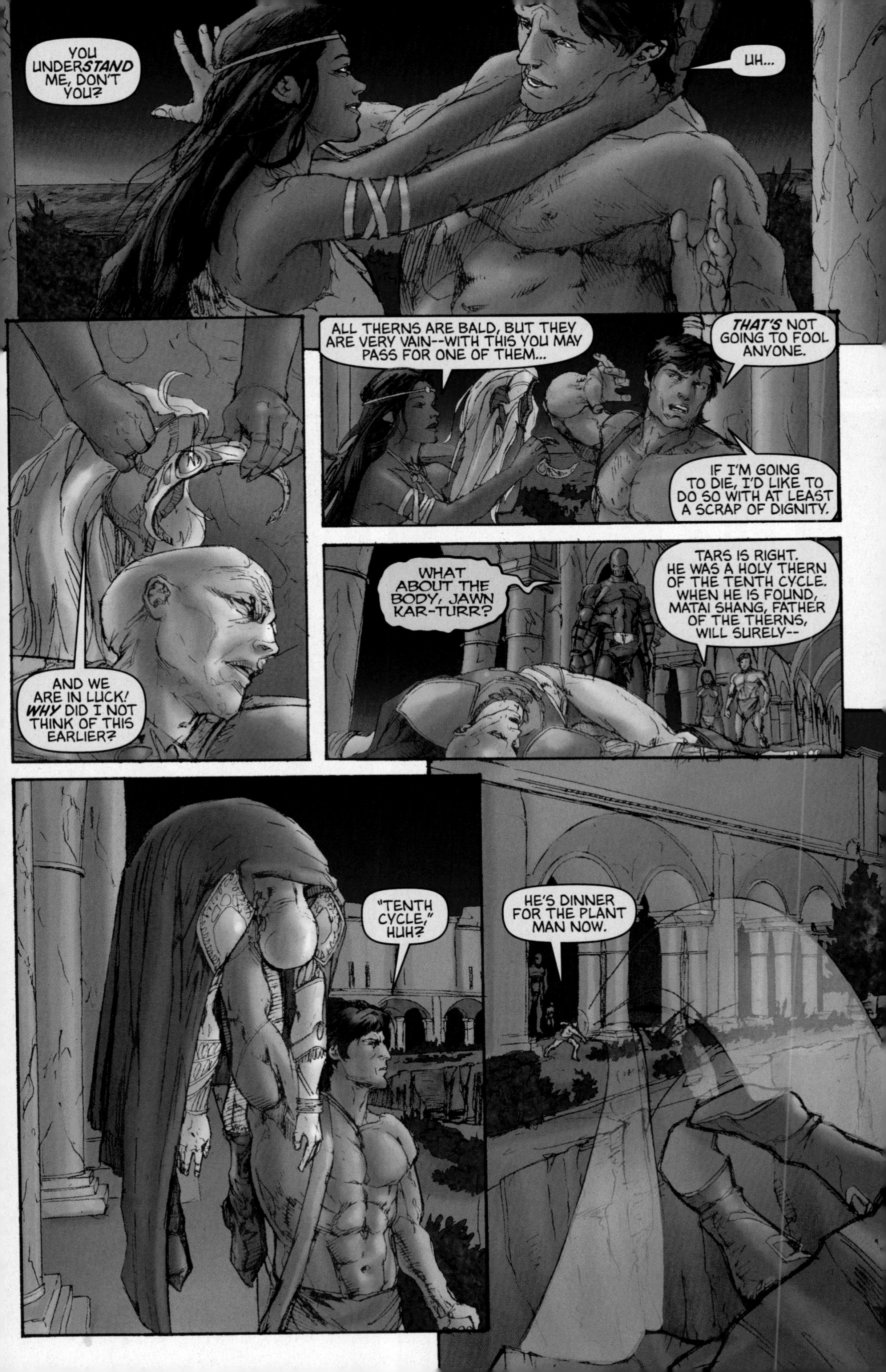
YOU UNDERSTAND ME, DON'T YOU?
UH...
AND WE ARE IN LUCK! WHY DID I NOT THINK OF THIS EARLIER?
ALL THERNS ARE BALD, BUT THEY ARE VERY VAIN--WITH THIS YOU MAY PASS FOR ONE OF THEM...
THAT'S NOT GOING TO FOOL ANYONE.
IF I'M GOING TO DIE, I'D LIKE TO DO SO WITH AT LEAST A SCRAP OF DIGNITY.
WHAT ABOUT THE BODY, JAWN KAR-TURR?
TARS IS RIGHT. HE WAS A HOLY THERN OF THE TENTH CYCLE. WHEN HE IS FOUND, MATAI SHANG, FATHER OF THE THERNS, WILL SURELY--
"TENTH CYCLE," HUH?
HE'S DINNER FOR THE PLANT MAN NOW.

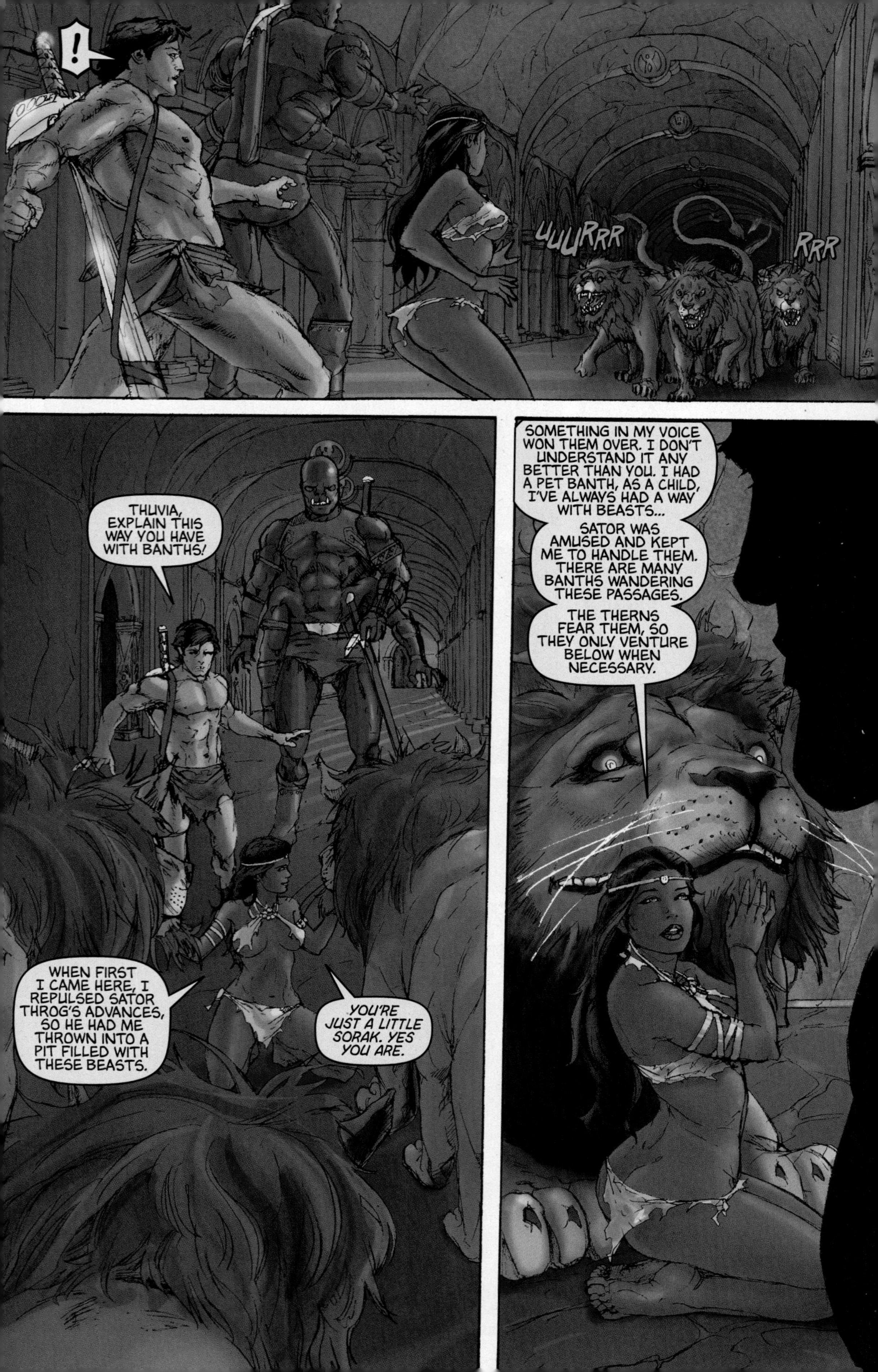
!
UUURRR
RRR
THUVIA, EXPLAIN THIS WAY YOU HAVE WITH BANTHS!
WHEN FIRST I CAME HERE, I REPULSED SATOR THROG'S ADVANCES, SO HE HAD ME THROWN INTO A PIT FILLED WITH THESE BEASTS.
YOU'RE JUST A LITTLE SORAK. YES YOU ARE.
SOMETHING IN MY VOICE WON THEM OVER. I DON'T UNDERSTAND IT ANY BETTER THAN YOU. I HAD A PET BANTH, AS A CHILD, I'VE ALWAYS HAD A WAY WITH BEASTS...
SATOR WAS AMUSED AND KEPT ME TO HANDLE THEM. THERE ARE MANY BANTHS WANDERING THESE PASSAGES.
THE THERNS FEAR THEM, SO THEY ONLY VENTURE BELOW WHEN NECESSARY.

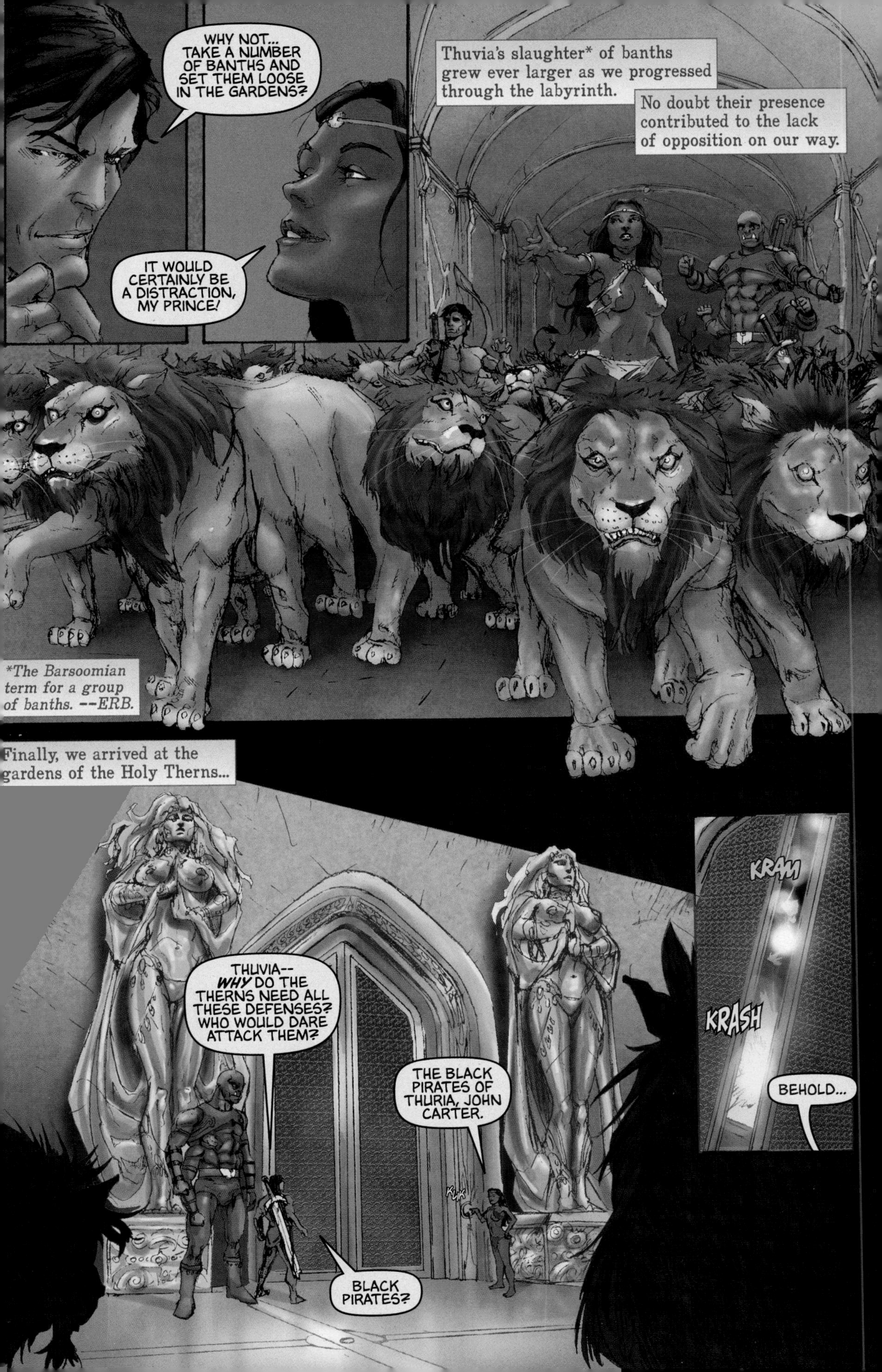
WHY NOT... TAKE A NUMBER OF BANTHS AND SET THEM LOOSE IN THE GARDENS?
IT WOULD CERTAINLY BE A DISTRACTION, MY PRINCE!
Thuvia's slaughter* of banths grew ever larger as we progressed through the labyrinth.
No doubt their presence contributed to the lack of opposition on our way.
*The Barsoomian term for a group of banths. --ERB.
Finally, we arrived at the gardens of the Holy Therns...
THUVIA-- *WHY* DO THE THERNS NEED ALL THESE DEFENSES? WHO WOULD DARE ATTACK THEM?
THE BLACK PIRATES OF THURIA, JOHN CARTER.
BLACK PIRATES?
KRAM
KRASH
BEHOLD...

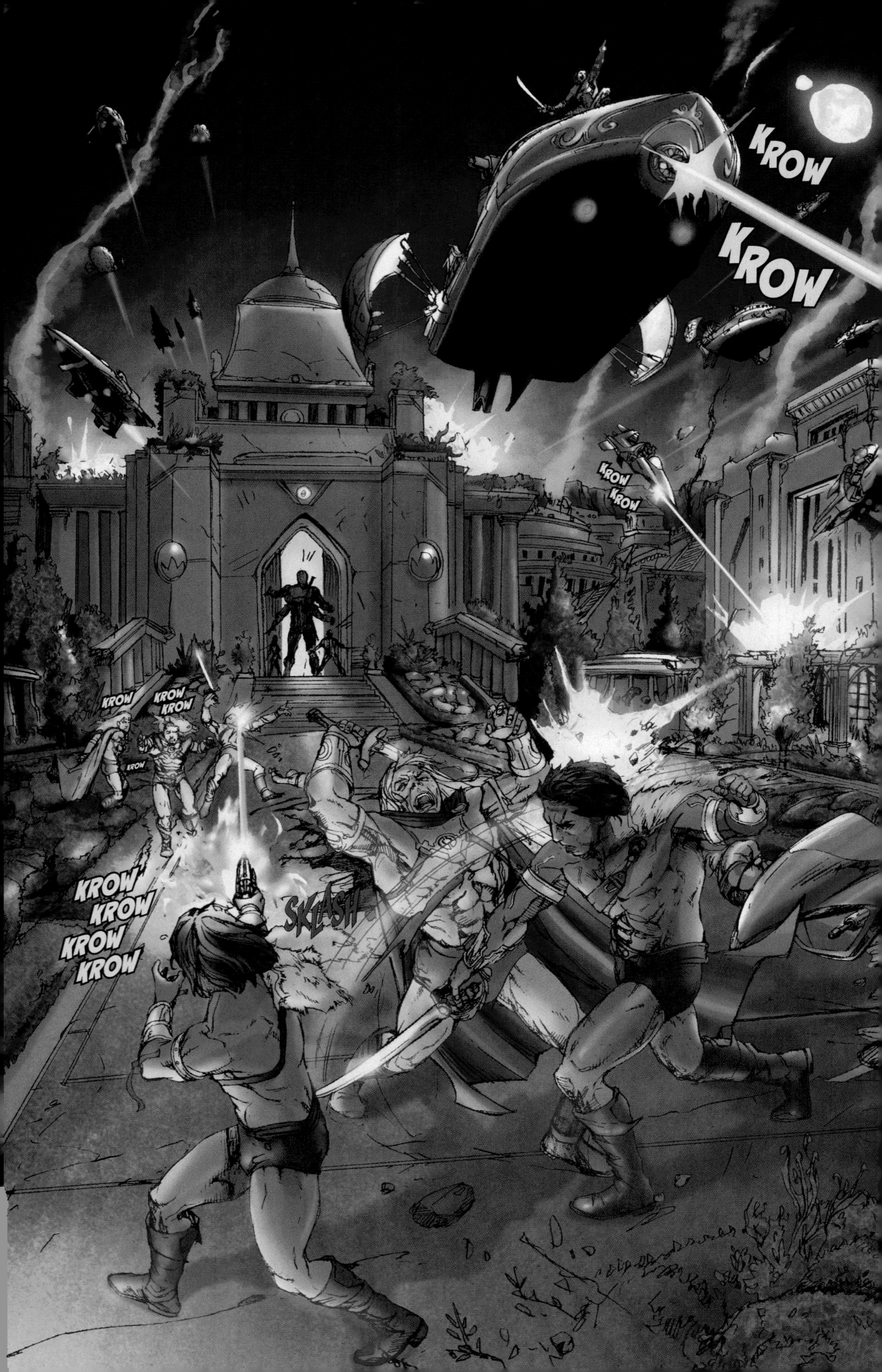
KROW
KROW
KROW
KROW
KROW
KROW
KROW
KROW
KROW
KROW
KROW
KROW
SKLASH

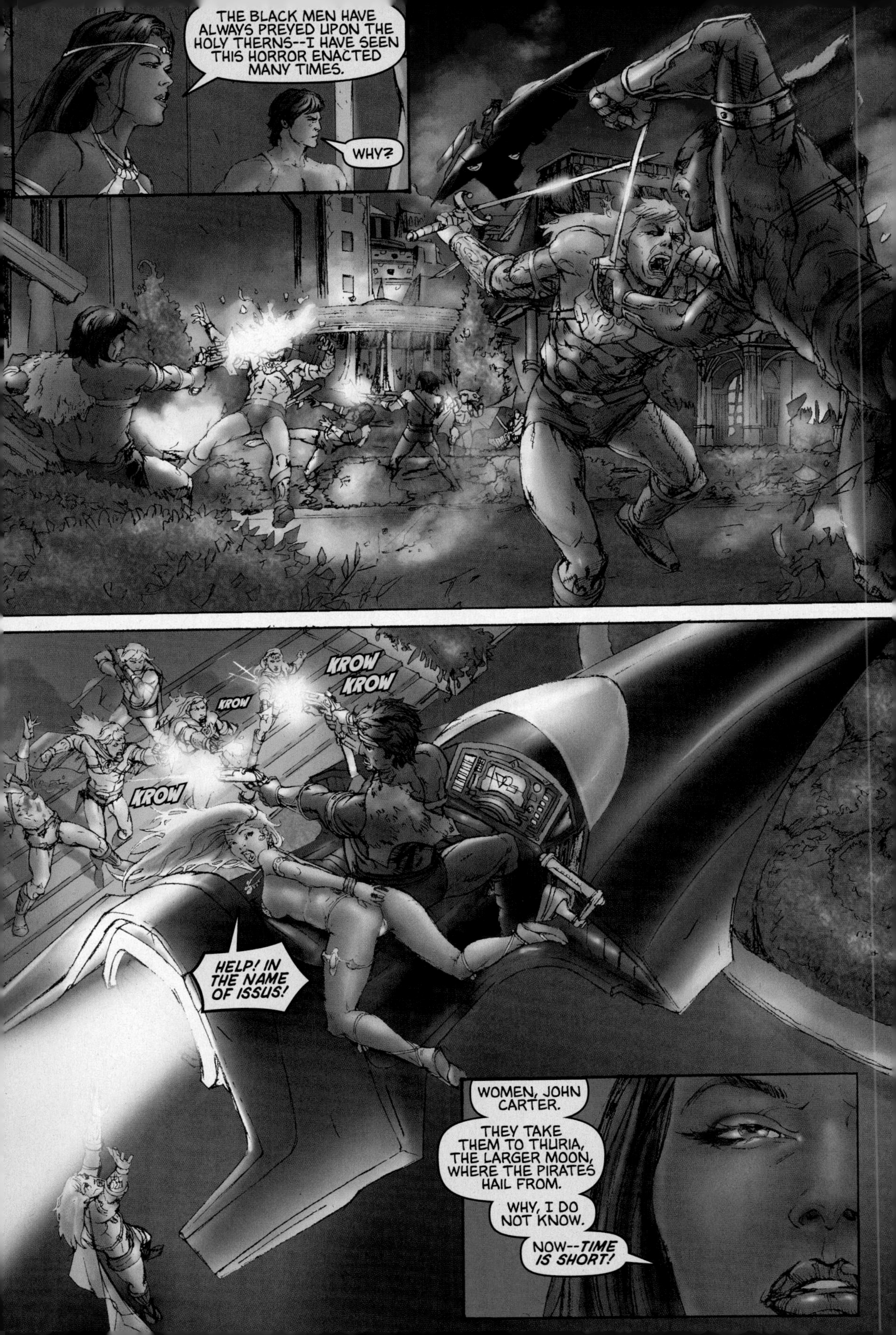
THE BLACK MEN HAVE ALWAYS PREYED UPON THE HOLY THERNS--I HAVE SEEN THIS HORROR ENACTED MANY TIMES.
WHY?
KROW
KROW
KROW
KROW
HELP! IN THE NAME OF ISSUS!
WOMEN, JOHN CARTER.
THEY TAKE THEM TO THURIA, THE LARGER MOON, WHERE THE PIRATES HAIL FROM.
WHY, I DO NOT KNOW.
NOW--*TIME IS SHORT!*

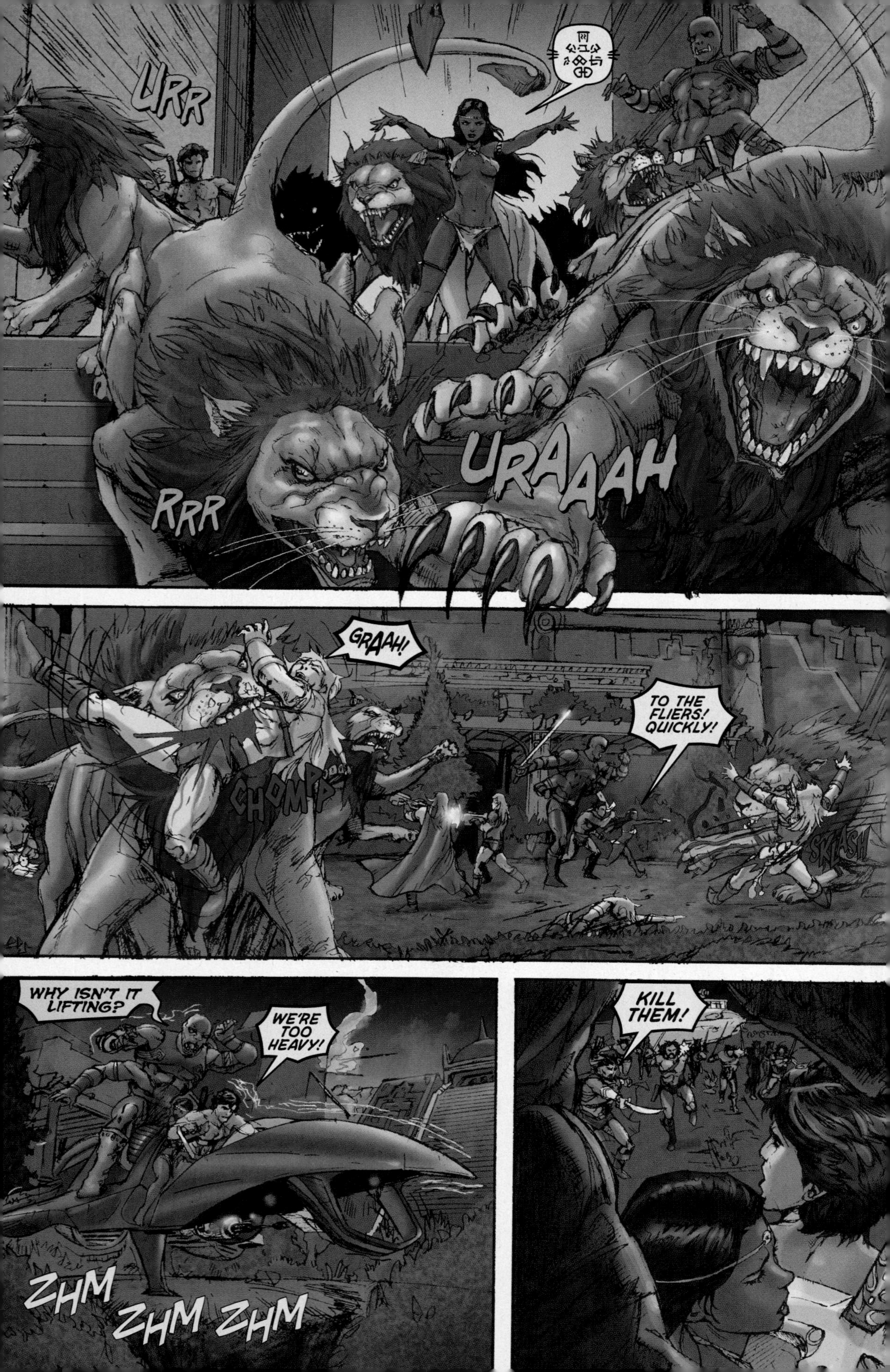
URR
URAAAH
RRR
GRAAH!
CHOMP
TO THE FLIERS! QUICKLY!
SKLASH
WHY ISN'T IT LIFTING?
WE'RE TOO HEAVY!
ZHM ZHM ZHM
KILL THEM!

WHAT ARE YOU DOING?
RANKK
FWREEE
TAKE CARE OF HER, TARS!
JAWN KAR-TURR, WAIT!
WASHH
NO, MY PRINCE! LET ME DIE WITH YOU!
DO NOT LEAVE ME!

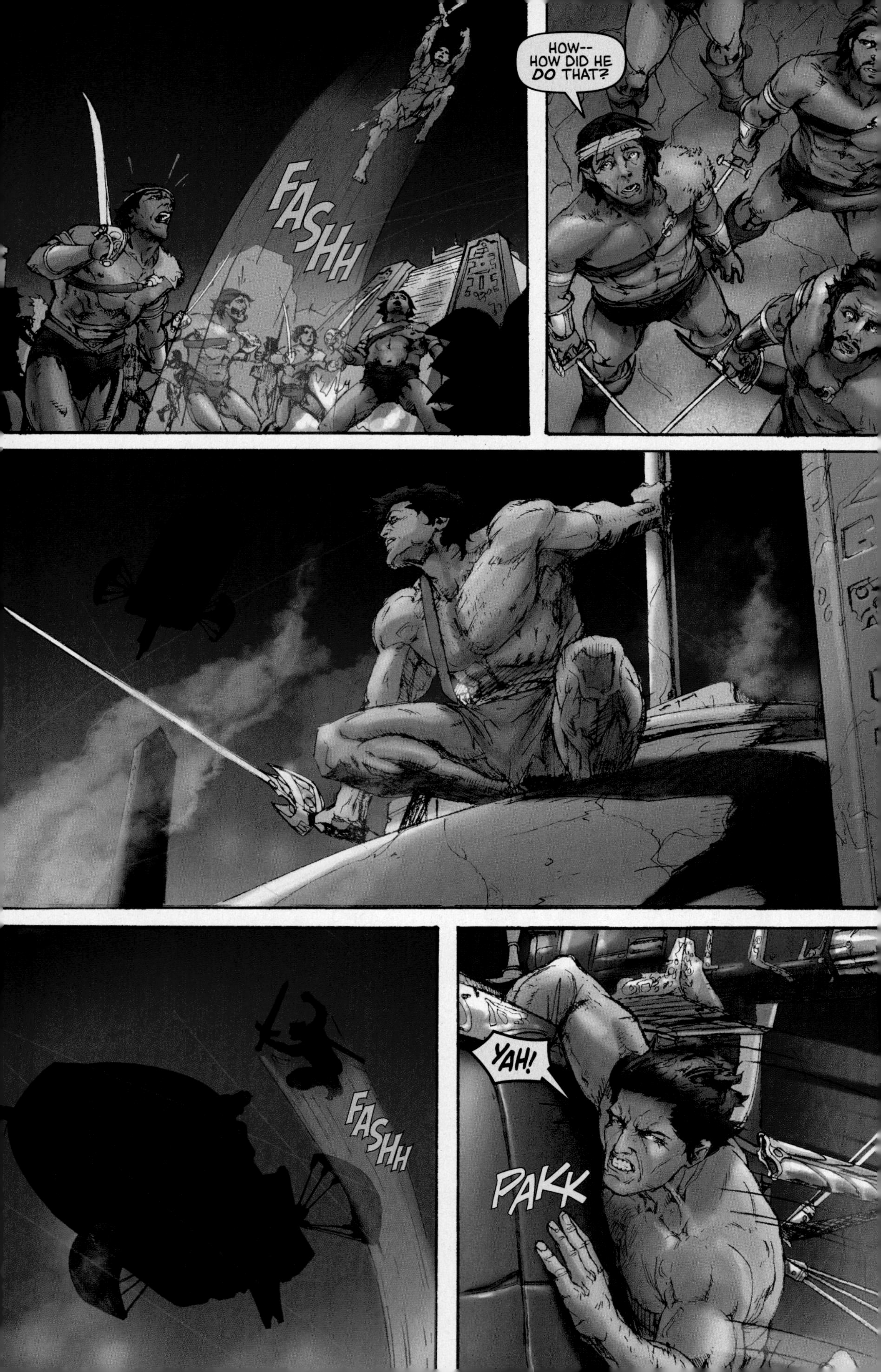
FASHH
HOW--
HOW DID HE
DO THAT?
FASHH
YAH!
PAKK

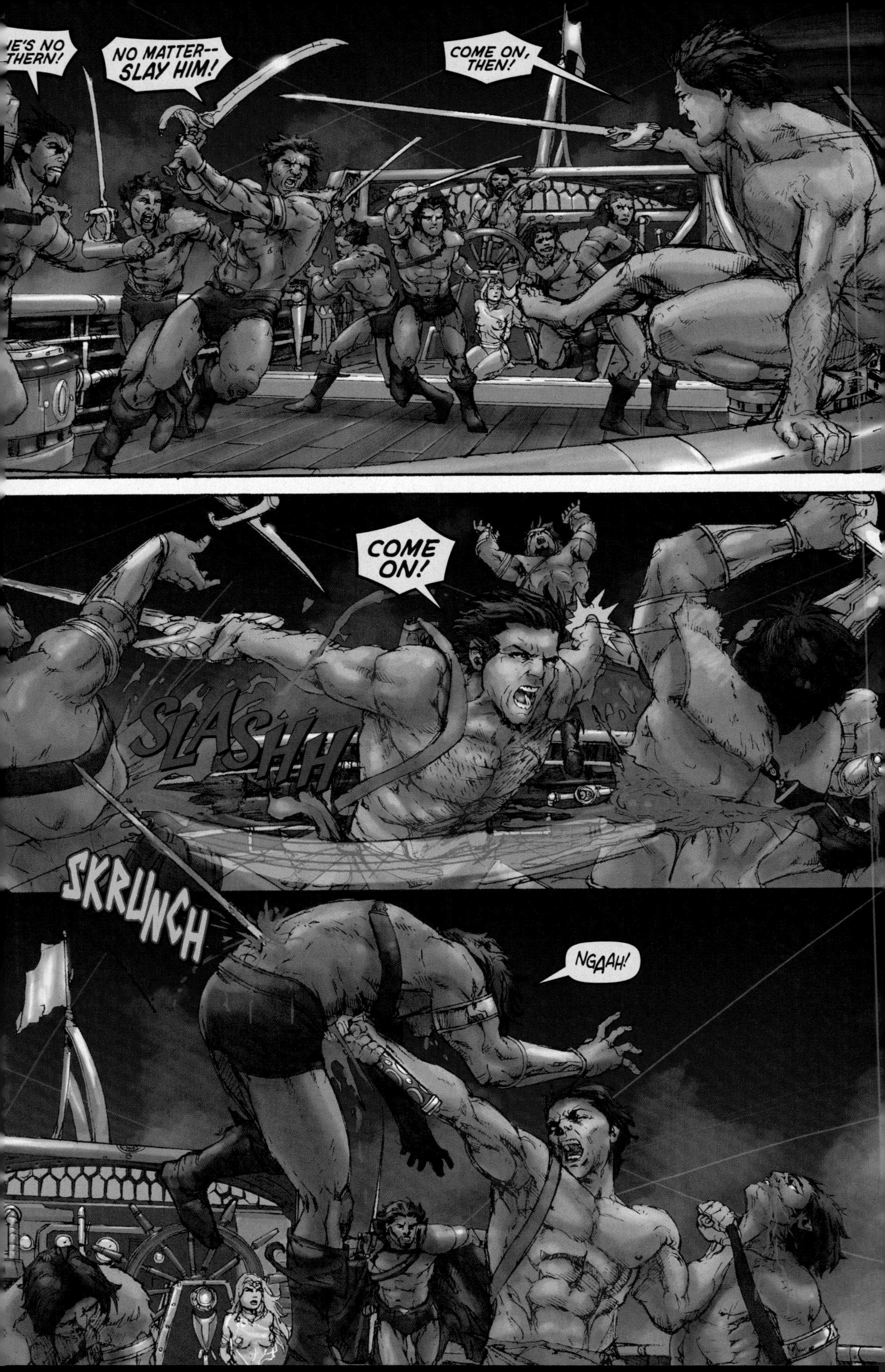
...E'S NO
...THERN!
NO MATTER--
SLAY HIM!
COME ON,
THEN!
COME
ON!
SLASHH
SKRUNCH
NGAAH!

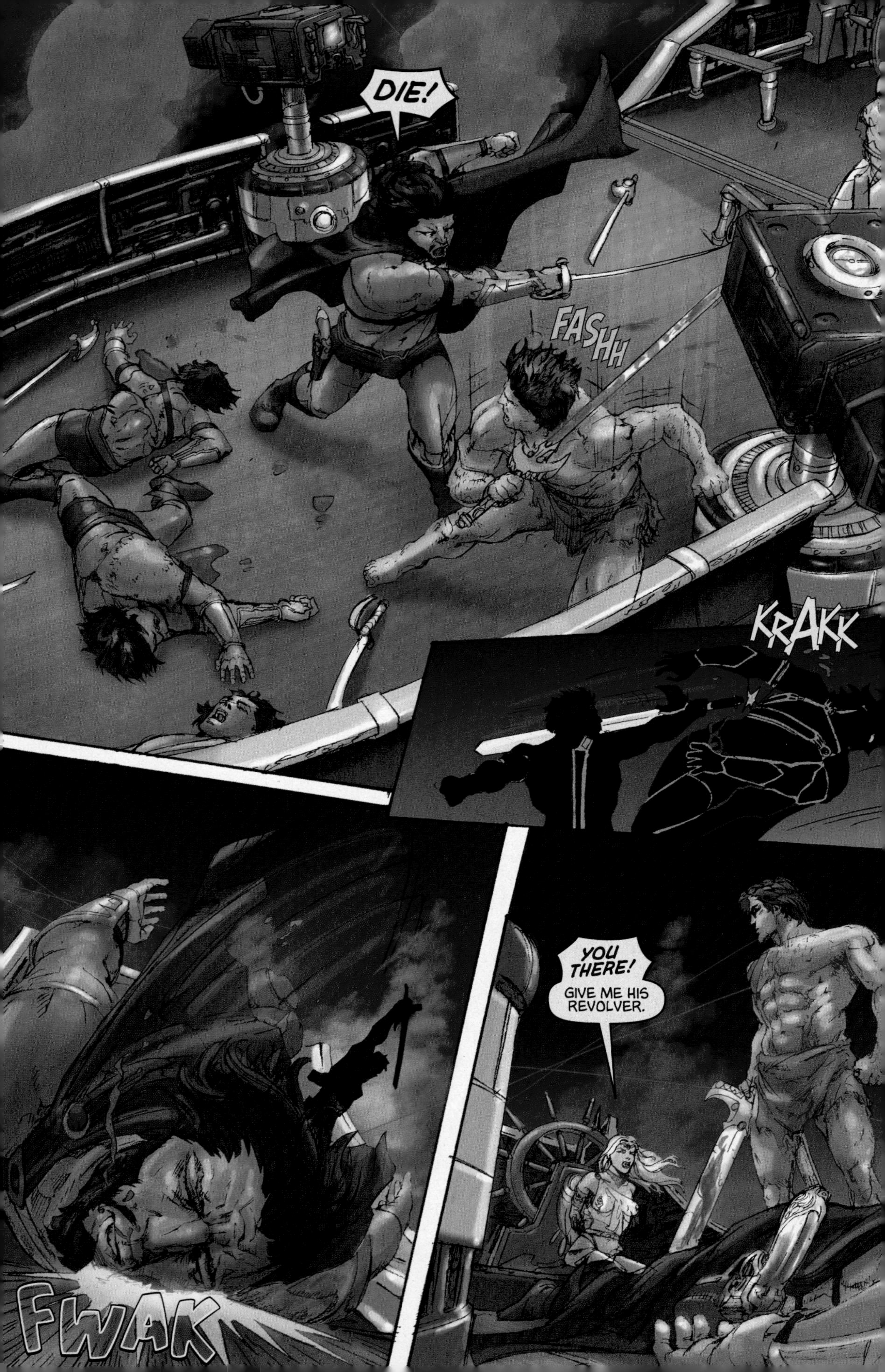
DIE!
FASHH
KRAKK
FWAK
YOU THERE!
GIVE ME HIS REVOLVER.

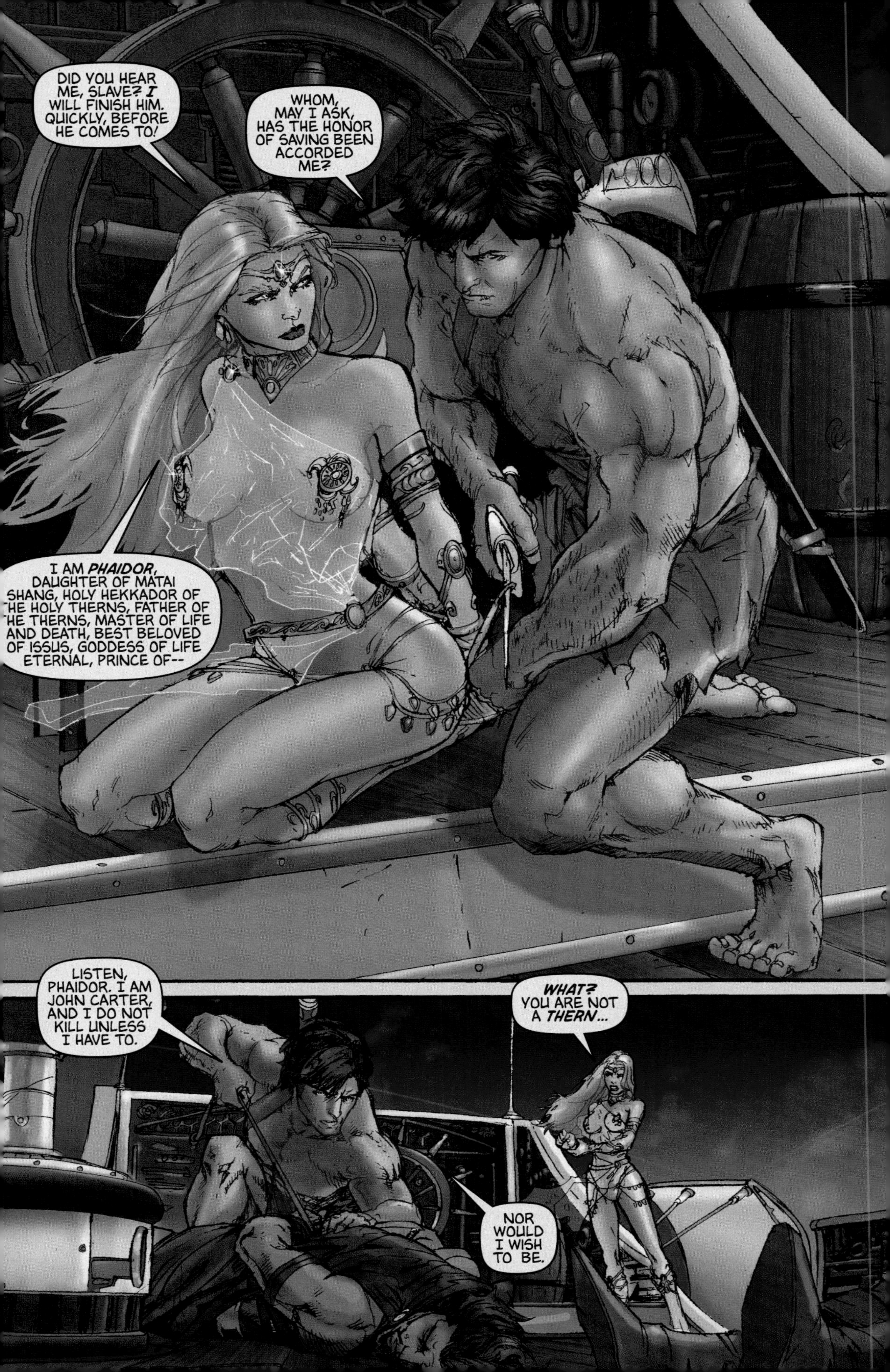
DID YOU HEAR ME, SLAVE? *I* WILL FINISH HIM. QUICKLY, BEFORE HE COMES TO!
WHOM, MAY I ASK, HAS THE HONOR OF SAVING BEEN ACCORDED ME?
I AM *PHAIDOR*, DAUGHTER OF MATAI SHANG, HOLY HEKKADOR OF THE HOLY THERNS, FATHER OF THE THERNS, MASTER OF LIFE AND DEATH, BEST BELOVED OF ISSUS, GODDESS OF LIFE ETERNAL, PRINCE OF--
LISTEN, PHAIDOR. I AM JOHN CARTER, AND I DO NOT KILL UNLESS I HAVE TO.
WHAT? YOU ARE NOT A *THERN*...
NOR WOULD I WISH TO BE.

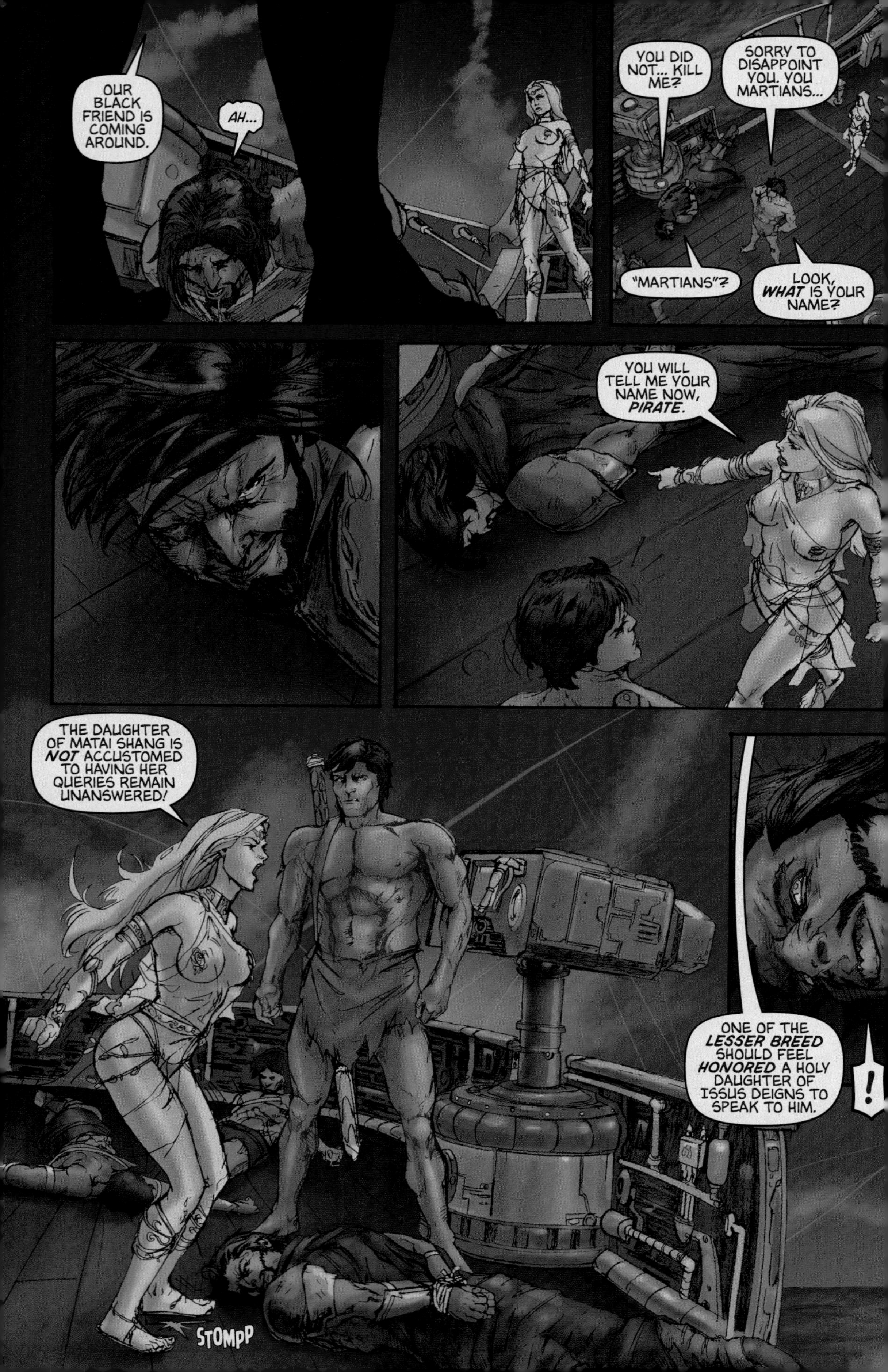
OUR BLACK FRIEND IS COMING AROUND.
AH...
YOU DID NOT... KILL ME?
SORRY TO DISAPPOINT YOU. YOU MARTIANS...
"MARTIANS"?
LOOK, **WHAT** IS YOUR NAME?
YOU WILL TELL ME YOUR NAME NOW, **PIRATE**.
THE DAUGHTER OF MATAI SHANG IS **NOT** ACCUSTOMED TO HAVING HER QUERIES REMAIN UNANSWERED!
ONE OF THE **LESSER BREED** SHOULD FEEL **HONORED** A HOLY DAUGHTER OF ISSUS DEIGNS TO SPEAK TO HIM.
!
STOMPP

I AM XODAR, DATOR OF THE FIRST BORN. I GIVE COMMANDS, I DO NOT TAKE THEM.

"FIRST BORN"? WHAT DRIVEL ARE YOU--

WHAT ARE YOUR INTENTIONS CONCERNING ME?

I'M TAKING YOU TO HELIUM, BOTH OF YOU.

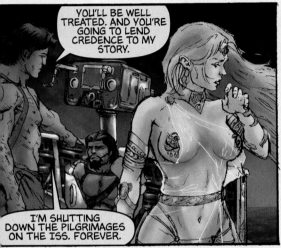

YOU'LL BE WELL TREATED. AND YOU'RE GOING TO LEND CREDENCE TO MY STORY.

I'M SHUTTING DOWN THE PILGRIMAGES ON THE ISS. FOREVER.

ARE YOU OF HELIUM?

I AM A PRINCE THERE. ORIGINALLY, I AM FROM EARTH.

EARTH! THAT EXPLAINS MUCH. NO WONDER YOU COULD BEST A DATOR. THEN THERE IS NO DISGRACE...

WHAT IS A "DATOR"?

NO. I AM DONE TALKING.

AND WHY IS THAT?

BECAUSE I HAVE DISTRACTED YOU LONG ENOUGH.

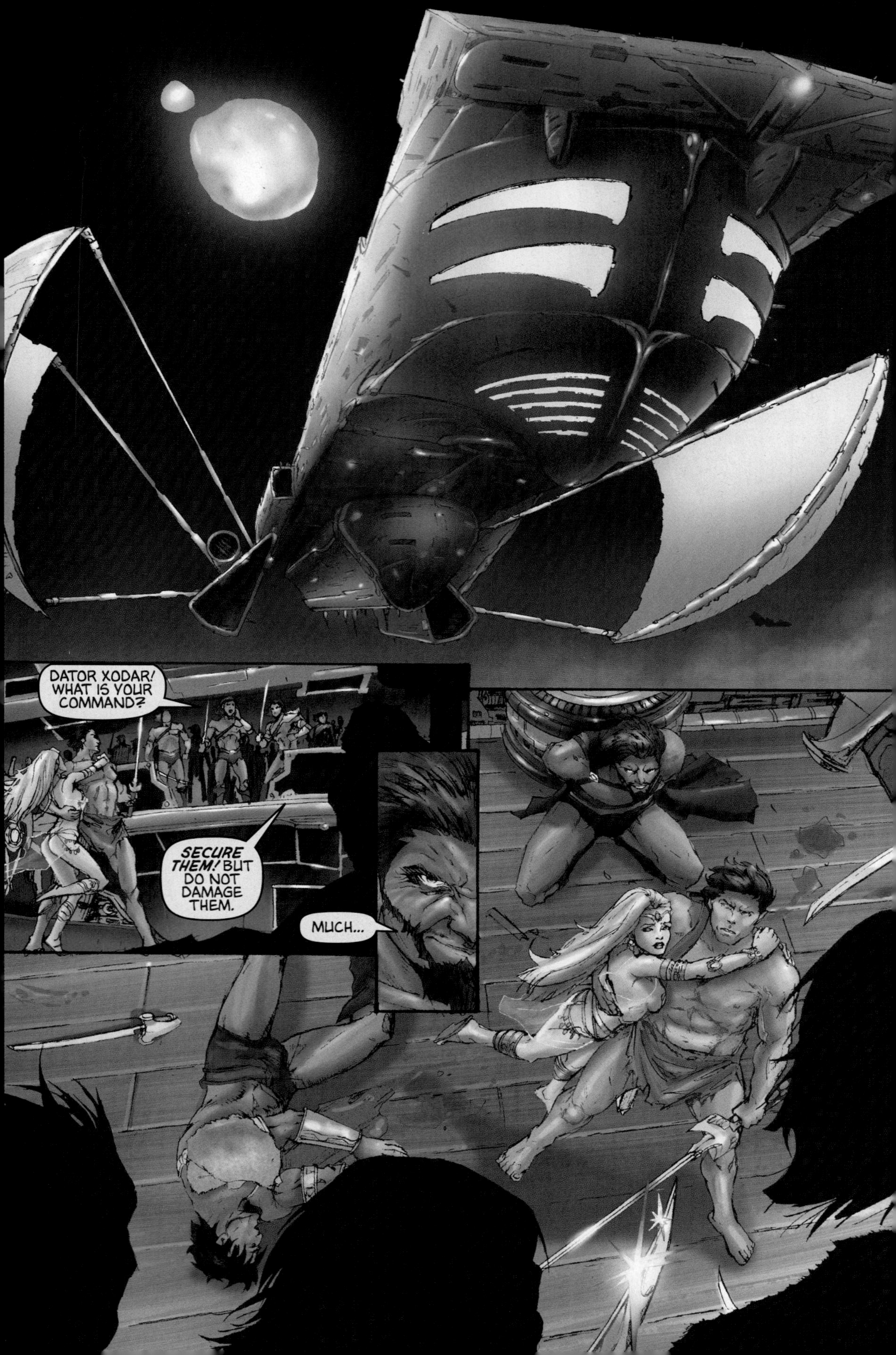
DATOR XODAR! WHAT IS YOUR COMMAND?
SECURE THEM! BUT DO NOT DAMAGE THEM.
MUCH...

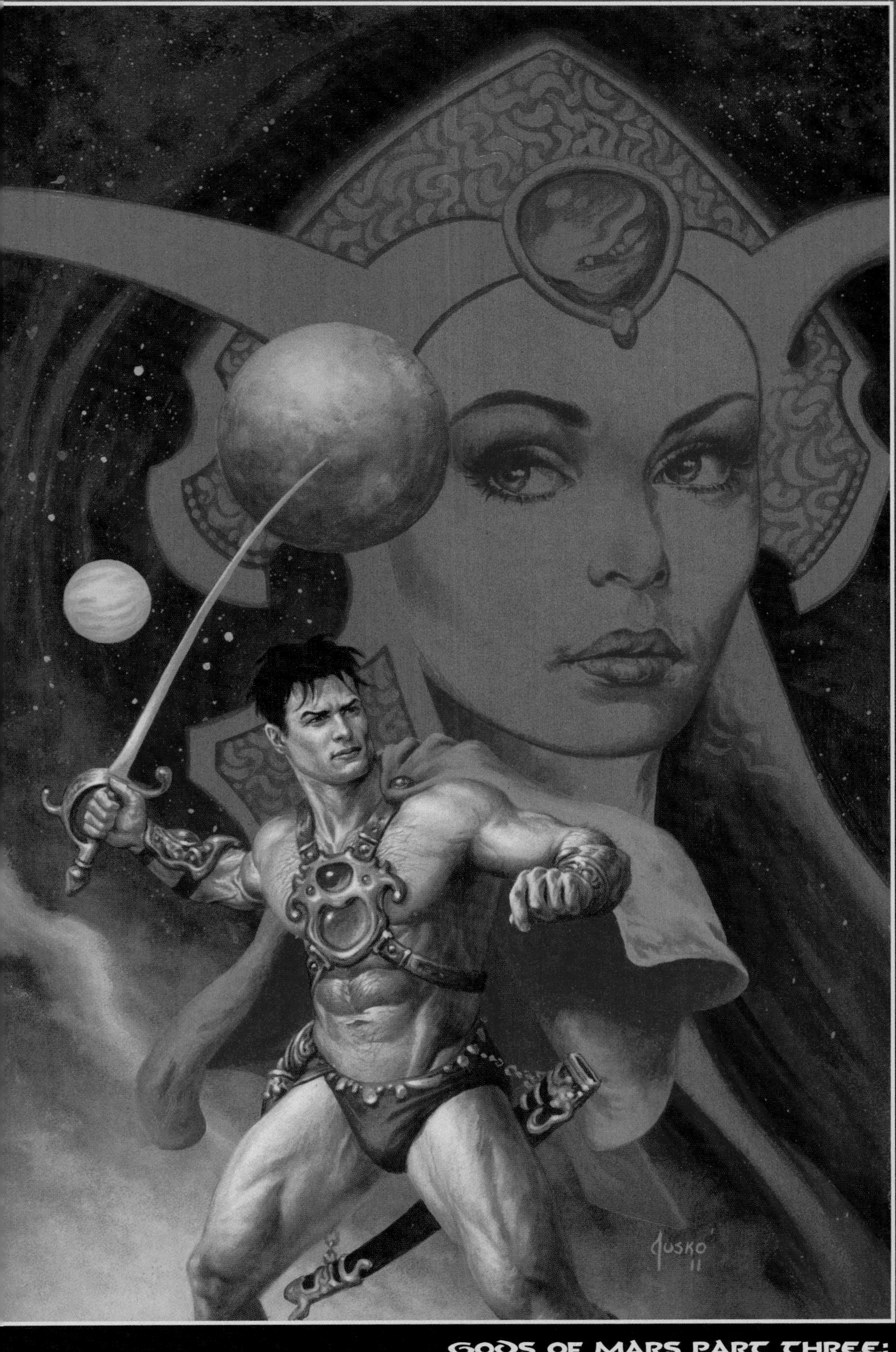
JUSKO 11

GODS OF MARS PART THREE:
ISSUS, GODDESS OF LIFE ETERNAL • Issue #15 cover by JOE JUSKO

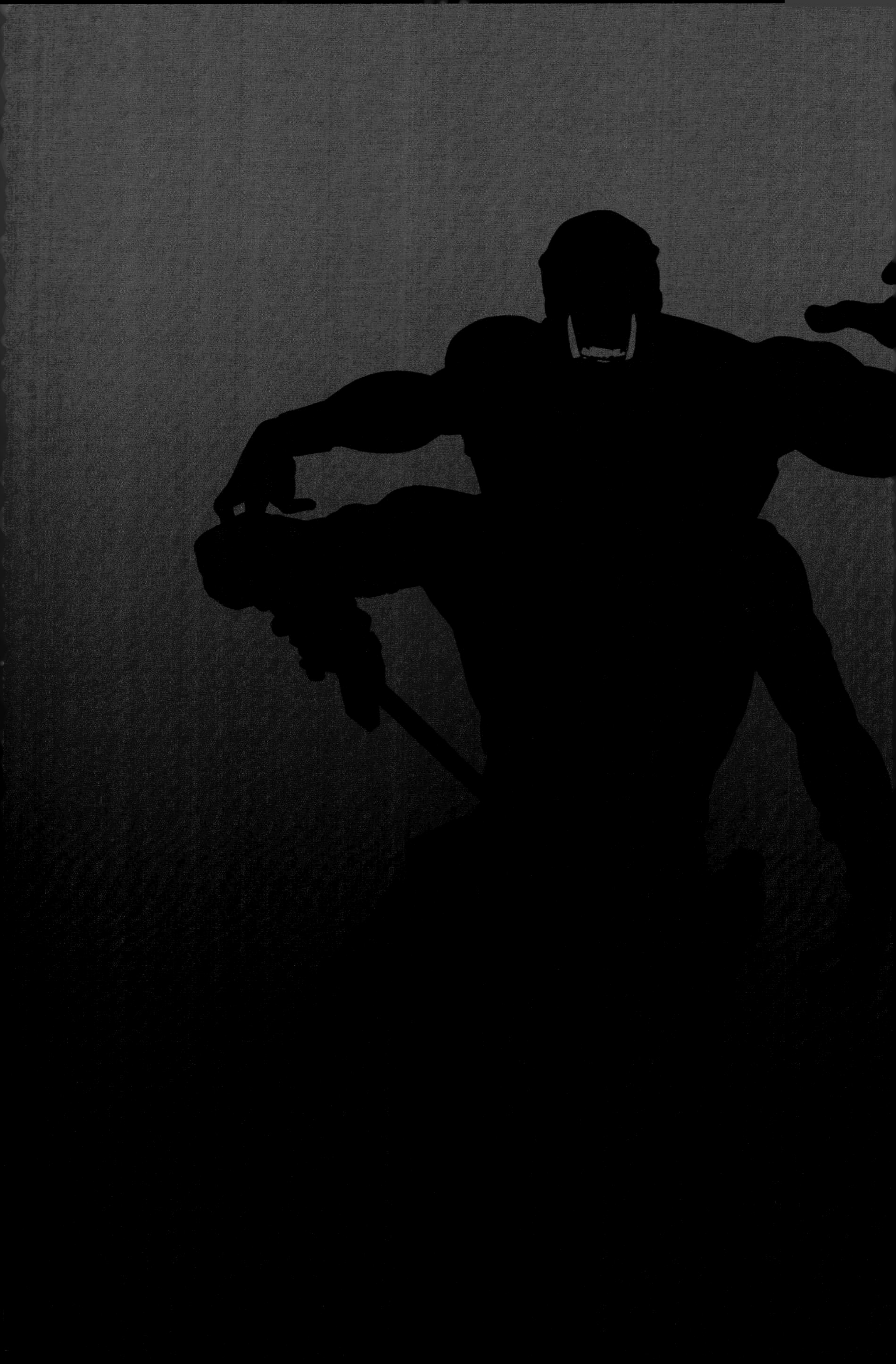

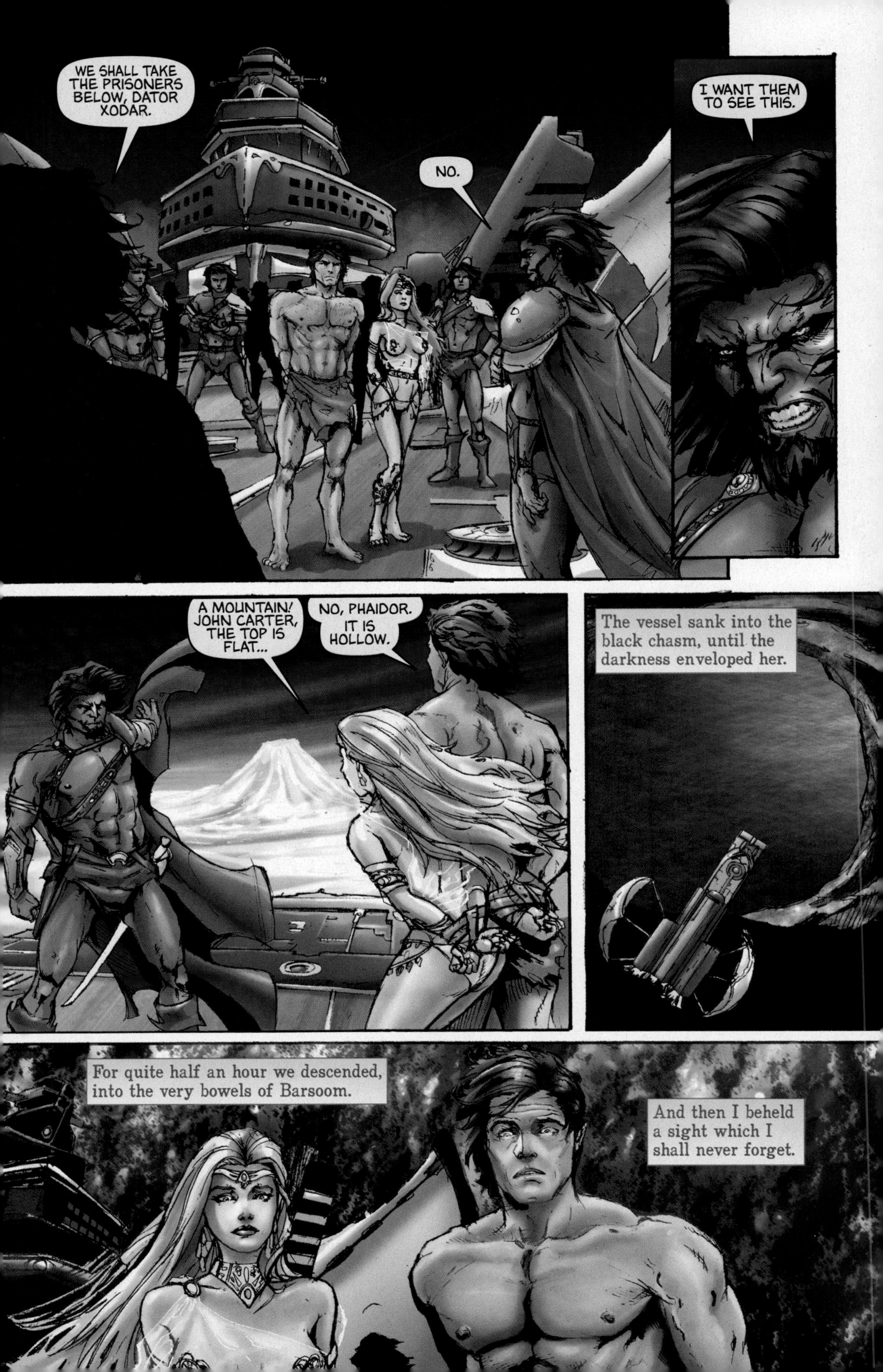
WE SHALL TAKE THE PRISONERS BELOW, DATOR XODAR.
NO.
I WANT THEM TO SEE THIS.
A MOUNTAIN! JOHN CARTER, THE TOP IS FLAT...
NO, PHAIDOR. IT IS HOLLOW.
The vessel sank into the black chasm, until the darkness enveloped her.
For quite half an hour we descended, into the very bowels of Barsoom.
And then I beheld a sight which I shall never forget.

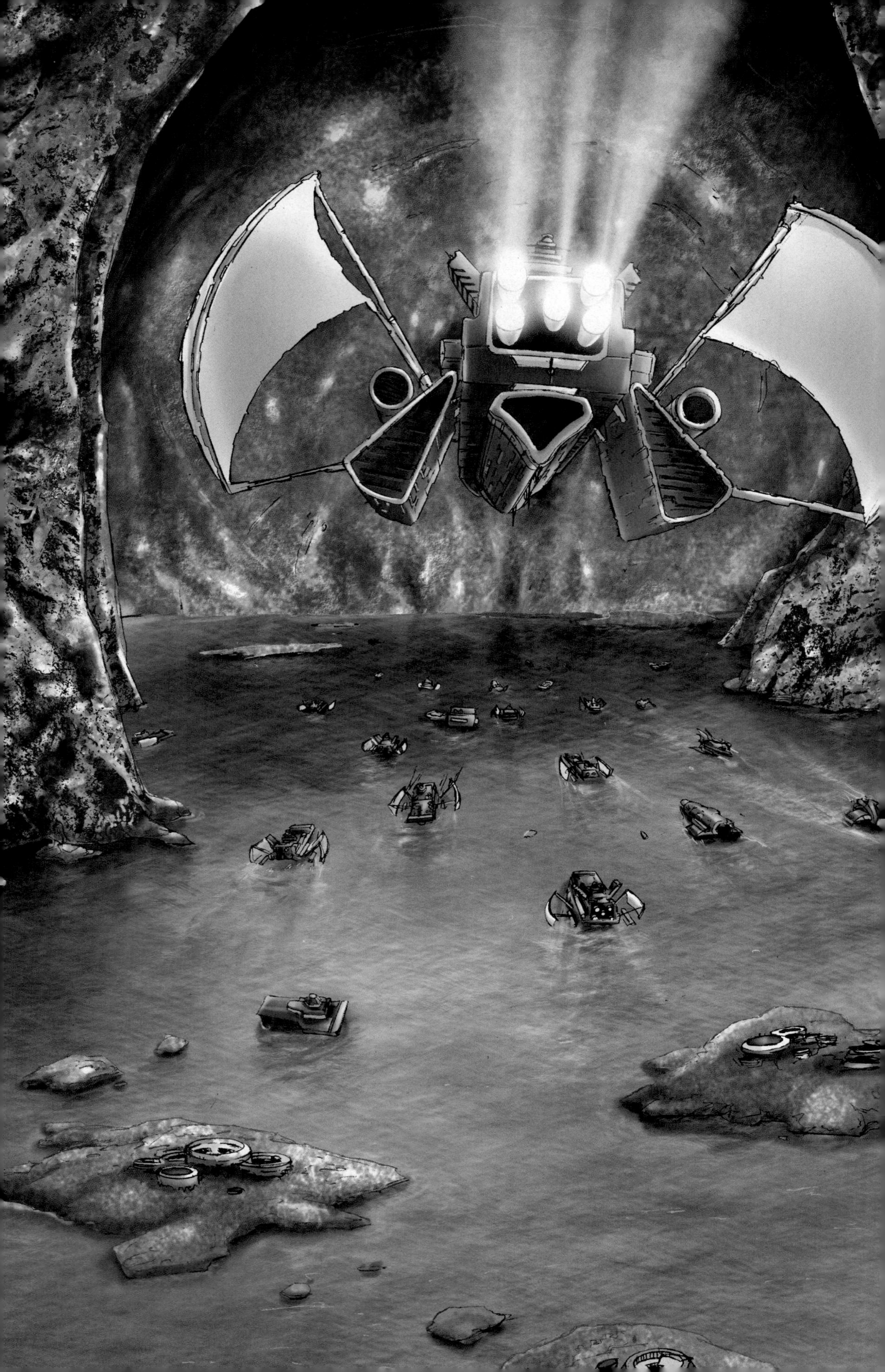

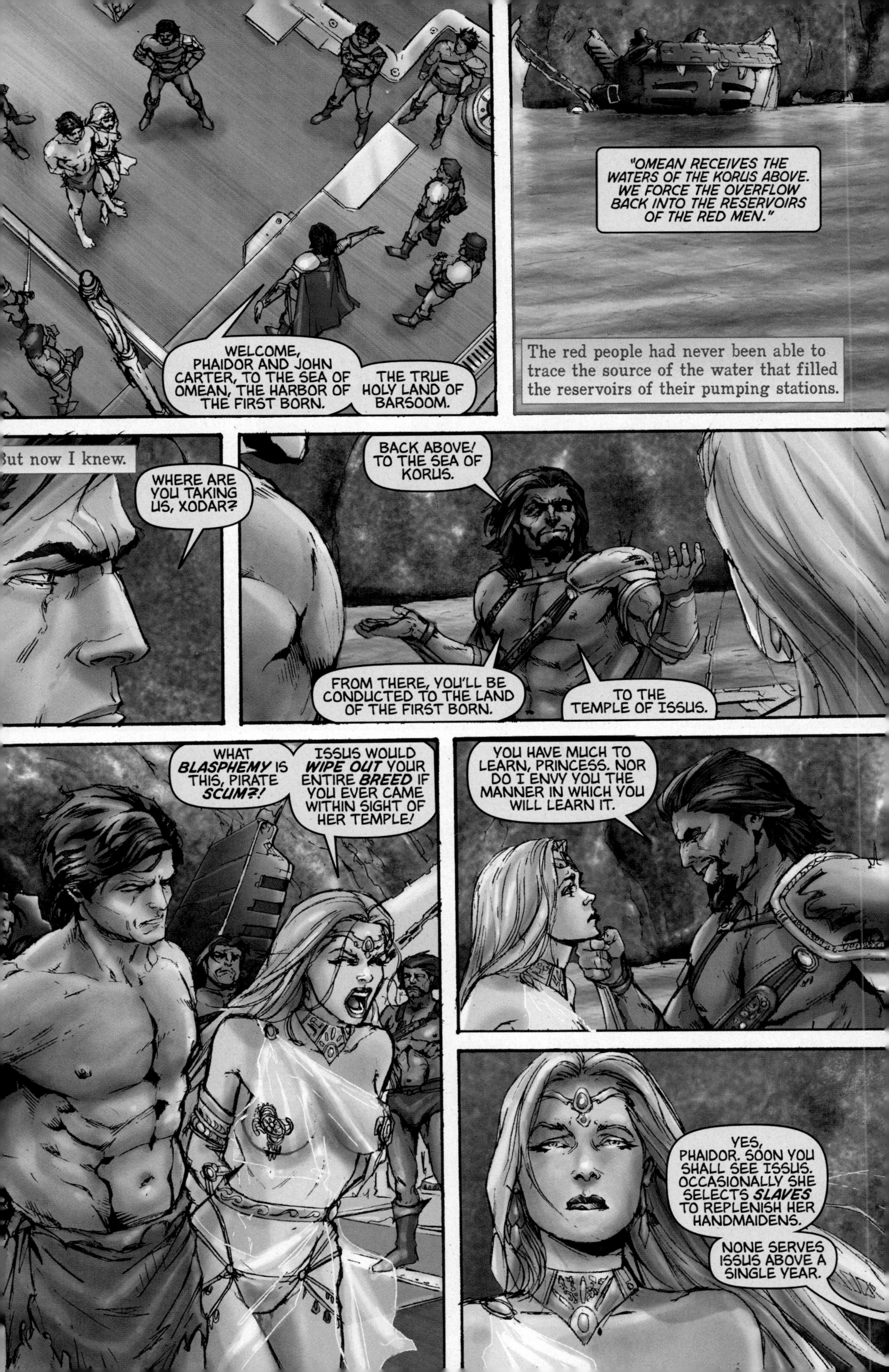
WELCOME, PHAIDOR AND JOHN CARTER, TO THE SEA OF OMEAN, THE HARBOR OF THE FIRST BORN.
THE TRUE HOLY LAND OF BARSOOM.
"OMEAN RECEIVES THE WATERS OF THE KORUS ABOVE. WE FORCE THE OVERFLOW BACK INTO THE RESERVOIRS OF THE RED MEN."
The red people had never been able to trace the source of the water that filled the reservoirs of their pumping stations.
But now I knew.
WHERE ARE YOU TAKING US, XODAR?
BACK ABOVE! TO THE SEA OF KORUS.
FROM THERE, YOU'LL BE CONDUCTED TO THE LAND OF THE FIRST BORN.
TO THE TEMPLE OF ISSUS.
WHAT BLASPHEMY IS THIS, PIRATE SCUM?!
ISSUS WOULD WIPE OUT YOUR ENTIRE BREED IF YOU EVER CAME WITHIN SIGHT OF HER TEMPLE!
YOU HAVE MUCH TO LEARN, PRINCESS. NOR DO I ENVY YOU THE MANNER IN WHICH YOU WILL LEARN IT.
YES, PHAIDOR. SOON YOU SHALL SEE ISSUS. OCCASIONALLY SHE SELECTS SLAVES TO REPLENISH HER HANDMAIDENS.
NONE SERVES ISSUS ABOVE A SINGLE YEAR.

HA HA HA

HA

HA

TAKE THEM AWAY.

HA HA

AH! YOU'RE HURTING ME!

SNAKK!

ENOUGH!

I HAVE HAD *QUITE ENOUGH* OF YOUR *BOORISH BEHAVIOR!* FIRST BORN, MOON PIRATES, *WHATEVER* YOU CALL YOURSELVES-- PHAIDOR IS UNDER *MY* PROTECTION NOW.

YOU MAY KILL ME, BUT I *PROMISE* YOU, WHOEVER LAYS A HAND ON HER AGAIN WILL DIE FIRST.

DID YOU SEE THAT?

THAT WAS... THAT WAS *THOAT* LEATHER, AND HE SNAPPED IT JUST LIKE--

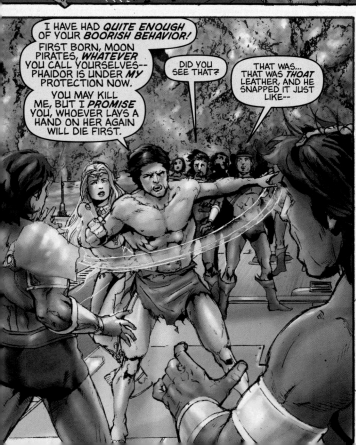

YOU--*CUT HER FREE!*

HA HA! VERY WELL. NEITHER OF THEM HAVE ANYWHERE TO ESCAPE TO.

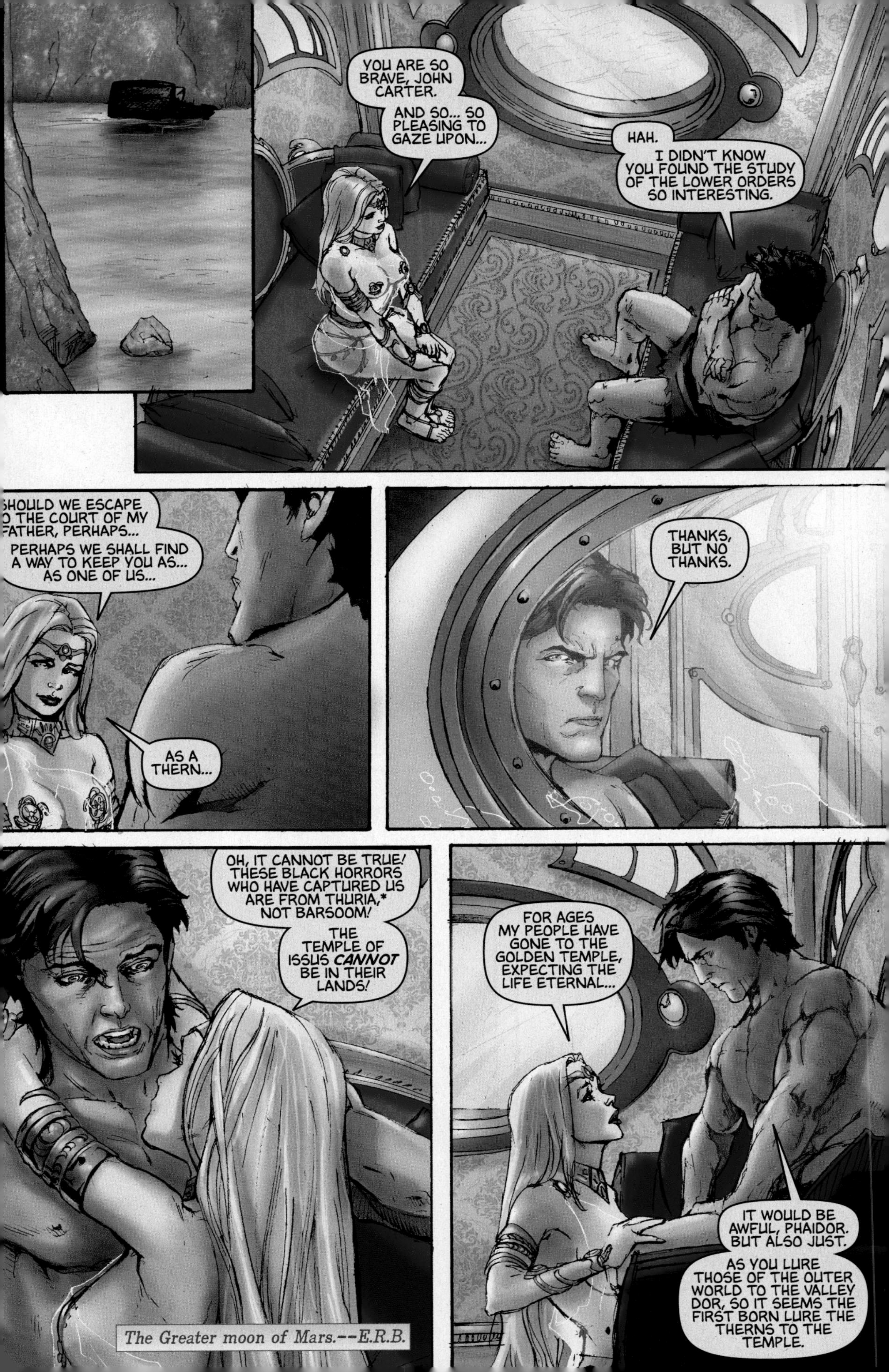
YOU ARE SO BRAVE, JOHN CARTER.
AND SO... SO PLEASING TO GAZE UPON...
HAH.
I DIDN'T KNOW YOU FOUND THE STUDY OF THE LOWER ORDERS SO INTERESTING.
SHOULD WE ESCAPE TO THE COURT OF MY FATHER, PERHAPS...
PERHAPS WE SHALL FIND A WAY TO KEEP YOU AS... AS ONE OF US...
AS A THERN...
THANKS, BUT NO THANKS.
OH, IT CANNOT BE TRUE! THESE BLACK HORRORS WHO HAVE CAPTURED US ARE FROM THURIA,* NOT BARSOOM!
THE TEMPLE OF ISSUS ***CANNOT*** BE IN THEIR LANDS!
The Greater moon of Mars.--E.R.B.
FOR AGES MY PEOPLE HAVE GONE TO THE GOLDEN TEMPLE, EXPECTING THE LIFE ETERNAL...
IT WOULD BE AWFUL, PHAIDOR. BUT ALSO JUST.
AS YOU LURE THOSE OF THE OUTER WORLD TO THE VALLEY DOR, SO IT SEEMS THE FIRST BORN LURE THE THERNS TO THE TEMPLE.

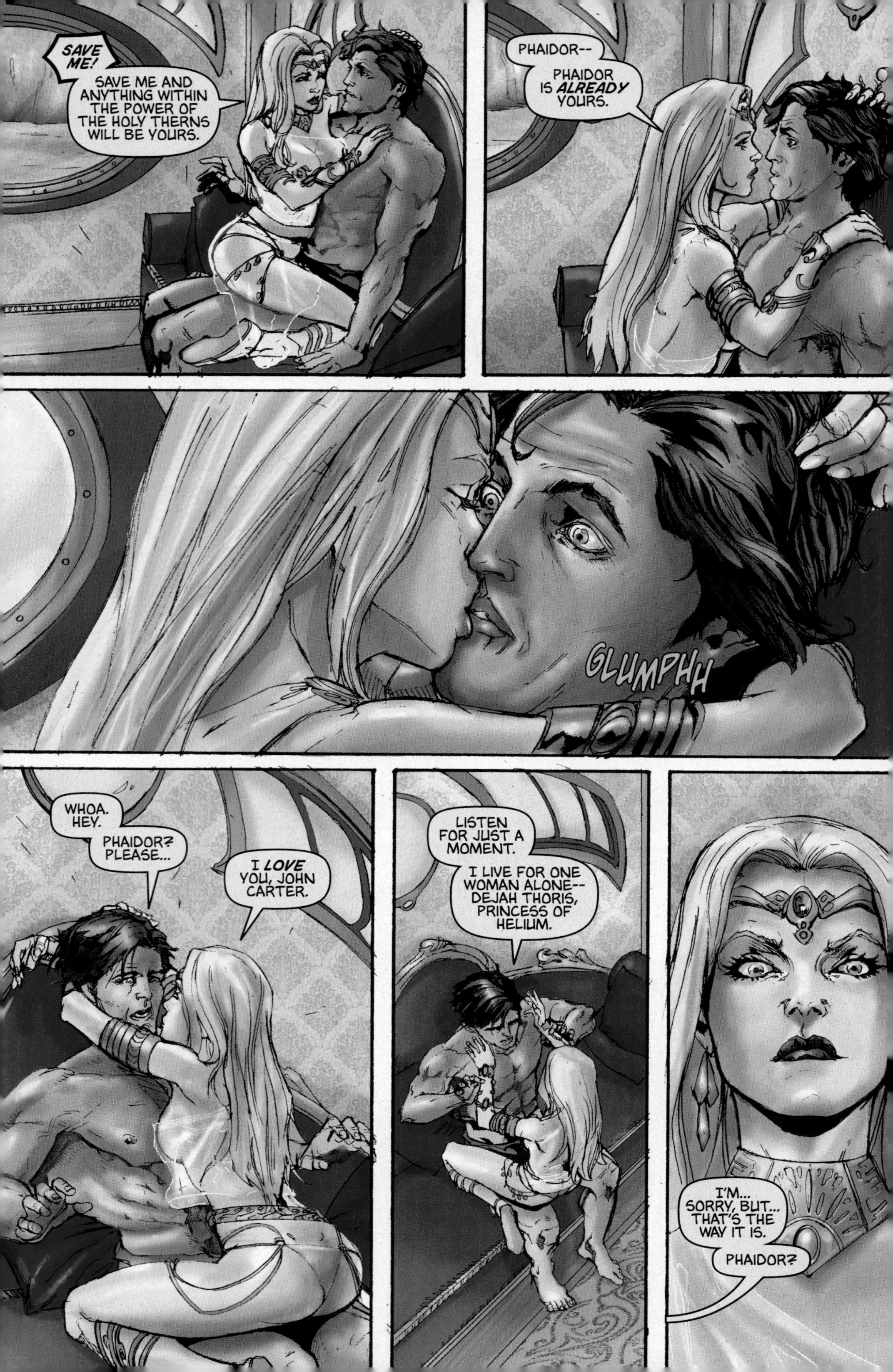

SAVE ME!
SAVE ME AND ANYTHING WITHIN THE POWER OF THE HOLY THERNS WILL BE YOURS.
PHAIDOR--
PHAIDOR IS ALREADY YOURS.
GLUMPHH
WHOA. HEY.
PHAIDOR? PLEASE...
I LOVE YOU, JOHN CARTER.
LISTEN FOR JUST A MOMENT.
I LIVE FOR ONE WOMAN ALONE-- DEJAH THORIS, PRINCESS OF HELIUM.
I'M... SORRY, BUT... THAT'S THE WAY IT IS.
PHAIDOR?

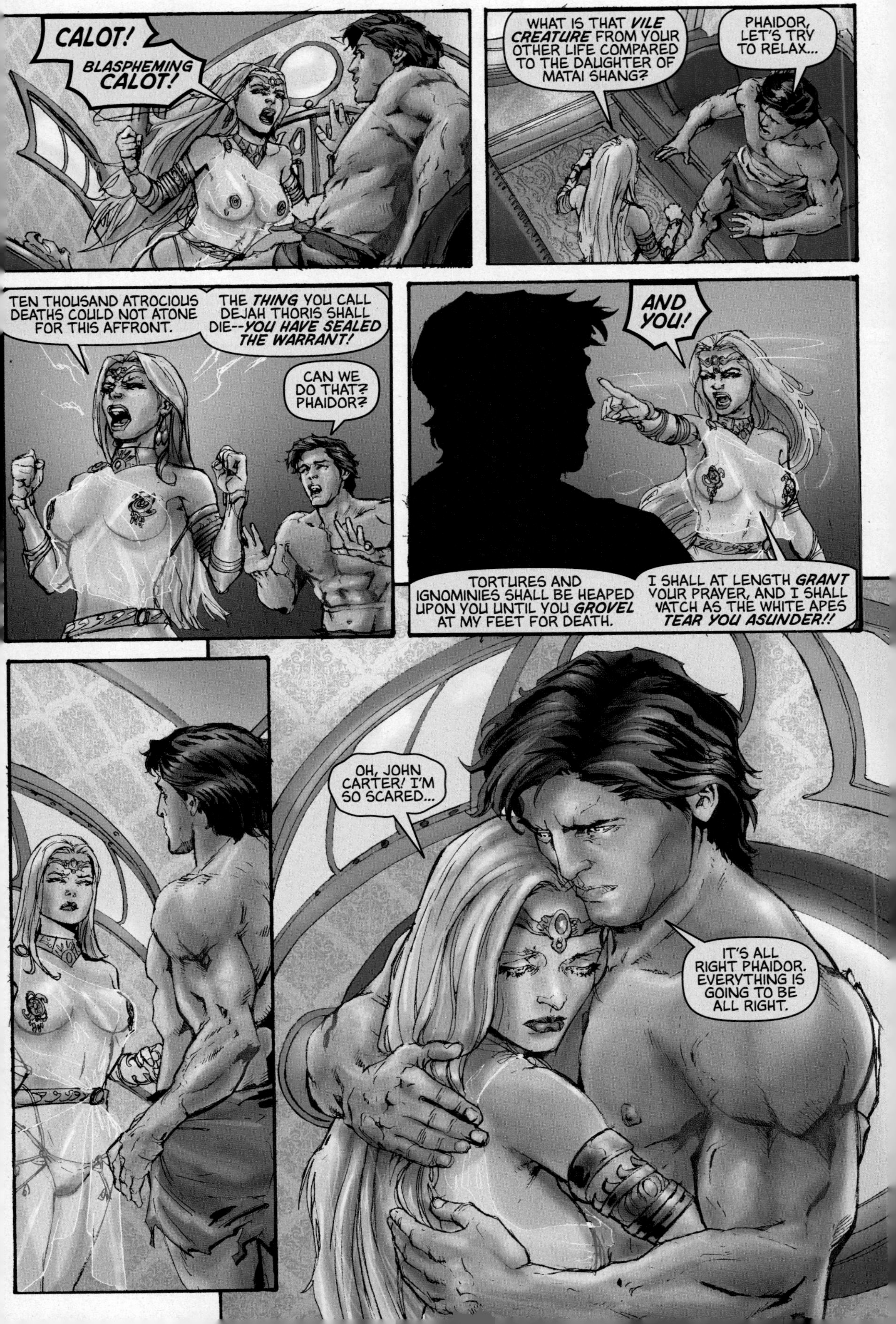
CALOT! BLASPHEMING CALOT!
WHAT IS THAT VILE CREATURE FROM YOUR OTHER LIFE COMPARED TO THE DAUGHTER OF MATAI SHANG?
PHAIDOR, LET'S TRY TO RELAX...
TEN THOUSAND ATROCIOUS DEATHS COULD NOT ATONE FOR THIS AFFRONT.
THE THING YOU CALL DEJAH THORIS SHALL DIE--YOU HAVE SEALED THE WARRANT!
CAN WE DO THAT? PHAIDOR?
AND YOU!
TORTURES AND IGNOMINIES SHALL BE HEAPED UPON YOU UNTIL YOU GROVEL AT MY FEET FOR DEATH.
I SHALL AT LENGTH GRANT YOUR PRAYER, AND I SHALL WATCH AS THE WHITE APES TEAR YOU ASUNDER!!
OH, JOHN CARTER! I'M SO SCARED...
IT'S ALL RIGHT PHAIDOR. EVERYTHING IS GOING TO BE ALL RIGHT.

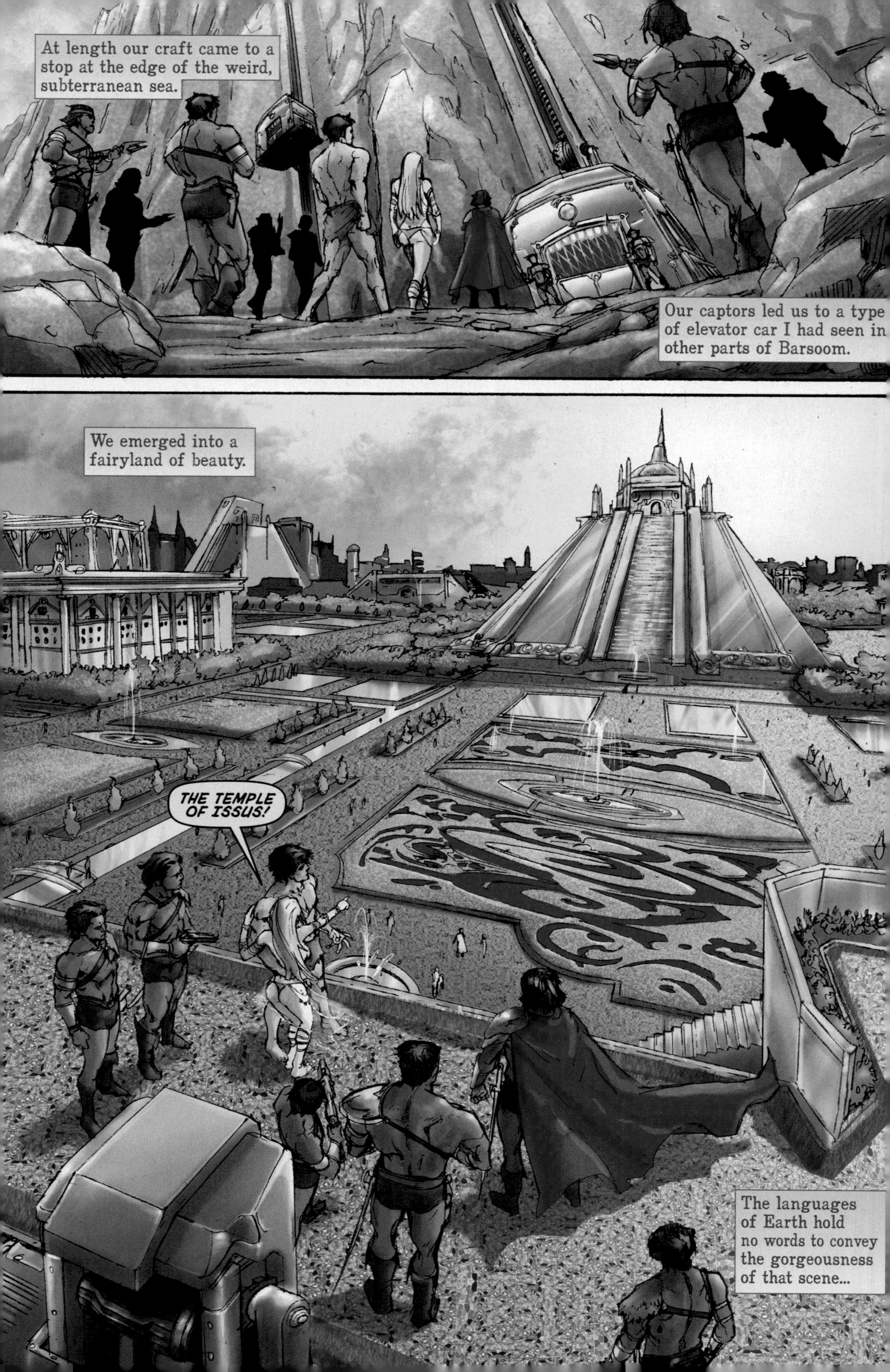

At length our craft came to a stop at the edge of the weird, subterranean sea.
Our captors led us to a type of elevator car I had seen in other parts of Barsoom.
We emerged into a fairyland of beauty.
THE TEMPLE OF ISSUS!
The languages of Earth hold no words to convey the gorgeousness of that scene...

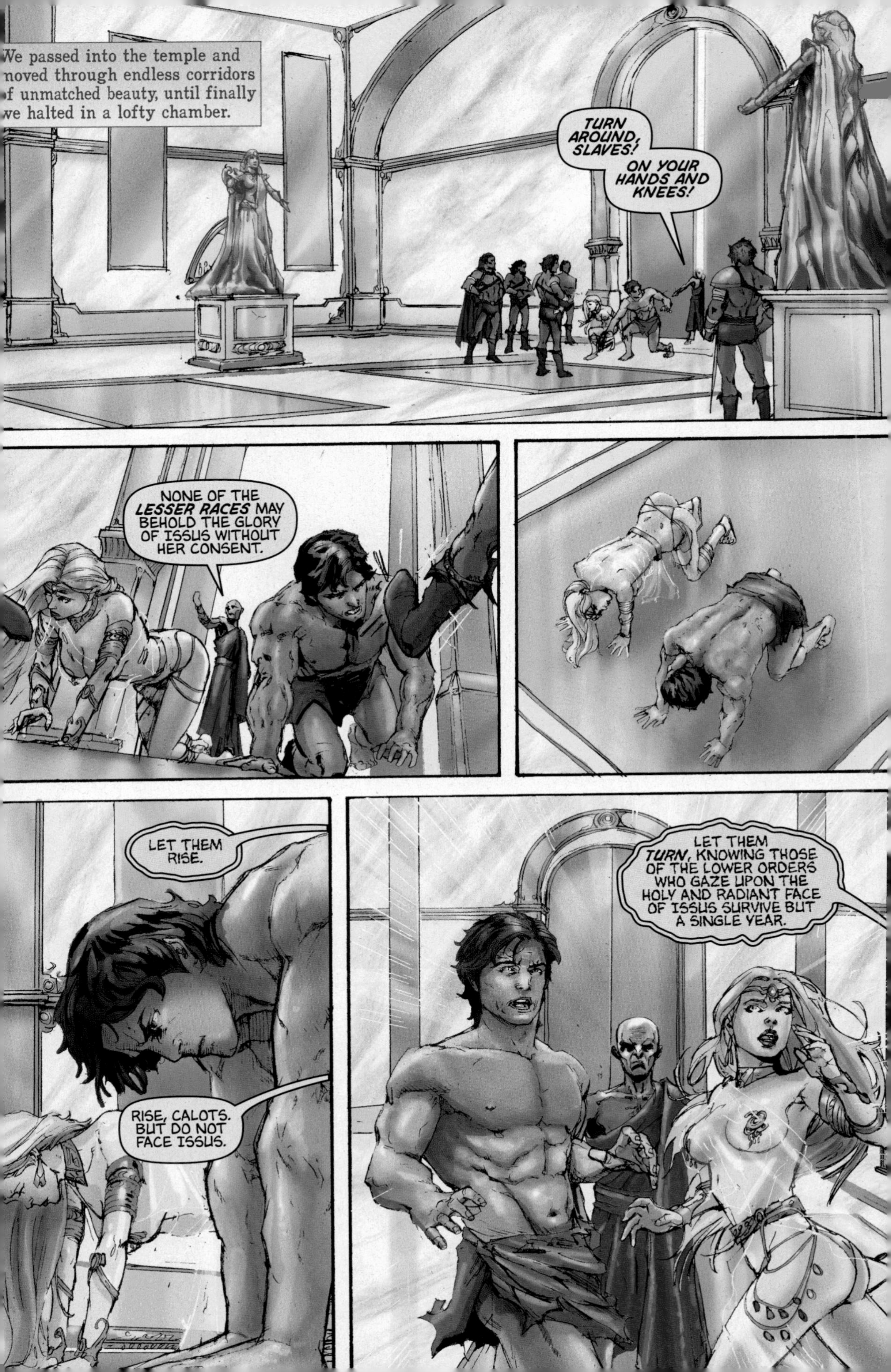
We passed into the temple and moved through endless corridors of unmatched beauty, until finally we halted in a lofty chamber.
TURN AROUND, SLAVES!
ON YOUR HANDS AND KNEES!
NONE OF THE LESSER RACES MAY BEHOLD THE GLORY OF ISSUS WITHOUT HER CONSENT.
LET THEM RISE.
RISE, CALOTS. BUT DO NOT FACE ISSUS.
LET THEM TURN, KNOWING THOSE OF THE LOWER ORDERS WHO GAZE UPON THE HOLY AND RADIANT FACE OF ISSUS SURVIVE BUT A SINGLE YEAR.

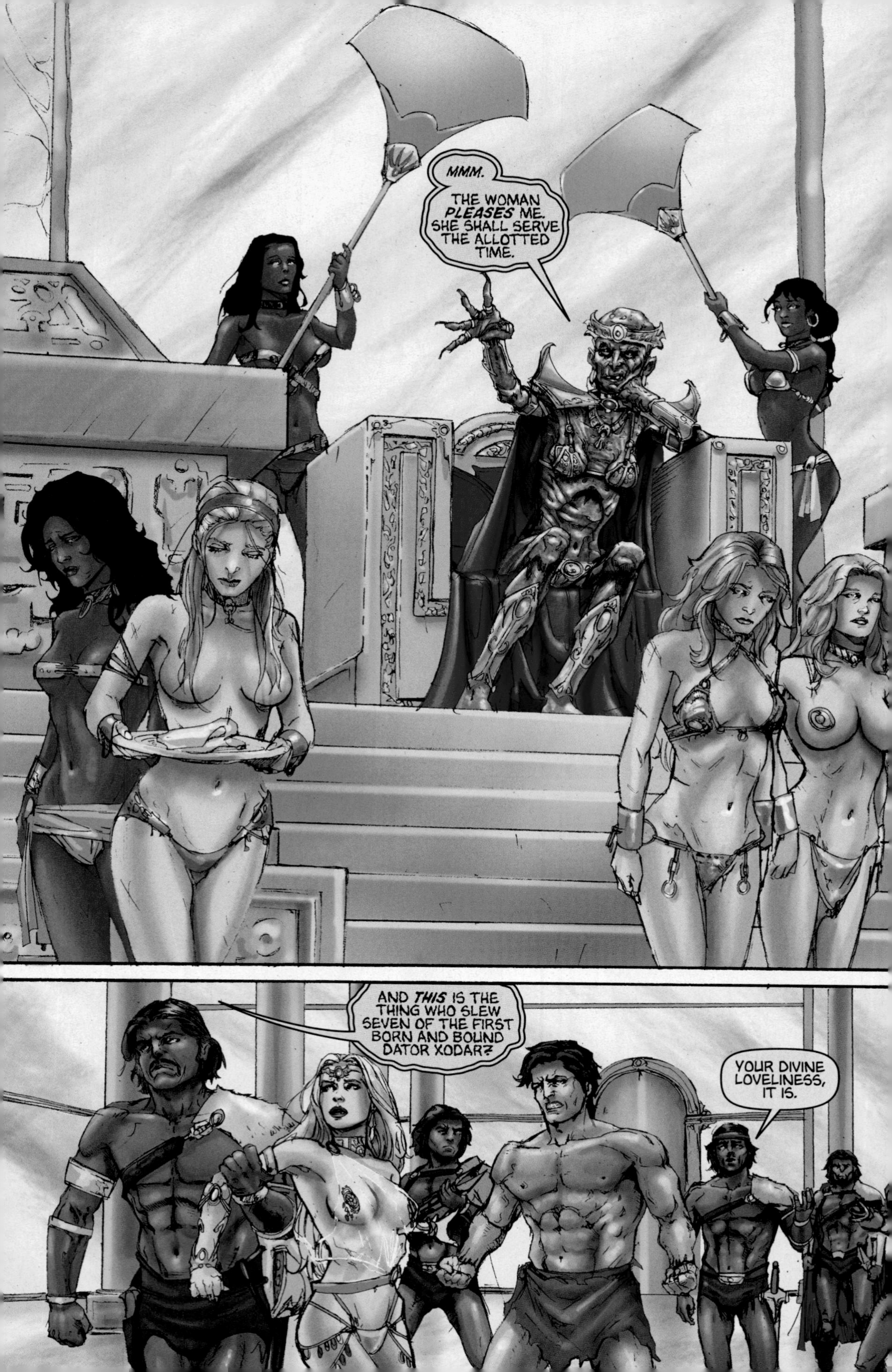
MMM.
THE WOMAN *PLEASES* ME. SHE SHALL SERVE THE ALLOTTED TIME.
AND *THIS* IS THE THING WHO SLEW SEVEN OF THE FIRST BORN AND BOUND DATOR XODAR?
YOUR DIVINE LOVELINESS, IT IS.

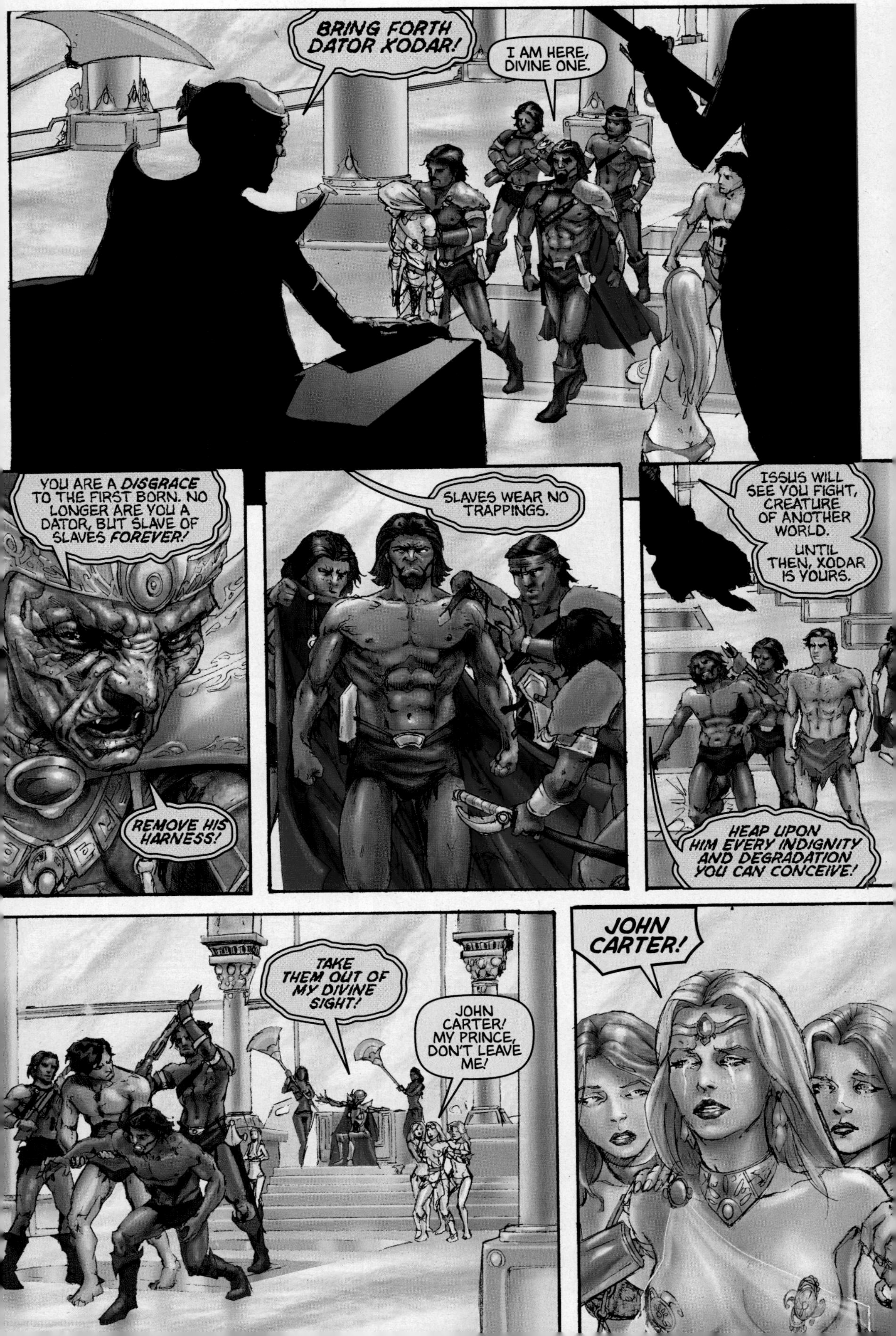
BRING FORTH DATOR XODAR!
I AM HERE, DIVINE ONE.
YOU ARE A DISGRACE TO THE FIRST BORN. NO LONGER ARE YOU A DATOR, BUT SLAVE OF SLAVES FOREVER!
REMOVE HIS HARNESS!
SLAVES WEAR NO TRAPPINGS.
ISSUS WILL SEE YOU FIGHT, CREATURE OF ANOTHER WORLD.
UNTIL THEN, XODAR IS YOURS.
HEAP UPON HIM EVERY INDIGNITY AND DEGRADATION YOU CAN CONCEIVE!
TAKE THEM OUT OF MY DIVINE SIGHT!
JOHN CARTER! MY PRINCE, DON'T LEAVE ME!
JOHN CARTER!

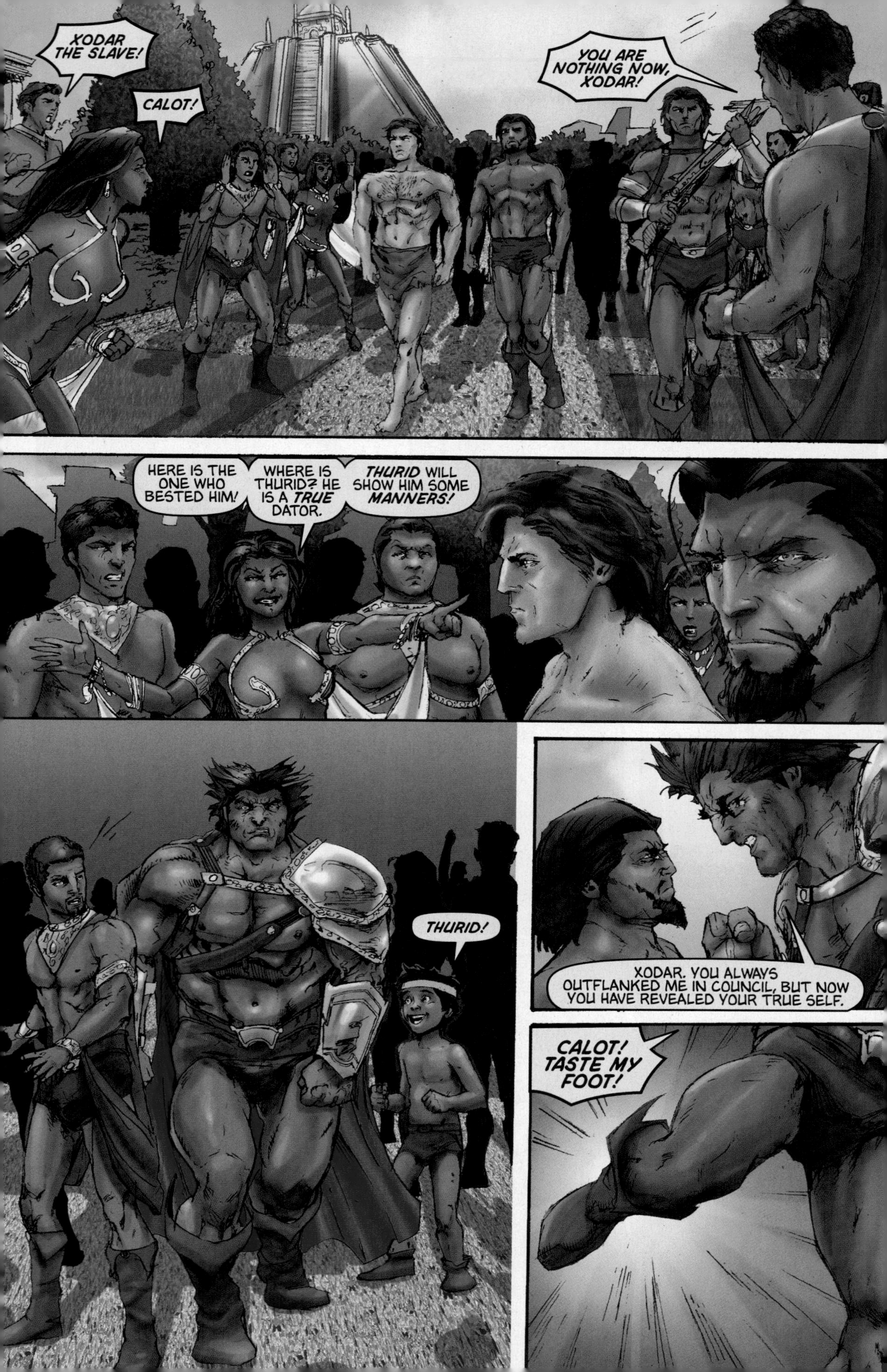
XODAR THE SLAVE!
CALOT!
YOU ARE NOTHING NOW, XODAR!
HERE IS THE ONE WHO BESTED HIM!
WHERE IS THURID? HE IS A TRUE DATOR.
THURID WILL SHOW HIM SOME MANNERS!
THURID!
XODAR. YOU ALWAYS OUTFLANKED ME IN COUNCIL, BUT NOW YOU HAVE REVEALED YOUR TRUE SELF.
CALOT! TASTE MY FOOT!

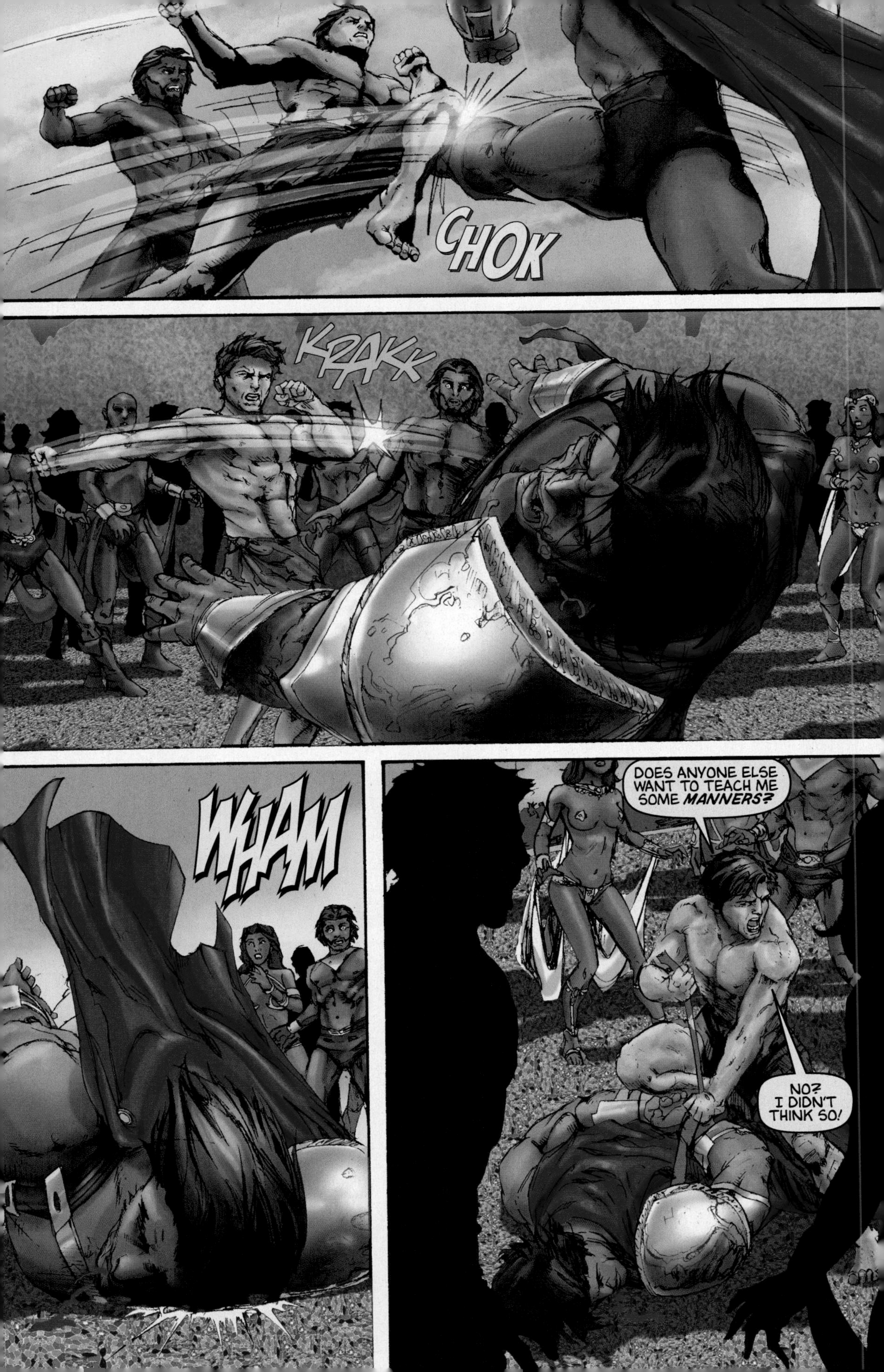
CHOK
KRAKK
WHAM
DOES ANYONE ELSE WANT TO TEACH ME SOME MANNERS?
NO? I DIDN'T THINK SO!

WELL, GO ON! HE IS BOUND IN HIS OWN HARNESS, LIKE XODAR.

TAKE HIM TO ISSUS! TELL HER THERE IS ONE WHO IS *GREATER* THAN THE FIRST BORN.

WHO *ARE* YOU?

I AM JOHN CARTER.

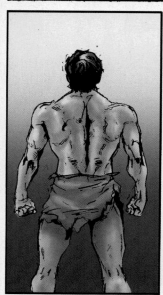

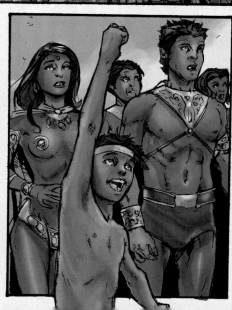

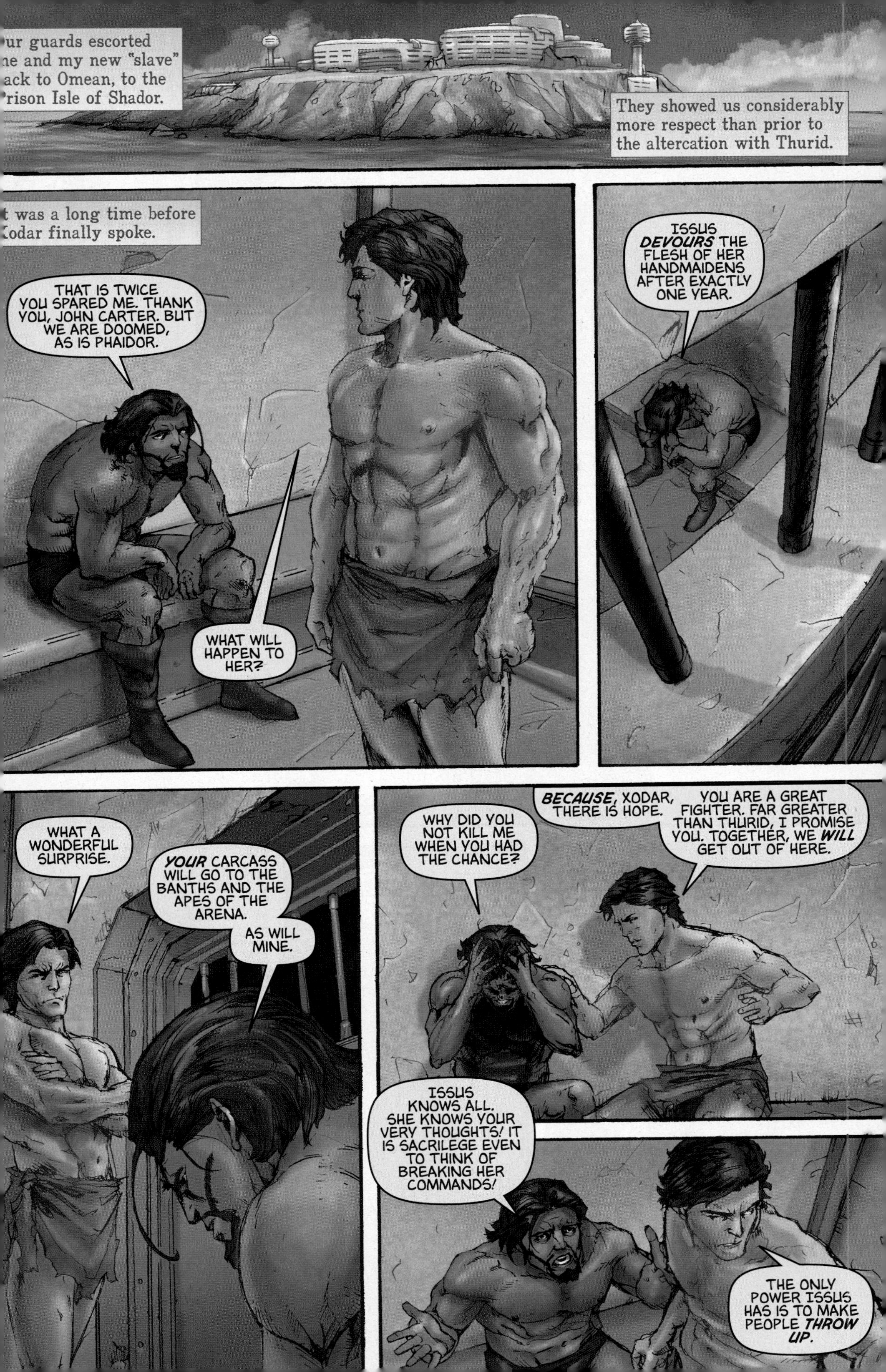
ur guards escorted
ne and my new "slave"
ack to Omean, to the
Prison Isle of Shador.
They showed us considerably more respect than prior to the altercation with Thurid.
t was a long time before
Xodar finally spoke.
THAT IS TWICE YOU SPARED ME. THANK YOU, JOHN CARTER. BUT WE ARE DOOMED, AS IS PHAIDOR.
WHAT WILL HAPPEN TO HER?
ISSUS *DEVOURS* THE FLESH OF HER HANDMAIDENS AFTER EXACTLY ONE YEAR.
WHAT A WONDERFUL SURPRISE.
YOUR CARCASS WILL GO TO THE BANTHS AND THE APES OF THE ARENA.
AS WILL MINE.
WHY DID YOU NOT KILL ME WHEN YOU HAD THE CHANCE?
BECAUSE, XODAR, THERE IS HOPE.
YOU ARE A GREAT FIGHTER. FAR GREATER THAN THURID, I PROMISE YOU. TOGETHER, WE *WILL* GET OUT OF HERE.
ISSUS KNOWS ALL. SHE KNOWS YOUR VERY THOUGHTS! IT IS SACRILEGE EVEN TO THINK OF BREAKING HER COMMANDS!
THE ONLY POWER ISSUS HAS IS TO MAKE PEOPLE *THROW UP*.

BLASPHEMER! IN ANOTHER INSTANT YOU WILL BE WRITHING IN YOUR DEATH THROES!

OH REALLY?

LISTEN UP, XODAR.

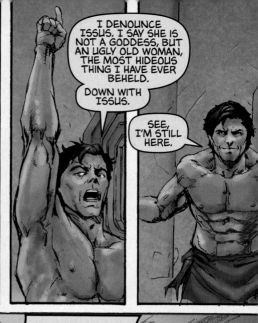

I DENOUNCE ISSUS. I SAY SHE IS NOT A GODDESS, BUT AN UGLY OLD WOMAN, THE MOST HIDEOUS THING I HAVE EVER BEHELD.

DOWN WITH ISSUS.

SEE, I'M STILL HERE.

BLASPHEMER!

XODAR, YOUR ISSUS IS A MORTAL OLD WOMAN!

NO!

ONCE YOU'RE OUT OF HER CLUTCHES, SHE CANNOT HARM YOU!

NO!

WHY DO I BOTHER?

ALL RIGHT. ISSUS IS AN OMNIPOTENT GODDESS, AND WE ALL BOW TO HER UNDYING GLORY.

AH!

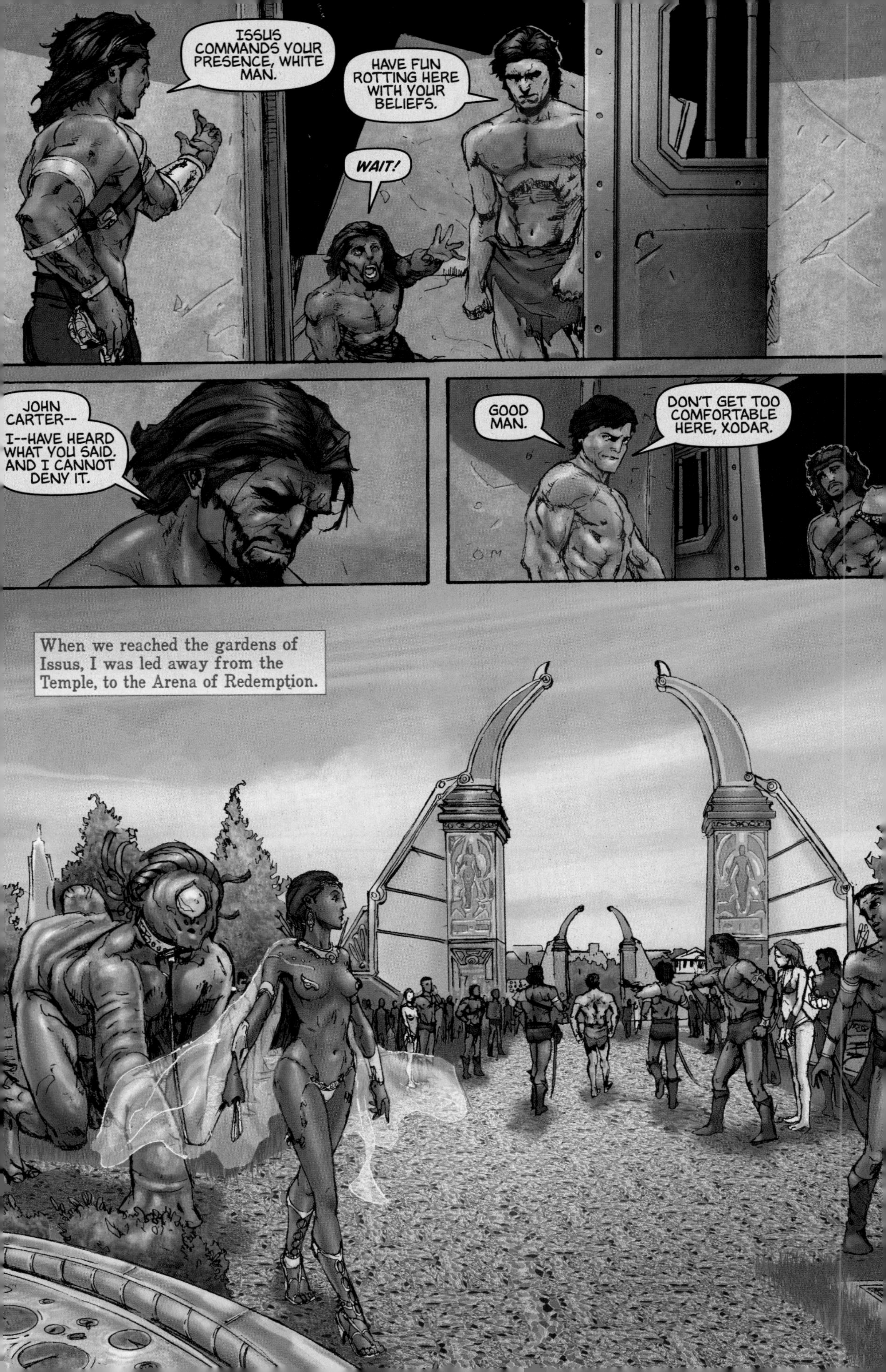
ISSUS COMMANDS YOUR PRESENCE, WHITE MAN.
HAVE FUN ROTTING HERE WITH YOUR BELIEFS.
WAIT!
JOHN CARTER--
I--HAVE HEARD WHAT YOU SAID. AND I CANNOT DENY IT.
GOOD MAN.
DON'T GET TOO COMFORTABLE HERE, XODAR.
When we reached the gardens of Issus, I was led away from the Temple, to the Arena of Redemption.

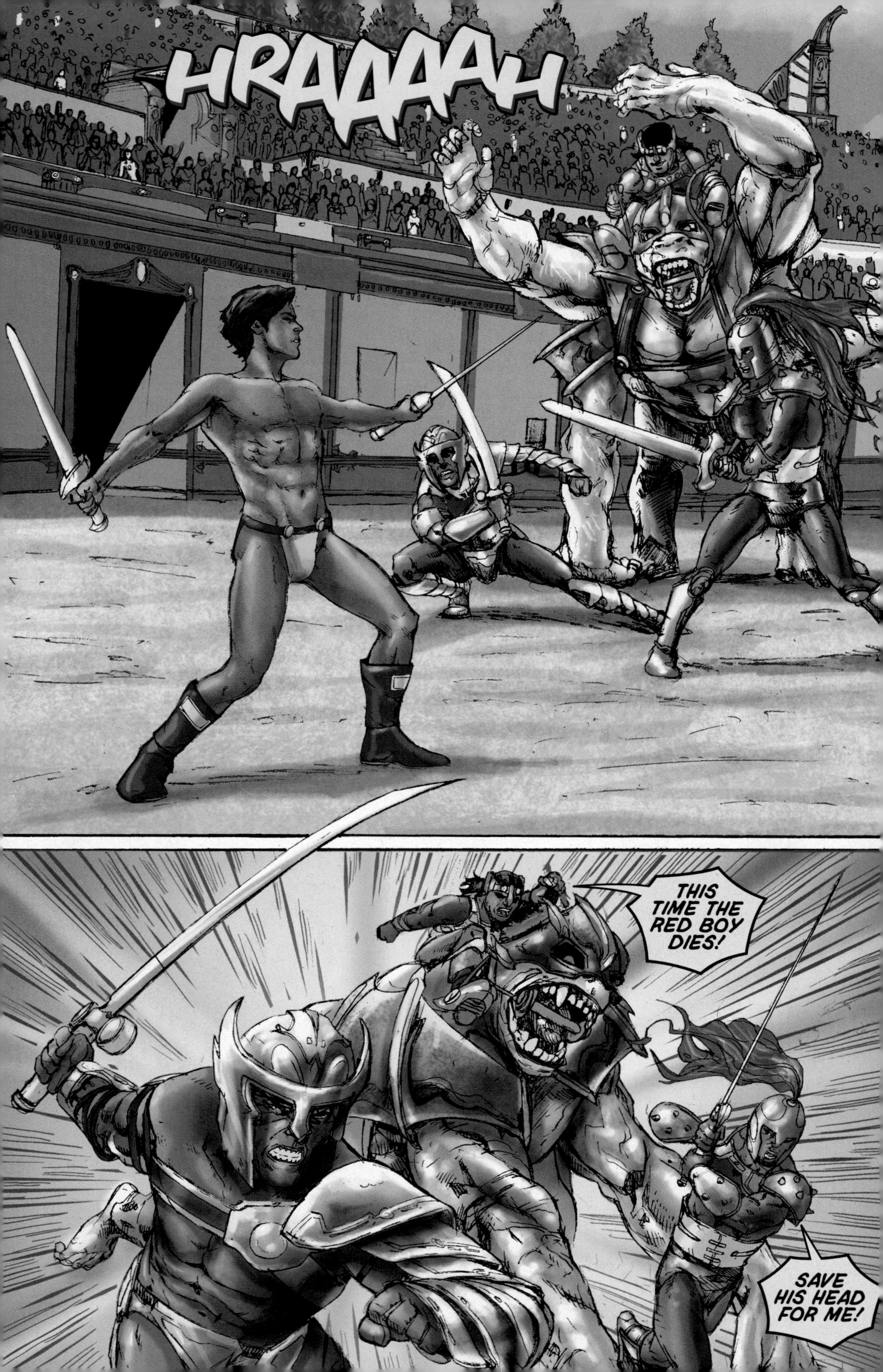
HRAAAAH
THIS TIME THE RED BOY DIES!
SAVE HIS HEAD FOR ME!

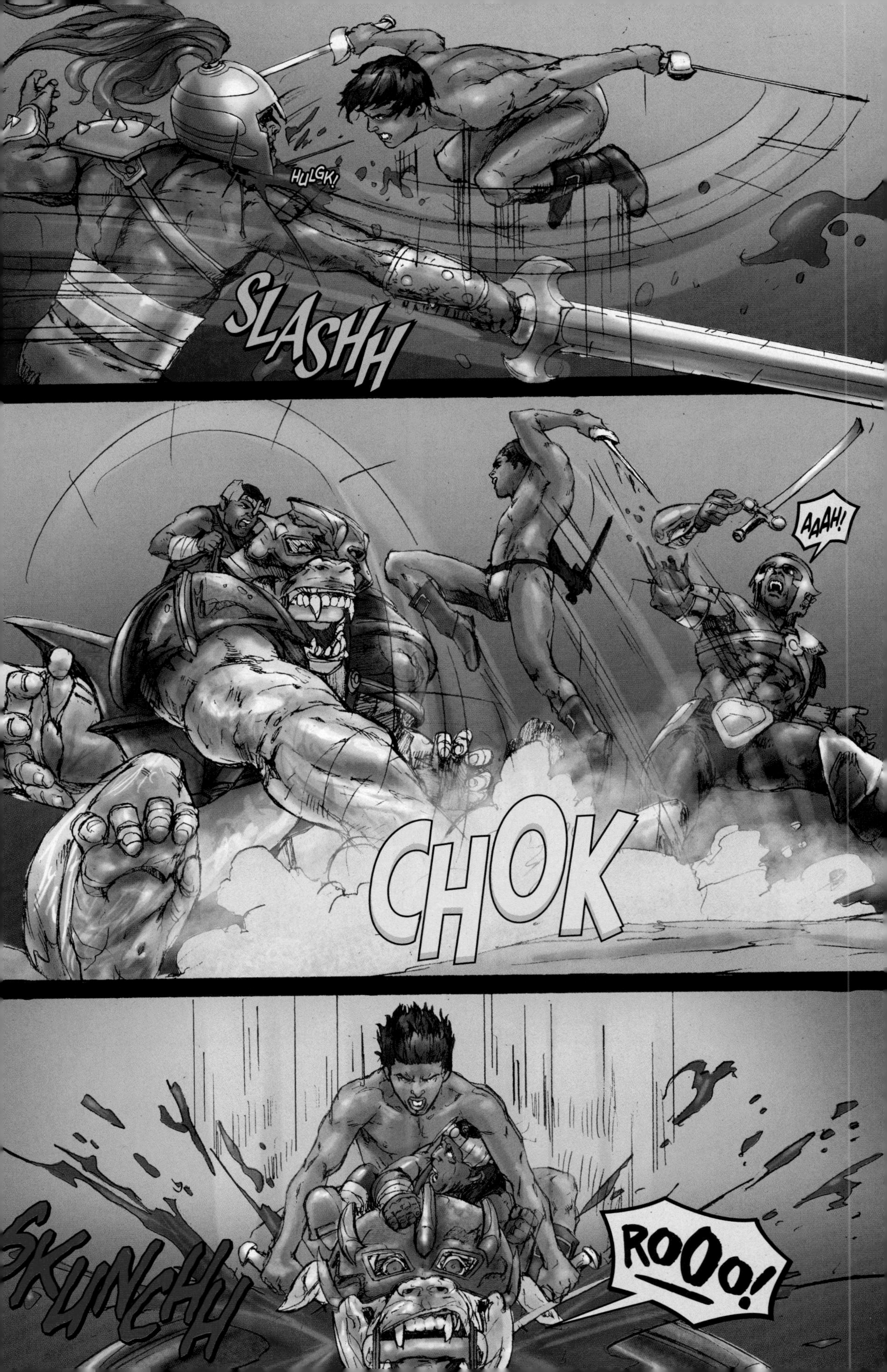
HULGK!
SLASHH
AAAH!
CHOK
SKUNCHH
ROOOO!

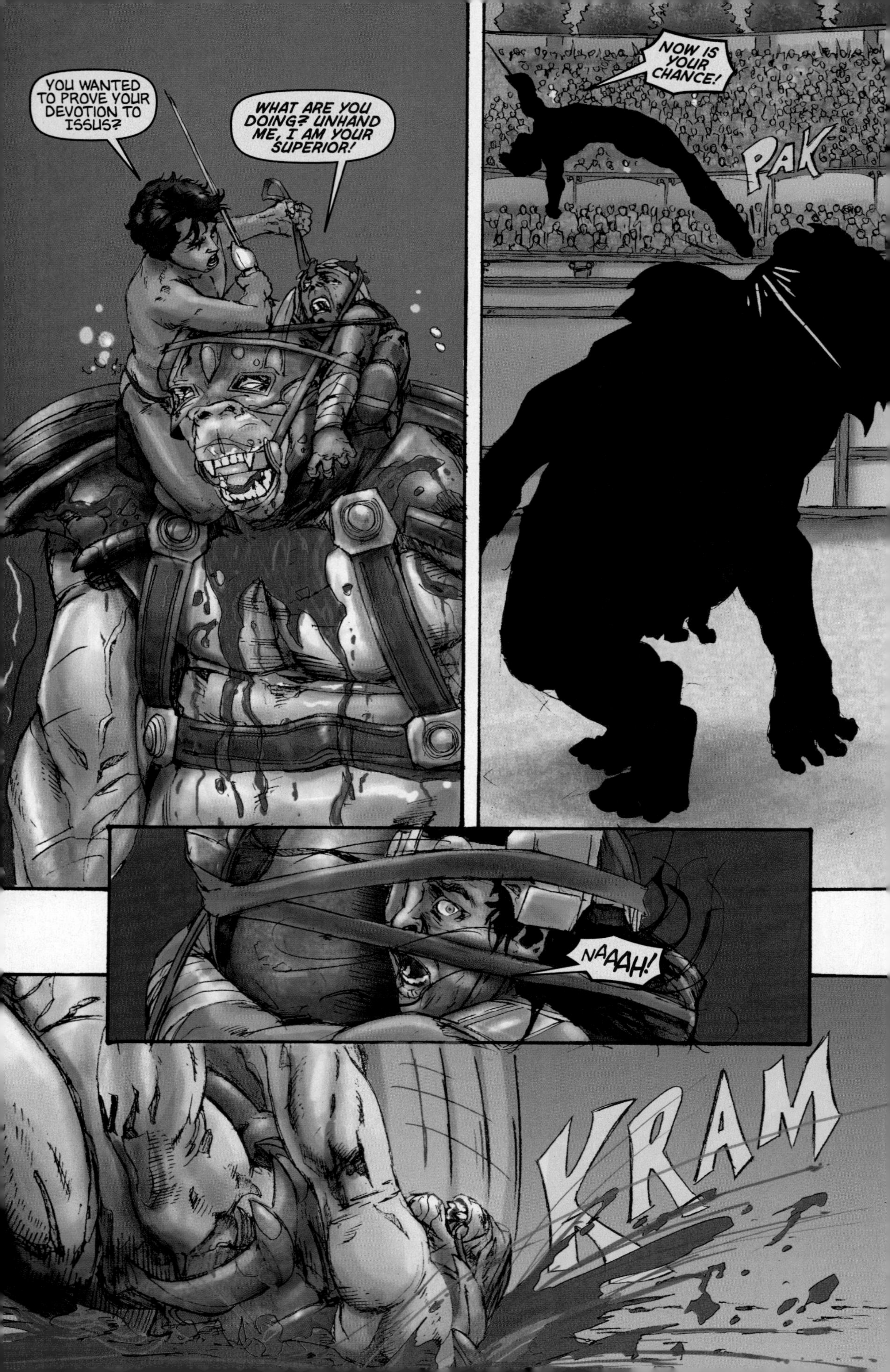
YOU WANTED TO PROVE YOUR DEVOTION TO ISSUS?
WHAT ARE YOU DOING? UNHAND ME, I AM YOUR SUPERIOR!
NOW IS YOUR CHANCE!
PAK
NAAAH!
KRAM

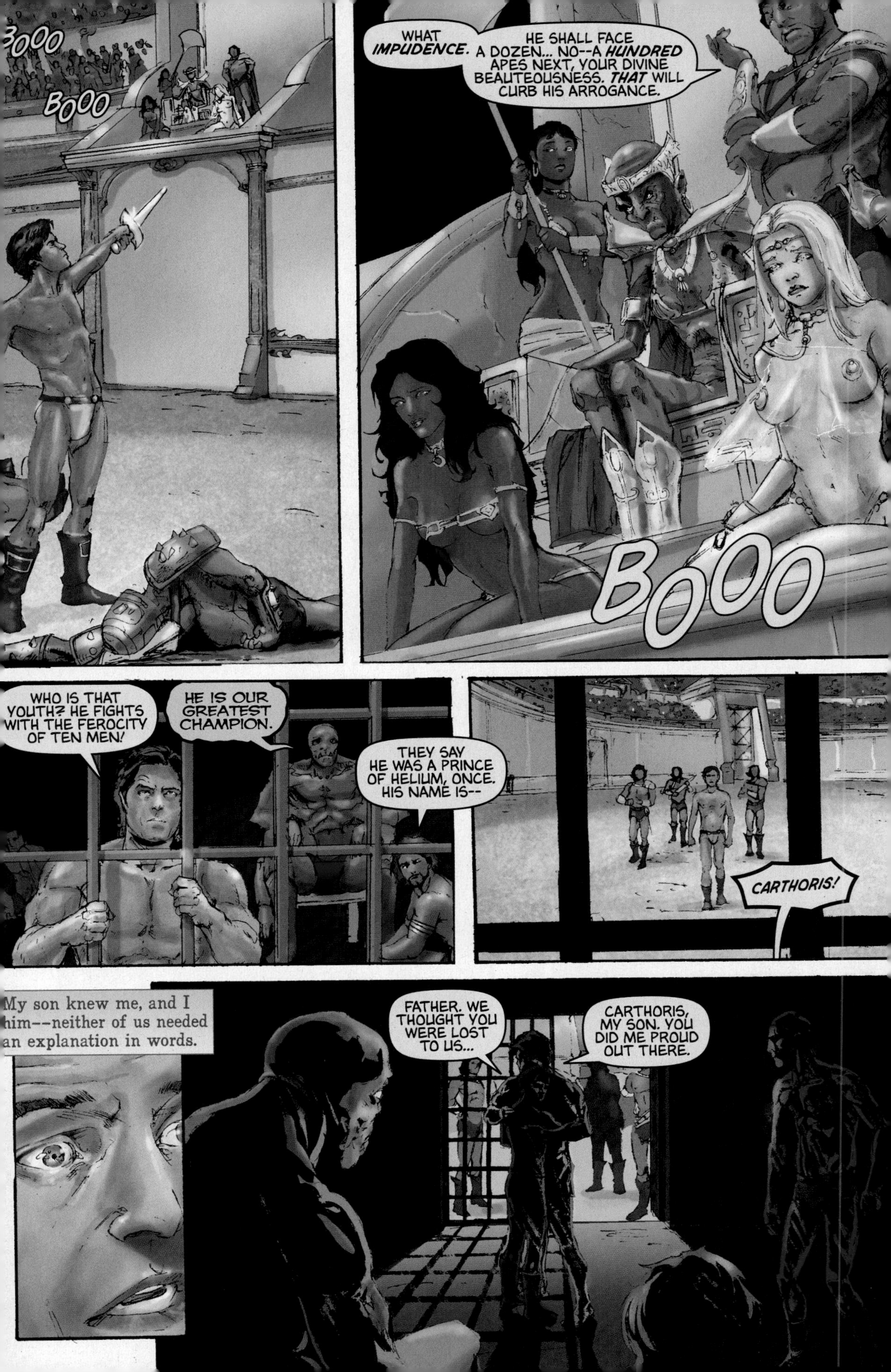
BOOO
BOOO
WHAT IMPUDENCE.
HE SHALL FACE A DOZEN... NO--A HUNDRED APES NEXT, YOUR DIVINE BEAUTEOUSNESS. THAT WILL CURB HIS ARROGANCE.
BOOO
WHO IS THAT YOUTH? HE FIGHTS WITH THE FEROCITY OF TEN MEN!
HE IS OUR GREATEST CHAMPION.
THEY SAY HE WAS A PRINCE OF HELIUM, ONCE. HIS NAME IS--
CARTHORIS!
My son knew me, and I him--neither of us needed an explanation in words.
FATHER. WE THOUGHT YOU WERE LOST TO US...
CARTHORIS, MY SON. YOU DID ME PROUD OUT THERE.

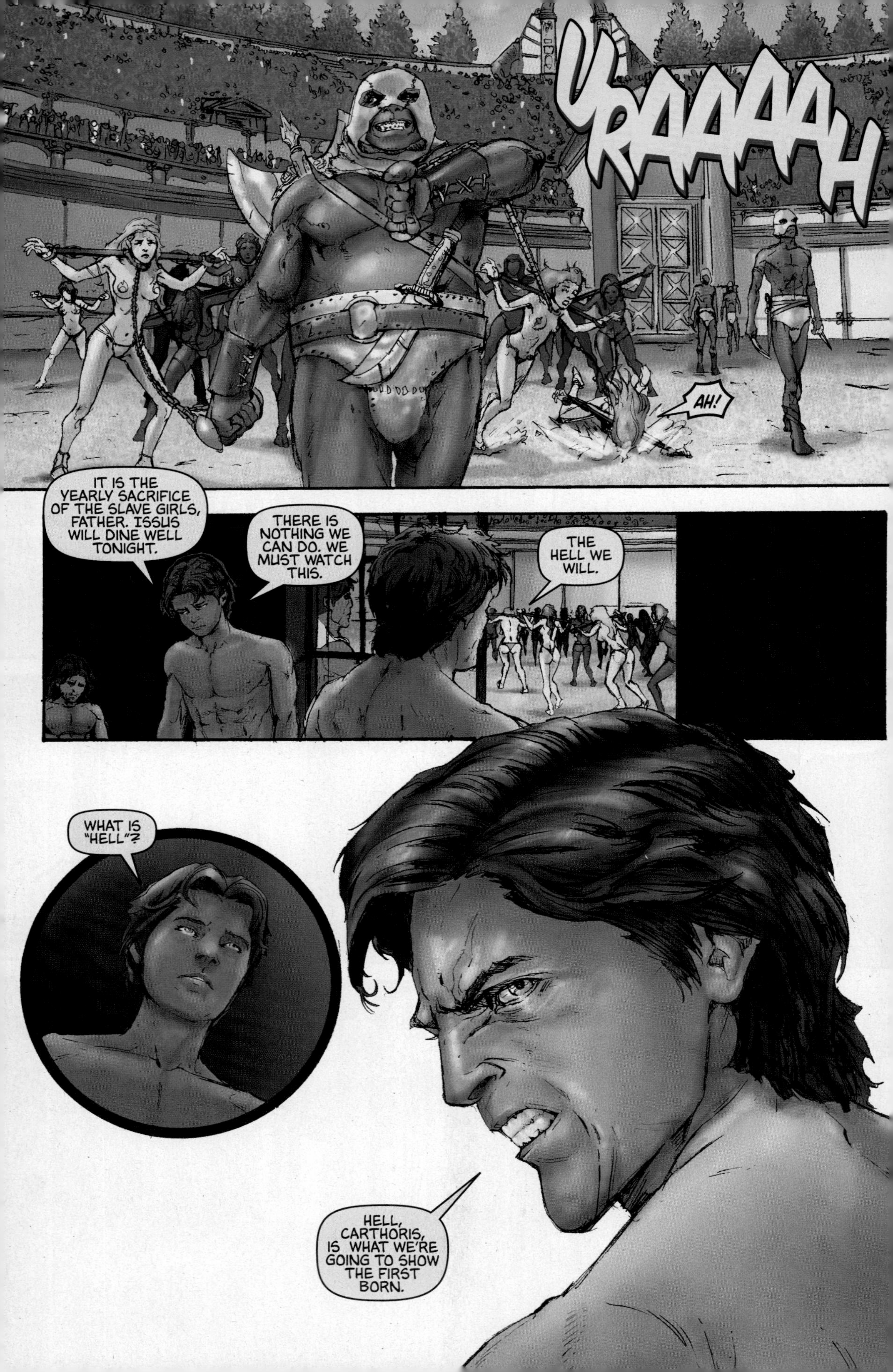
URAAAAAH
AH!
IT IS THE YEARLY SACRIFICE OF THE SLAVE GIRLS, FATHER. ISSUS WILL DINE WELL TONIGHT.
THERE IS NOTHING WE CAN DO. WE MUST WATCH THIS.
THE HELL WE WILL.
WHAT IS "HELL"?
HELL, CARTHORIS, IS WHAT WE'RE GOING TO SHOW THE FIRST BORN.

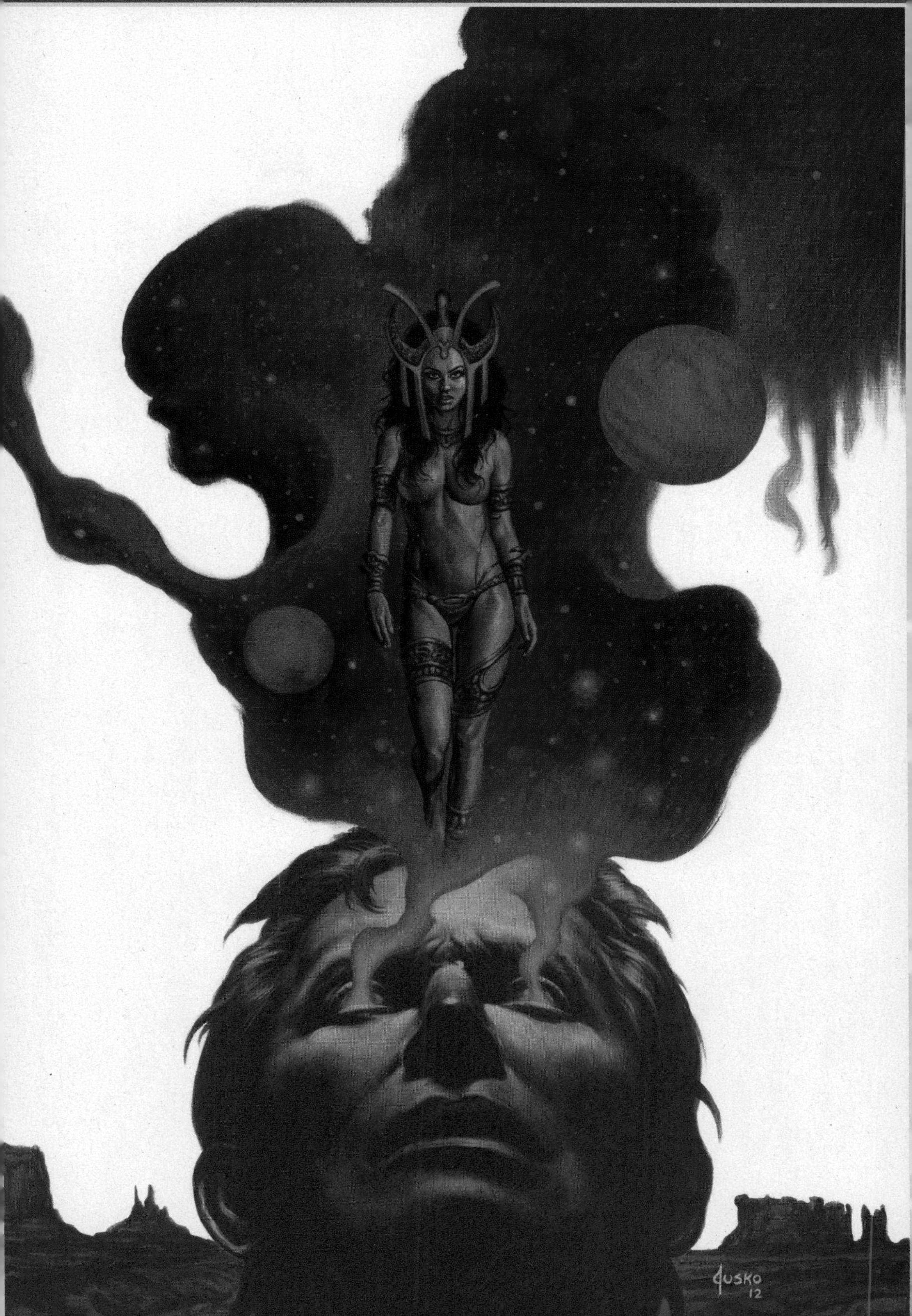
JUSKO
12

ARS PAR
#16 cover by

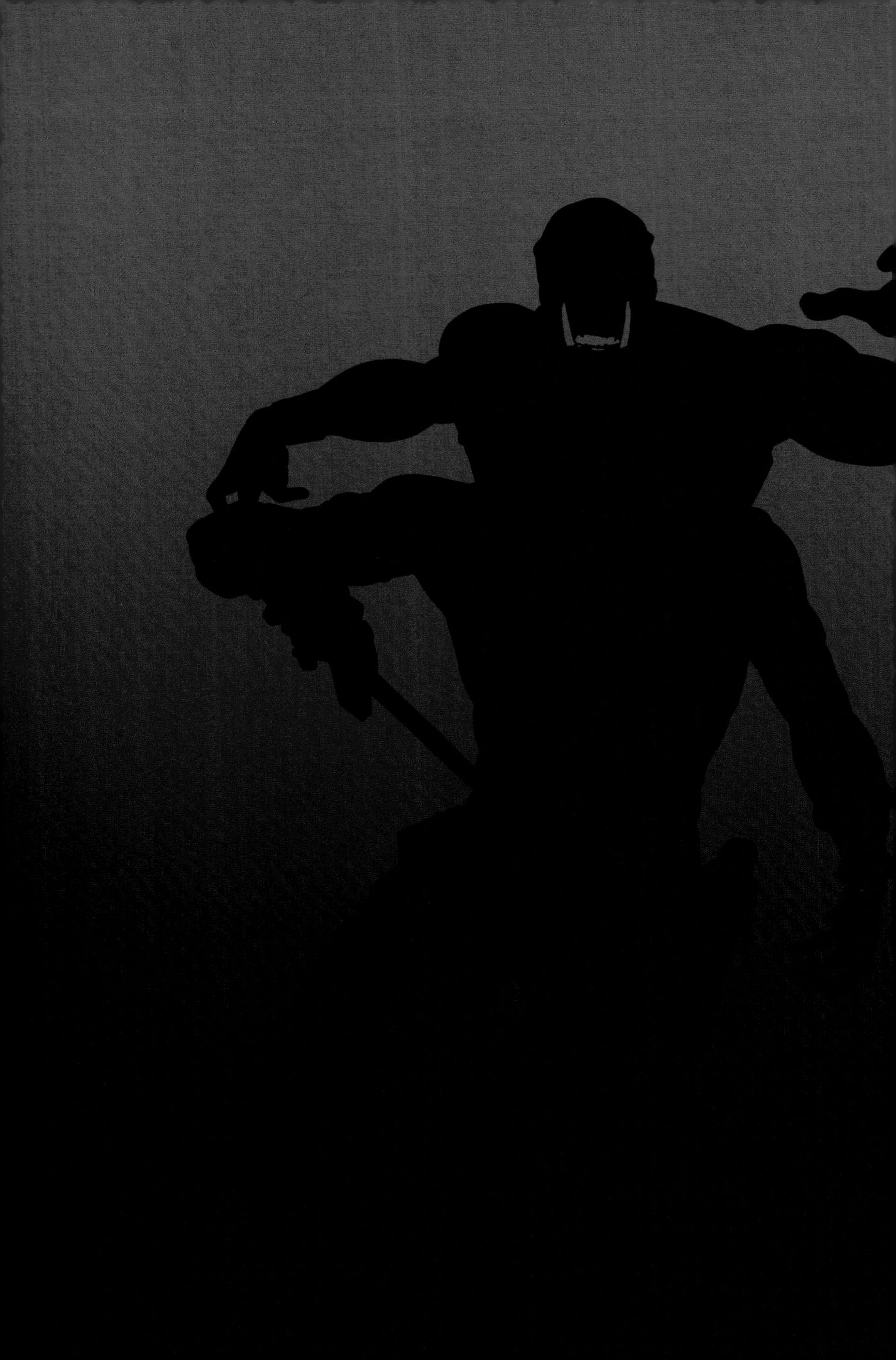

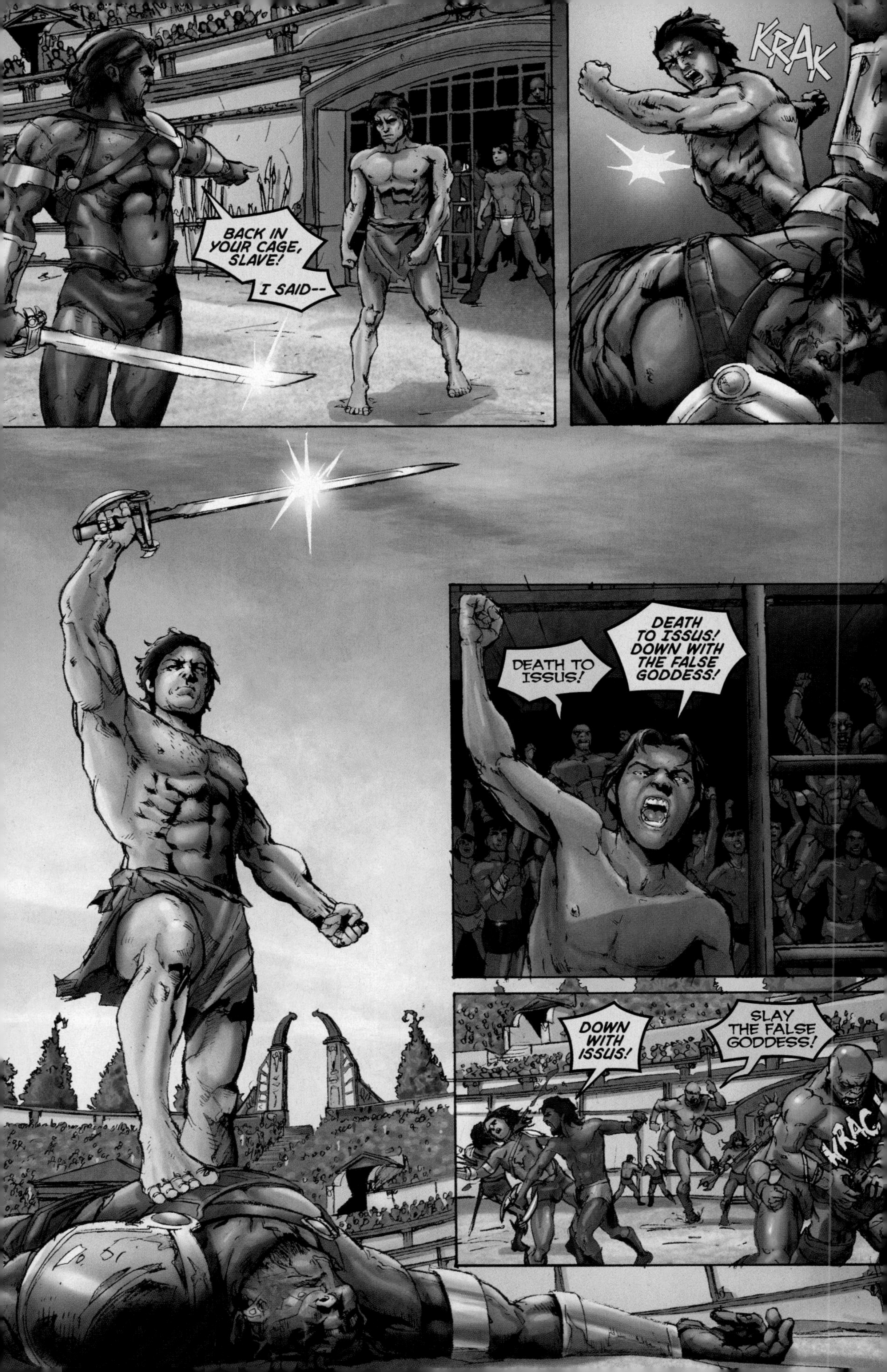
BACK IN YOUR CAGE, SLAVE!
I SAID--
KRAK
DEATH TO ISSUS!
DEATH TO ISSUS! DOWN WITH THE FALSE GODDESS!
DOWN WITH ISSUS!
SLAY THE FALSE GODDESS!

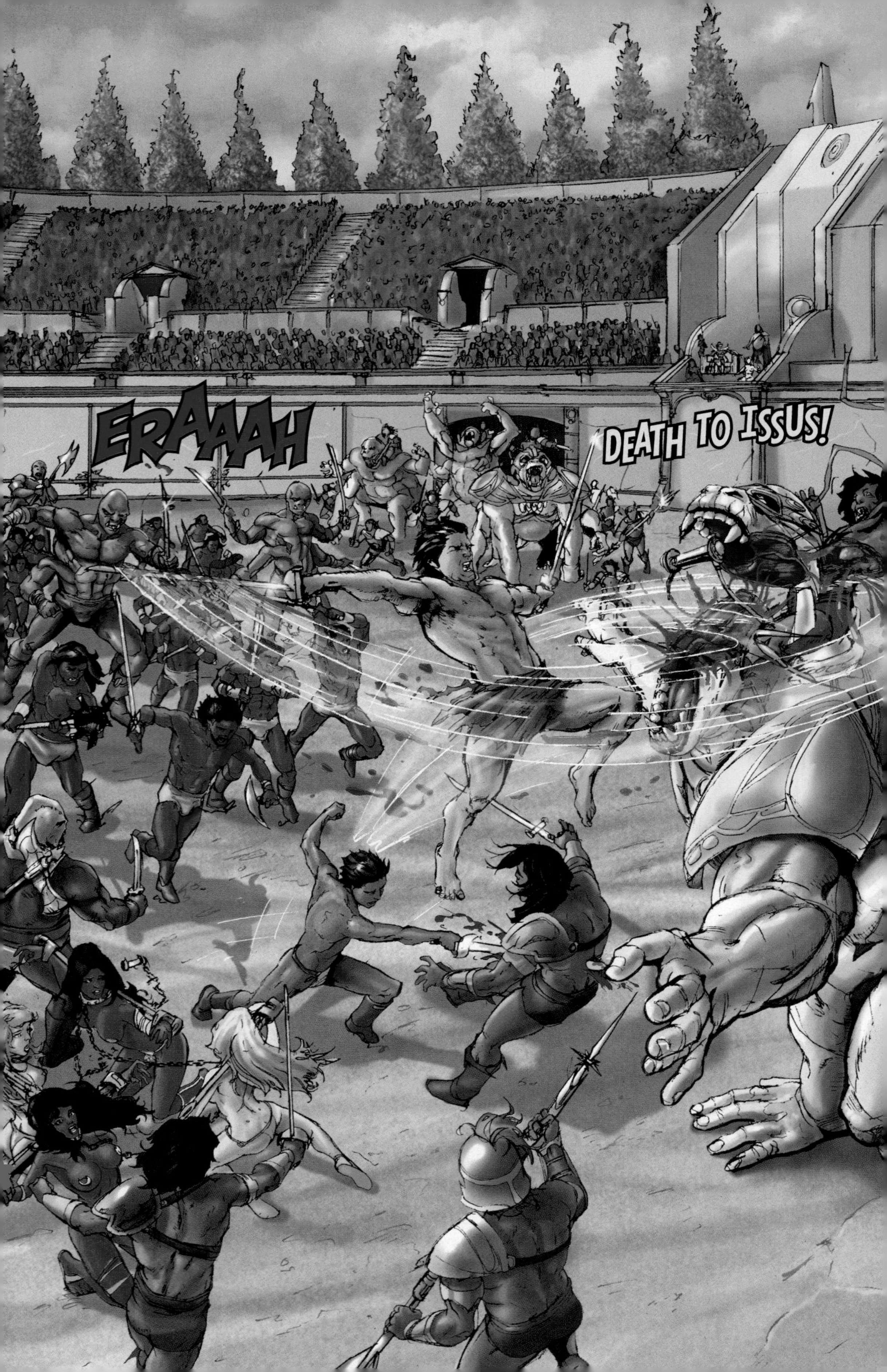
ERAAAH
DEATH TO ISSUS!

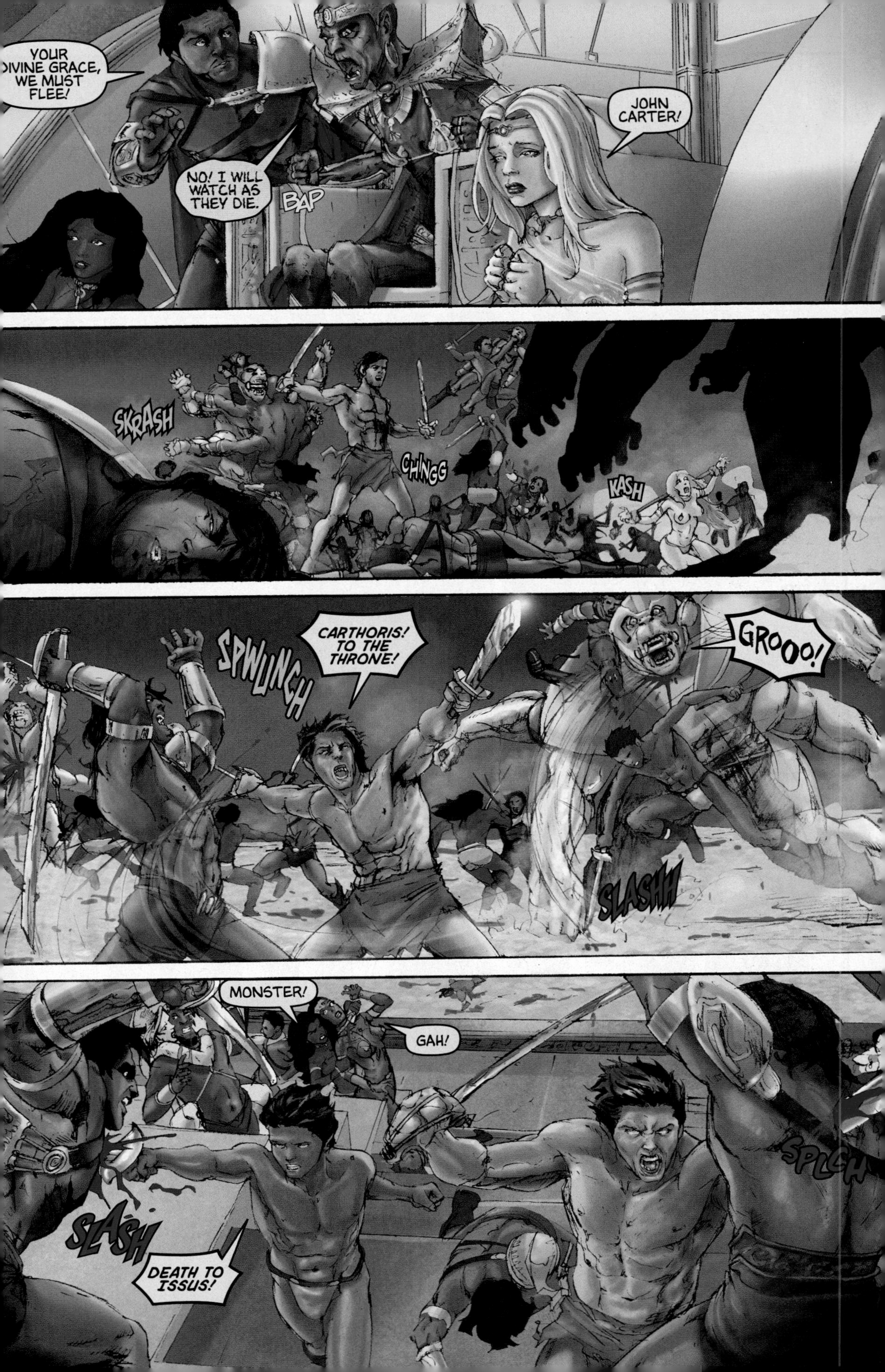
YOUR DIVINE GRACE, WE MUST FLEE!
NO! I WILL WATCH AS THEY DIE.
BAP
JOHN CARTER!
SKRASH
CHINGG
KASH
SPWUNCH
CARTHORIS! TO THE THRONE!
GROOO!
SLASHH
MONSTER!
GAH!
SPLCH
SLASH
DEATH TO ISSUS!

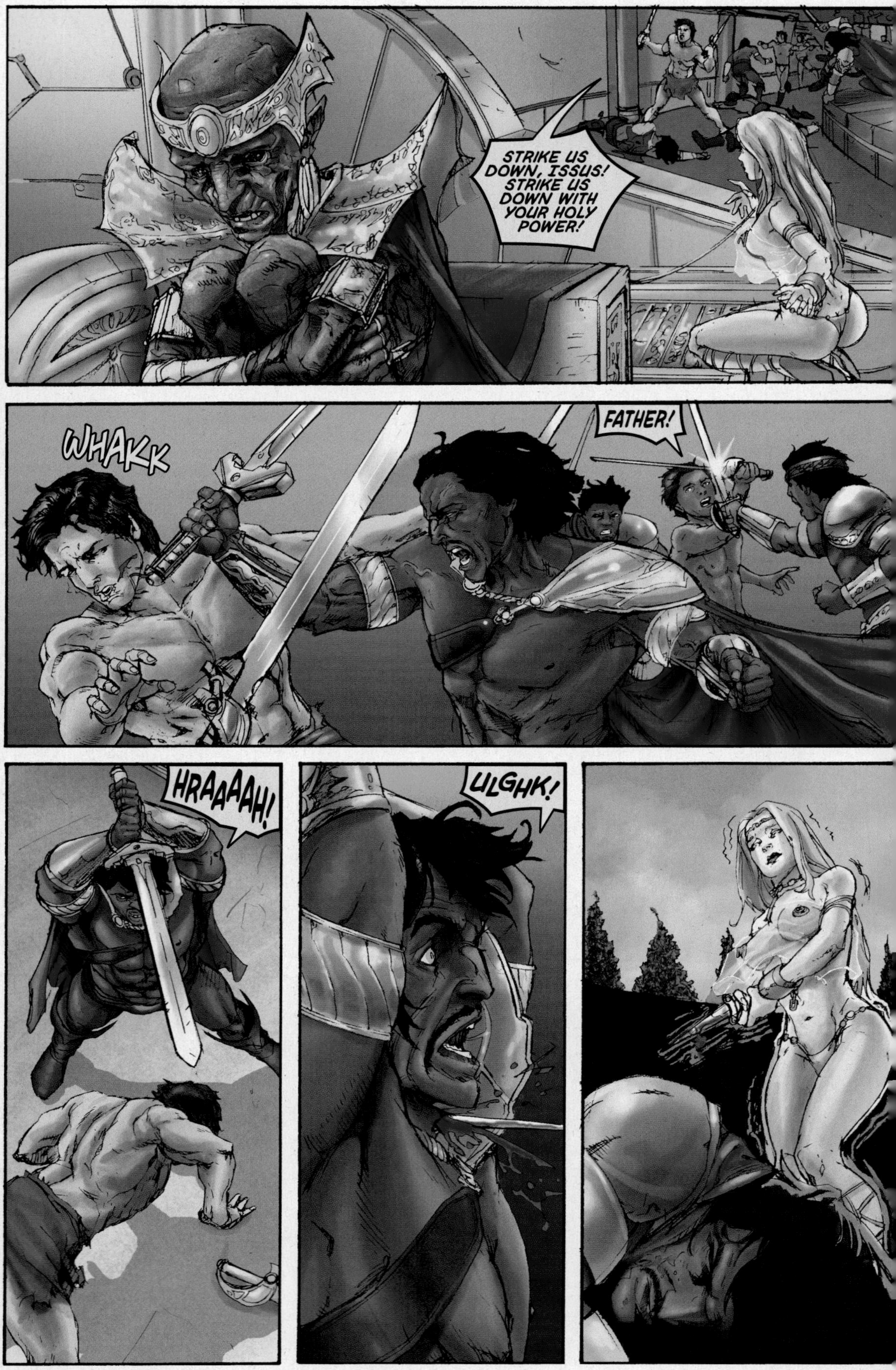
STRIKE US DOWN, ISSUS! STRIKE US DOWN WITH YOUR HOLY POWER!
WHAKK
FATHER!
HRAAAAH!
ULGHK!

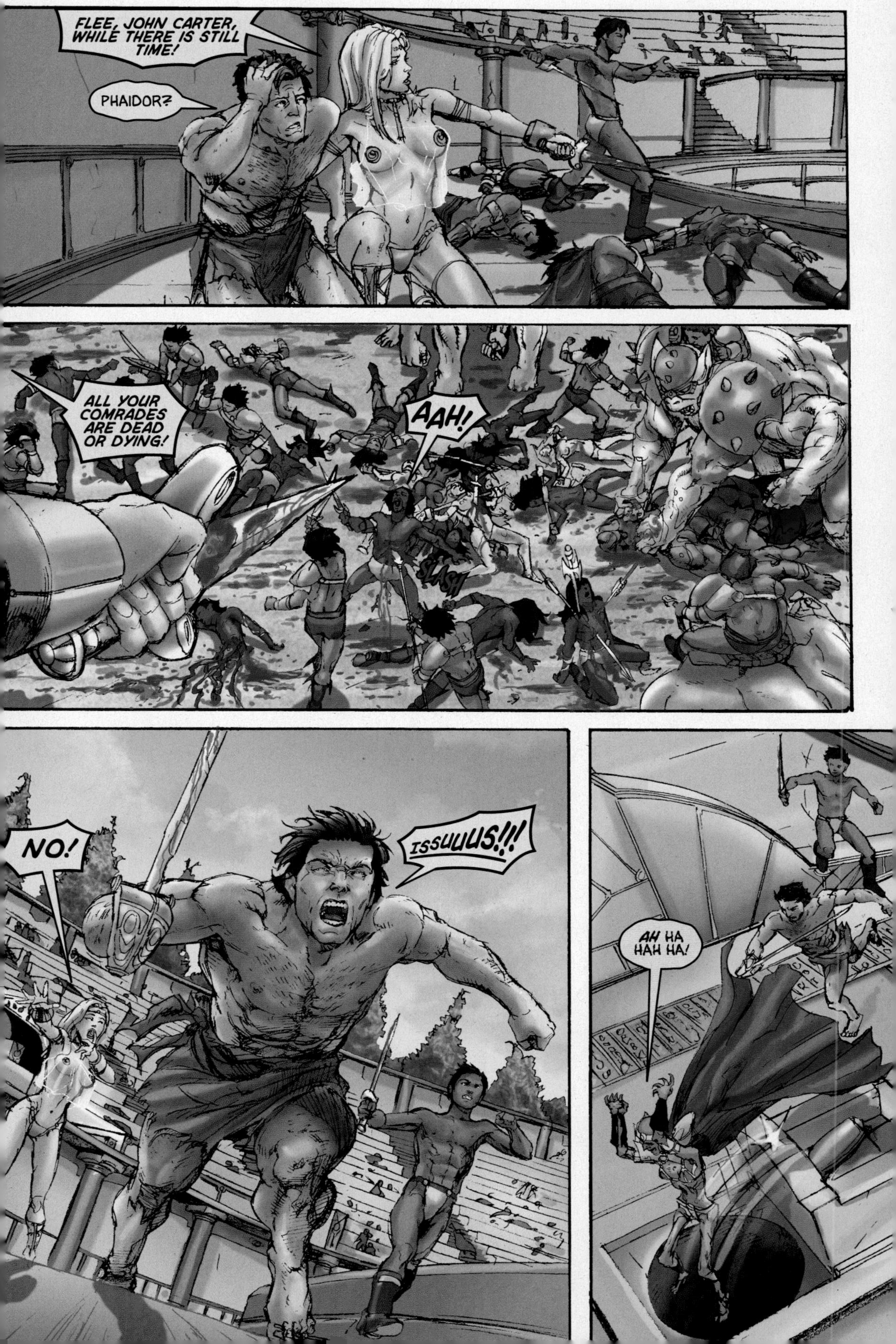
FLEE, JOHN CARTER, WHILE THERE IS STILL TIME!
PHAIDOR?
ALL YOUR COMRADES ARE DEAD OR DYING!
AAH!
SLASH
NO!
ISSUUUS!!!
AH HA HAH HA!

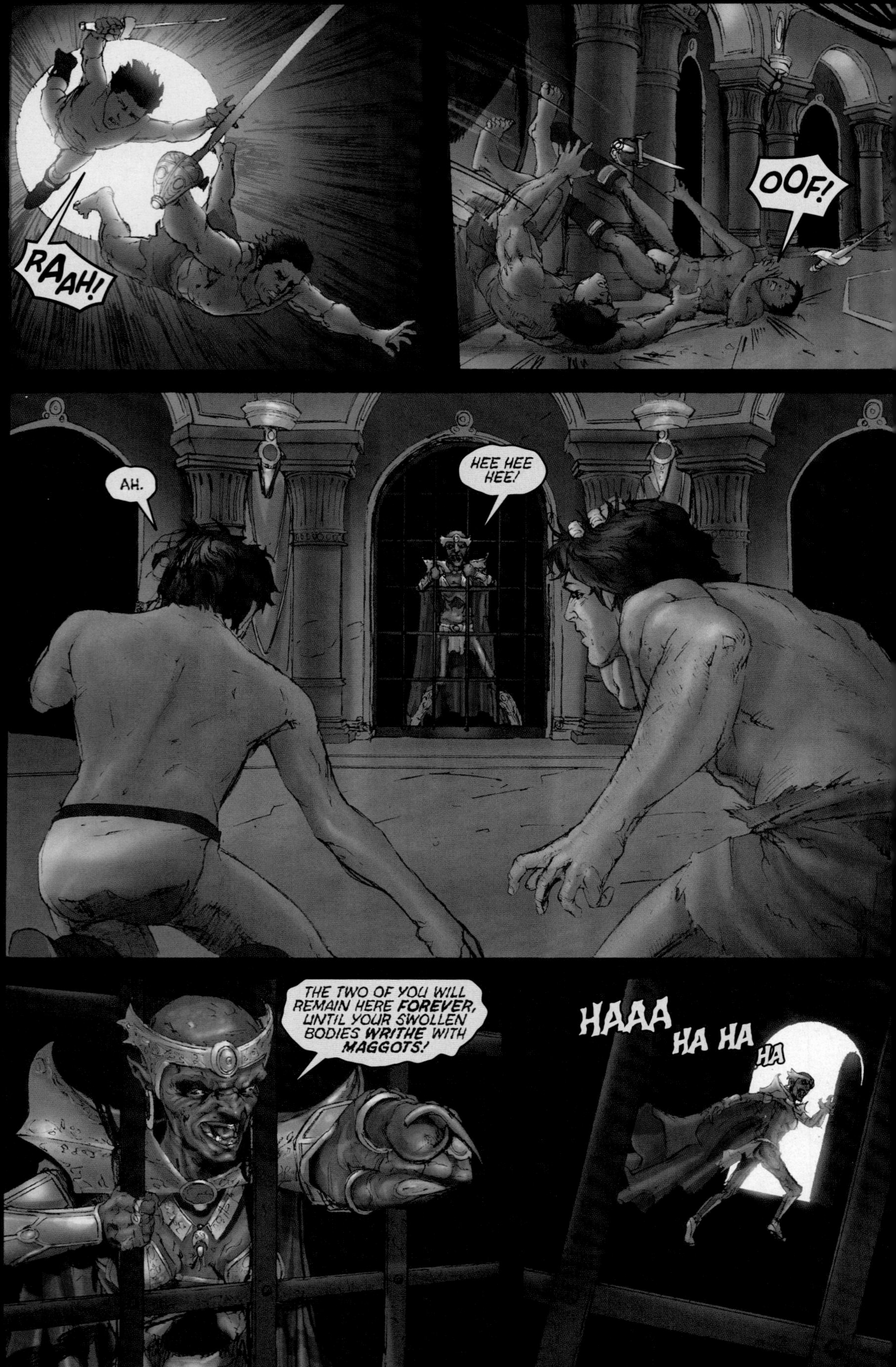
RAAH!
OOF!
AH.
HEE HEE HEE!
THE TWO OF YOU WILL REMAIN HERE FOREVER, UNTIL YOUR SWOLLEN BODIES WRITHE WITH MAGGOTS!
HAAA HA HA HA

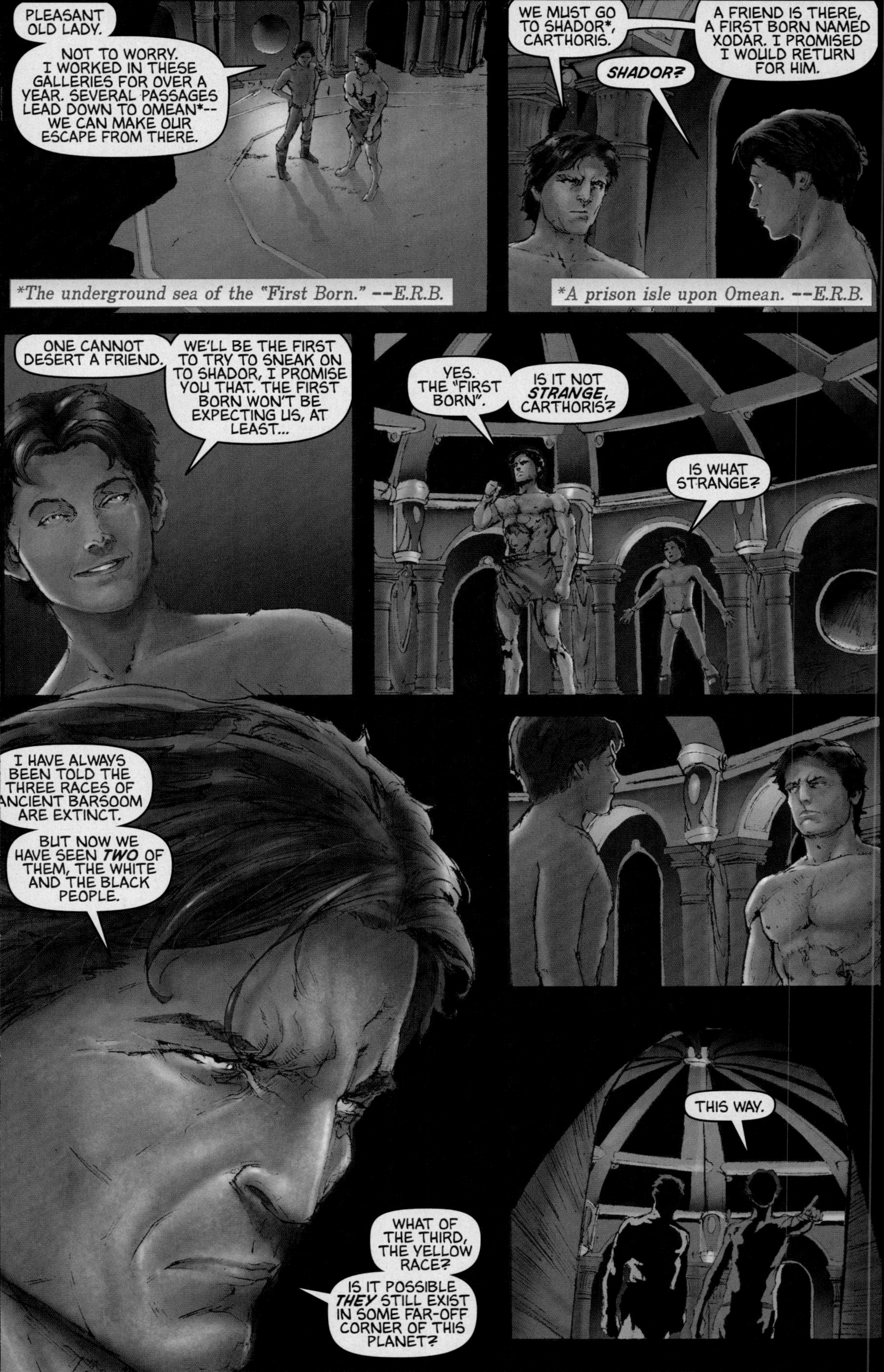
PLEASANT OLD LADY.
NOT TO WORRY. I WORKED IN THESE GALLERIES FOR OVER A YEAR. SEVERAL PASSAGES LEAD DOWN TO OMEAN*-- WE CAN MAKE OUR ESCAPE FROM THERE.
*The underground sea of the "First Born." --E.R.B.
WE MUST GO TO SHADOR*, CARTHORIS.
SHADOR?
A FRIEND IS THERE, A FIRST BORN NAMED XODAR. I PROMISED I WOULD RETURN FOR HIM.
*A prison isle upon Omean. --E.R.B.
ONE CANNOT DESERT A FRIEND.
WE'LL BE THE FIRST TO TRY TO SNEAK ON TO SHADOR, I PROMISE YOU THAT. THE FIRST BORN WON'T BE EXPECTING US, AT LEAST...
YES. THE "FIRST BORN".
IS IT NOT STRANGE, CARTHORIS?
IS WHAT STRANGE?
I HAVE ALWAYS BEEN TOLD THE THREE RACES OF ANCIENT BARSOOM ARE EXTINCT.
BUT NOW WE HAVE SEEN TWO OF THEM, THE WHITE AND THE BLACK PEOPLE.
WHAT OF THE THIRD, THE YELLOW RACE?
IS IT POSSIBLE THEY STILL EXIST IN SOME FAR-OFF CORNER OF THIS PLANET?
THIS WAY.

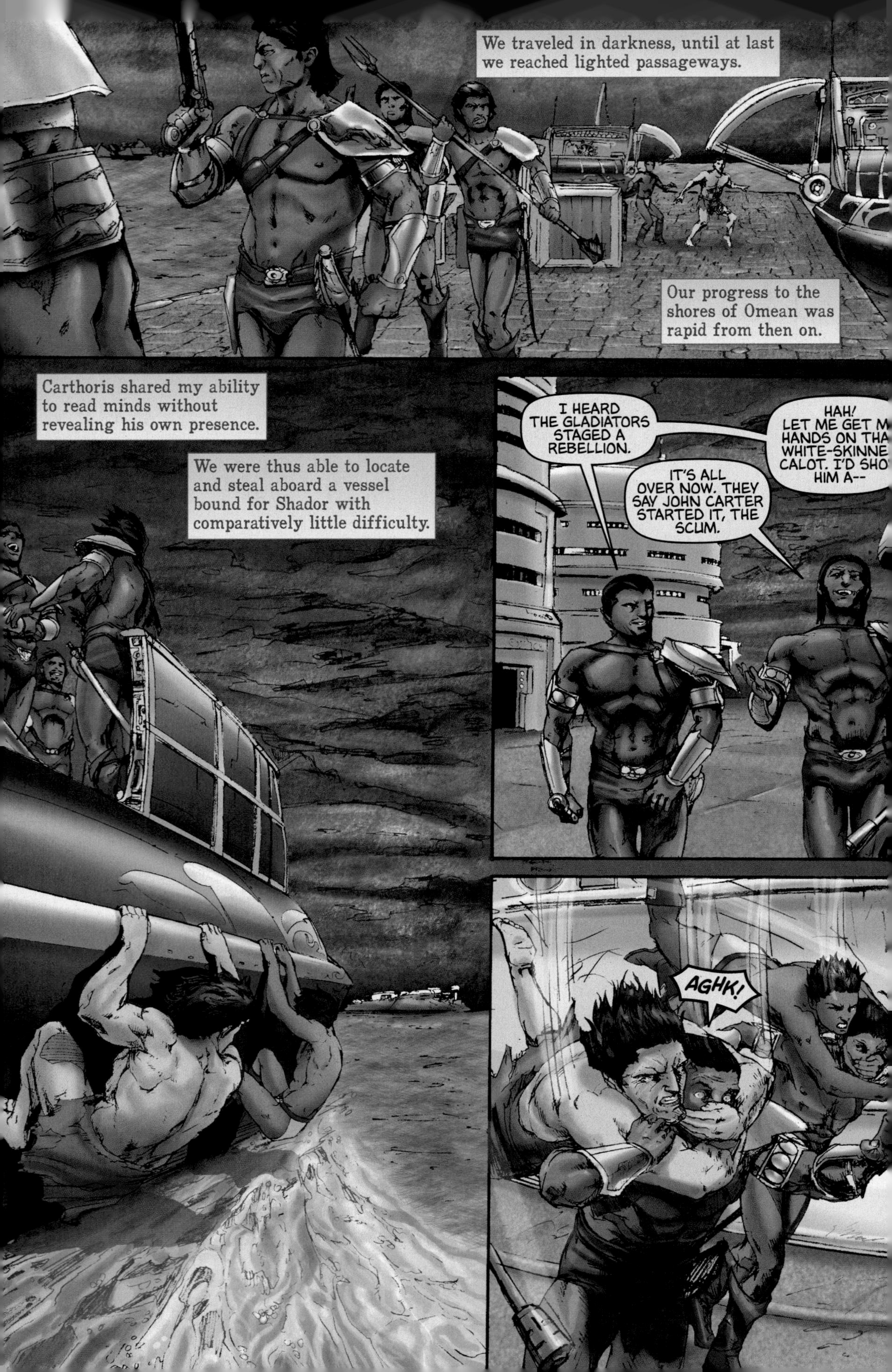

We traveled in darkness, until at last we reached lighted passageways.
Our progress to the shores of Omean was rapid from then on.
Carthoris shared my ability to read minds without revealing his own presence.
We were thus able to locate and steal aboard a vessel bound for Shador with comparatively little difficulty.
I HEARD THE GLADIATORS STAGED A REBELLION.
IT'S ALL OVER NOW. THEY SAY JOHN CARTER STARTED IT, THE SCUM.
HAH! LET ME GET M HANDS ON THA WHITE-SKINNE CALOT. I'D SHO HIM A--
AGHK!

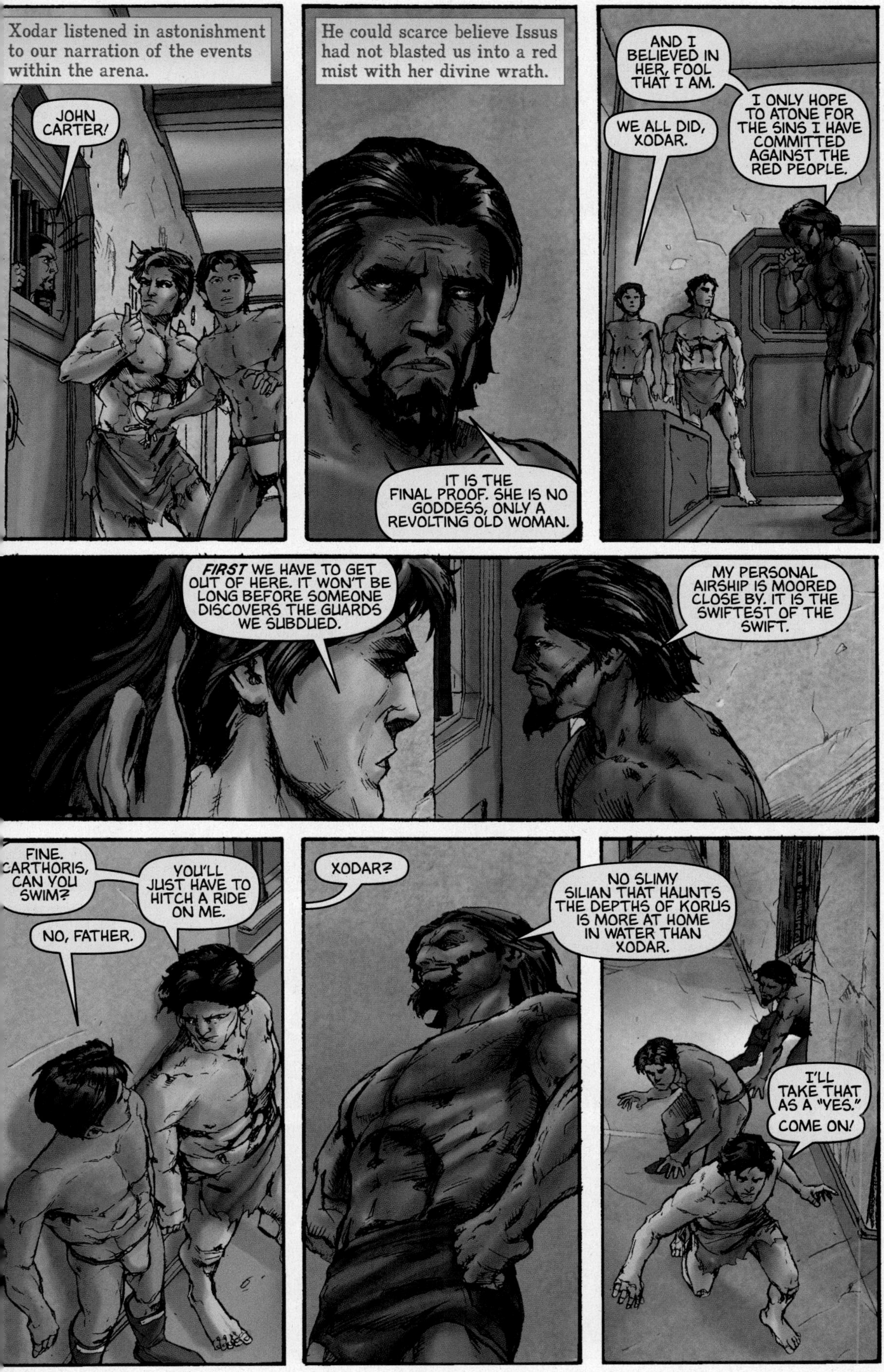
Xodar listened in astonishment to our narration of the events within the arena.
JOHN CARTER!
He could scarce believe Issus had not blasted us into a red mist with her divine wrath.
IT IS THE FINAL PROOF. SHE IS NO GODDESS, ONLY A REVOLTING OLD WOMAN.
AND I BELIEVED IN HER, FOOL THAT I AM.
WE ALL DID, XODAR.
I ONLY HOPE TO ATONE FOR THE SINS I HAVE COMMITTED AGAINST THE RED PEOPLE.
FIRST WE HAVE TO GET OUT OF HERE. IT WON'T BE LONG BEFORE SOMEONE DISCOVERS THE GUARDS WE SUBDUED.
MY PERSONAL AIRSHIP IS MOORED CLOSE BY. IT IS THE SWIFTEST OF THE SWIFT.
FINE. CARTHORIS, CAN YOU SWIM?
NO, FATHER.
YOU'LL JUST HAVE TO HITCH A RIDE ON ME.
XODAR?
NO SLIMY SILIAN THAT HAUNTS THE DEPTHS OF KORUS IS MORE AT HOME IN WATER THAN XODAR.
I'LL TAKE THAT AS A "YES."
COME ON!

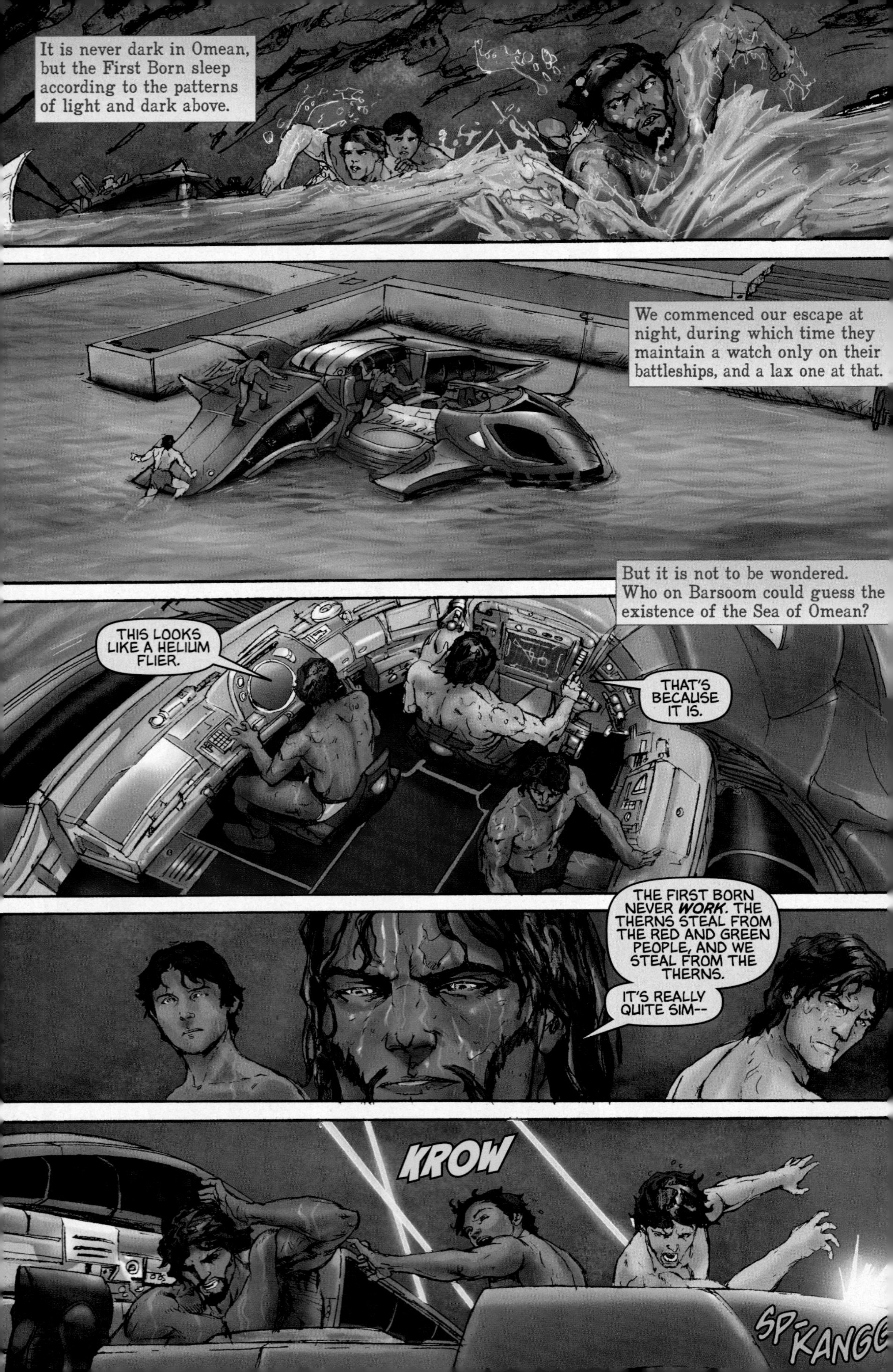
It is never dark in Omean, but the First Born sleep according to the patterns of light and dark above.
We commenced our escape at night, during which time they maintain a watch only on their battleships, and a lax one at that.
But it is not to be wondered. Who on Barsoom could guess the existence of the Sea of Omean?
THIS LOOKS LIKE A HELIUM FLIER.
THAT'S BECAUSE IT IS.
THE FIRST BORN NEVER WORK. THE THERNS STEAL FROM THE RED AND GREEN PEOPLE, AND WE STEAL FROM THE THERNS.
IT'S REALLY QUITE SIM--
KROW
SP-KANGG

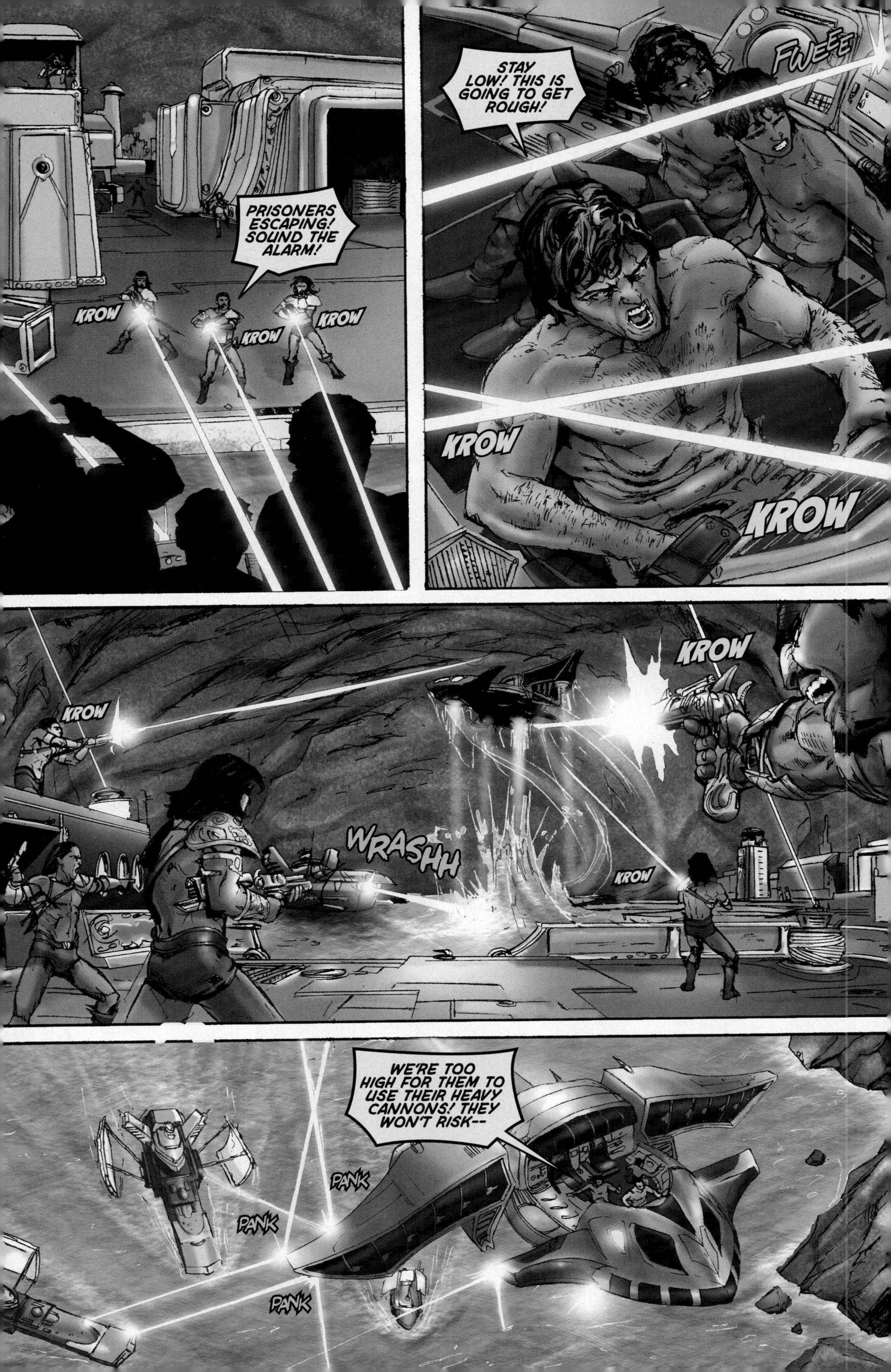
PRISONERS ESCAPING! SOUND THE ALARM!
KROW
KROW
KROW
STAY LOW! THIS IS GOING TO GET ROUGH!
FWEEE
KROW
KROW
KROW
KROW
WRASHH
KROW
WE'RE TOO HIGH FOR THEM TO USE THEIR HEAVY CANNONS! THEY WON'T RISK--
PANK
PANK
PANK

KROOM

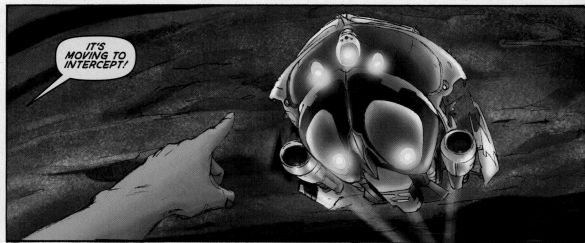

YOU WERE SAYING?!

FATHER! ABOVE US!

IT'S MOVING TO INTERCEPT!

WE'LL BE SMASHED TO PIECES!

NO WE WON'T! I KNOW A LITTLE TRICK--I'M GOING TO OVER-THROTTLE THE REPULSORS!

IS IT SAFE?

OF COURSE NOT! HOLD ON!

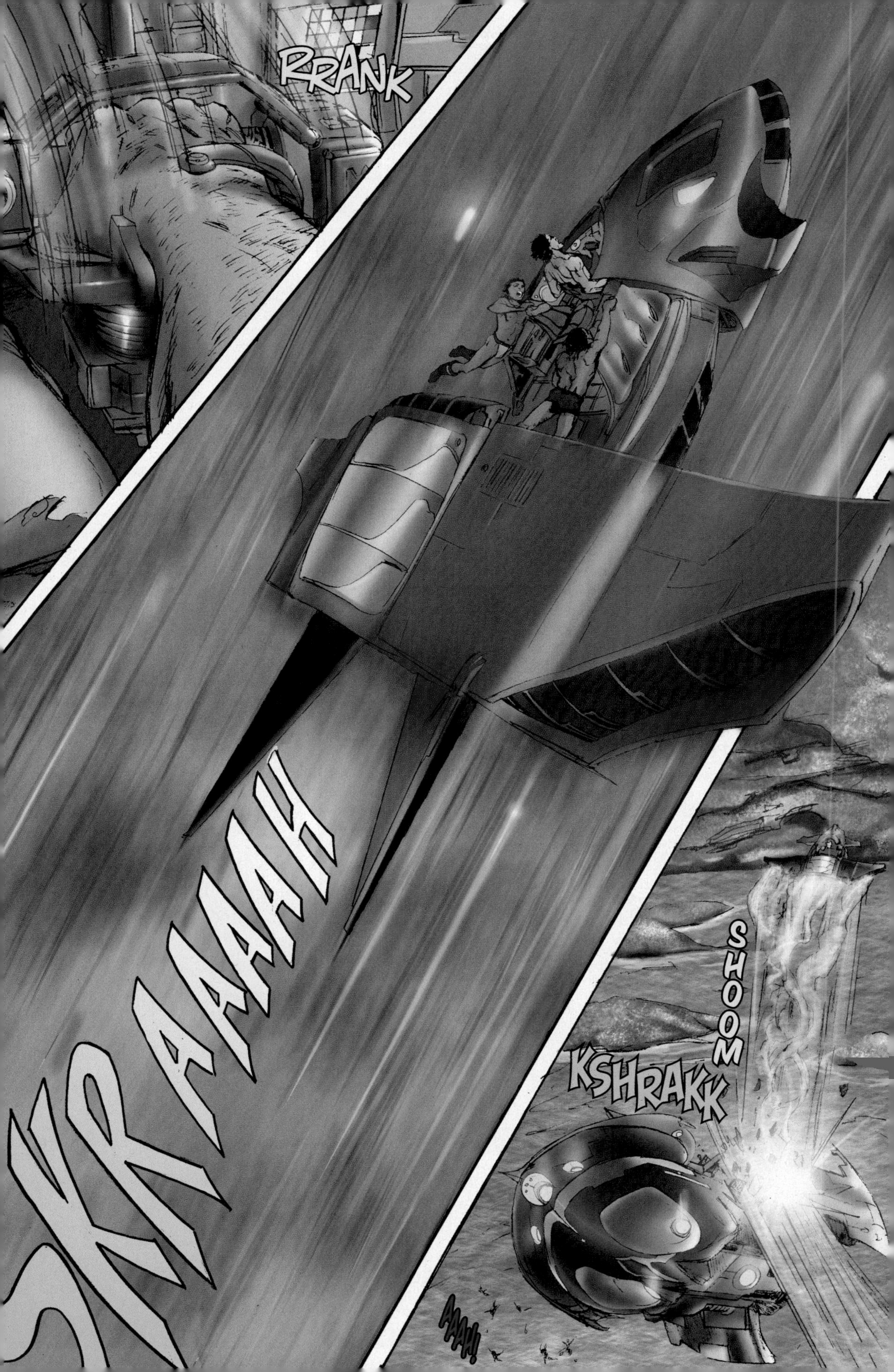
RRANK
SKRAAAAH
KSHRAKK
SHOOM
AAAH!

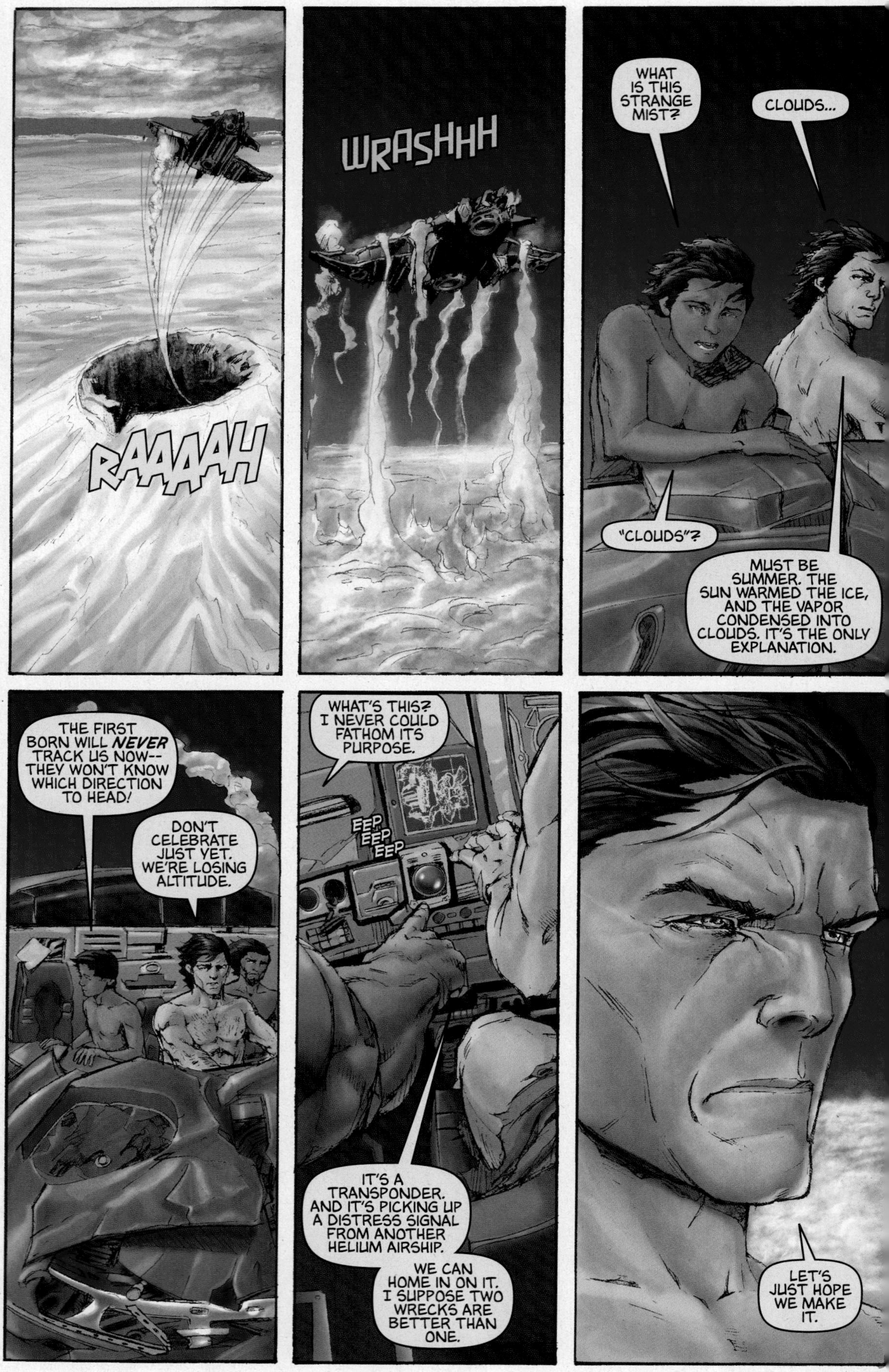
RAAAAH
WRASHHH
WHAT IS THIS STRANGE MIST?
CLOUDS...
"CLOUDS"?
MUST BE SUMMER. THE SUN WARMED THE ICE, AND THE VAPOR CONDENSED INTO CLOUDS. IT'S THE ONLY EXPLANATION.
THE FIRST BORN WILL NEVER TRACK US NOW-- THEY WON'T KNOW WHICH DIRECTION TO HEAD!
DON'T CELEBRATE JUST YET. WE'RE LOSING ALTITUDE.
WHAT'S THIS? I NEVER COULD FATHOM ITS PURPOSE.
EEP EEP EEP
IT'S A TRANSPONDER. AND IT'S PICKING UP A DISTRESS SIGNAL FROM ANOTHER HELIUM AIRSHIP.
WE CAN HOME IN ON IT. I SUPPOSE TWO WRECKS ARE BETTER THAN ONE.
LET'S JUST HOPE WE MAKE IT.

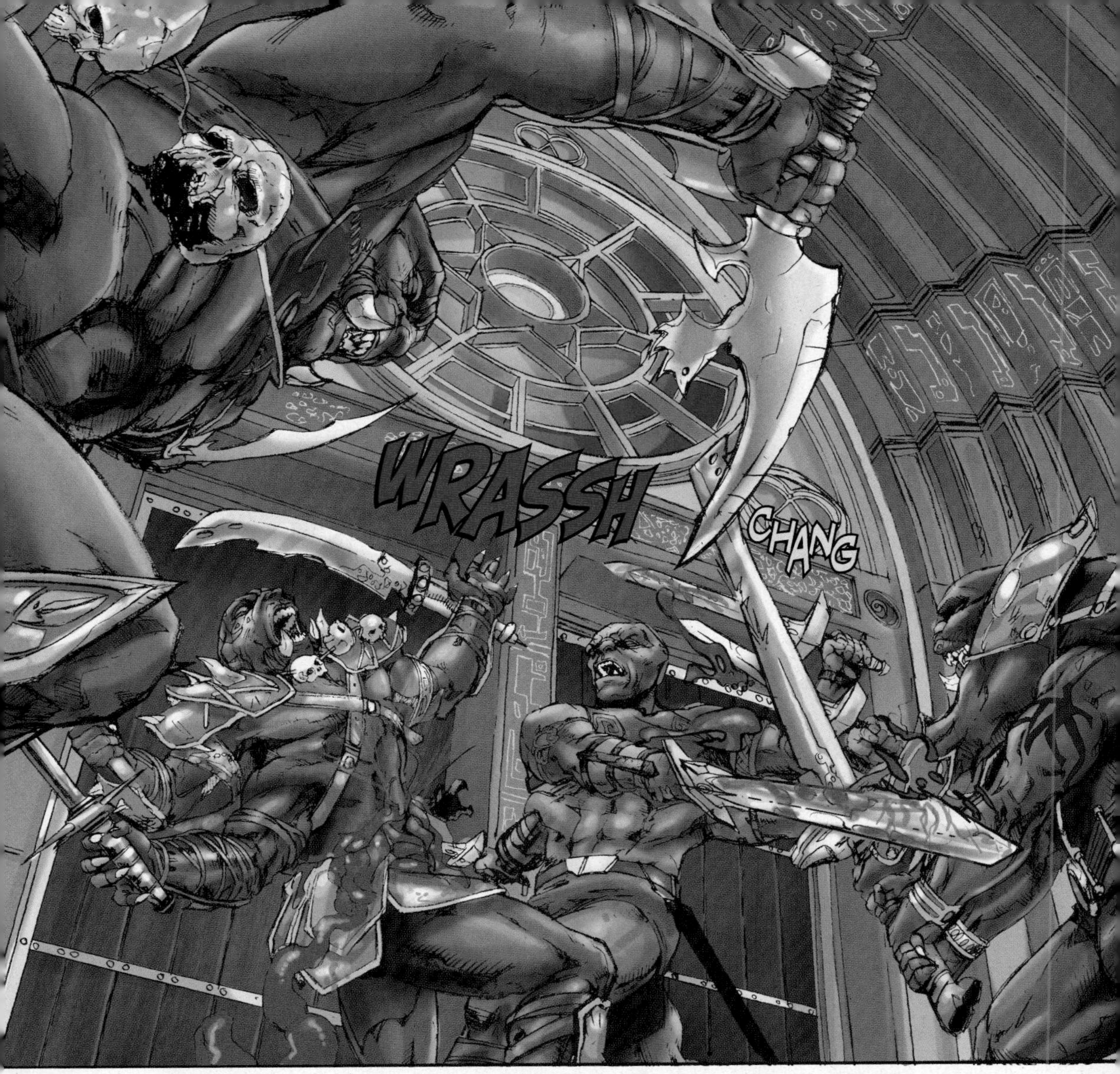
WRASSH
CHANG

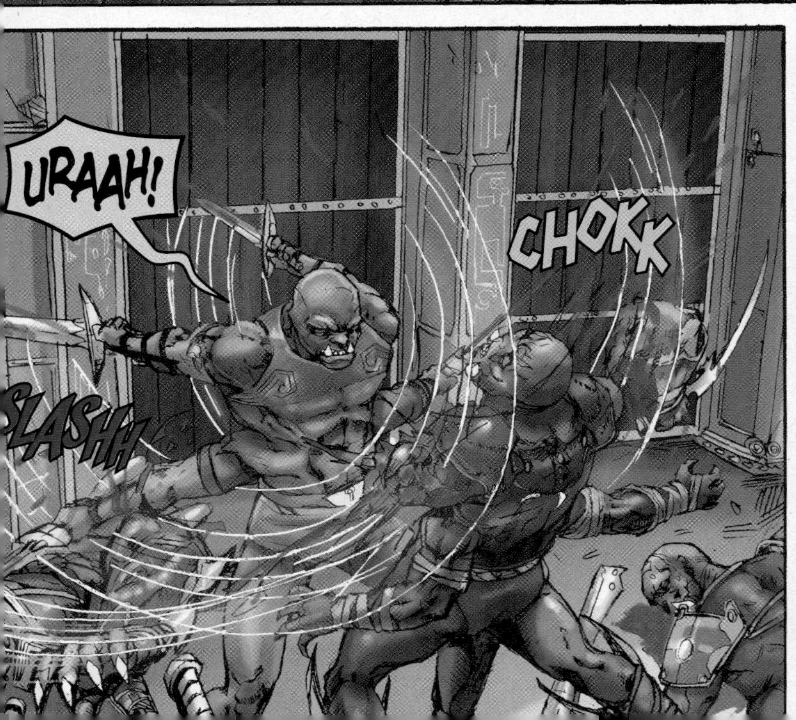
URAAH!
CHOKK
SLASHH

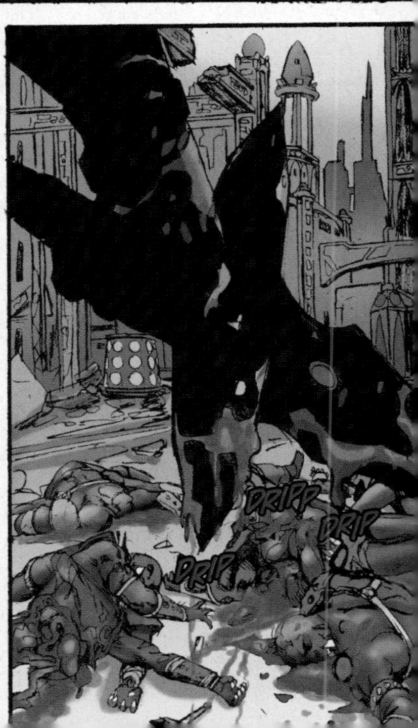
DRIPP
DRIP
DRIP

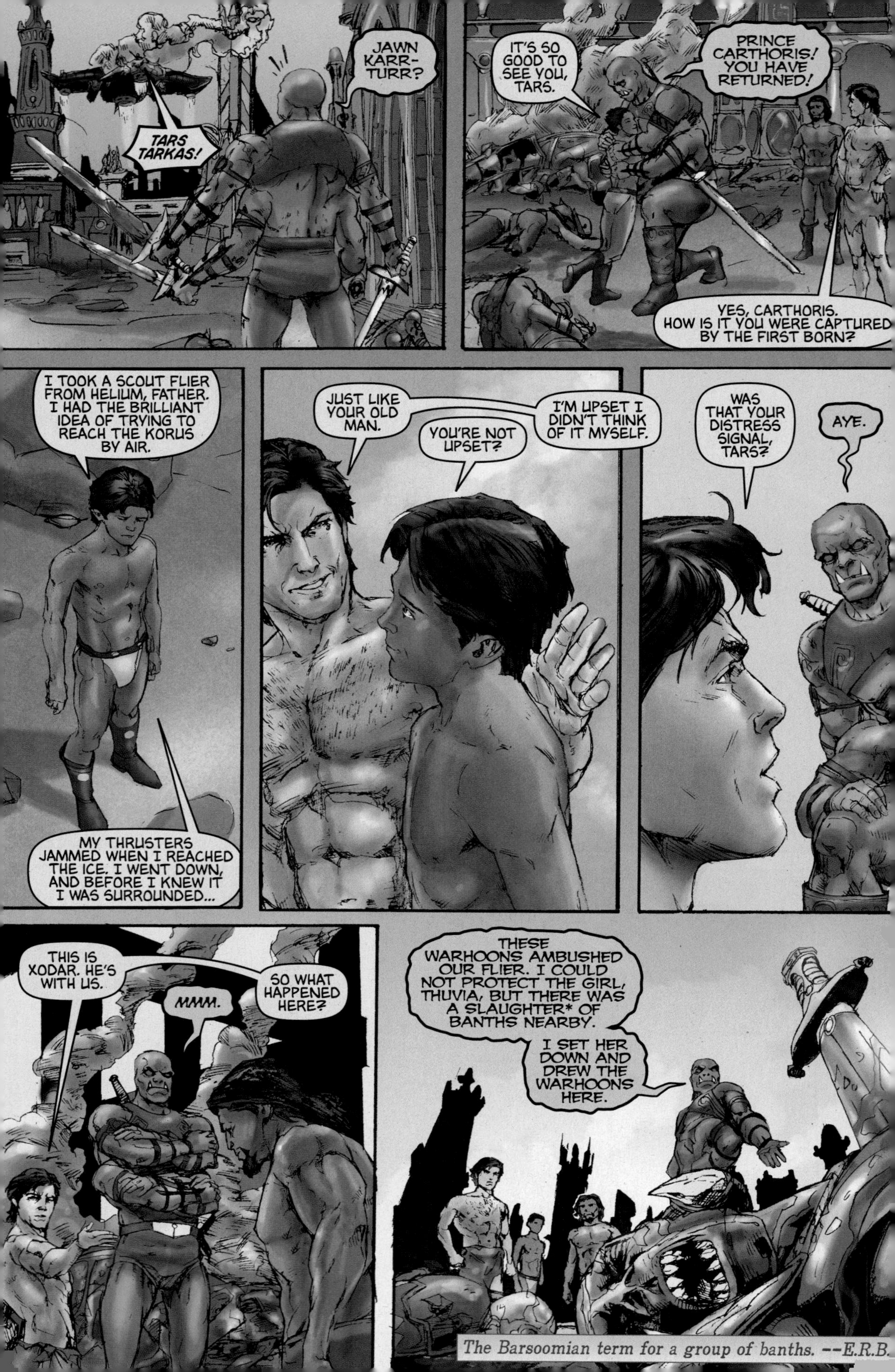
TARS TARKAS!
JAWN KARR-TURR?
IT'S SO GOOD TO SEE YOU, TARS.
PRINCE CARTHORIS! YOU HAVE RETURNED!
YES, CARTHORIS. HOW IS IT YOU WERE CAPTURED BY THE FIRST BORN?
I TOOK A SCOUT FLIER FROM HELIUM, FATHER. I HAD THE BRILLIANT IDEA OF TRYING TO REACH THE KORUS BY AIR.
MY THRUSTERS JAMMED WHEN I REACHED THE ICE. I WENT DOWN, AND BEFORE I KNEW IT I WAS SURROUNDED...
JUST LIKE YOUR OLD MAN.
YOU'RE NOT UPSET?
I'M UPSET I DIDN'T THINK OF IT MYSELF.
WAS THAT YOUR DISTRESS SIGNAL, TARS?
AYE.
THIS IS XODAR. HE'S WITH US.
MMM.
SO WHAT HAPPENED HERE?
THESE WARHOONS AMBUSHED OUR FLIER. I COULD NOT PROTECT THE GIRL, THUVIA, BUT THERE WAS A SLAUGHTER* OF BANTHS NEARBY.
I SET HER DOWN AND DREW THE WARHOONS HERE.
*The Barsoomian term for a group of banths. --E.R.B.

YOU WERE ALL SHE WOULD TALK ABOUT, JAWN KAR-TURR. IT WAS MOST ANNOYING.

I STILL DON'T UNDERSTAND THIS OBSESSION YOU TWO-ARMS HAVE WITH PROCREATION.

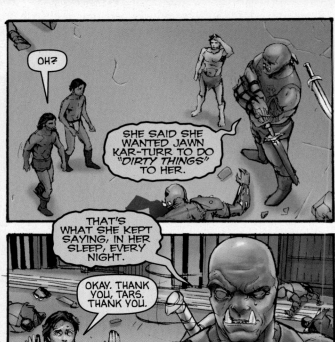

OH?

SHE SAID SHE WANTED JAWN KAR-TURR TO DO "*DIRTY THINGS*" TO HER.

THAT'S WHAT SHE KEPT SAYING, IN HER SLEEP, EVERY NIGHT.

OKAY. THANK YOU, TARS. THANK YOU.

"JAWN KAR-TURR, I WANT YOU TO DO DIRTY THINGS TO ME!"

WE GET THE IDEA, TARS.

"I WANT YOU TO DO DIRTY THINGS TO ME, FOR I AM A DIRTY LITTLE GIRL!"

TARS...

WHAT... *KIND* OF DIRTY THINGS?

THAT IS THE STRANGEST *PART!* PERHAPS IT IS BECAUSE OF OUR TUSKS, BUT WE THARKS WOULD *NEVER* USE OUR MOUTH-HOLES TO STIMULATE OUR--

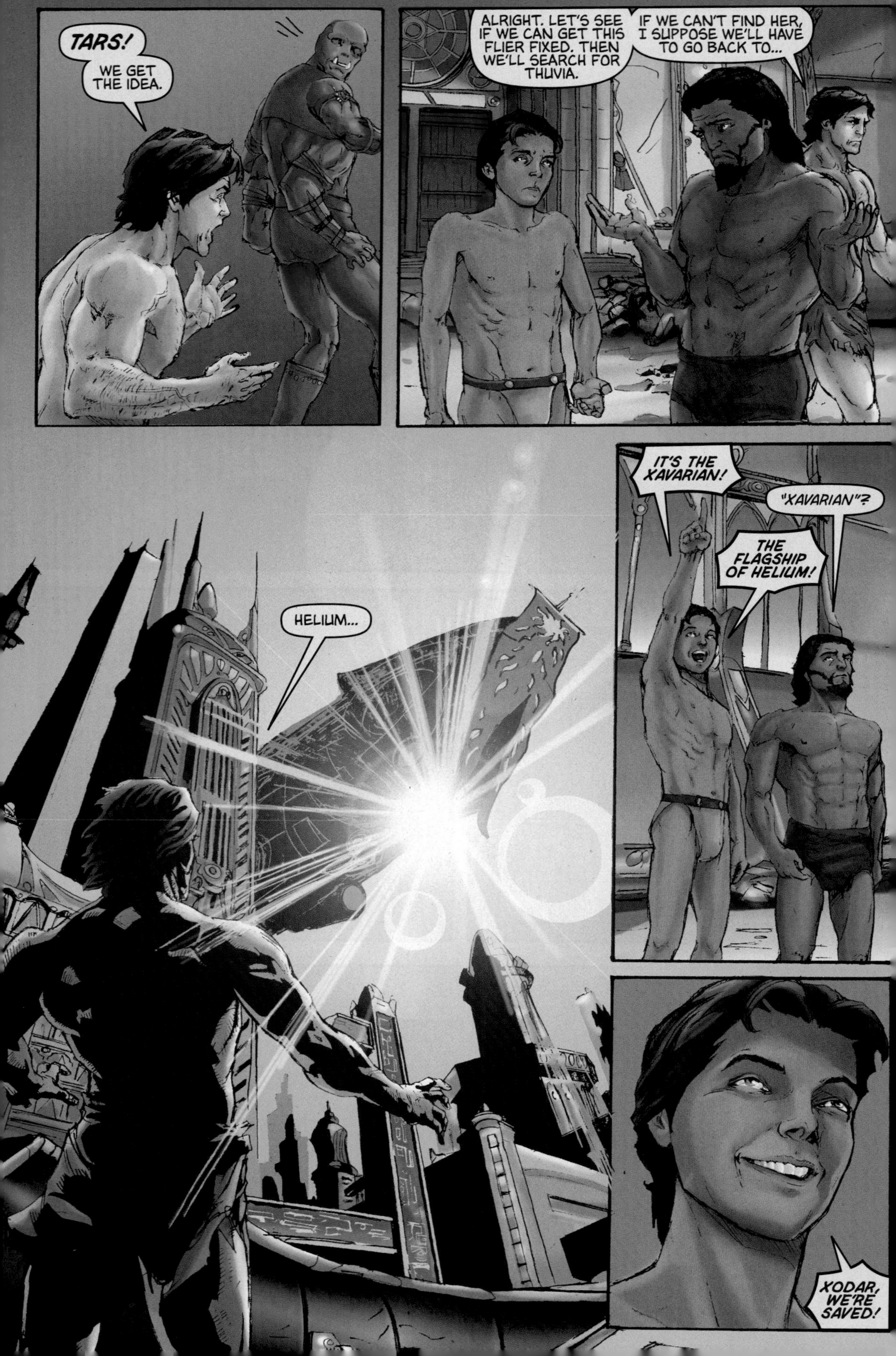
TARS!
WE GET THE IDEA.
ALRIGHT. LET'S SEE IF WE CAN GET THIS FLIER FIXED. THEN WE'LL SEARCH FOR THUVIA.
IF WE CAN'T FIND HER, I SUPPOSE WE'LL HAVE TO GO BACK TO...
HELIUM...
IT'S THE XAVARIAN!
"XAVARIAN"?
THE FLAGSHIP OF HELIUM!
XODAR, WE'RE SAVED!

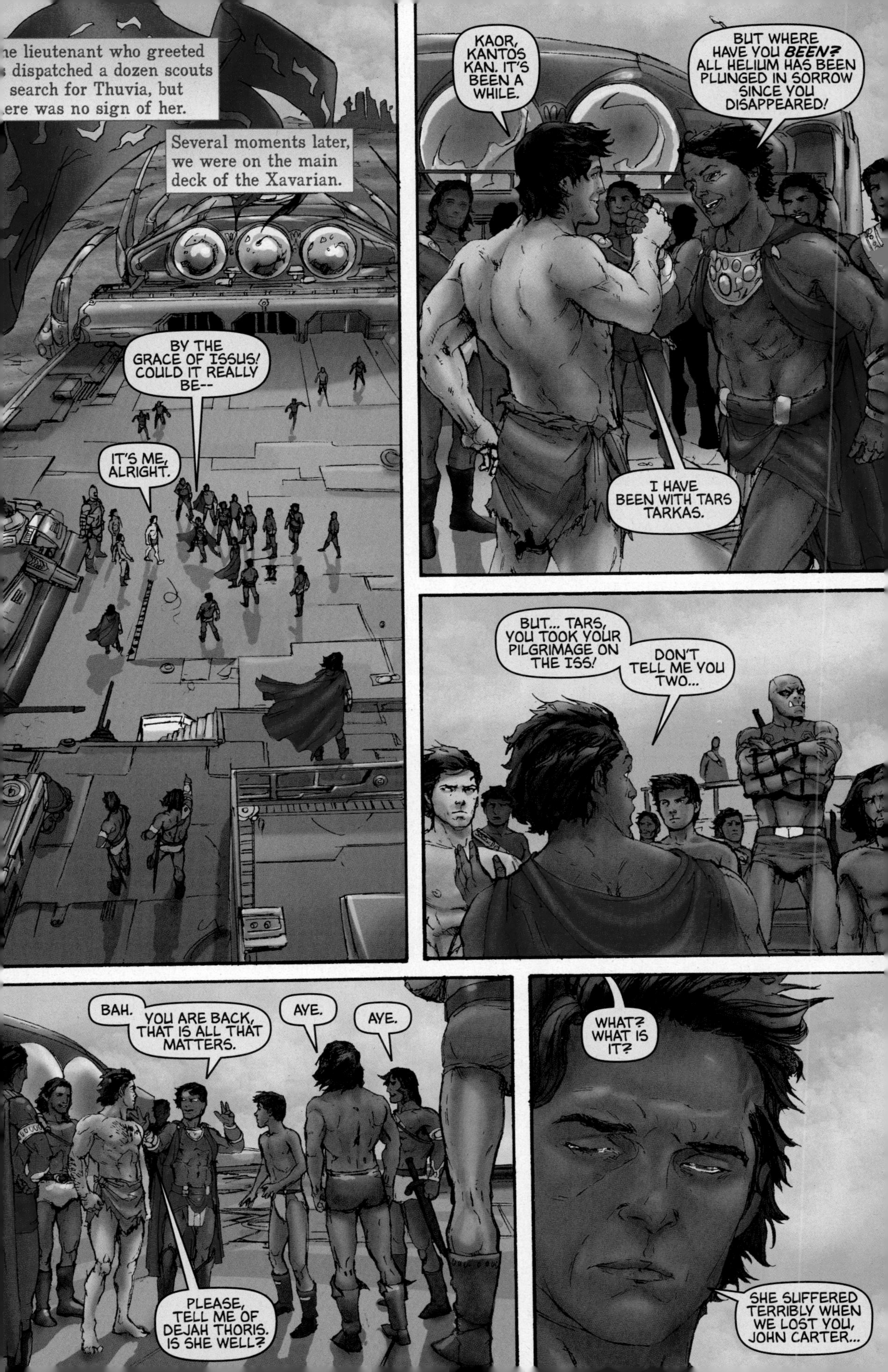

he lieutenant who greeted
s dispatched a dozen scouts
search for Thuvia, but
ere was no sign of her.
Several moments later, we were on the main deck of the Xavarian.
BY THE GRACE OF ISSUS! COULD IT REALLY BE--
IT'S ME, ALRIGHT.
KAOR, KANTOS KAN. IT'S BEEN A WHILE.
BUT WHERE HAVE YOU BEEN? ALL HELIUM HAS BEEN PLUNGED IN SORROW SINCE YOU DISAPPEARED!
I HAVE BEEN WITH TARS TARKAS.
BUT... TARS, YOU TOOK YOUR PILGRIMAGE ON THE ISS!
DON'T TELL ME YOU TWO...
BAH.
YOU ARE BACK, THAT IS ALL THAT MATTERS.
AYE.
AYE.
PLEASE, TELL ME OF DEJAH THORIS. IS SHE WELL?
WHAT? WHAT IS IT?
SHE SUFFERED TERRIBLY WHEN WE LOST YOU, JOHN CARTER...

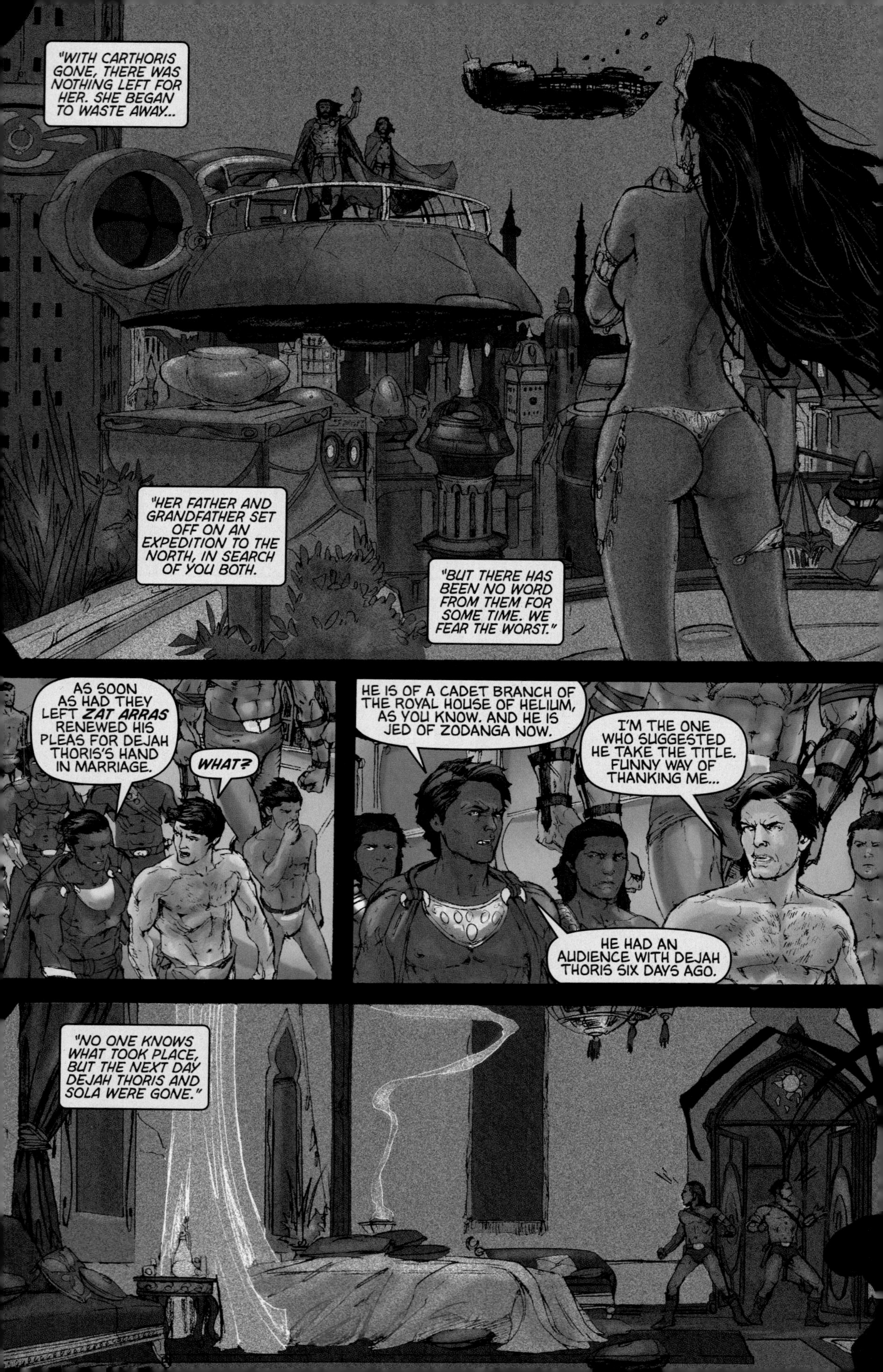
"WITH CARTHORIS GONE, THERE WAS NOTHING LEFT FOR HER. SHE BEGAN TO WASTE AWAY...
"HER FATHER AND GRANDFATHER SET OFF ON AN EXPEDITION TO THE NORTH, IN SEARCH OF YOU BOTH.
"BUT THERE HAS BEEN NO WORD FROM THEM FOR SOME TIME. WE FEAR THE WORST."
AS SOON AS HAD THEY LEFT ZAT ARRAS RENEWED HIS PLEAS FOR DEJAH THORIS'S HAND IN MARRIAGE.
WHAT?
HE IS OF A CADET BRANCH OF THE ROYAL HOUSE OF HELIUM, AS YOU KNOW. AND HE IS JED OF ZODANGA NOW.
I'M THE ONE WHO SUGGESTED HE TAKE THE TITLE. FUNNY WAY OF THANKING ME...
HE HAD AN AUDIENCE WITH DEJAH THORIS SIX DAYS AGO.
"NO ONE KNOWS WHAT TOOK PLACE, BUT THE NEXT DAY DEJAH THORIS AND SOLA WERE GONE."

SOLA? WHAT OF MY DAUGHTER?

I'M SORRY, TARS TARKAS. WE JUST DON'T KNOW. BUT IT IS ALWAYS THUS WHEN SOMEONE TAKES TO THE ISS.

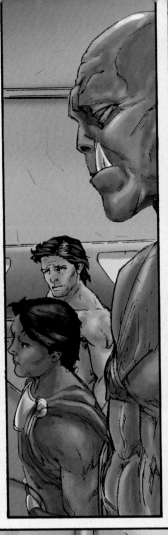

AND WHERE IS ZAT ARRAS?

HE IS ABOARD THIS SHIP, JOHN CARTER. HE WISHES TO SPEAK WITH YOU.

DOES HE NOW.

KAOR, ZAT ARRAS.

YOU'VE GOT SOME EXPLAINING--

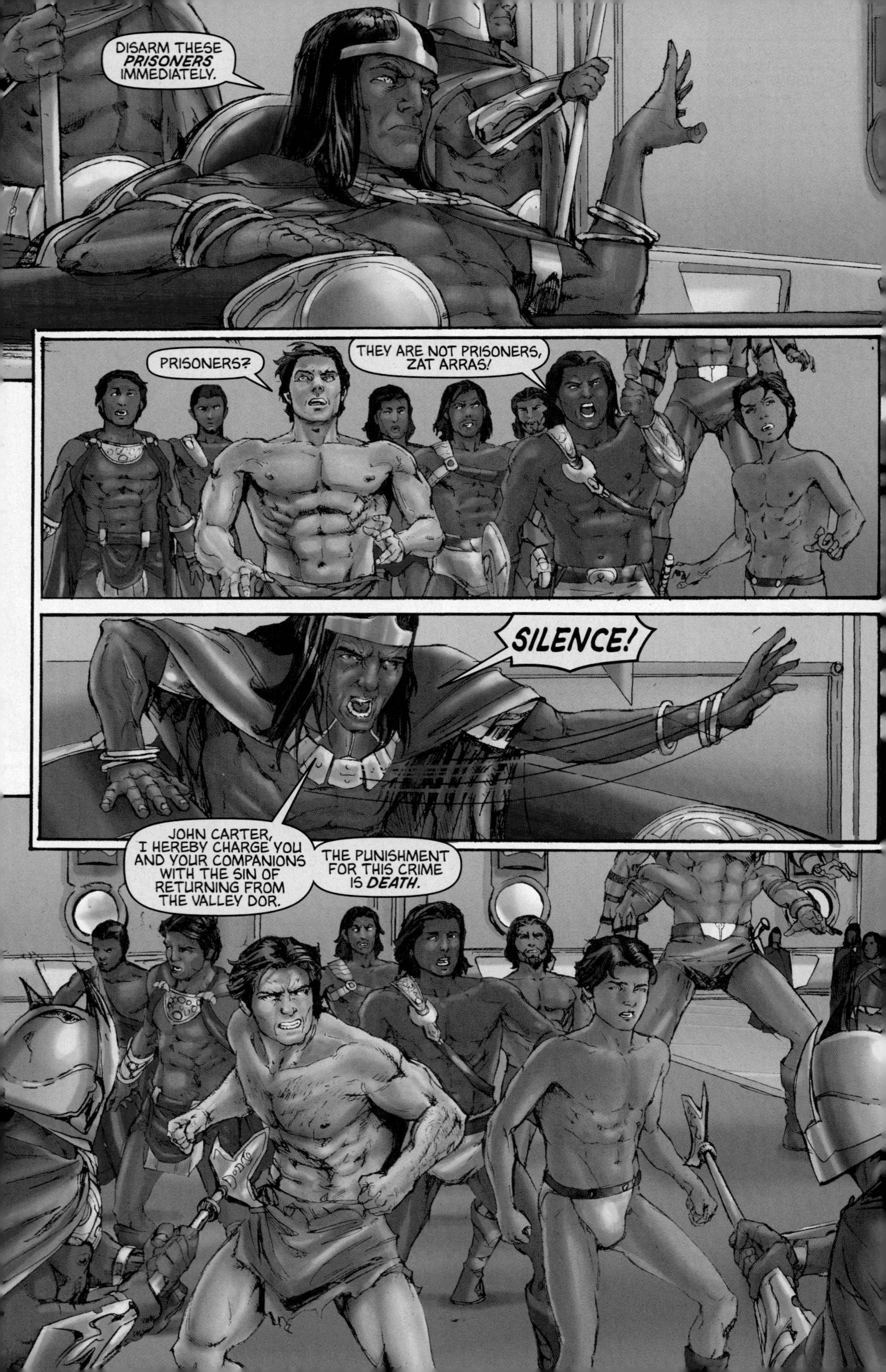
DISARM THESE *PRISONERS* IMMEDIATELY.
PRISONERS?
THEY ARE NOT PRISONERS, ZAT ARRAS!
SILENCE!
JOHN CARTER, I HEREBY CHARGE YOU AND YOUR COMPANIONS WITH THE SIN OF RETURNING FROM THE VALLEY DOR.
THE PUNISHMENT FOR THIS CRIME IS *DEATH*.

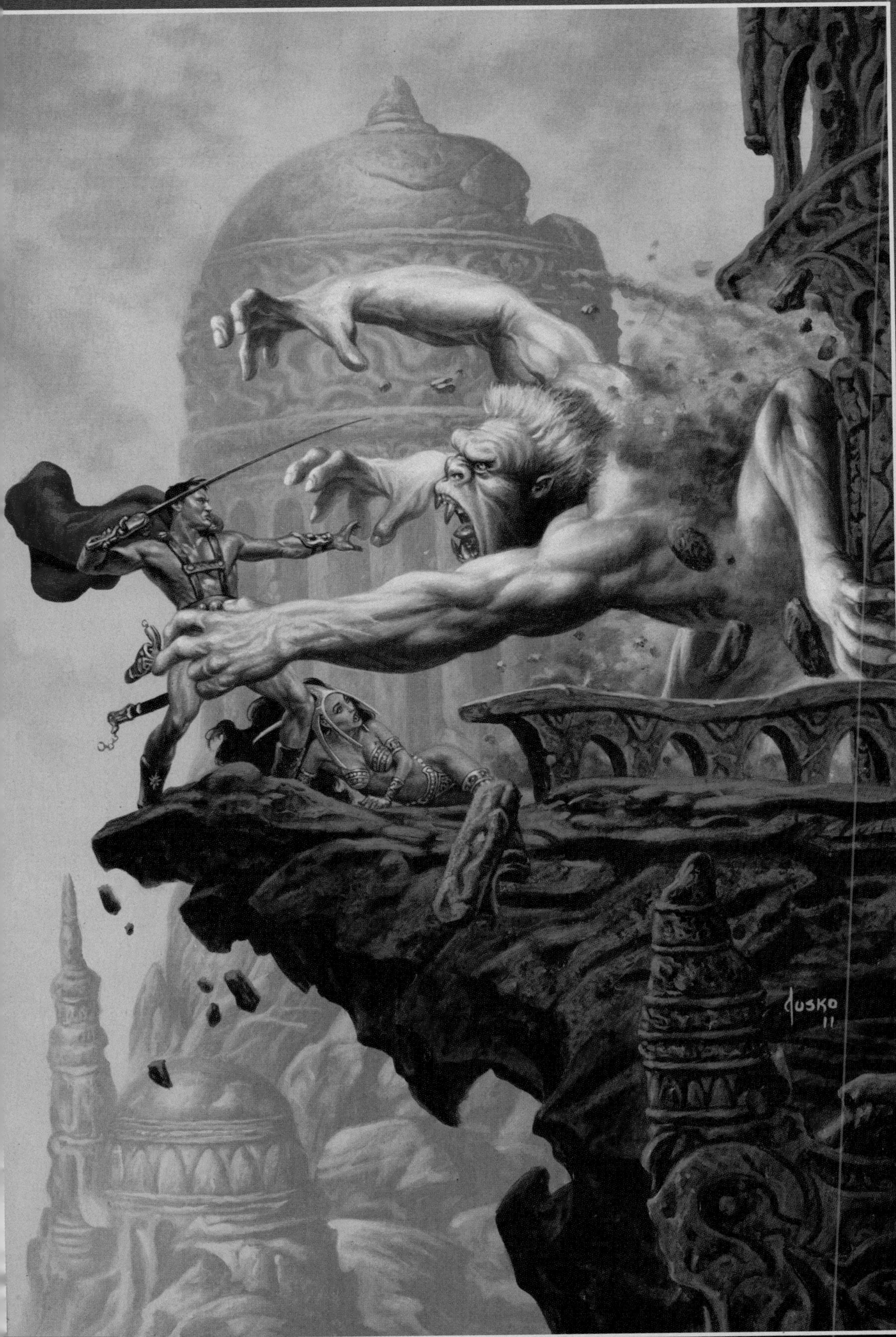
Jusko
11

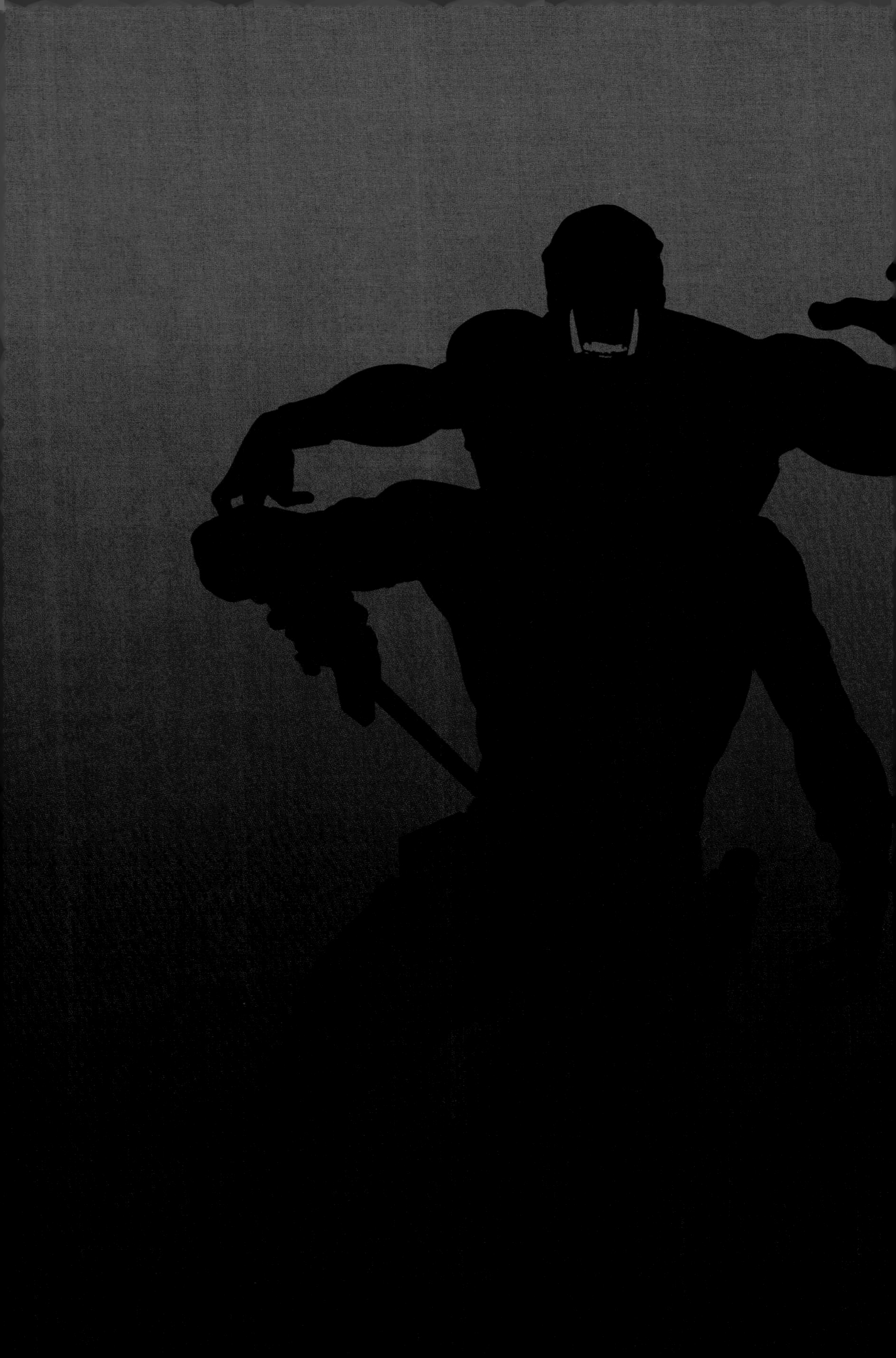

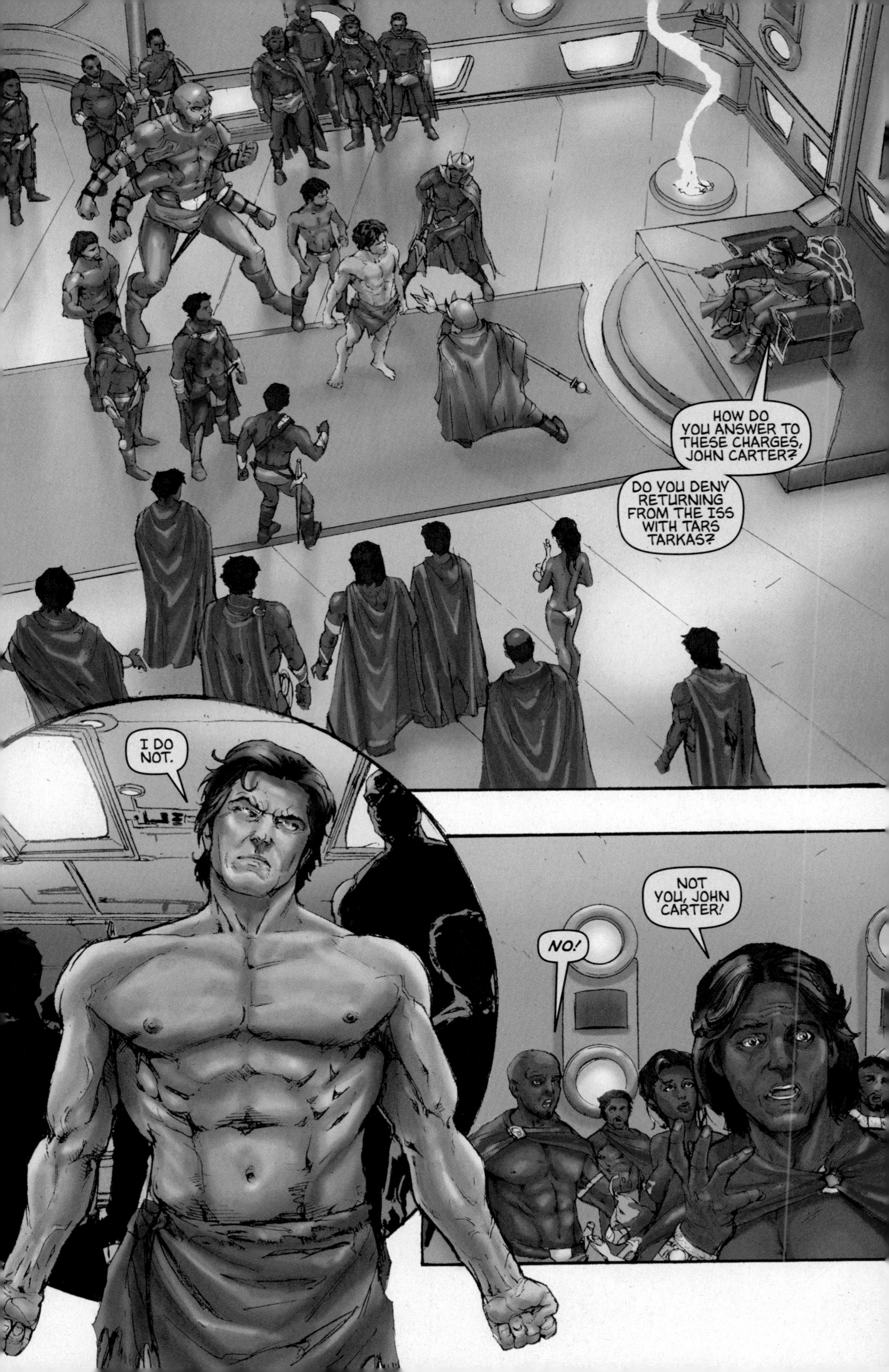
HOW DO YOU ANSWER TO THESE CHARGES, JOHN CARTER?
DO YOU DENY RETURNING FROM THE ISS WITH TARS TARKAS?
I DO NOT.
NO!
NOT YOU, JOHN CARTER!

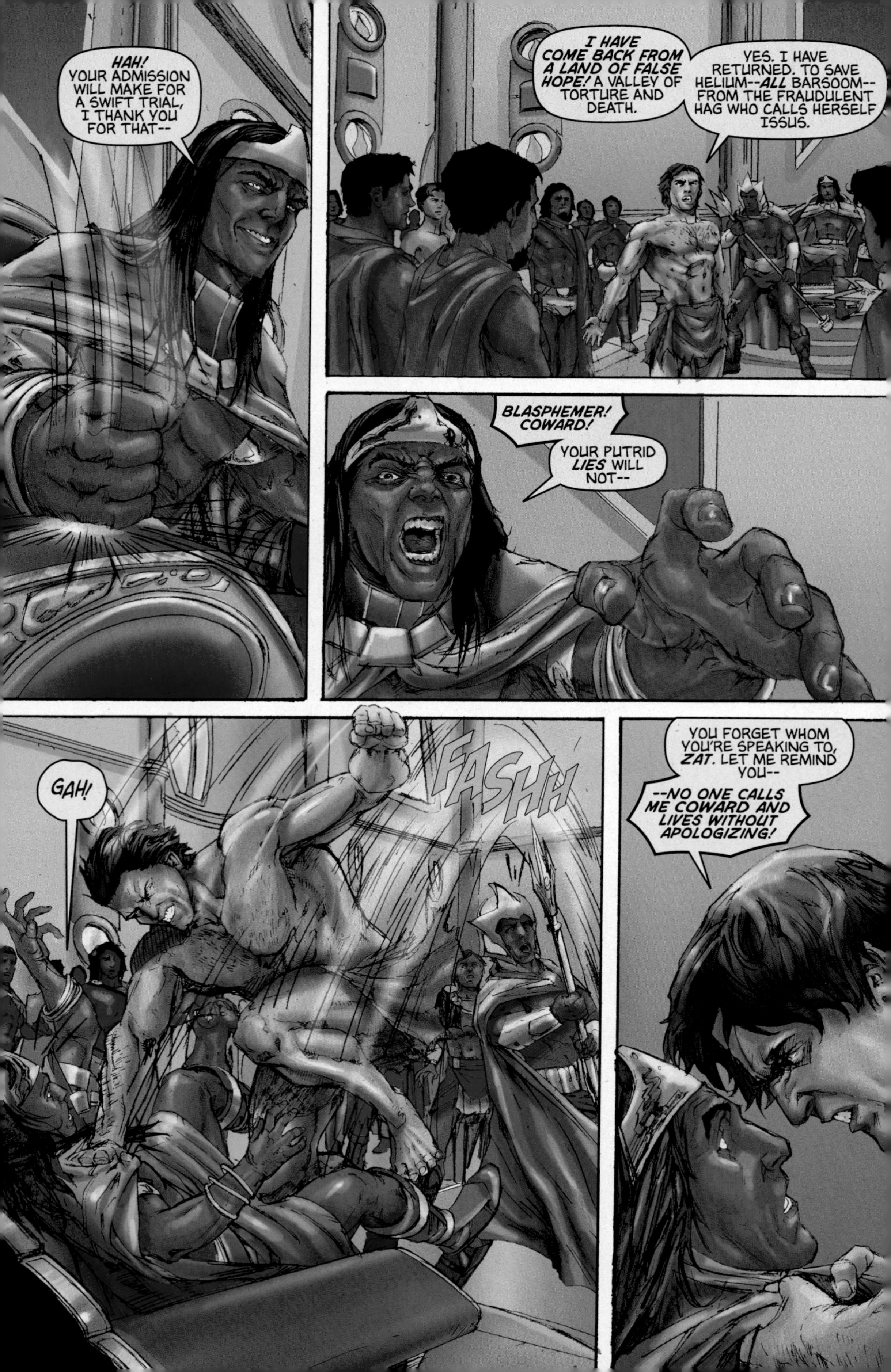
HAH! YOUR ADMISSION WILL MAKE FOR A SWIFT TRIAL, I THANK YOU FOR THAT--
I HAVE COME BACK FROM A LAND OF FALSE HOPE! A VALLEY OF TORTURE AND DEATH.
YES. I HAVE RETURNED. TO SAVE HELIUM--ALL BARSOOM--FROM THE FRAUDULENT HAG WHO CALLS HERSELF ISSUS.
BLASPHEMER! COWARD!
YOUR PUTRID LIES WILL NOT--
GAH!
FASHH
YOU FORGET WHOM YOU'RE SPEAKING TO, ZAT. LET ME REMIND YOU--
--NO ONE CALLS ME COWARD AND LIVES WITHOUT APOLOGIZING!

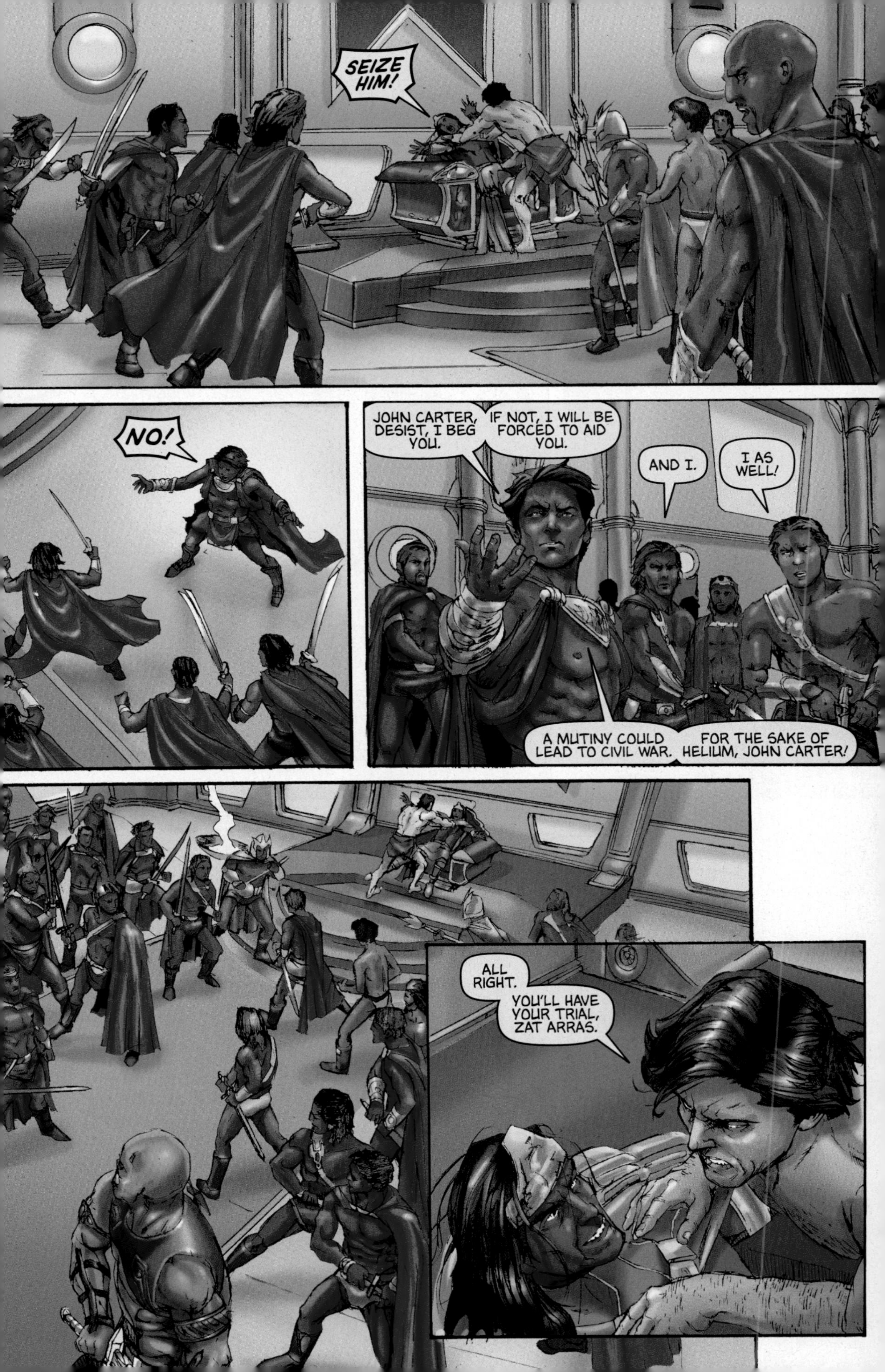
SEIZE HIM!
NO!
JOHN CARTER, DESIST, I BEG YOU.
IF NOT, I WILL BE FORCED TO AID YOU.
AND I.
I AS WELL!
A MUTINY COULD LEAD TO CIVIL WAR.
FOR THE SAKE OF HELIUM, JOHN CARTER!
ALL RIGHT.
YOU'LL HAVE YOUR TRIAL, ZAT ARRAS.

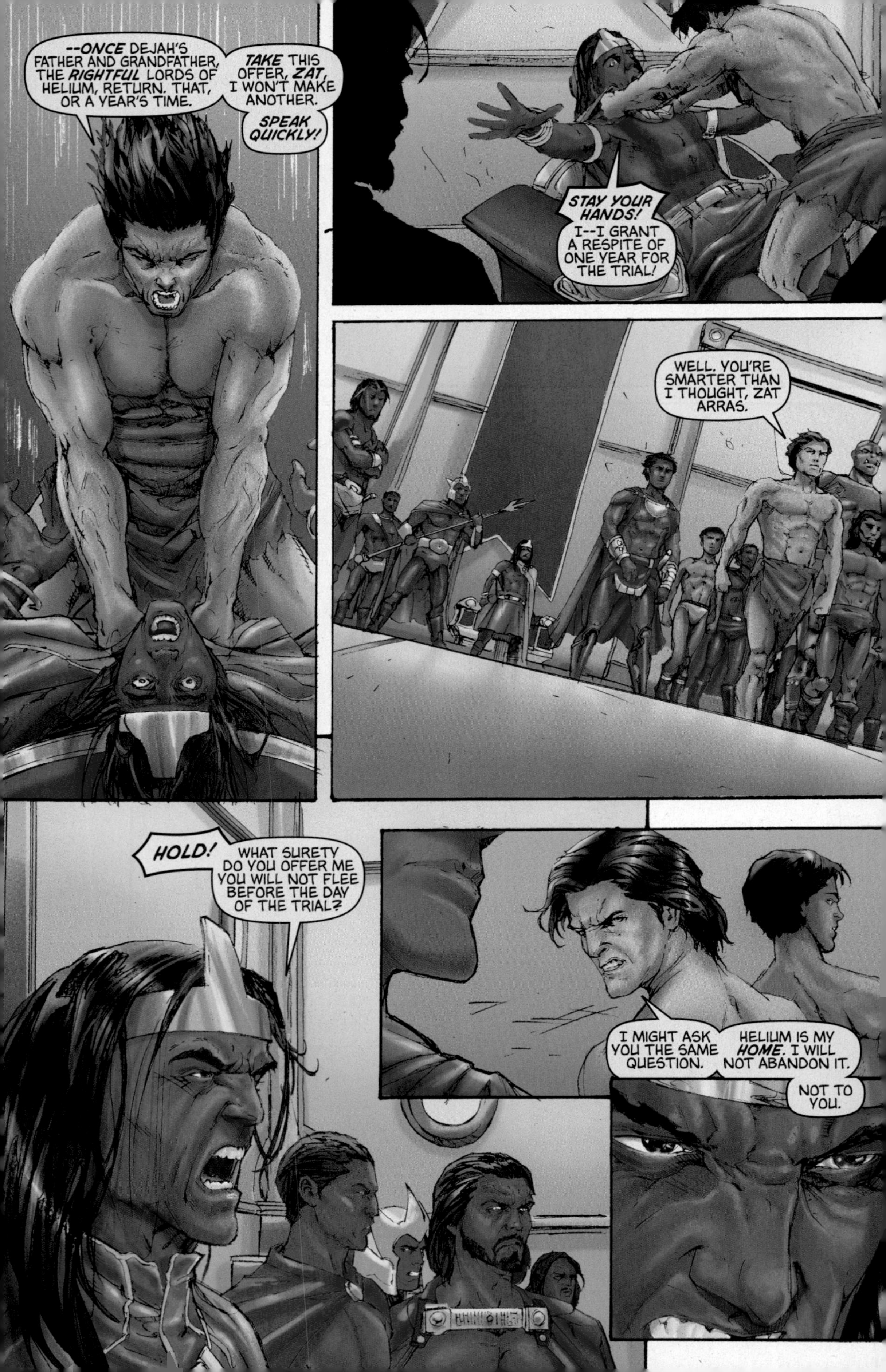
--ONCE DEJAH'S FATHER AND GRANDFATHER, THE RIGHTFUL LORDS OF HELIUM, RETURN. THAT, OR A YEAR'S TIME.
TAKE THIS OFFER, ZAT, I WON'T MAKE ANOTHER.
SPEAK QUICKLY!
STAY YOUR HANDS!
I--I GRANT A RESPITE OF ONE YEAR FOR THE TRIAL!
WELL. YOU'RE SMARTER THAN I THOUGHT, ZAT ARRAS.
HOLD!
WHAT SURETY DO YOU OFFER ME YOU WILL NOT FLEE BEFORE THE DAY OF THE TRIAL?
I MIGHT ASK YOU THE SAME QUESTION.
HELIUM IS MY HOME. I WILL NOT ABANDON IT.
NOT TO YOU.

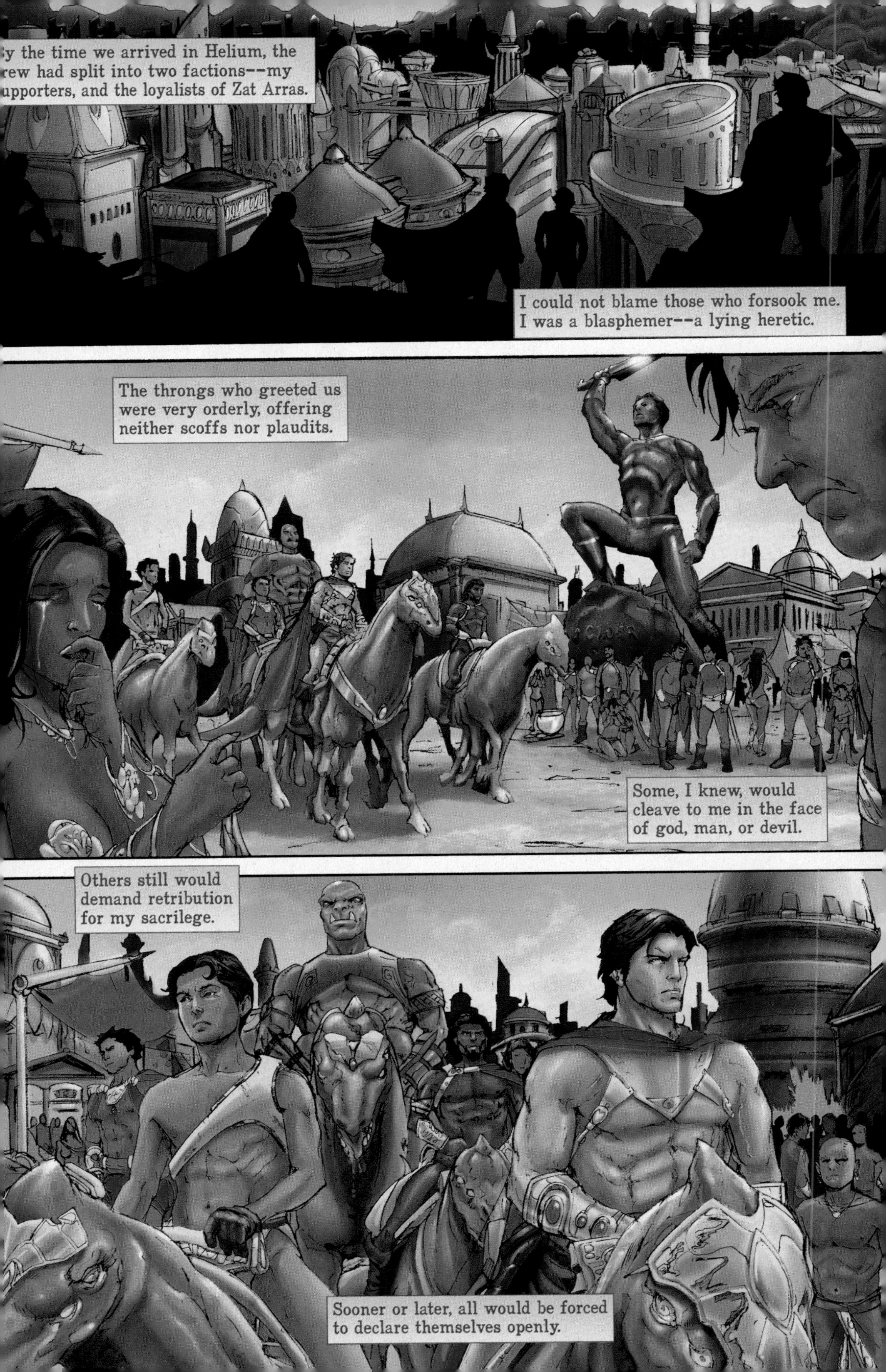
y the time we arrived in Helium, the
rew had split into two factions--my
upporters, and the loyalists of Zat Arras.
I could not blame those who forsook me.
I was a blasphemer--a lying heretic.
The throngs who greeted us
were very orderly, offering
neither scoffs nor plaudits.
Some, I knew, would
cleave to me in the face
of god, man, or devil.
Others still would
demand retribution
for my sacrilege.
Sooner or later, all would be forced
to declare themselves openly.

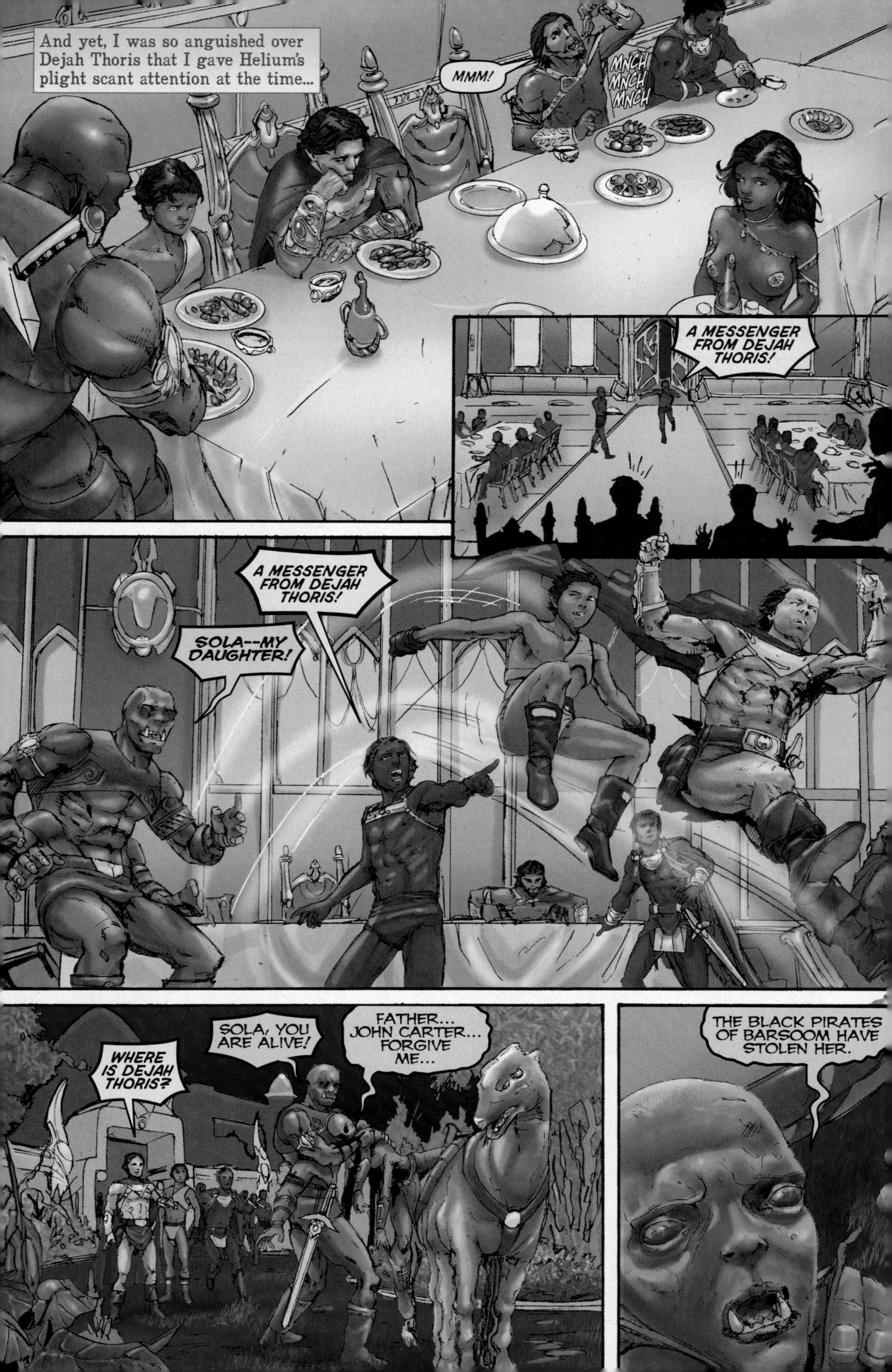
And yet, I was so anguished over Dejah Thoris that I gave Helium's plight scant attention at the time...
MMM!
MNCH MNCH MNCH
A MESSENGER FROM DEJAH THORIS!
A MESSENGER FROM DEJAH THORIS!
SOLA--MY DAUGHTER!
WHERE IS DEJAH THORIS?
SOLA, YOU ARE ALIVE!
FATHER... JOHN CARTER... FORGIVE ME...
THE BLACK PIRATES OF BARSOOM HAVE STOLEN HER.

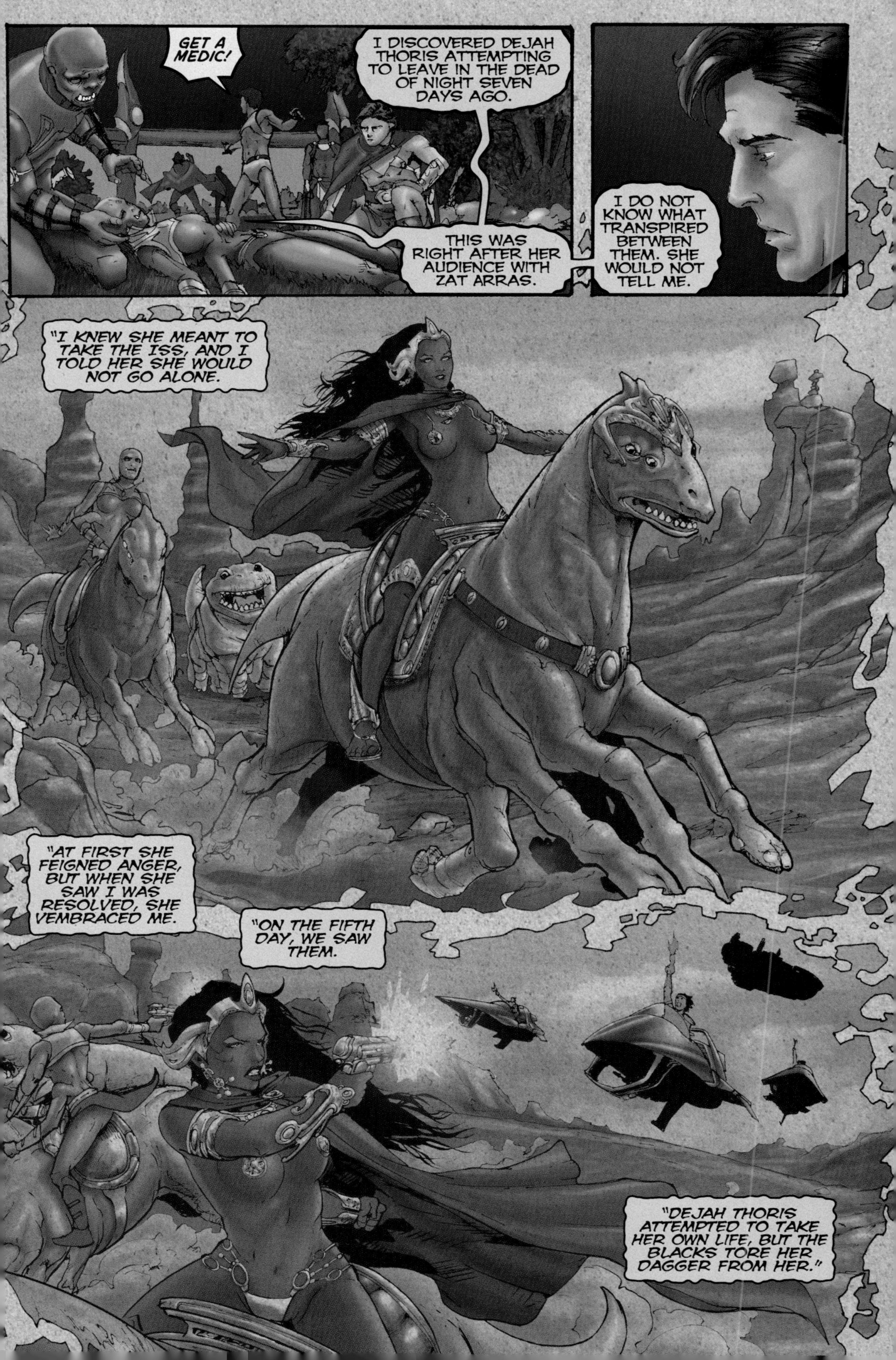
GET A MEDIC!
I DISCOVERED DEJAH THORIS ATTEMPTING TO LEAVE IN THE DEAD OF NIGHT SEVEN DAYS AGO.
THIS WAS RIGHT AFTER HER AUDIENCE WITH ZAT ARRAS.
I DO NOT KNOW WHAT TRANSPIRED BETWEEN THEM. SHE WOULD NOT TELL ME.
"I KNEW SHE MEANT TO TAKE THE ISS, AND I TOLD HER SHE WOULD NOT GO ALONE.
"AT FIRST SHE FEIGNED ANGER, BUT WHEN SHE SAW I WAS RESOLVED, SHE VEMBRACED ME.
"ON THE FIFTH DAY, WE SAW THEM.
"DEJAH THORIS ATTEMPTED TO TAKE HER OWN LIFE, BUT THE BLACKS TORE HER DAGGER FROM HER."

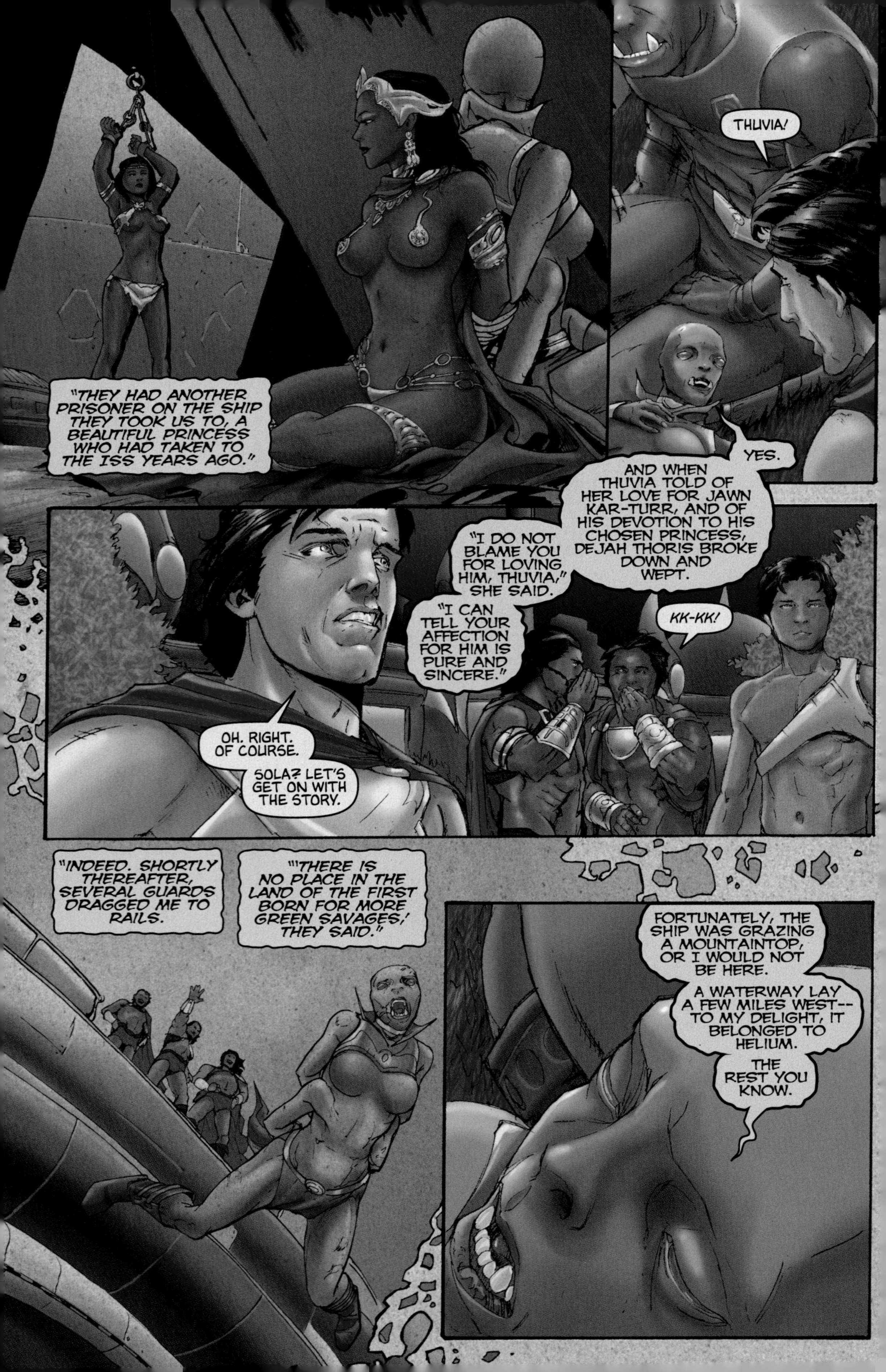
"THEY HAD ANOTHER PRISONER ON THE SHIP THEY TOOK US TO, A BEAUTIFUL PRINCESS WHO HAD TAKEN TO THE ISS YEARS AGO."
THUVIA!
YES.
AND WHEN THUVIA TOLD OF HER LOVE FOR JAWN KAR-TURR, AND OF HIS DEVOTION TO HIS CHOSEN PRINCESS, DEJAH THORIS BROKE DOWN AND WEPT.
"I DO NOT BLAME YOU FOR LOVING HIM, THUVIA," SHE SAID.
"I CAN TELL YOUR AFFECTION FOR HIM IS PURE AND SINCERE."
KK-KK!
OH. RIGHT. OF COURSE.
SOLA? LET'S GET ON WITH THE STORY.
"INDEED. SHORTLY THEREAFTER, SEVERAL GUARDS DRAGGED ME TO RAILS.
"'THERE IS NO PLACE IN THE LAND OF THE FIRST BORN FOR MORE GREEN SAVAGES,' THEY SAID."
FORTUNATELY, THE SHIP WAS GRAZING A MOUNTAINTOP, OR I WOULD NOT BE HERE.
A WATERWAY LAY A FEW MILES WEST-- TO MY DELIGHT, IT BELONGED TO HELIUM.
THE REST YOU KNOW.

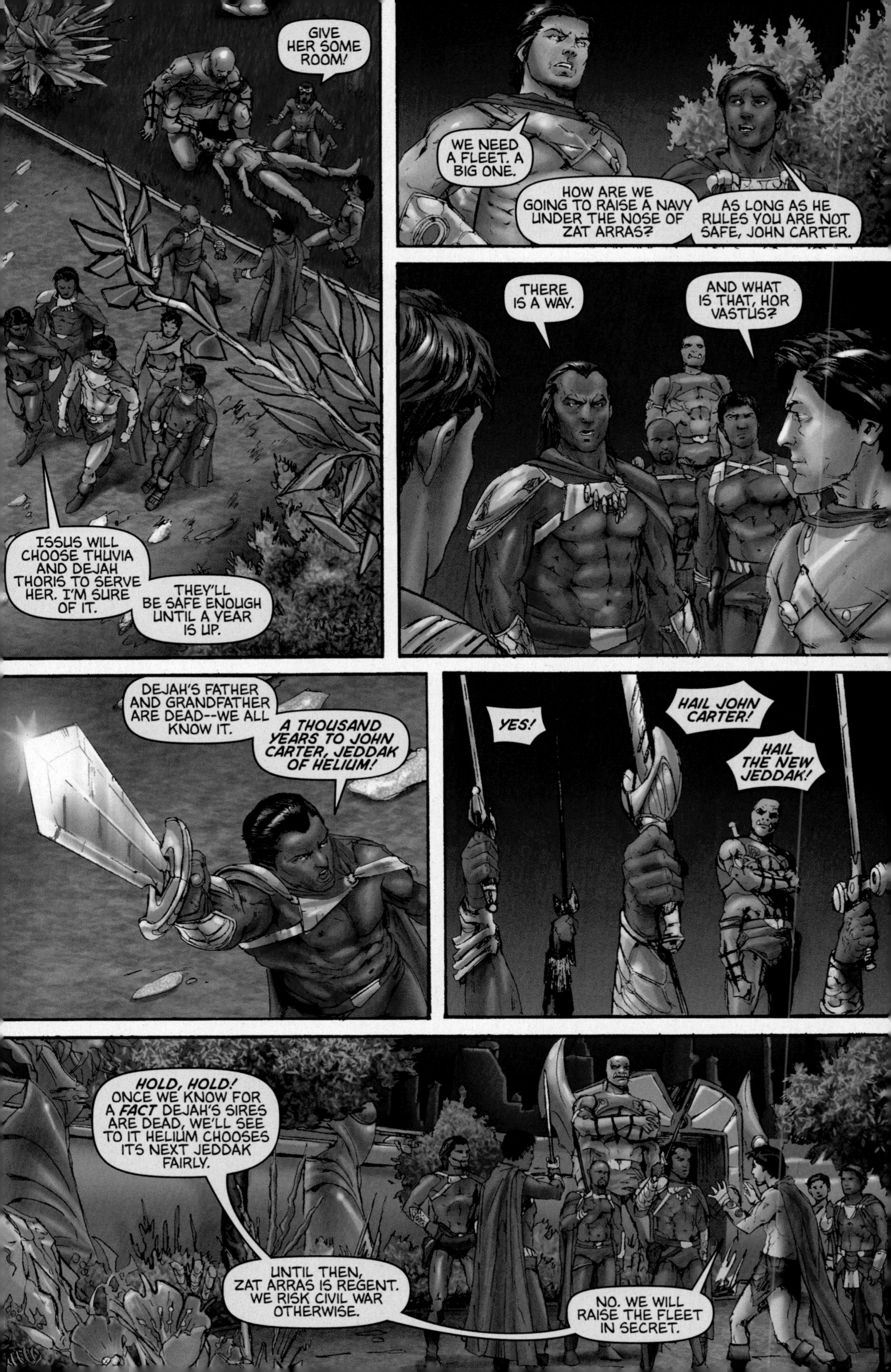
GIVE HER SOME ROOM!
ISSUS WILL CHOOSE THUVIA AND DEJAH THORIS TO SERVE HER. I'M SURE OF IT.
THEY'LL BE SAFE ENOUGH UNTIL A YEAR IS UP.
WE NEED A FLEET. A BIG ONE.
HOW ARE WE GOING TO RAISE A NAVY UNDER THE NOSE OF ZAT ARRAS?
AS LONG AS HE RULES YOU ARE NOT SAFE, JOHN CARTER.
THERE IS A WAY.
AND WHAT IS THAT, HOR VASTUS?
DEJAH'S FATHER AND GRANDFATHER ARE DEAD--WE ALL KNOW IT.
A THOUSAND YEARS TO JOHN CARTER, JEDDAK OF HELIUM!
YES!
HAIL JOHN CARTER!
HAIL THE NEW JEDDAK!
HOLD, HOLD! ONCE WE KNOW FOR A FACT DEJAH'S SIRES ARE DEAD, WE'LL SEE TO IT HELIUM CHOOSES ITS NEXT JEDDAK FAIRLY.
UNTIL THEN, ZAT ARRAS IS REGENT. WE RISK CIVIL WAR OTHERWISE.
NO. WE WILL RAISE THE FLEET IN SECRET.

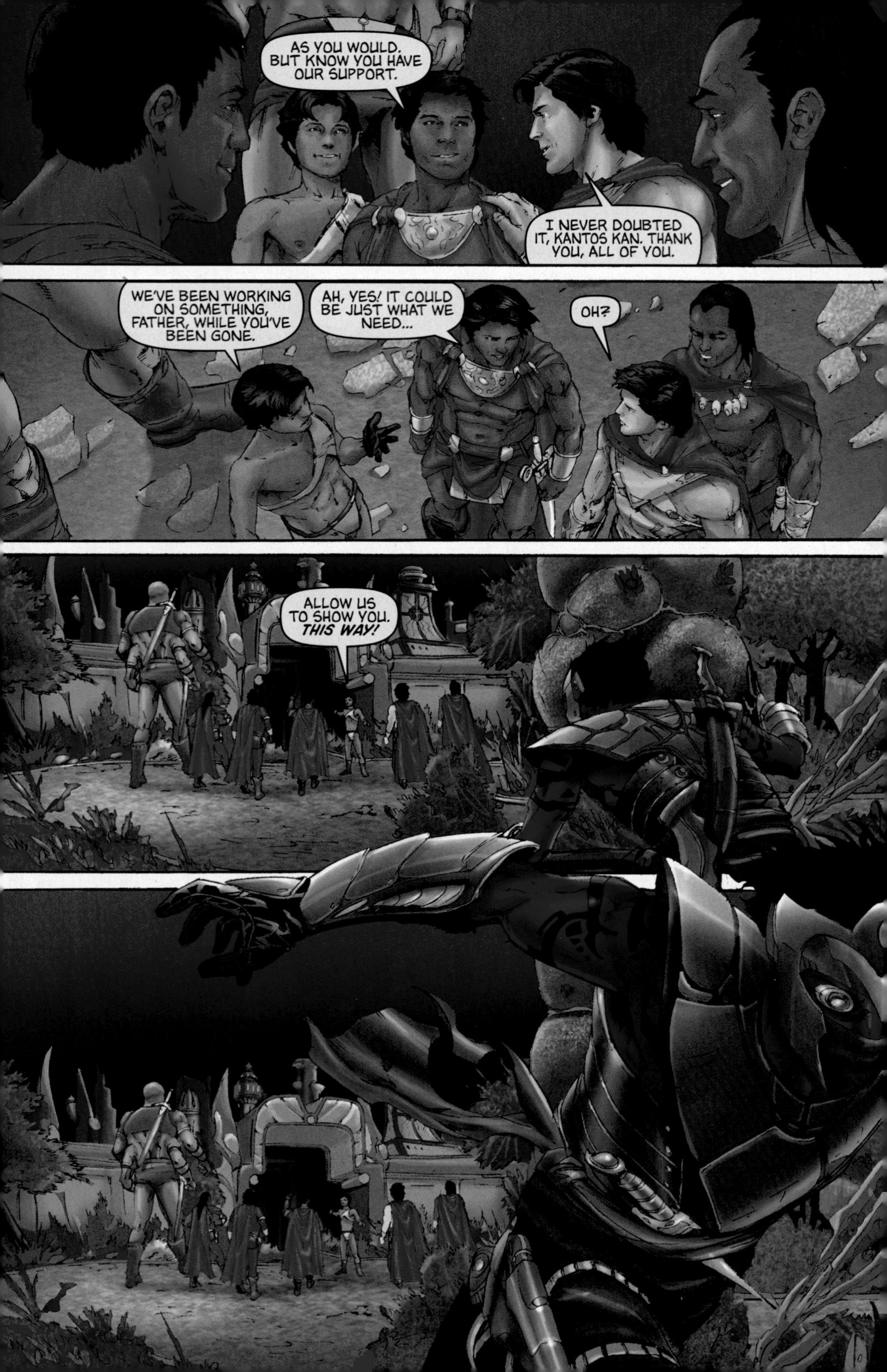
AS YOU WOULD. BUT KNOW YOU HAVE OUR SUPPORT.
I NEVER DOUBTED IT, KANTOS KAN. THANK YOU, ALL OF YOU.
WE'VE BEEN WORKING ON SOMETHING, FATHER, WHILE YOU'VE BEEN GONE.
AH, YES! IT COULD BE JUST WHAT WE NEED...
OH?
ALLOW US TO SHOW YOU. THIS WAY!

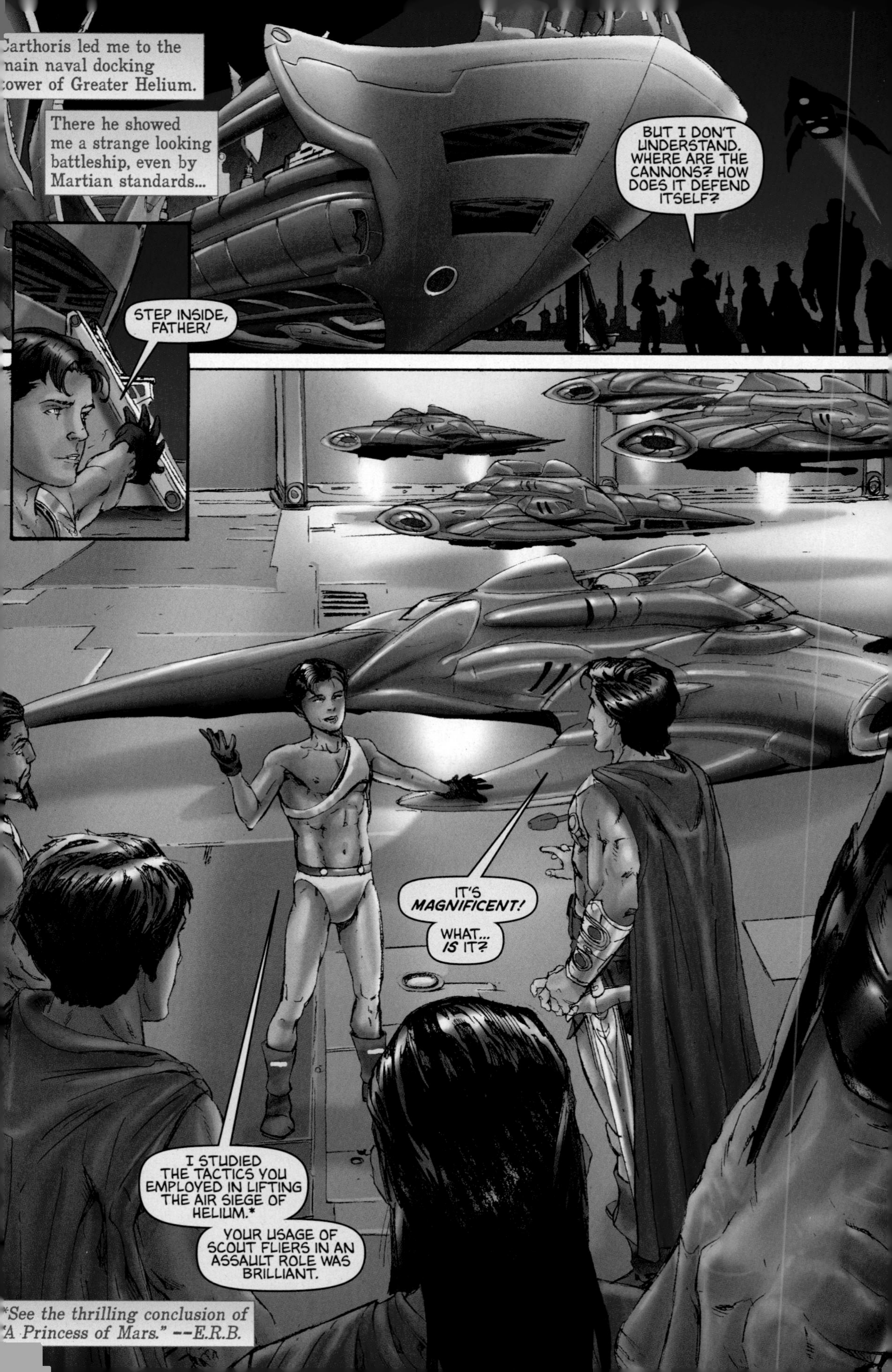
Carthoris led me to the main naval docking tower of Greater Helium.
There he showed me a strange looking battleship, even by Martian standards...
BUT I DON'T UNDERSTAND. WHERE ARE THE CANNONS? HOW DOES IT DEFEND ITSELF?
STEP INSIDE, FATHER!
IT'S MAGNIFICENT!
WHAT... IS IT?
I STUDIED THE TACTICS YOU EMPLOYED IN LIFTING THE AIR SIEGE OF HELIUM.*
YOUR USAGE OF SCOUT FLIERS IN AN ASSAULT ROLE WAS BRILLIANT.
*See the thrilling conclusion of "A Princess of Mars." --E.R.B.

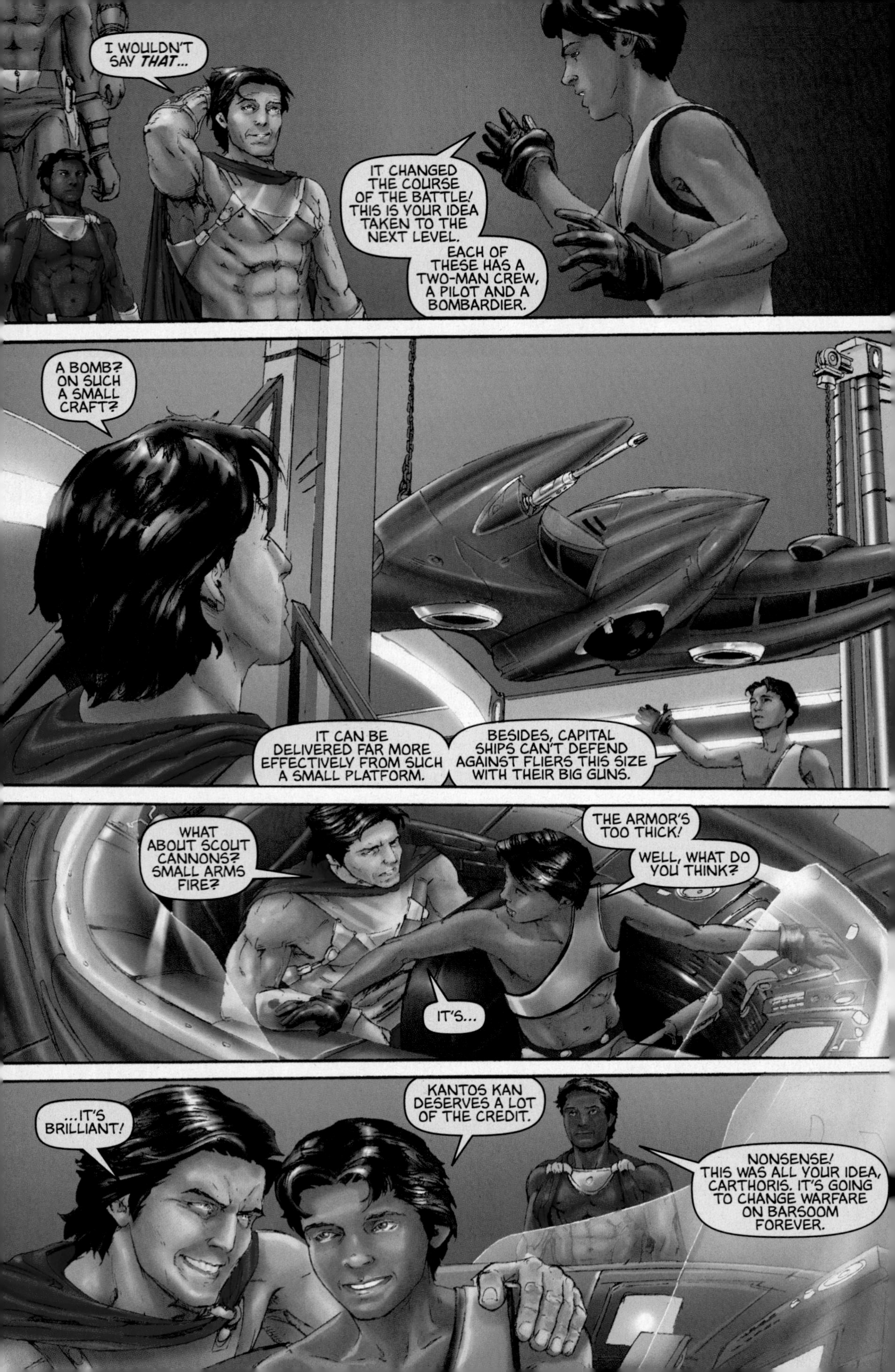
I WOULDN'T SAY *THAT*...
IT CHANGED THE COURSE OF THE BATTLE! THIS IS YOUR IDEA TAKEN TO THE NEXT LEVEL.
EACH OF THESE HAS A TWO-MAN CREW, A PILOT AND A BOMBARDIER.
A BOMB? ON SUCH A SMALL CRAFT?
IT CAN BE DELIVERED FAR MORE EFFECTIVELY FROM SUCH A SMALL PLATFORM.
BESIDES, CAPITAL SHIPS CAN'T DEFEND AGAINST FLIERS THIS SIZE WITH THEIR BIG GUNS.
WHAT ABOUT SCOUT CANNONS? SMALL ARMS FIRE?
THE ARMOR'S TOO THICK!
WELL, WHAT DO YOU THINK?
IT'S...
...IT'S BRILLIANT!
KANTOS KAN DESERVES A LOT OF THE CREDIT.
NONSENSE! THIS WAS ALL YOUR IDEA, CARTHORIS. IT'S GOING TO CHANGE WARFARE ON BARSOOM FOREVER.

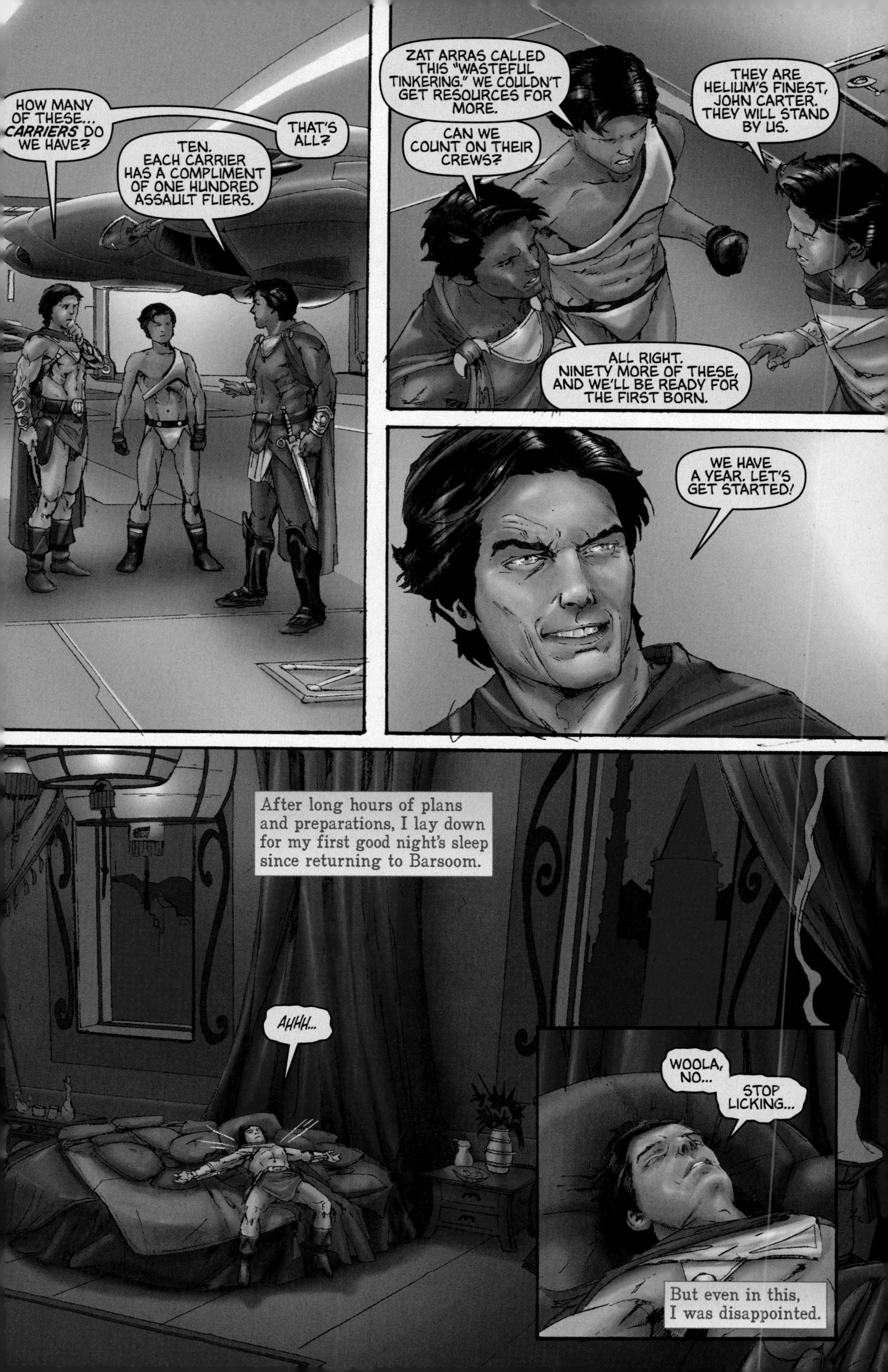
HOW MANY OF THESE... CARRIERS DO WE HAVE?
TEN. EACH CARRIER HAS A COMPLIMENT OF ONE HUNDRED ASSAULT FLIERS.
THAT'S ALL?
ZAT ARRAS CALLED THIS "WASTEFUL TINKERING." WE COULDN'T GET RESOURCES FOR MORE.
CAN WE COUNT ON THEIR CREWS?
THEY ARE HELIUM'S FINEST, JOHN CARTER. THEY WILL STAND BY US.
ALL RIGHT. NINETY MORE OF THESE, AND WE'LL BE READY FOR THE FIRST BORN.
WE HAVE A YEAR. LET'S GET STARTED!
After long hours of plans and preparations, I lay down for my first good night's sleep since returning to Barsoom.
AHHH...
WOOLA, NO...
STOP LICKING...
But even in this, I was disappointed.

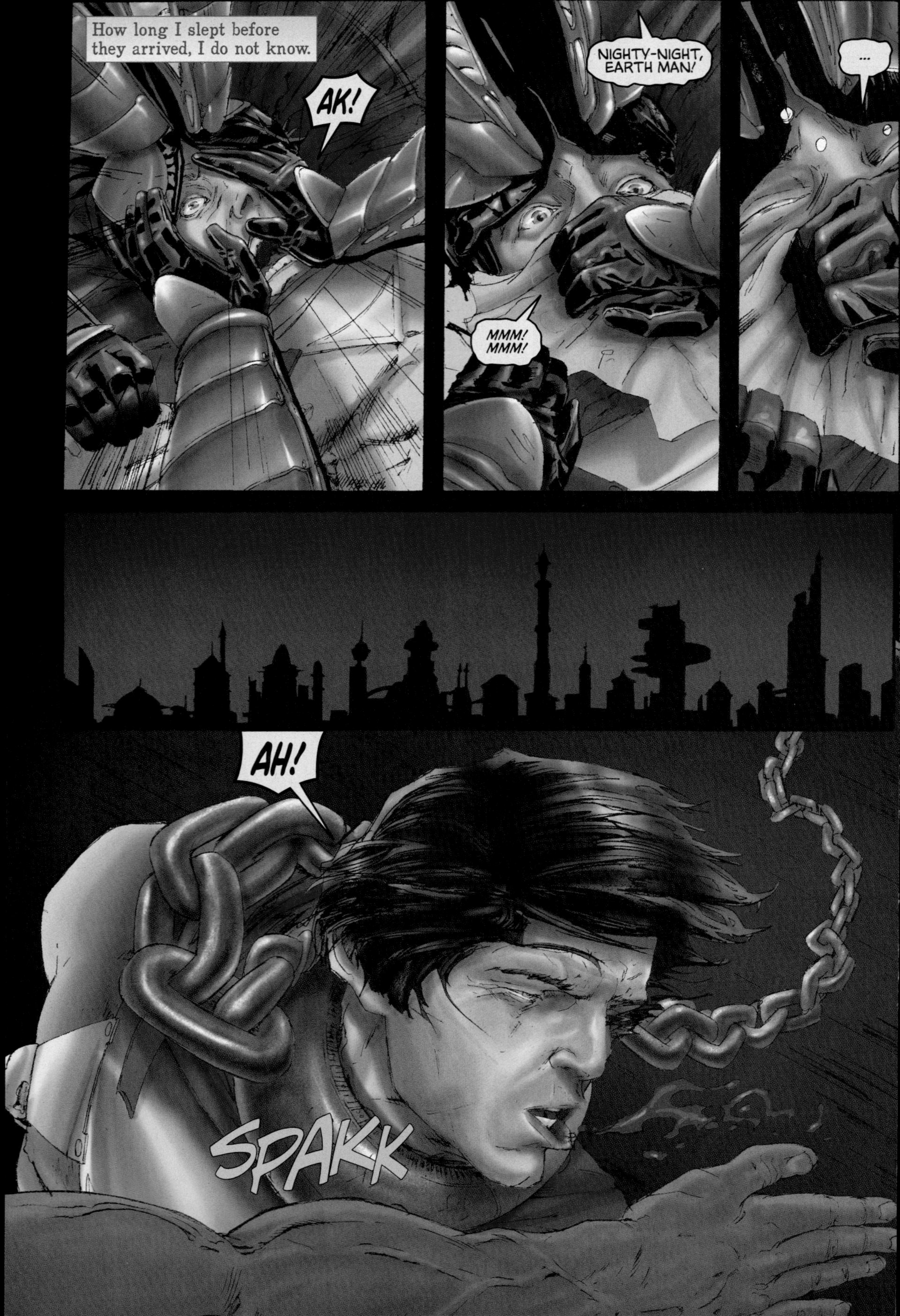
How long I slept before they arrived, I do not know.
AK!
NIGHTY-NIGHT, EARTH MAN!
MMM! MMM!
...
AH!
SPAKK

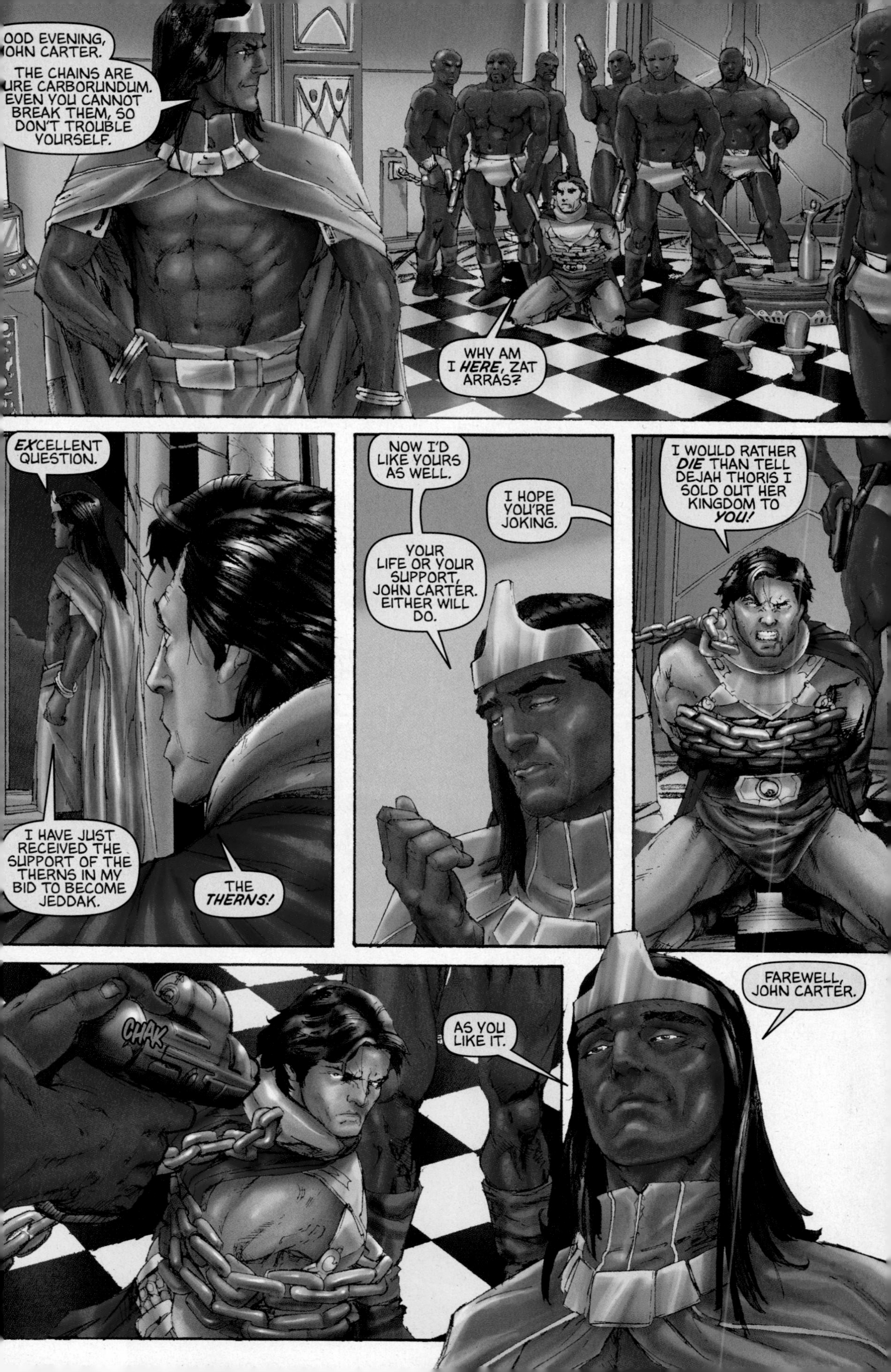
OOD EVENING, JOHN CARTER.
THE CHAINS ARE URE CARBORUNDUM. EVEN YOU CANNOT BREAK THEM, SO DON'T TROUBLE YOURSELF.
WHY AM I *HERE*, ZAT ARRAS?
*EX*CELLENT QUESTION.
I HAVE JUST RECEIVED THE SUPPORT OF THE THERNS IN MY BID TO BECOME JEDDAK.
THE *THERNS!*
NOW I'D LIKE YOURS AS WELL.
I HOPE YOU'RE JOKING.
YOUR LIFE OR YOUR SUPPORT, JOHN CARTER. EITHER WILL DO.
I WOULD RATHER *DIE* THAN TELL DEJAH THORIS I SOLD OUT HER KINGDOM TO *YOU!*
CHAK
AS YOU LIKE IT.
FAREWELL, JOHN CARTER.

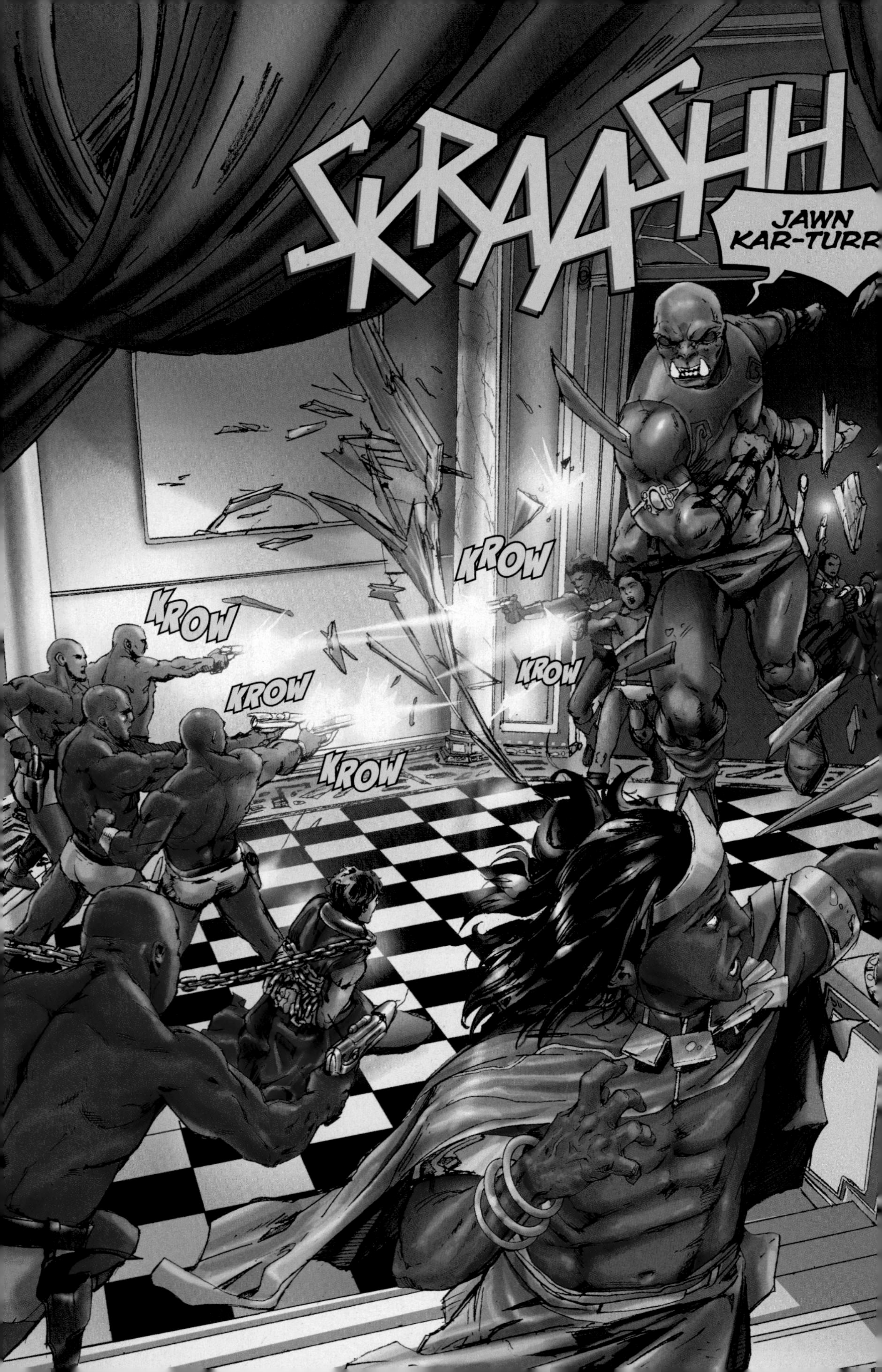
SKRAASHH
JAWN KAR-TURR
KROW
KROW
KROW
KROW
KROW

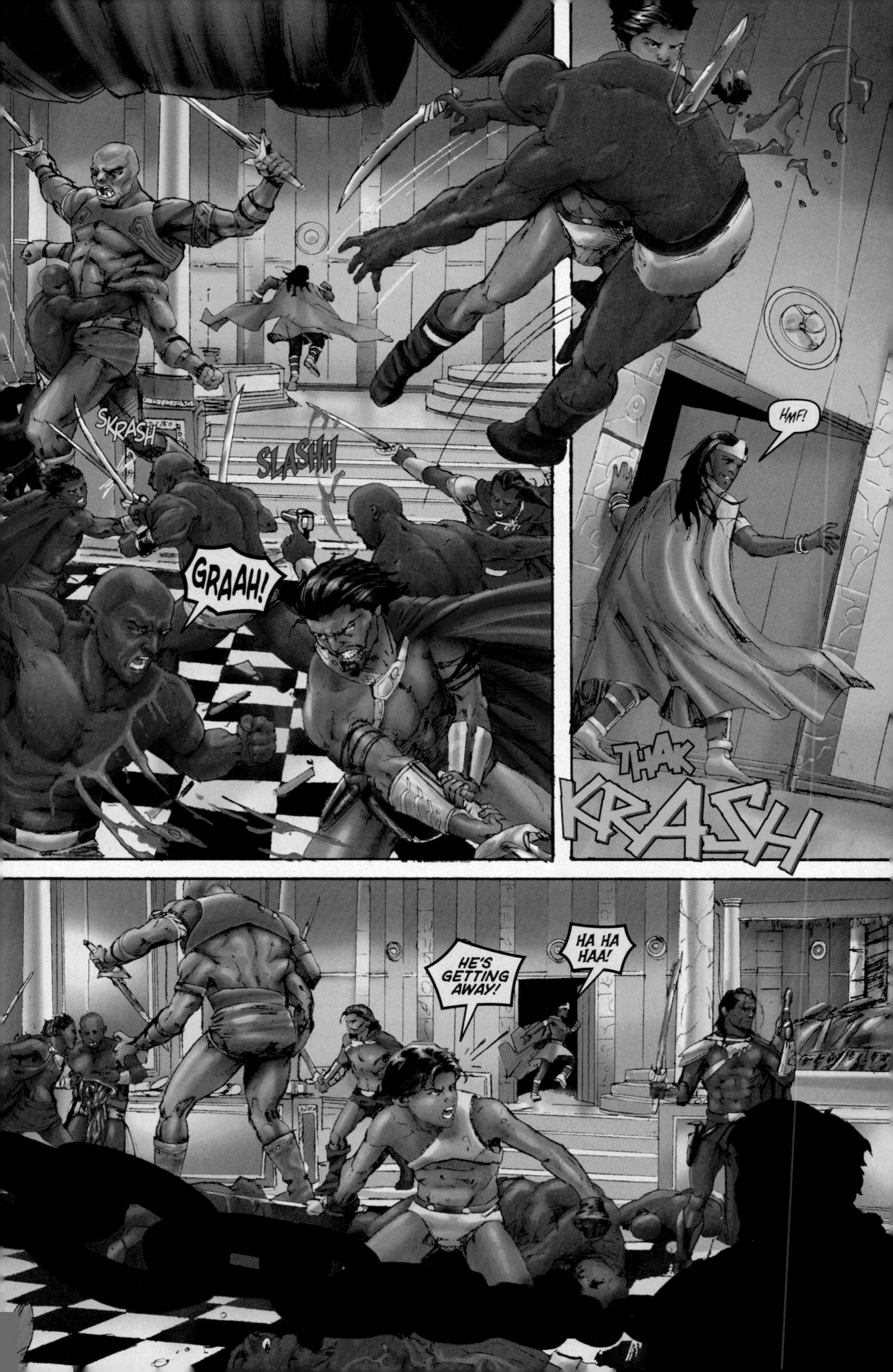
SKRASH
SLASHH
GRAAH!
HMF!
THAK
KRASH
HE'S GETTING AWAY!
HA HA HAA!

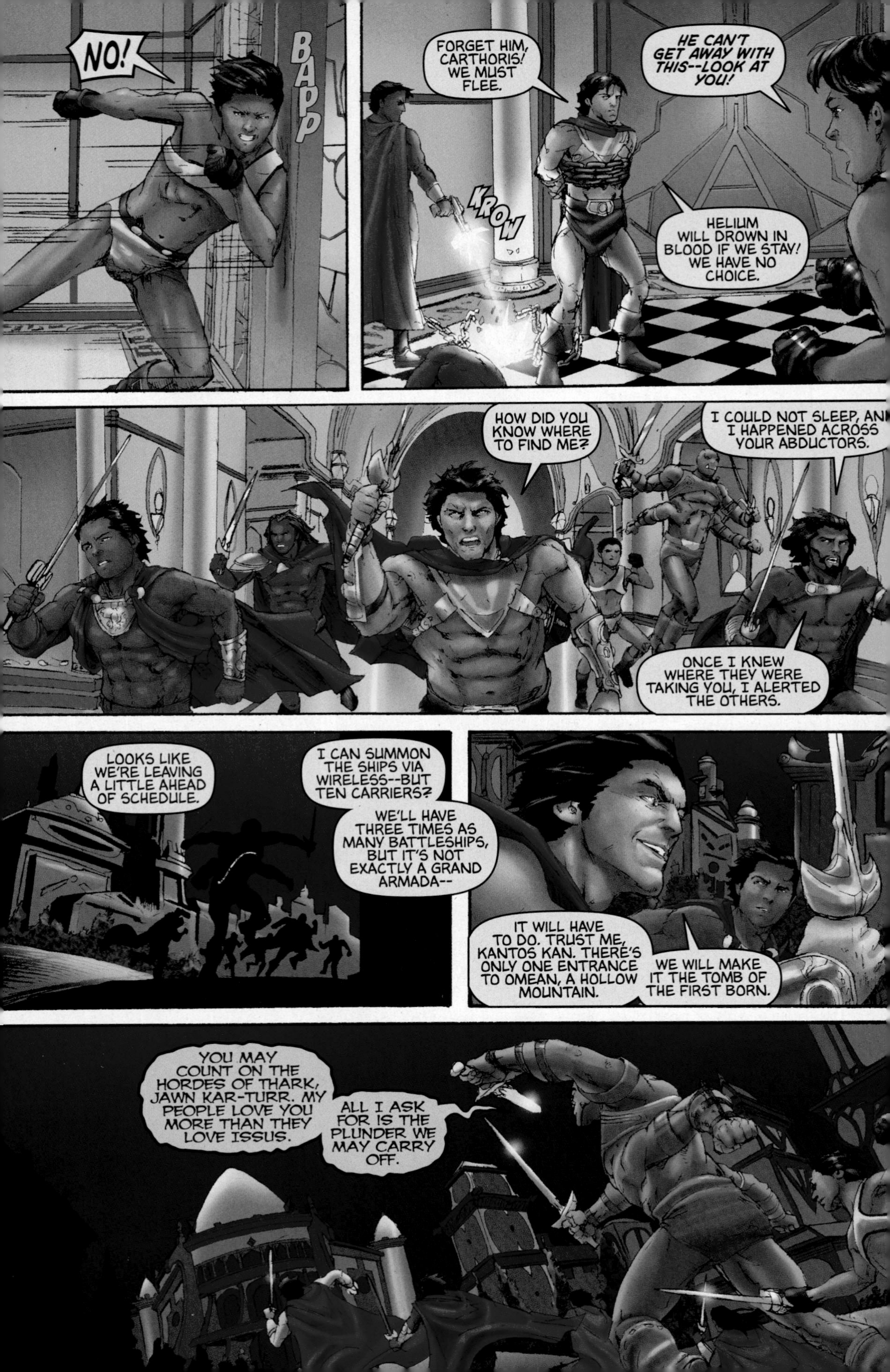
NO!
BAPP
FORGET HIM, CARTHORIS! WE MUST FLEE.
HE CAN'T GET AWAY WITH THIS--LOOK AT YOU!
KROW
HELIUM WILL DROWN IN BLOOD IF WE STAY! WE HAVE NO CHOICE.
HOW DID YOU KNOW WHERE TO FIND ME?
I COULD NOT SLEEP, AN
I HAPPENED ACROSS YOUR ABDUCTORS.
ONCE I KNEW WHERE THEY WERE TAKING YOU, I ALERTED THE OTHERS.
LOOKS LIKE WE'RE LEAVING A LITTLE AHEAD OF SCHEDULE.
I CAN SUMMON THE SHIPS VIA WIRELESS--BUT TEN CARRIERS?
WE'LL HAVE THREE TIMES AS MANY BATTLESHIPS, BUT IT'S NOT EXACTLY A GRAND ARMADA--
IT WILL HAVE TO DO. TRUST ME, KANTOS KAN. THERE'S ONLY ONE ENTRANCE TO OMEAN, A HOLLOW MOUNTAIN.
WE WILL MAKE IT THE TOMB OF THE FIRST BORN.
YOU MAY COUNT ON THE HORDES OF THARK, JAWN KAR-TURR. MY PEOPLE LOVE YOU MORE THAN THEY LOVE ISSUS.
ALL I ASK FOR IS THE PLUNDER WE MAY CARRY OFF.

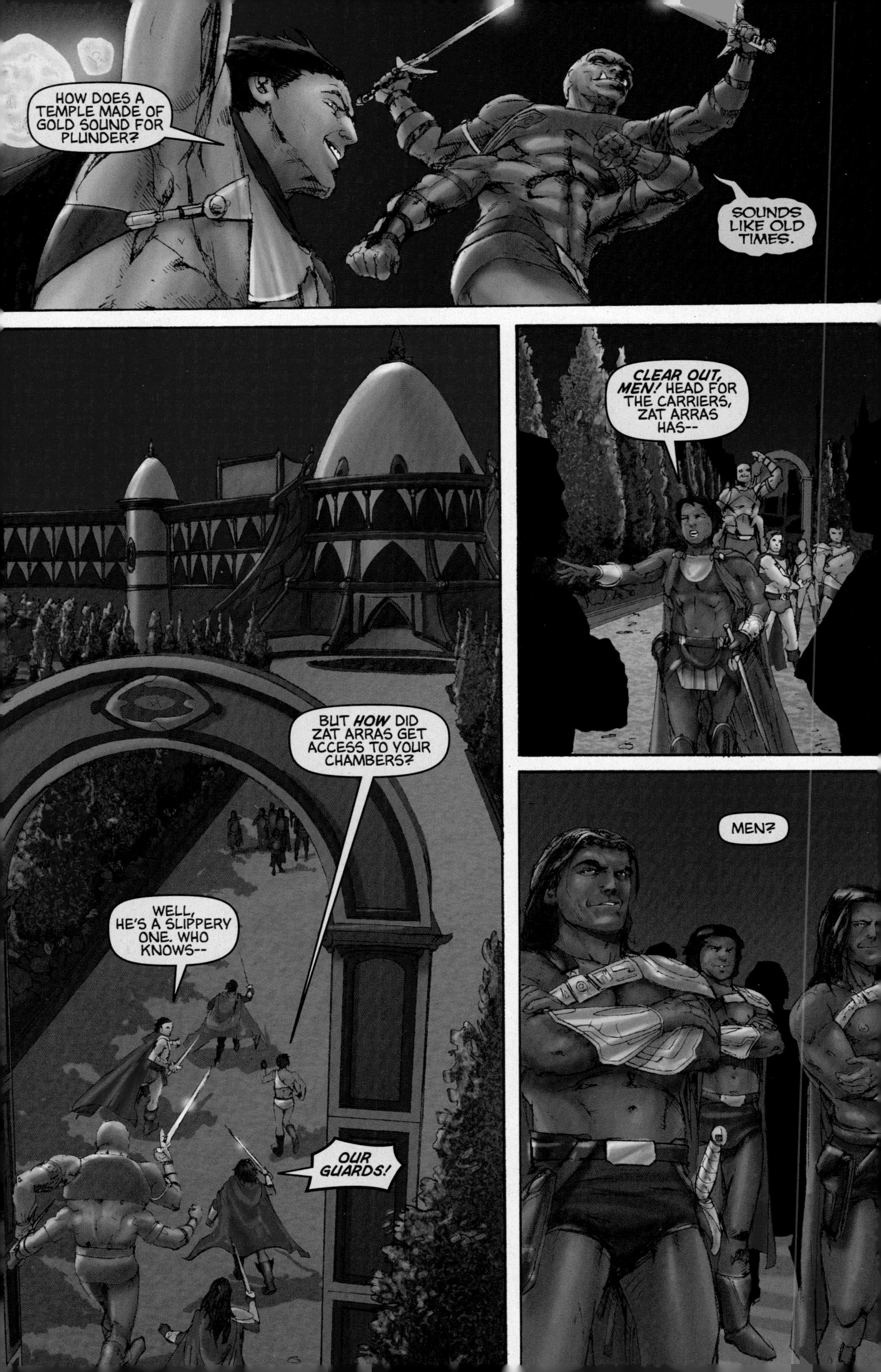
HOW DOES A TEMPLE MADE OF GOLD SOUND FOR PLUNDER?
SOUNDS LIKE OLD TIMES.
BUT *HOW* DID ZAT ARRAS GET ACCESS TO YOUR CHAMBERS?
WELL, HE'S A SLIPPERY ONE. WHO KNOWS--
OUR GUARDS!
CLEAR OUT, MEN! HEAD FOR THE CARRIERS, ZAT ARRAS HAS--
MEN?

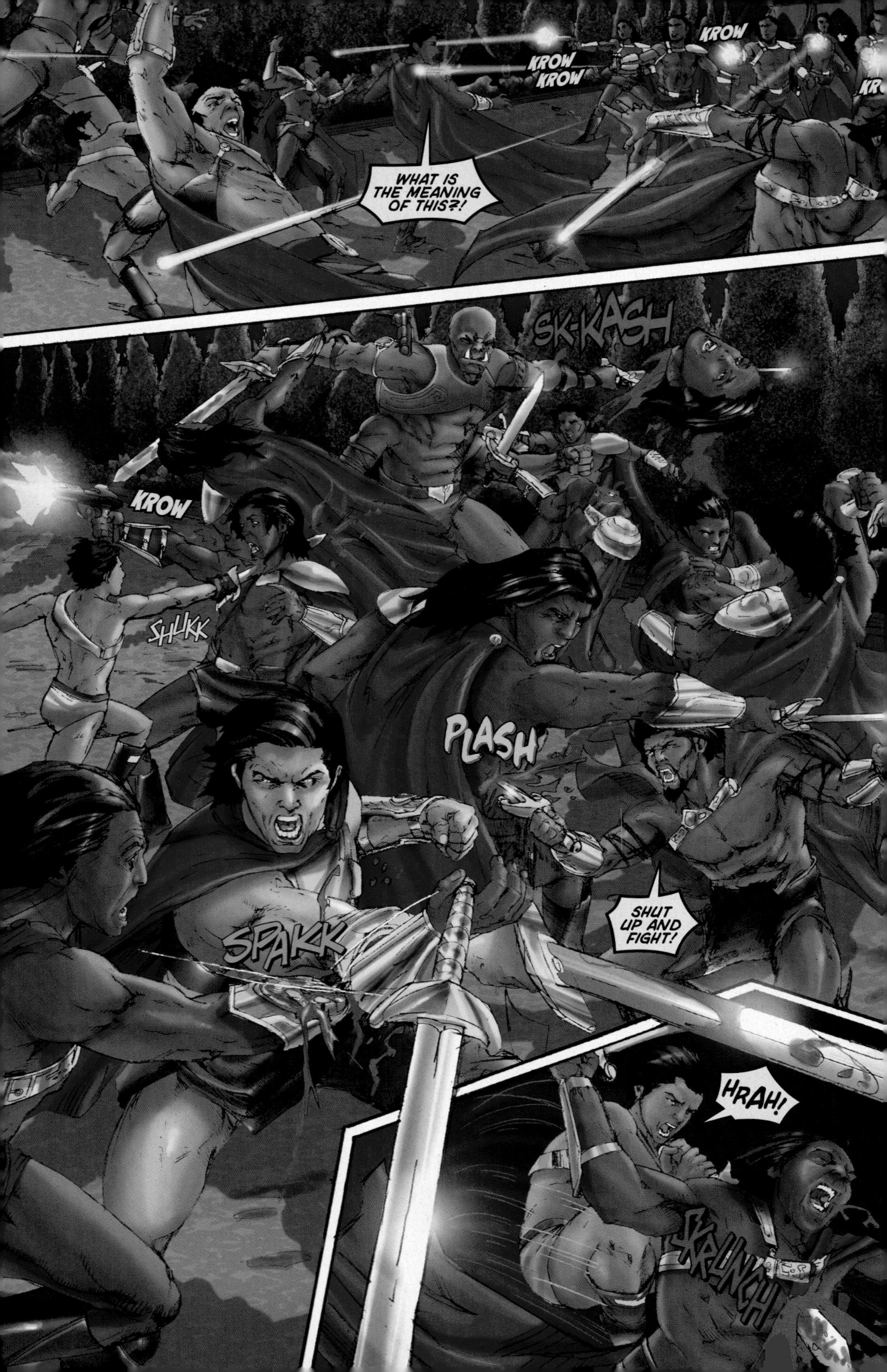
KROW
KROW
KROW
KRO
WHAT IS THE MEANING OF THIS?!
SK-KASH
KROW
SHUKK
PLASH
SPAKK
SHUT UP AND FIGHT!
HRAH!
SKRUNCH

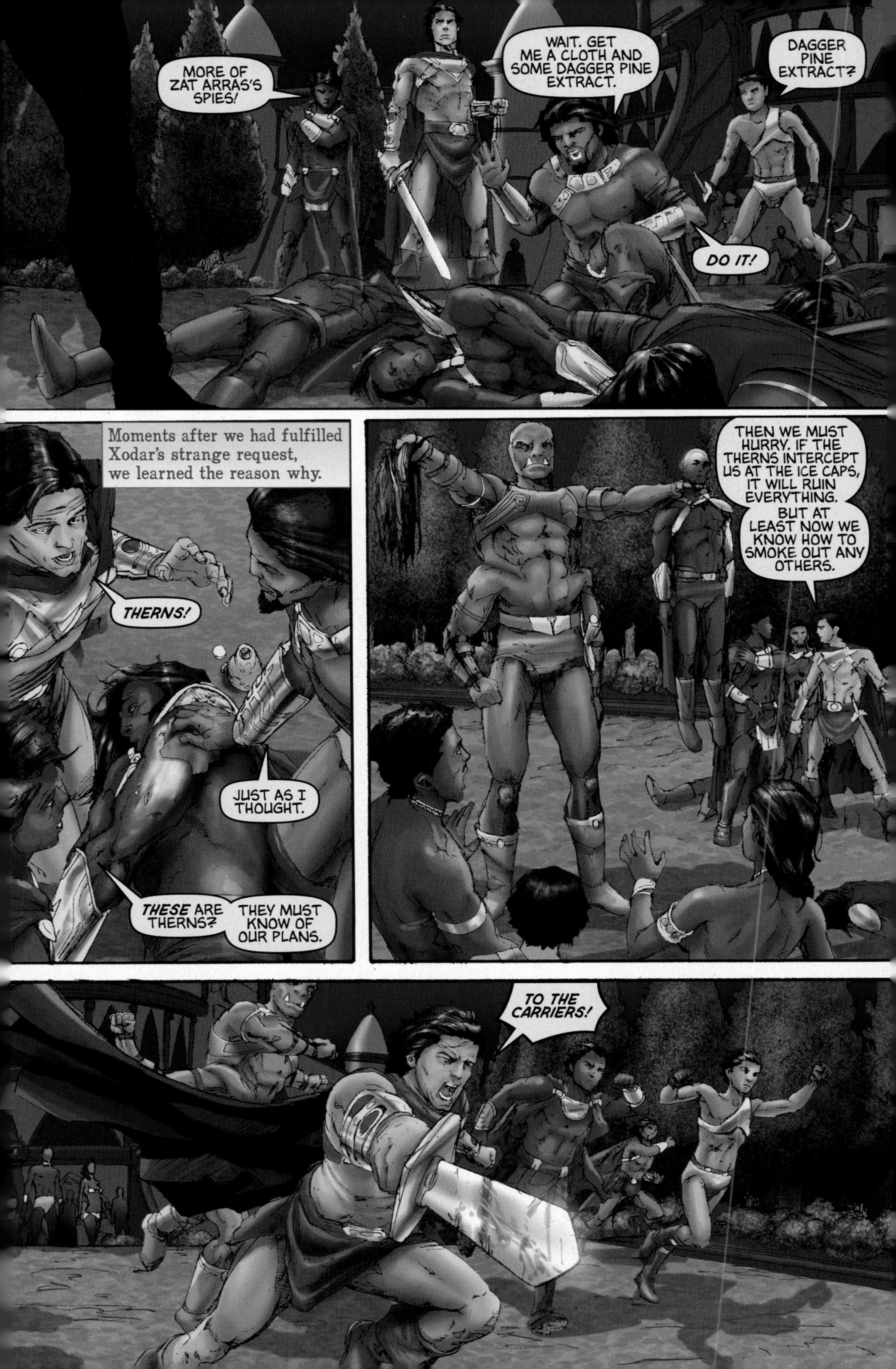
MORE OF ZAT ARRAS'S SPIES!
WAIT. GET ME A CLOTH AND SOME DAGGER PINE EXTRACT.
DAGGER PINE EXTRACT?
DO IT!
Moments after we had fulfilled Xodar's strange request, we learned the reason why.
THERNS!
JUST AS I THOUGHT.
THESE ARE THERNS?
THEY MUST KNOW OF OUR PLANS.
THEN WE MUST HURRY. IF THE THERNS INTERCEPT US AT THE ICE CAPS, IT WILL RUIN EVERYTHING.
BUT AT LEAST NOW WE KNOW HOW TO SMOKE OUT ANY OTHERS.
TO THE CARRIERS!

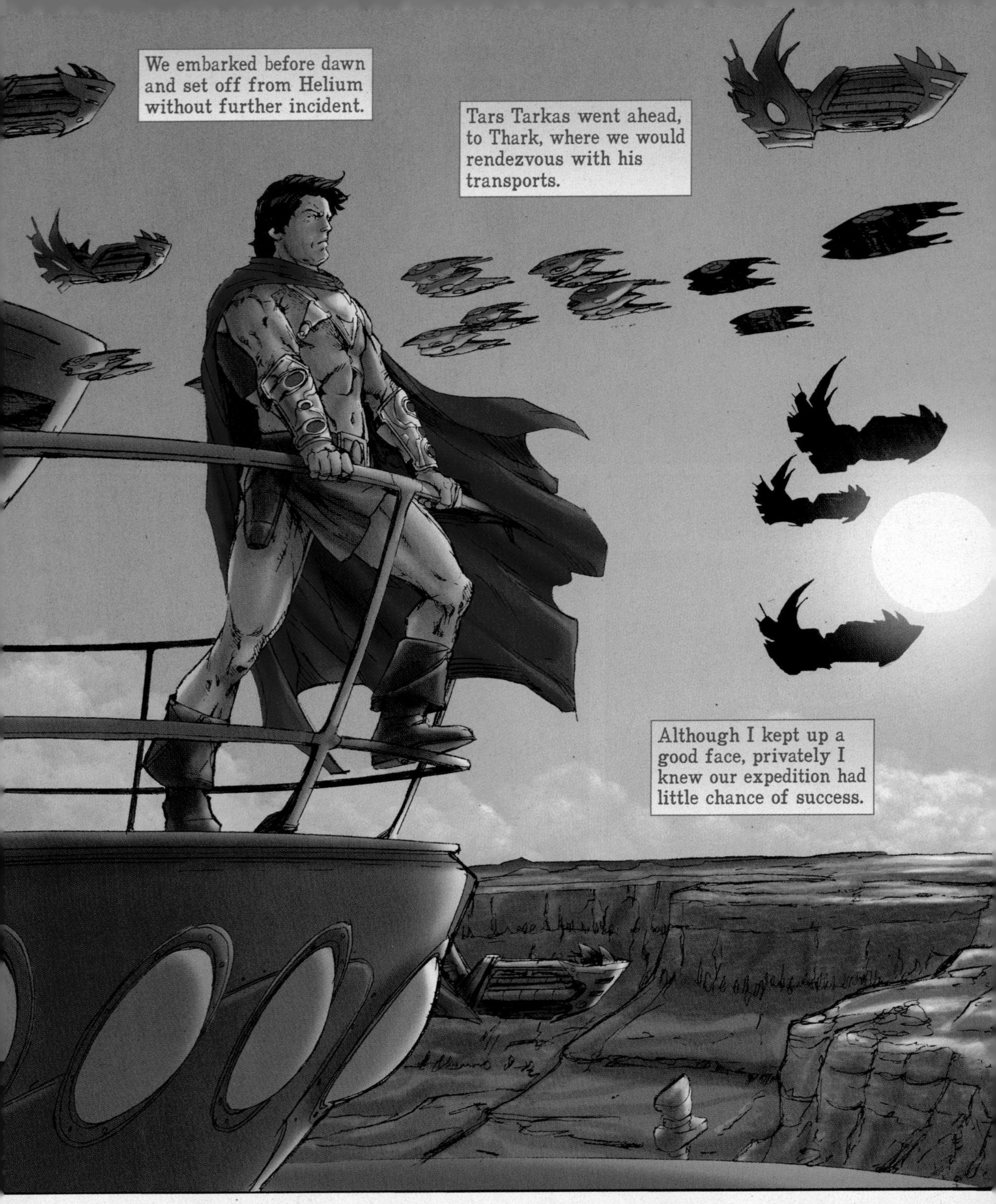
We embarked before dawn and set off from Helium without further incident.
Tars Tarkas went ahead, to Thark, where we would rendezvous with his transports.
Although I kept up a good face, privately I knew our expedition had little chance of success.

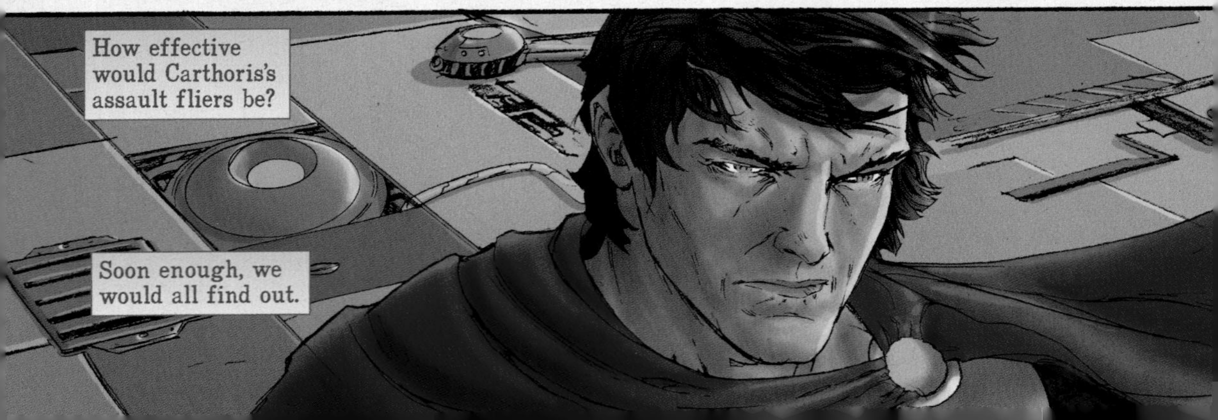
How effective would Carthoris's assault fliers be?
Soon enough, we would all find out.

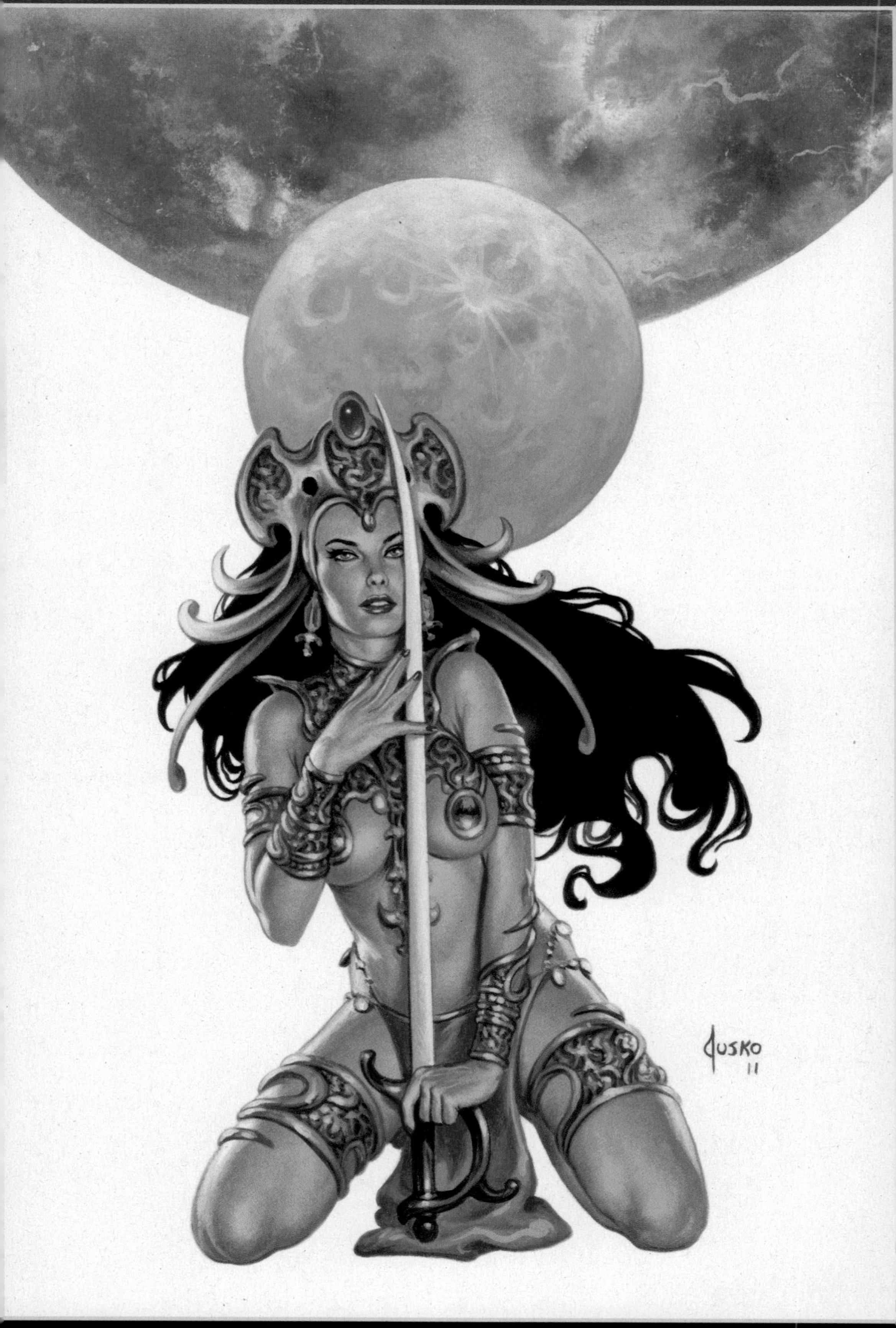
JUSKO
11

GODS OF MARS PART SIX:
THROUGH FLOOD AND FLAME • Issue #18 cover by JOE JUSKO

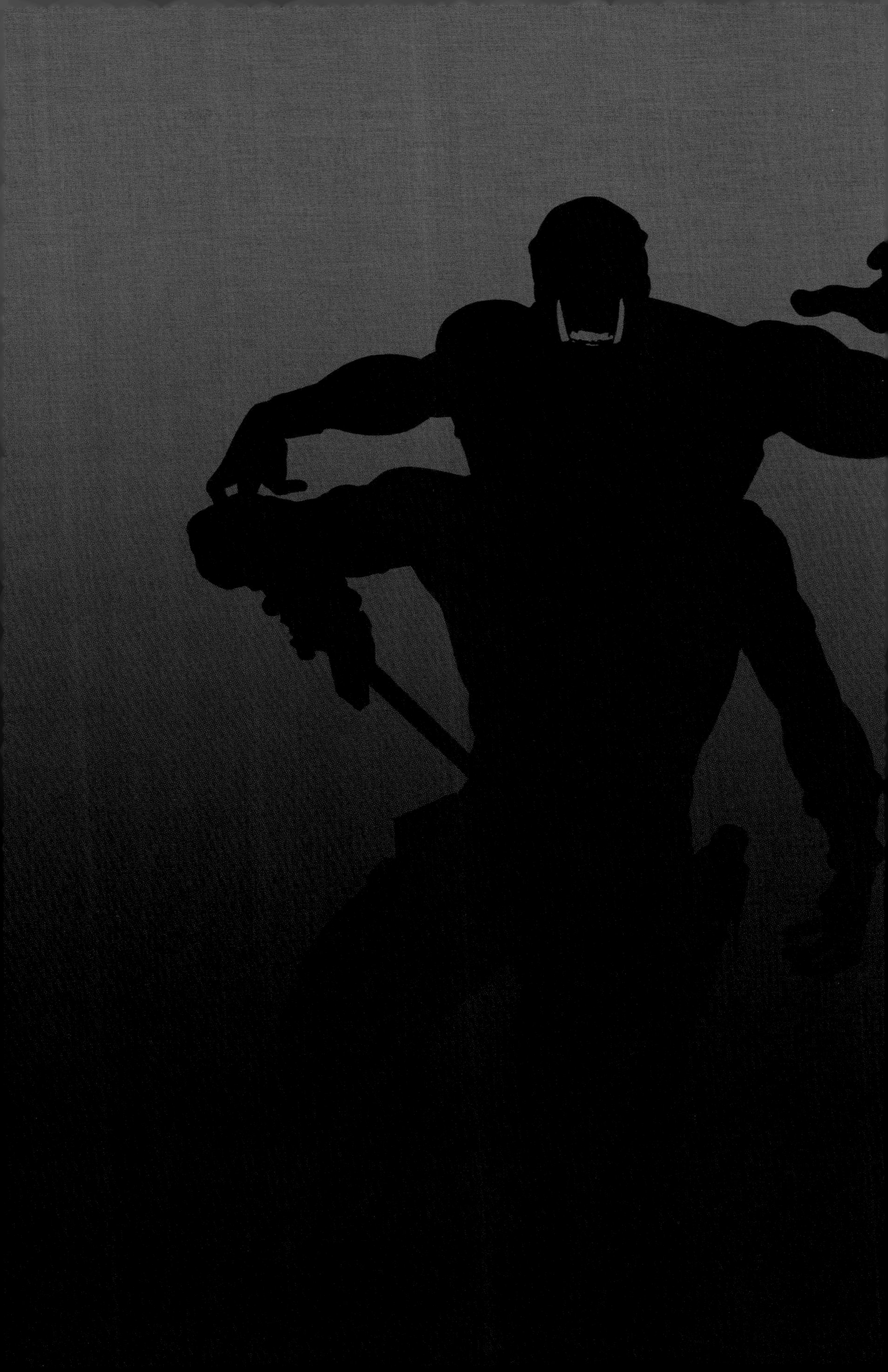

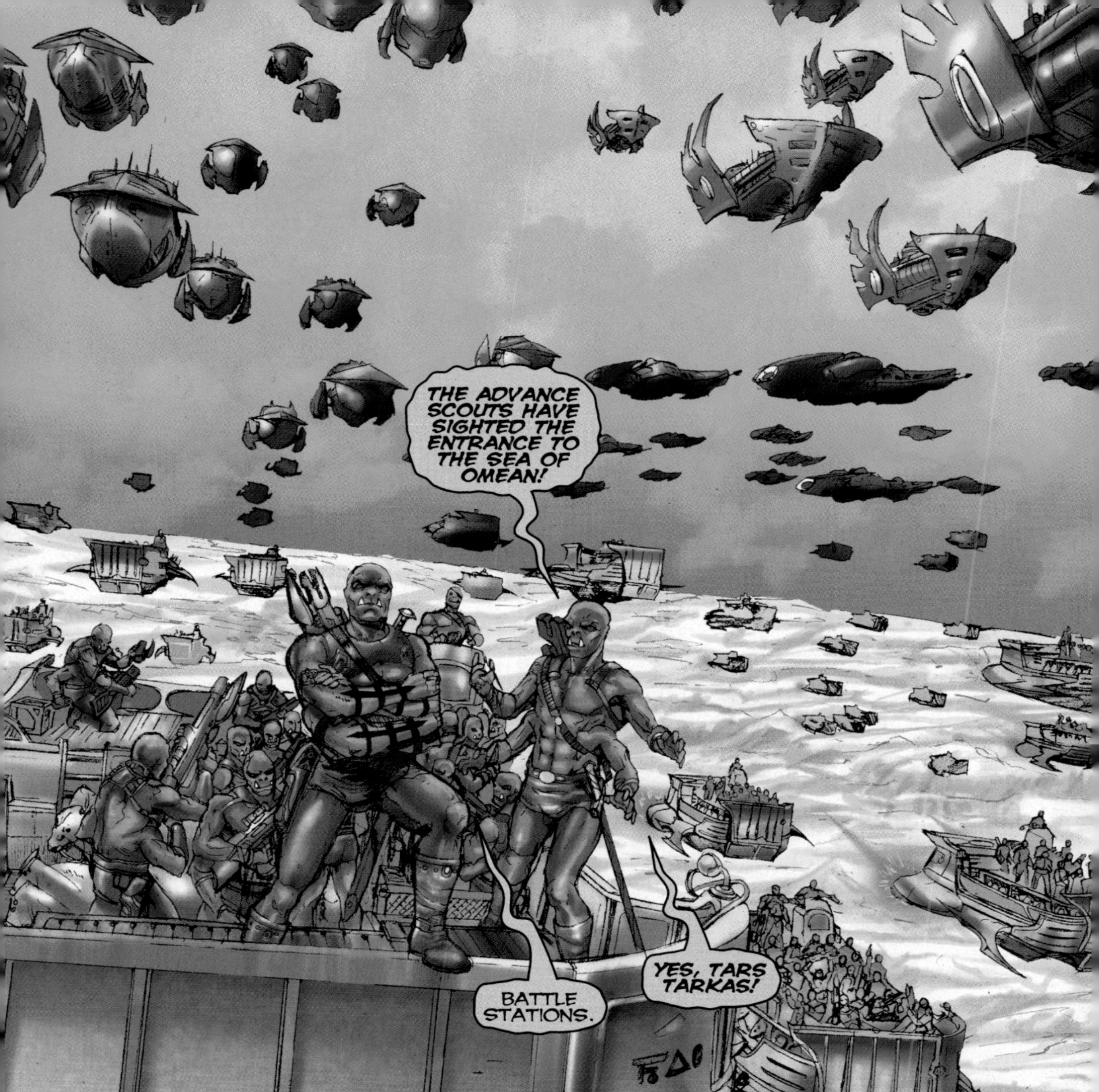
THE ADVANCE SCOUTS HAVE SIGHTED THE ENTRANCE TO THE SEA OF OMEAN!
BATTLE STATIONS.
YES, TARS TARKAS!
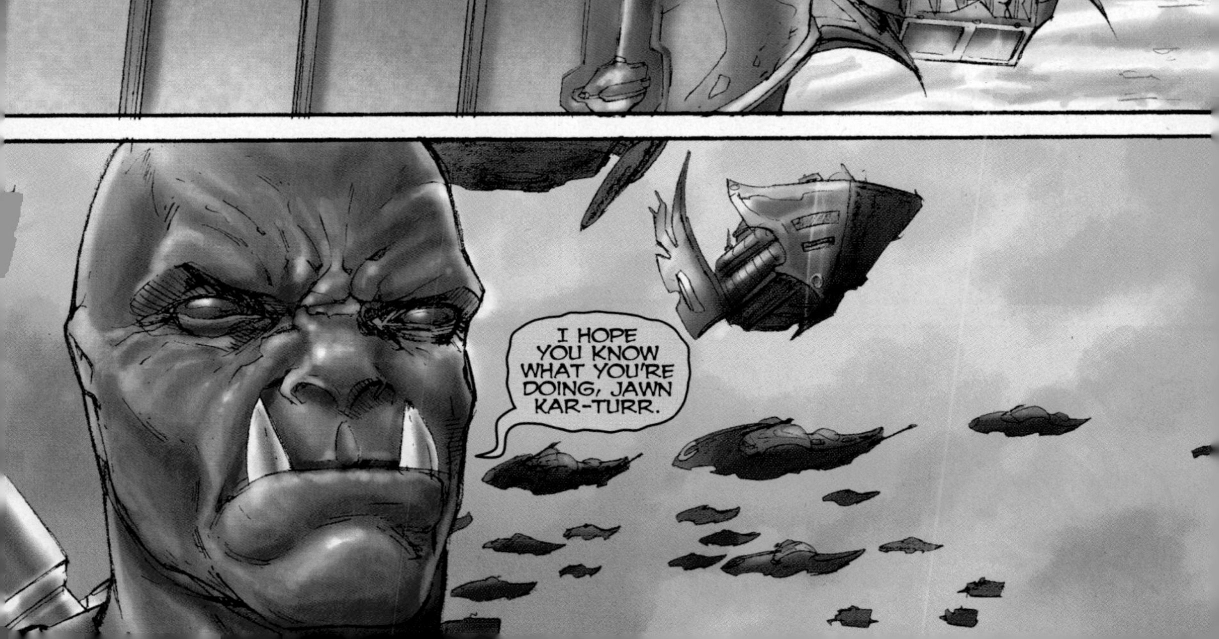
I HOPE YOU KNOW WHAT YOU'RE DOING, JAWN KAR-TURR.

THERE IT IS, FATHER! OMEAN! ENEMY BATTLESHIPS ARE RISING FROM THE ENTRANCE!

MANEUVER FOR INTERCEPT.

WE'LL TRAP THEM LIKE ULSIOS.

I HAVE VISUAL CONTACT WITH ANOTHER FLEET!

SEVERAL HUNDRED VESSELS BEARING SOUTH-SOUTHEAST!

FROM THE SOUTH? IT COULD ONLY BE...

...THERNS. THEY KNEW WE WERE COMING AFTER ALL.

WE CAN'T POSSIBLY HOPE TO ENGAGE AN ENEMY THAT SIZE!

DIVIDE THE FLEET.

DIVIDE IT? WE ARE ALREADY OUTNUMBERED TEN TO ONE!

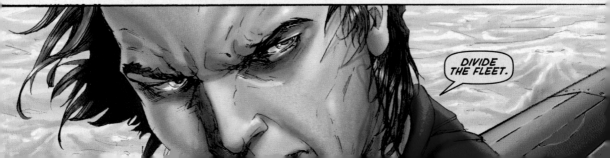

DIVIDE THE FLEET.

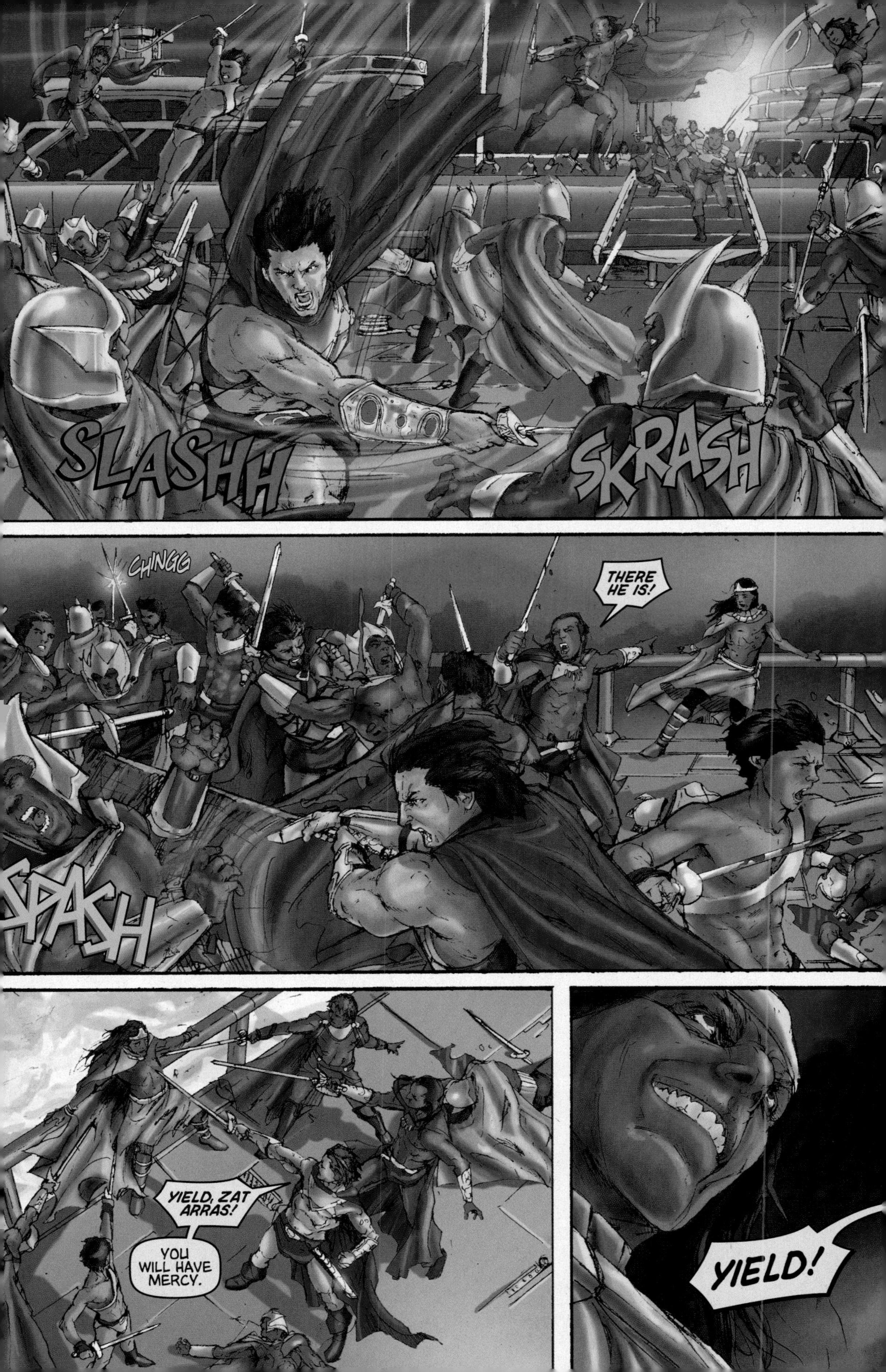
SLASHH
SKRASH
CHINGG
THERE HE IS!
SPASH
YIELD, ZAT ARRAS!
YOU WILL HAVE MERCY.
YIELD!

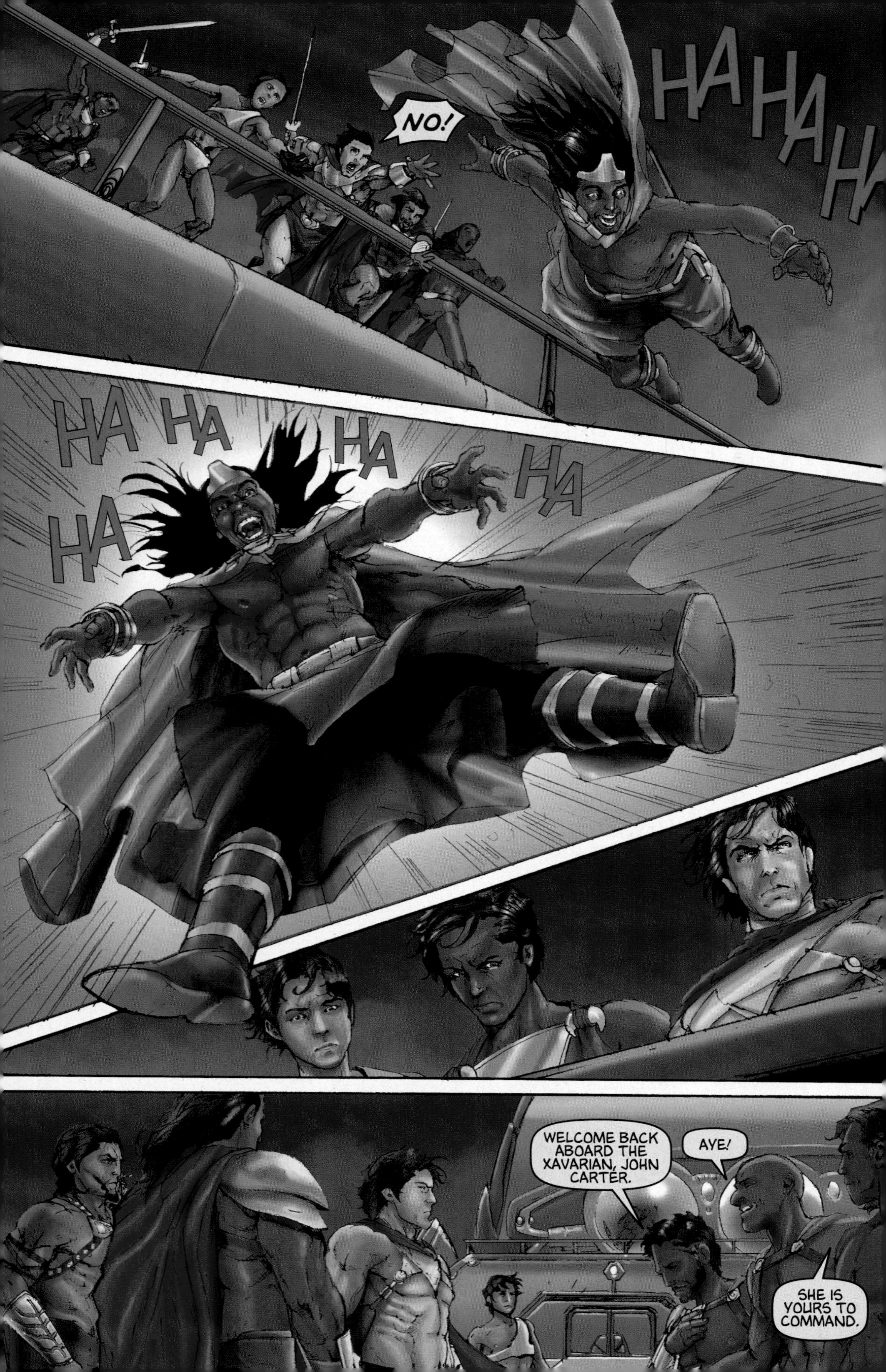
NO!
HA HA HA HA
HA HA HA HA HA
WELCOME BACK ABOARD THE XAVARIAN, JOHN CARTER.
AYE!
SHE IS YOURS TO COMMAND.

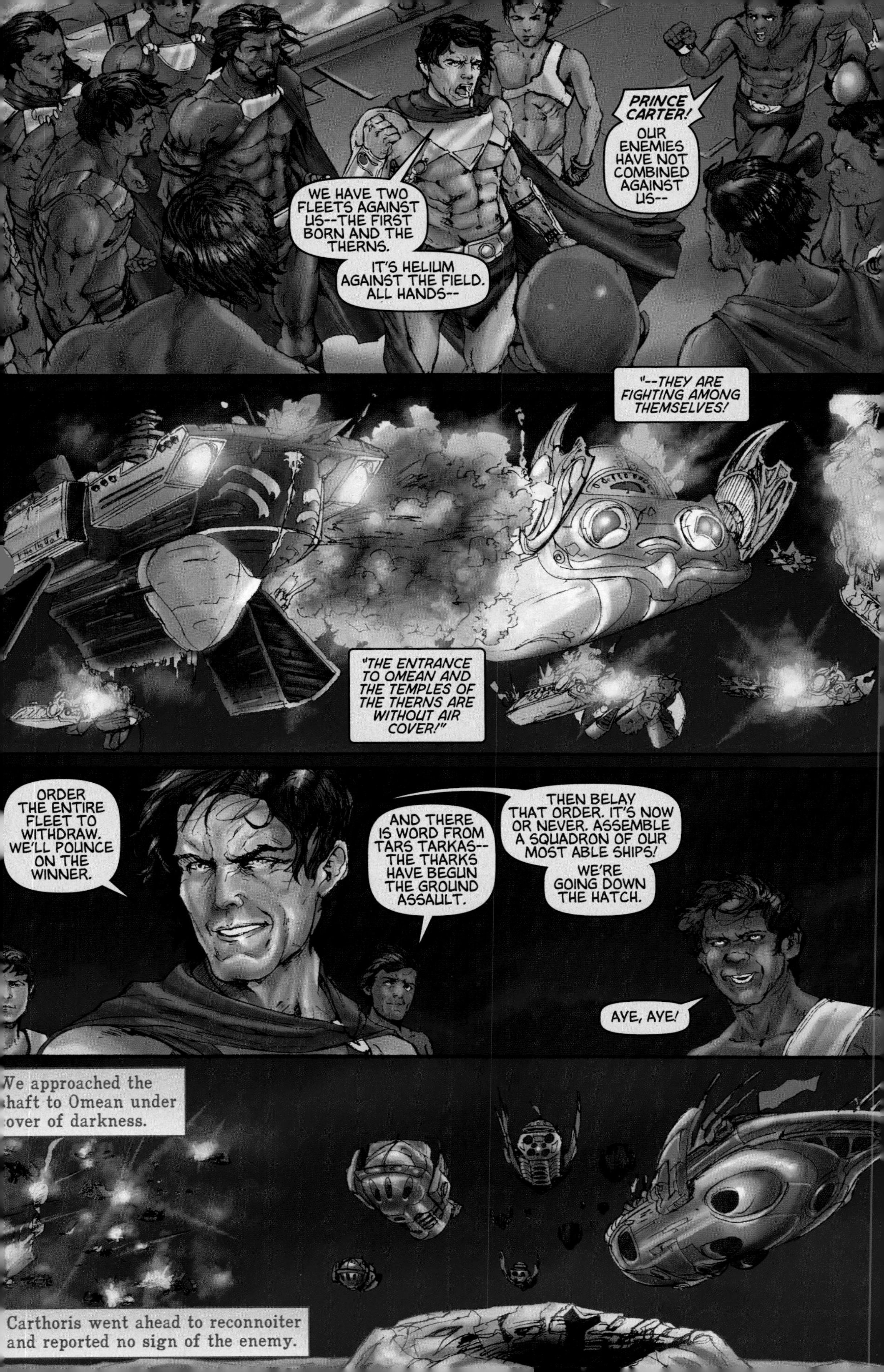
WE HAVE TWO FLEETS AGAINST US--THE FIRST BORN AND THE THERNS.
IT'S HELIUM AGAINST THE FIELD. ALL HANDS--
PRINCE CARTER!
OUR ENEMIES HAVE NOT COMBINED AGAINST US--
"--THEY ARE FIGHTING AMONG THEMSELVES!
"THE ENTRANCE TO OMEAN AND THE TEMPLES OF THE THERNS ARE WITHOUT AIR COVER!"
ORDER THE ENTIRE FLEET TO WITHDRAW. WE'LL POUNCE ON THE WINNER.
AND THERE IS WORD FROM TARS TARKAS--THE THARKS HAVE BEGUN THE GROUND ASSAULT.
THEN BELAY THAT ORDER. IT'S NOW OR NEVER. ASSEMBLE A SQUADRON OF OUR MOST ABLE SHIPS!
WE'RE GOING DOWN THE HATCH.
AYE, AYE!
We approached the shaft to Omean under cover of darkness.
Carthoris went ahead to reconnoiter and reported no sign of the enemy.

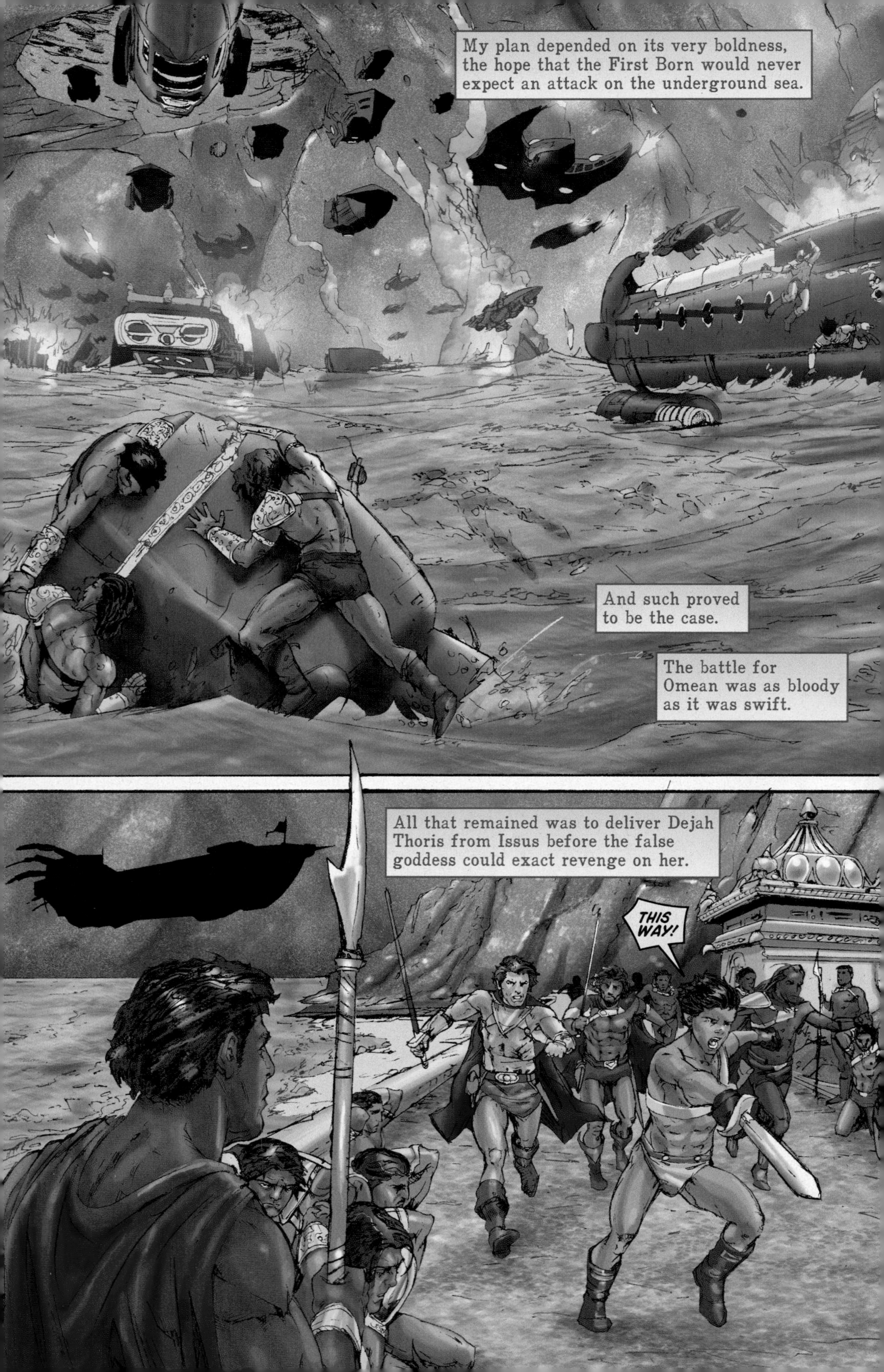
My plan depended on its very boldness, the hope that the First Born would never expect an attack on the underground sea.
And such proved to be the case.
The battle for Omean was as bloody as it was swift.
All that remained was to deliver Dejah Thoris from Issus before the false goddess could exact revenge on her.
THIS WAY!

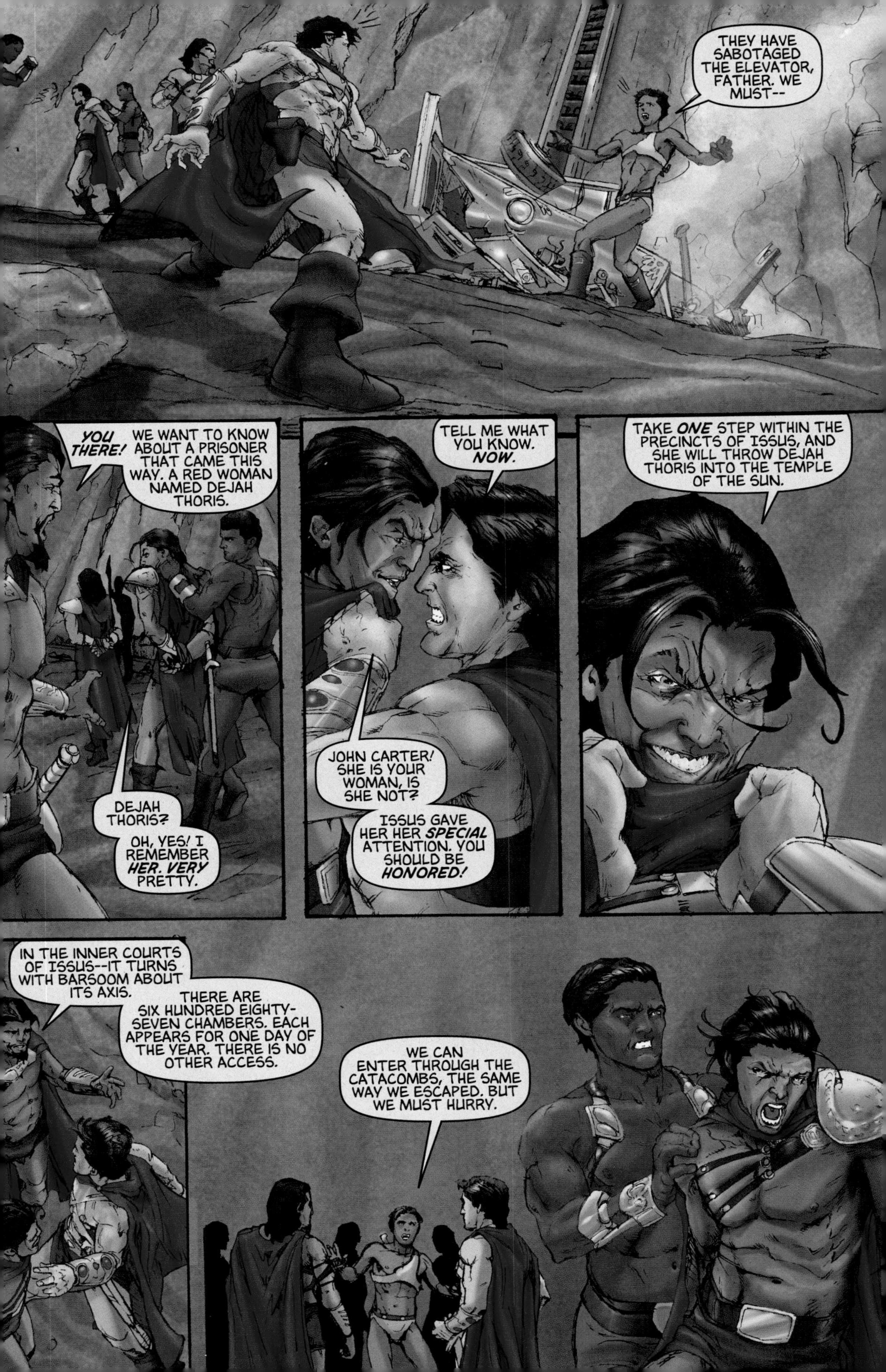

THEY HAVE SABOTAGED THE ELEVATOR, FATHER. WE MUST--
YOU THERE! WE WANT TO KNOW ABOUT A PRISONER THAT CAME THIS WAY. A RED WOMAN NAMED DEJAH THORIS.
DEJAH THORIS?
OH, YES! I REMEMBER HER. VERY PRETTY.
TELL ME WHAT YOU KNOW. NOW.
JOHN CARTER! SHE IS YOUR WOMAN, IS SHE NOT?
ISSUS GAVE HER HER SPECIAL ATTENTION. YOU SHOULD BE HONORED!
TAKE ONE STEP WITHIN THE PRECINCTS OF ISSUS, AND SHE WILL THROW DEJAH THORIS INTO THE TEMPLE OF THE SUN.
IN THE INNER COURTS OF ISSUS--IT TURNS WITH BARSOOM ABOUT ITS AXIS.
THERE ARE SIX HUNDRED EIGHTY-SEVEN CHAMBERS. EACH APPEARS FOR ONE DAY OF THE YEAR. THERE IS NO OTHER ACCESS.
WE CAN ENTER THROUGH THE CATACOMBS, THE SAME WAY WE ESCAPED. BUT WE MUST HURRY.

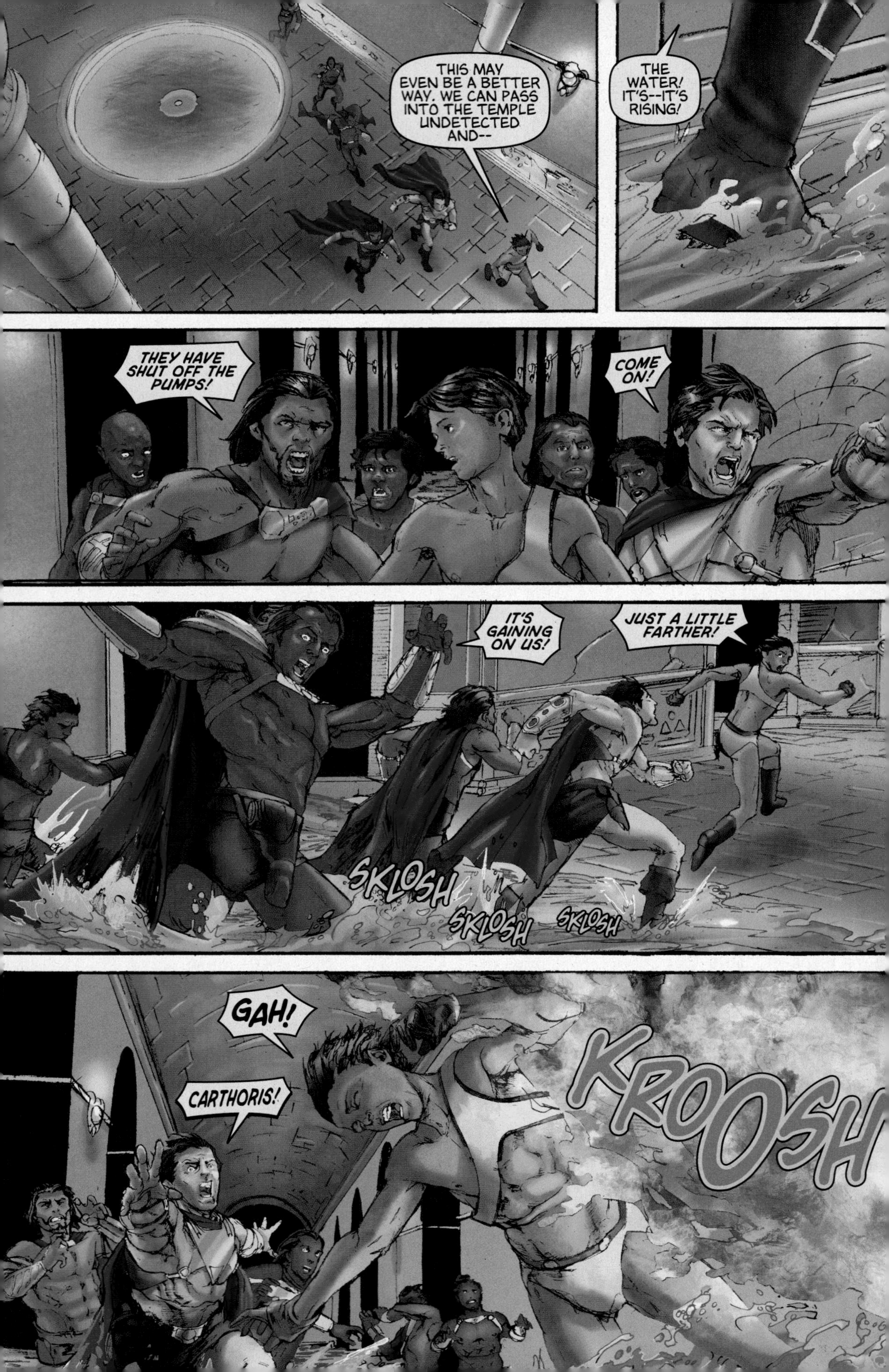
THIS MAY EVEN BE A BETTER WAY. WE CAN PASS INTO THE TEMPLE UNDETECTED AND--
THE WATER! IT'S--IT'S RISING!
THEY HAVE SHUT OFF THE PUMPS!
COME ON!
IT'S GAINING ON US!
JUST A LITTLE FARTHER!
SKLOSH
SKLOSH
SKLOSH
GAH!
CARTHORIS!
KROOSH

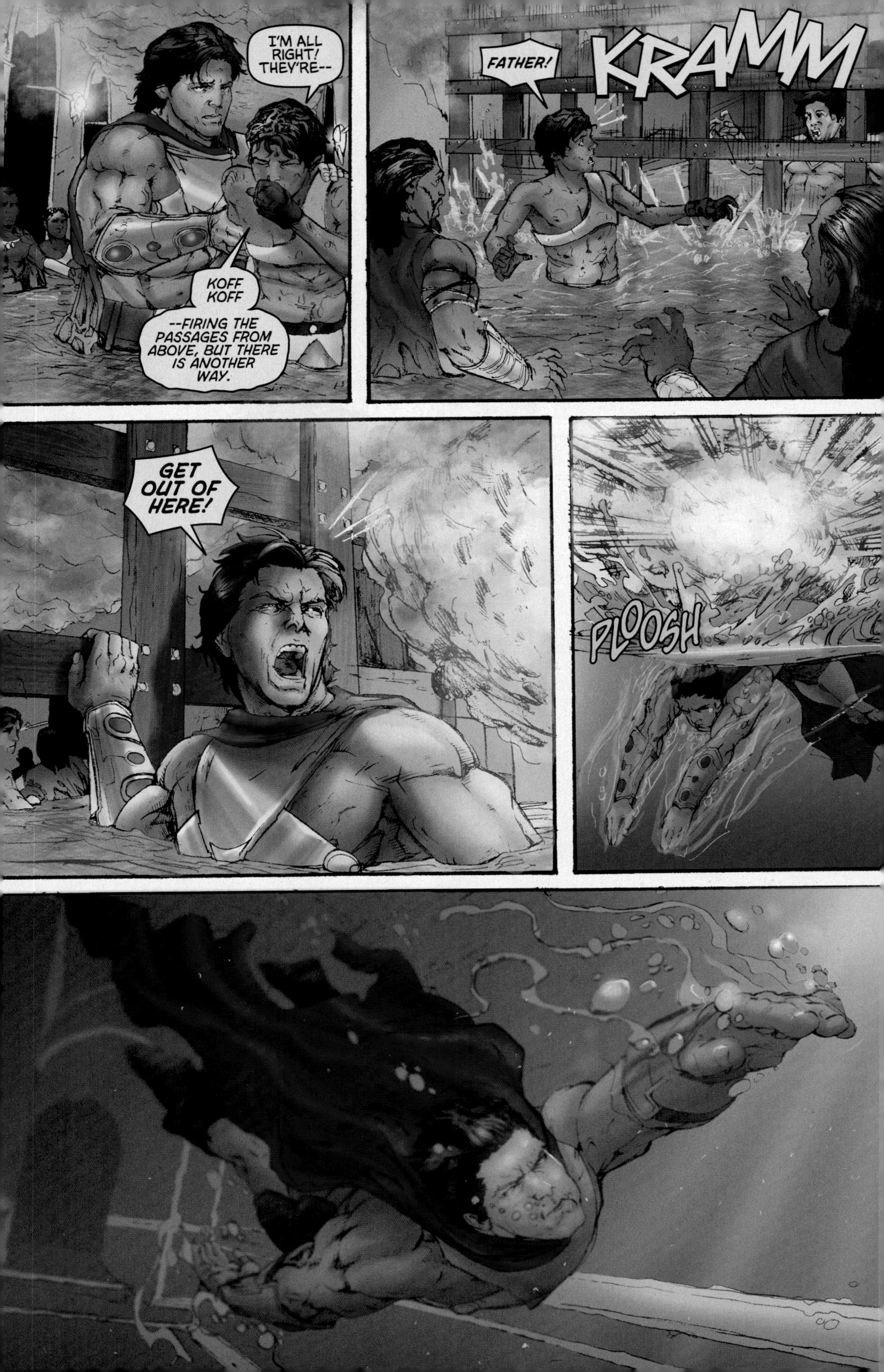

I'M ALL RIGHT! THEY'RE--
KOFF KOFF
--FIRING THE PASSAGES FROM ABOVE, BUT THERE IS ANOTHER WAY.
FATHER!
KRAMM
GET OUT OF HERE!
PLOOSH

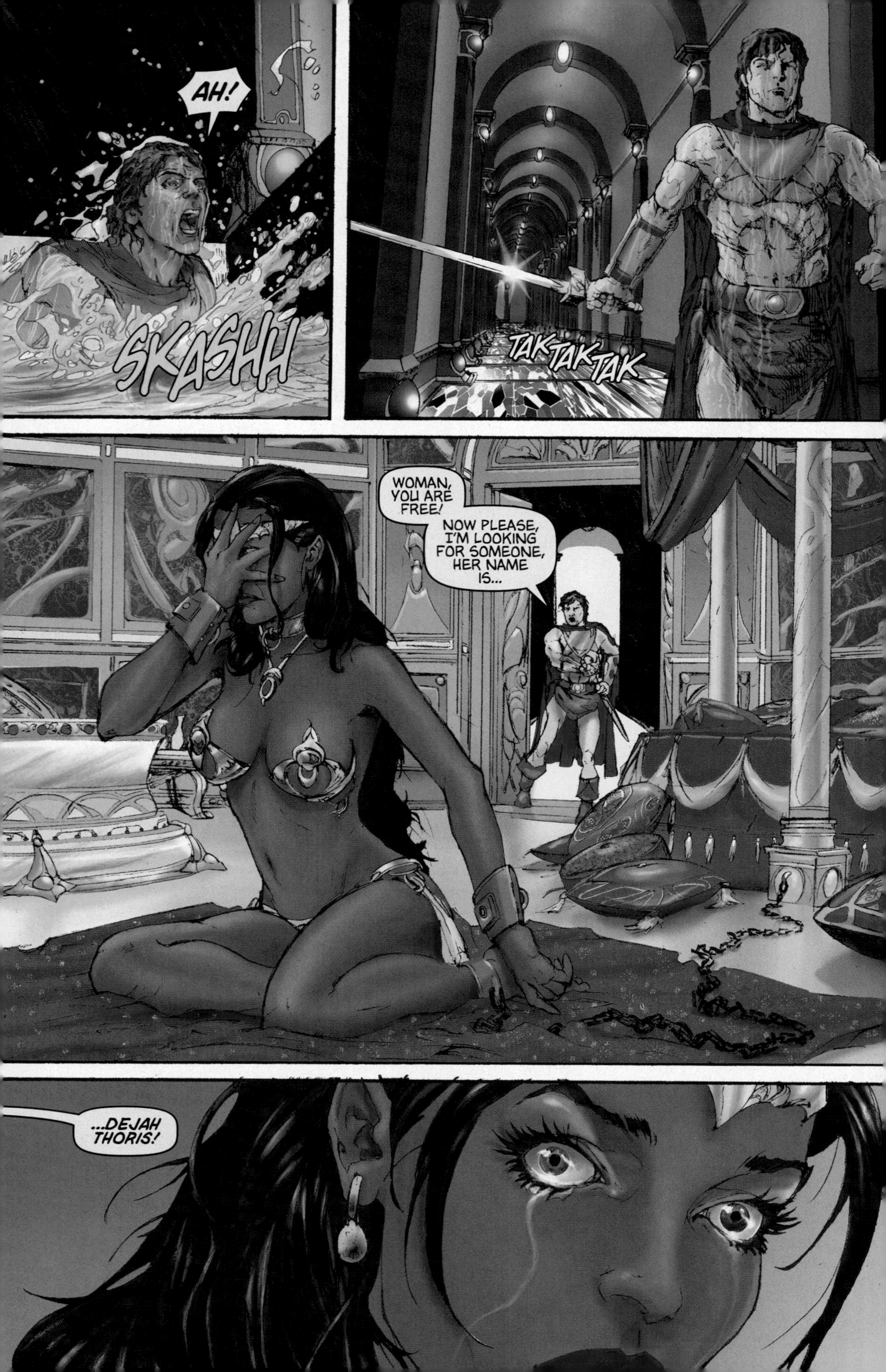
AH!
SKASHH
TAK TAK TAK
WOMAN, YOU ARE FREE!
NOW PLEASE, I'M LOOKING FOR SOMEONE, HER NAME IS...
...DEJAH THORIS!

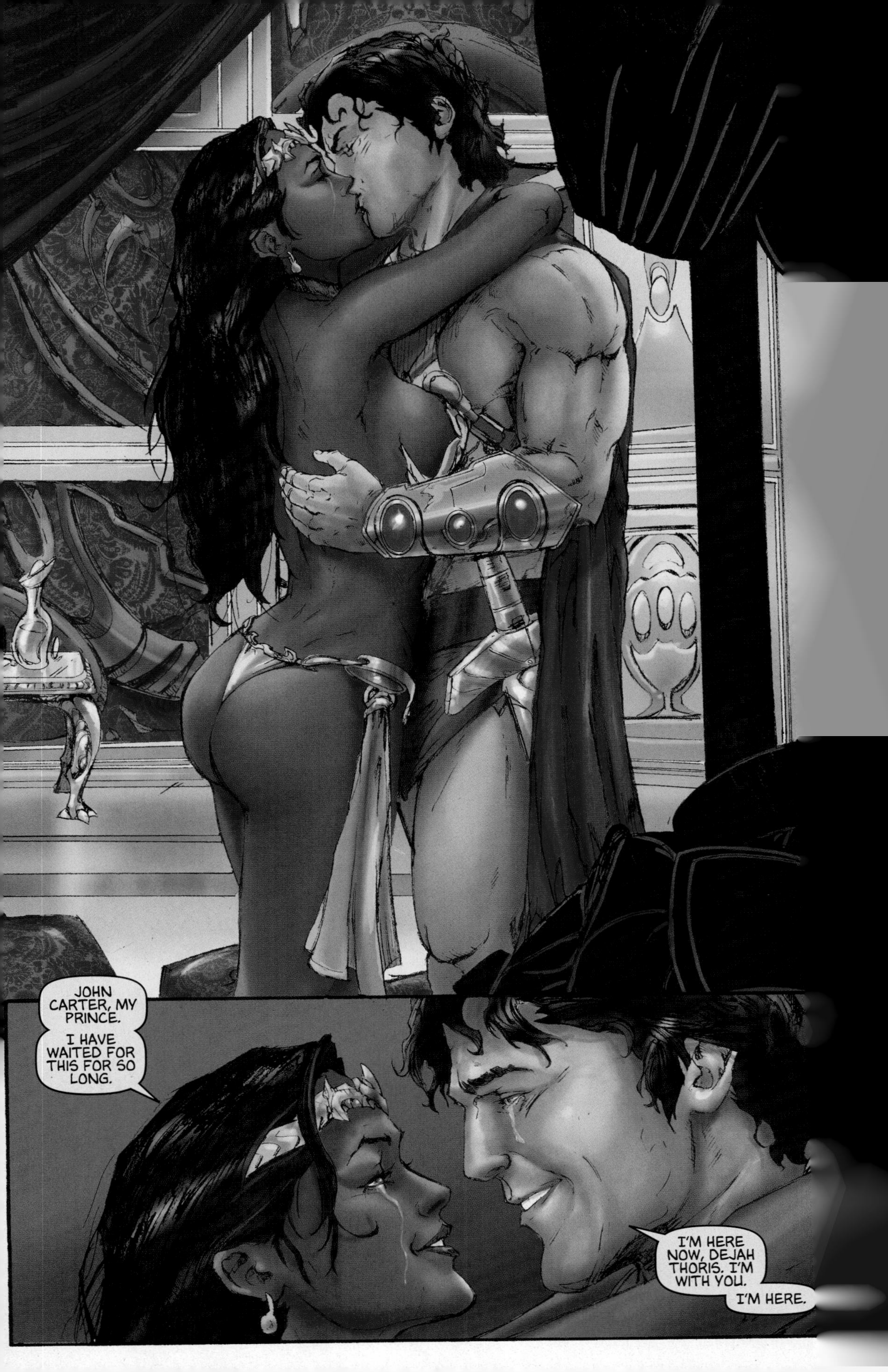
JOHN CARTER, MY PRINCE.
I HAVE WAITED FOR THIS FOR SO LONG.
I'M HERE NOW, DEJAH THORIS. I'M WITH YOU.
I'M HERE.

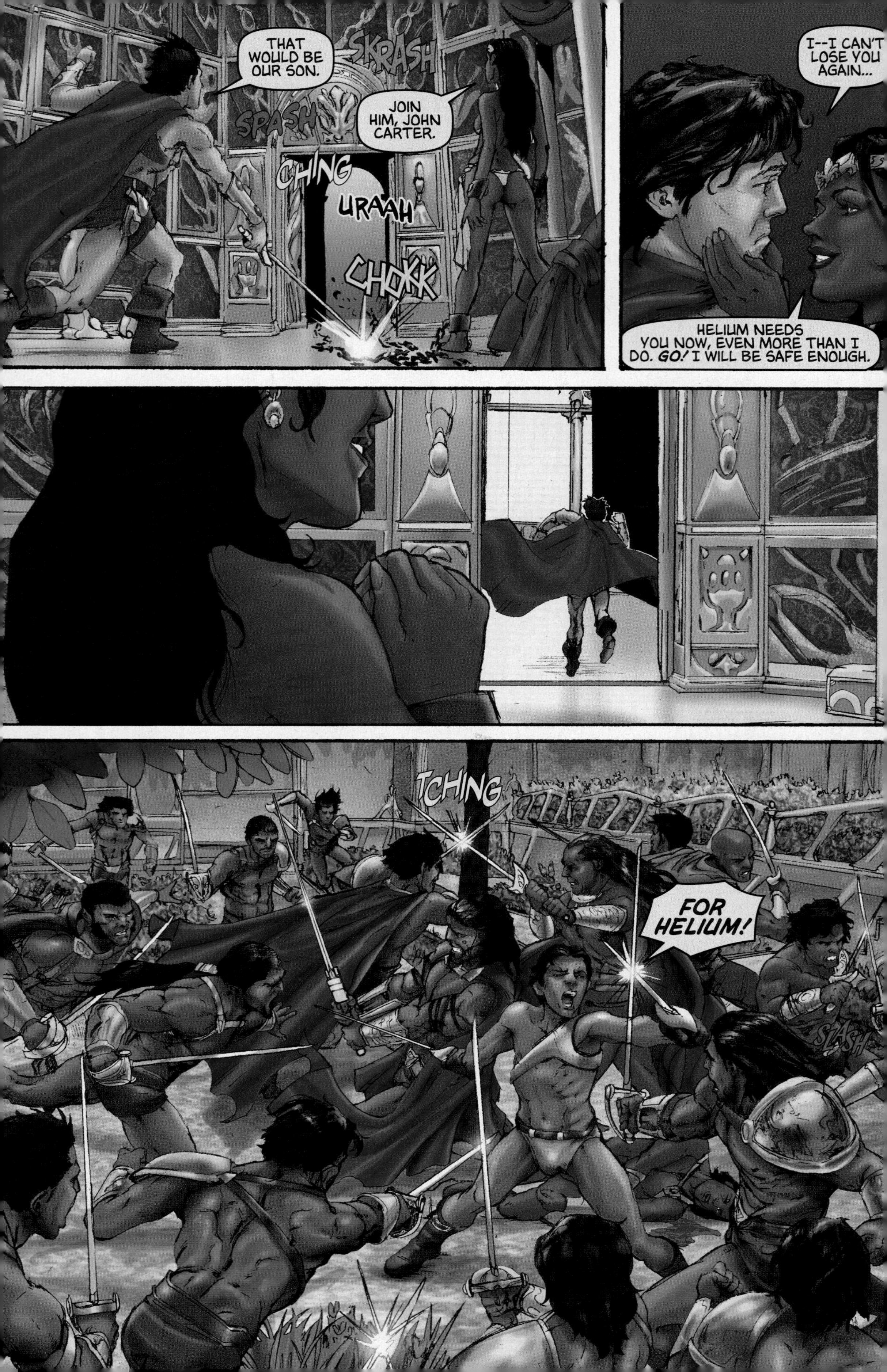

THAT WOULD BE OUR SON.
SKRASH
SPASH
JOIN HIM, JOHN CARTER.
CHING
URAAH
CHOKK
I--I CAN'T LOSE YOU AGAIN...
HELIUM NEEDS YOU NOW, EVEN MORE THAN I DO. GO! I WILL BE SAFE ENOUGH.
TCHING
FOR HELIUM!
SLASH

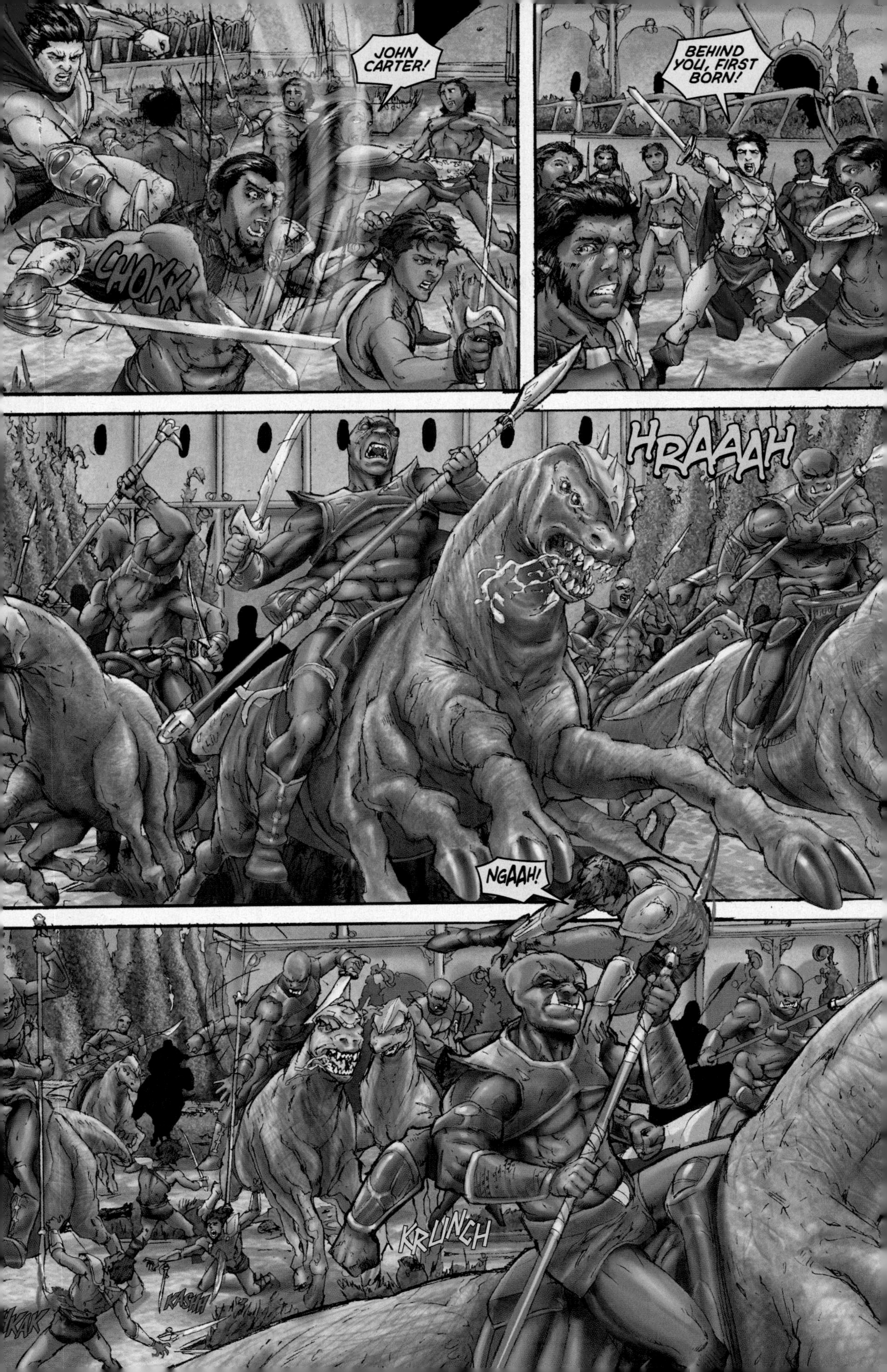
JOHN CARTER!
CHOKK
BEHIND YOU, FIRST BORN!
HRAAAH
NGAAH!
KRUNCH
KASH
KAK

We returned to Dejah Thoris's chambers to find her vanished amidst signs of struggle.

FIND ISSUS, AND WE FIND THE PRINCESS!

I think in that instant I hovered on the verge of insanity.

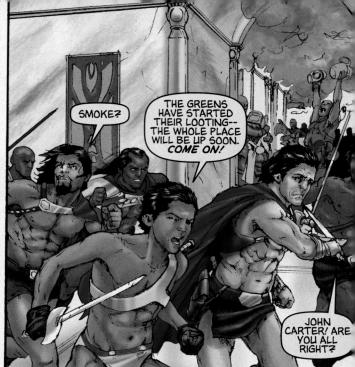

SMOKE?

THE GREENS HAVE STARTED THEIR LOOTING-- THE WHOLE PLACE WILL BE UP SOON. COME ON!

JOHN CARTER! ARE YOU ALL RIGHT?

THERE SHE IS! THE FALSE GODDESS!

INFIDELS! DEFILERS! YOU SHALL NOT--

FASSH

GAK!

HALT!

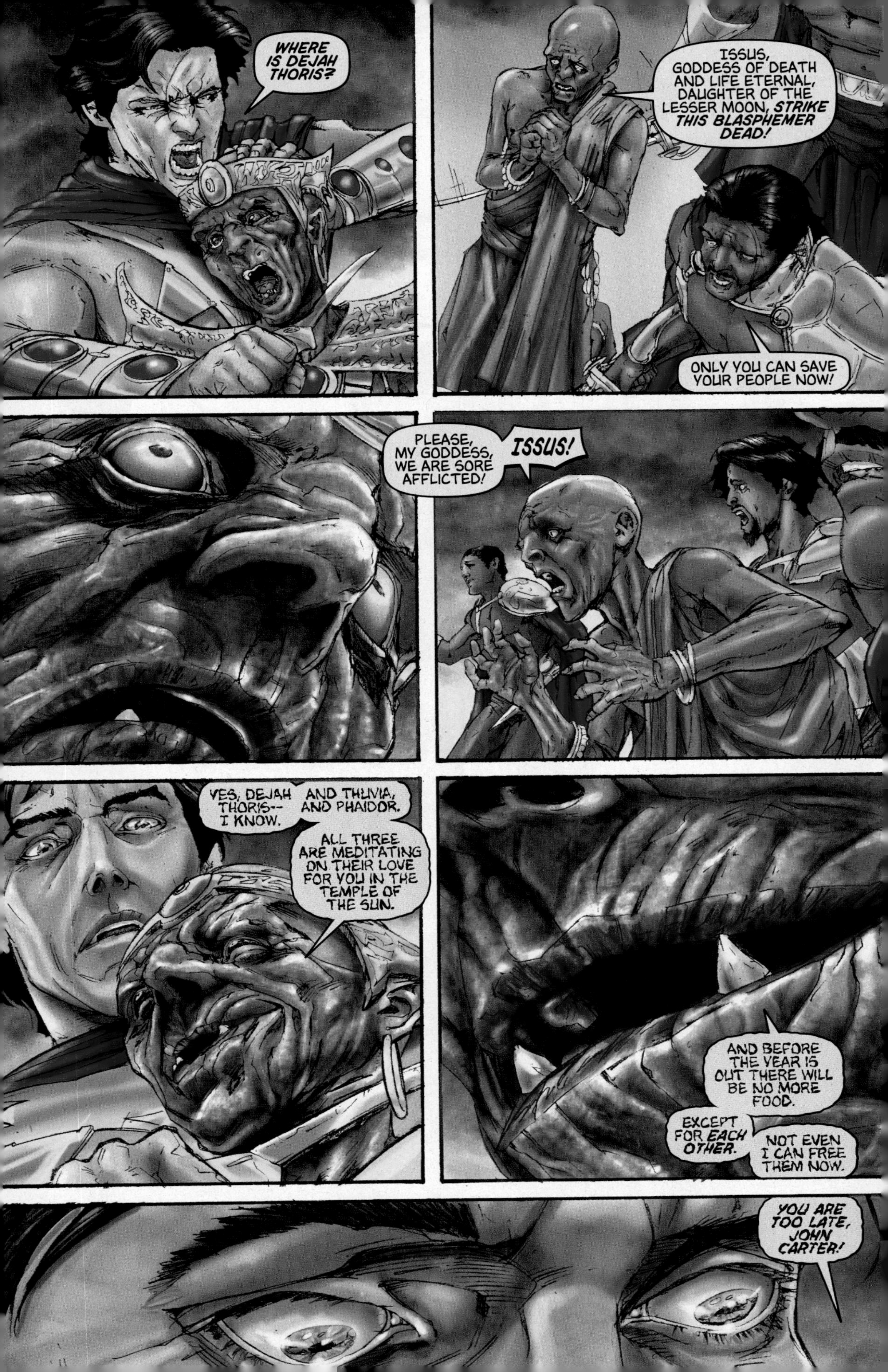
WHERE IS DEJAH THORIS?
ISSUS, GODDESS OF DEATH AND LIFE ETERNAL, DAUGHTER OF THE LESSER MOON, STRIKE THIS BLASPHEMER DEAD!
ONLY YOU CAN SAVE YOUR PEOPLE NOW!
PLEASE, MY GODDESS, WE ARE SORE AFFLICTED!
ISSUS!
YES, DEJAH THORIS-- I KNOW.
AND THUVIA, AND PHAIDOR.
ALL THREE ARE MEDITATING ON THEIR LOVE FOR YOU IN THE TEMPLE OF THE SUN.
AND BEFORE THE YEAR IS OUT THERE WILL BE NO MORE FOOD.
EXCEPT FOR EACH OTHER.
NOT EVEN I CAN FREE THEM NOW.
YOU ARE TOO LATE, JOHN CARTER!

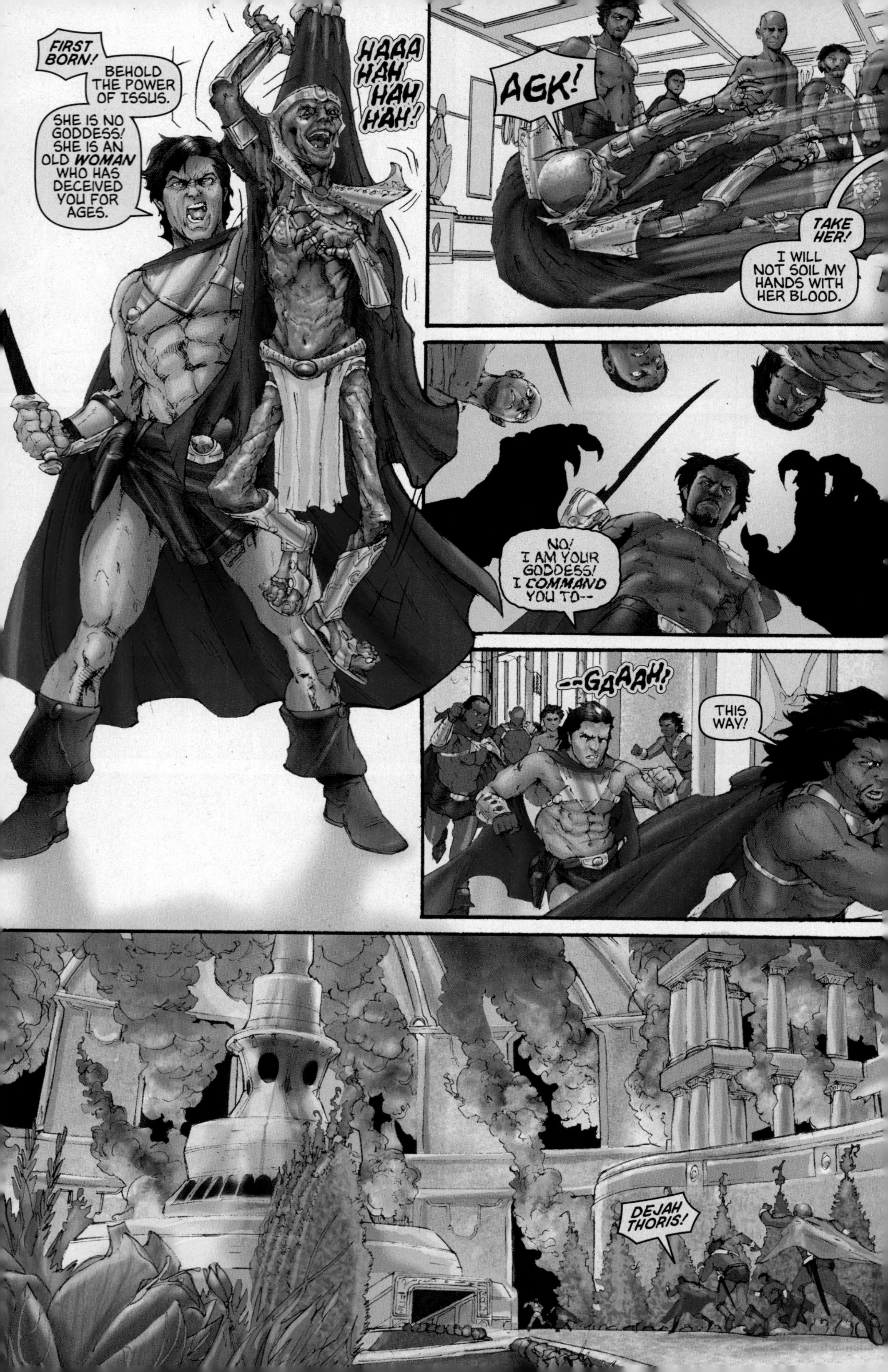
FIRST BORN!
BEHOLD THE POWER OF ISSUS.
SHE IS NO GODDESS! SHE IS AN OLD WOMAN WHO HAS DECEIVED YOU FOR AGES.
HAAA HAH HAH HAH!
AGK!
TAKE HER!
I WILL NOT SOIL MY HANDS WITH HER BLOOD.
NO! I AM YOUR GODDESS! I COMMAND YOU TO--
--GAAAH!
THIS WAY!
DEJAH THORIS!

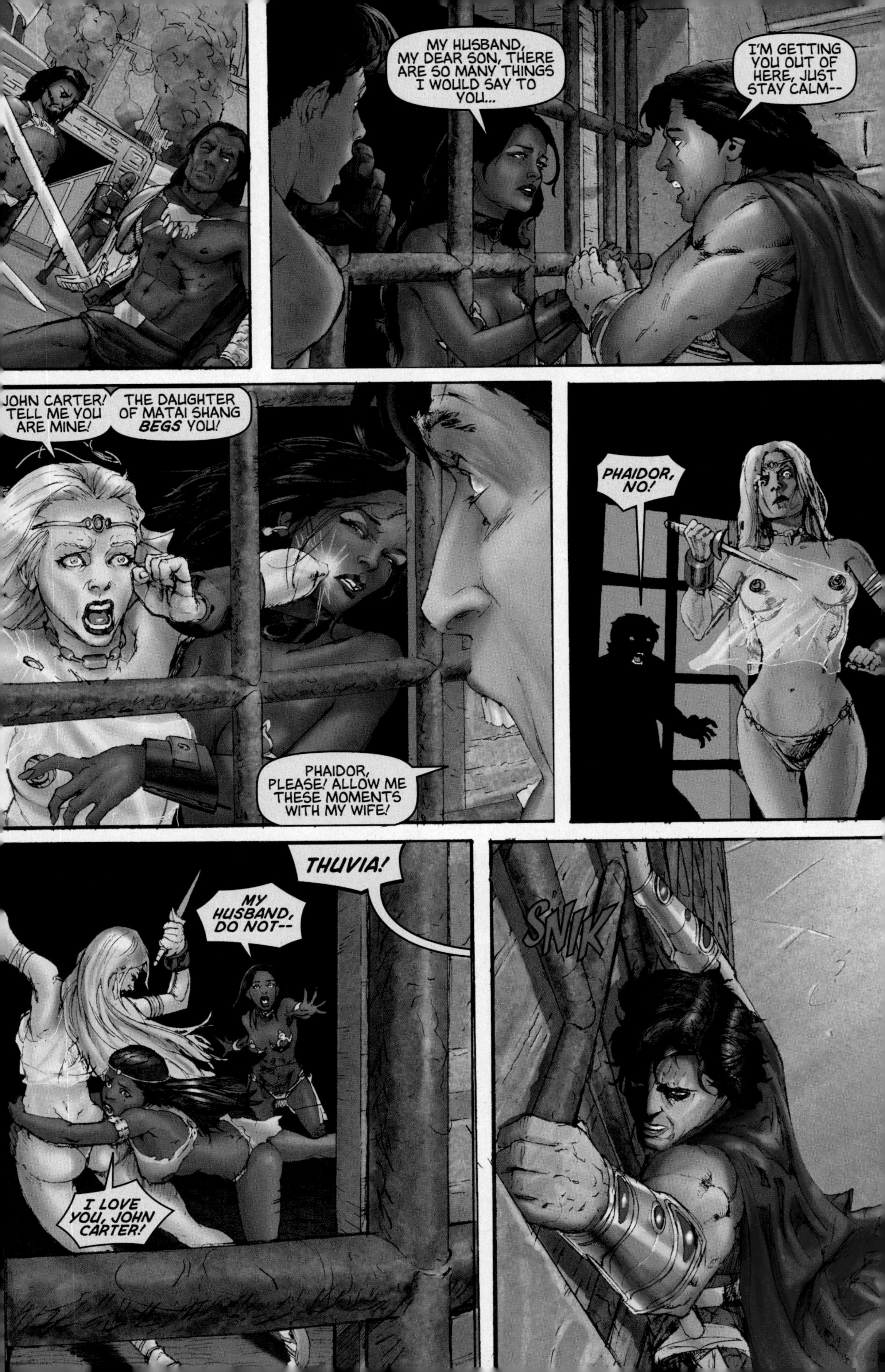
MY HUSBAND, MY DEAR SON, THERE ARE SO MANY THINGS I WOULD SAY TO YOU...
I'M GETTING YOU OUT OF HERE, JUST STAY CALM--
JOHN CARTER! TELL ME YOU ARE MINE!
THE DAUGHTER OF MATAI SHANG BEGS YOU!
PHAIDOR, PLEASE! ALLOW ME THESE MOMENTS WITH MY WIFE!
PHAIDOR, NO!
THUVIA!
MY HUSBAND, DO NOT--
I LOVE YOU, JOHN CARTER!
SNIK

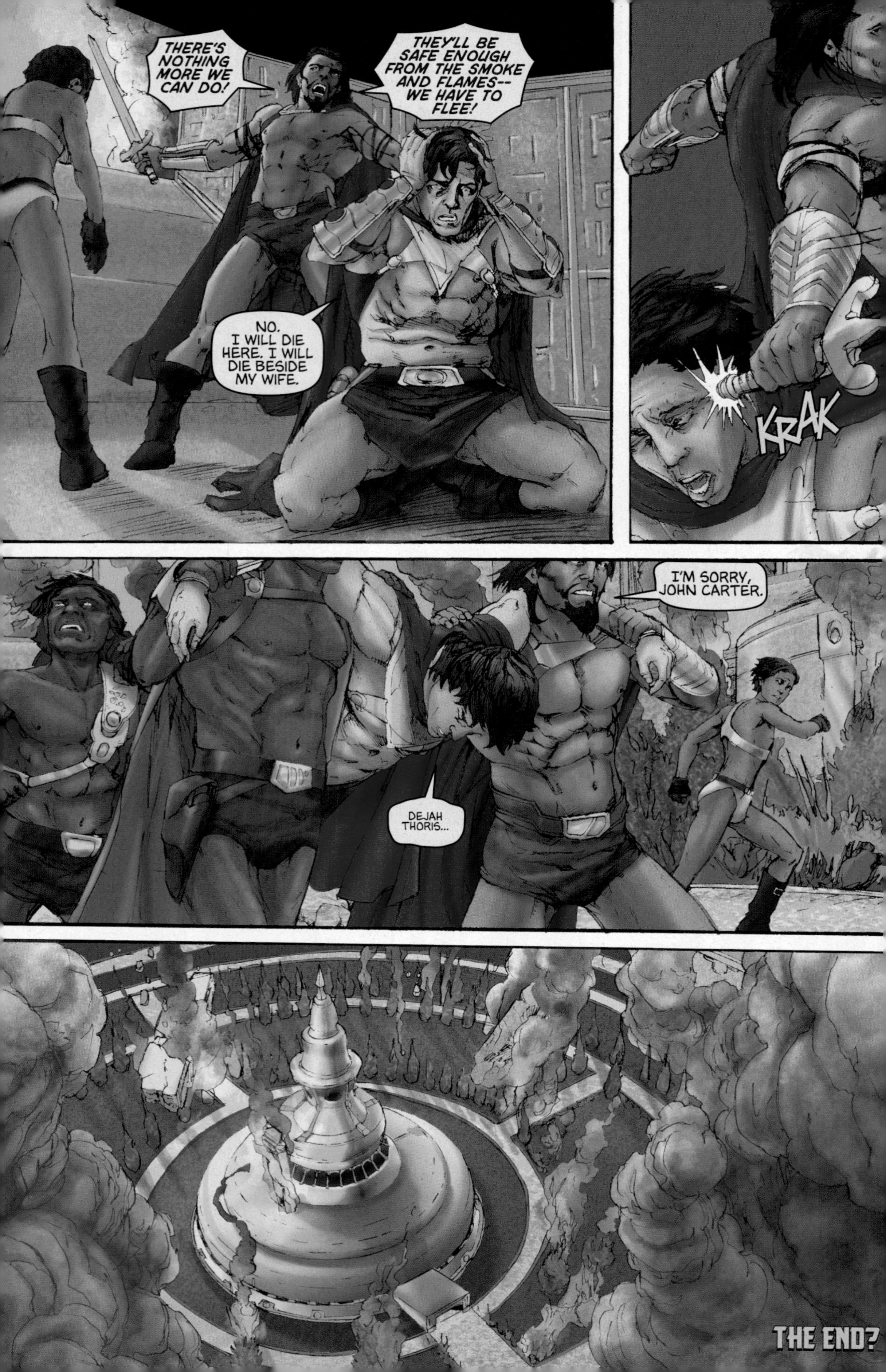
THERE'S NOTHING MORE WE CAN DO!
THEY'LL BE SAFE ENOUGH FROM THE SMOKE AND FLAMES-- WE HAVE TO FLEE!
NO. I WILL DIE HERE. I WILL DIE BESIDE MY WIFE.
KRAK
I'M SORRY, JOHN CARTER.
DEJAH THORIS...
THE END?

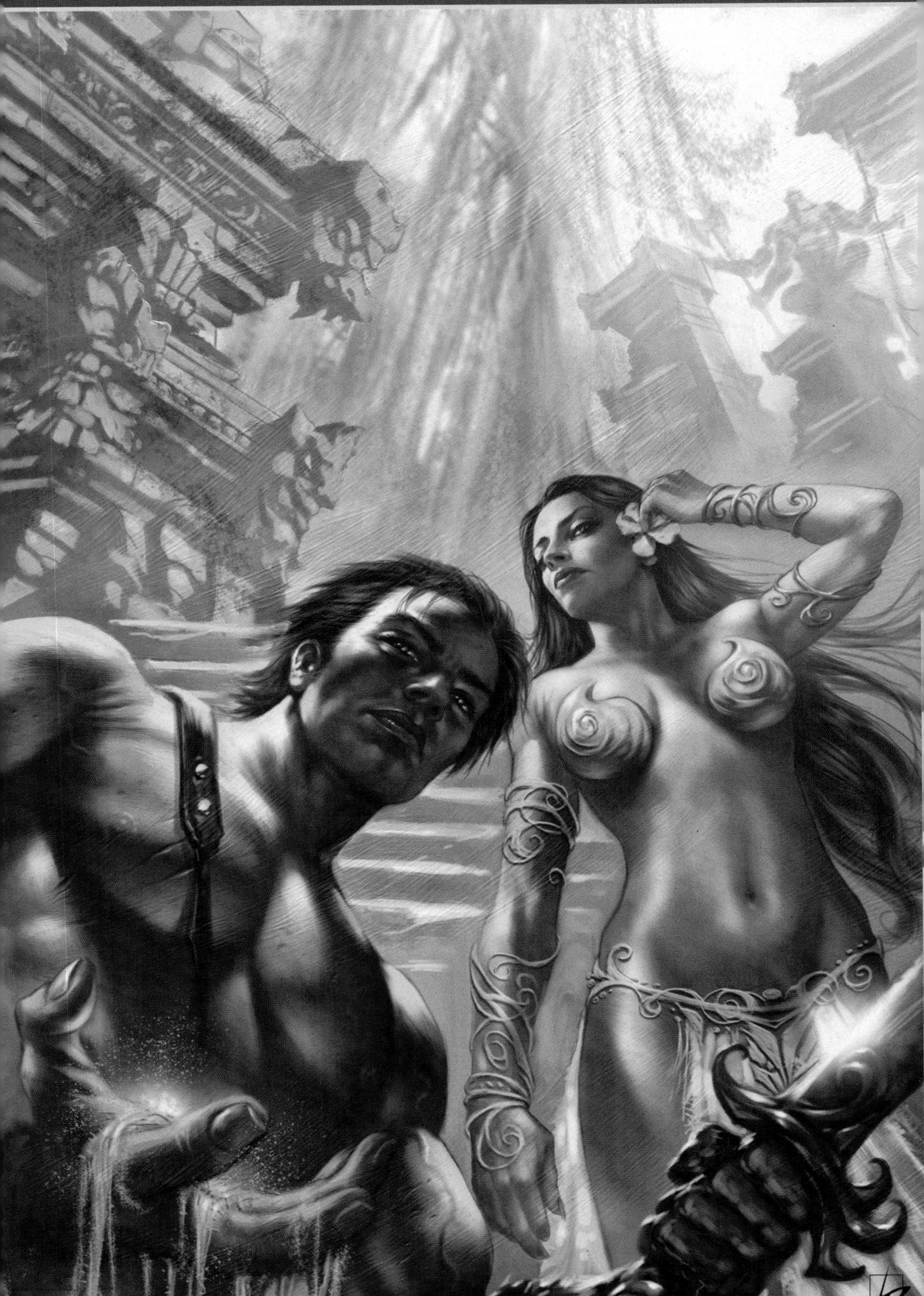

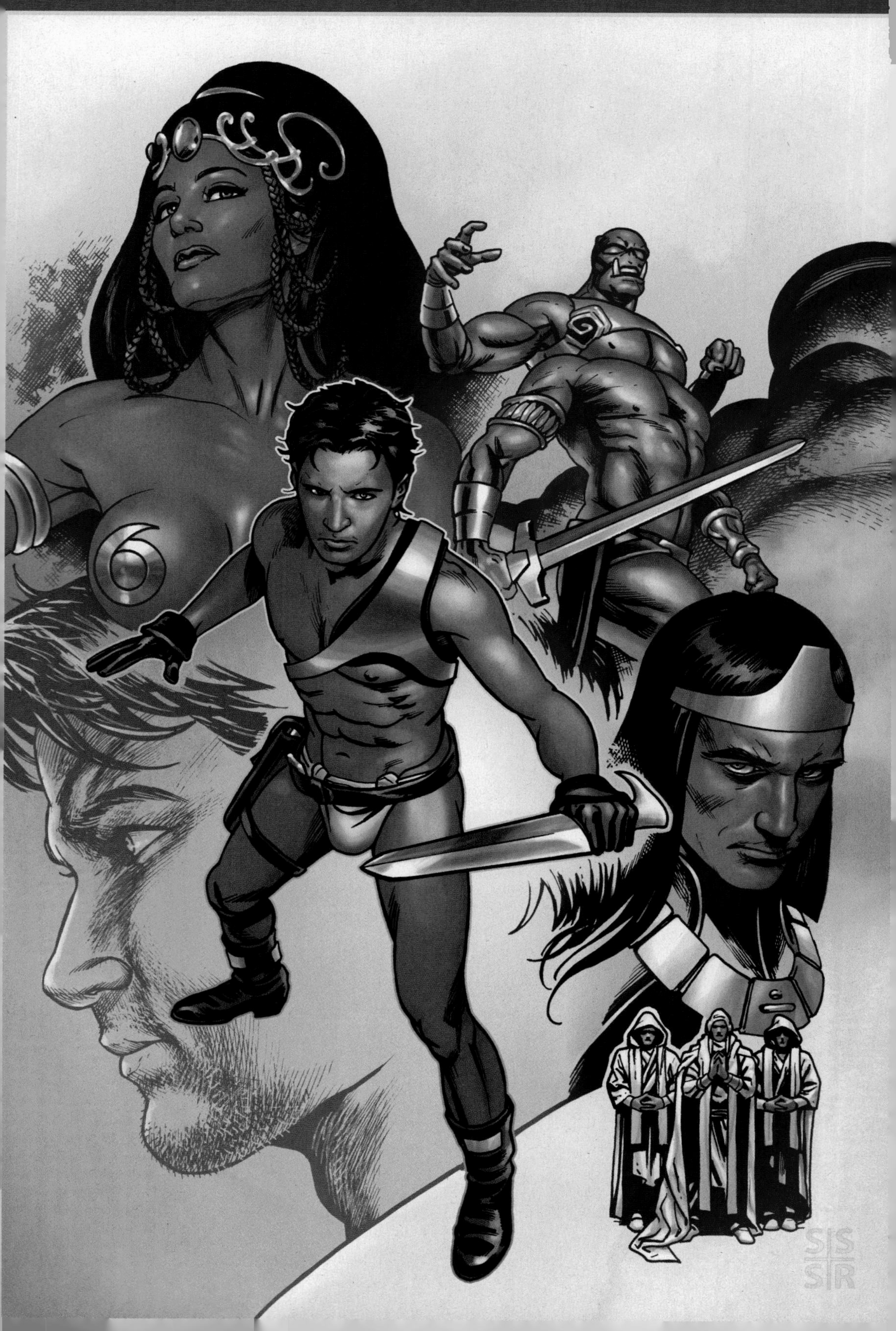

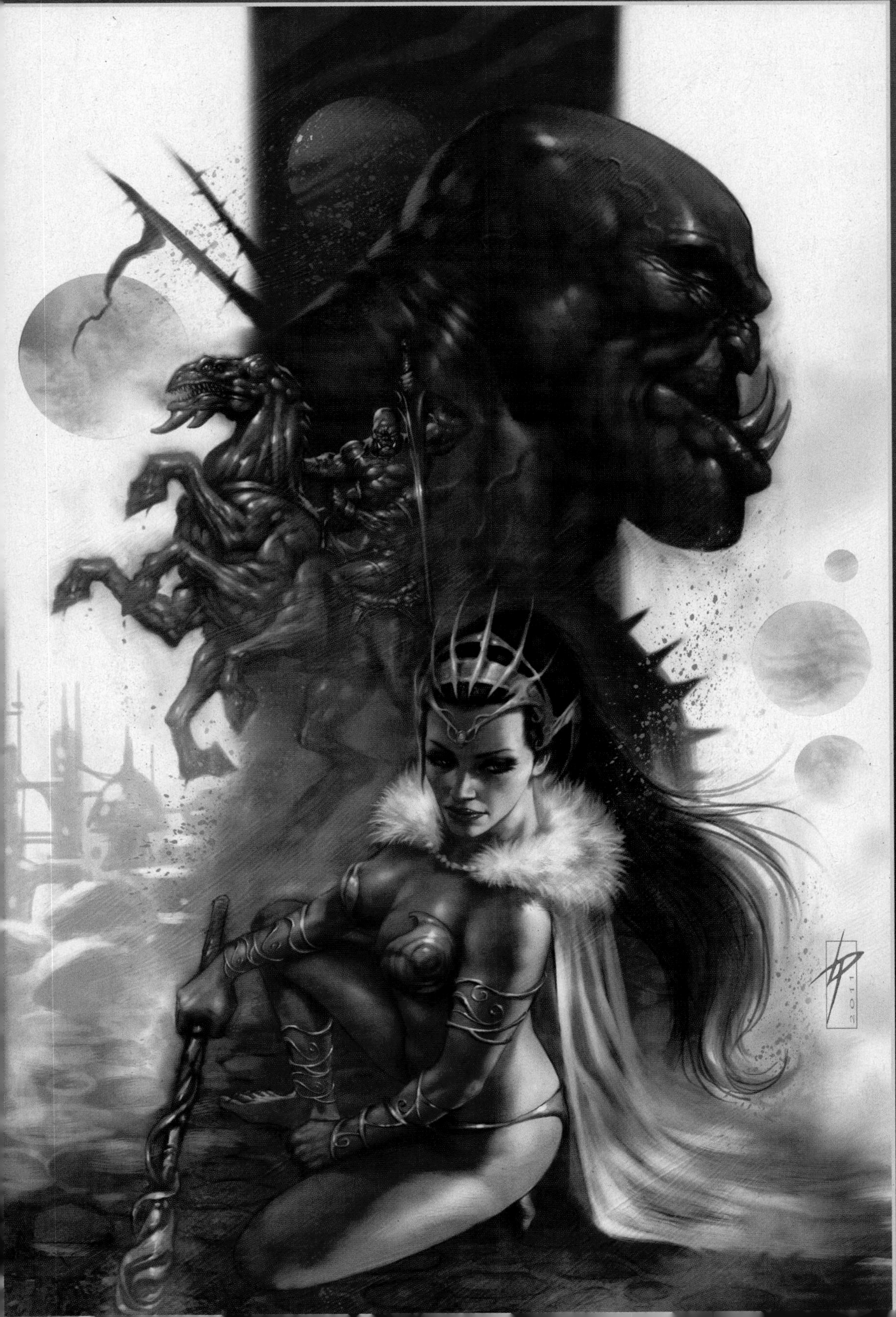

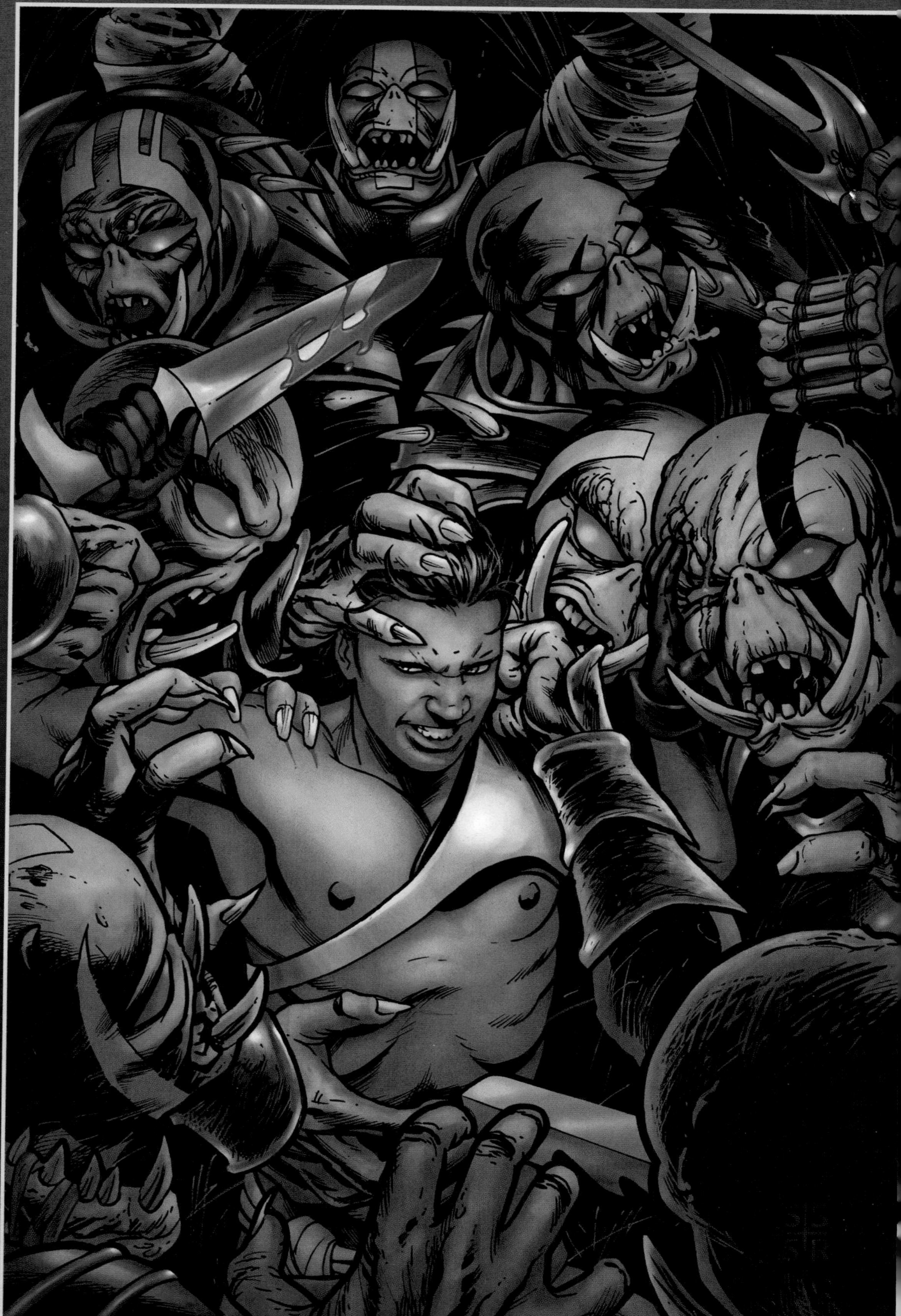

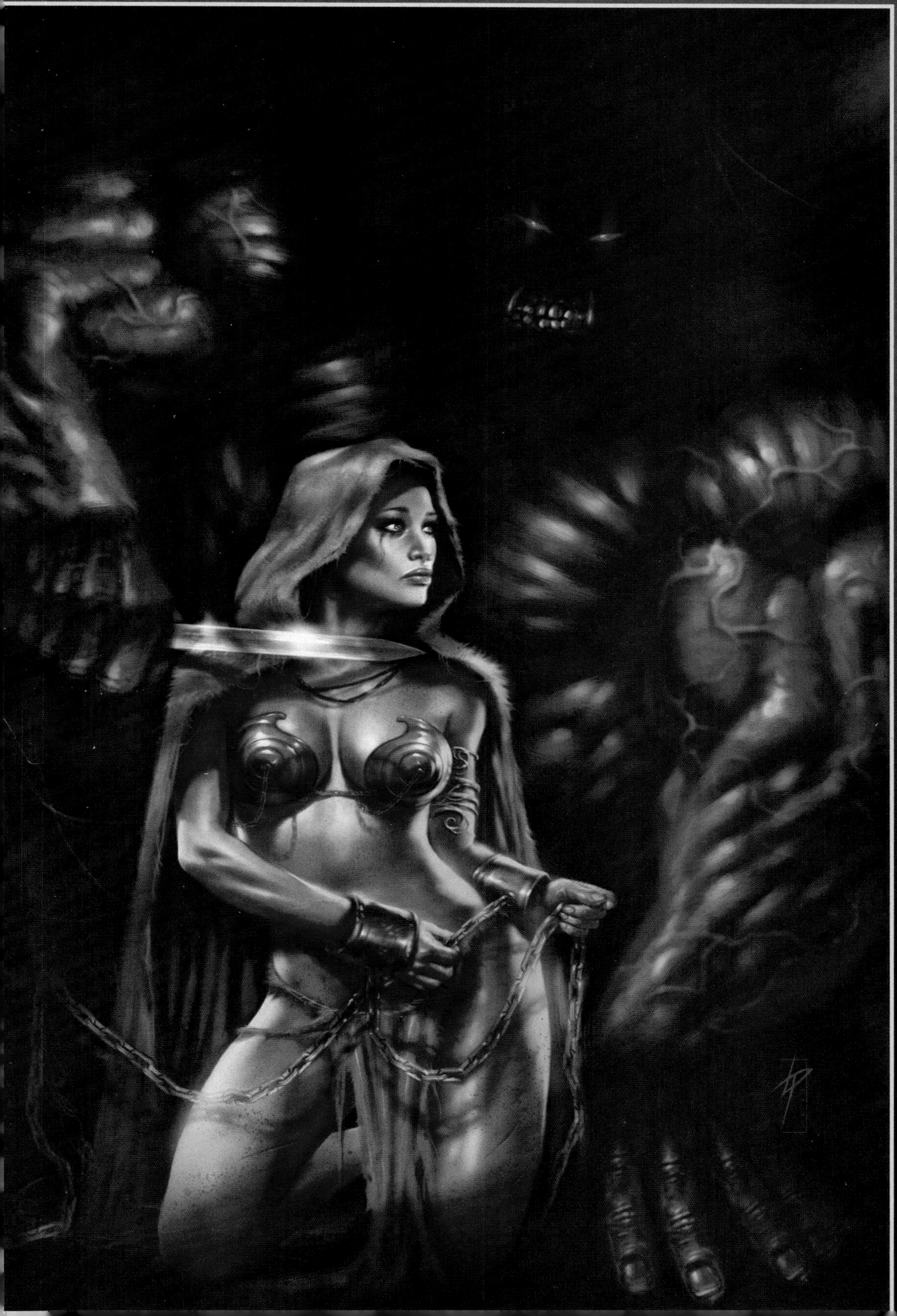

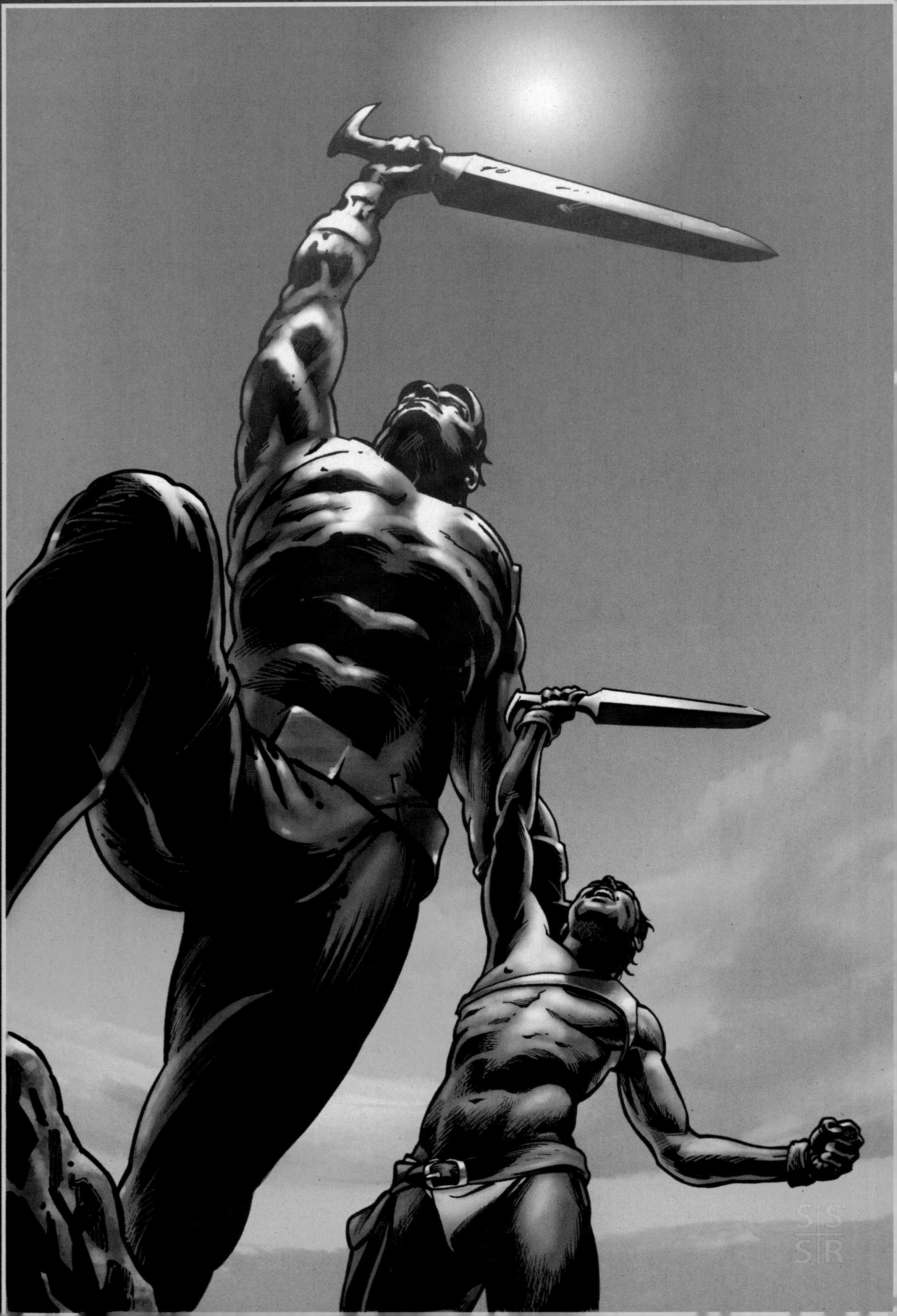

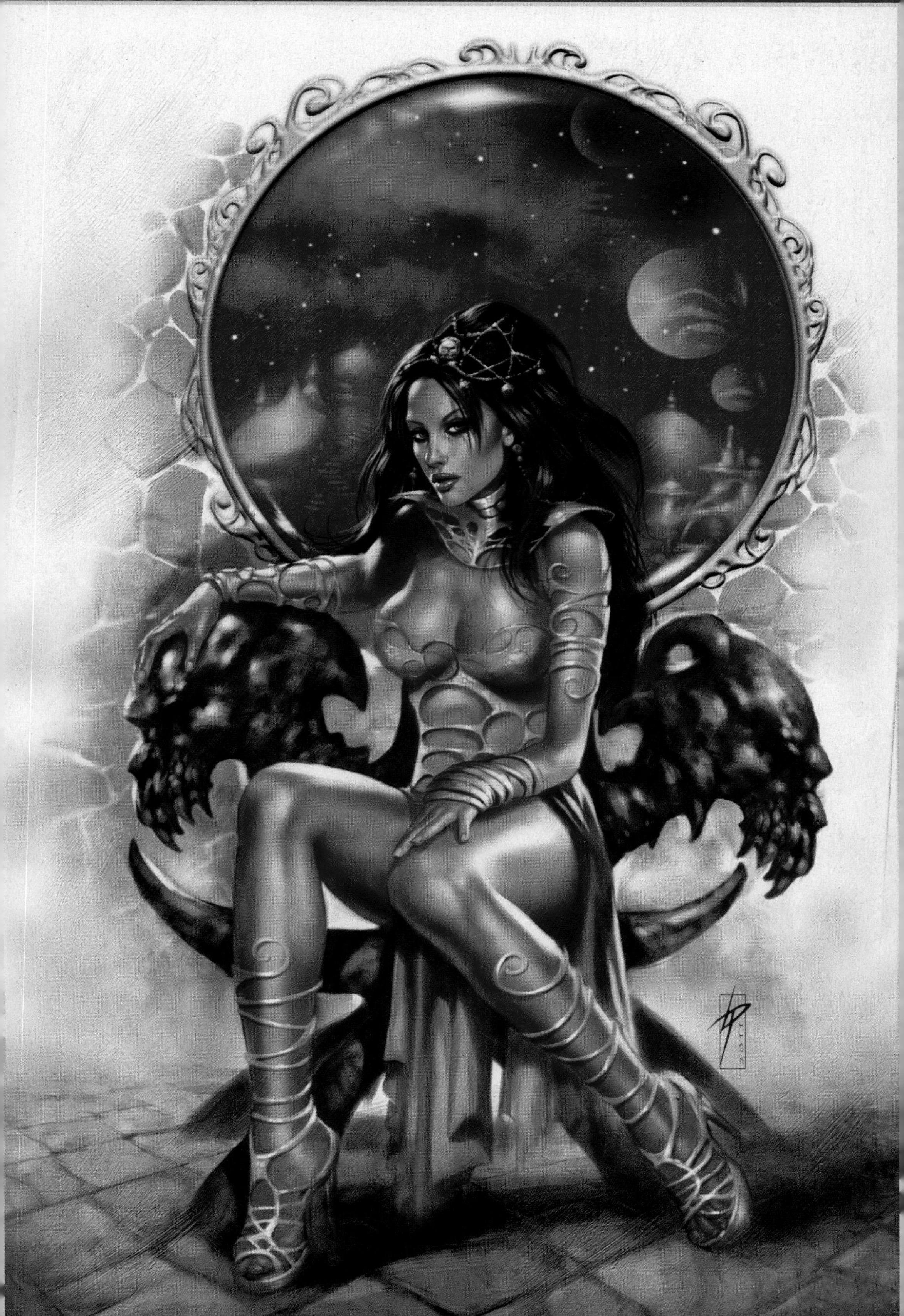

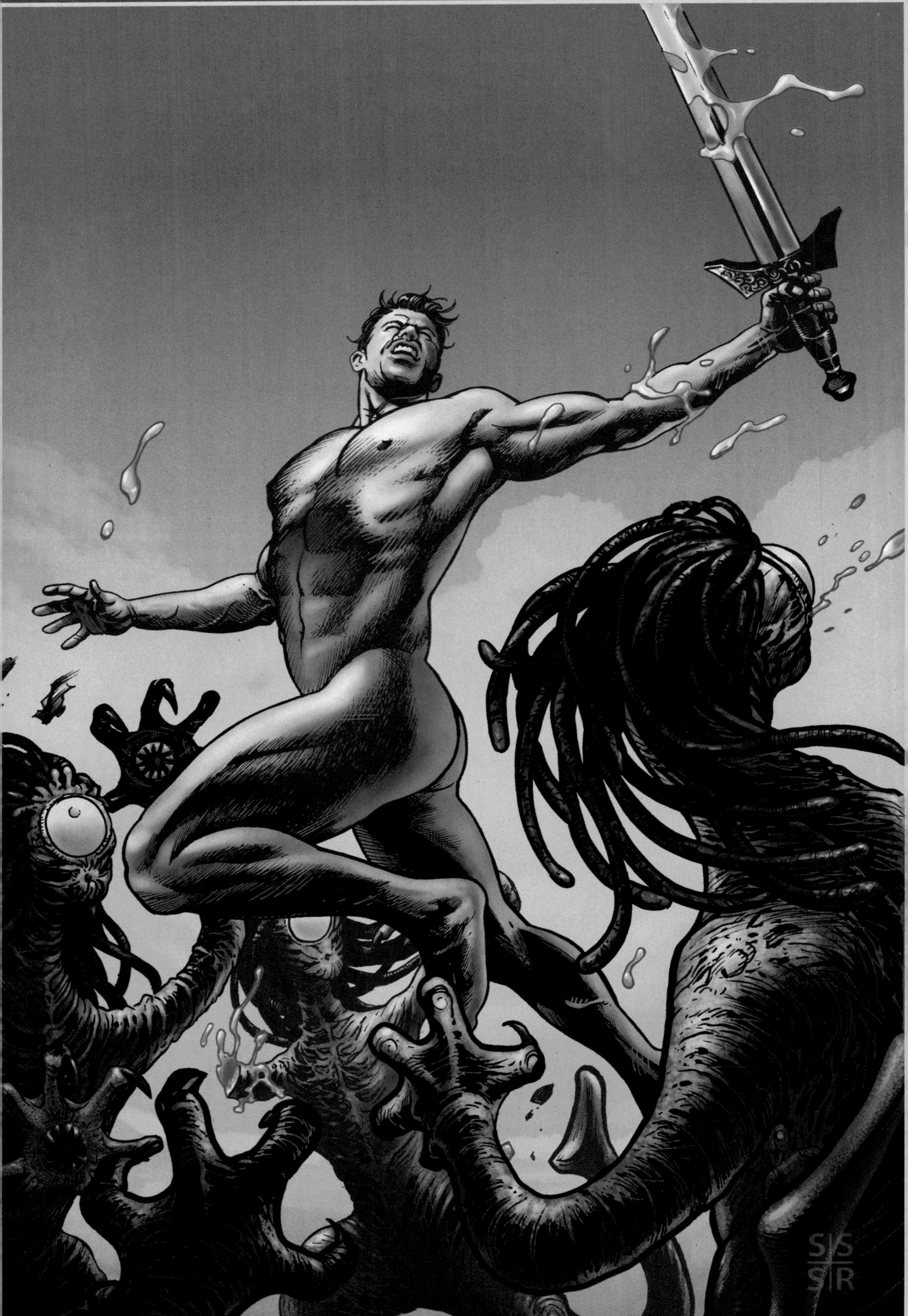

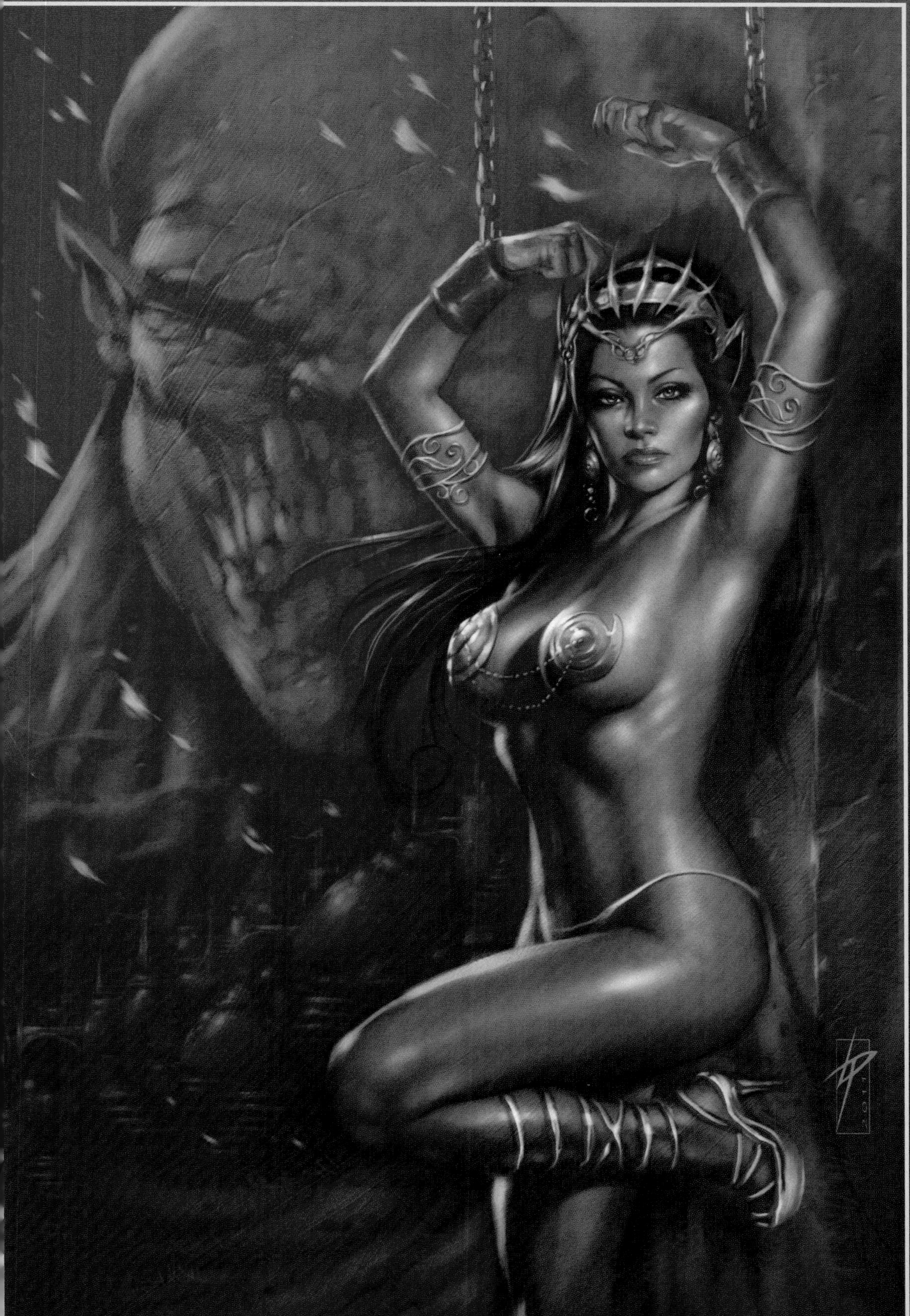

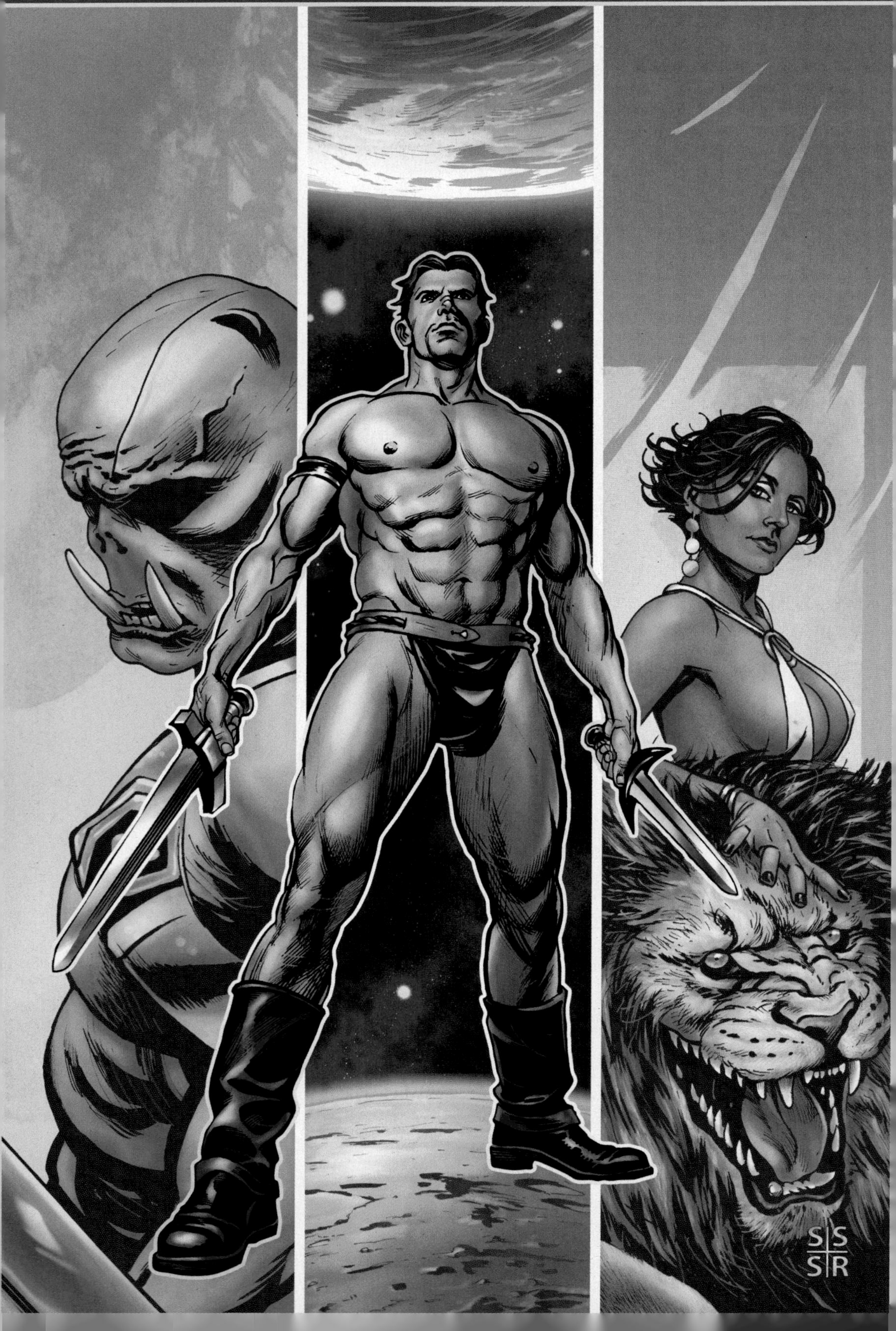

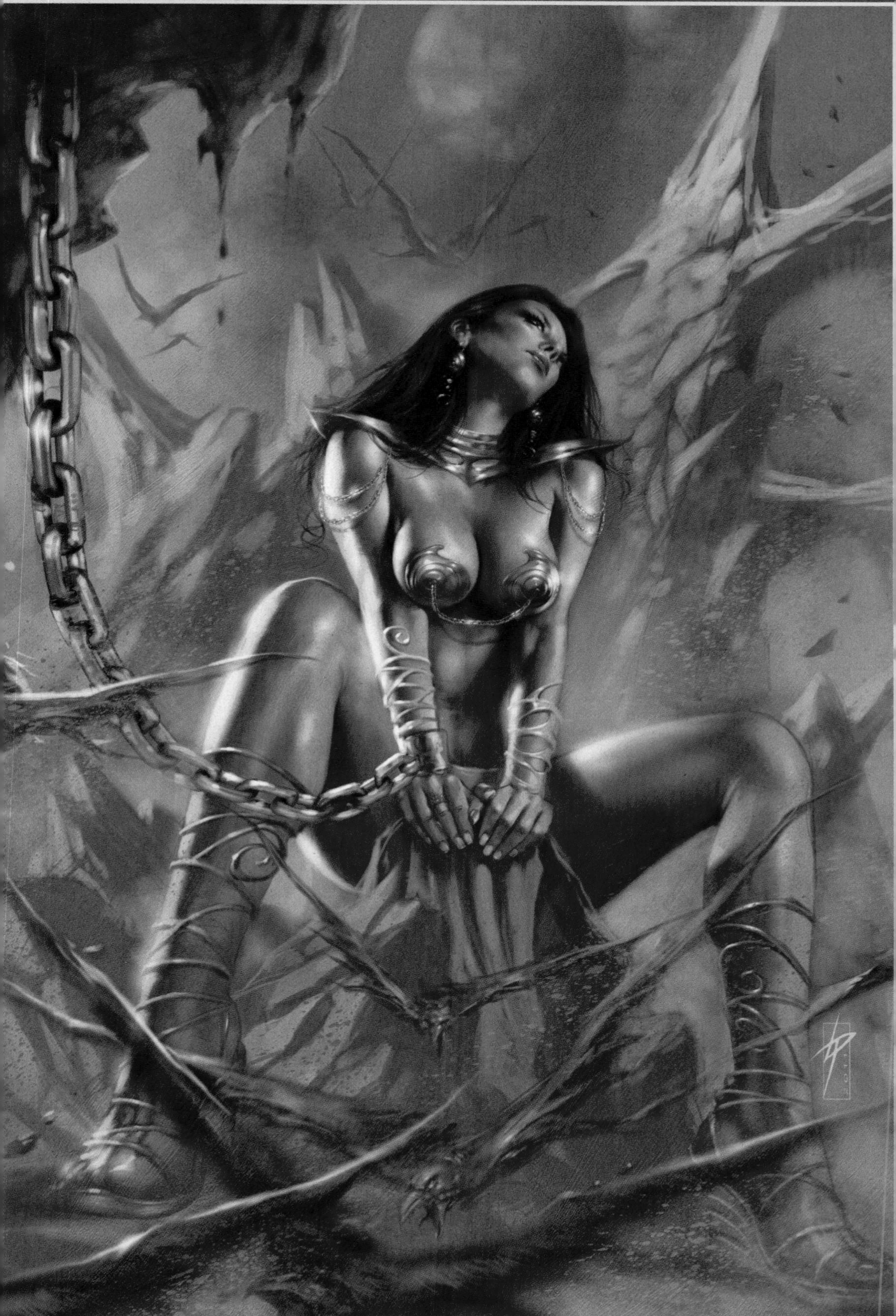

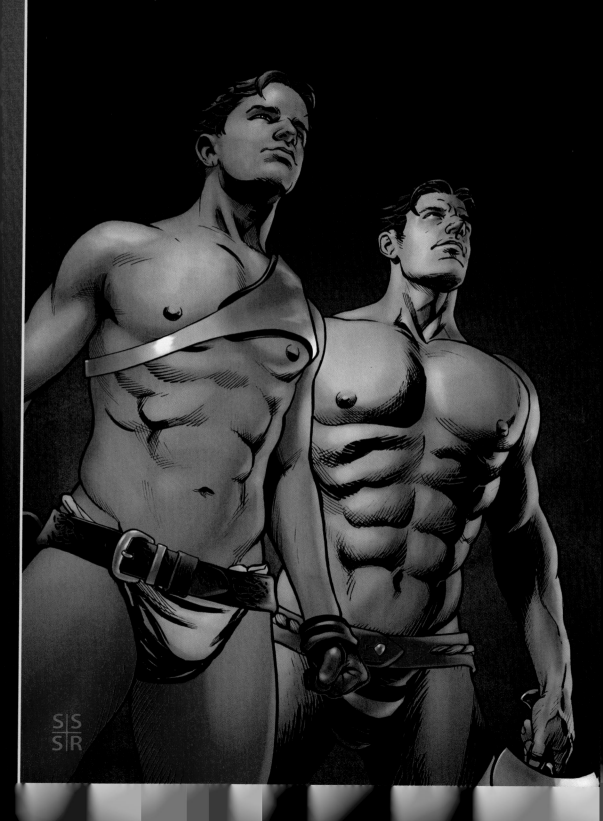

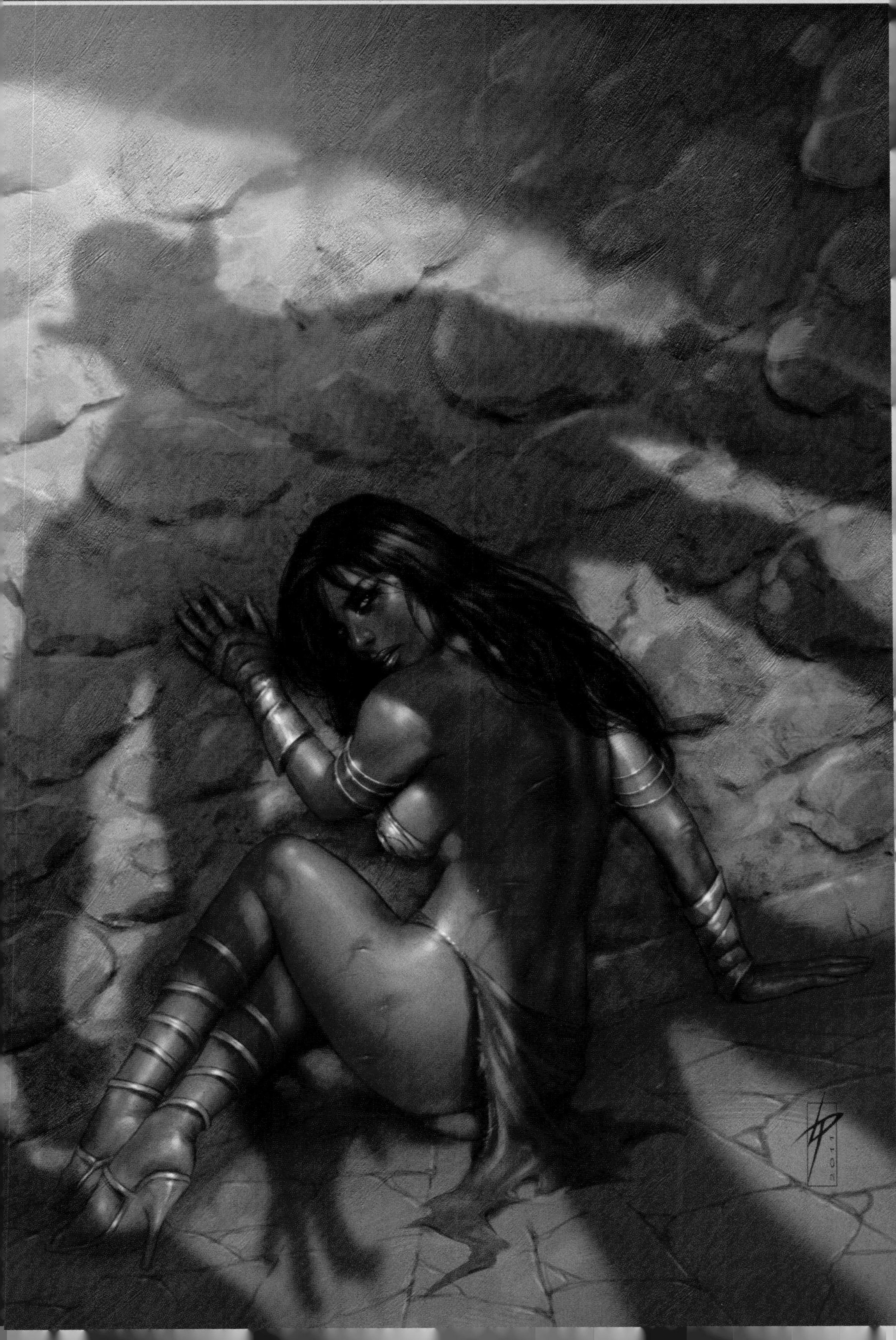

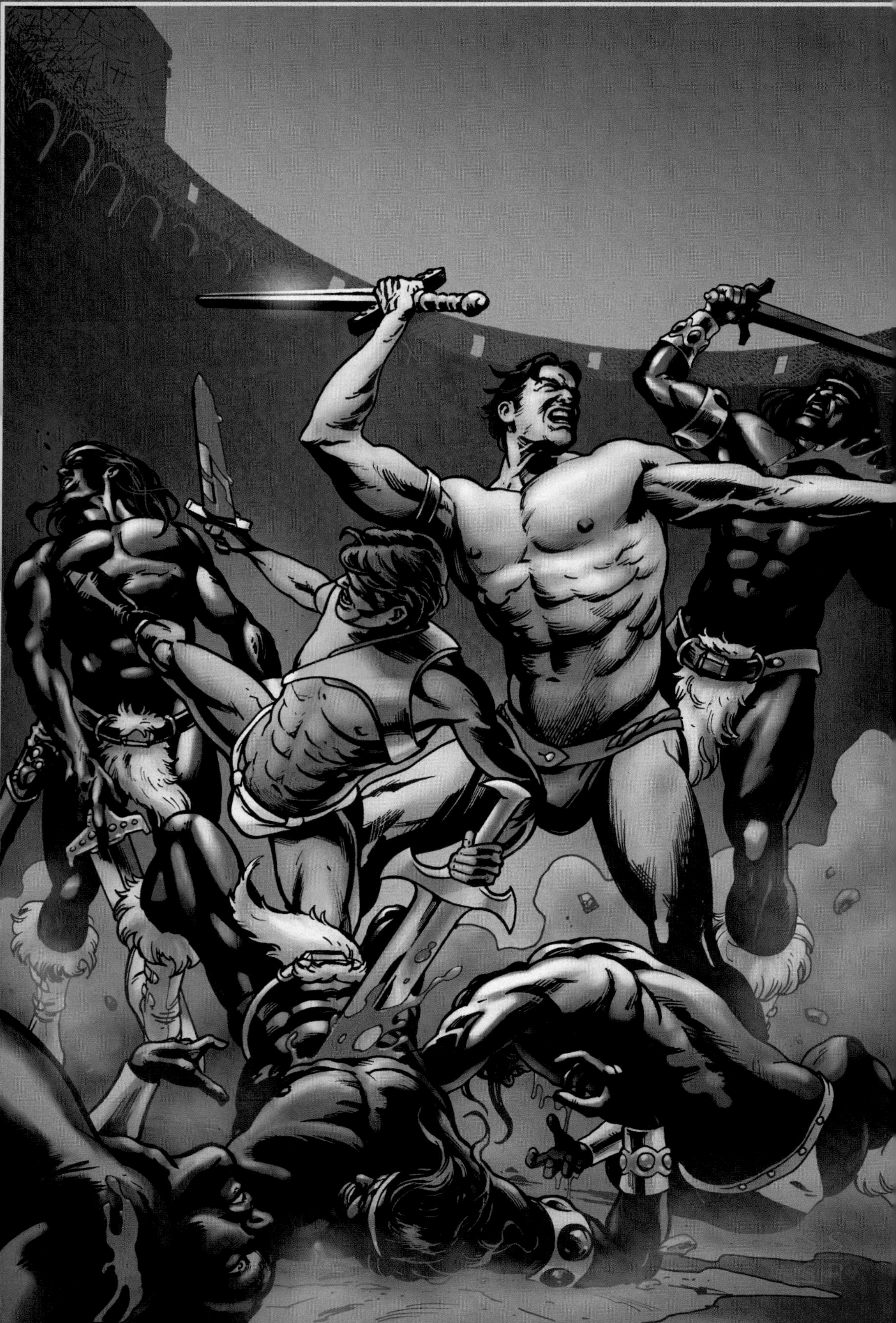

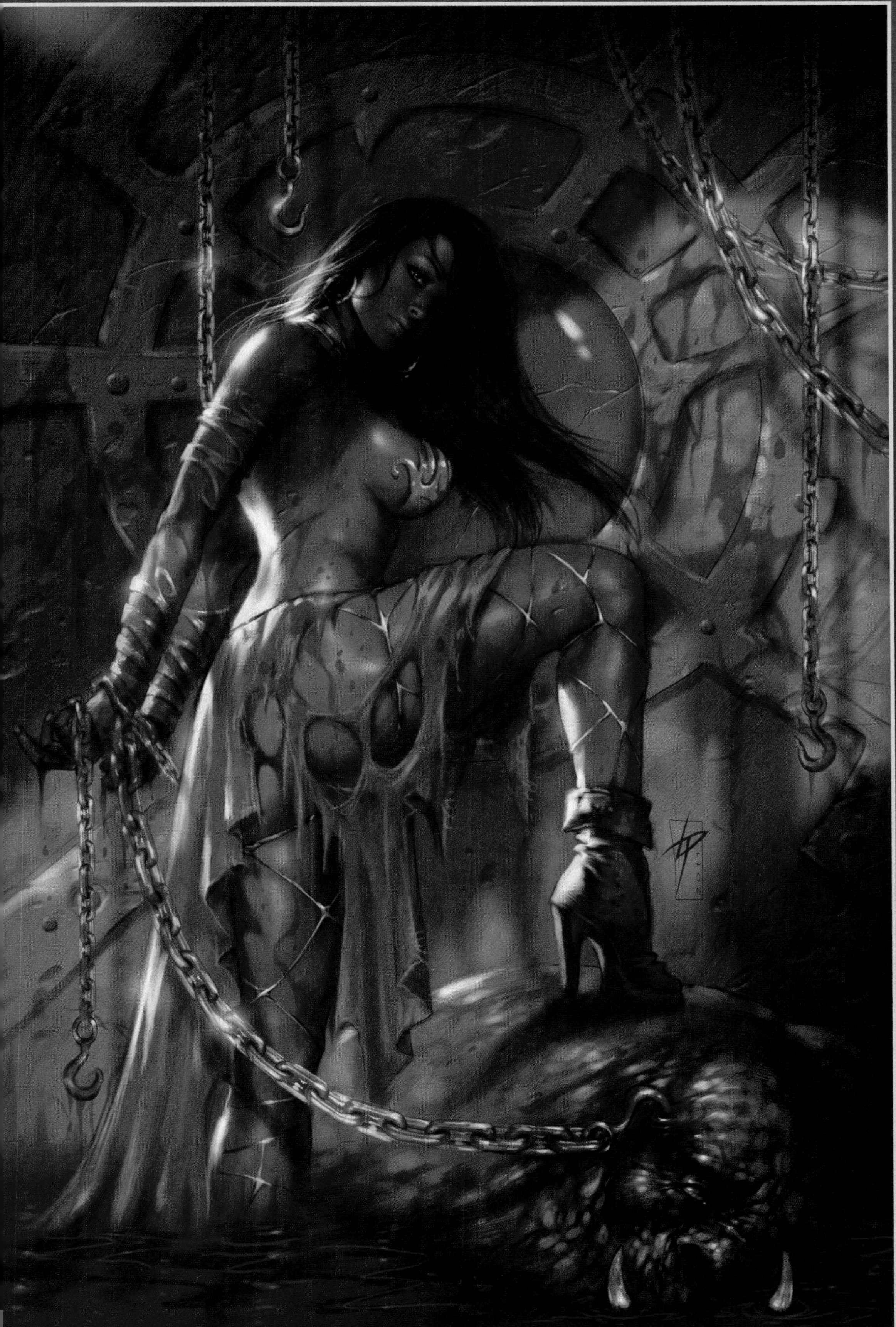

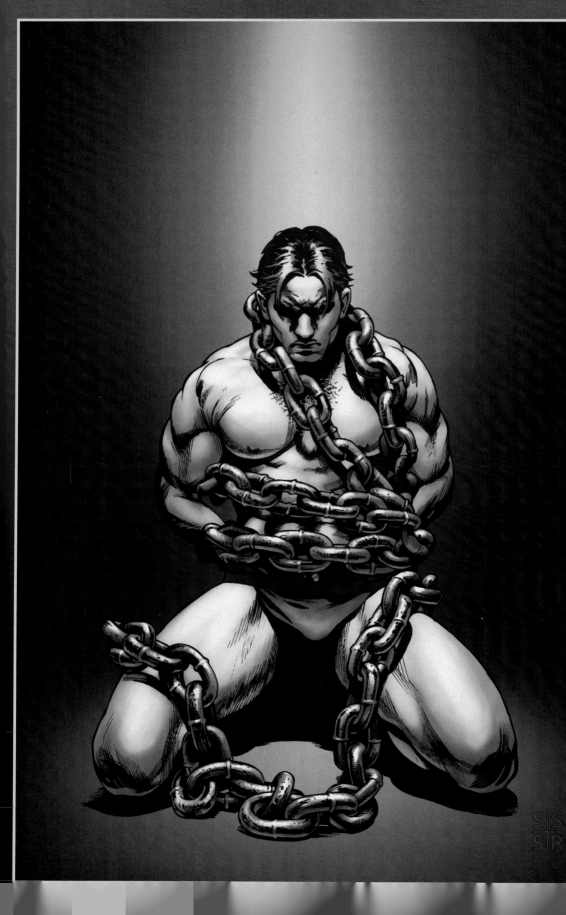

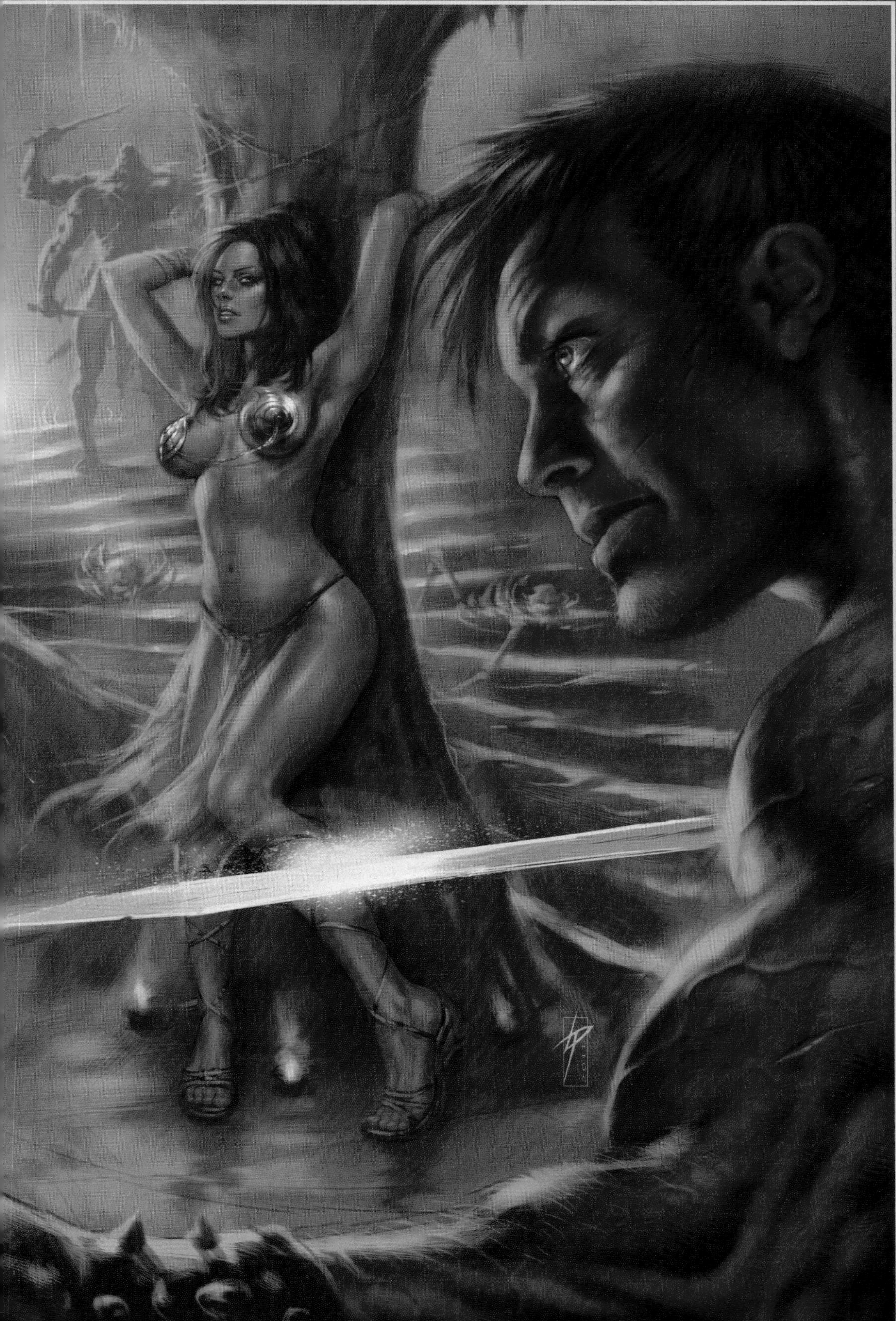

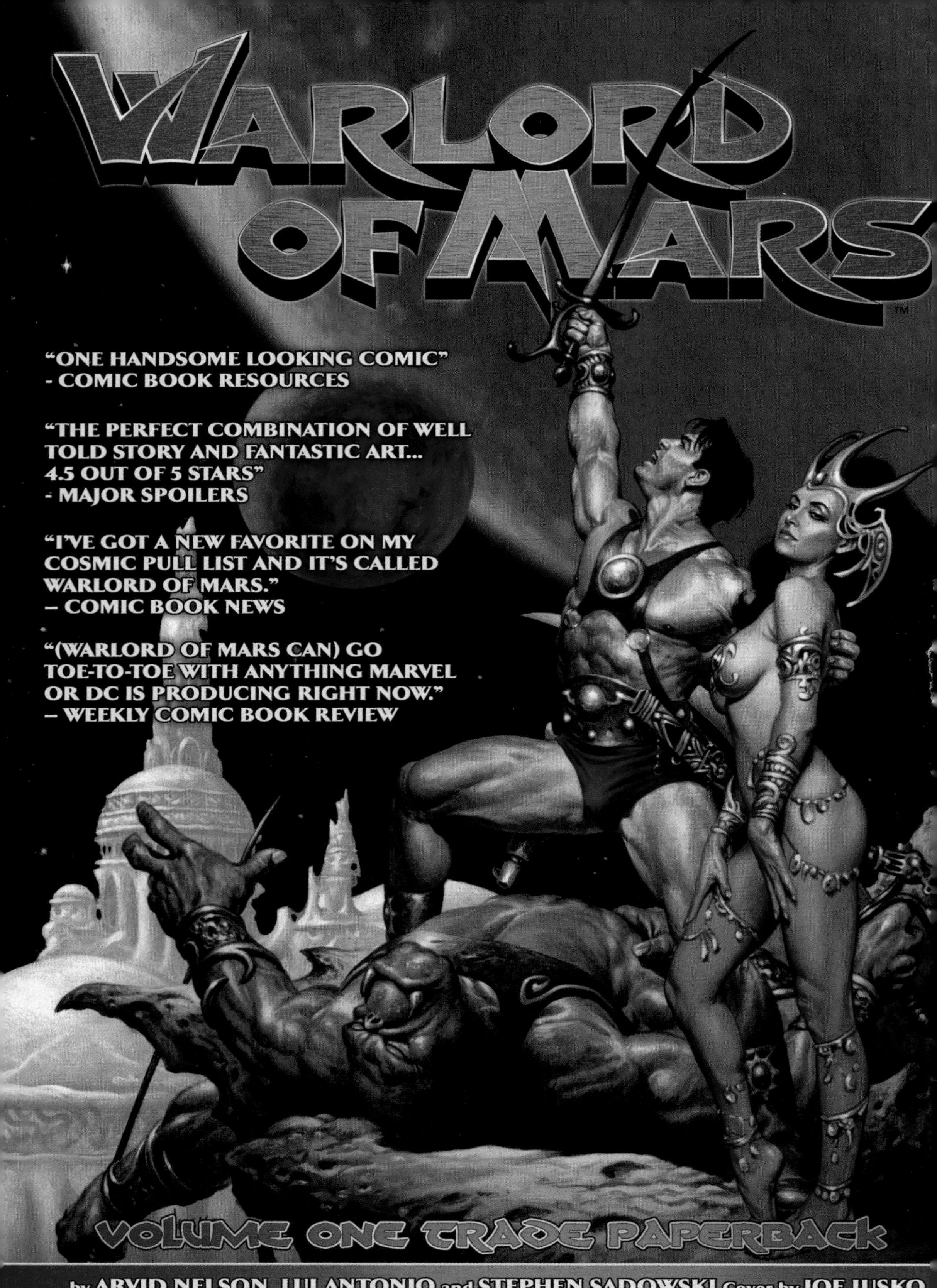
WARLORD OF MARS ™
"ONE HANDSOME LOOKING COMIC"
- COMIC BOOK RESOURCES
"THE PERFECT COMBINATION OF WELL TOLD STORY AND FANTASTIC ART... 4.5 OUT OF 5 STARS"
- MAJOR SPOILERS
"I'VE GOT A NEW FAVORITE ON MY COSMIC PULL LIST AND IT'S CALLED WARLORD OF MARS."
– COMIC BOOK NEWS
"(WARLORD OF MARS CAN) GO TOE-TO-TOE WITH ANYTHING MARVEL OR DC IS PRODUCING RIGHT NOW."
– WEEKLY COMIC BOOK REVIEW
VOLUME ONE TRADE PAPERBACK